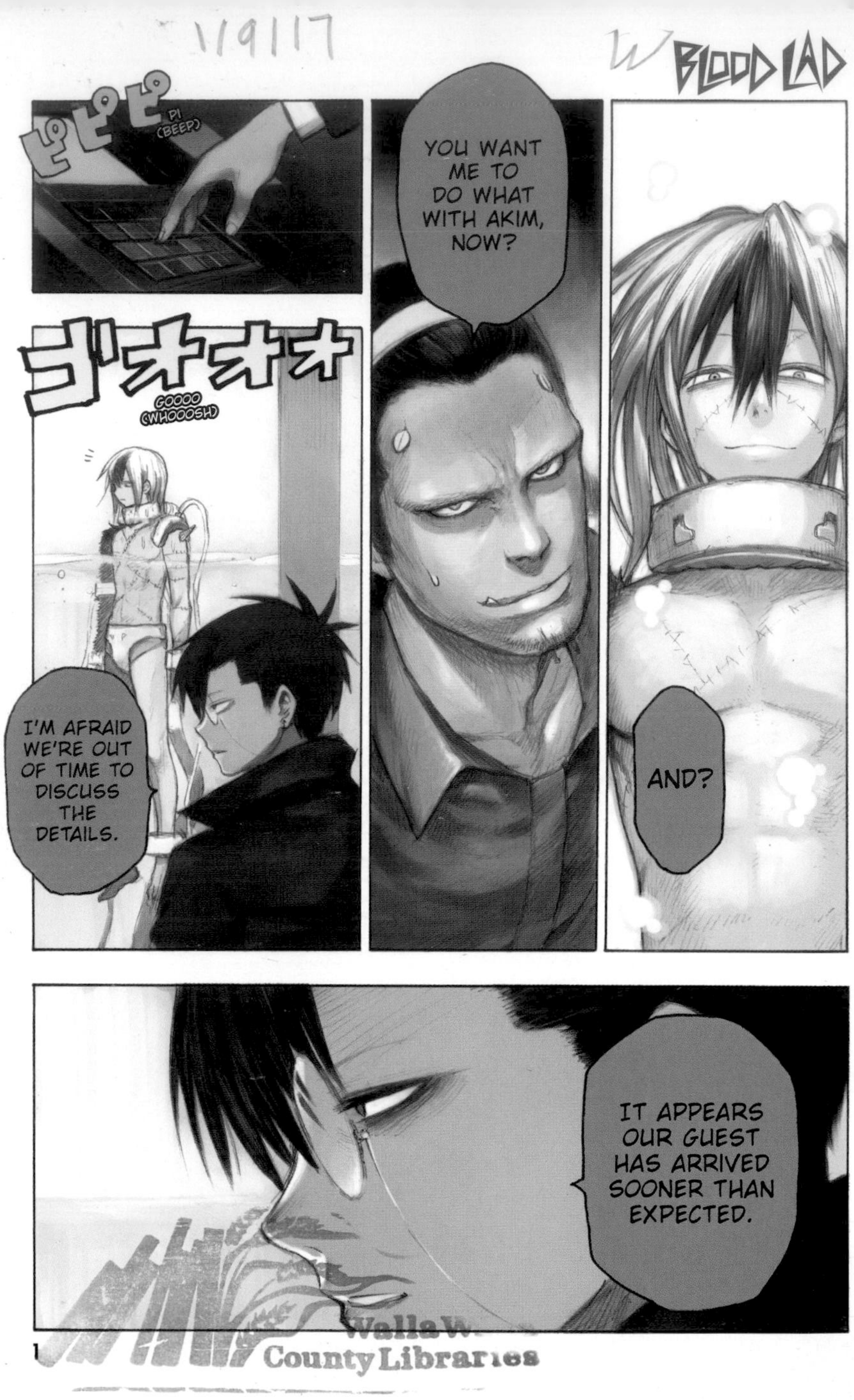
AND?
YOU WANT ME TO DO WHAT WITH AKIM, NOW?
ピピピ
PI (BEEP)
ゴオオオ
GOOOO (WHOOOSH)
I'M AFRAID WE'RE OUT OF TIME TO DISCUSS THE DETAILS.
IT APPEARS OUR GUEST HAS ARRIVED SOONER THAN EXPECTED.

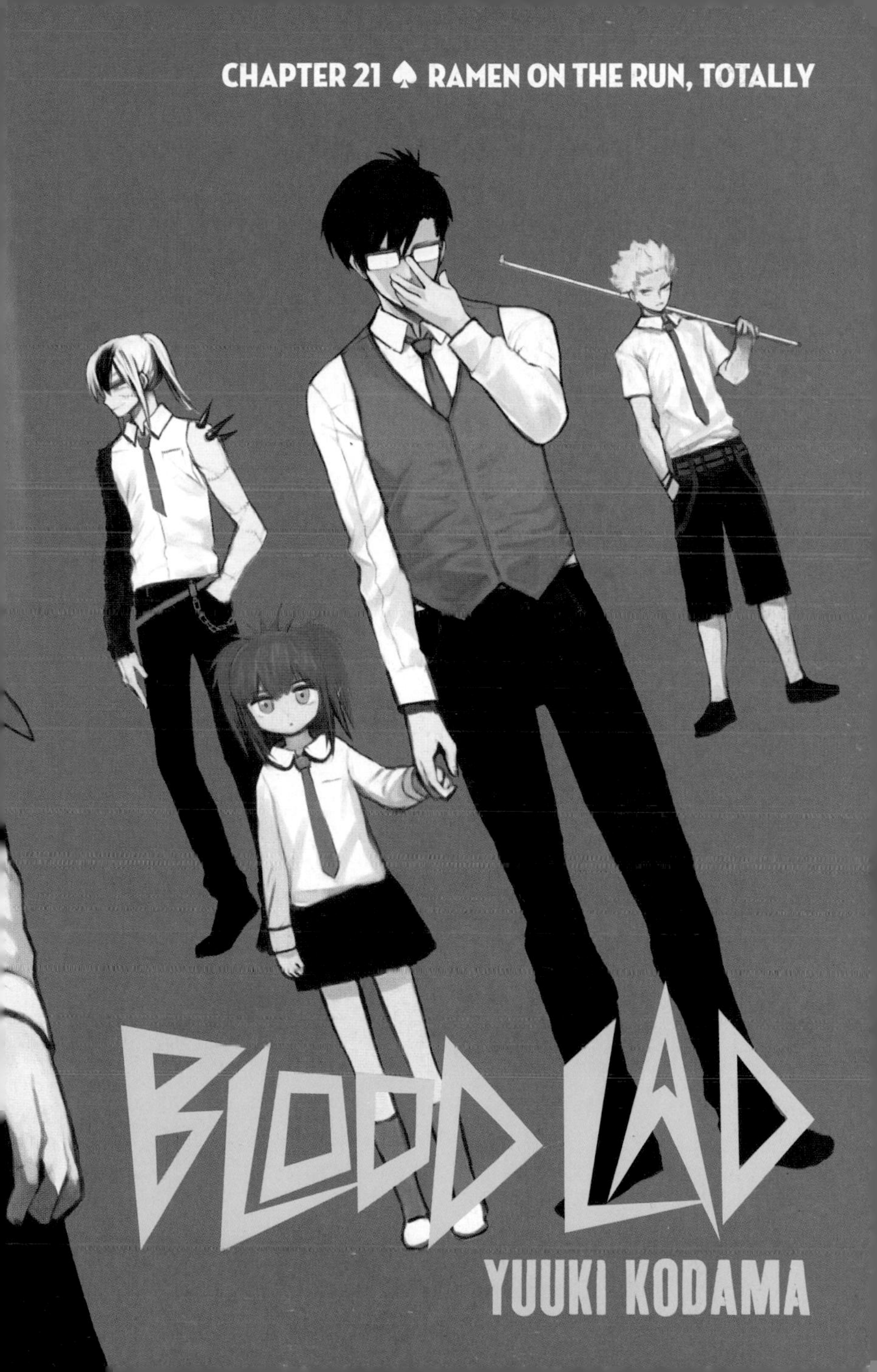
CHAPTER 21 ♠ RAMEN ON THE RUN, TOTALLY
BLOOD LAD
YUUKI KODAMA

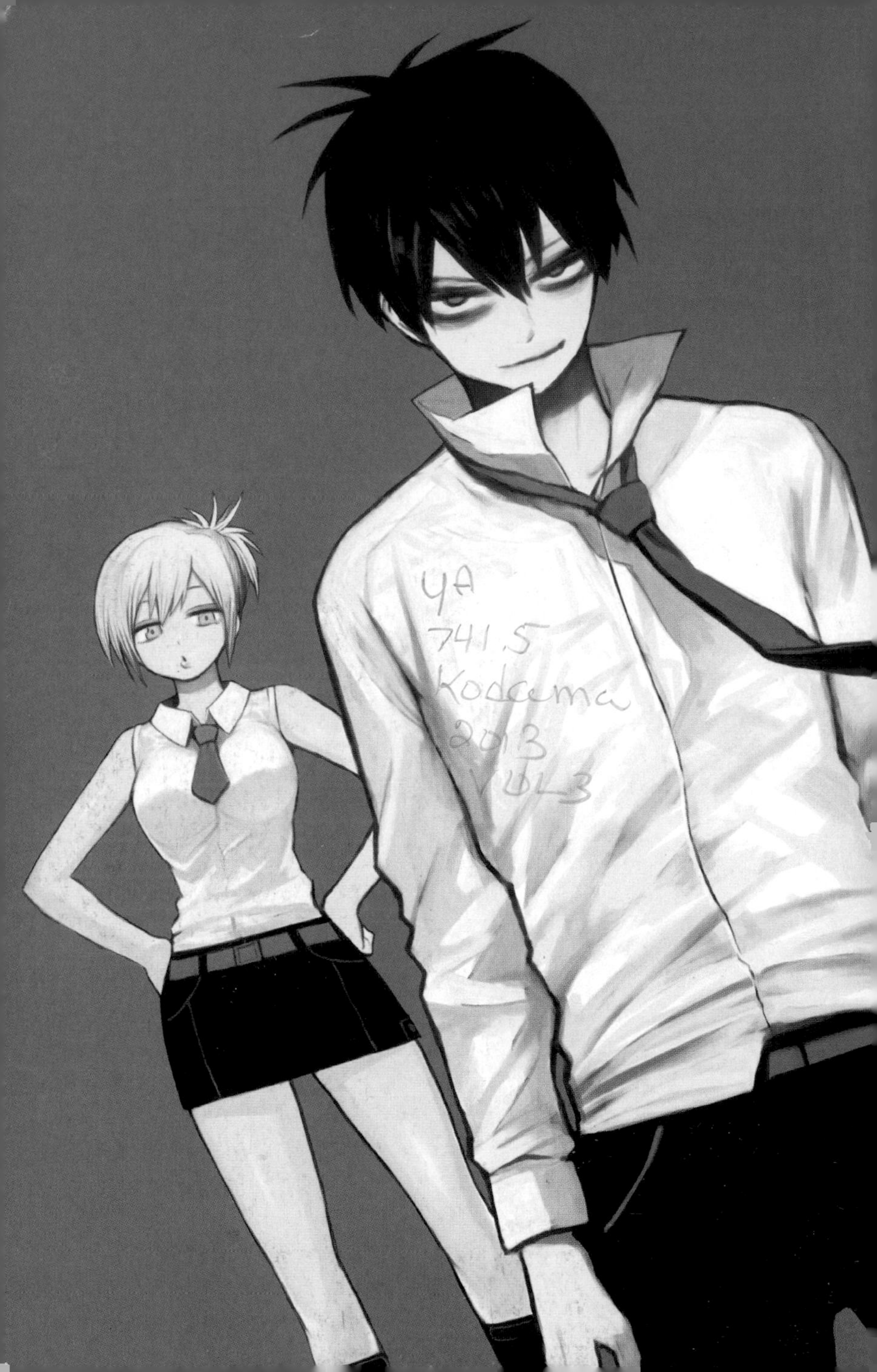

CONTENTS

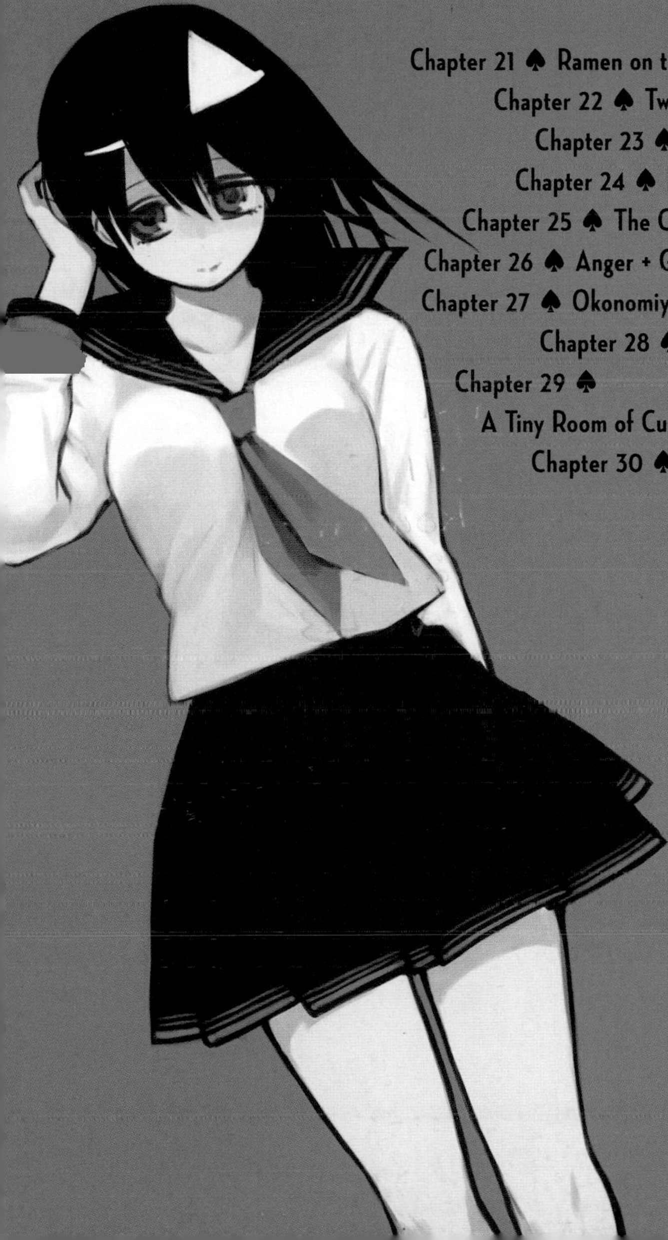

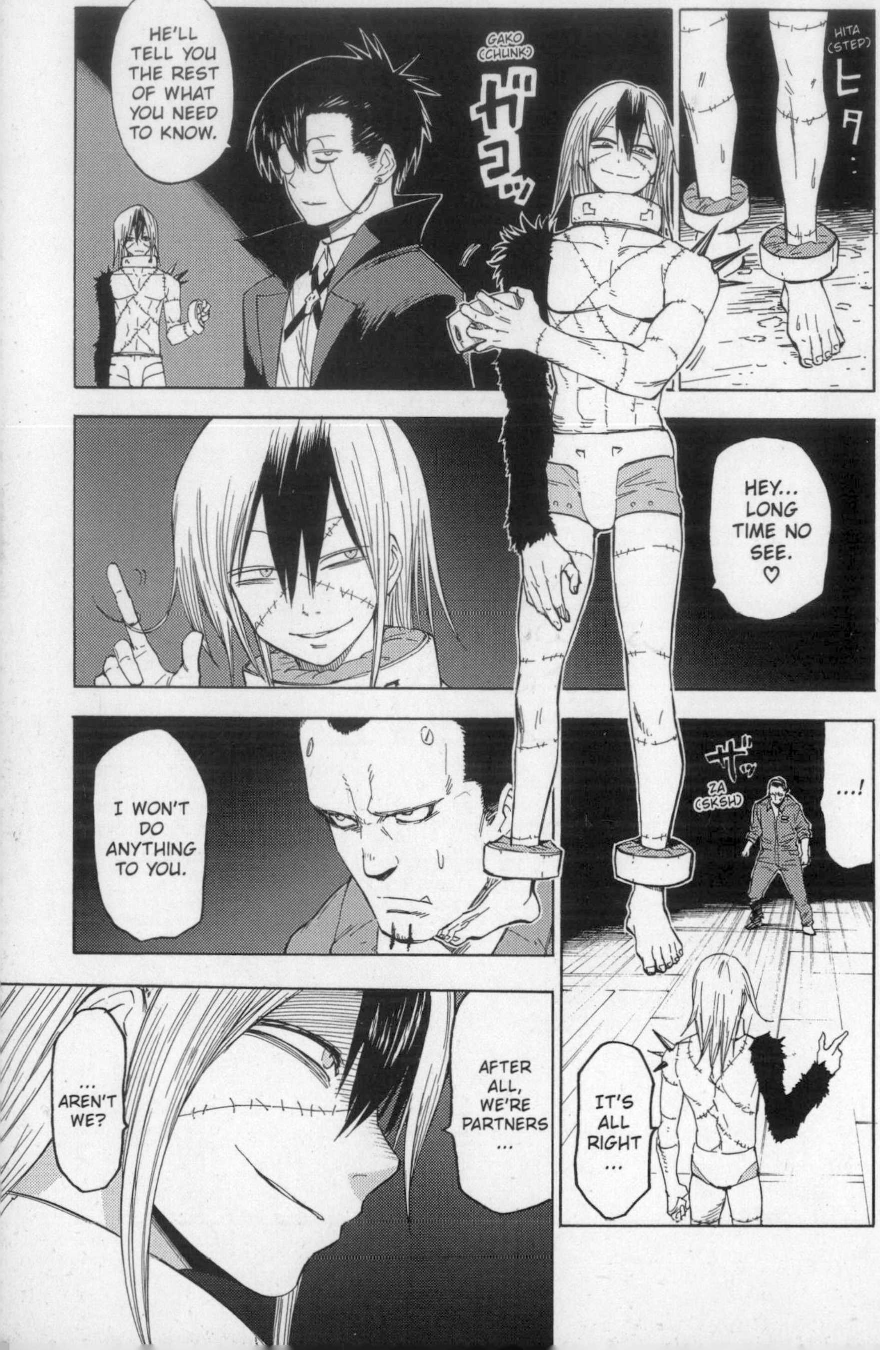
HITA (STEP)
ヒタ・・
GAKO (CHUNK)
ガゴッ
HE'LL TELL YOU THE REST OF WHAT YOU NEED TO KNOW.
HEY... LONG TIME NO SEE. ♡
...!
ZA (SKSH)
ザッ
I WON'T DO ANYTHING TO YOU.
IT'S ALL RIGHT ...
AFTER ALL, WE'RE PARTNERS ...
... AREN'T WE?

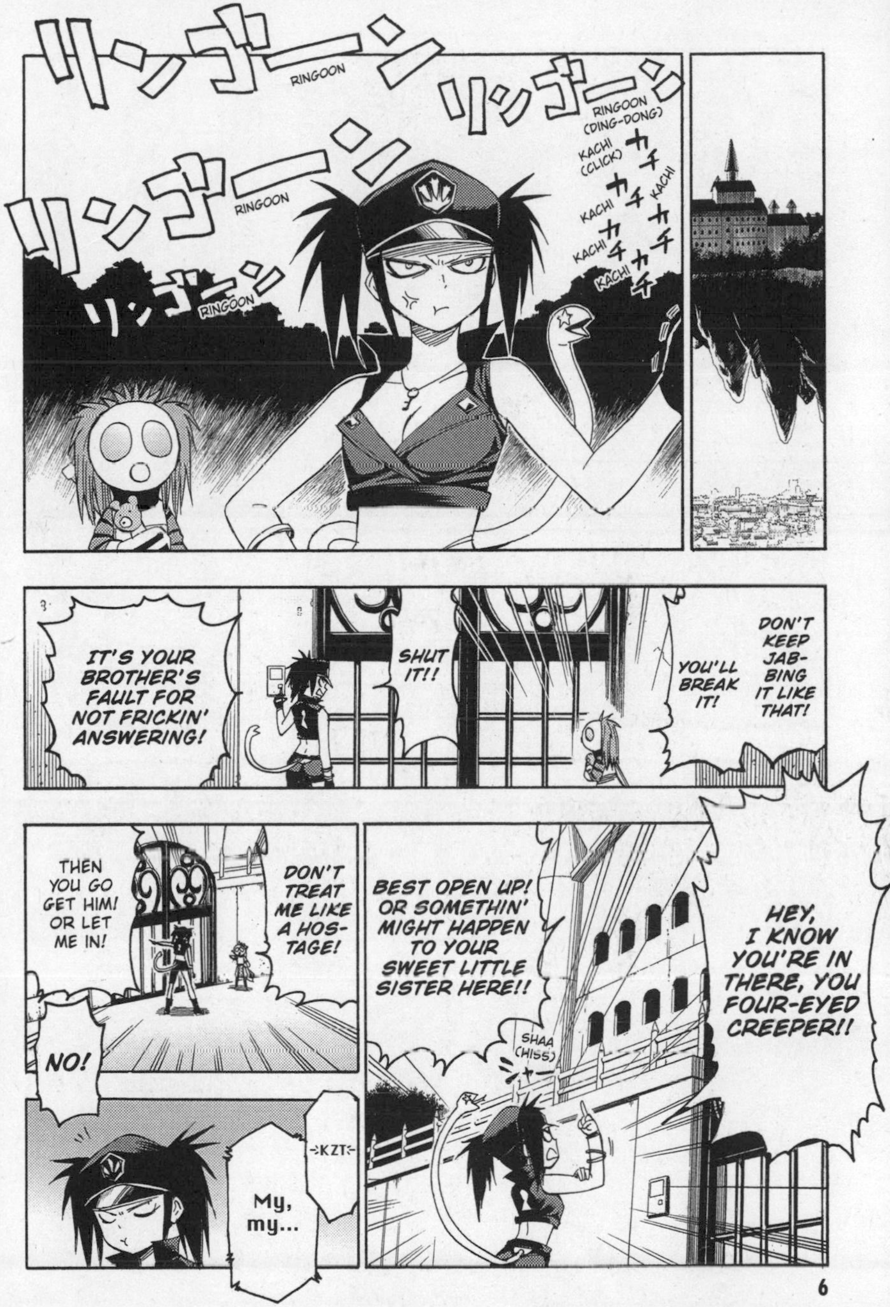
リンゴーン
RINGOON
リンゴーン
RINGOON (DING-DONG)
リンゴーン
RINGOON
リンゴーン
RINGOON
カチ
KACHI (CLICK)
カチ
KACHI
カチ
KACHI
カチ
KACHI
カチ
KACHI
DON'T KEEP JAB-BING IT LIKE THAT!
YOU'LL BREAK IT!
SHUT IT!!
IT'S YOUR BROTHER'S FAULT FOR NOT FRICKIN' ANSWERING!
HEY, I KNOW YOU'RE IN THERE, YOU FOUR-EYED CREEPER!!
BEST OPEN UP! OR SOMETHIN' MIGHT HAPPEN TO YOUR SWEET LITTLE SISTER HERE!!
SHAA (HISS)
DON'T TREAT ME LIKE A HOS-TAGE!
THEN YOU GO GET HIM! OR LET ME IN!
NO!
-KZT-
My, my...

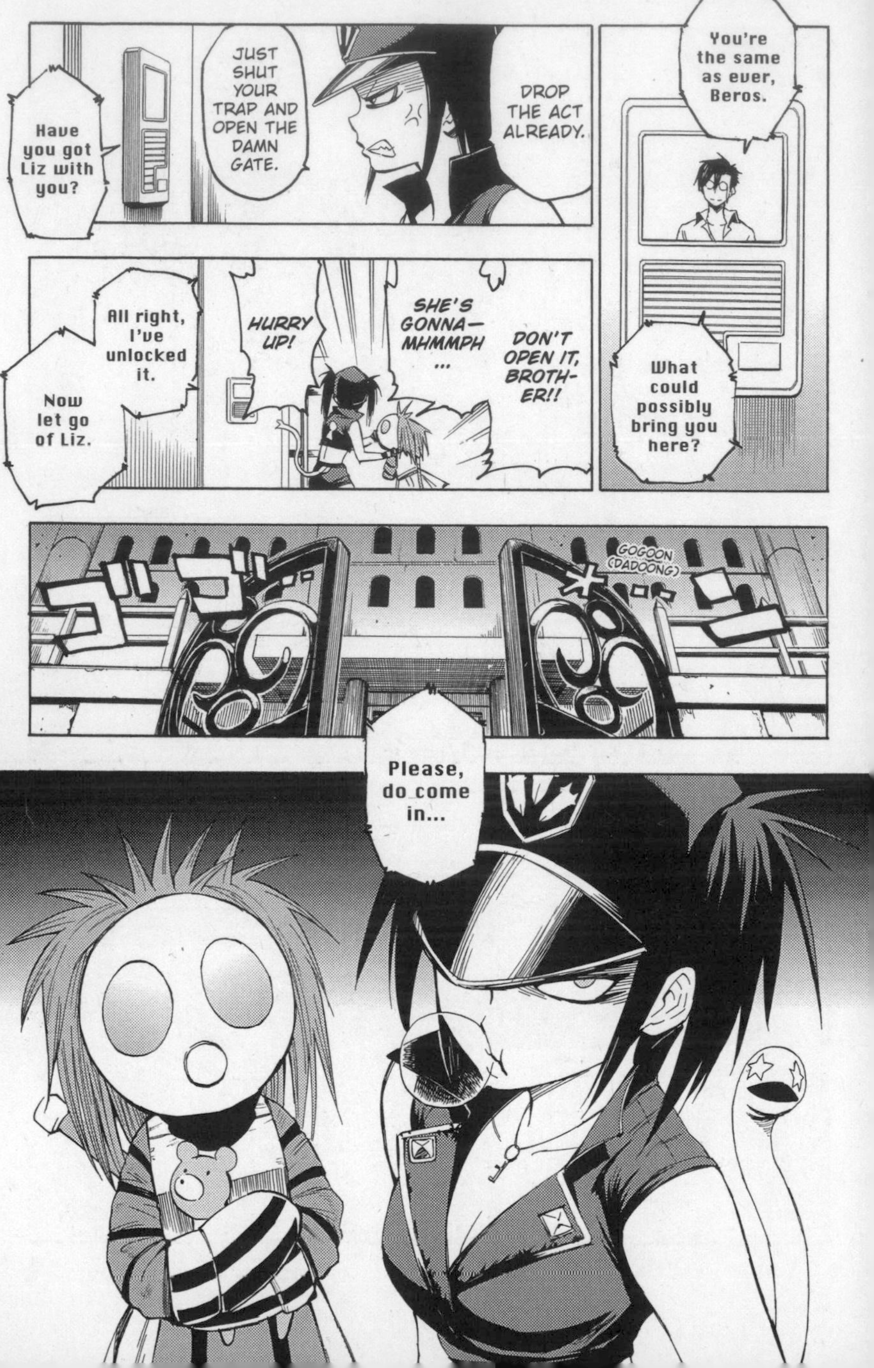
You're the same as ever, Beros.
What could possibly bring you here?
DROP THE ACT ALREADY.
JUST SHUT YOUR TRAP AND OPEN THE DAMN GATE.
Have you got Liz with you?
DON'T OPEN IT, BROTHER!!
SHE'S GONNA—MHMMPH ...
HURRY UP!
All right, I've unlocked it.
Now let go of Liz.
GOGOON (DADOONG)
Please, do come in...

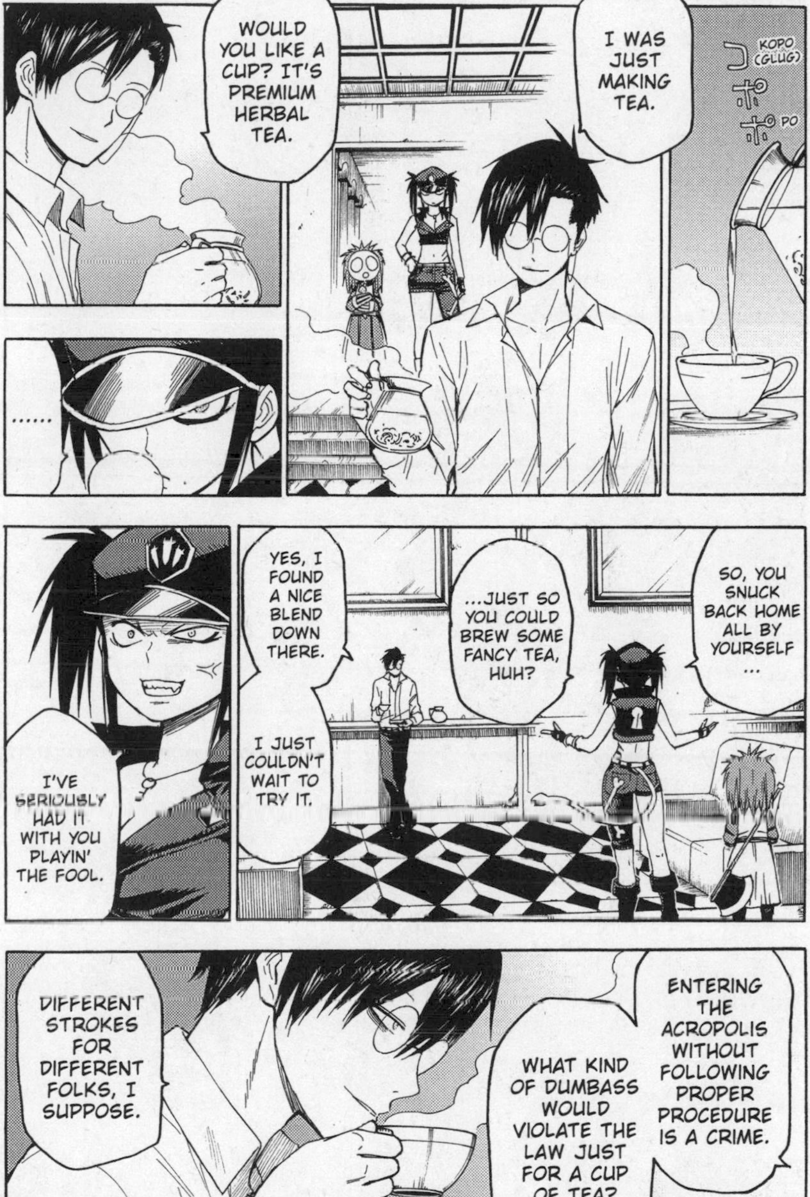
KOPO (GLUG)
PO
I WAS JUST MAKING TEA.
WOULD YOU LIKE A CUP? IT'S PREMIUM HERBAL TEA.
......
SO, YOU SNUCK BACK HOME ALL BY YOURSELF ...
...JUST SO YOU COULD BREW SOME FANCY TEA, HUH?
YES, I FOUND A NICE BLEND DOWN THERE.
I JUST COULDN'T WAIT TO TRY IT.
I'VE SERIOUSLY HAD IT WITH YOU PLAYIN' THE FOOL.
ENTERING THE ACROPOLIS WITHOUT FOLLOWING PROPER PROCEDURE IS A CRIME.
WHAT KIND OF DUMBASS WOULD VIOLATE THE LAW JUST FOR A CUP OF TEA?
DIFFERENT STROKES FOR DIFFERENT FOLKS, I SUPPOSE.

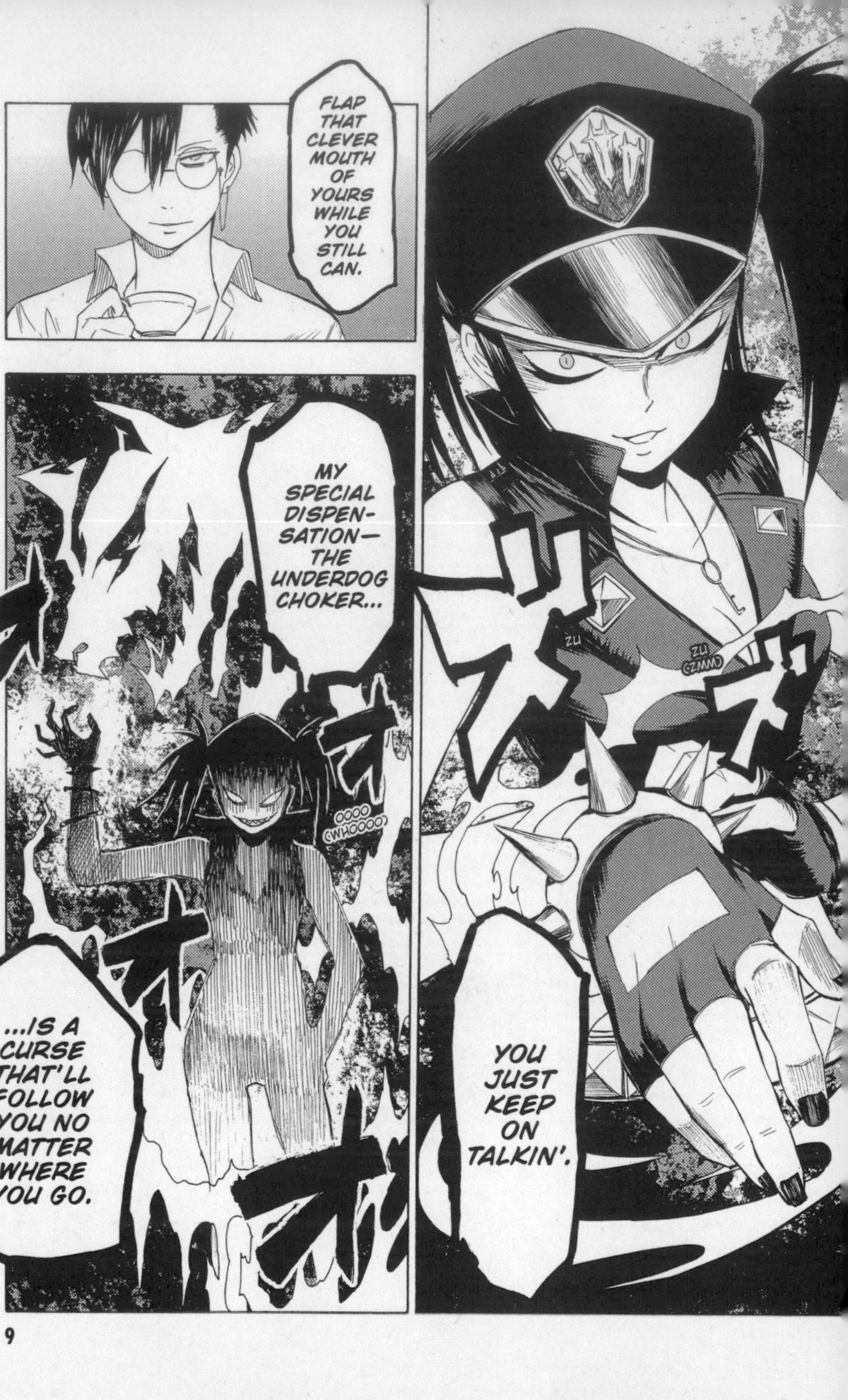
ZU
ZU (ZMM)
YOU JUST KEEP ON TALKIN'.
FLAP THAT CLEVER MOUTH OF YOURS WHILE YOU STILL CAN.
MY SPECIAL DISPEN-SATION—THE UNDERDOG CHOKER...
OOOO (WHOOOO)
...IS A CURSE THAT'LL FOLLOW YOU NO MATTER WHERE YOU GO.

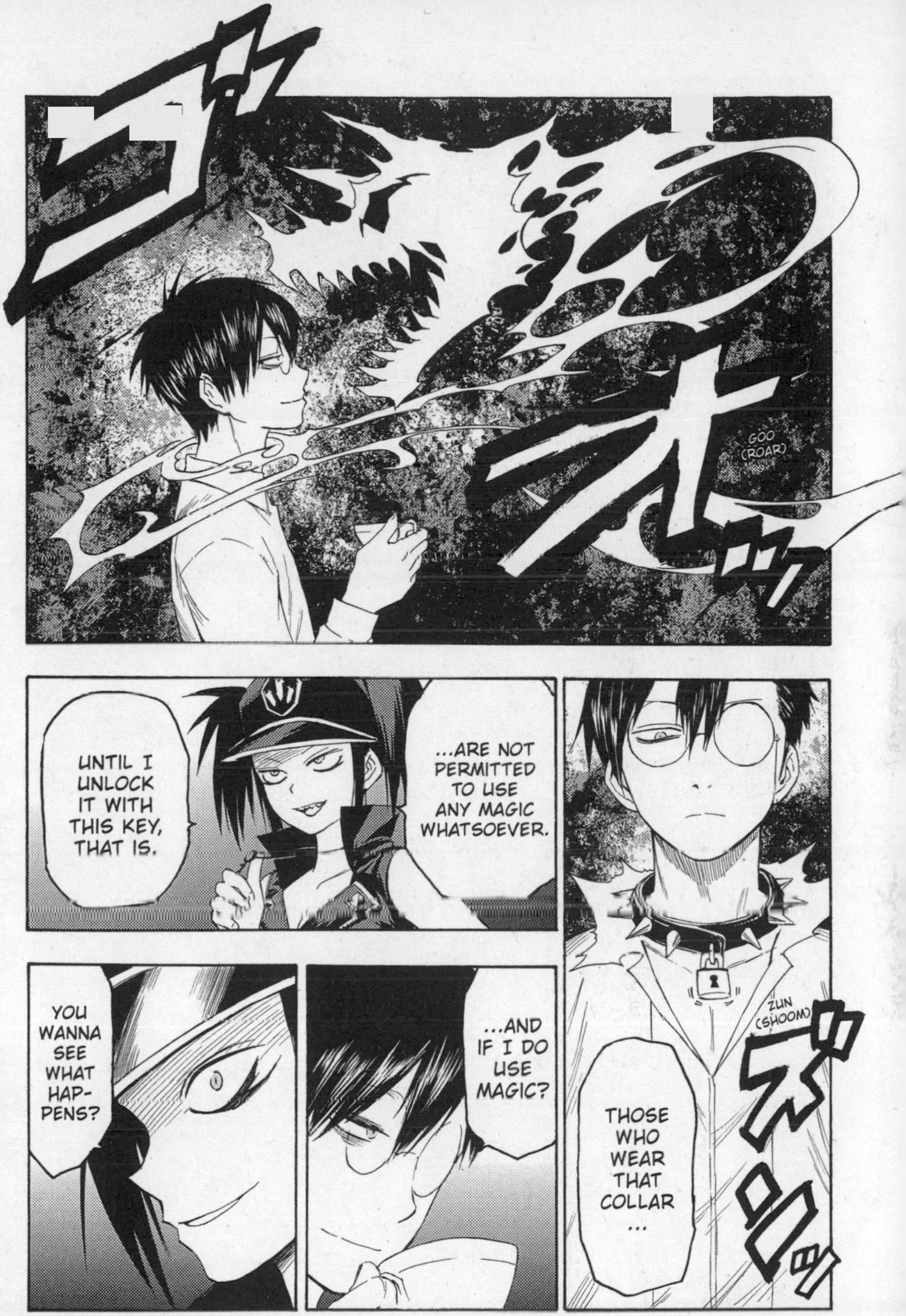
GOO (ROAR)
ZUN (SHOOM)
THOSE WHO WEAR THAT COLLAR ...
...ARE NOT PERMITTED TO USE ANY MAGIC WHATSOEVER.
UNTIL I UNLOCK IT WITH THIS KEY, THAT IS.
...AND IF I DO USE MAGIC?
YOU WANNA SEE WHAT HAP-PENS?

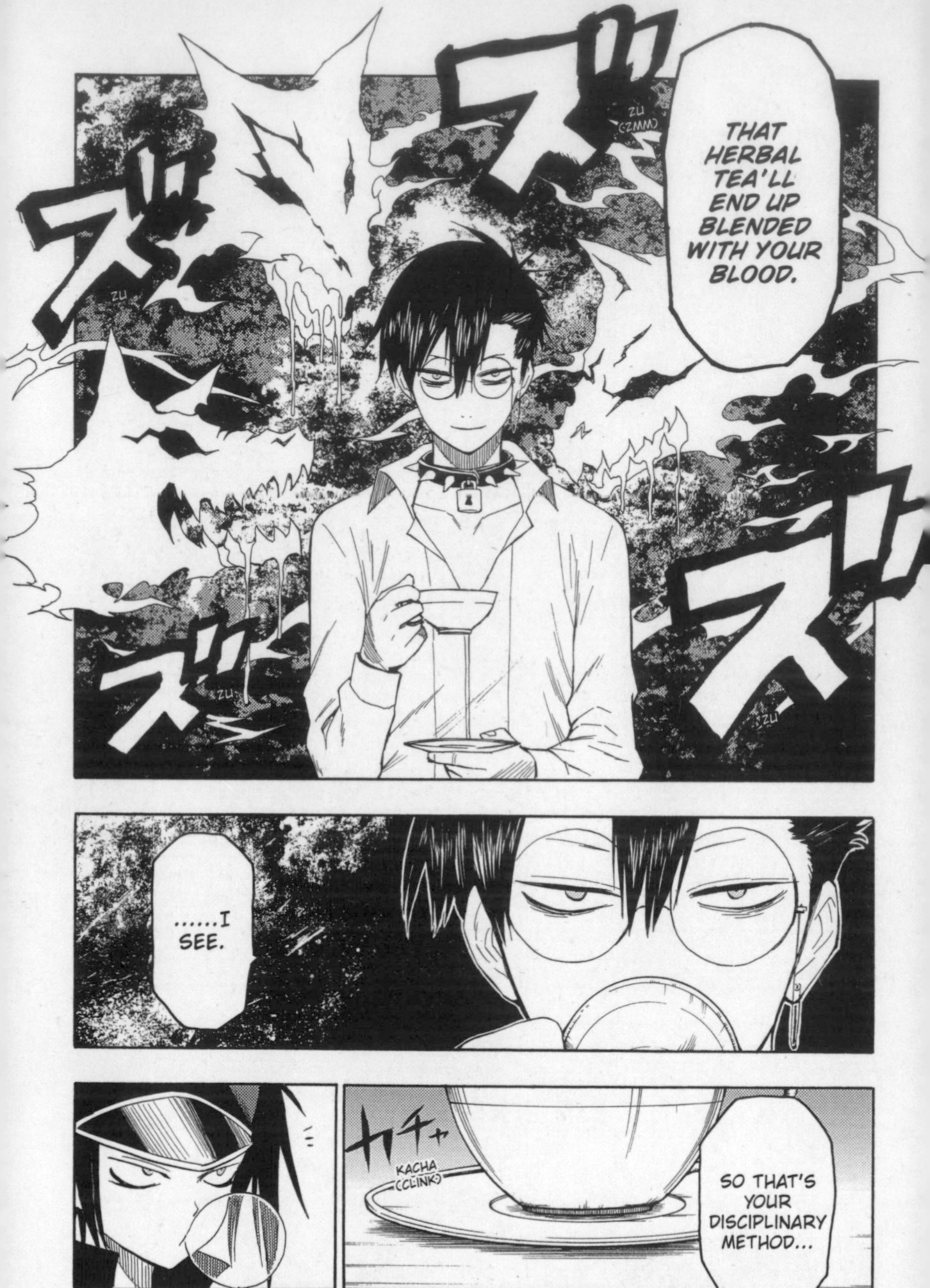
THAT HERBAL TEA'LL END UP BLENDED WITH YOUR BLOOD.
ZU (ZMMM)
ZU
ZU
ZU
......I SEE.
SO THAT'S YOUR DISCIPLINARY METHOD...
カチャ
KACHA (CLINK)

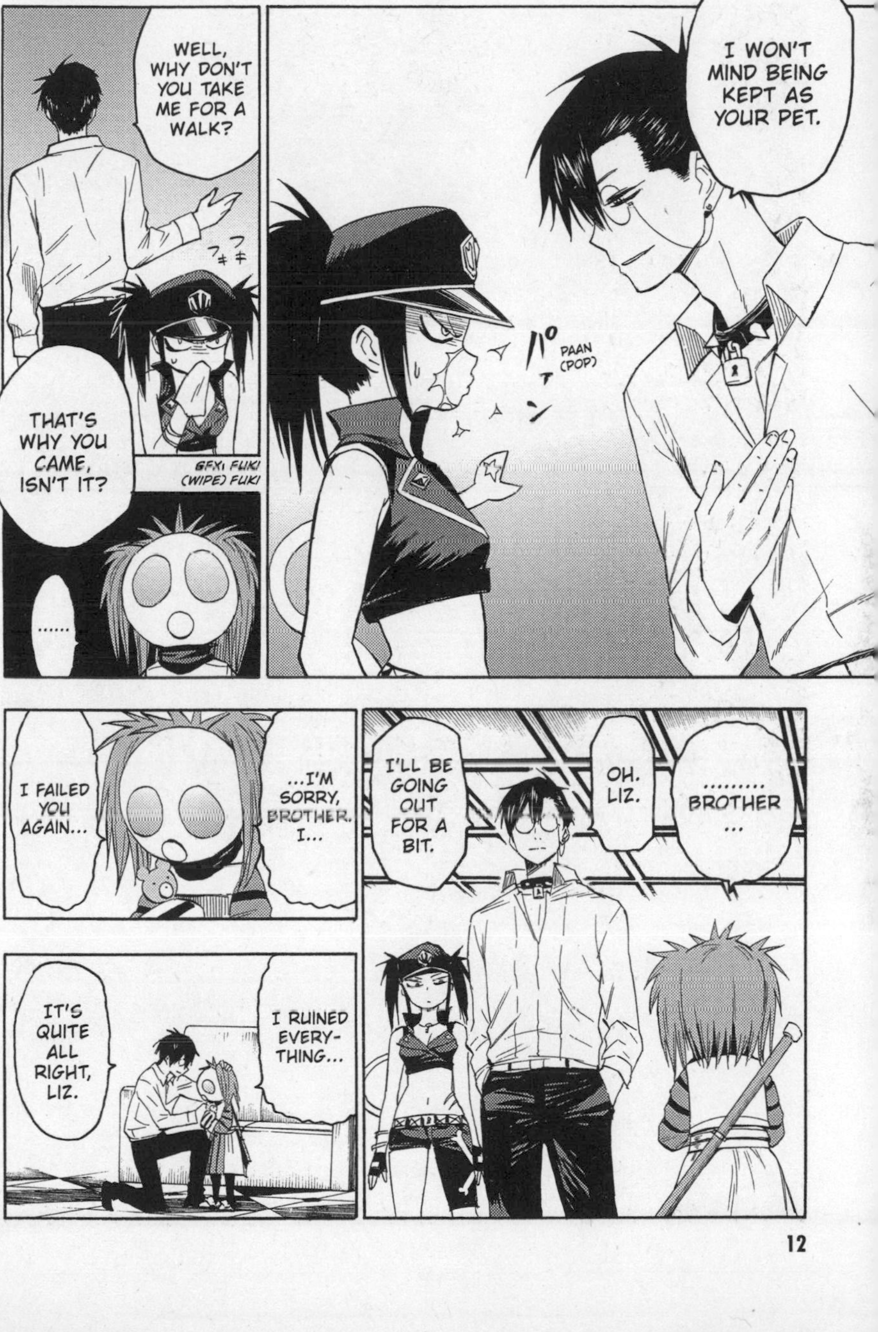
I WON'T MIND BEING KEPT AS YOUR PET.
PAAN (POP)
WELL, WHY DON'T YOU TAKE ME FOR A WALK?
SFX: FUKI (WIPE) FUKI
THAT'S WHY YOU CAME, ISN'T IT?
......
.... BROTHER ...
OH. LIZ.
I'LL BE GOING OUT FOR A BIT.
...I'M SORRY, BROTHER. I...
I FAILED YOU AGAIN...
I RUINED EVERY-THING...
IT'S QUITE ALL RIGHT, LIZ.

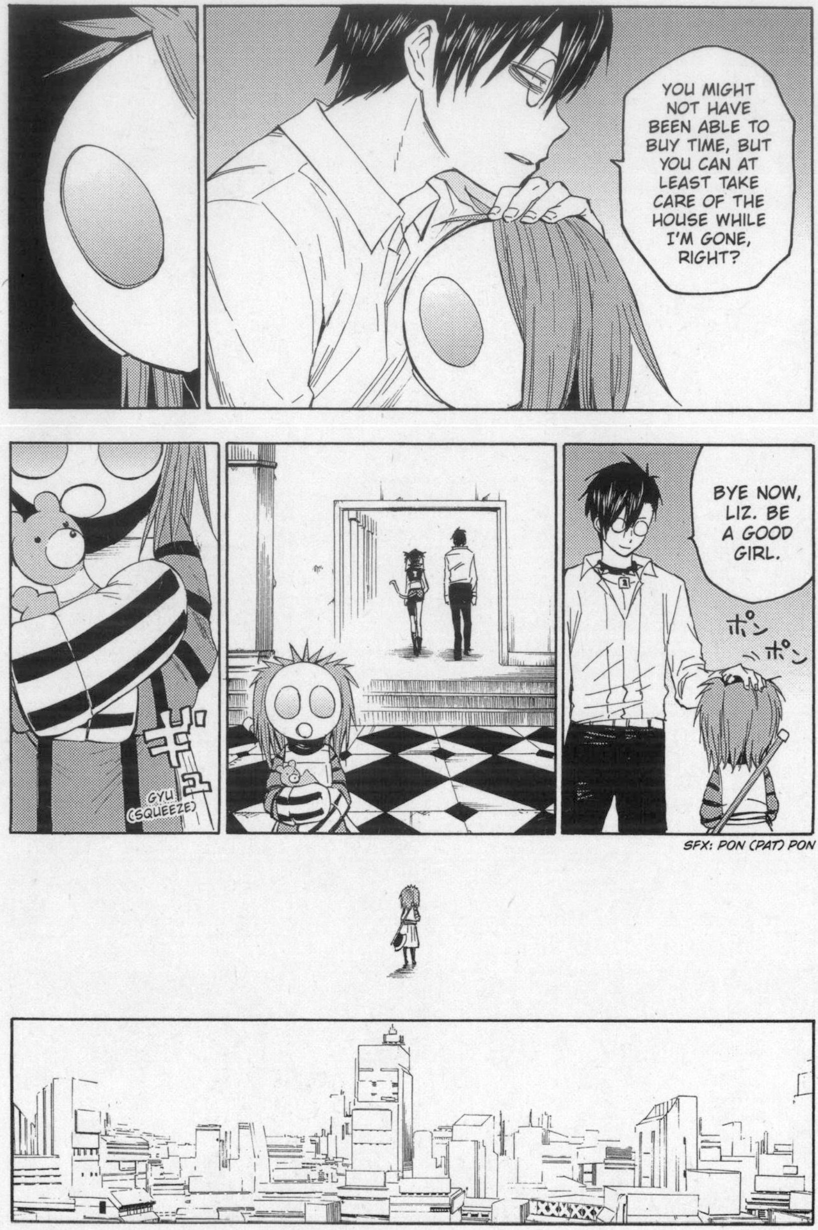
YOU MIGHT NOT HAVE BEEN ABLE TO BUY TIME, BUT YOU CAN AT LEAST TAKE CARE OF THE HOUSE WHILE I'M GONE, RIGHT?
BYE NOW, LIZ. BE A GOOD GIRL.
ポン ポン
SFX: PON (PAT) PON
ギュ
GYU (SQUEEZE)

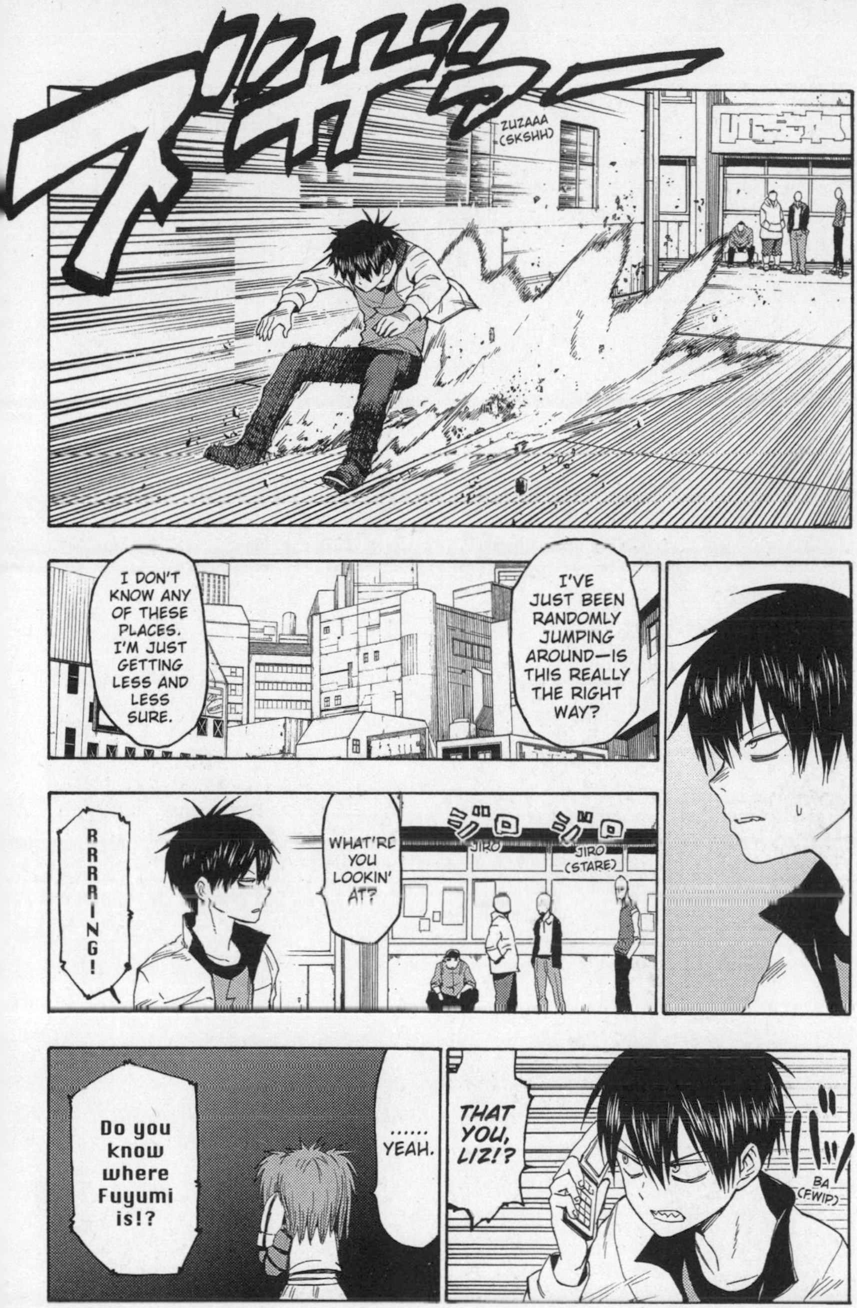
ZUZAAA
(SKSHH)
I'VE JUST BEEN RANDOMLY JUMPING AROUND—IS THIS REALLY THE RIGHT WAY?
I DON'T KNOW ANY OF THESE PLACES. I'M JUST GETTING LESS AND LESS SURE.
JIRO
JIRO
(STARE)
WHAT'RE YOU LOOKIN' AT?
RRRRING!
BA
(FWIP)
THAT YOU, LIZ!?
...... YEAH.
Do you know where Fuyumi is!?

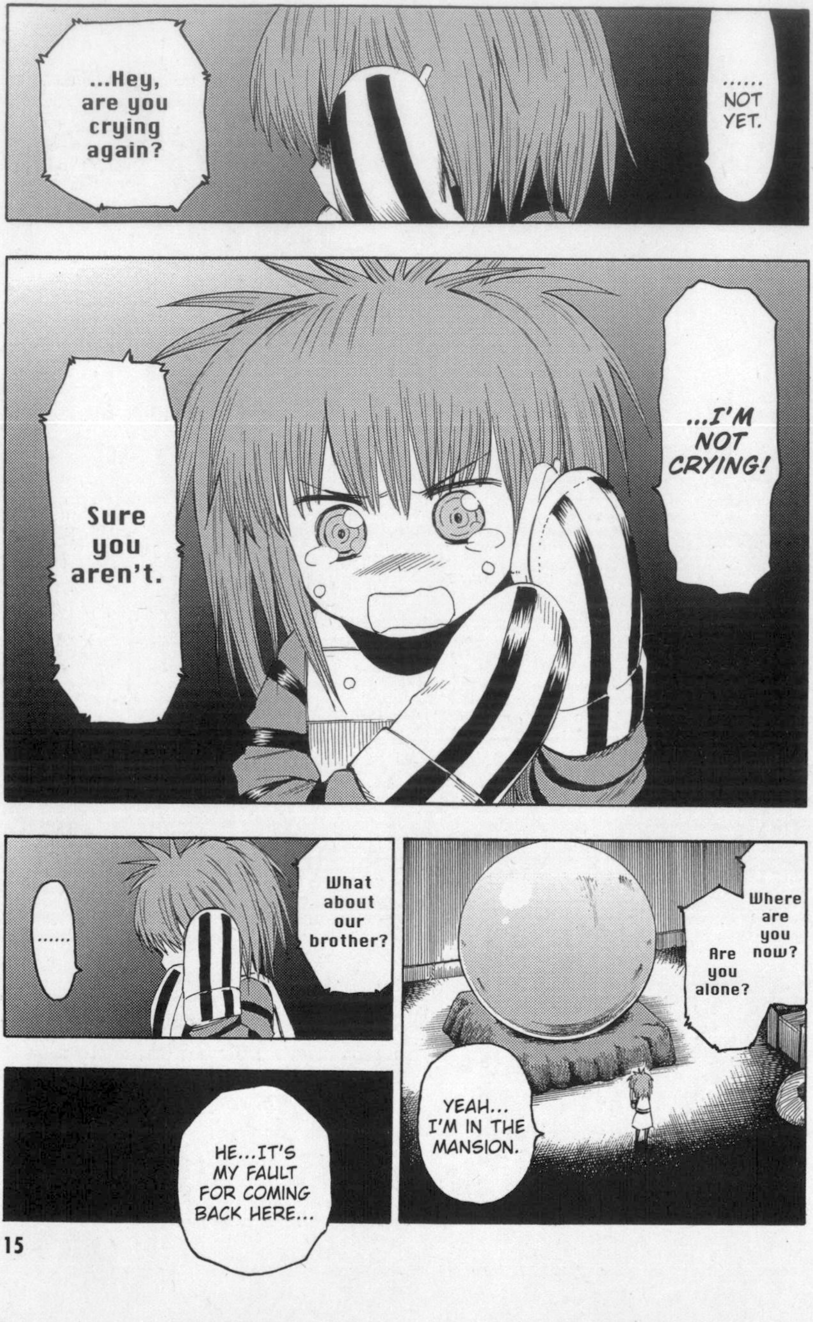

...... NOT YET.
...Hey, are you crying again?
...I'M NOT CRYING!
Sure you aren't.
Where are you now?
Are you alone?
YEAH... I'M IN THE MANSION.
What about our brother?
......
HE...IT'S MY FAULT FOR COMING BACK HERE...

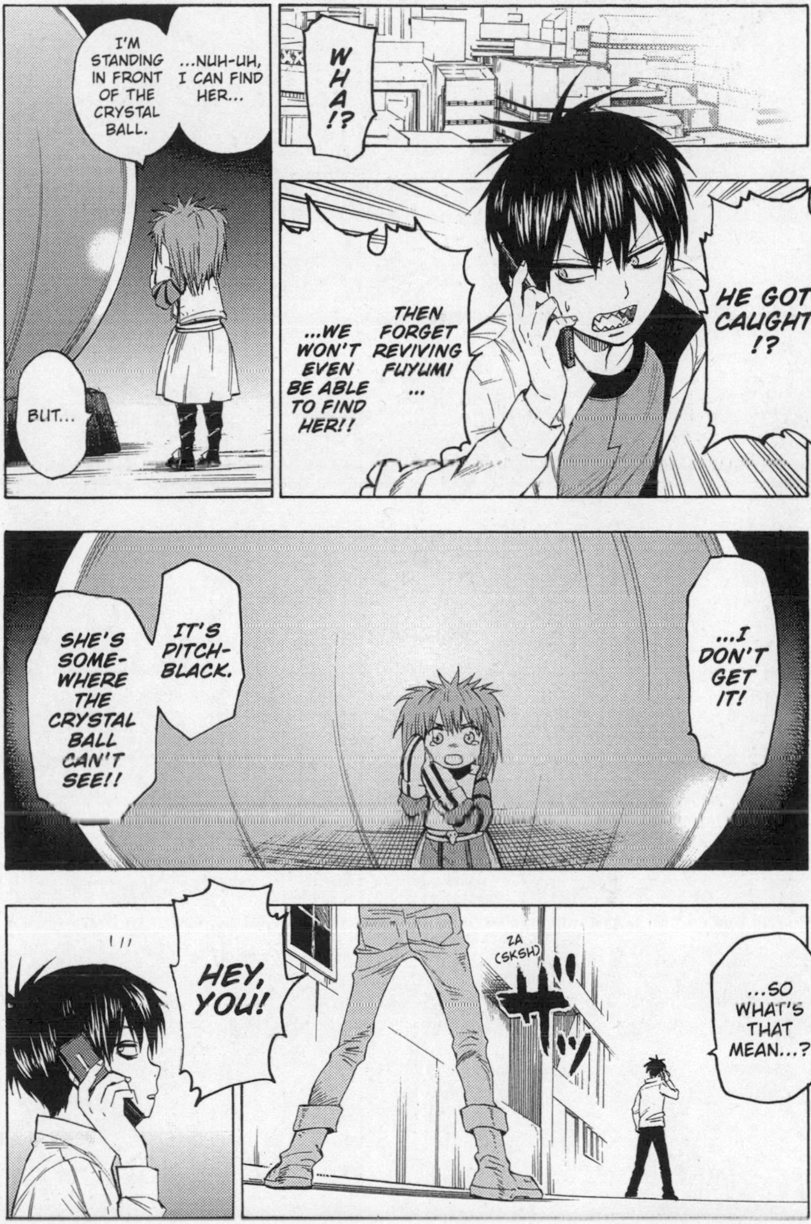
WHA!?
HE GOT CAUGHT!?
THEN FORGET REVIVING FUYUMI...
...WE WON'T EVEN BE ABLE TO FIND HER!!
...NUH-UH, I CAN FIND HER...
I'M STANDING IN FRONT OF THE CRYSTAL BALL.
BUT...
...I DON'T GET IT!
IT'S PITCH-BLACK.
SHE'S SOMEWHERE THE CRYSTAL BALL CAN'T SEE!!
...SO WHAT'S THAT MEAN...?
ZA (SKSH)
HEY, YOU!

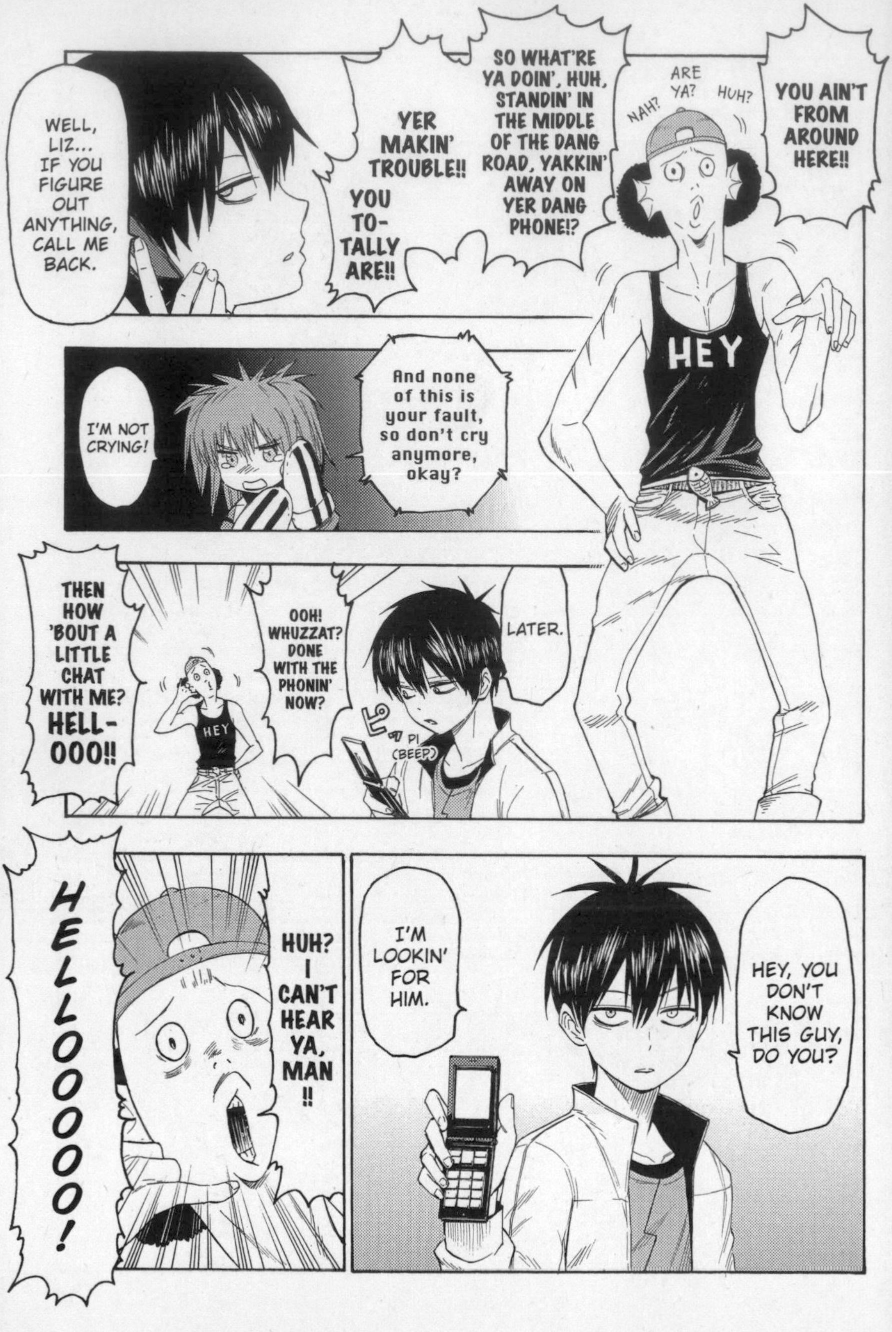
YOU AIN'T FROM AROUND HERE!!
NAH?
ARE YA?
HUH?
SO WHAT'RE YA DOIN', HUH, STANDIN' IN THE MIDDLE OF THE DANG ROAD, YAKKIN' AWAY ON YER DANG PHONE!?
YER MAKIN' TROUBLE!!
YOU TO-TALLY ARE!!
WELL, LIZ... IF YOU FIGURE OUT ANYTHING, CALL ME BACK.
And none of this is your fault, so don't cry anymore, okay?
I'M NOT CRYING!
LATER.
PI (BEEP)
OOH! WHUZZAT? DONE WITH THE PHONIN' NOW?
THEN HOW 'BOUT A LITTLE CHAT WITH ME? HELL-OOO!!
HEY
HEY
HEY, YOU DON'T KNOW THIS GUY, DO YOU?
I'M LOOKIN' FOR HIM.
HUH? I CAN'T HEAR YA, MAN!!
HELLOOOOOO!

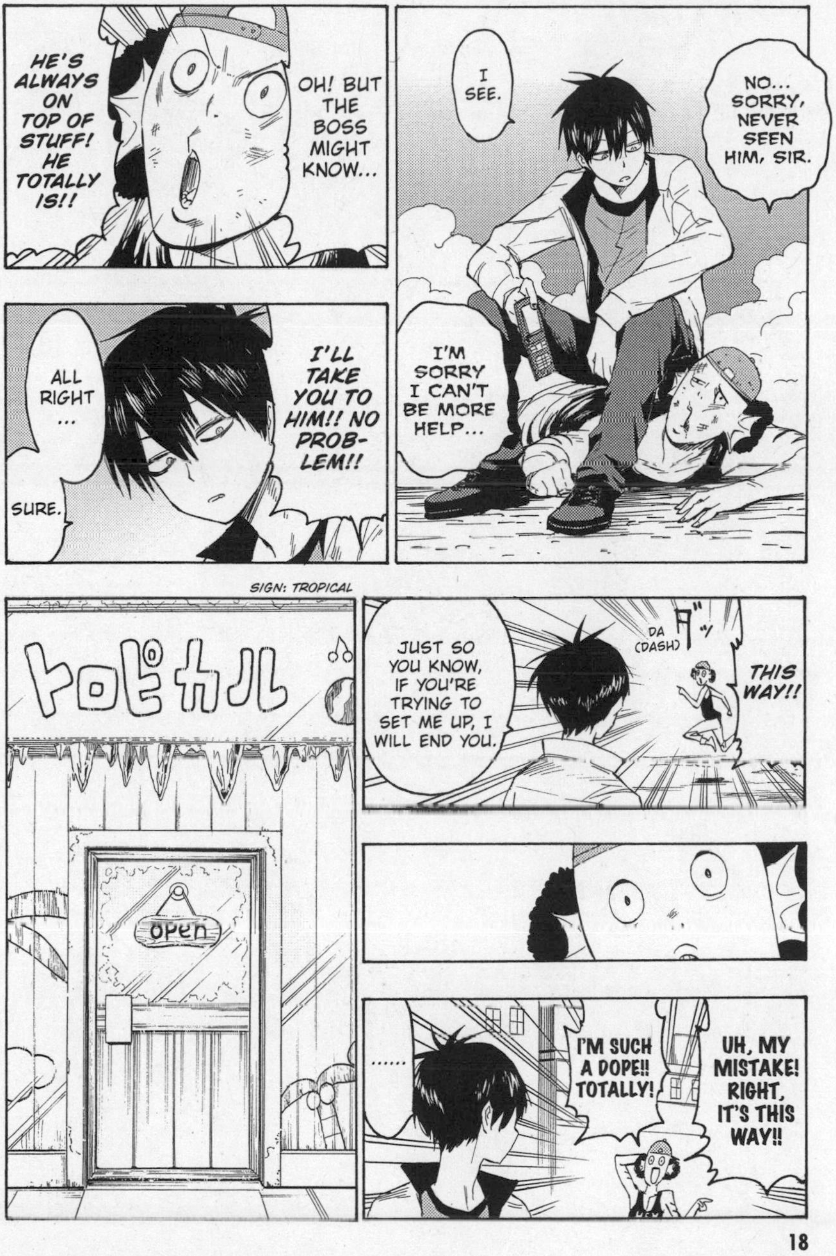
NO... SORRY, NEVER SEEN HIM, SIR.
I SEE.
I'M SORRY I CAN'T BE MORE HELP...
OH! BUT THE BOSS MIGHT KNOW...
HE'S ALWAYS ON TOP OF STUFF! HE TOTALLY IS!!
I'LL TAKE YOU TO HIM!! NO PROB-LEM!!
ALL RIGHT...
SURE.
THIS WAY!!
ダッ
DA (DASH)
JUST SO YOU KNOW, IF YOU'RE TRYING TO SET ME UP, I WILL END YOU.
UH, MY MISTAKE! RIGHT, IT'S THIS WAY!!
I'M SUCH A DOPE!! TOTALLY!
......
SIGN: TROPICAL
トロピカル
open

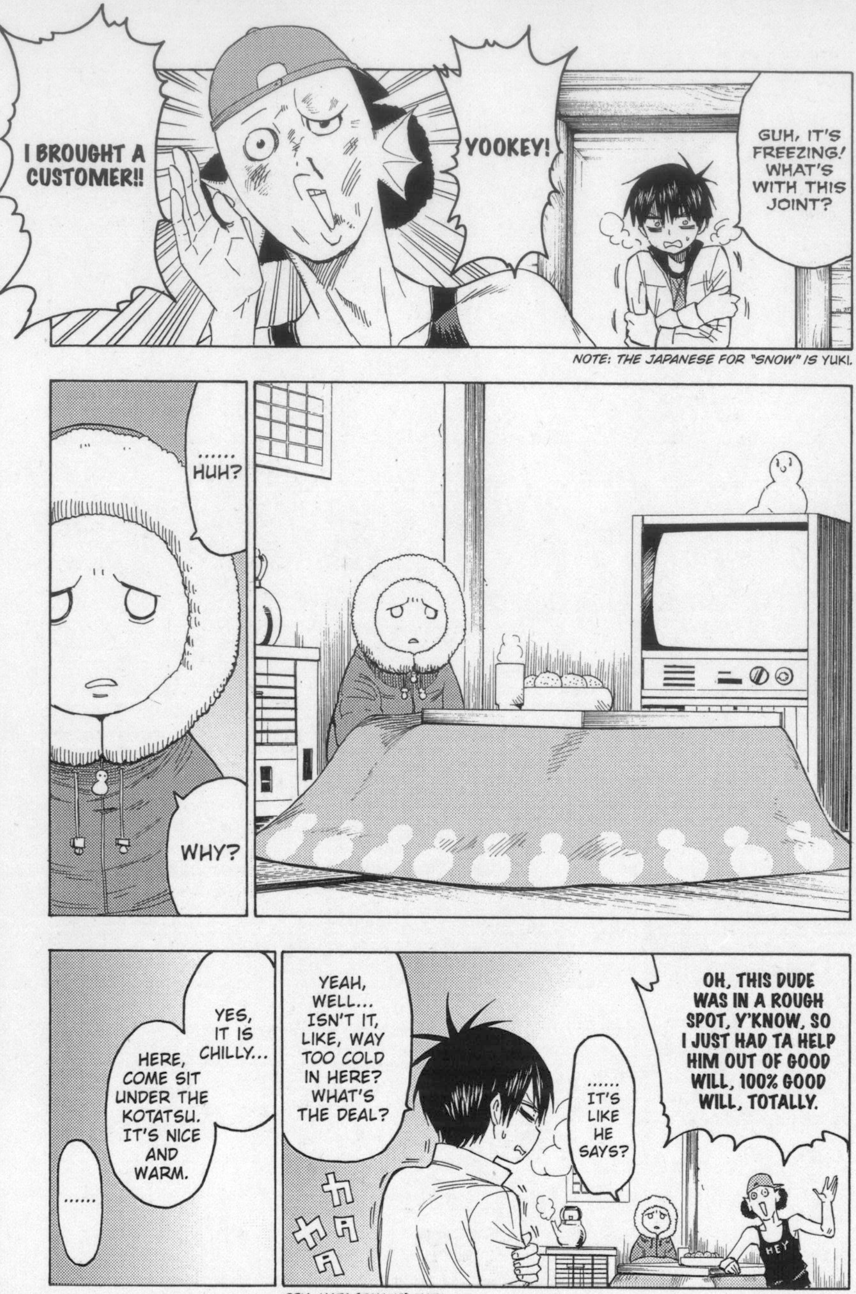
GUH, IT'S FREEZING! WHAT'S WITH THIS JOINT?
YOOKEY!
I BROUGHT A CUSTOMER!!
...... HUH?
WHY?
OH, THIS DUDE WAS IN A ROUGH SPOT, Y'KNOW, SO I JUST HAD TA HELP HIM OUT OF GOOD WILL, 100% GOOD WILL, TOTALLY.
HEY
...... IT'S LIKE HE SAYS?
YEAH, WELL... ISN'T IT, LIKE, WAY TOO COLD IN HERE? WHAT'S THE DEAL?
カタカタ
YES, IT IS CHILLY...
HERE, COME SIT UNDER THE KOTATSU. IT'S NICE AND WARM.
......

NOTE: THE JAPANESE FOR "SNOW" IS *YUKI*.

SFX: KATA (SHAKE) KATA

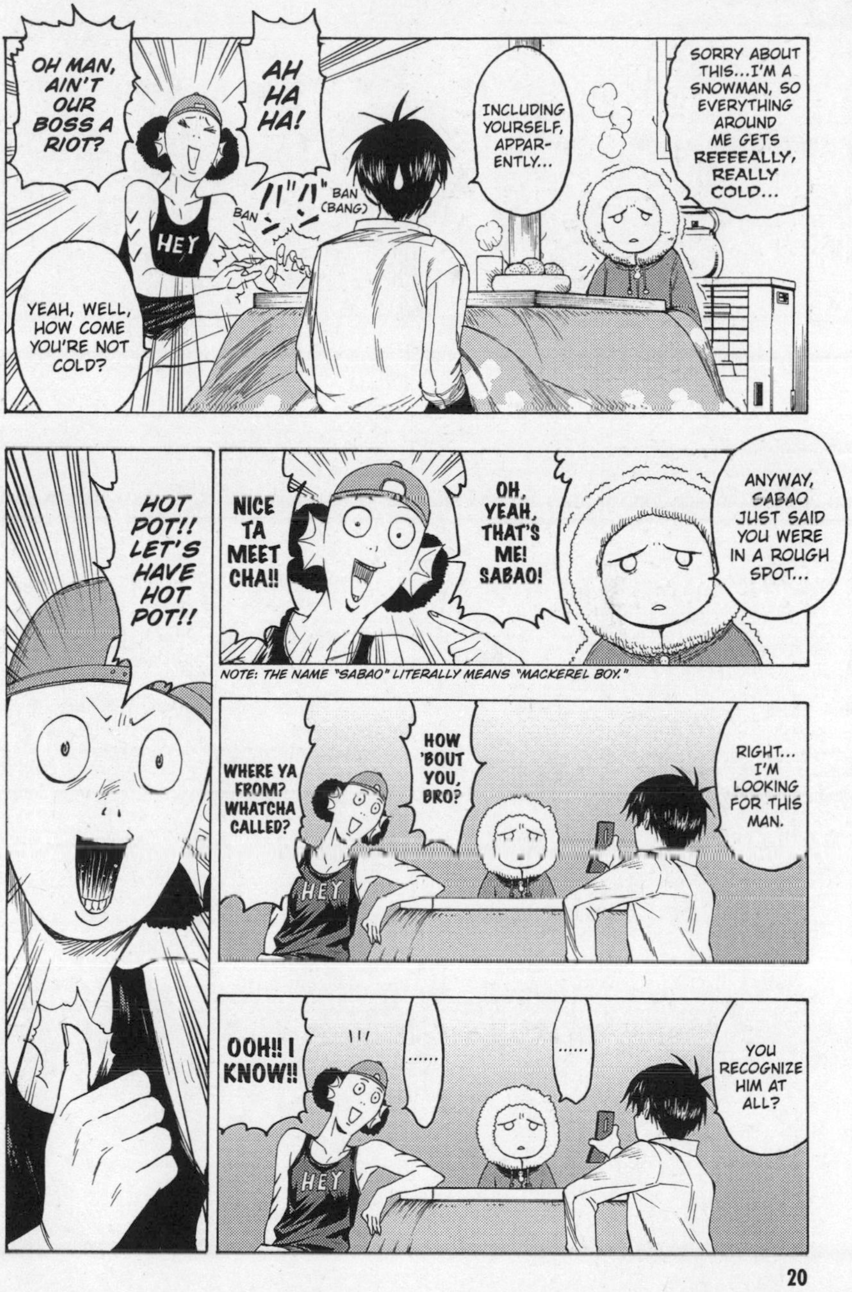
SORRY ABOUT THIS...I'M A SNOWMAN, SO EVERYTHING AROUND ME GETS REEEEALLY, REALLY COLD...
INCLUDING YOURSELF, APPARENTLY...
AH HA HA!
OH MAN, AIN'T OUR BOSS A RIOT?
BAN (BANG)
BAN
YEAH, WELL, HOW COME YOU'RE NOT COLD?
ANYWAY, SABAO JUST SAID YOU WERE IN A ROUGH SPOT...
OH, YEAH, THAT'S ME! SABAO!
NICE TA MEET CHA!!
RIGHT... I'M LOOKING FOR THIS MAN.
HOW 'BOUT YOU, BRO?
WHERE YA FROM? WHATCHA CALLED?
YOU RECOGNIZE HIM AT ALL?
......
......
OOH!! I KNOW!!
HOT POT!! LET'S HAVE HOT POT!!

NOTE: THE NAME "SABAO" LITERALLY MEANS "MACKEREL BOY."

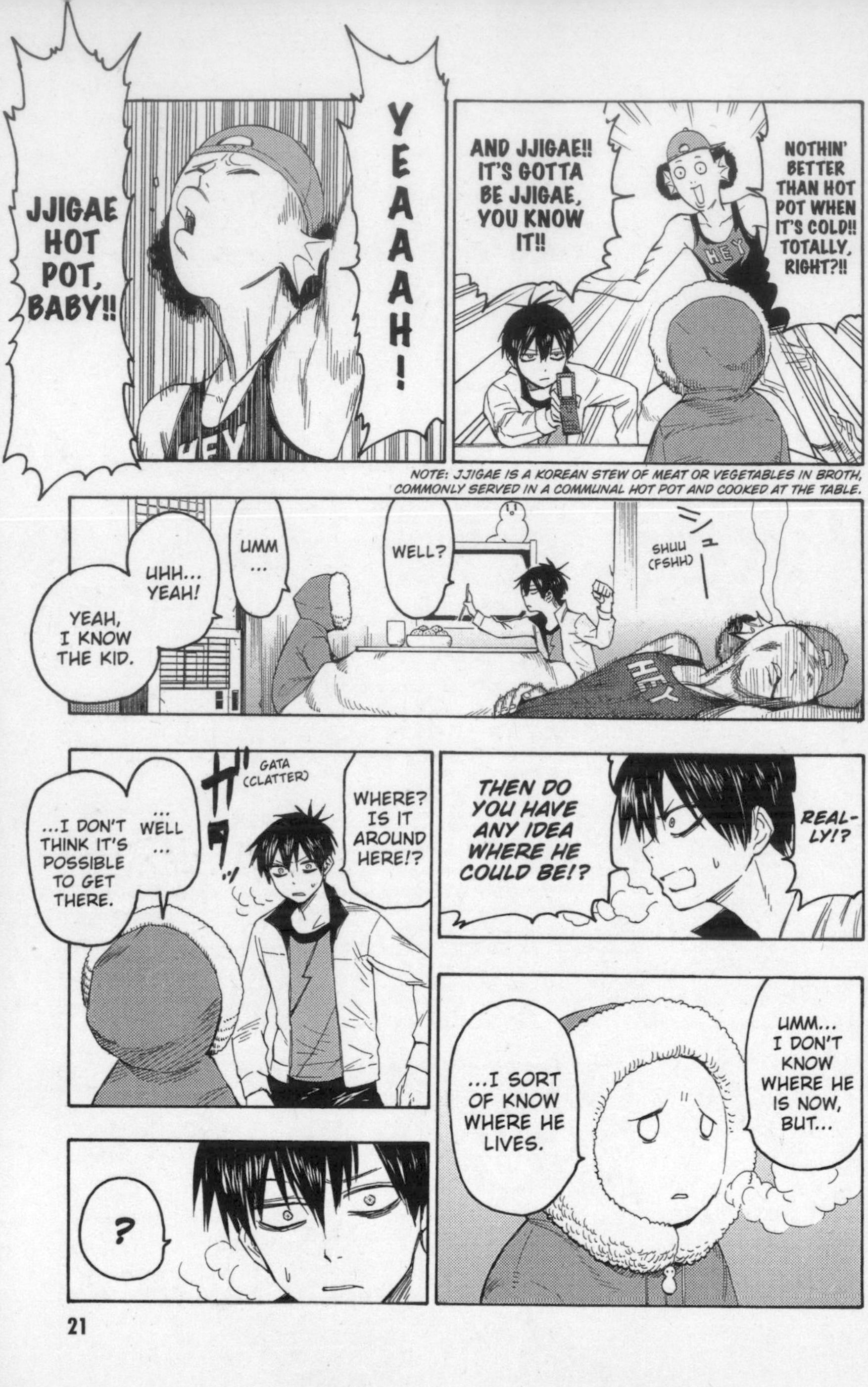
NOTHIN' BETTER THAN HOT POT WHEN IT'S COLD!! TOTALLY, RIGHT?!!
AND JJIGAE!! IT'S GOTTA BE JJIGAE, YOU KNOW IT!!
YEAAAAH!
JJIGAE HOT POT, BABY!!
HEY
NOTE: JJIGAE IS A KOREAN STEW OF MEAT OR VEGETABLES IN BROTH, COMMONLY SERVED IN A COMMUNAL HOT POT AND COOKED AT THE TABLE.
SHUU (FSHH)
HEY
WELL?
UMM ...
UHH... YEAH!
YEAH, I KNOW THE KID.
REAL-LY!?
THEN DO YOU HAVE ANY IDEA WHERE HE COULD BE!?
WHERE? IS IT AROUND HERE!?
GATA (CLATTER)
... WELL ...
...I DON'T THINK IT'S POSSIBLE TO GET THERE.
UMM... I DON'T KNOW WHERE HE IS NOW, BUT...
...I SORT OF KNOW WHERE HE LIVES.
?

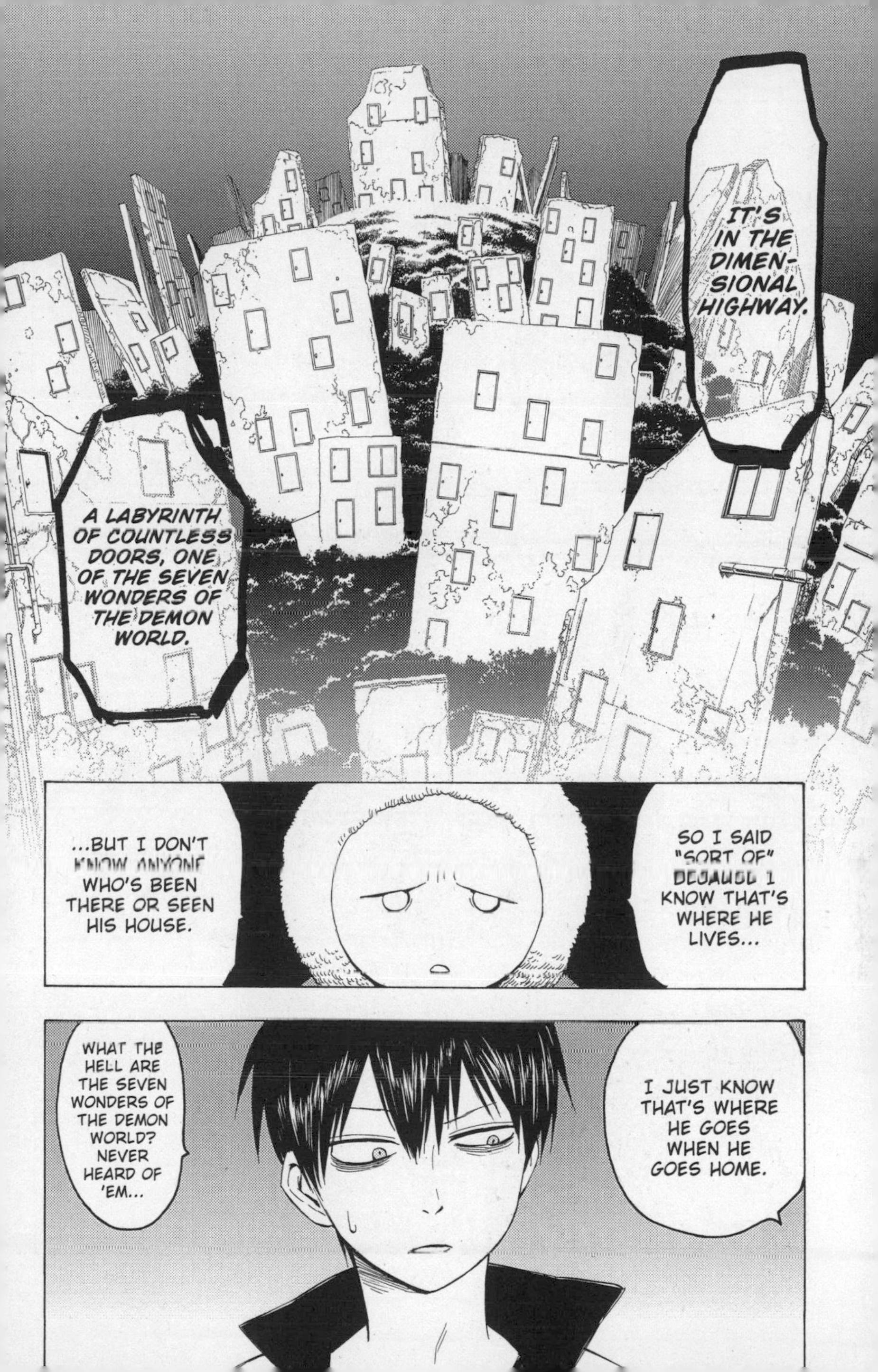
IT'S IN THE DIMENSIONAL HIGHWAY.
A LABYRINTH OF COUNTLESS DOORS, ONE OF THE SEVEN WONDERS OF THE DEMON WORLD.
SO I SAID "SORT OF" BECAUSE I KNOW THAT'S WHERE HE LIVES...
...BUT I DON'T KNOW ANYONE WHO'S BEEN THERE OR SEEN HIS HOUSE.
I JUST KNOW THAT'S WHERE HE GOES WHEN HE GOES HOME.
WHAT THE HELL ARE THE SEVEN WONDERS OF THE DEMON WORLD? NEVER HEARD OF 'EM...

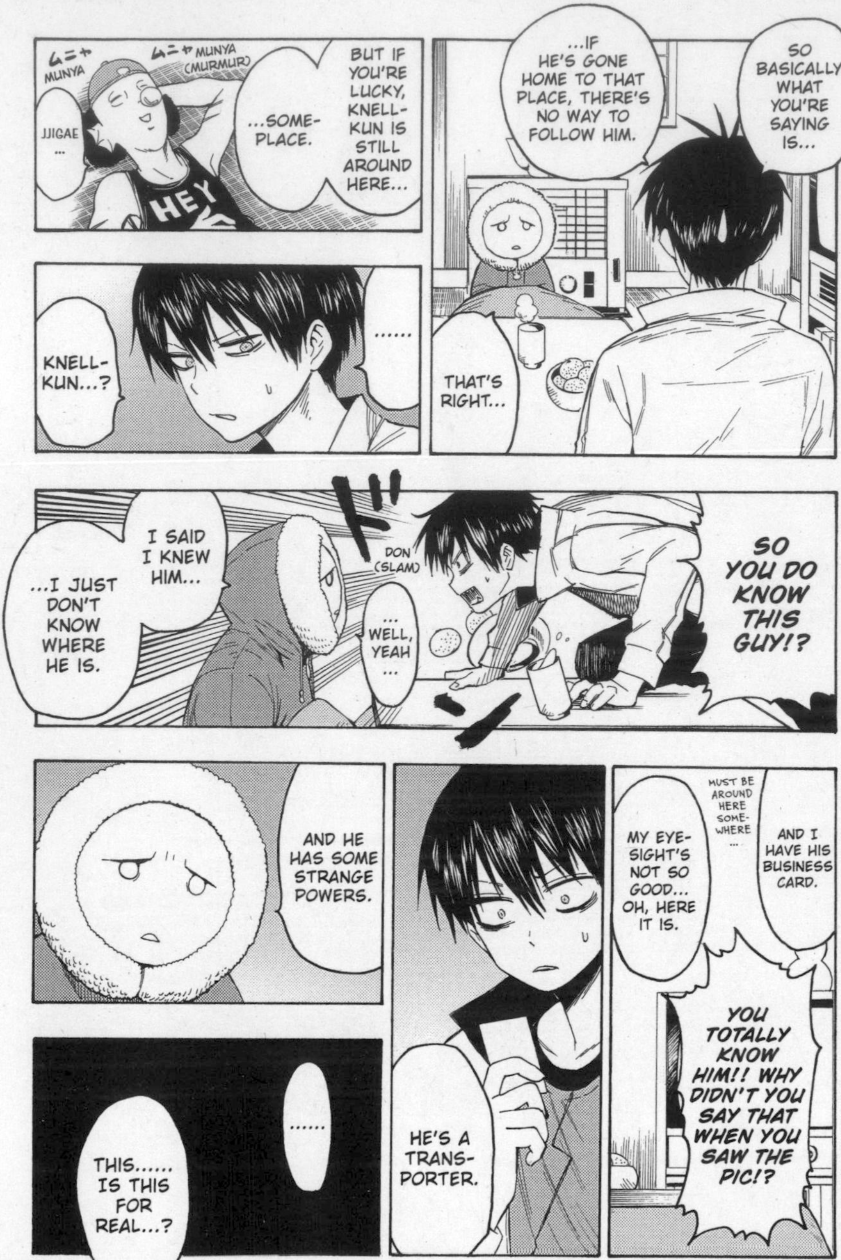
SO BASICALLY WHAT YOU'RE SAYING IS...
...IF HE'S GONE HOME TO THAT PLACE, THERE'S NO WAY TO FOLLOW HIM.
THAT'S RIGHT...
BUT IF YOU'RE LUCKY, KNELL-KUN IS STILL AROUND HERE...
...SOME-PLACE.
ムニャ MUNYA (MURMUR)
ムニャ MUNYA
JJIGAE...
......
KNELL-KUN...?
SO YOU DO KNOW THIS GUY!?
DON (SLAM)
...WELL, YEAH...
I SAID I KNEW HIM...
...I JUST DON'T KNOW WHERE HE IS.
AND I HAVE HIS BUSINESS CARD.
MUST BE AROUND HERE SOME-WHERE...
MY EYE-SIGHT'S NOT SO GOOD... OH, HERE IT IS.
YOU TOTALLY KNOW HIM!! WHY DIDN'T YOU SAY THAT WHEN YOU SAW THE PIC!?
HE'S A TRANS-PORTER.
AND HE HAS SOME STRANGE POWERS.
......
THIS...... IS THIS FOR REAL...?

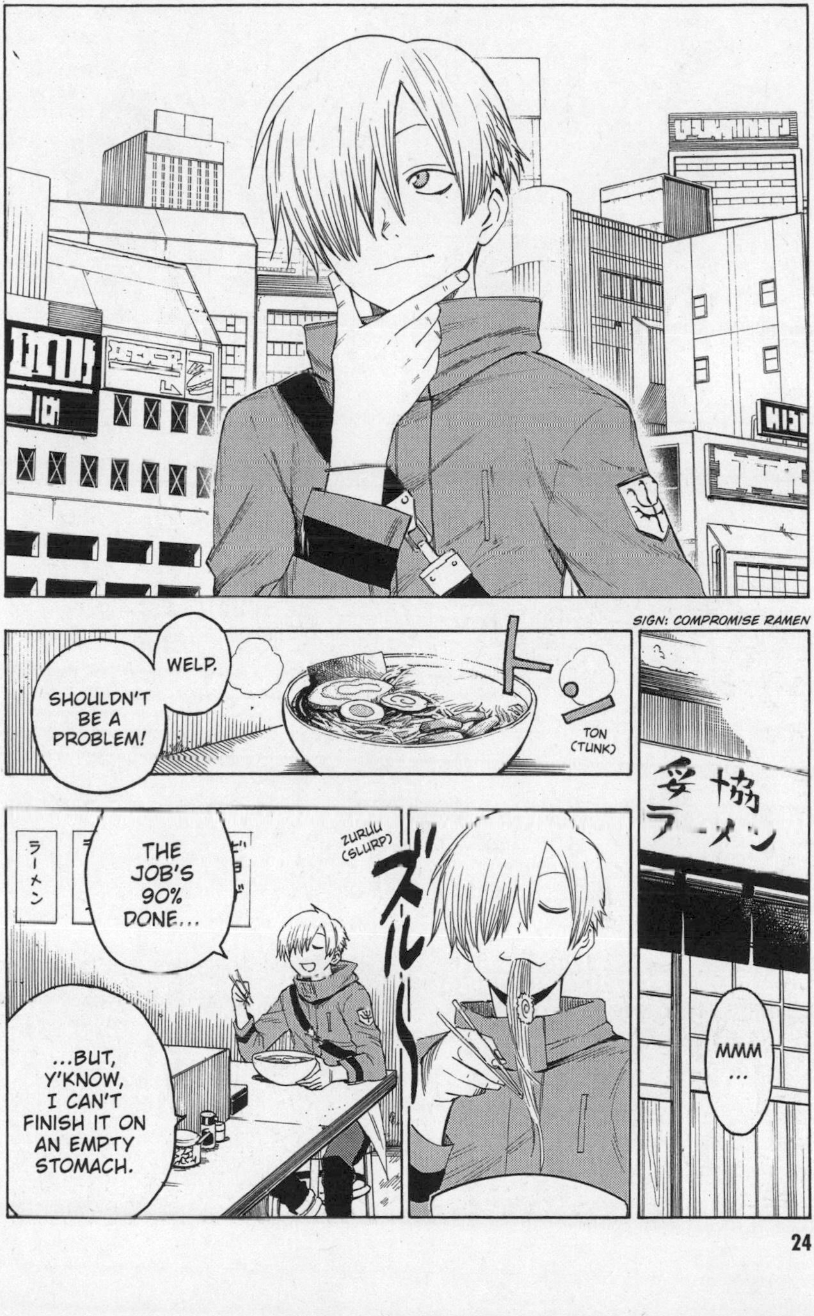
SIGN: COMPROMISE RAMEN
妥協ラーメン
MMM…
WELP.
SHOULDN'T BE A PROBLEM!
TON (TUNK)
ZURUU (SLURP)
ズルー
THE JOB'S 90% DONE…
…BUT, Y'KNOW, I CAN'T FINISH IT ON AN EMPTY STOMACH.
ラーメン

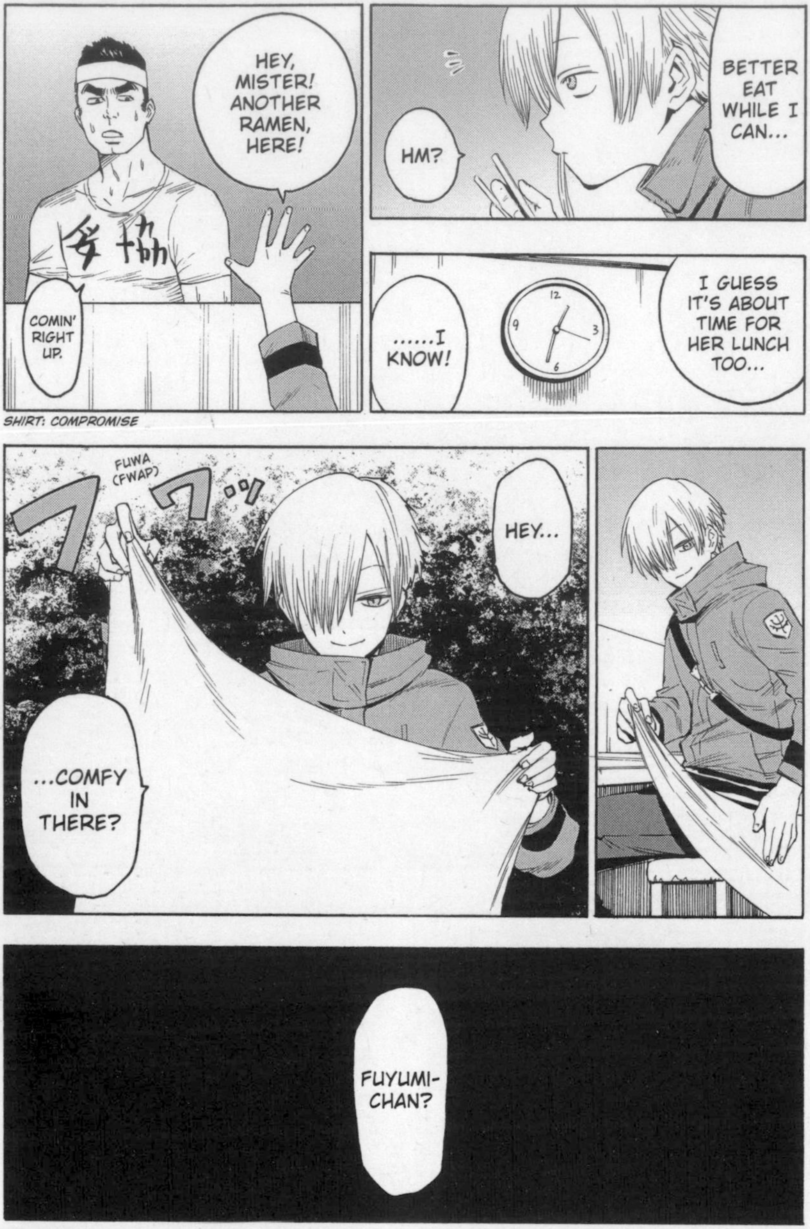
BETTER EAT WHILE I CAN...
HM?
I GUESS IT'S ABOUT TIME FOR HER LUNCH TOO...
......I KNOW!
HEY, MISTER! ANOTHER RAMEN, HERE!
妥協
COMIN' RIGHT UP.
HEY...
フワッ
FUWA (FWAP)
...COMFY IN THERE?
FUYUMI-CHAN?
SHIRT: COMPROMISE

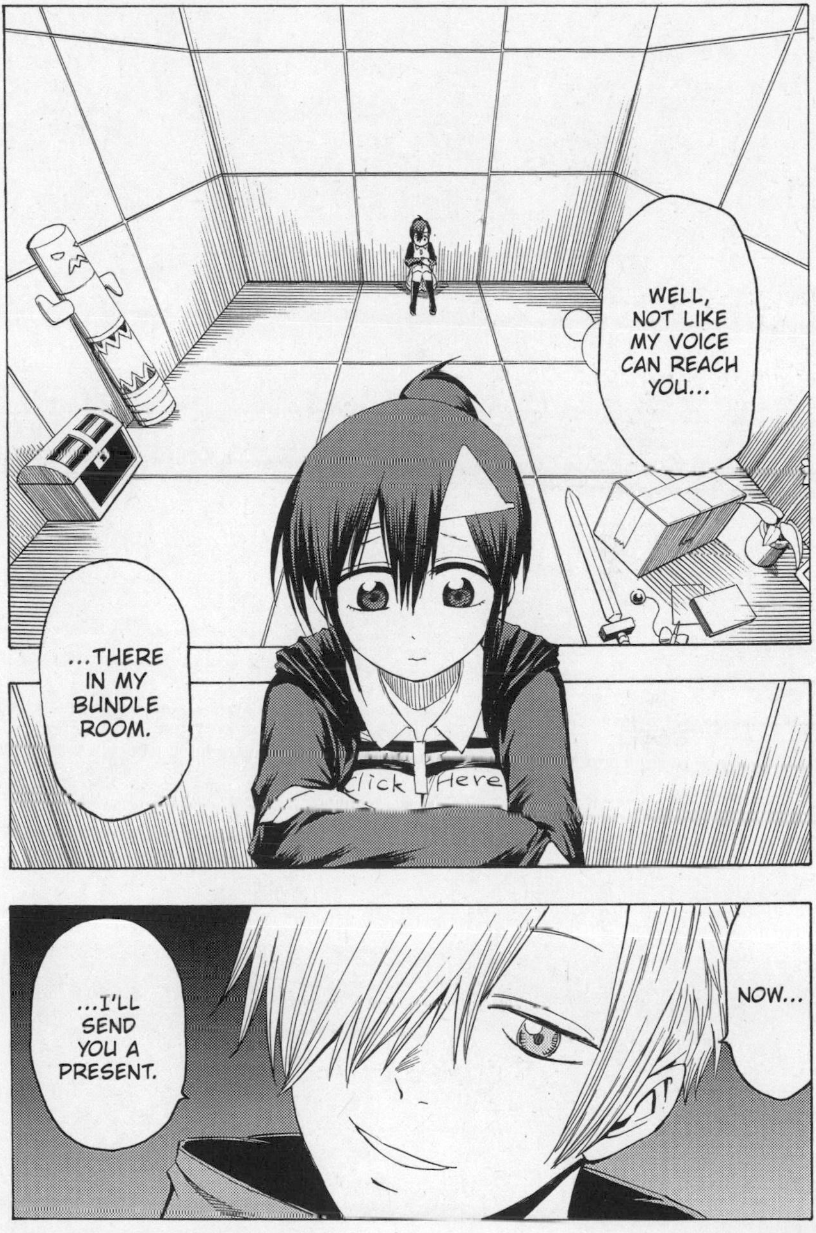
WELL, NOT LIKE MY VOICE CAN REACH YOU...
...THERE IN MY BUNDLE ROOM.
Click Here
NOW...
...I'LL SEND YOU A PRESENT.

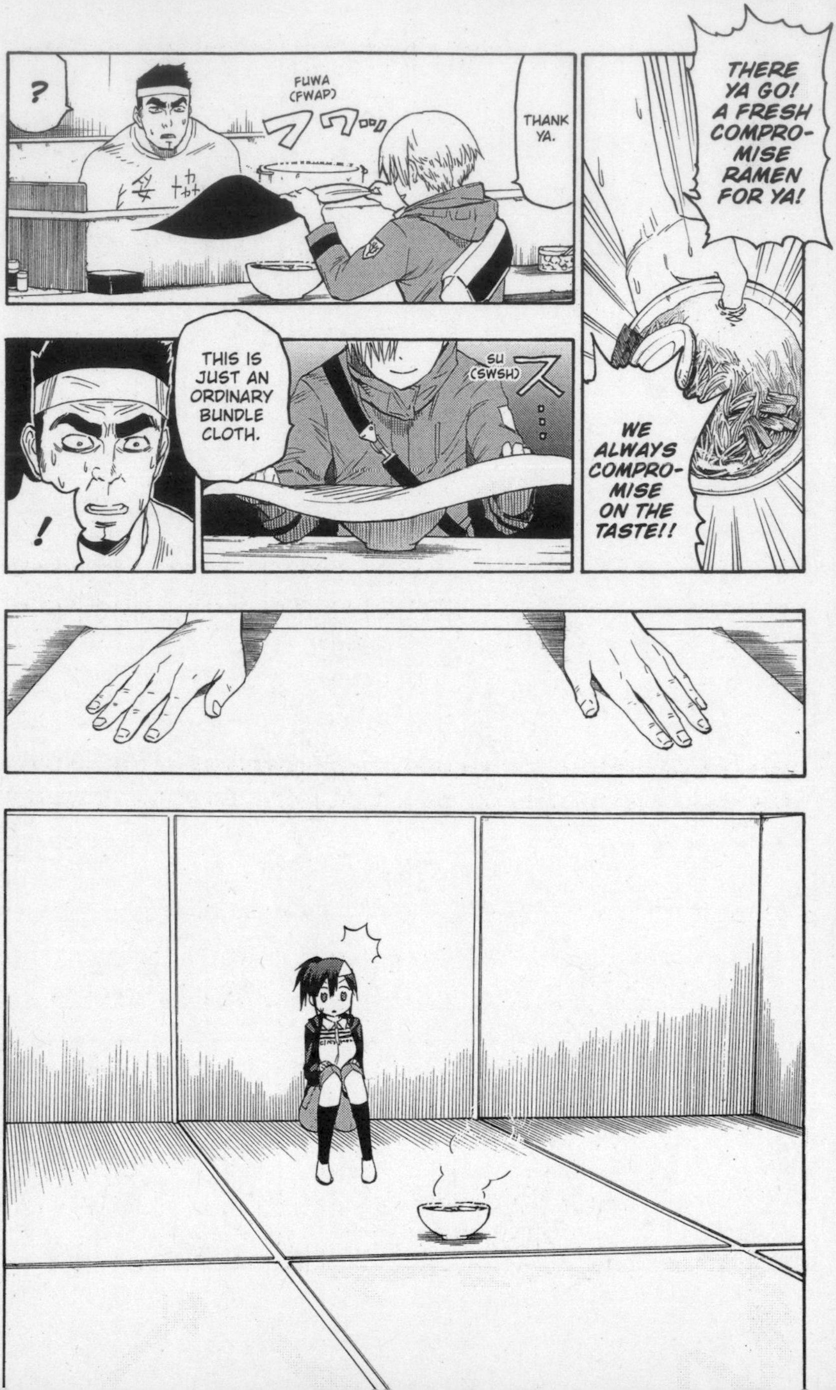
THERE YA GO! A FRESH COMPRO-MISE RAMEN FOR YA!
WE ALWAYS COMPRO-MISE ON THE TASTE!!
THANK YA.
FUWA (FWAP)
フワッ
?
SU (SWSH)
ス
...
THIS IS JUST AN ORDINARY BUNDLE CLOTH.
!

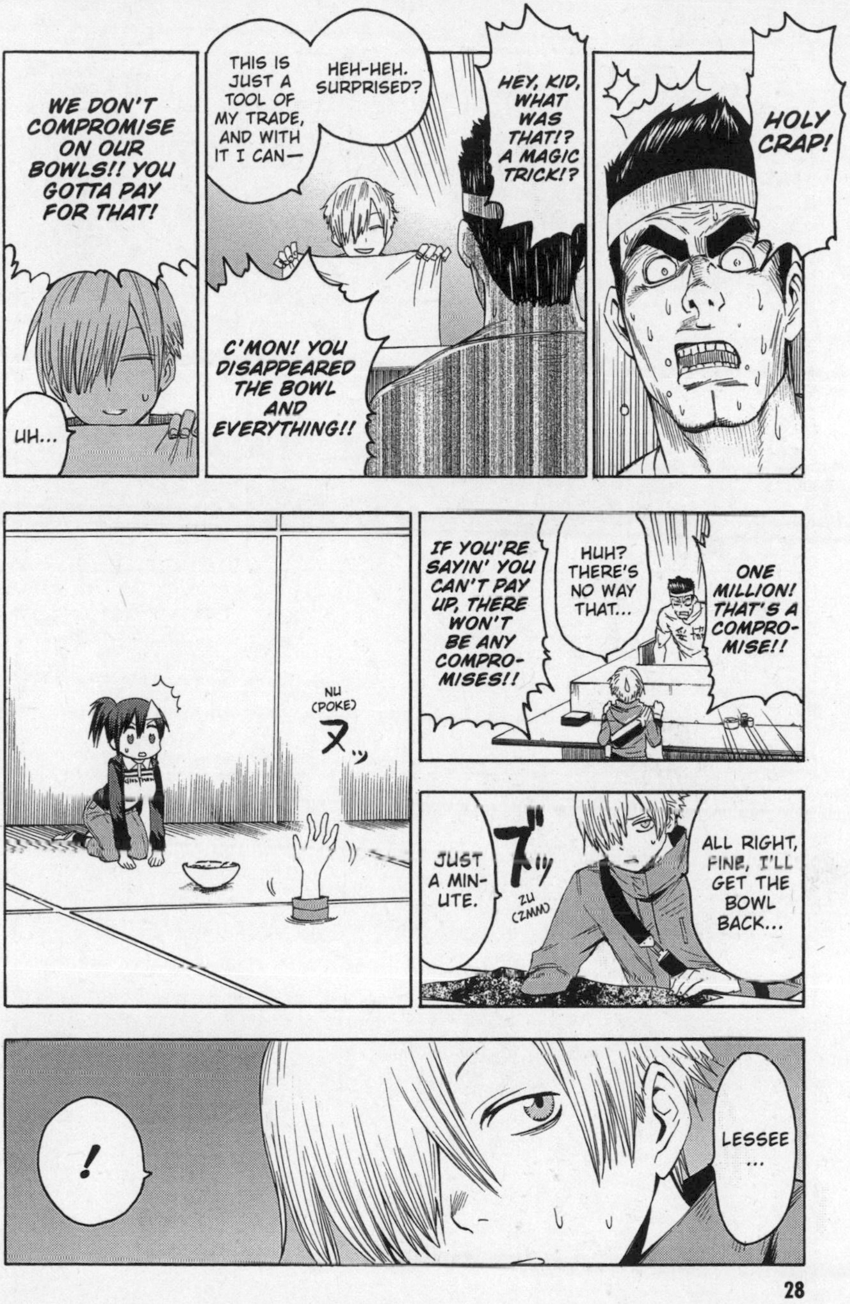
HOLY CRAP!
HEY, KID, WHAT WAS THAT!? A MAGIC TRICK!?
HEH-HEH. SURPRISED?
THIS IS JUST A TOOL OF MY TRADE, AND WITH IT I CAN—
C'MON! YOU DISAPPEARED THE BOWL AND EVERYTHING!!
WE DON'T COMPROMISE ON OUR BOWLS!! YOU GOTTA PAY FOR THAT!
UH...
ONE MILLION! THAT'S A COMPRO-MISE!!
HUH? THERE'S NO WAY THAT...
IF YOU'RE SAYIN' YOU CAN'T PAY UP, THERE WON'T BE ANY COMPRO-MISES!!
ALL RIGHT, FINE, I'LL GET THE BOWL BACK...
ズッ
ZU (ZMMM)
JUST A MIN-UTE.
NU (POKE)
ヌッ
LESSEE ...
!

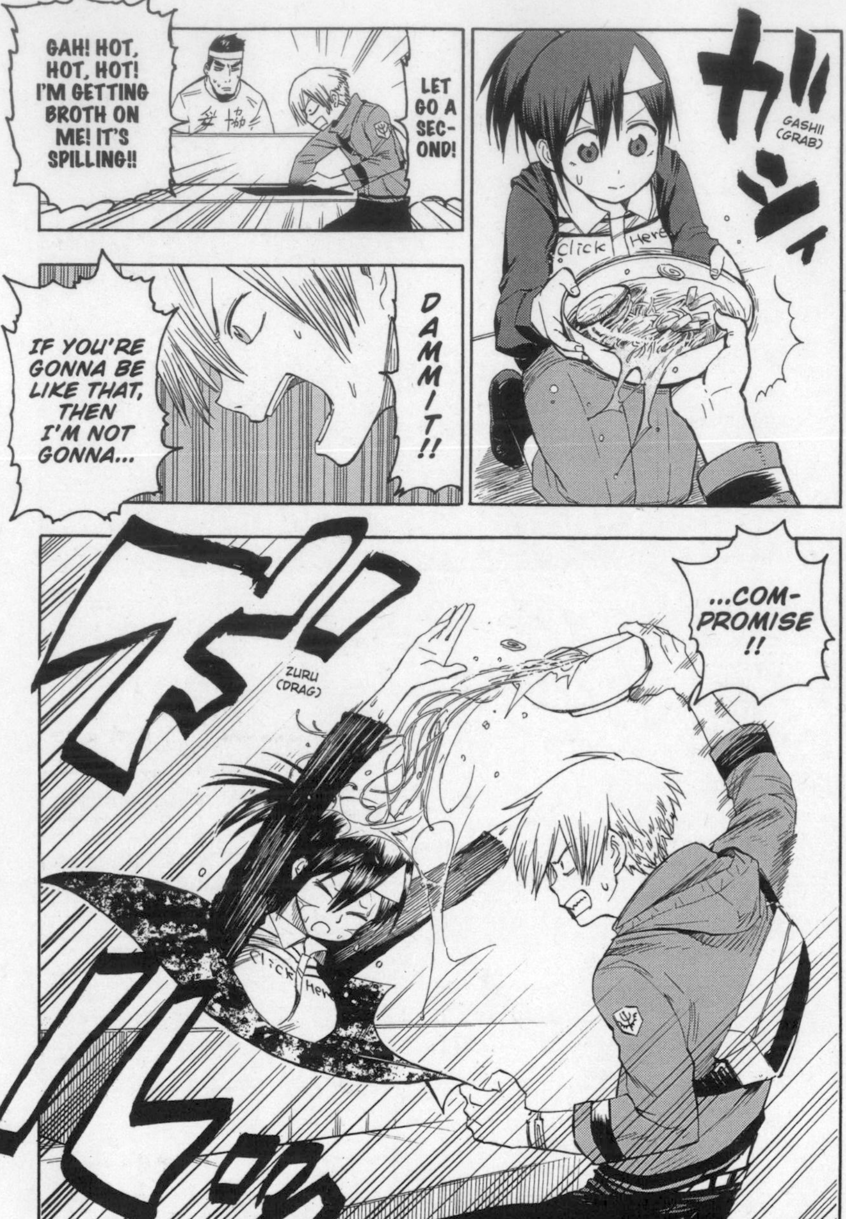
GASHII (GRAB)
LET GO A SEC-OND!
GAH! HOT, HOT, HOT! I'M GETTING BROTH ON ME! IT'S SPILLING!!
DAMMIT!!
IF YOU'RE GONNA BE LIKE THAT, THEN I'M NOT GONNA...
...COM-PROMISE!!
ZURU (DRAG)

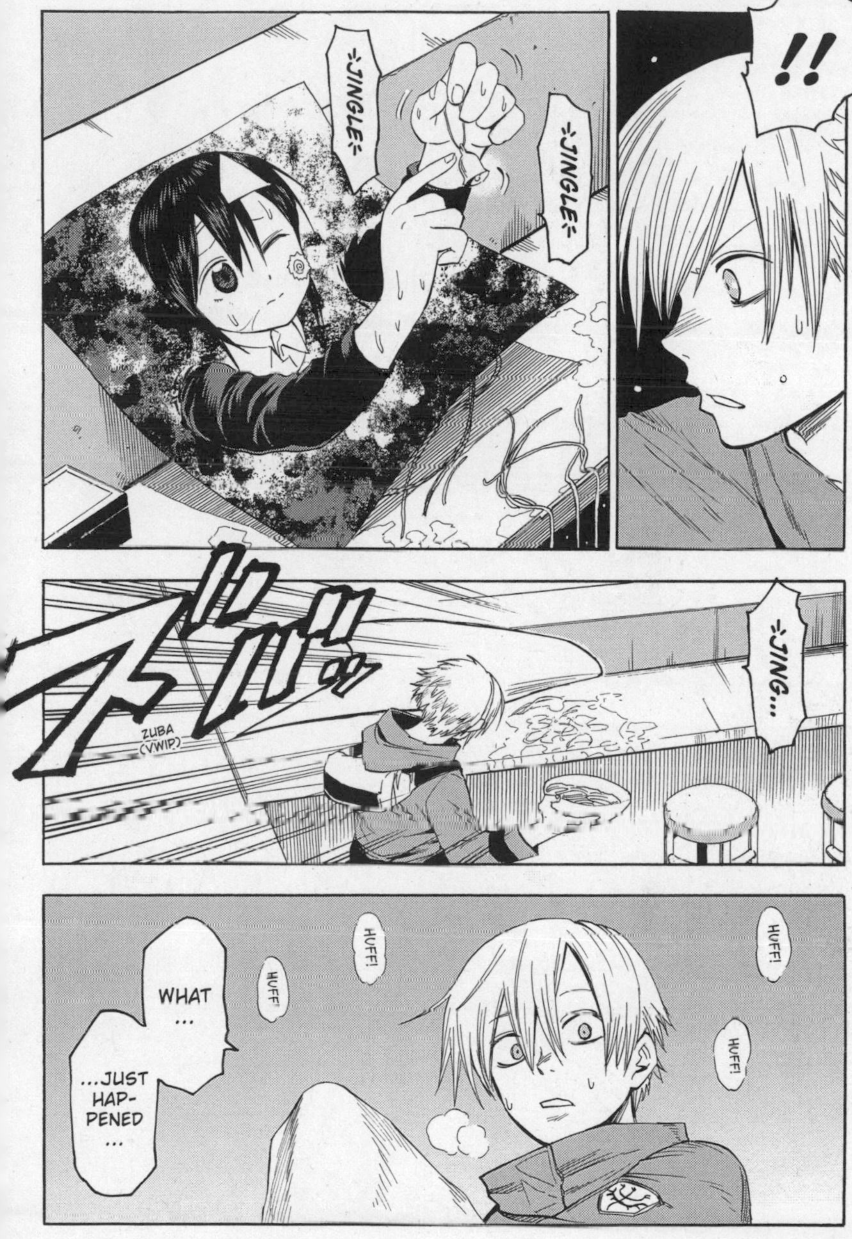
!!
JINGLE
JINGLE
JING...
ZUBA (VWIP)
HUFF!
HUFF!
HUFF!
HUFF!
WHAT ...
...JUST HAP-PENED ...

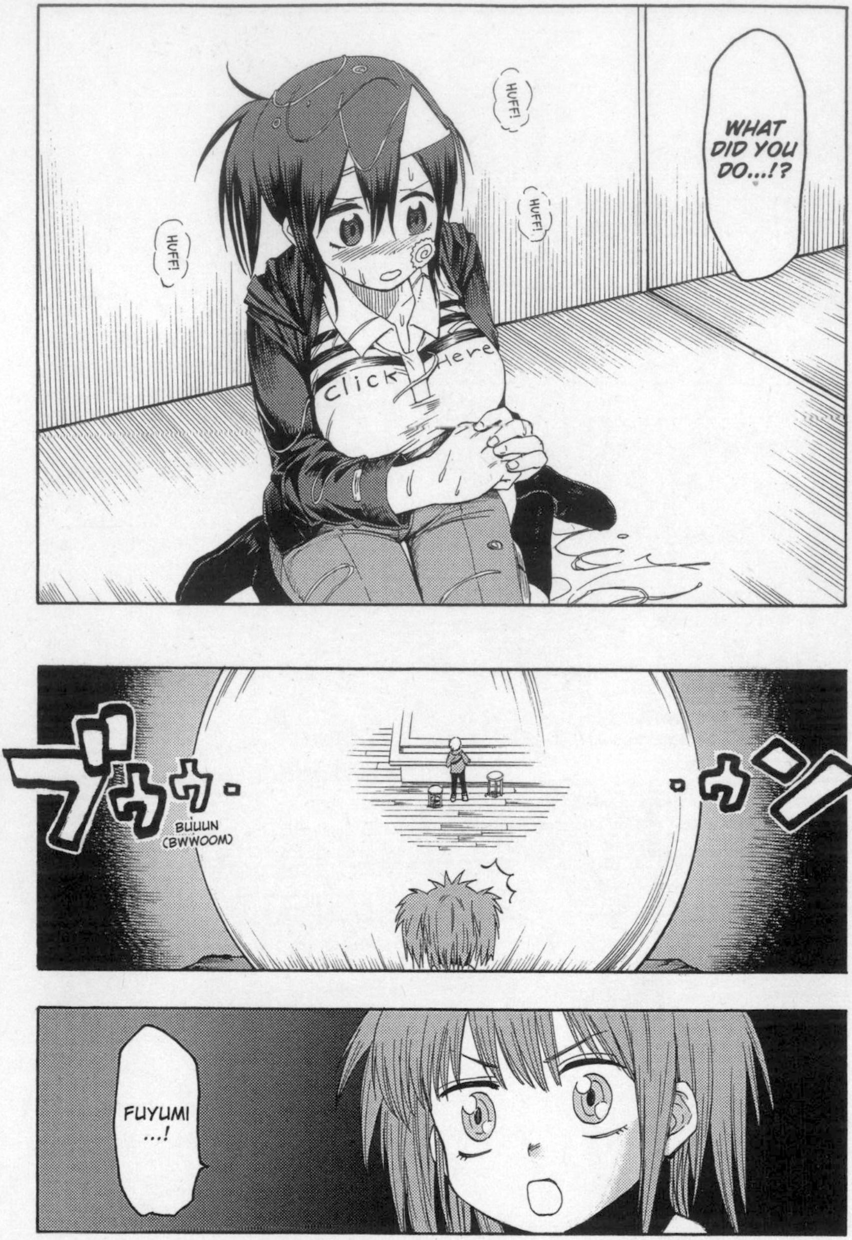
WHAT DID YOU DO...!?
HUFF!
HUFF!
HUFF!
ブゥゥ・・ゥン
BUUUN (BWWOOM)
FUYUMI ...!

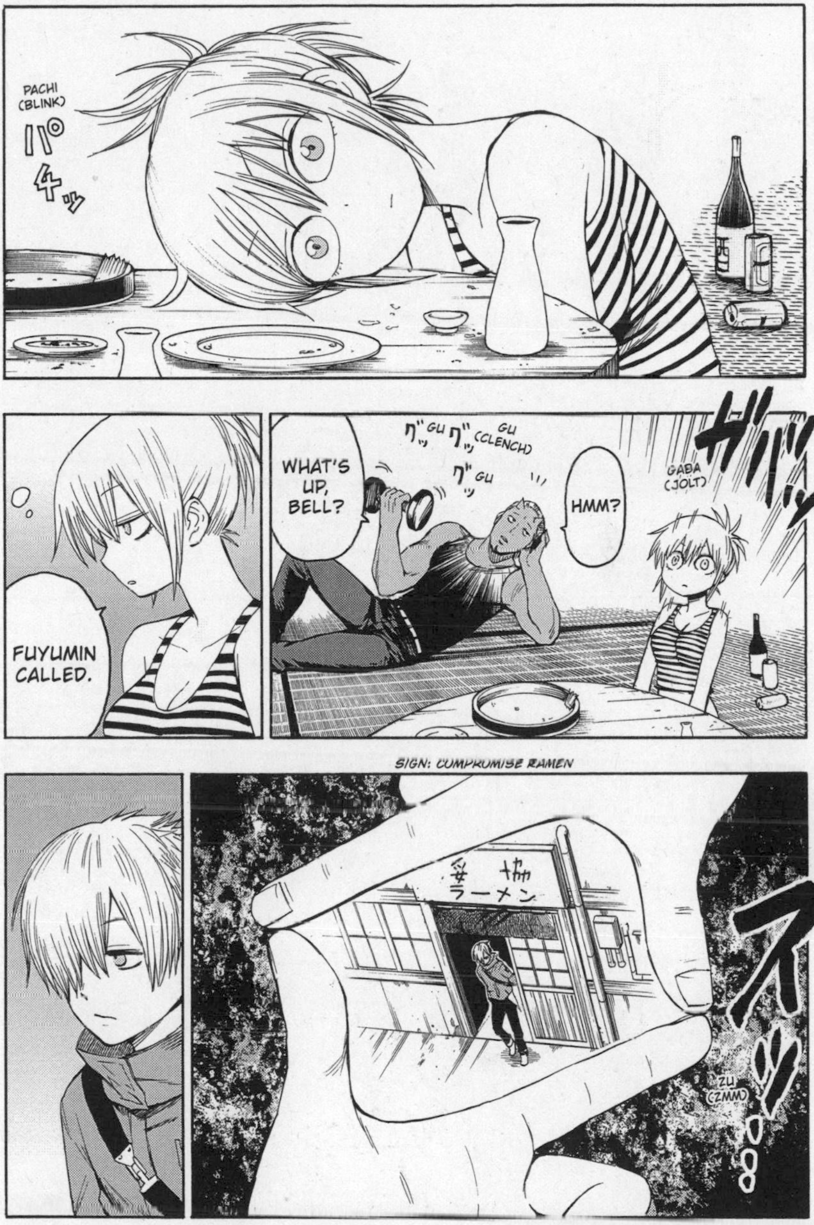
PACHI (BLINK)
パチッ
ザバッ
GABA (JOLT)
HMM?
グッ グッ グッ
GU GU GU (CLENCH)
WHAT'S UP, BELL?
FUYUMIN CALLED.
SIGN: COMPROMISE RAMEN
妥協ラーメン
ズッ
ZU (ZMM)

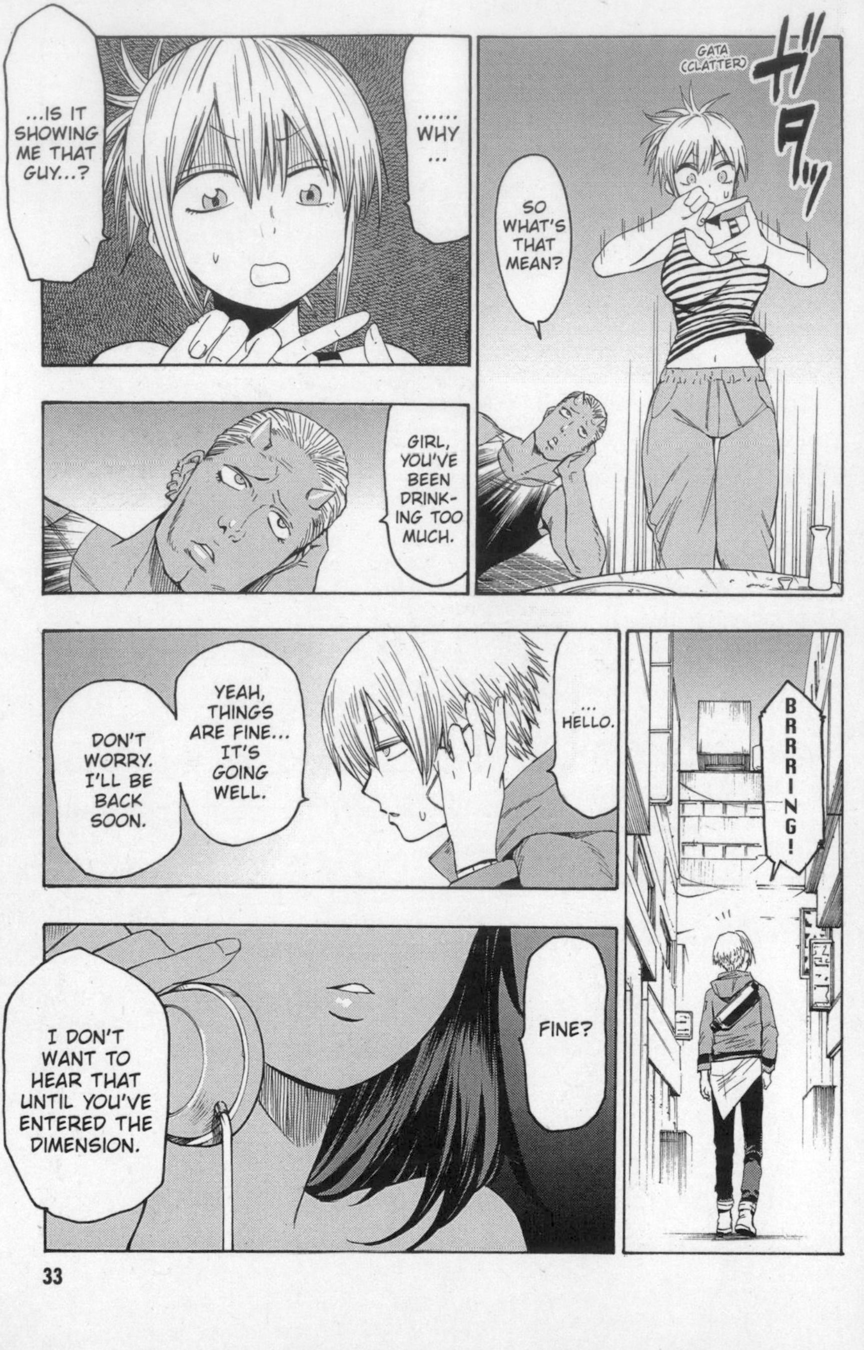
GATA (CLATTER)
SO WHAT'S THAT MEAN?
......WHY...
...IS IT SHOWING ME THAT GUY...?
GIRL, YOU'VE BEEN DRINK-ING TOO MUCH.
BRRRING!
...HELLO.
YEAH, THINGS ARE FINE... IT'S GOING WELL.
DON'T WORRY. I'LL BE BACK SOON.
FINE?
I DON'T WANT TO HEAR THAT UNTIL YOU'VE ENTERED THE DIMENSION.

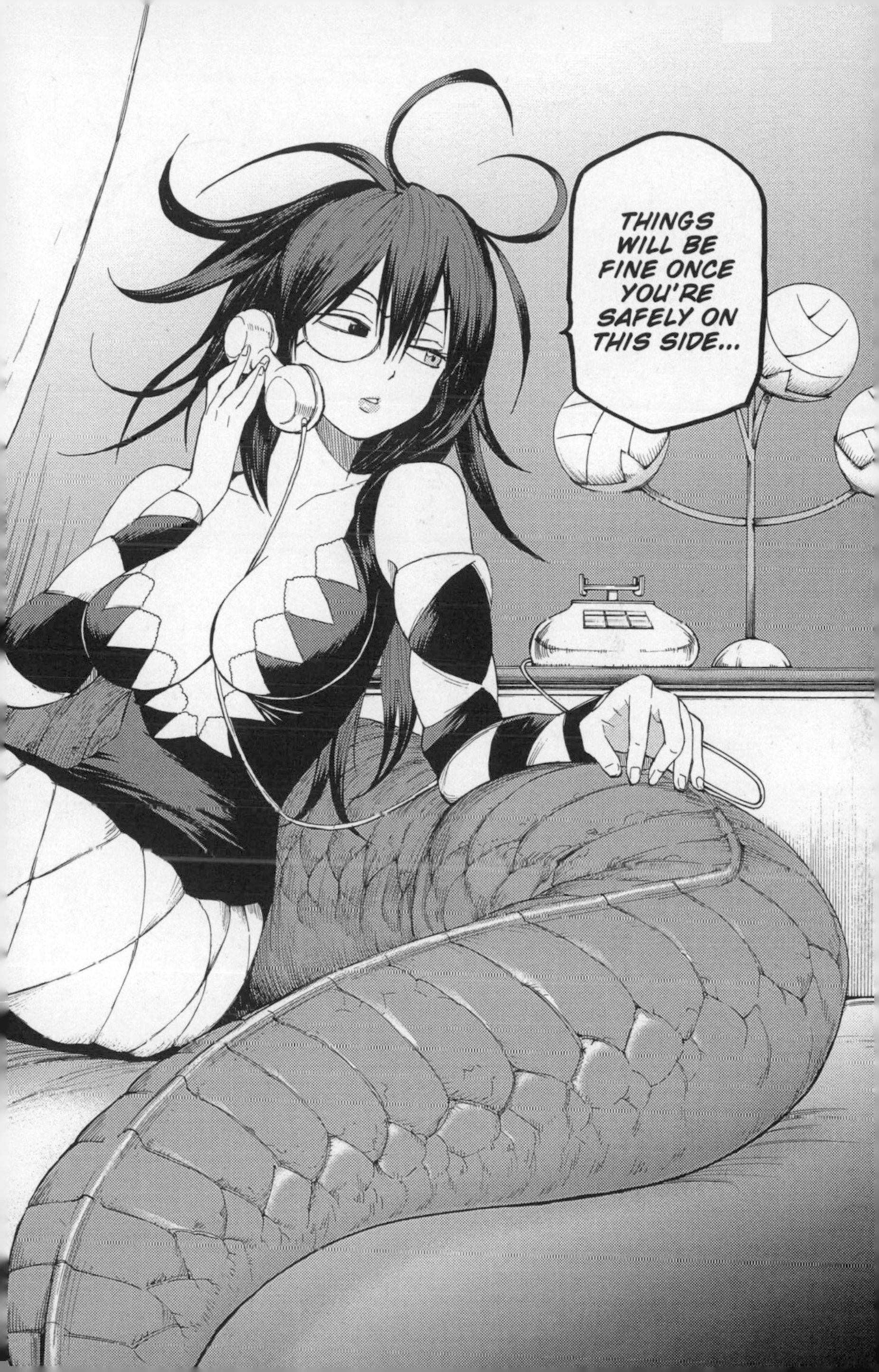
THINGS WILL BE FINE ONCE YOU'RE SAFELY ON THIS SIDE...

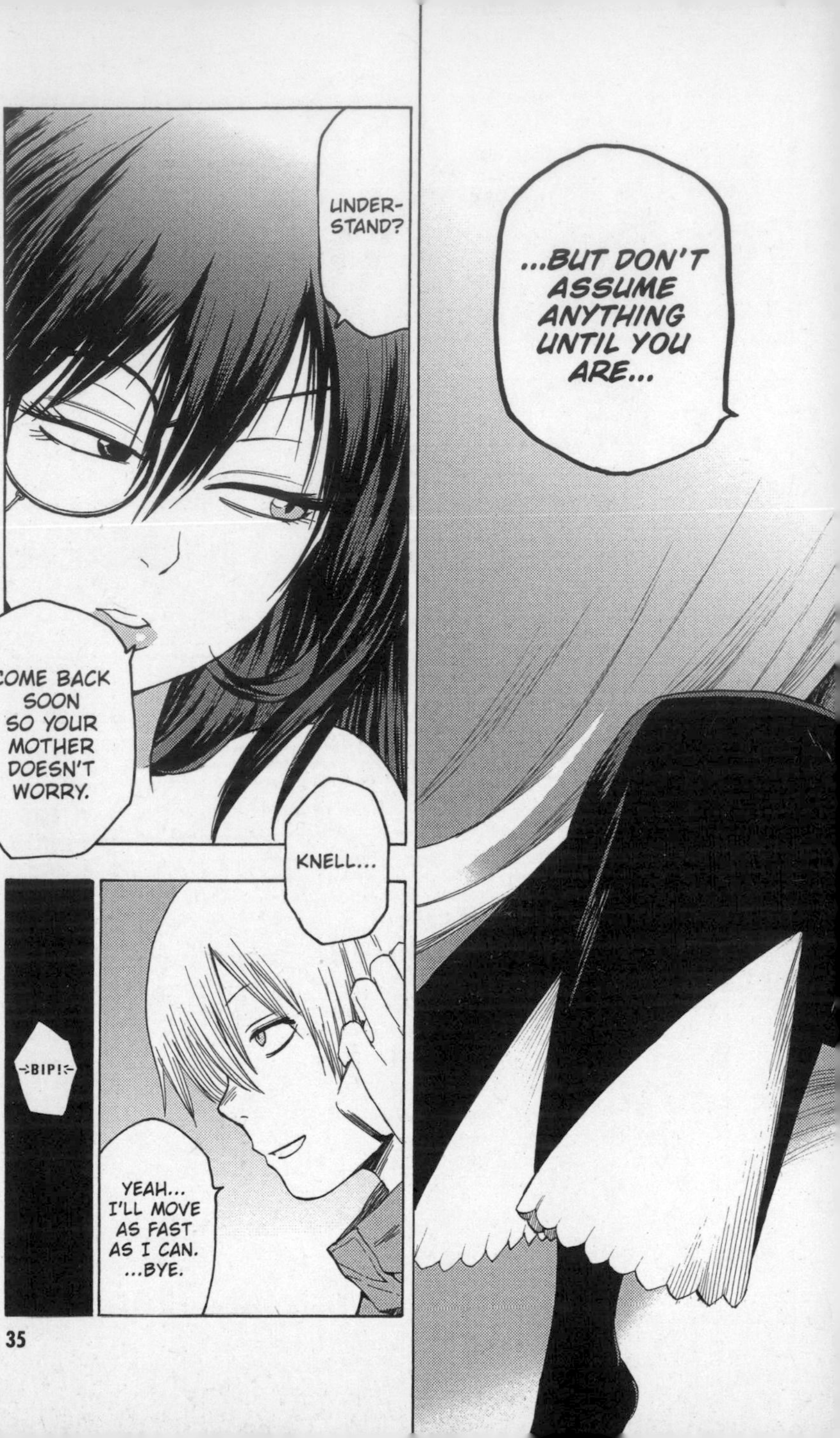
...BUT DON'T ASSUME ANYTHING UNTIL YOU ARE...
UNDER-STAND?
COME BACK SOON SO YOUR MOTHER DOESN'T WORRY.
KNELL...
BIP!
YEAH... I'LL MOVE AS FAST AS I CAN. ...BYE.

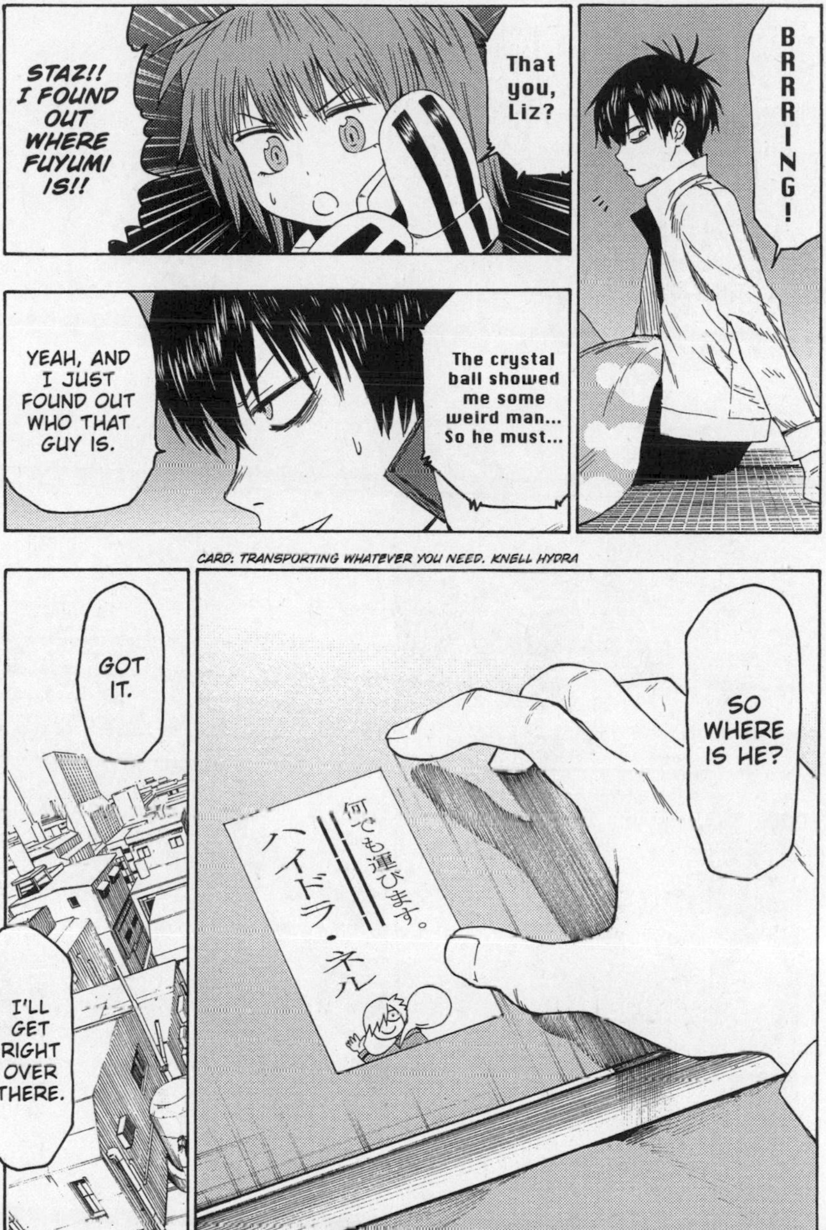
BRRRING!
That you, Liz?
STAZ!! I FOUND OUT WHERE FUYUMI IS!!
The crystal ball showed me some weird man... So he must...
YEAH, AND I JUST FOUND OUT WHO THAT GUY IS.
CARD: TRANSPORTING WHATEVER YOU NEED. KNELL HYDRA
SO WHERE IS HE?
何でも運びます。
ハイドラ・ネル
GOT IT.
I'LL GET RIGHT OVER THERE.

♠ To Be Continued ♠

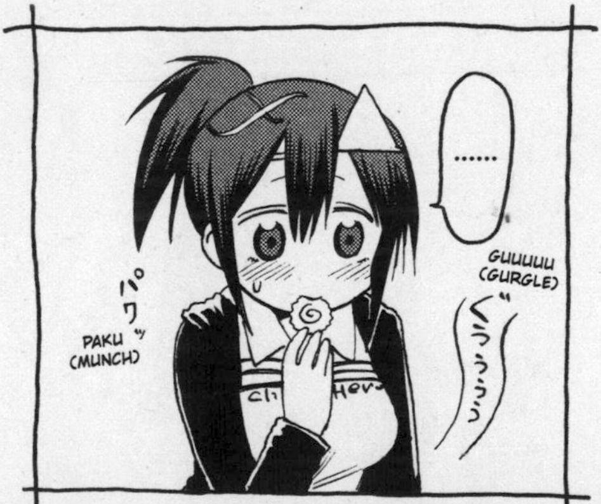
......
GUUUUU
(GURGLE)
PAKU
(MUNCH)

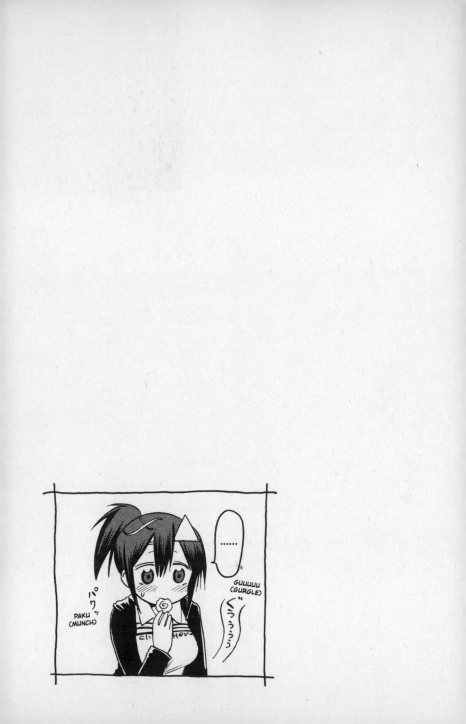

BLOOD LAD

CHAPTER 22 ♠ TWO IS A TREASURE

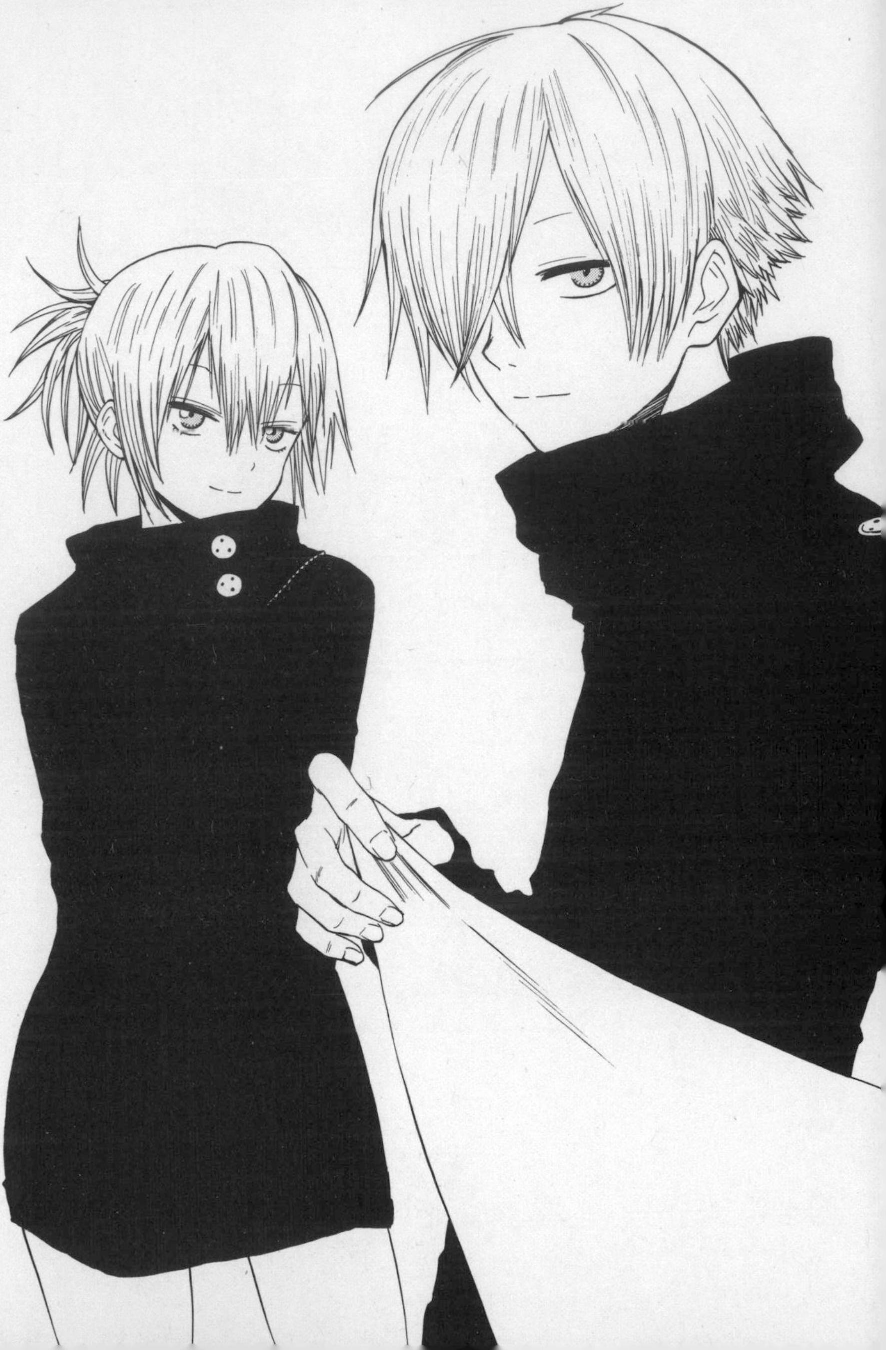

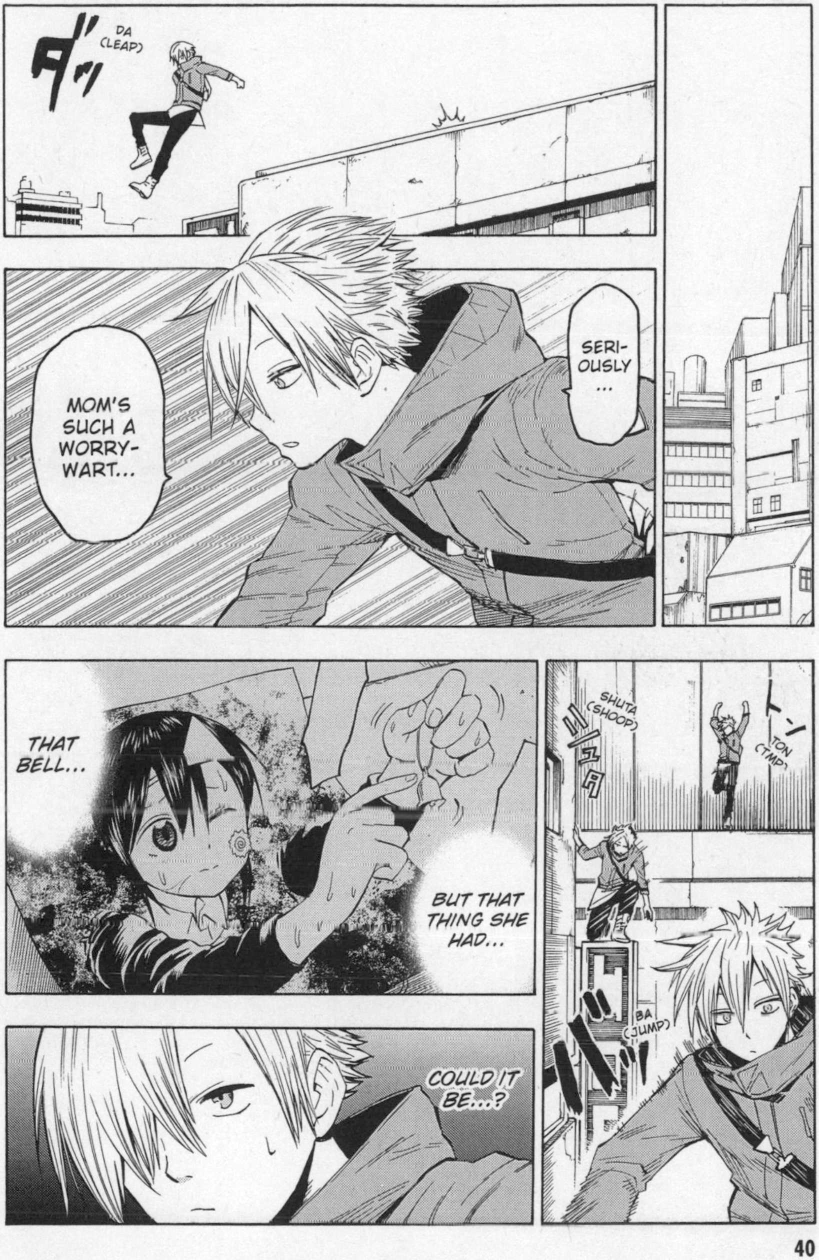
ダッ
DA (LEAP)
SERI-OUSLY...
MOM'S SUCH A WORRY-WART...
トン
TON (TMP)
シュタ
SHUTA (SHOOP)
バッ
BA (JUMP)
THAT BELL...
BUT THAT THING SHE HAD...
COULD IT BE...?

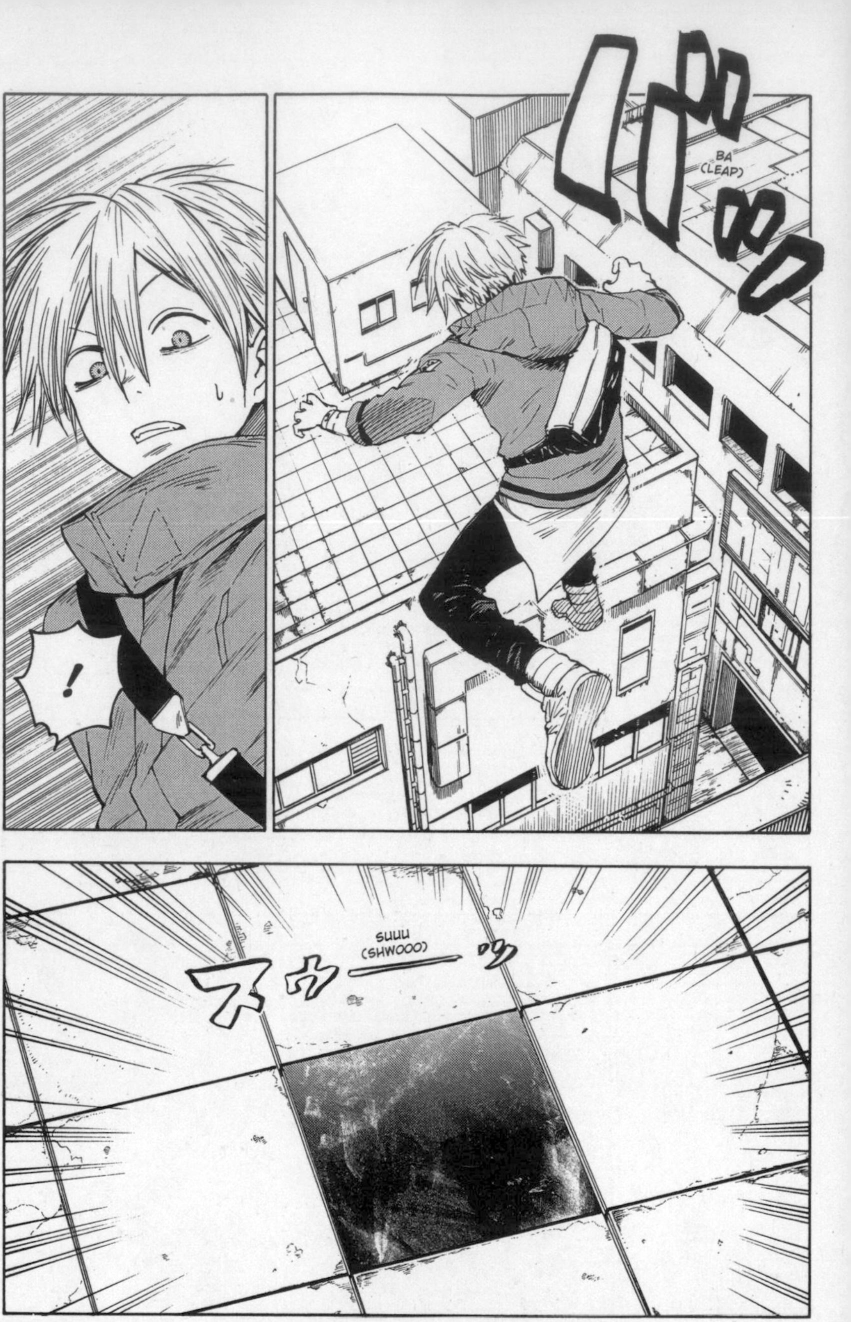
BA (LEAP)
!
SUUU (SHWOOO)

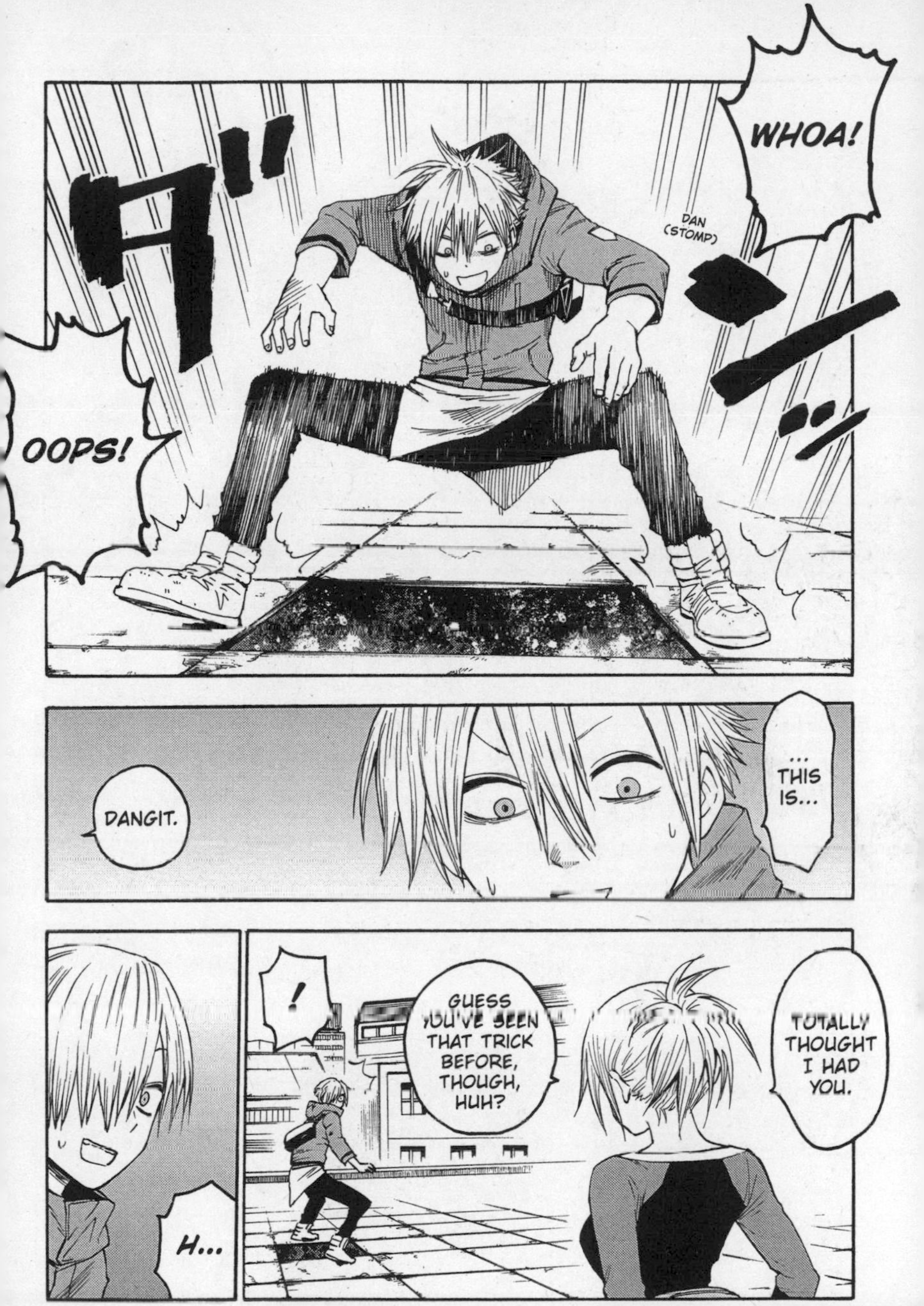
WHOA!
DAN (STOMP)
OOPS!
... THIS IS...
DANGIT.
TOTALLY THOUGHT I HAD YOU.
GUESS YOU'VE SEEN THAT TRICK BEFORE, THOUGH, HUH?
!
H...

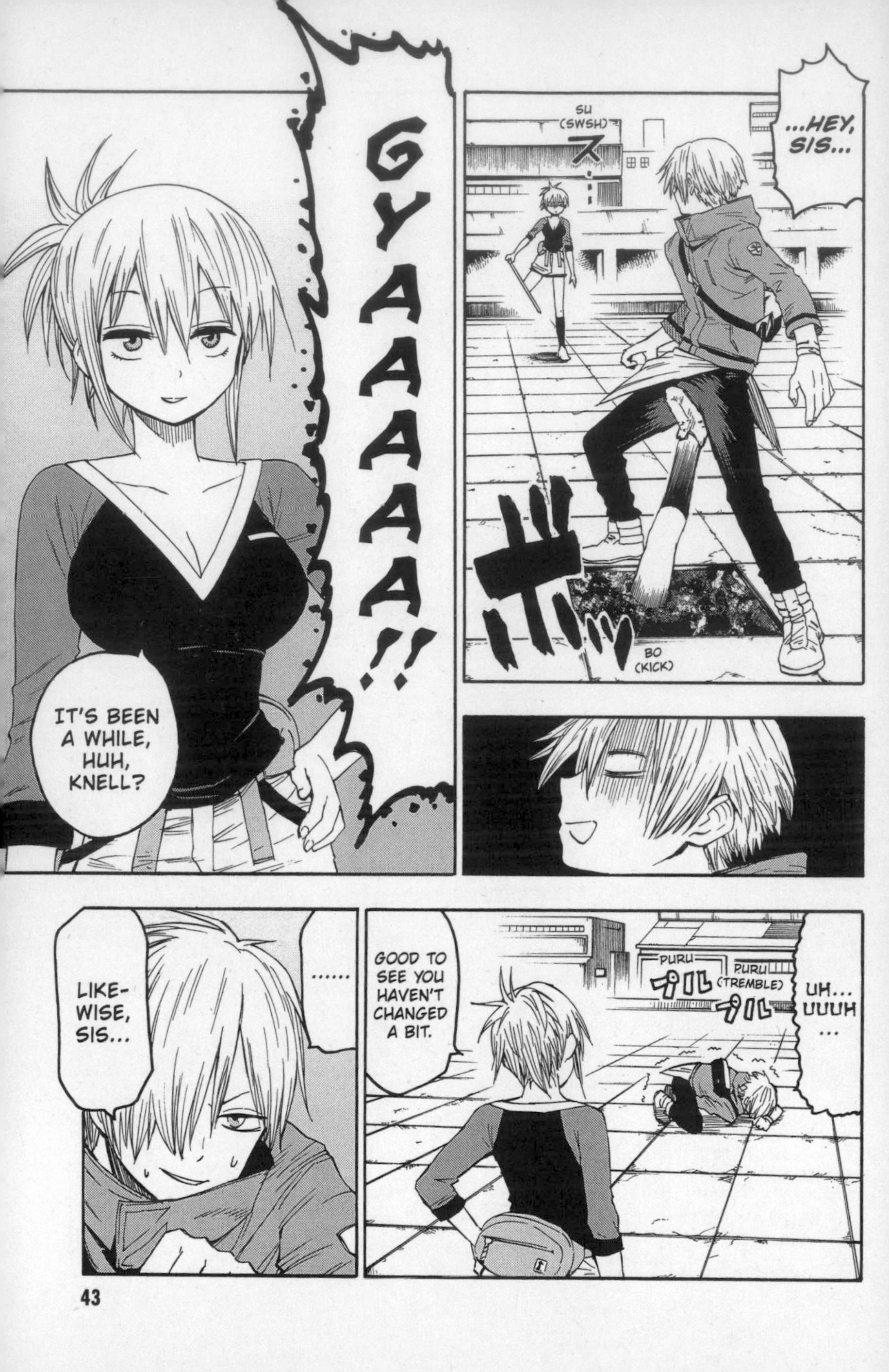
...HEY, SIS...
SU (SWSH)
ス
BO (KICK)
GYAAAAA!!
IT'S BEEN A WHILE, HUH, KNELL?
UH... UUUH...
PURU
イル
PURU (TREMBLE)
イル
GOOD TO SEE YOU HAVEN'T CHANGED A BIT.
......
LIKE-WISE, SIS...

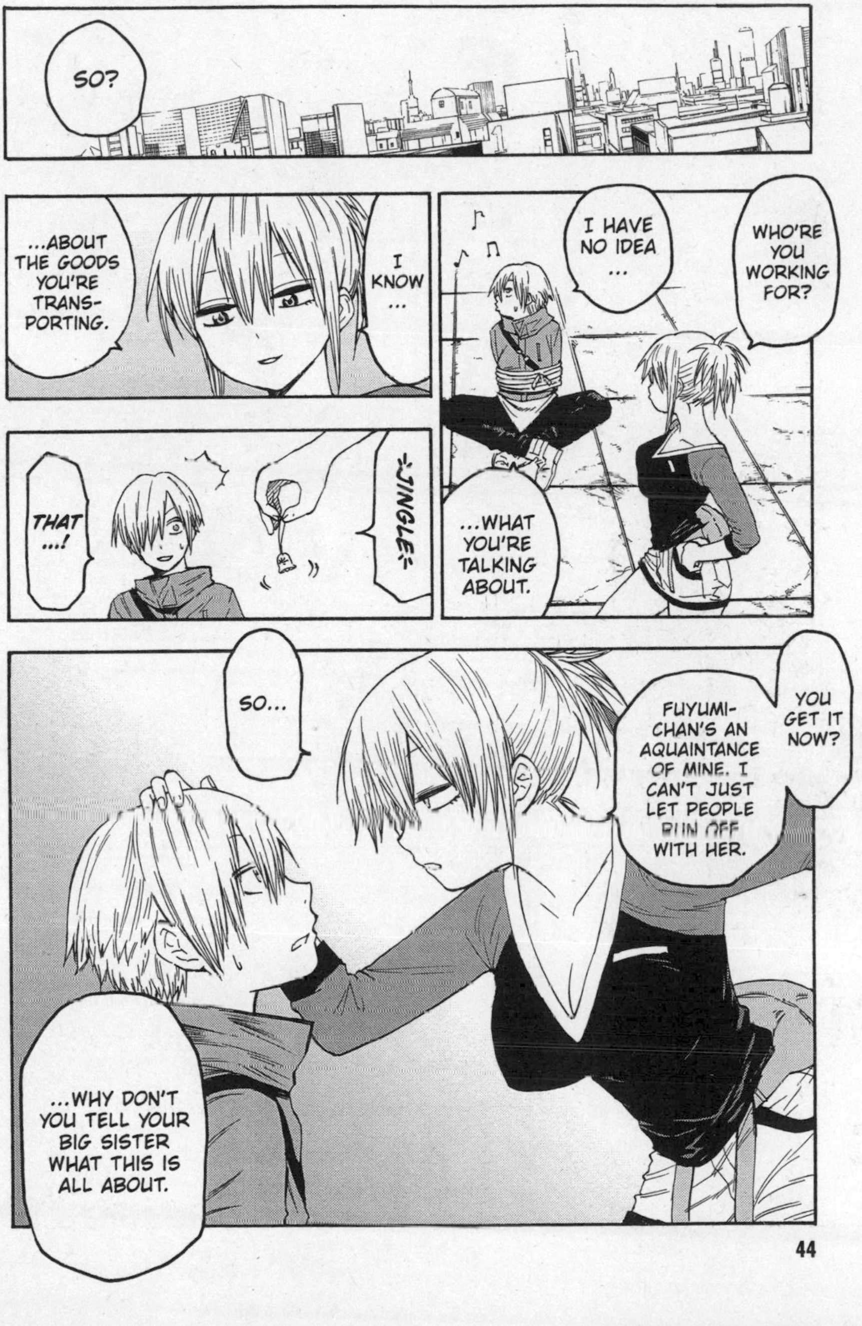
SO?
WHO'RE YOU WORKING FOR?
I HAVE NO IDEA ...
...WHAT YOU'RE TALKING ABOUT.
I KNOW ...
...ABOUT THE GOODS YOU'RE TRANS-PORTING.
JINGLE
THAT ...!
YOU GET IT NOW?
FUYUMI-CHAN'S AN AQUAINTANCE OF MINE. I CAN'T JUST LET PEOPLE RUN OFF WITH HER.
SO...
...WHY DON'T YOU TELL YOUR BIG SISTER WHAT THIS IS ALL ABOUT.

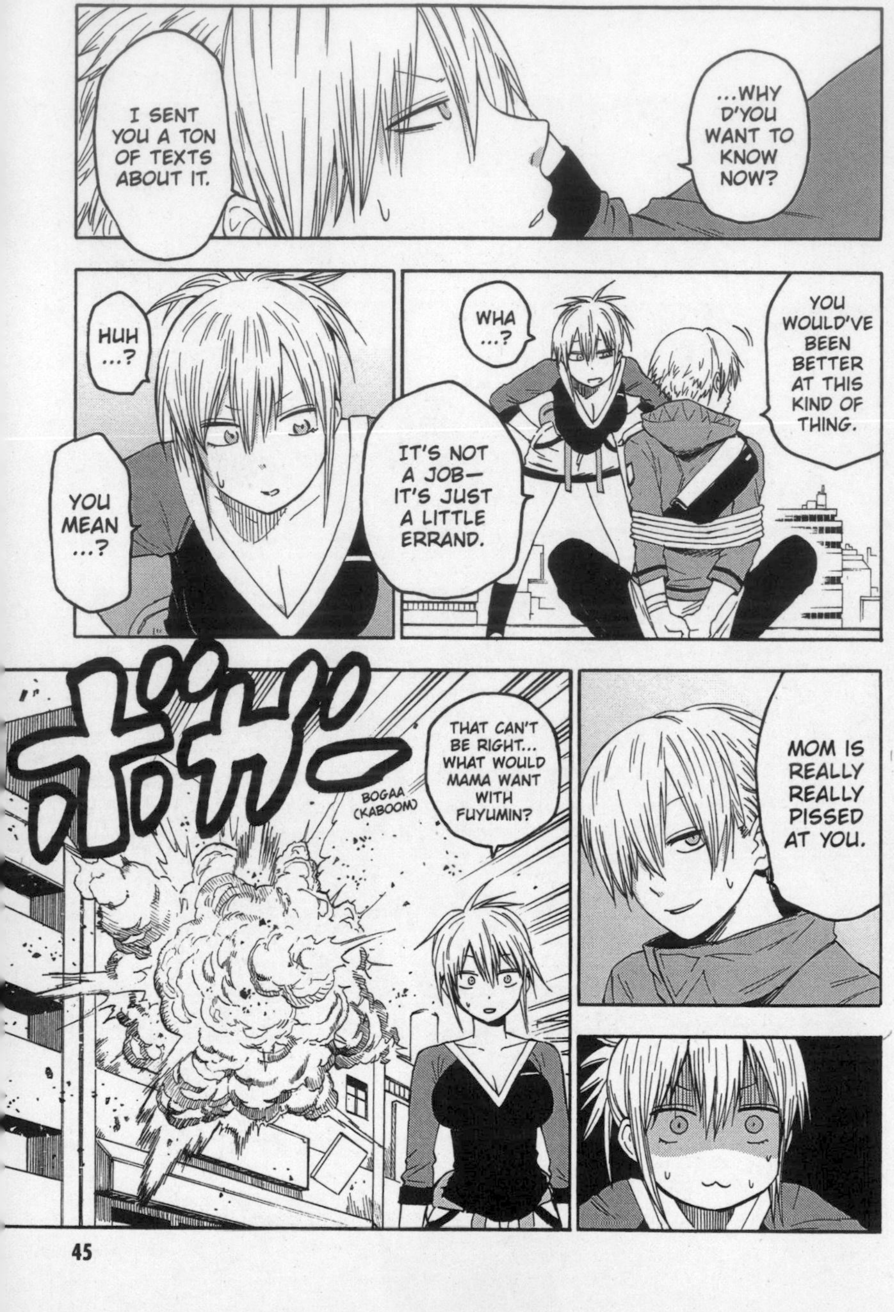
...WHY D'YOU WANT TO KNOW NOW?
I SENT YOU A TON OF TEXTS ABOUT IT.
YOU WOULD'VE BEEN BETTER AT THIS KIND OF THING.
WHA ...?
IT'S NOT A JOB— IT'S JUST A LITTLE ERRAND.
HUH ...?
YOU MEAN ...?
MOM IS REALLY REALLY PISSED AT YOU.
THAT CAN'T BE RIGHT... WHAT WOULD MAMA WANT WITH FUYUMIN?
BOGAA (KABOOM)

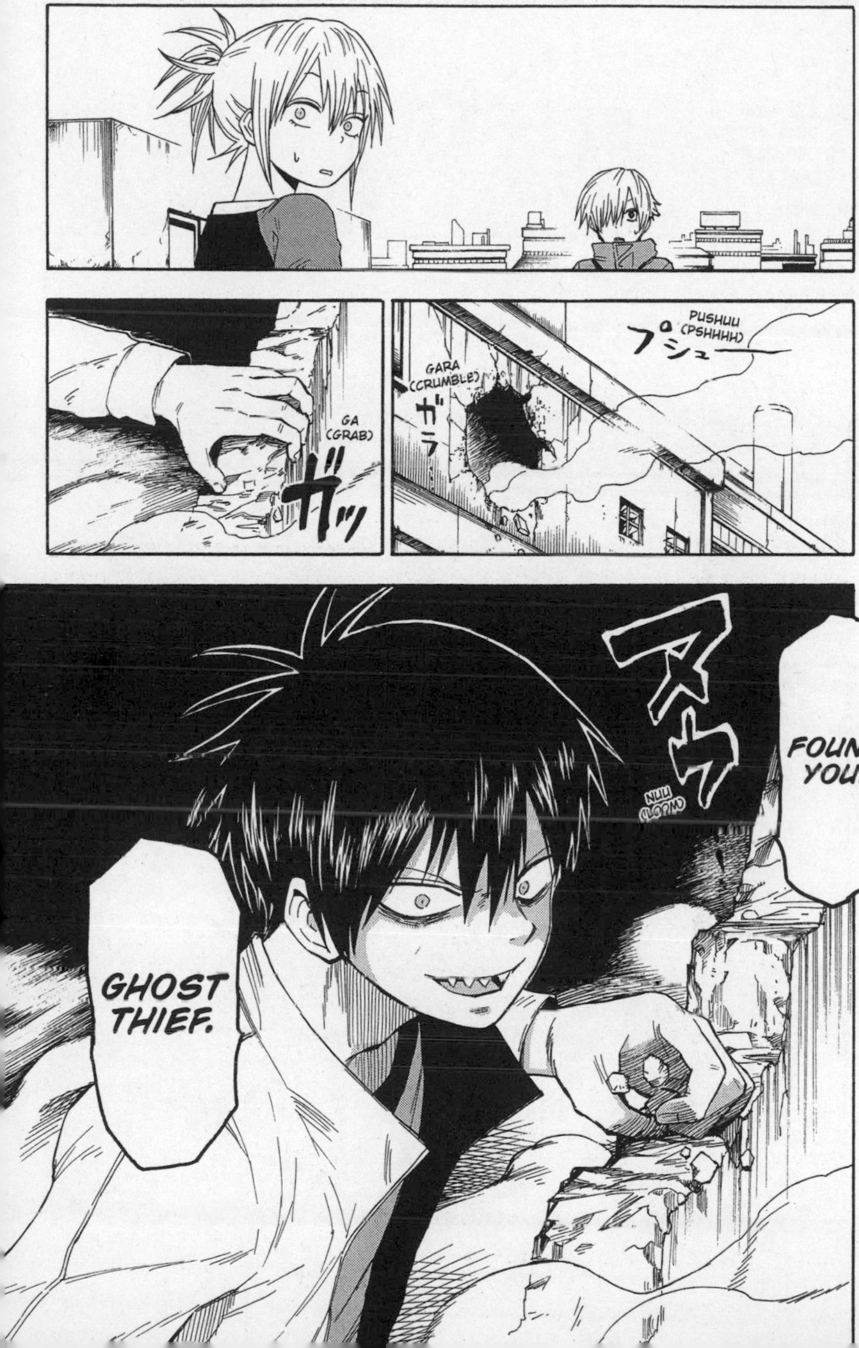
PUSHUU (PSHHHH)
プシュー
GARA (CRUMBLE)
ガラ
GA (GRAB)
ガッ
FOUND YOU.
NUU (LOOM)
ヌゥ
GHOST THIEF.

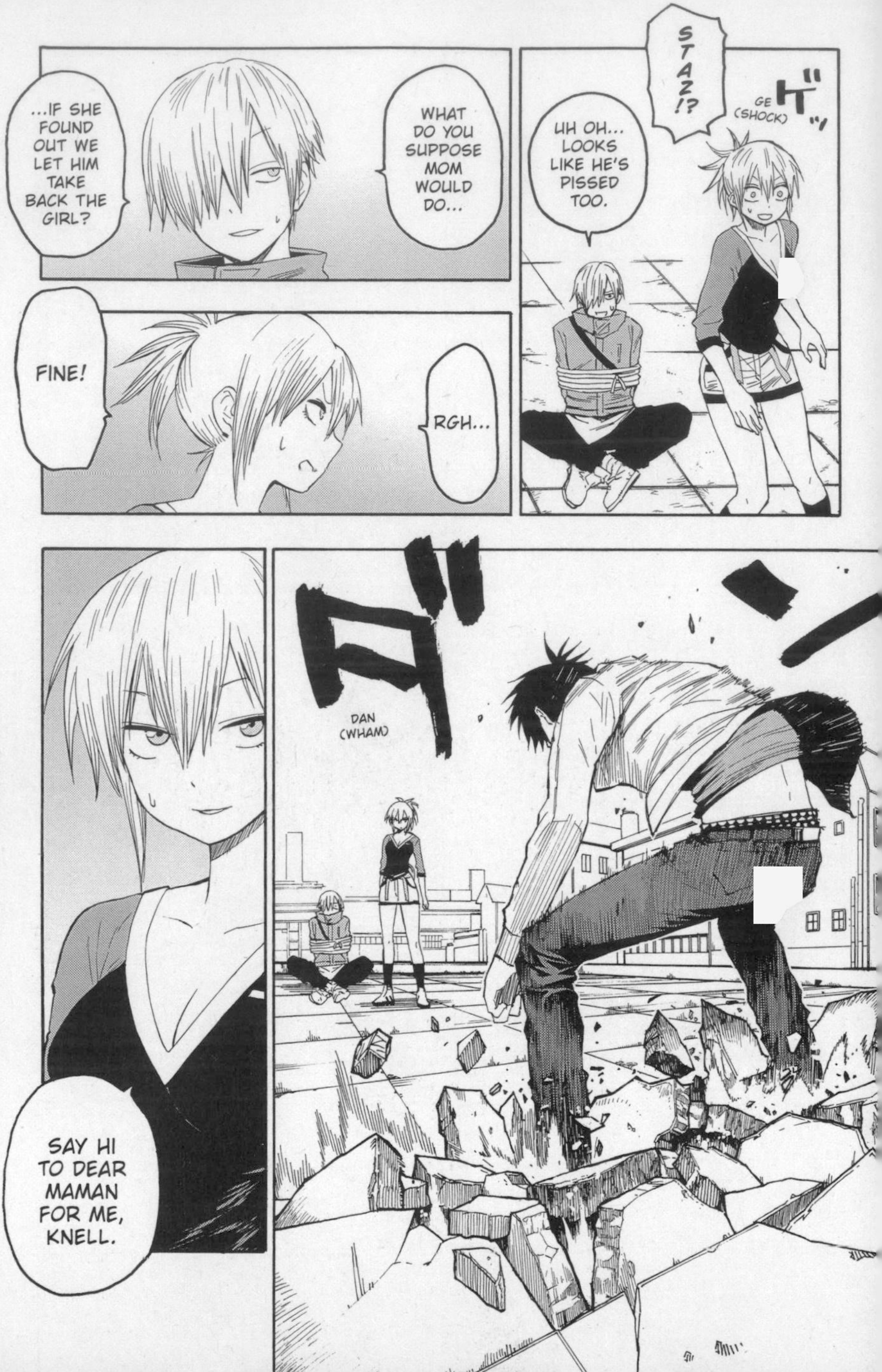
STAZ!?
GE (SHOCK)
UH OH... LOOKS LIKE HE'S PISSED TOO.
WHAT DO YOU SUPPOSE MOM WOULD DO...
...IF SHE FOUND OUT WE LET HIM TAKE BACK THE GIRL?
RGH...
FINE!
DAN (WHAM)
SAY HI TO DEAR MAMAN FOR ME, KNELL.

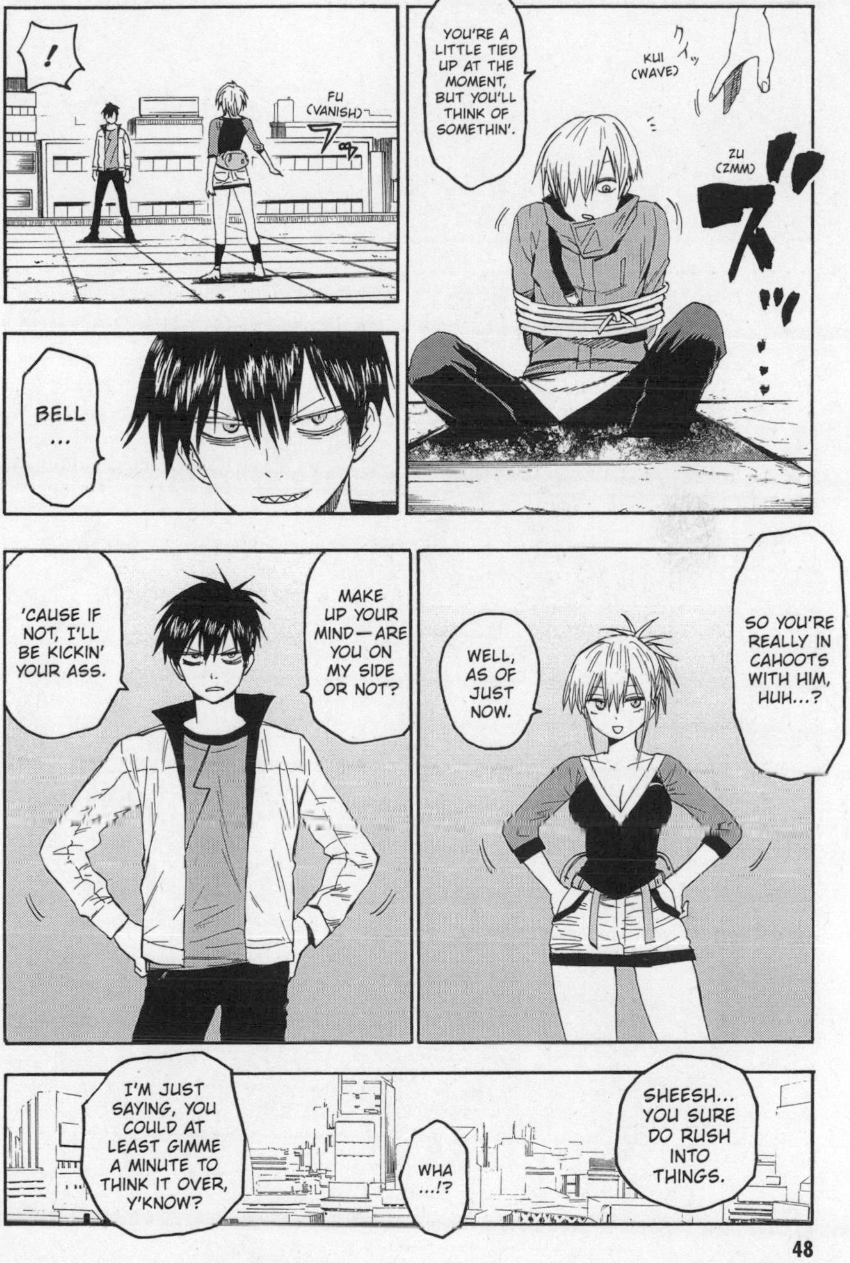
KUI (WAVE)
YOU'RE A LITTLE TIED UP AT THE MOMENT, BUT YOU'LL THINK OF SOMETHIN'.
ZU (ZMM)
!
FU (VANISH)
BELL ...
SO YOU'RE REALLY IN CAHOOTS WITH HIM, HUH...?
WELL, AS OF JUST NOW.
MAKE UP YOUR MIND—ARE YOU ON MY SIDE OR NOT?
'CAUSE IF NOT, I'LL BE KICKIN' YOUR ASS.
SHEESH... YOU SURE DO RUSH INTO THINGS.
WHA ...!?
I'M JUST SAYING, YOU COULD AT LEAST GIMME A MINUTE TO THINK IT OVER, Y'KNOW?

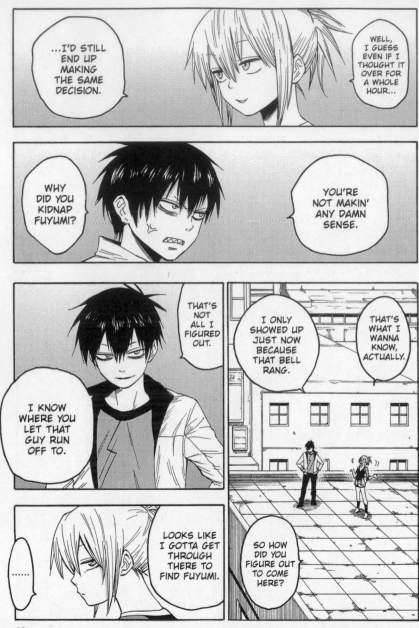

WELL, I GUESS EVEN IF I THOUGHT IT OVER FOR A WHOLE HOUR...
...I'D STILL END UP MAKING THE SAME DECISION.
YOU'RE NOT MAKIN' ANY DAMN SENSE.
WHY DID YOU KIDNAP FUYUMI?
THAT'S WHAT I WANNA KNOW, ACTUALLY.
I ONLY SHOWED UP JUST NOW BECAUSE THAT BELL RANG.
SO HOW DID YOU FIGURE OUT TO COME HERE?
THAT'S NOT ALL I FIGURED OUT.
I KNOW WHERE YOU LET THAT GUY RUN OFF TO.
LOOKS LIKE I GOTTA GET THROUGH THERE TO FIND FUYUMI.
......

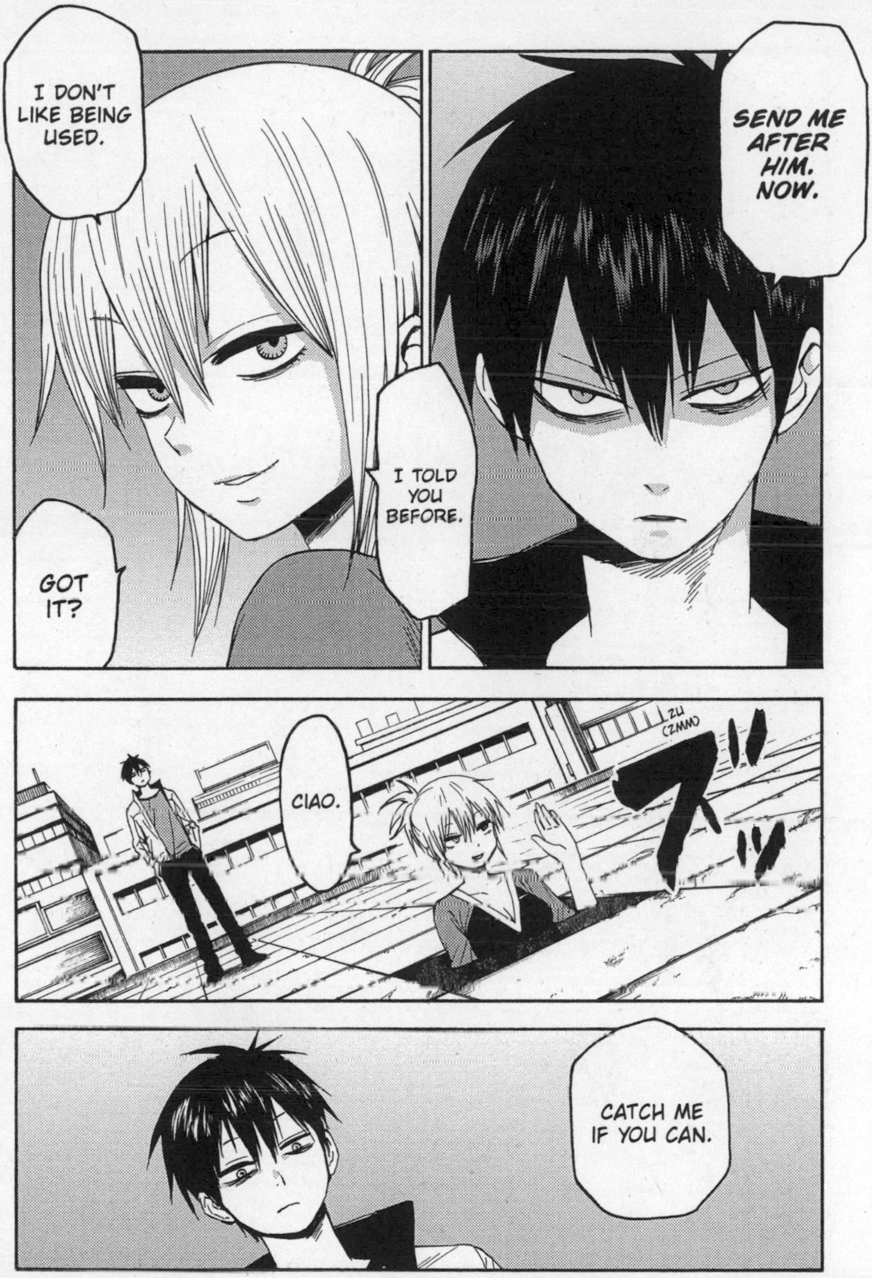
SEND ME AFTER HIM. NOW.
I TOLD YOU BEFORE.
I DON'T LIKE BEING USED.
GOT IT?
ZU (ZMM)
CIAO.
CATCH ME IF YOU CAN.

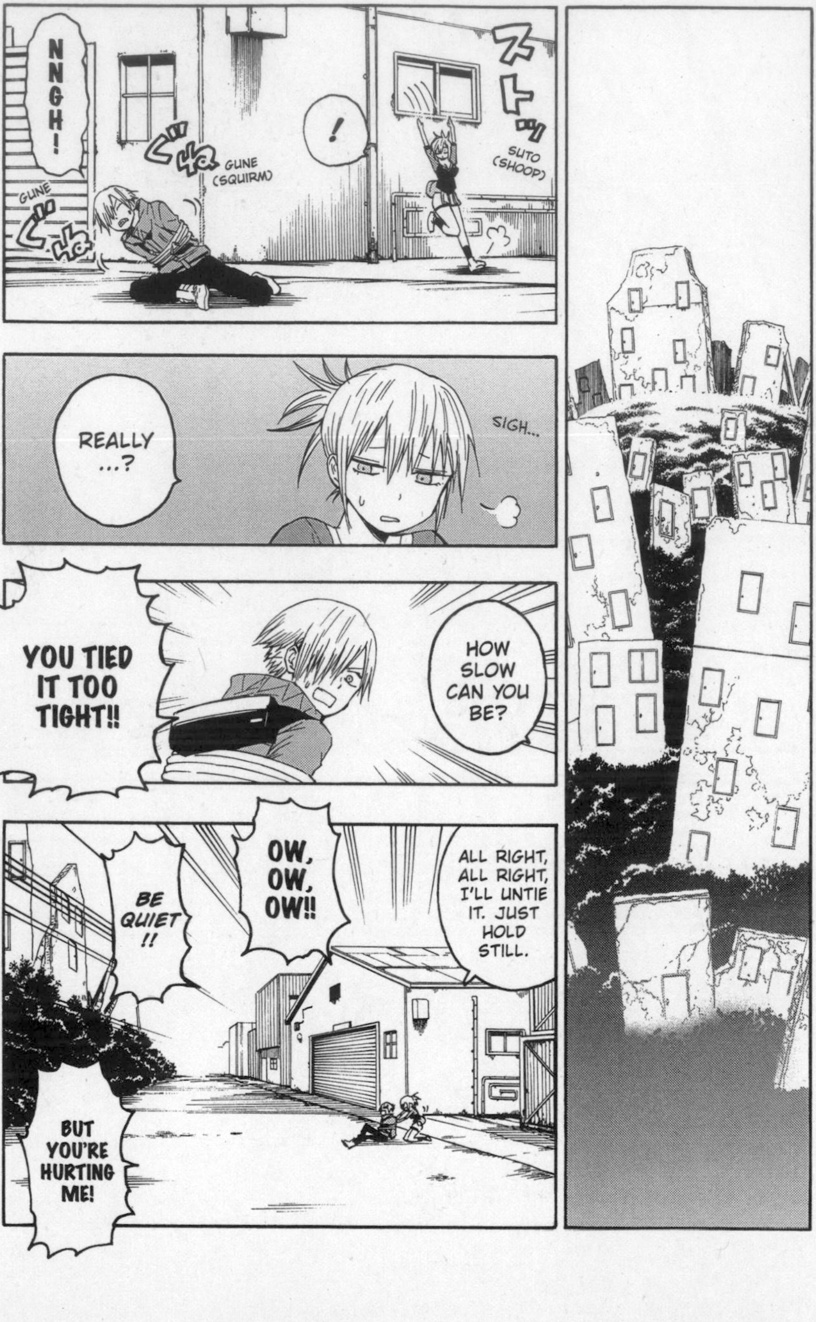
SUTO (SHOOP)
!
GUNE (SQUIRM)
NNGH!
GUNE
SIGH...
REALLY ...?
HOW SLOW CAN YOU BE?
YOU TIED IT TOO TIGHT!!
ALL RIGHT, ALL RIGHT, I'LL UNTIE IT. JUST HOLD STILL.
OW, OW, OW!!
BE QUIET!!
BUT YOU'RE HURTING ME!

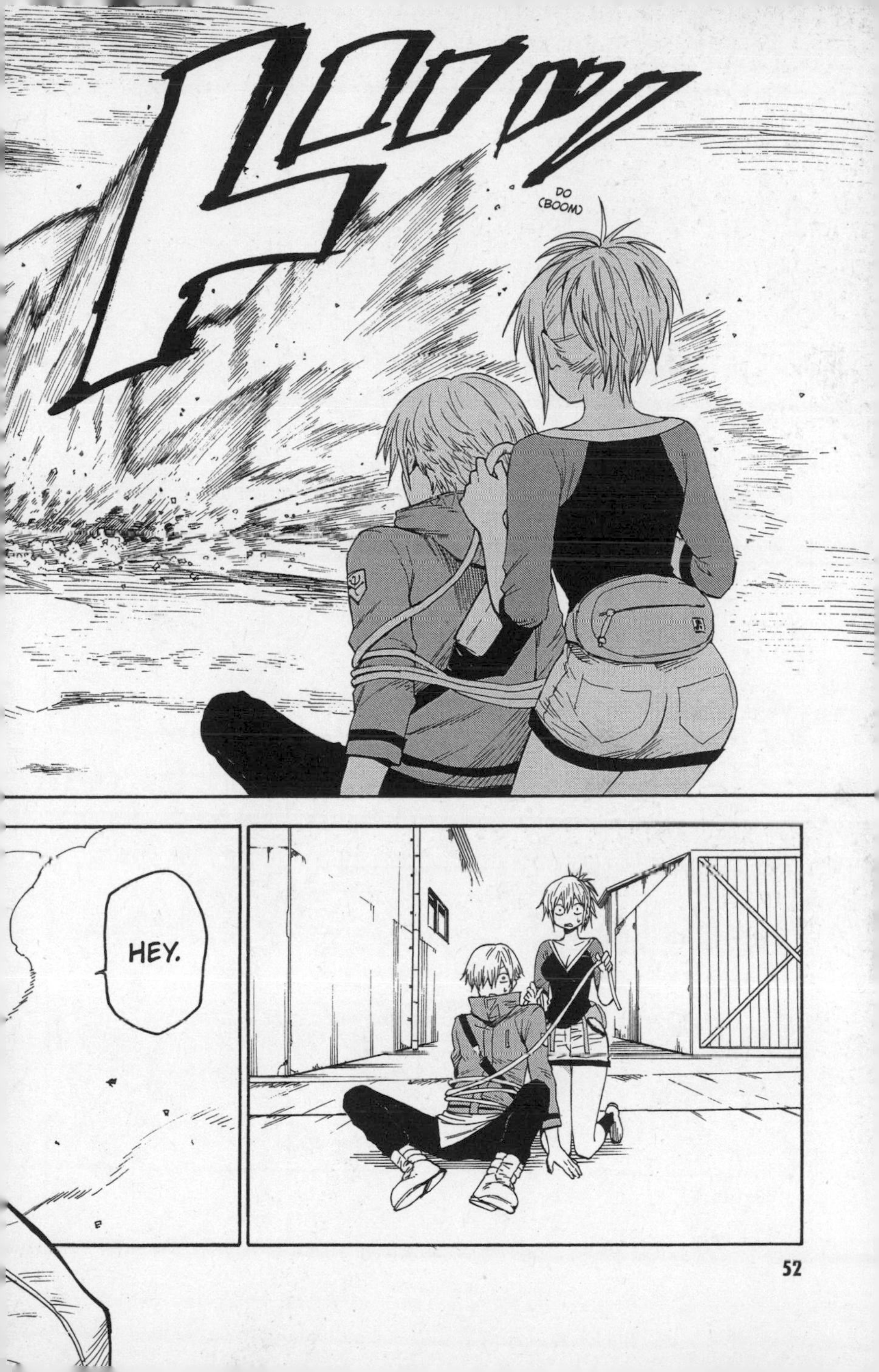
DO
(BOOM)
HEY.

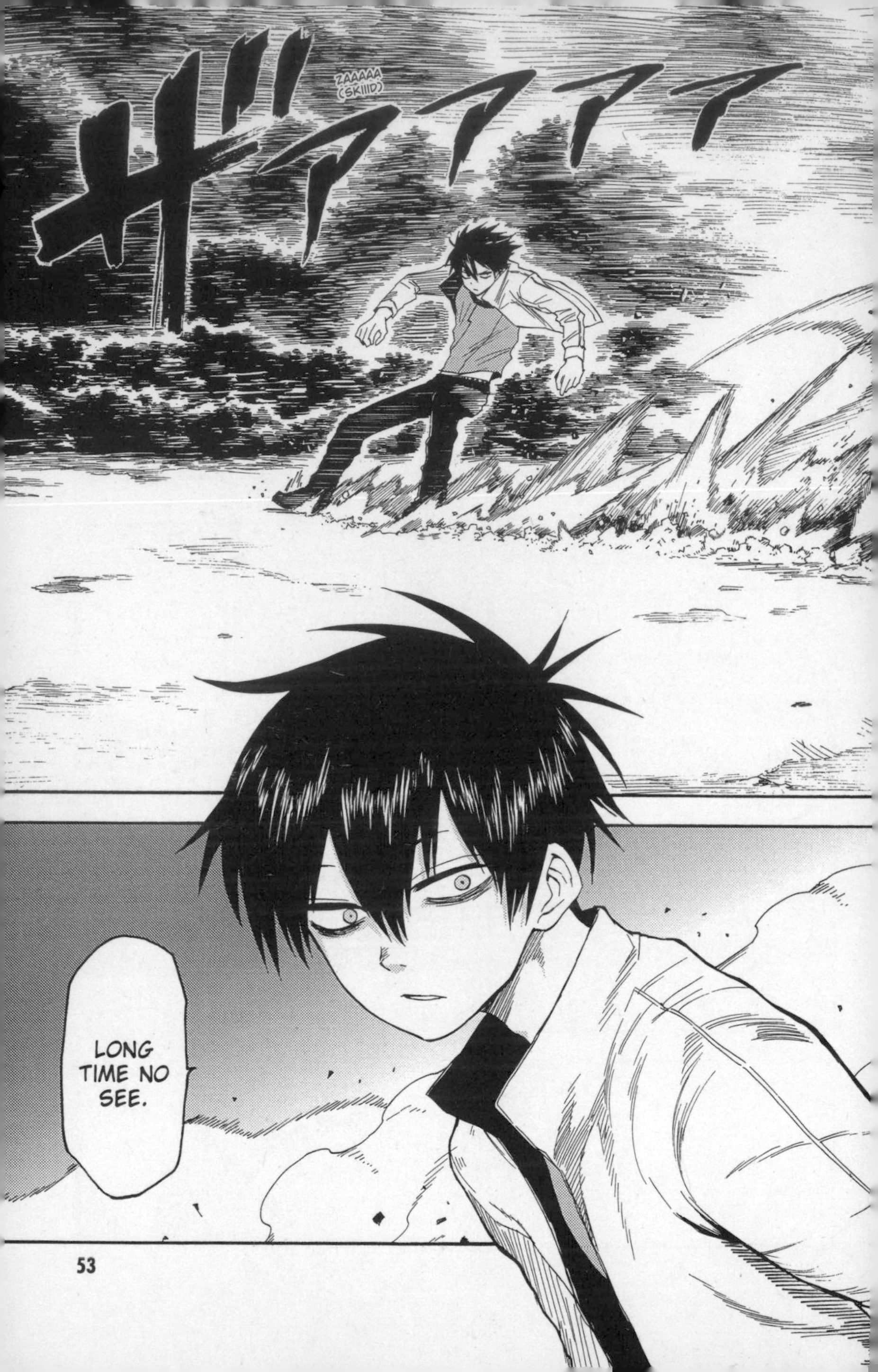
ZAAAAA (SKIIID)
LONG TIME NO SEE.

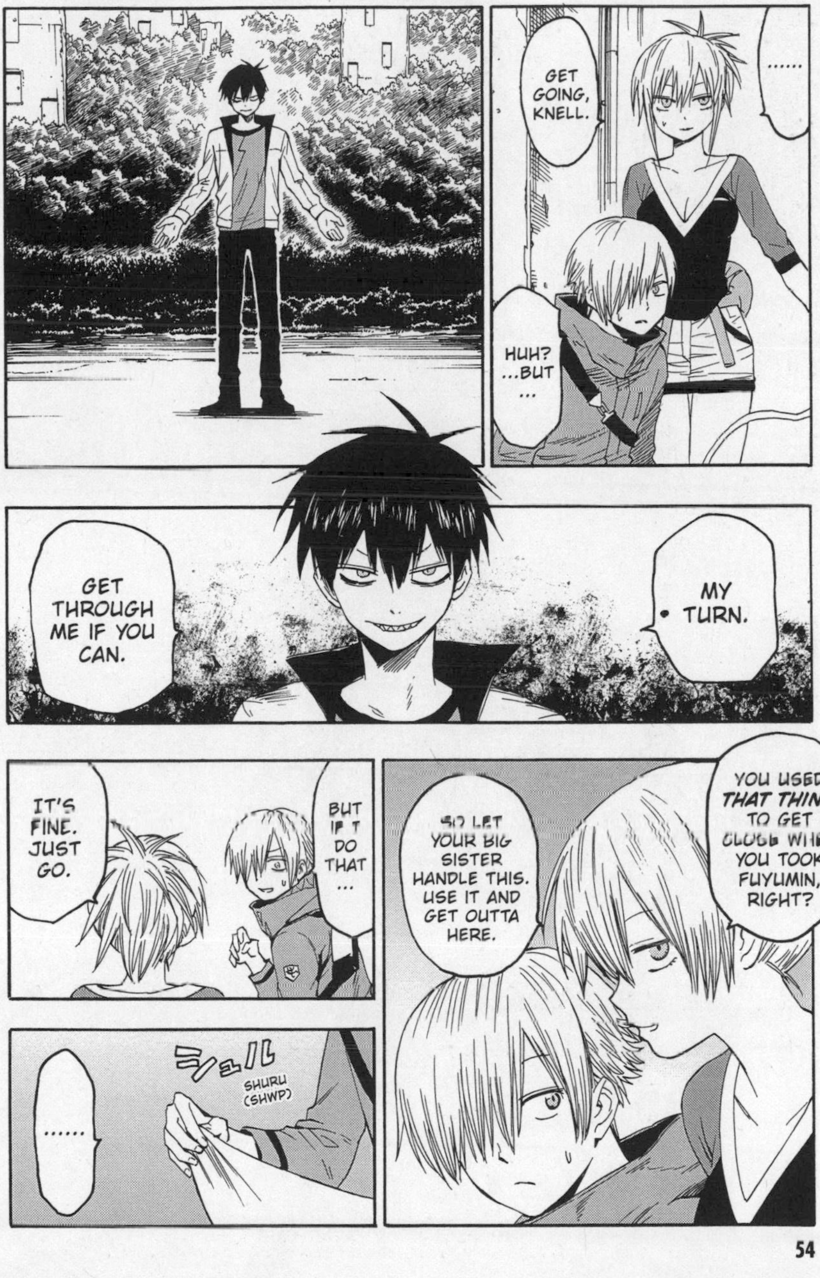
......
GET GOING, KNELL.
HUH? ...BUT ...
MY TURN.
GET THROUGH ME IF YOU CAN.
YOU USED *THAT THING* TO GET CLOSE WHEN YOU TOOK FUYUMIN, RIGHT?
SO LET YOUR BIG SISTER HANDLE THIS. USE IT AND GET OUTTA HERE.
BUT IF I DO THAT ...
IT'S FINE. JUST GO.
シュル
SHURU (SHWP)
......

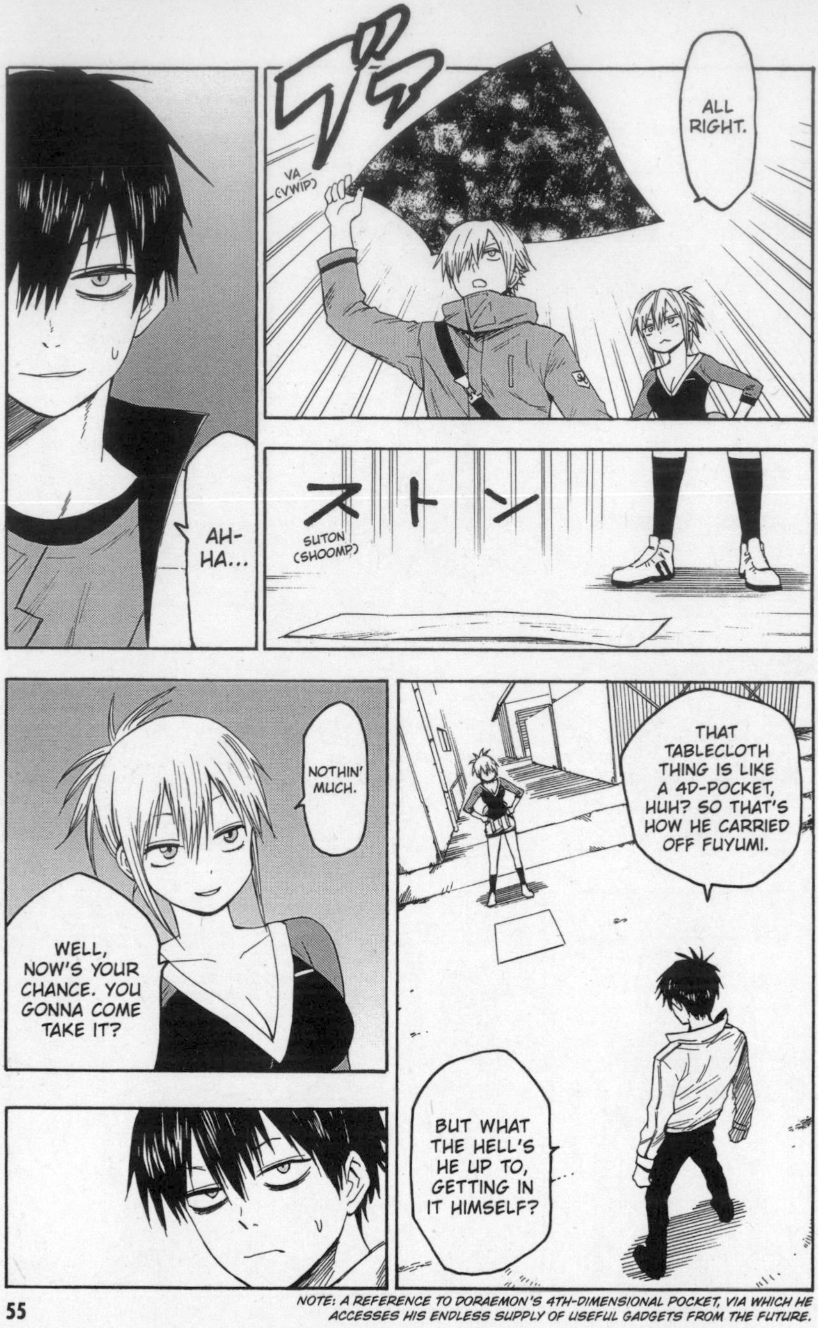
ブァ
VA (VWIP)
ALL RIGHT.
ストン
SUTON (SHOOMP)
AH- HA...
THAT TABLECLOTH THING IS LIKE A 4D-POCKET, HUH? SO THAT'S HOW HE CARRIED OFF FUYUMI.
BUT WHAT THE HELL'S HE UP TO, GETTING IN IT HIMSELF?
NOTHIN' MUCH.
WELL, NOW'S YOUR CHANCE. YOU GONNA COME TAKE IT?

NOTE: A REFERENCE TO DORAEMON'S 4TH-DIMENSIONAL POCKET, VIA WHICH HE ACCESSES HIS ENDLESS SUPPLY OF USEFUL GADGETS FROM THE FUTURE.

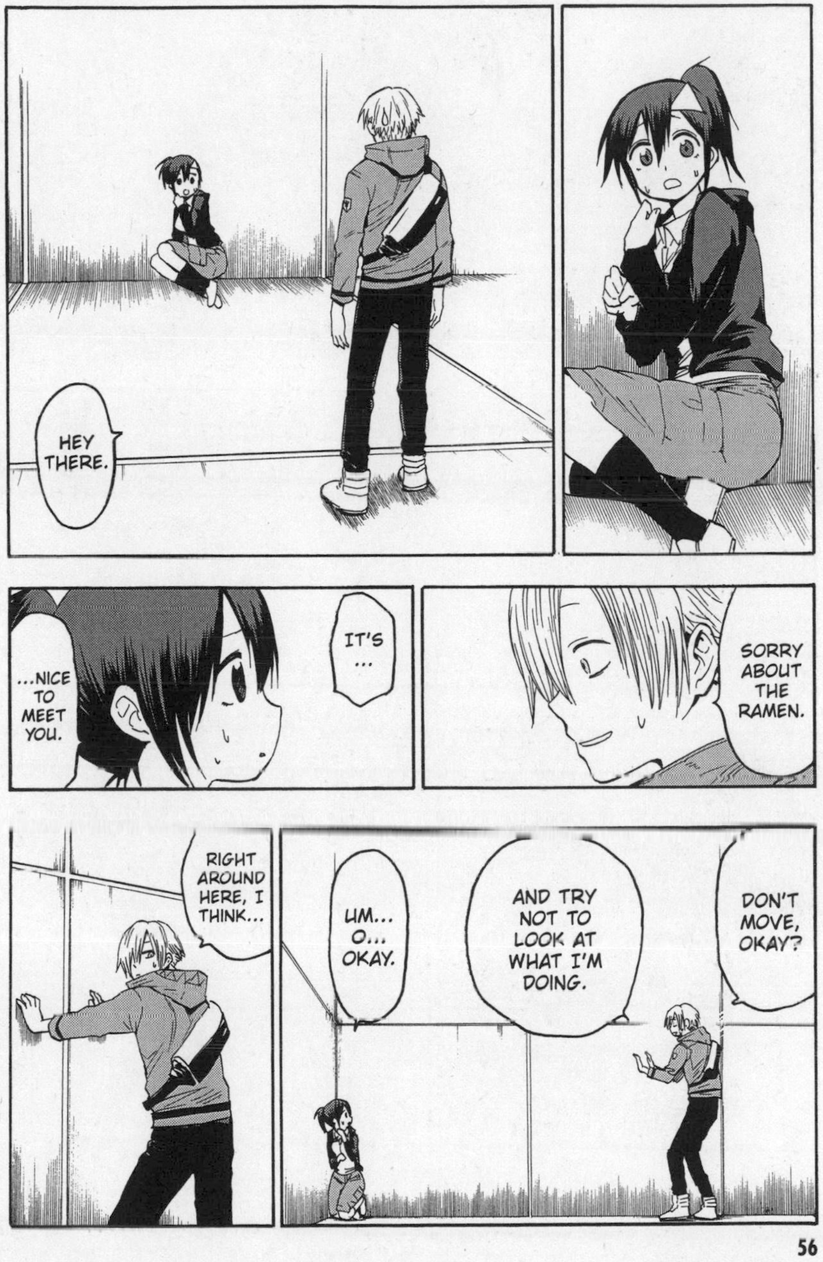
HEY THERE.
SORRY ABOUT THE RAMEN.
IT'S ...
...NICE TO MEET YOU.
DON'T MOVE, OKAY?
AND TRY NOT TO LOOK AT WHAT I'M DOING.
UM... O... OKAY.
RIGHT AROUND HERE, I THINK...

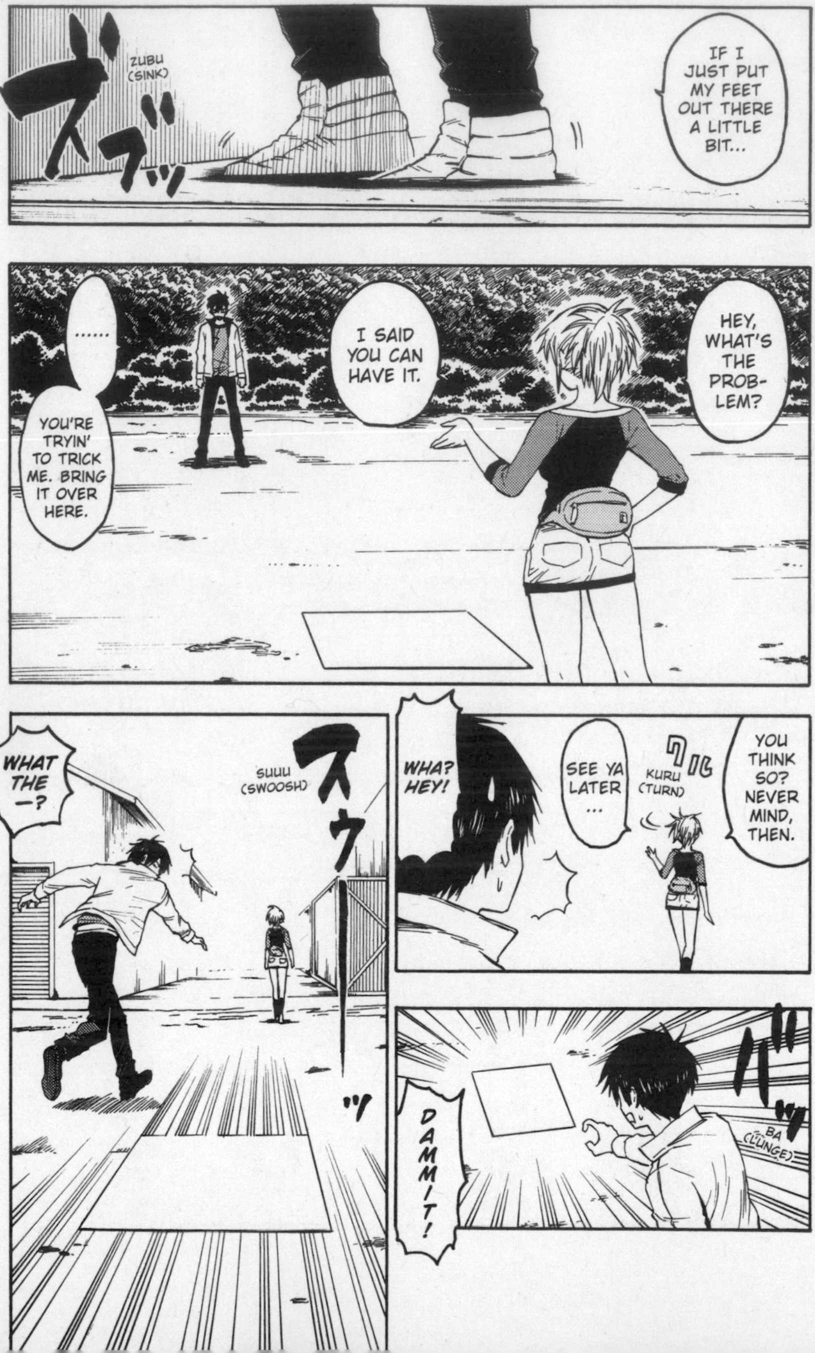
IF I JUST PUT MY FEET OUT THERE A LITTLE BIT...
ZUBU (SINK)
HEY, WHAT'S THE PROB-LEM?
I SAID YOU CAN HAVE IT.
......
YOU'RE TRYIN' TO TRICK ME. BRING IT OVER HERE.
YOU THINK SO? NEVER MIND, THEN.
KURU (TURN)
SEE YA LATER ...
WHA? HEY!
BA (LUNGE)
DAMMIT!
SUUU (SWOOSH)
WHAT THE —?

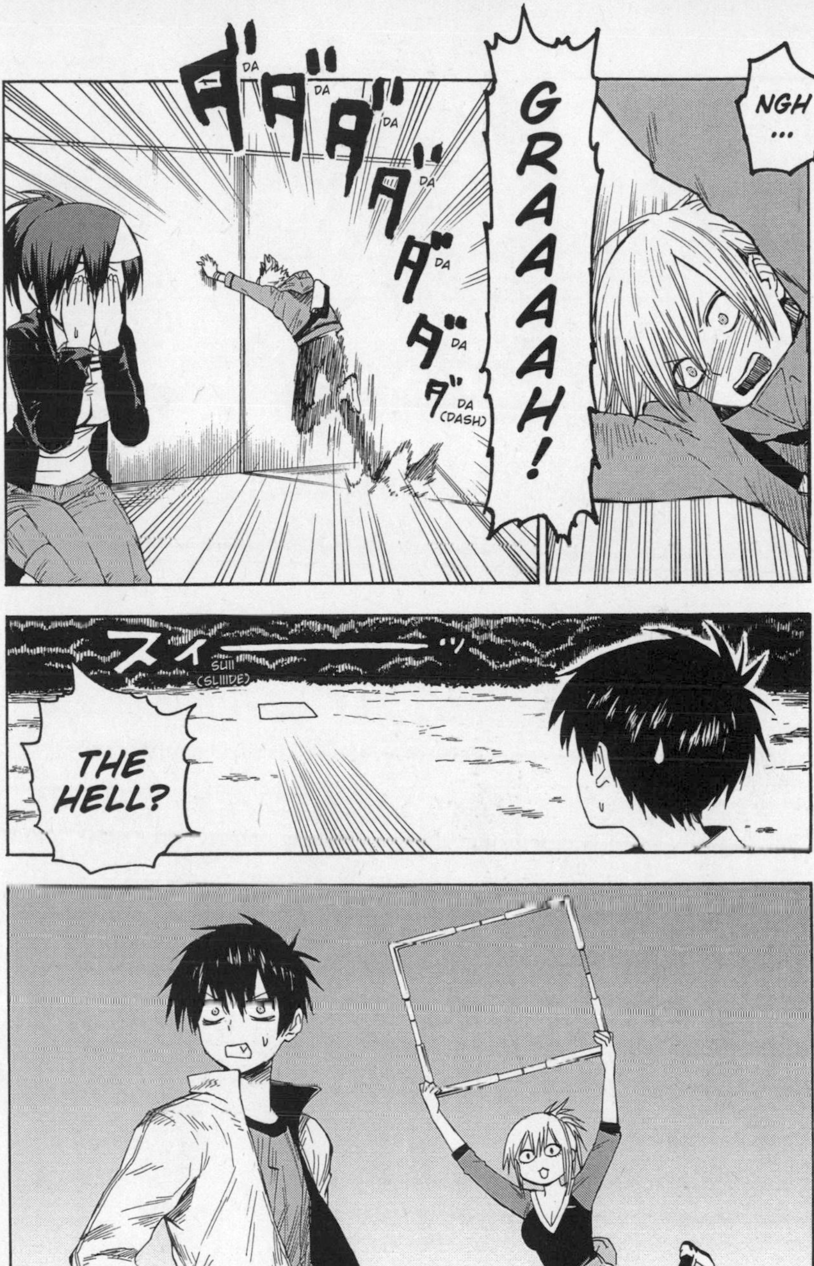
NGH ...
GRAAAAAH!
ダダダダダダダ
DA DA DA DA DA DA DA (DASH)
スィーーーーッ
SUII (SLIIIDE)
THE HELL?

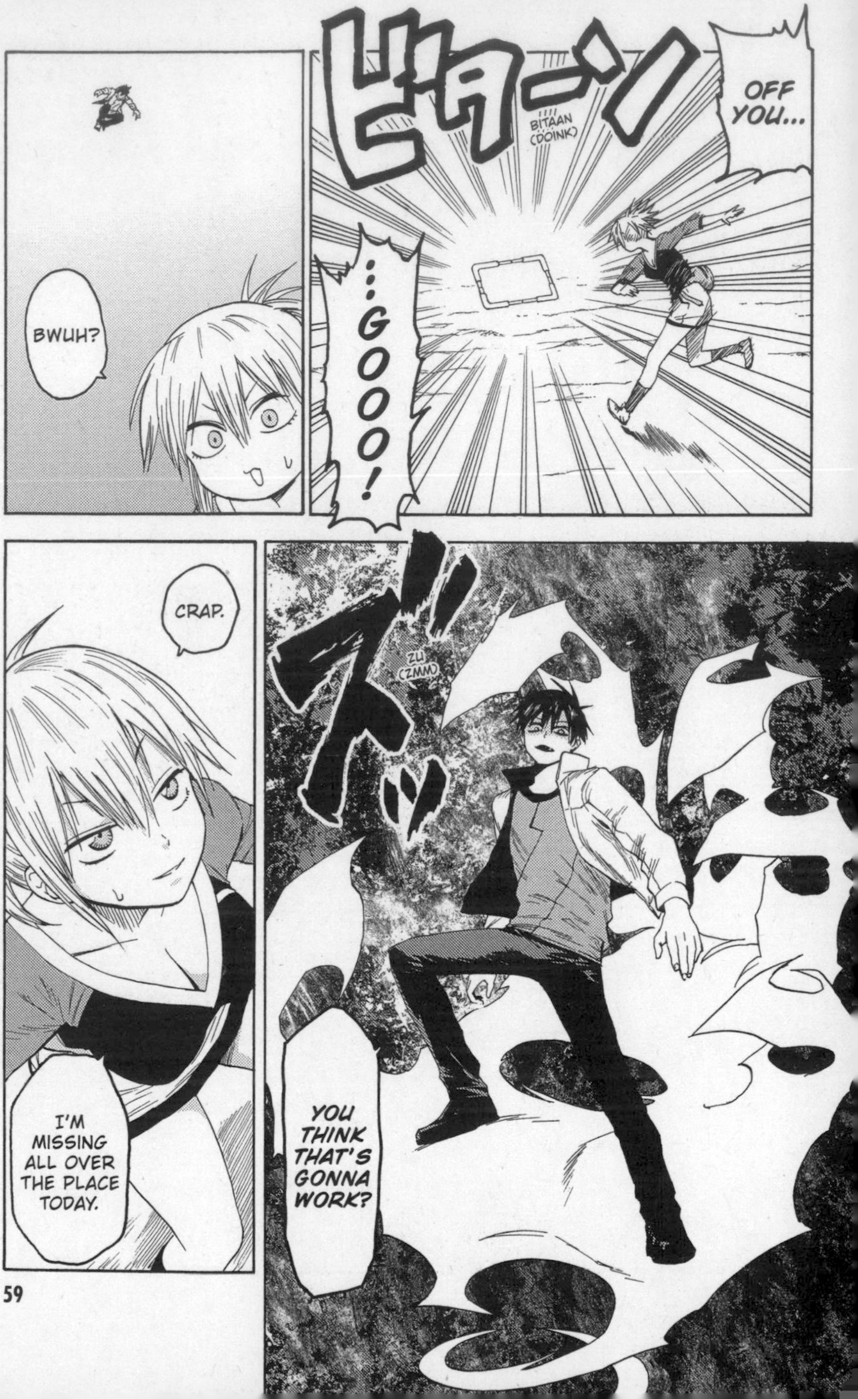
OFF YOU...
BITAAN (DOINK)
...GOOOO!
BWUH?
ZU (ZMM)
YOU THINK THAT'S GONNA WORK?
CRAP.
I'M MISSING ALL OVER THE PLACE TODAY.

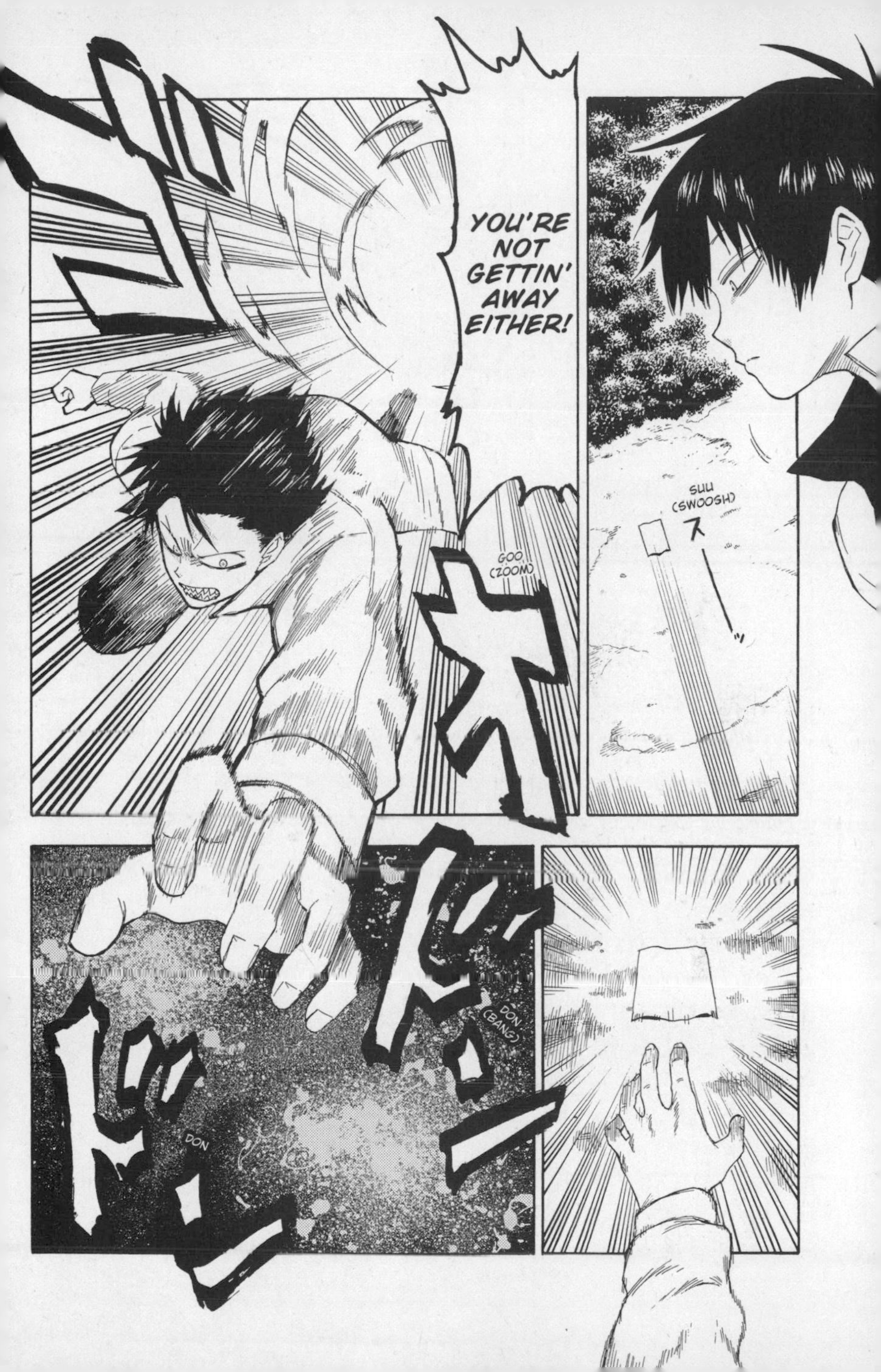
SUU (SWOOSH)
YOU'RE NOT GETTIN' AWAY EITHER!
GOO (ZOOM)
DON (BANG)
DON

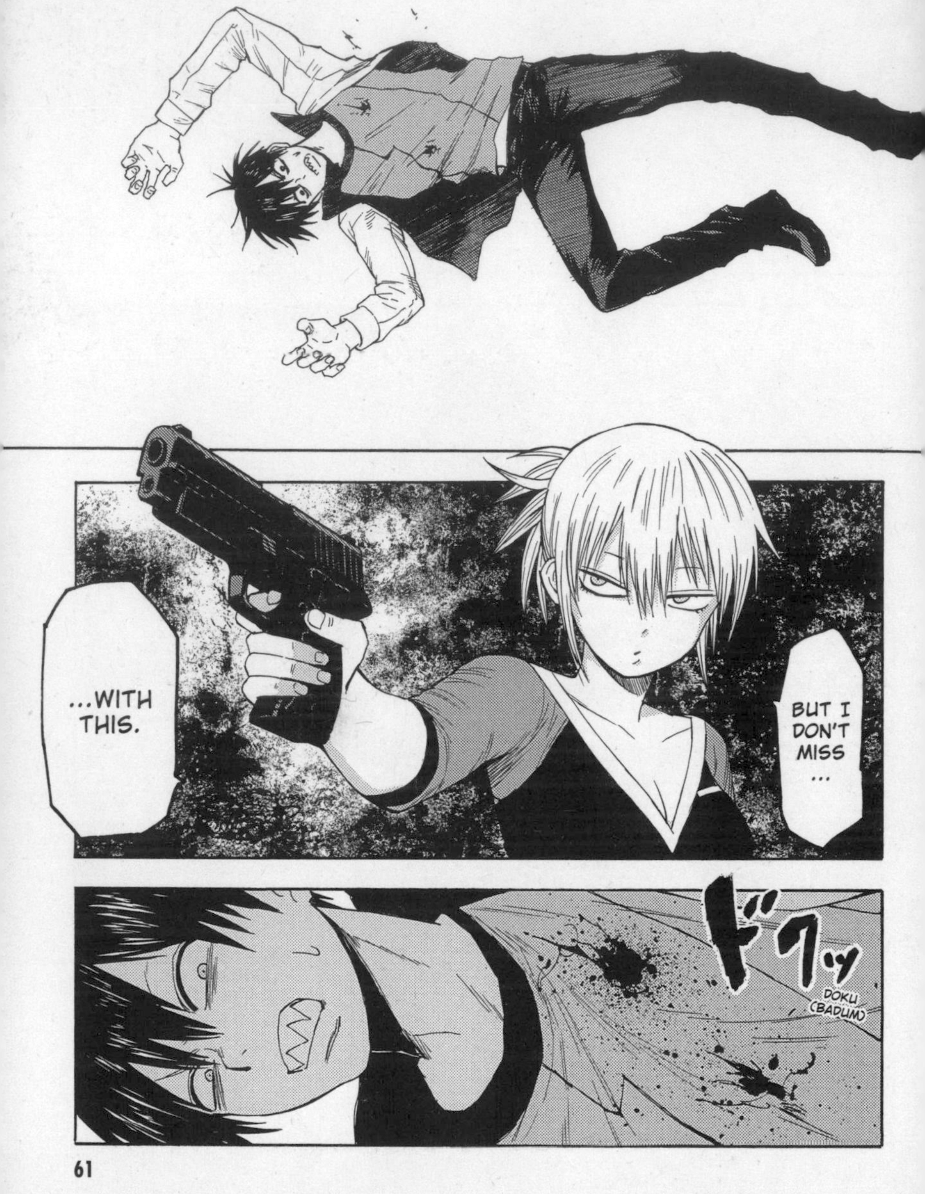
BUT I DON'T MISS ...
...WITH THIS.
ドクッ
DOKU (BADUM)

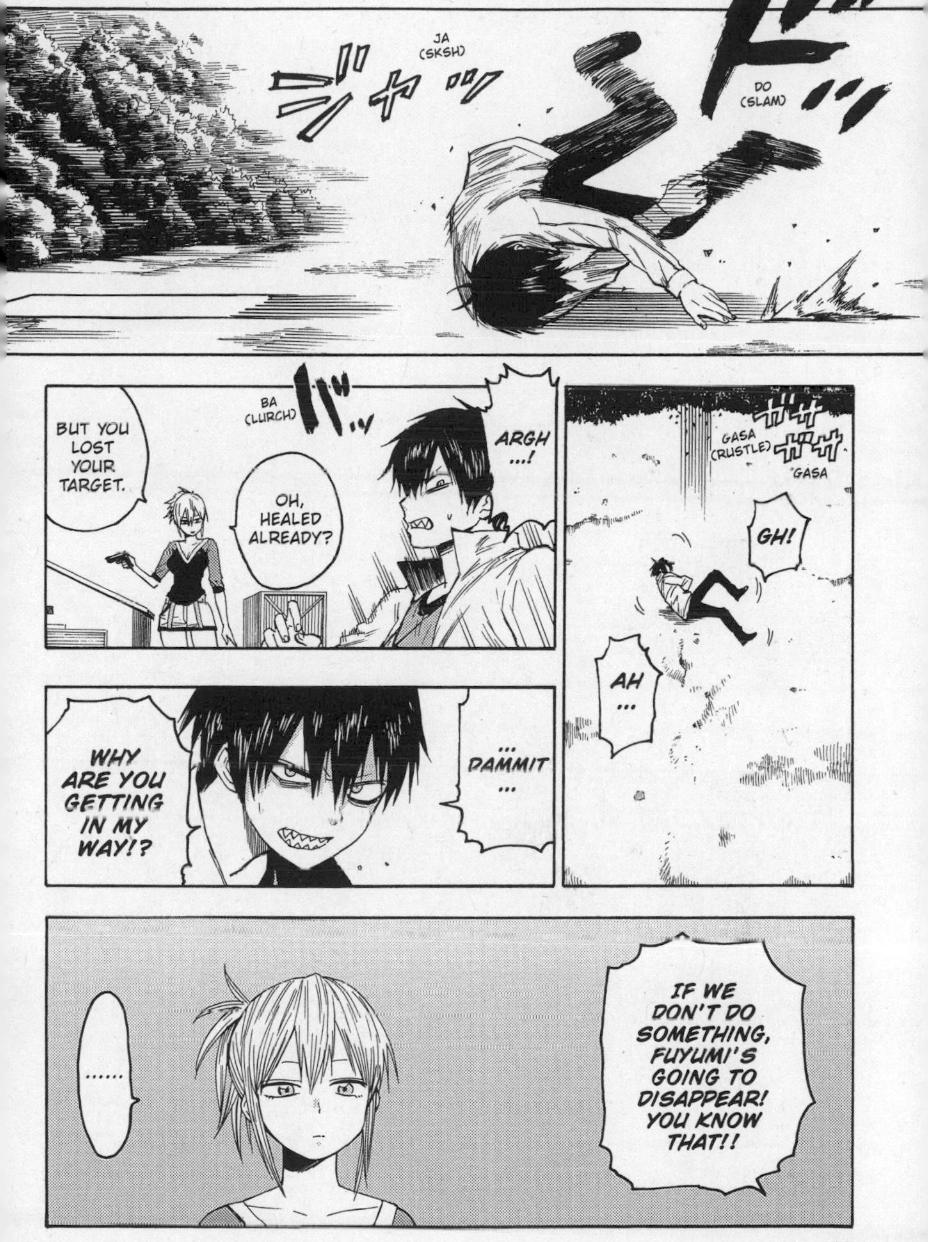
DO (SLAM)
JA (SKSH)
GASA (RUSTLE)
GASA
GH!
AH ...
ARGH ...!
BA (LURCH)
OH, HEALED ALREADY?
BUT YOU LOST YOUR TARGET.
... DAMMIT ...
WHY ARE YOU GETTING IN MY WAY!?
IF WE DON'T DO SOMETHING, FUYUMI'S GOING TO DISAPPEAR! YOU KNOW THAT!!
......

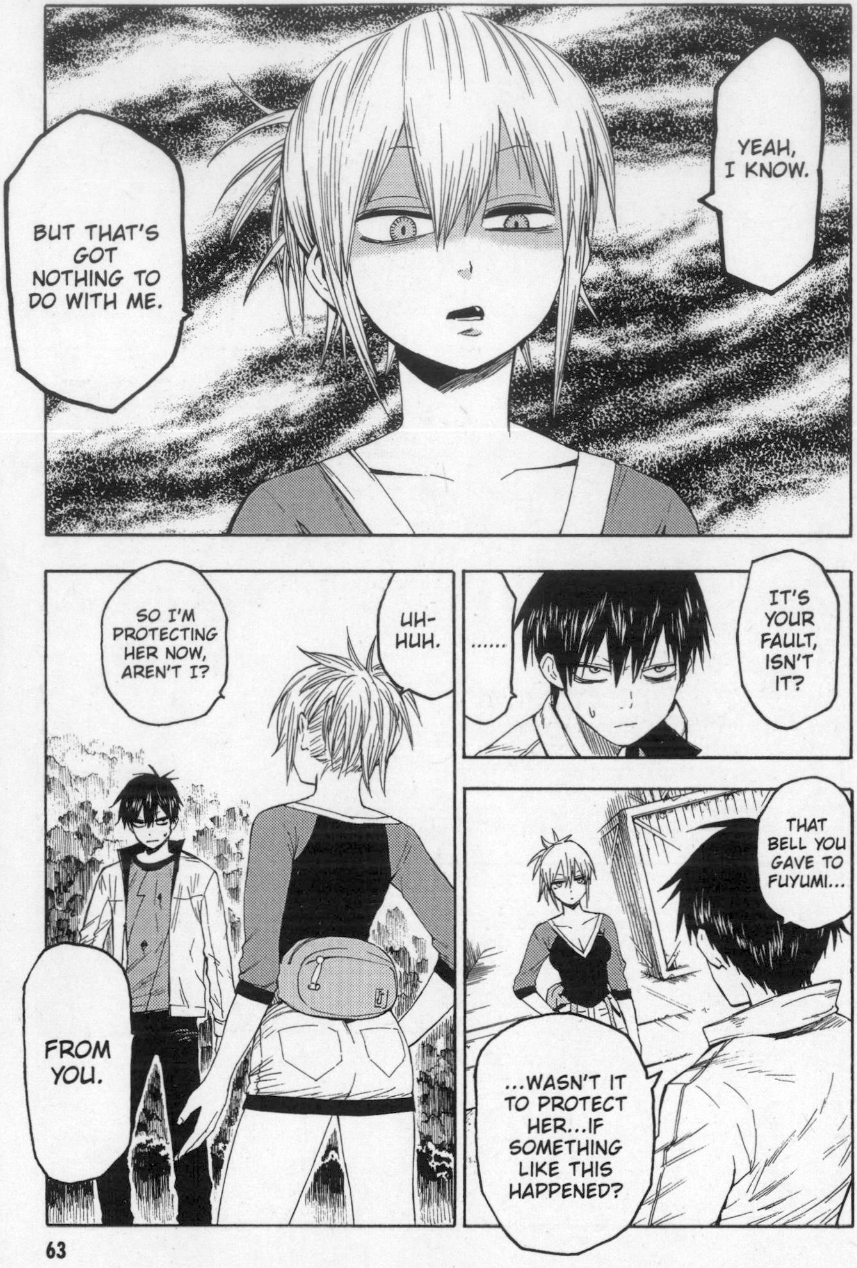
YEAH, I KNOW.
BUT THAT'S GOT NOTHING TO DO WITH ME.
IT'S YOUR FAULT, ISN'T IT?
......
THAT BELL YOU GAVE TO FUYUMI...
...WASN'T IT TO PROTECT HER...IF SOMETHING LIKE THIS HAPPENED?
UH-HUH.
SO I'M PROTECTING HER NOW, AREN'T I?
FROM YOU.

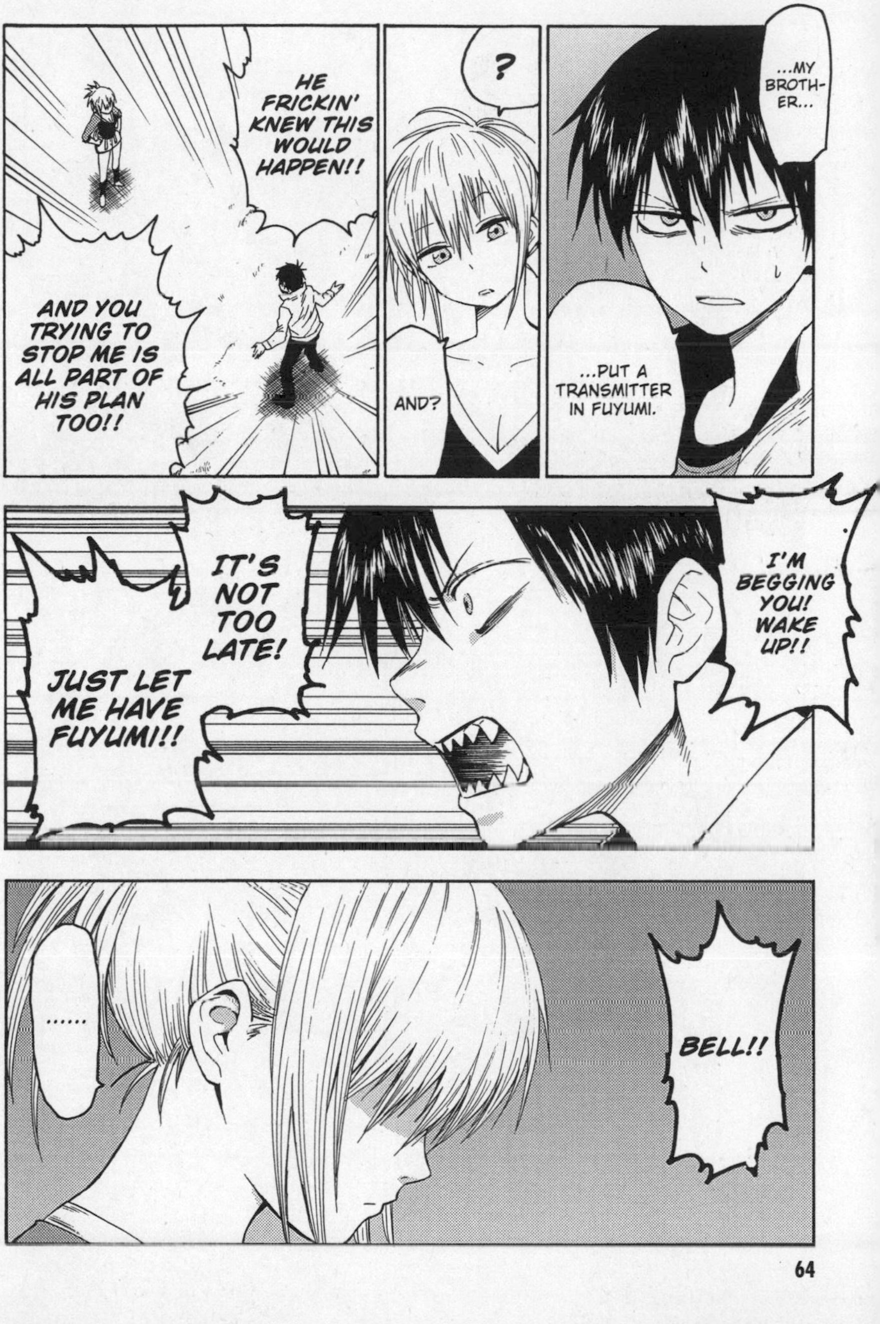
...MY BROTH-ER...
...PUT A TRANSMITTER IN FUYUMI.
?
AND?
HE FRICKIN' KNEW THIS WOULD HAPPEN!!
AND YOU TRYING TO STOP ME IS ALL PART OF HIS PLAN TOO!!
I'M BEGGING YOU! WAKE UP!!
IT'S NOT TOO LATE!
JUST LET ME HAVE FUYUMI!!
BELL!!
......

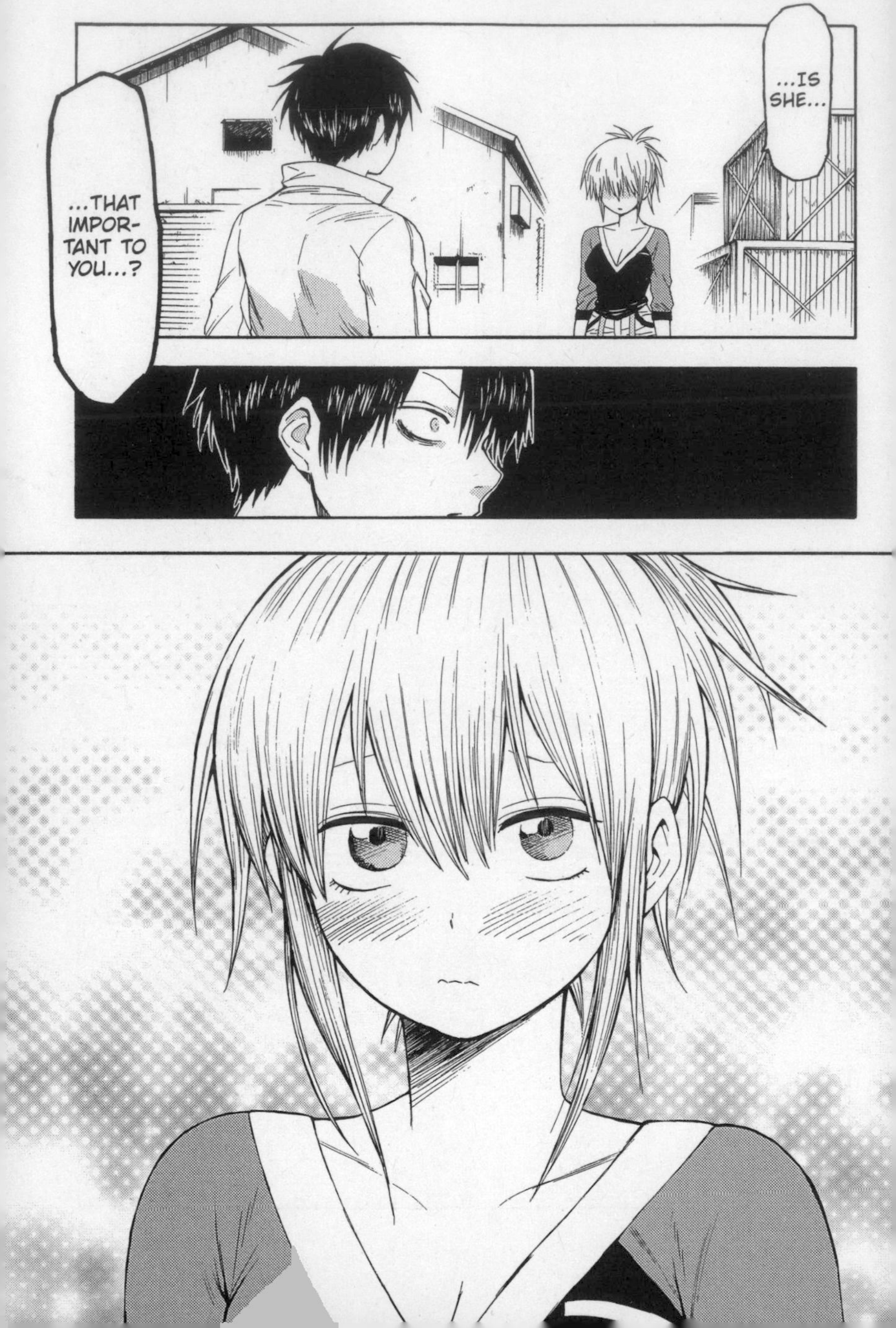
...IS SHE...
...THAT IMPORTANT TO YOU...?

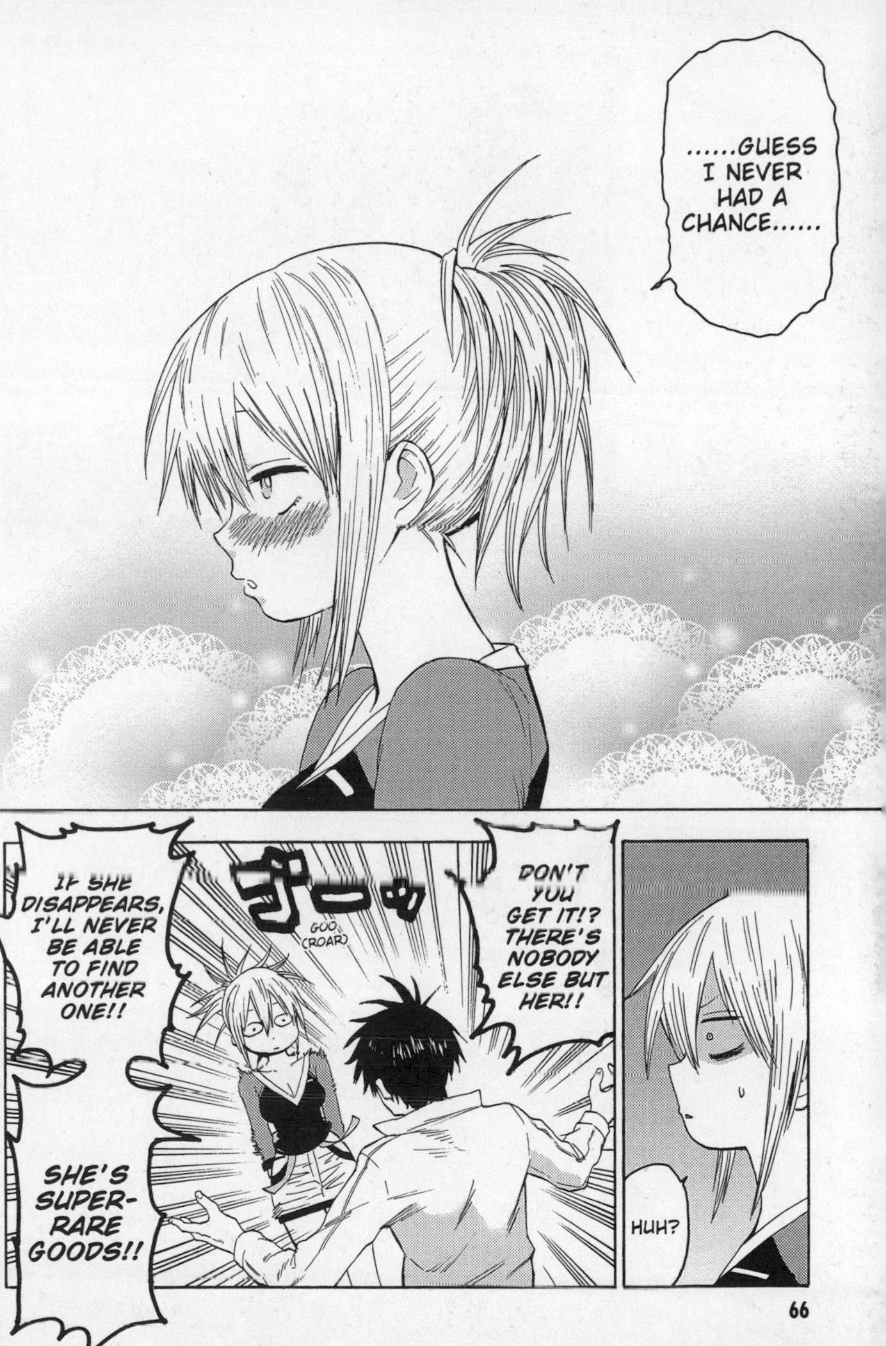
......GUESS I NEVER HAD A CHANCE......
HUH?
DON'T YOU GET IT!? THERE'S NOBODY ELSE BUT HER!!
GOO (ROAR)
IF SHE DISAPPEARS, I'LL NEVER BE ABLE TO FIND ANOTHER ONE!!
SHE'S SUPER-RARE GOODS!!

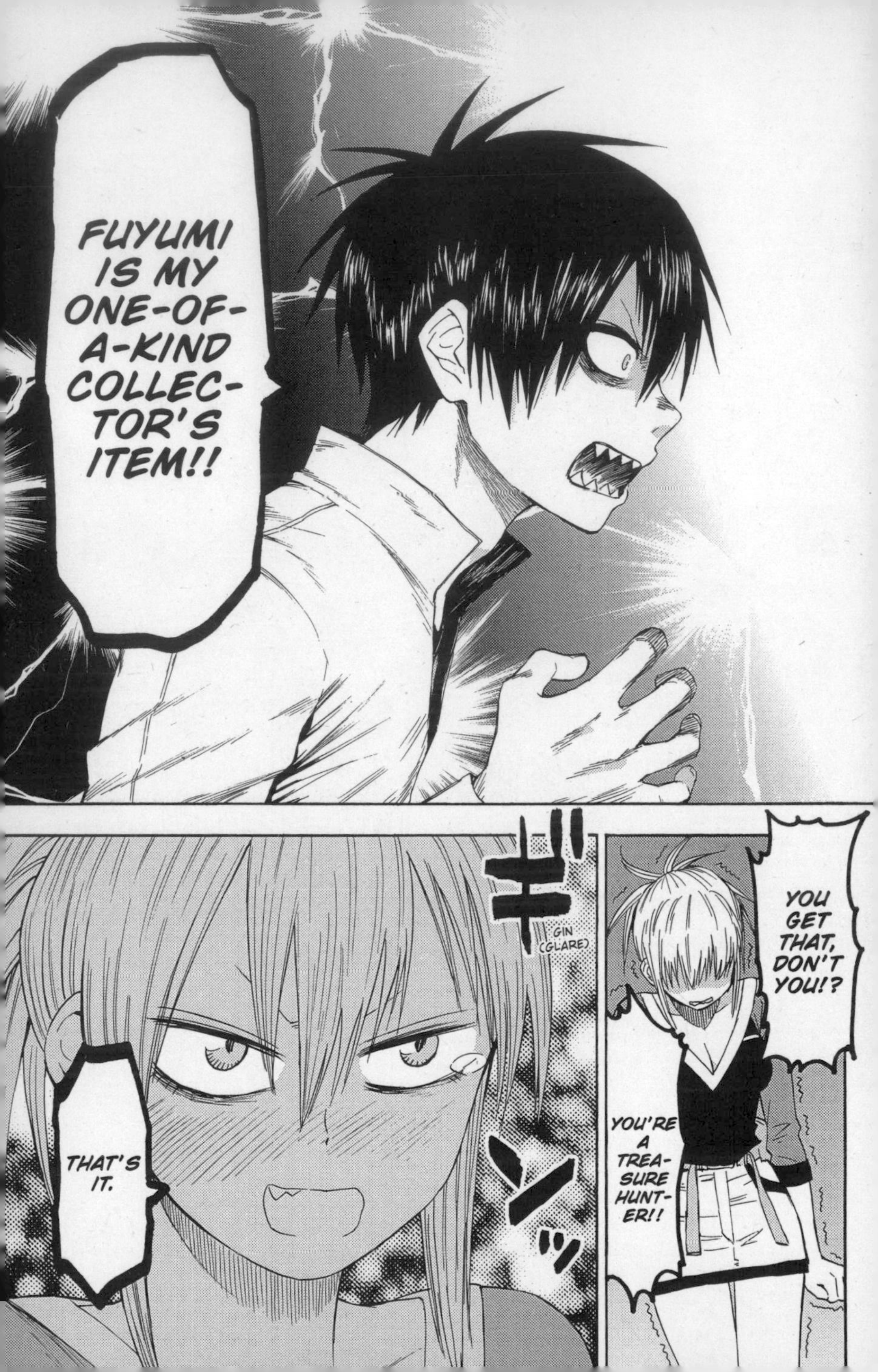
FUYUMI IS MY ONE-OF-A-KIND COLLECTOR'S ITEM!!
YOU GET THAT, DON'T YOU!?
YOU'RE A TREASURE HUNTER!!
GIN (GLARE)
THAT'S IT.

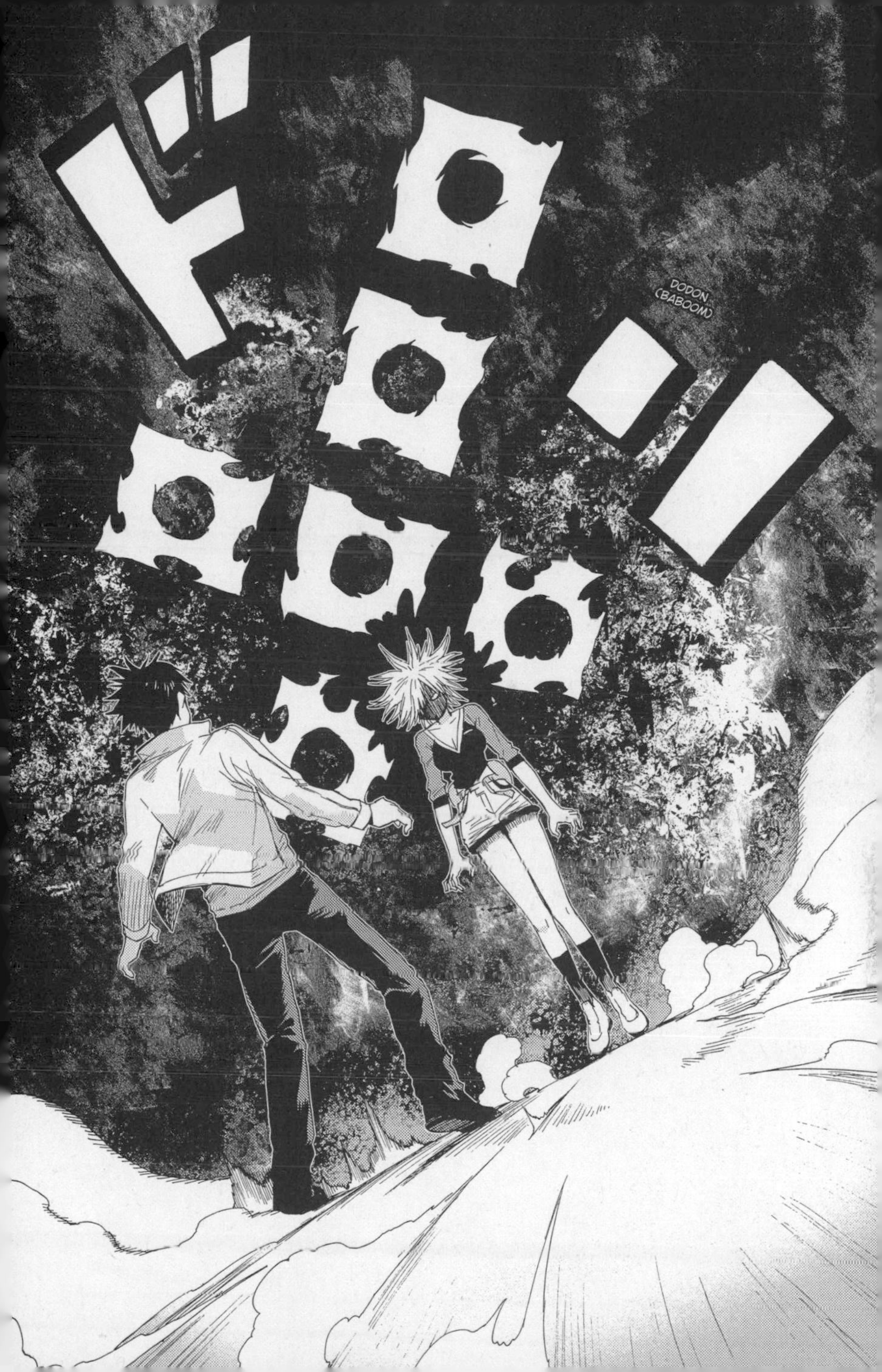
DODON
(BABOOM)

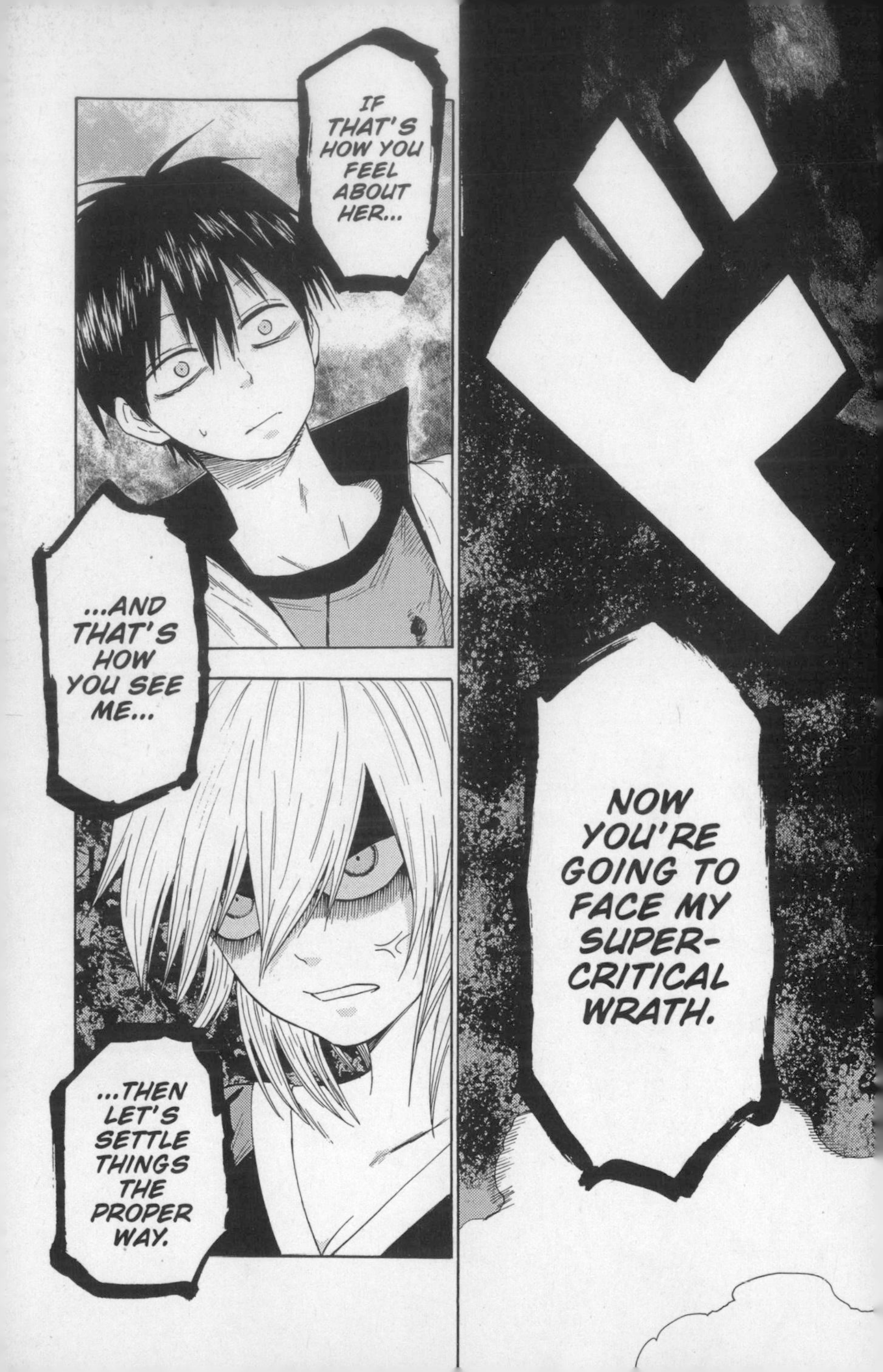
NOW YOU'RE GOING TO FACE MY SUPER-CRITICAL WRATH.
IF THAT'S HOW YOU FEEL ABOUT HER...
...AND THAT'S HOW YOU SEE ME...
...THEN LET'S SETTLE THINGS THE PROPER WAY.

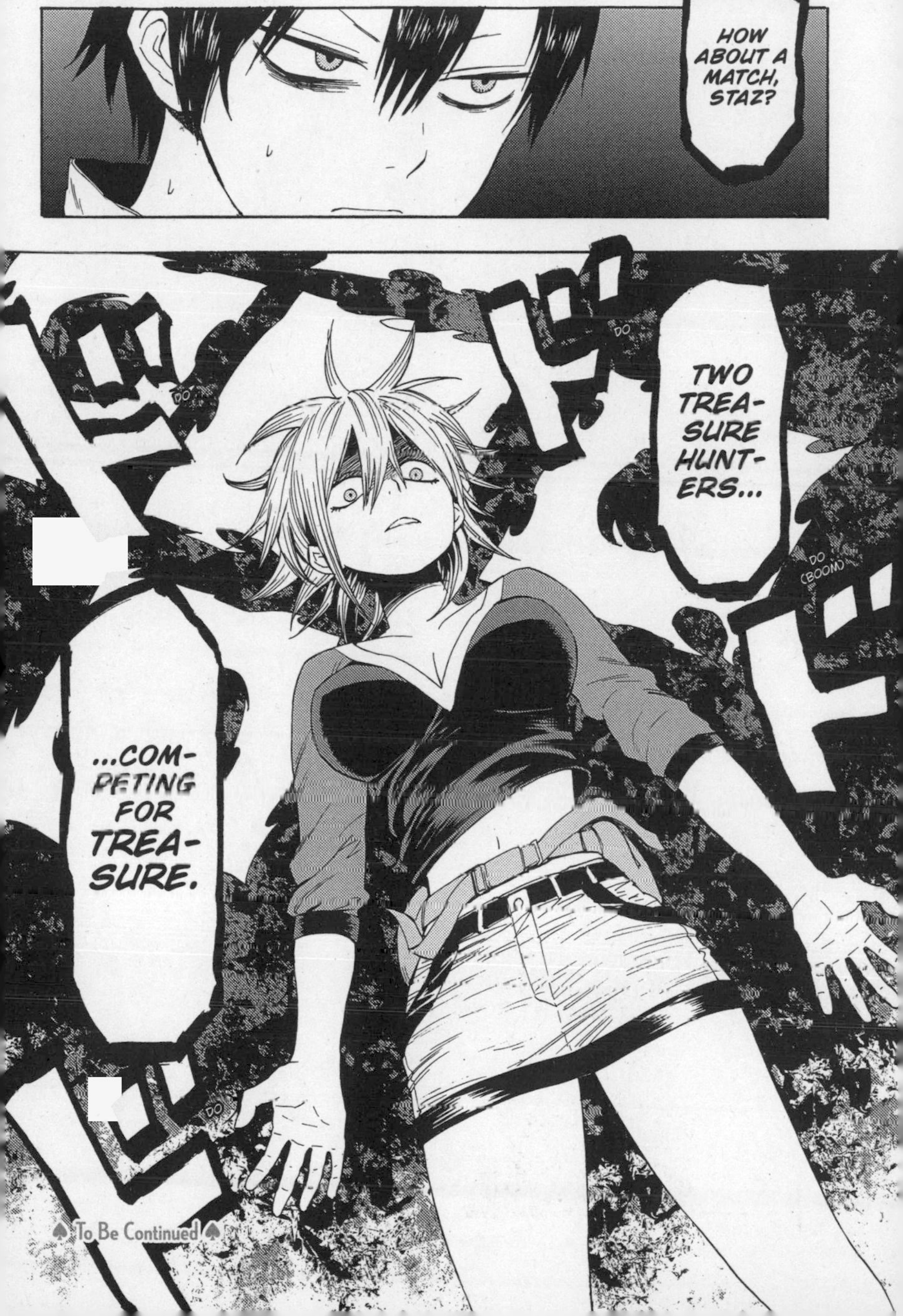
HOW ABOUT A MATCH, STAZ?
DO
TWO TREA-SURE HUNT-ERS...
DO (BOOM)
DO
...COM-PETING FOR TREA-SURE.
DO
To Be Continued

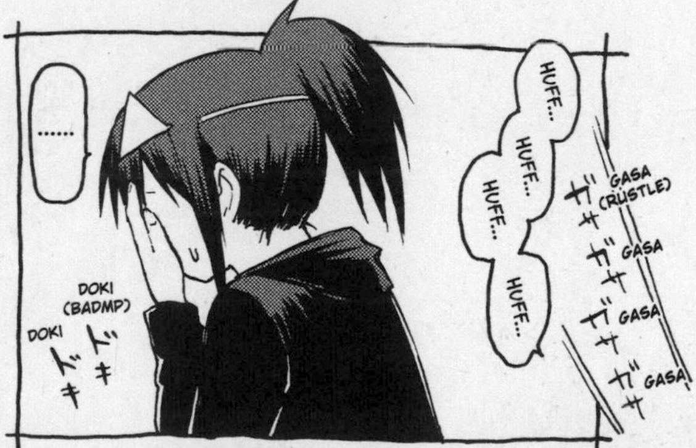
HUFF... HUFF... HUFF... HUFF...
GASA (RUSTLE)
GASA
GASA
GASA
......
DOKI (BADMP)
DOKI

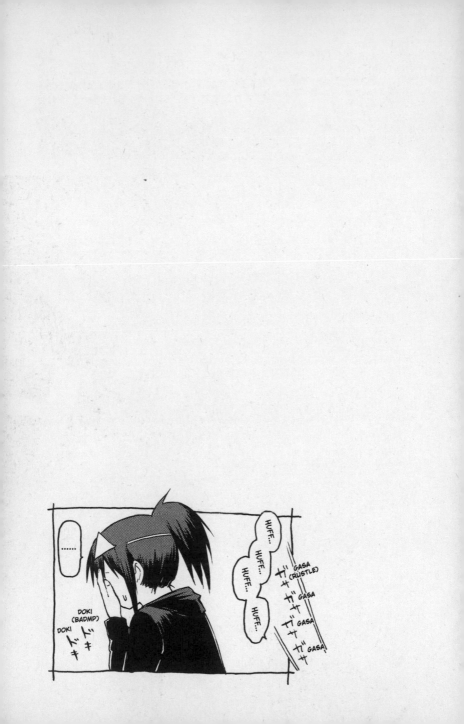

BLOOD LAD

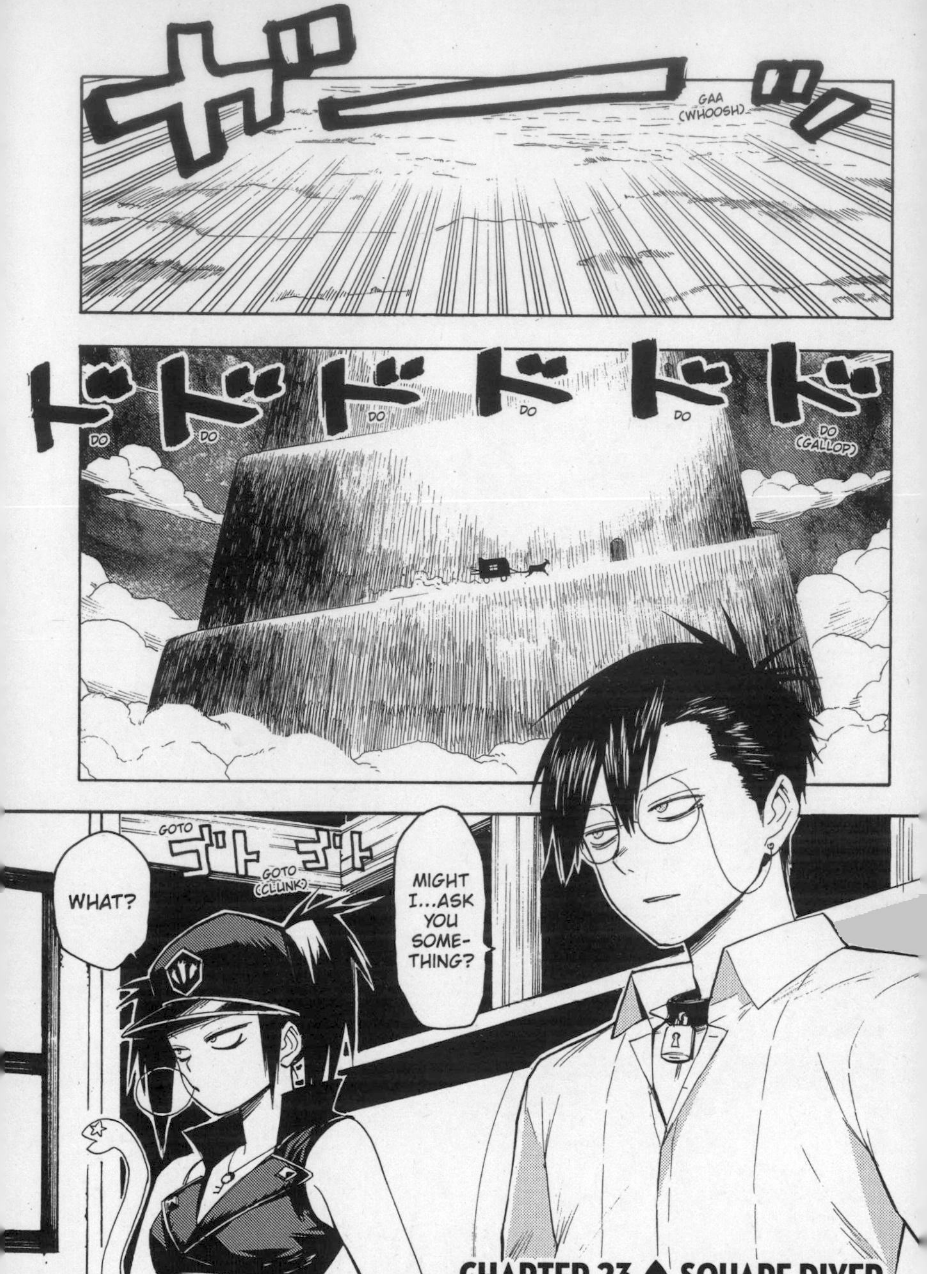
GAA (WHOOSH)
DO (GALLOP)
DO
DO
DO
DO
DO
MIGHT I...ASK YOU SOME-THING?
GOTO
GOTO (CLUNK)
WHAT?
CHAPTER 23 ♠ SQUARE DIVER

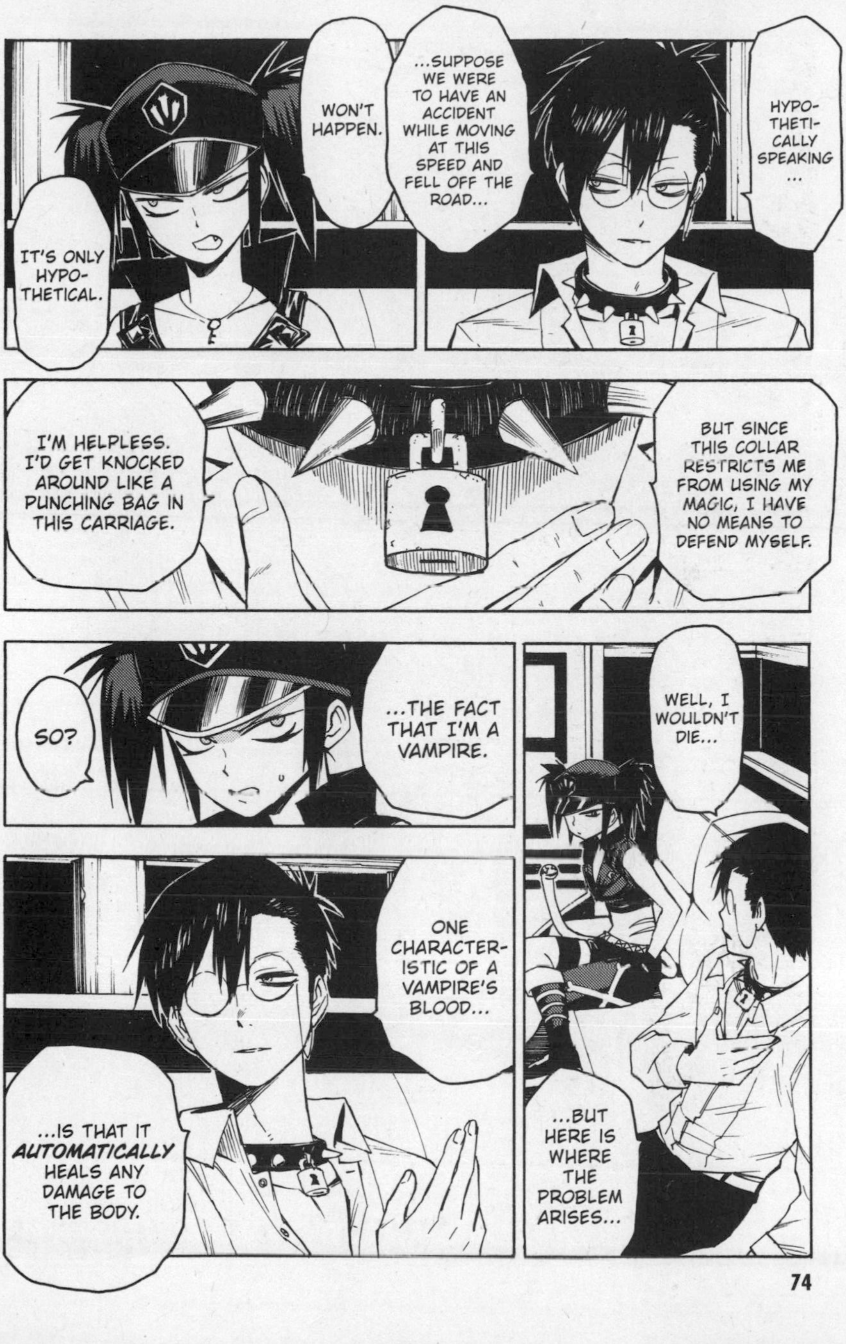
HYPOTHETICALLY SPEAKING...
...SUPPOSE WE WERE TO HAVE AN ACCIDENT WHILE MOVING AT THIS SPEED AND FELL OFF THE ROAD...
WON'T HAPPEN.
IT'S ONLY HYPOTHETICAL.
BUT SINCE THIS COLLAR RESTRICTS ME FROM USING MY MAGIC, I HAVE NO MEANS TO DEFEND MYSELF.
I'M HELPLESS. I'D GET KNOCKED AROUND LIKE A PUNCHING BAG IN THIS CARRIAGE.
WELL, I WOULDN'T DIE...
...BUT HERE IS WHERE THE PROBLEM ARISES...
...THE FACT THAT I'M A VAMPIRE.
SO?
ONE CHARACTERISTIC OF A VAMPIRE'S BLOOD...
...IS THAT IT *AUTOMATICALLY* HEALS ANY DAMAGE TO THE BODY.

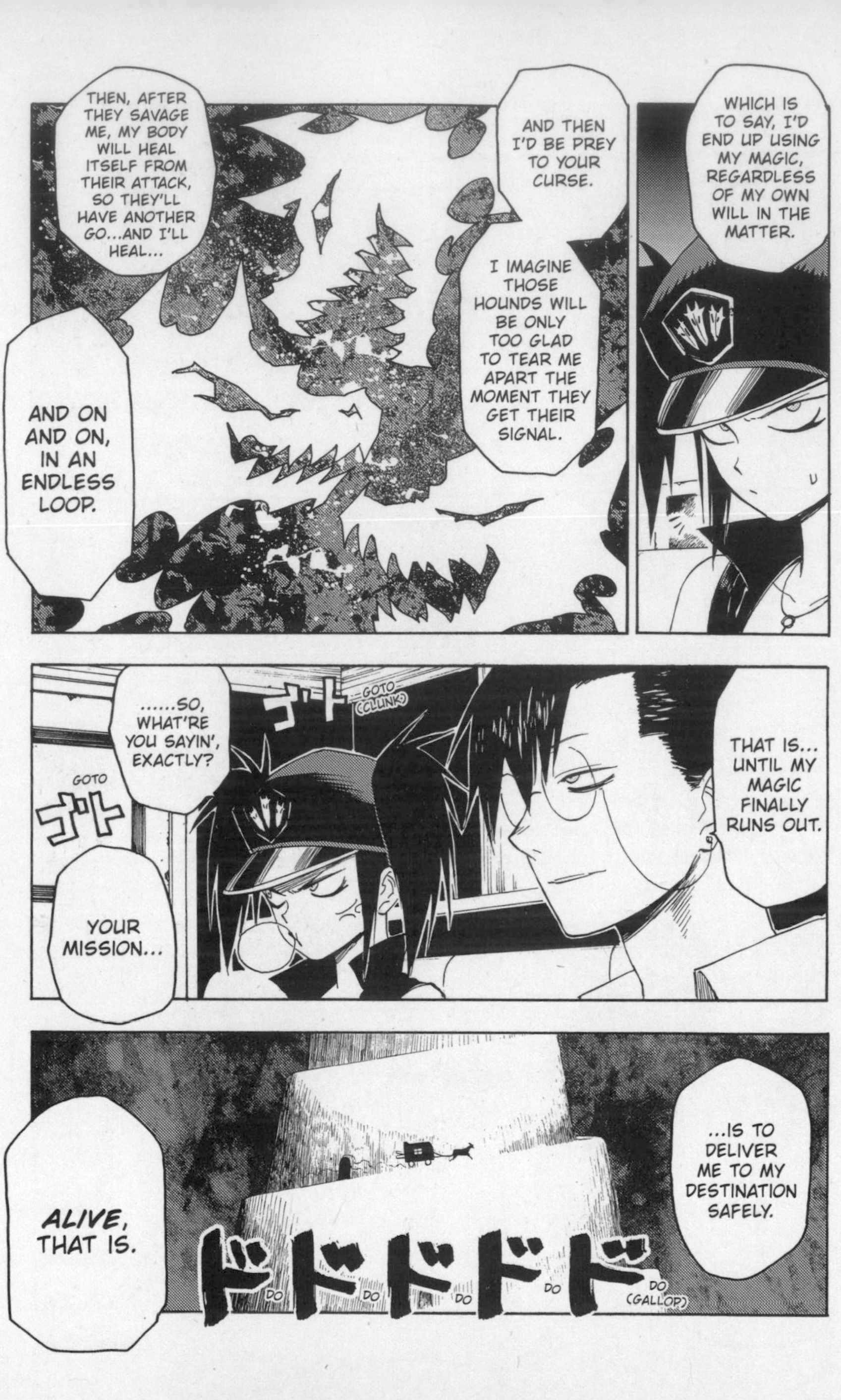
I IMAGINE THOSE HOUNDS WILL BE ONLY TOO GLAD TO TEAR ME APART THE MOMENT THEY GET THEIR SIGNAL.
THEN, AFTER THEY SAVAGE ME, MY BODY WILL HEAL ITSELF FROM THEIR ATTACK, SO THEY'LL HAVE ANOTHER GO...AND I'LL HEAL...
AND ON AND ON, IN AN ENDLESS LOOP.
AND THEN I'D BE PREY TO YOUR CURSE.
WHICH IS TO SAY, I'D END UP USING MY MAGIC, REGARDLESS OF MY OWN WILL IN THE MATTER.
THAT IS... UNTIL MY MAGIC FINALLY RUNS OUT.
ゴト GOTO (CLUNK)
......SO, WHAT'RE YOU SAYIN', EXACTLY?
ゴト GOTO
YOUR MISSION...
...IS TO DELIVER ME TO MY DESTINATION SAFELY.
ALIVE, THAT IS.
ドッドッドッドッドッ DO DO DO DO DO (GALLOP)

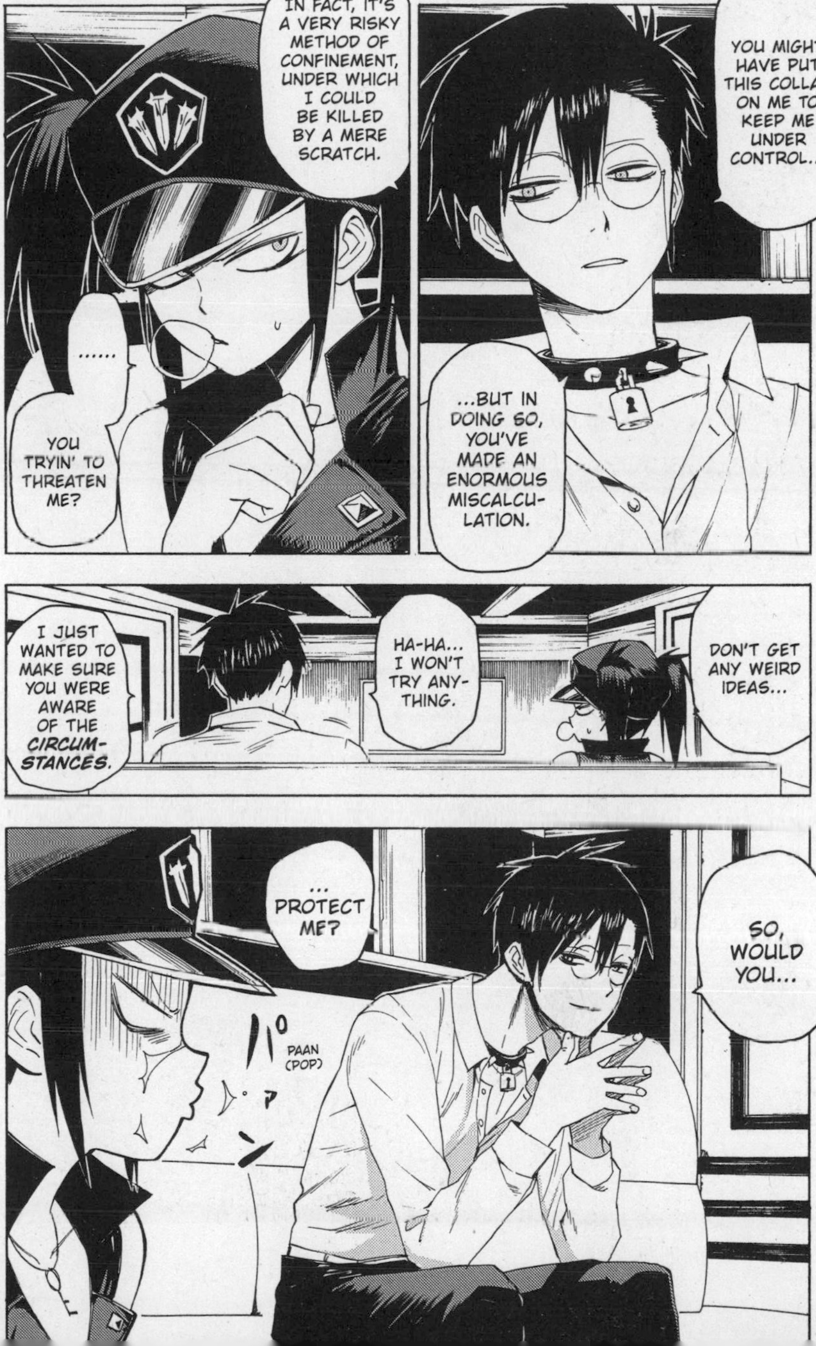
YOU MIGHT HAVE PUT THIS COLLAR ON ME TO KEEP ME UNDER CONTROL...
...BUT IN DOING SO, YOU'VE MADE AN ENORMOUS MISCALCULATION.
IN FACT, IT'S A VERY RISKY METHOD OF CONFINEMENT, UNDER WHICH I COULD BE KILLED BY A MERE SCRATCH.
......
YOU TRYIN' TO THREATEN ME?
DON'T GET ANY WEIRD IDEAS...
HA-HA... I WON'T TRY ANYTHING.
I JUST WANTED TO MAKE SURE YOU WERE AWARE OF THE *CIRCUMSTANCES*.
SO, WOULD YOU...
...PROTECT ME?
PAAN (POP)

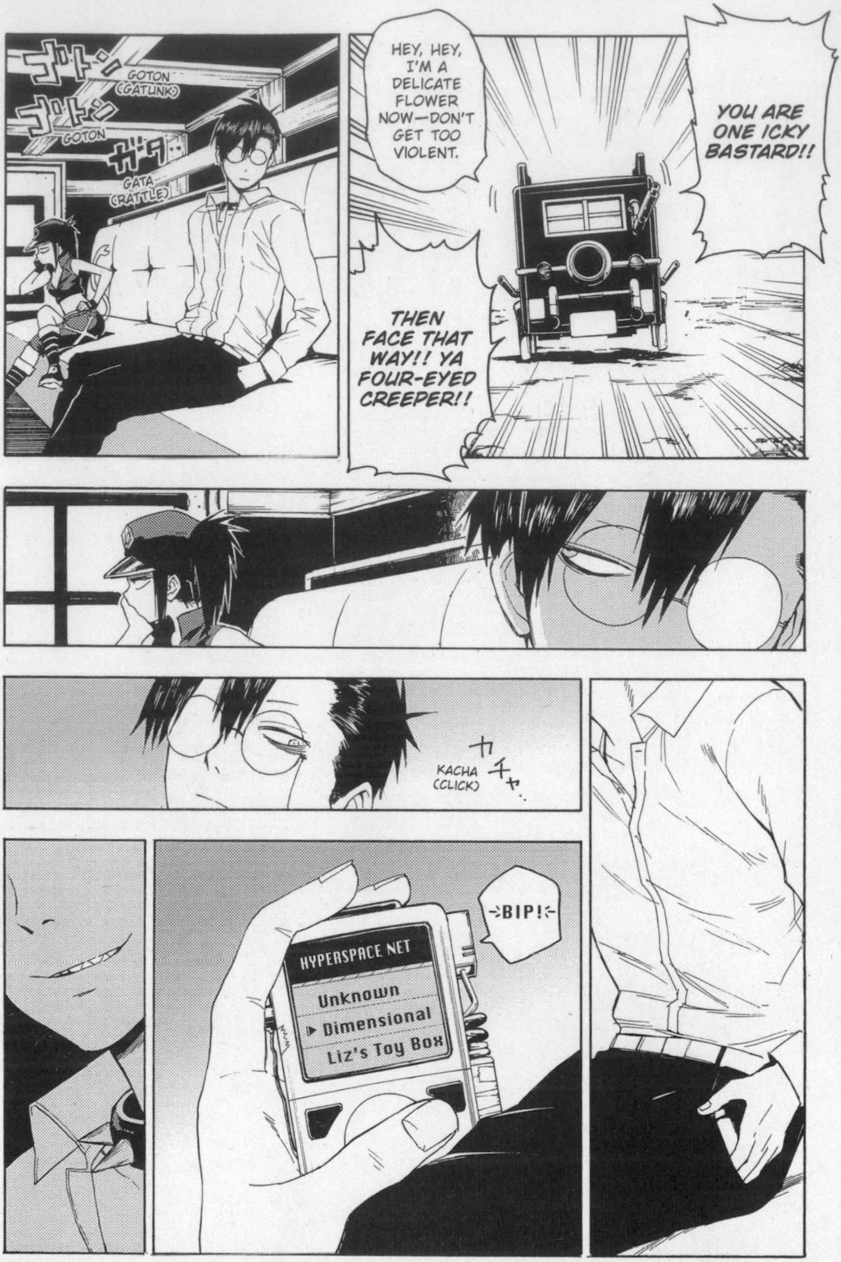
YOU ARE ONE ICKY BASTARD!!
HEY, HEY, I'M A DELICATE FLOWER NOW—DON'T GET TOO VIOLENT.
THEN FACE THAT WAY!! YA FOUR-EYED CREEPER!!
ゴトン
GOTON (GATUNK)
ゴトン
GOTON
ガタ
GATA (RATTLE)
カチャ…
KACHA (CLICK)
BIP!
HYPERSPACE NET
Unknown
Dimensional
Liz's Toy Box

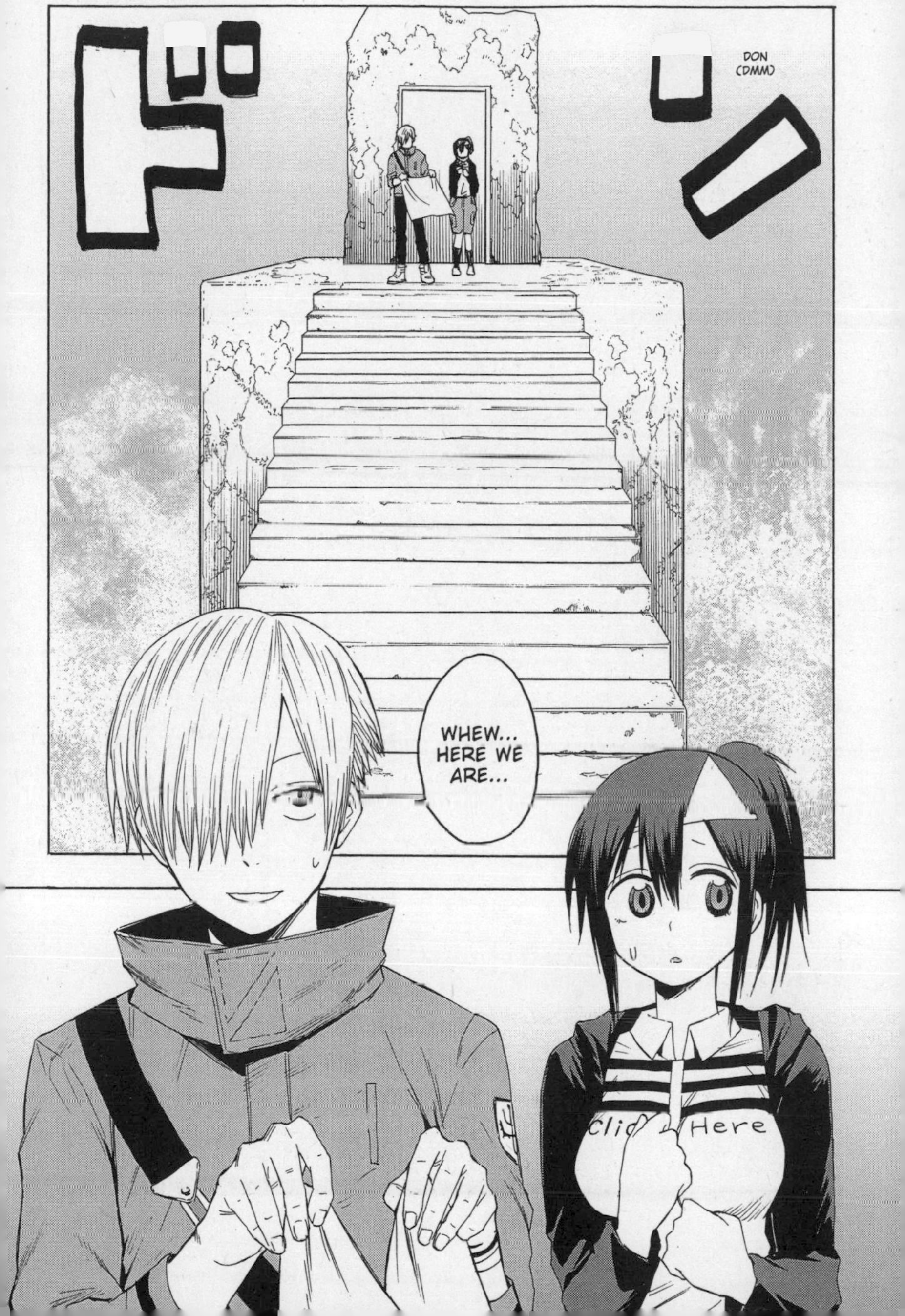
DON
(DMM)
WHEW... HERE WE ARE...

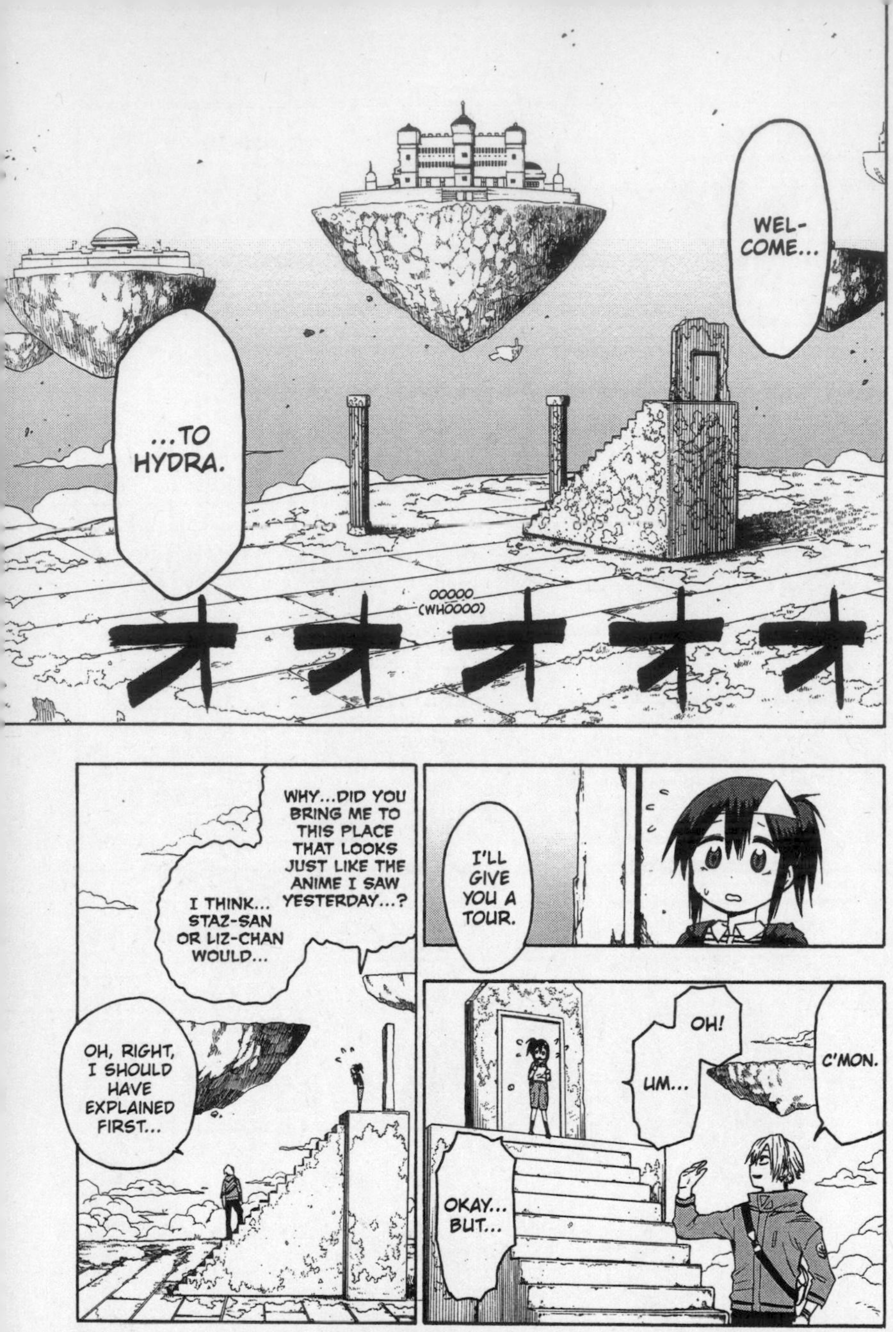
WEL-COME...
...TO HYDRA.
OOOOO (WHOOOO)
I'LL GIVE YOU A TOUR.
C'MON.
OH!
UM...
OKAY... BUT...
WHY...DID YOU BRING ME TO THIS PLACE THAT LOOKS JUST LIKE THE ANIME I SAW YESTERDAY...?
I THINK... STAZ-SAN OR LIZ-CHAN WOULD...
OH, RIGHT, I SHOULD HAVE EXPLAINED FIRST...

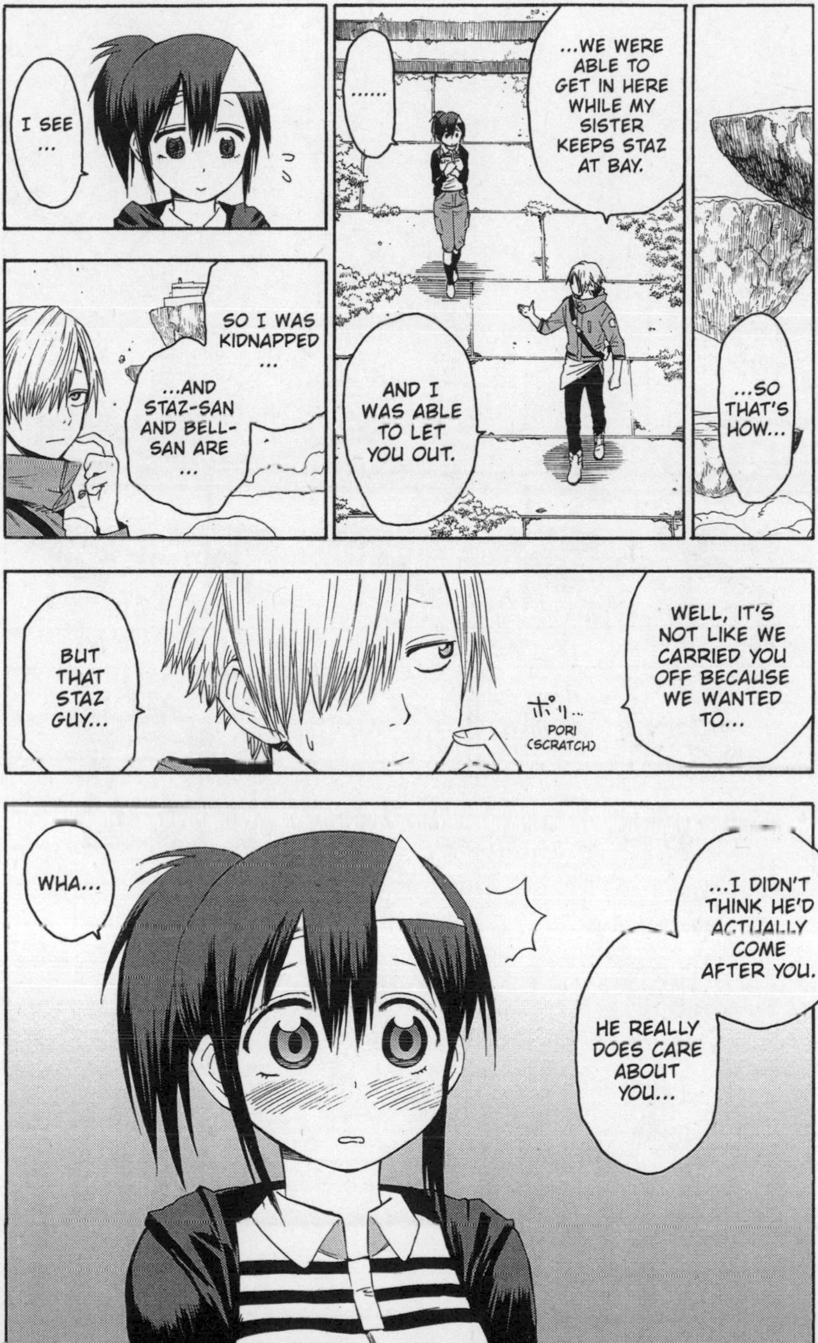
...SO THAT'S HOW...
...WE WERE ABLE TO GET IN HERE WHILE MY SISTER KEEPS STAZ AT BAY.
......
AND I WAS ABLE TO LET YOU OUT.
I SEE ...
SO I WAS KIDNAPPED ...
...AND STAZ-SAN AND BELL-SAN ARE ...
WELL, IT'S NOT LIKE WE CARRIED YOU OFF BECAUSE WE WANTED TO...
ポリ... PORI (SCRATCH)
BUT THAT STAZ GUY...
...I DIDN'T THINK HE'D ACTUALLY COME AFTER YOU.
HE REALLY DOES CARE ABOUT YOU...
WHA...

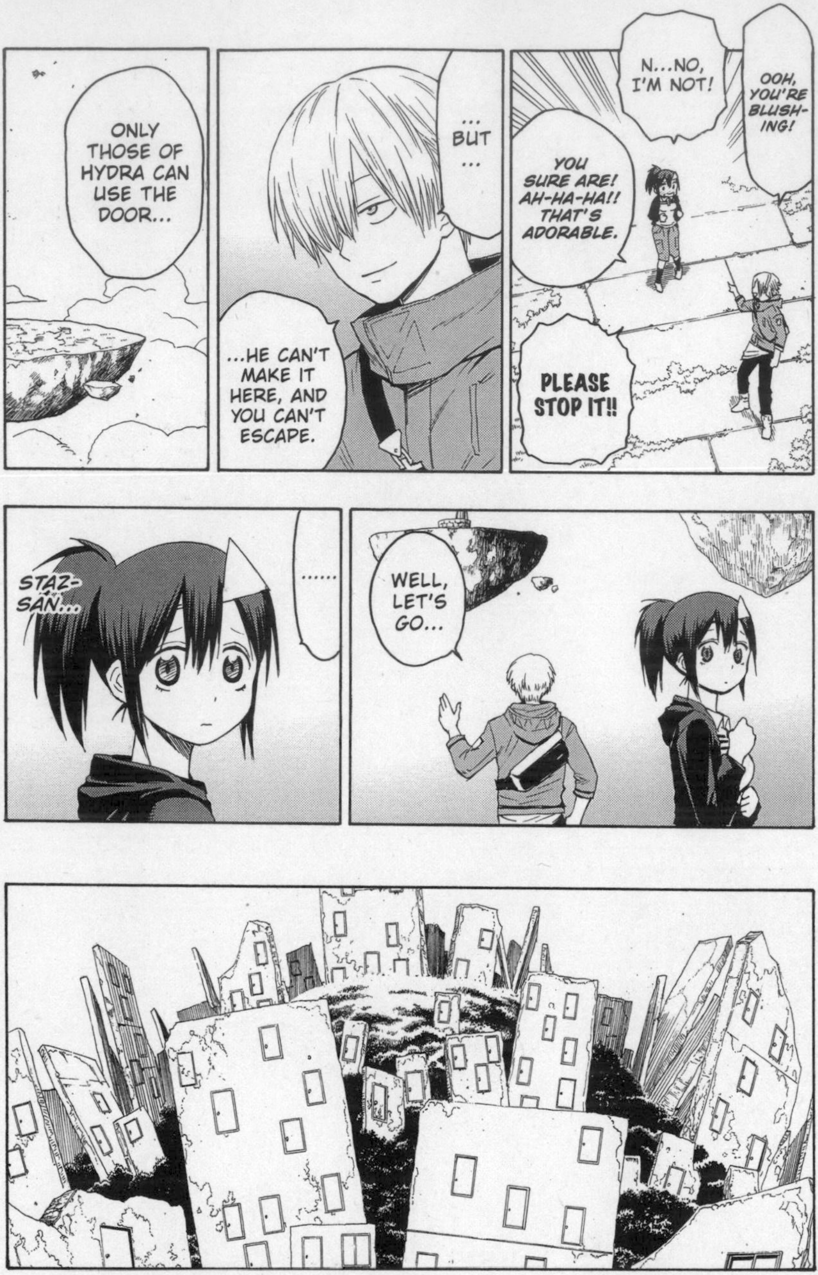
OOH, YOU'RE BLUSHING!
N...NO, I'M NOT!
YOU SURE ARE! AH-HA-HA!! THAT'S ADORABLE.
PLEASE STOP IT!!
... BUT ...
...HE CAN'T MAKE IT HERE, AND YOU CAN'T ESCAPE.
ONLY THOSE OF HYDRA CAN USE THE DOOR...
WELL, LET'S GO...
......
STAZ-SAN...

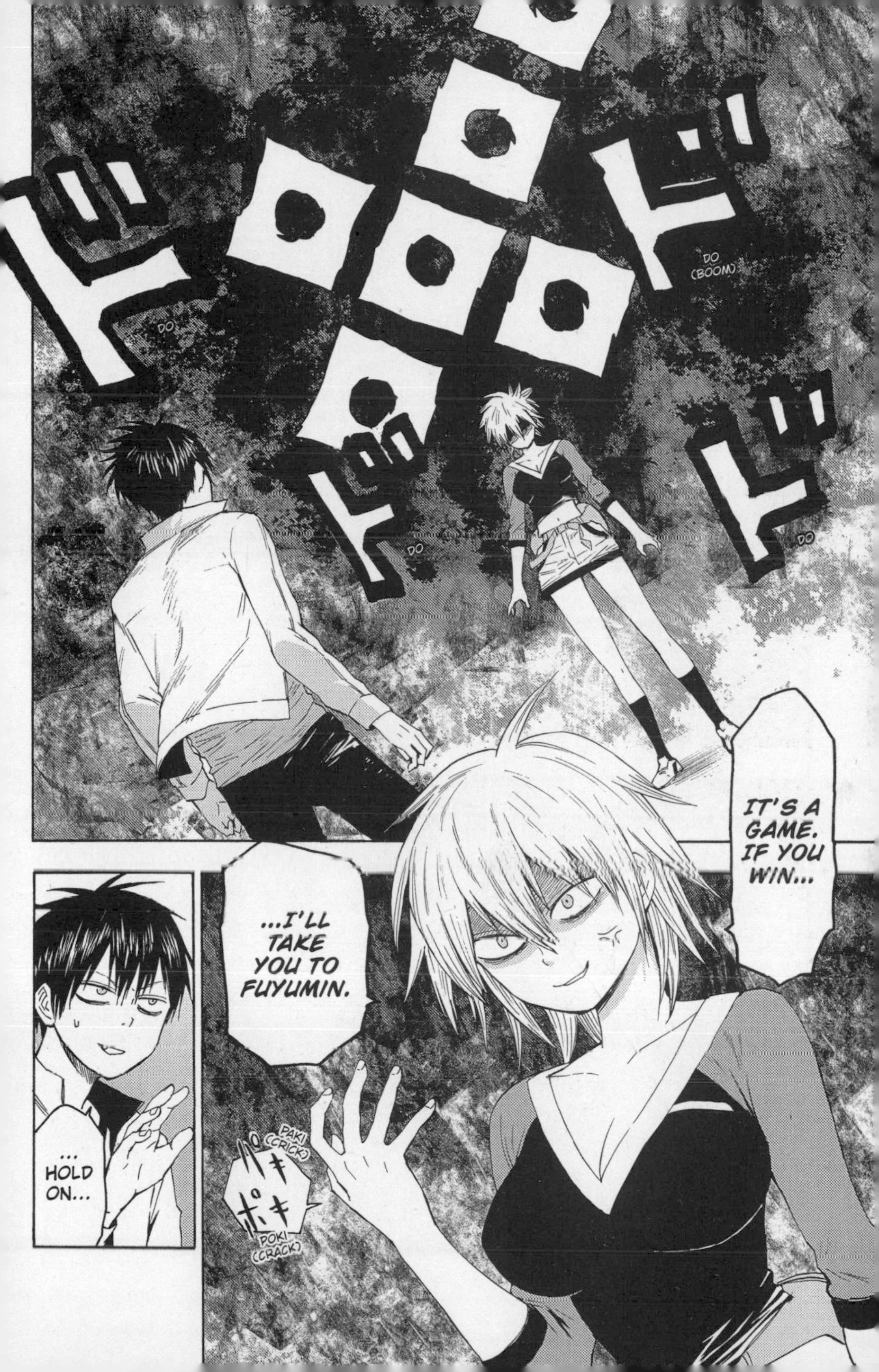
DO (BOOM)
DO
DO
DO
IT'S A GAME. IF YOU WIN...
...I'LL TAKE YOU TO FUYUMIN.
パキ
PAKI (CRICK)
ポキ
POKI (CRACK)
... HOLD ON...

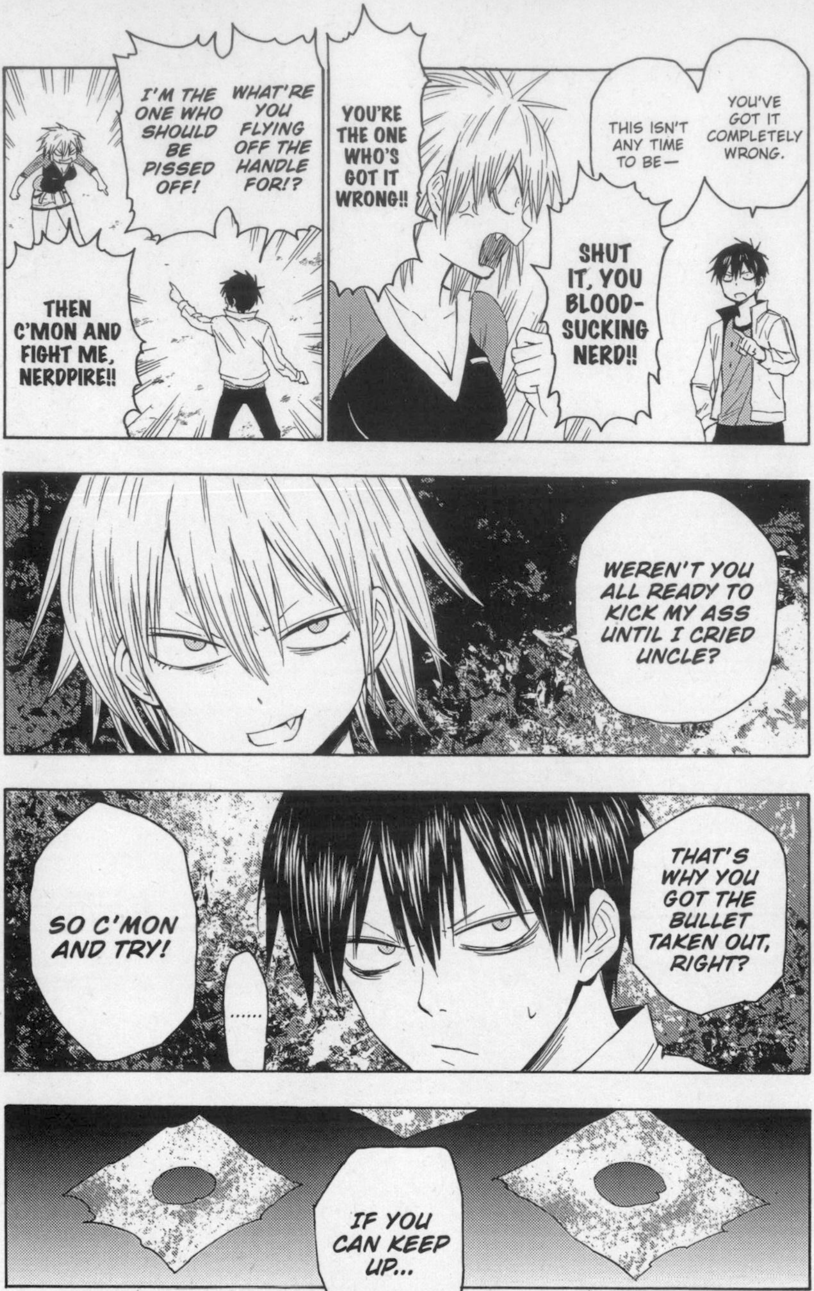
YOU'VE GOT IT COMPLETELY WRONG.
THIS ISN'T ANY TIME TO BE—
SHUT IT, YOU BLOOD-SUCKING NERD!!
YOU'RE THE ONE WHO'S GOT IT WRONG!!
WHAT'RE YOU FLYING OFF THE HANDLE FOR!?
I'M THE ONE WHO SHOULD BE PISSED OFF!
THEN C'MON AND FIGHT ME, NERDPIRE!!
WEREN'T YOU ALL READY TO KICK MY ASS UNTIL I CRIED UNCLE?
THAT'S WHY YOU GOT THE BULLET TAKEN OUT, RIGHT?
......
SO C'MON AND TRY!
IF YOU CAN KEEP UP...

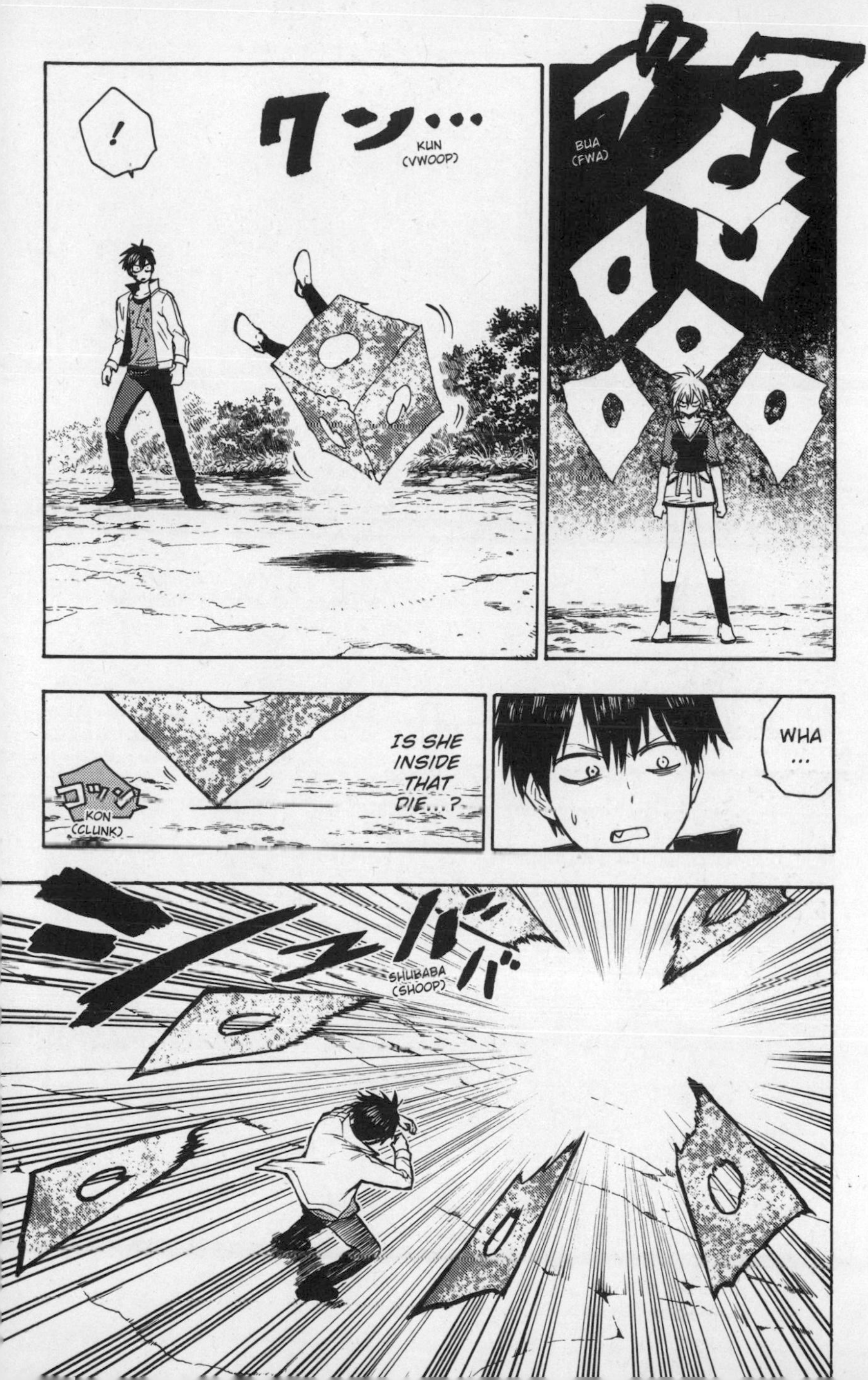
BUA
(FWA)
KUN
(VWOOP)
!
WHA
...
IS SHE INSIDE THAT DIE...?
KON
(CLUNK)
SHUBABA
(SHOOP)

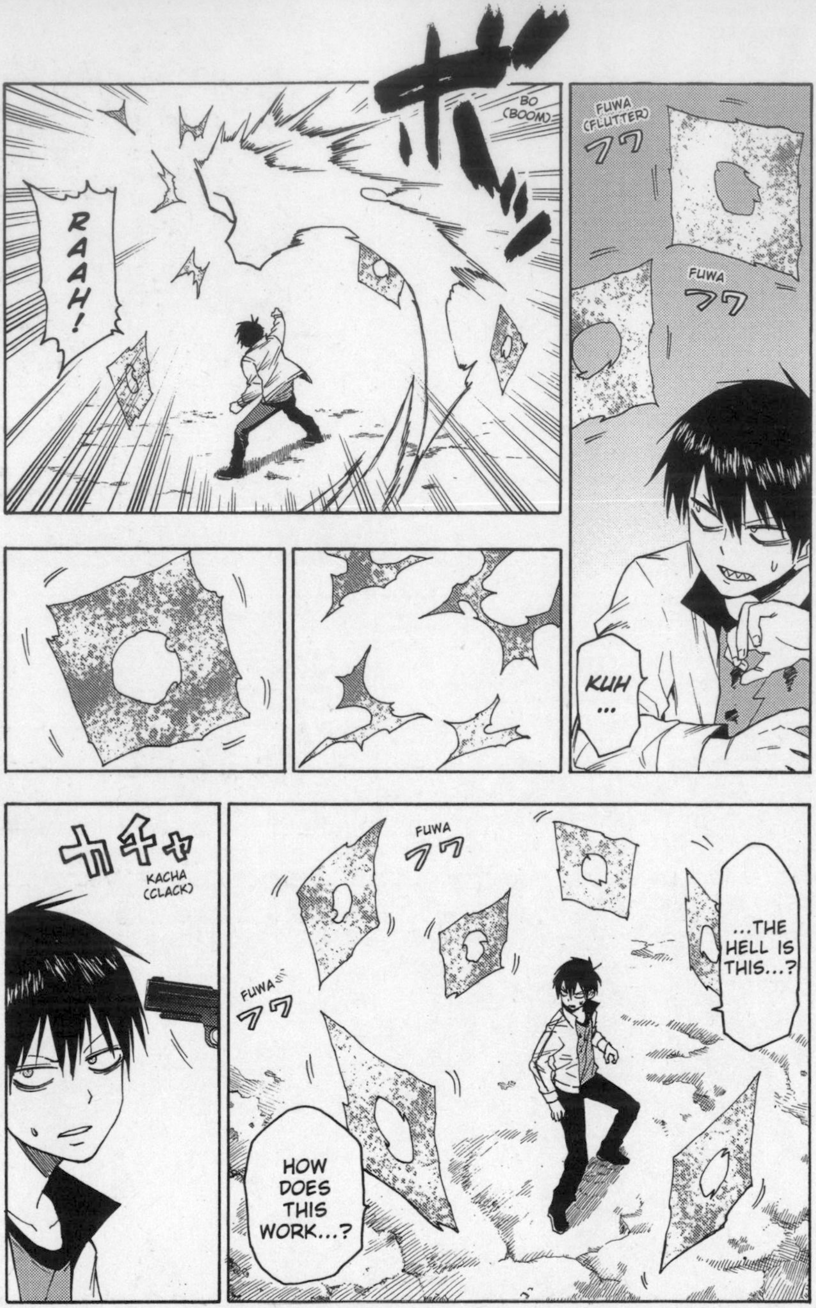
FUWA (FLUTTER)
フワ
FUWA
フワ
KUH...
ボッ
BO (BOOM)
RAAH!
FUWA
フワ
...THE HELL IS THIS...?
FUWA
フワ
HOW DOES THIS WORK...?
カチャ
KACHA (CLACK)

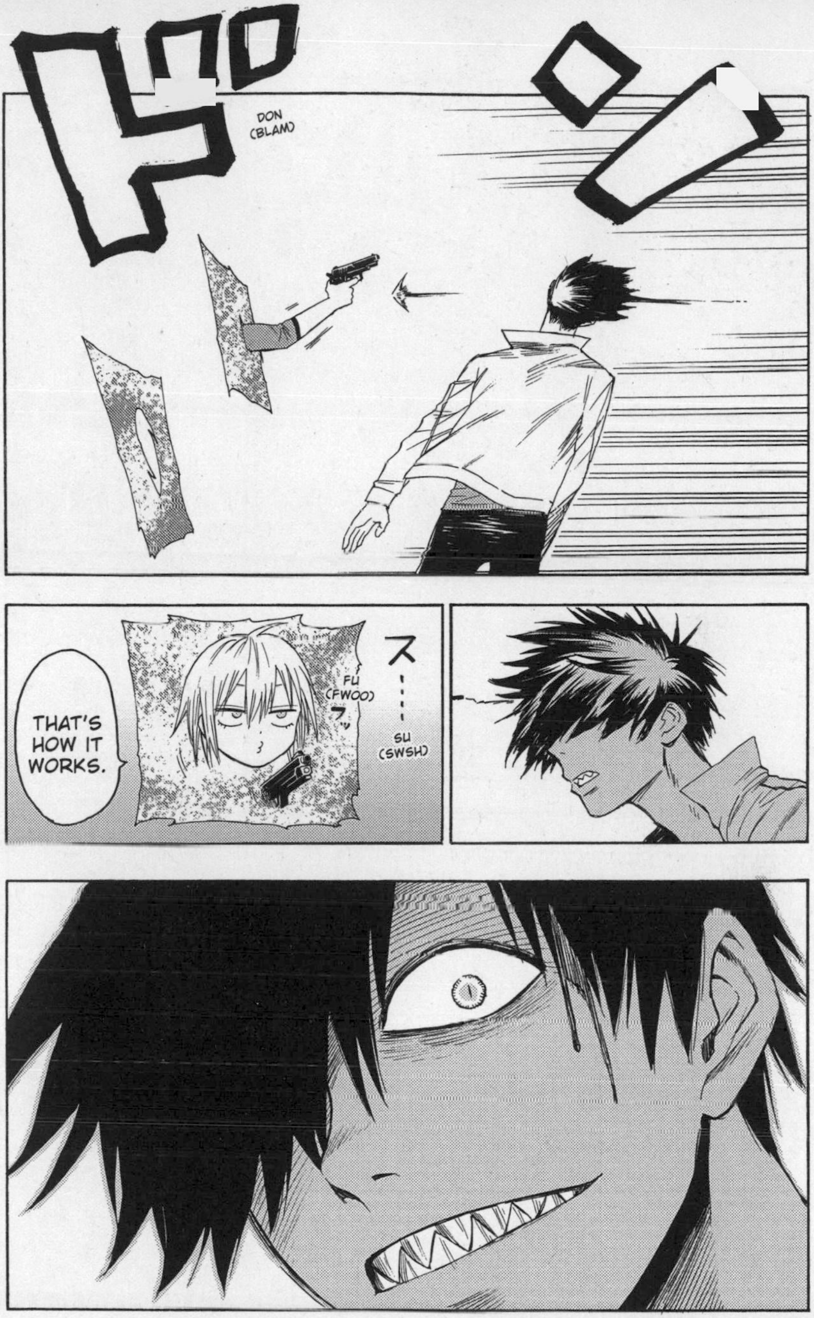
DON (BLAM)
SU (SWSH)
FU (FWOO)
THAT'S HOW IT WORKS.

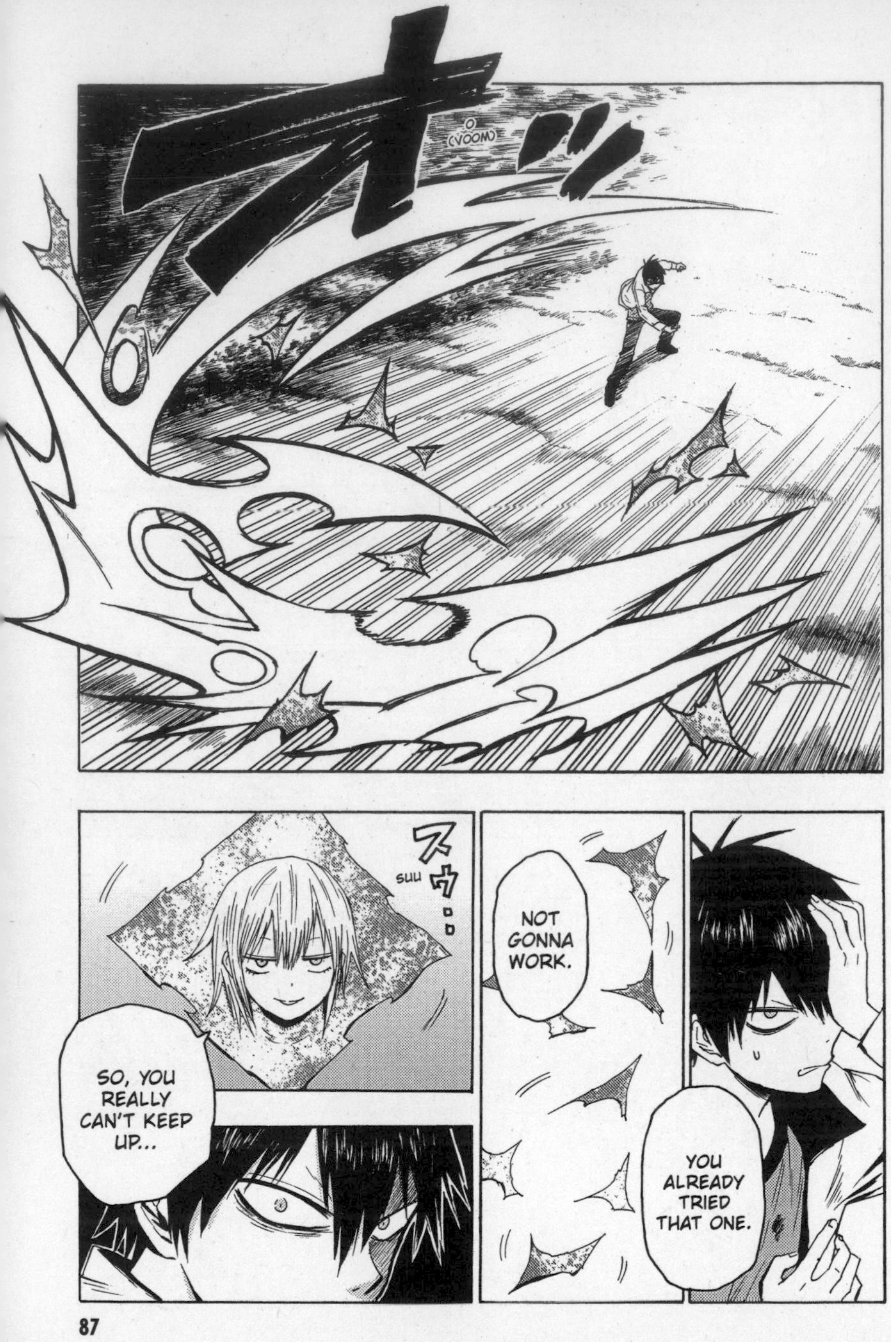
O (VOOM)
NOT GONNA WORK.
YOU ALREADY TRIED THAT ONE.
SUU
SO, YOU REALLY CAN'T KEEP UP...

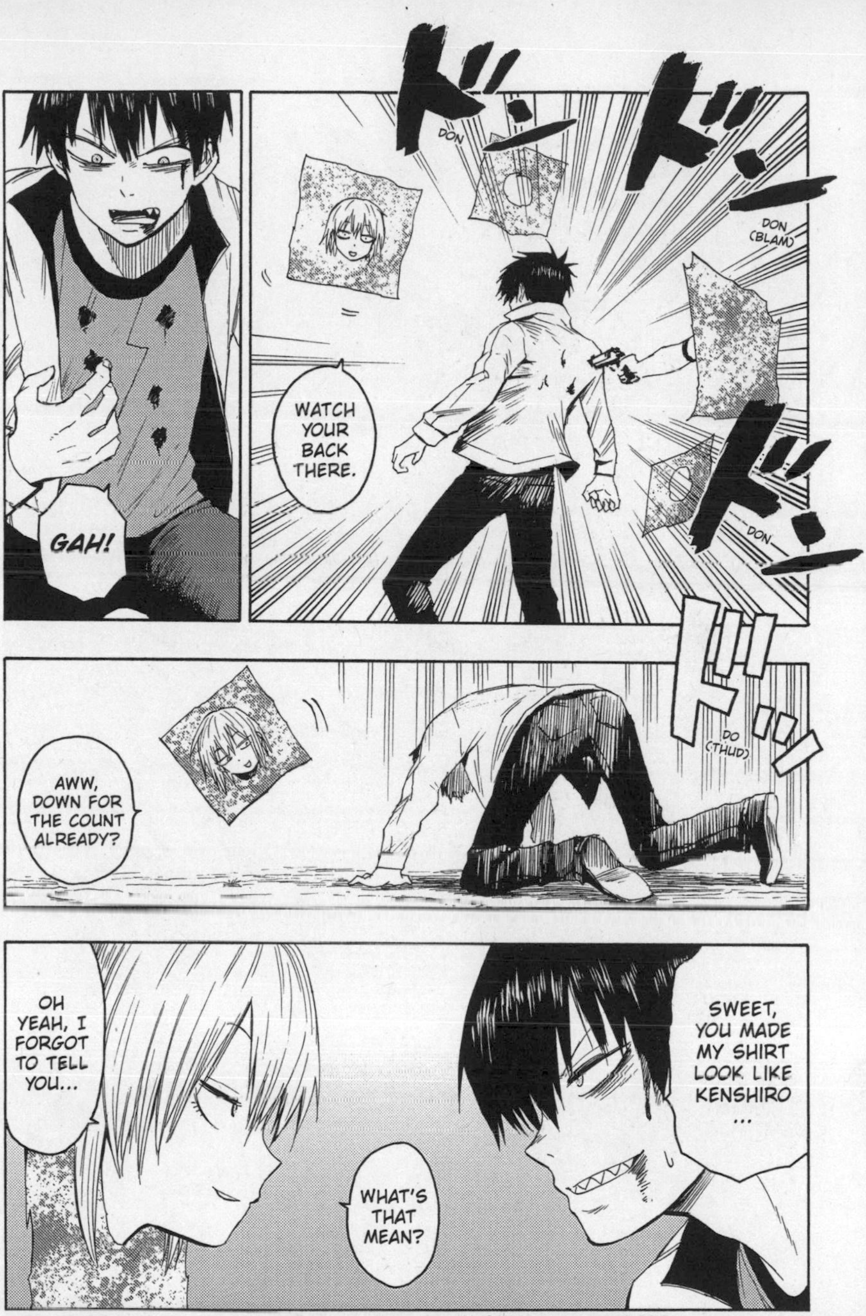
DON
DON (BLAM)
WATCH YOUR BACK THERE.
DON
GAH!
DO (THUD)
AWW, DOWN FOR THE COUNT ALREADY?
SWEET, YOU MADE MY SHIRT LOOK LIKE KENSHIRO ...
WHAT'S THAT MEAN?
OH YEAH, I FORGOT TO TELL YOU...

NOTE: A REFERENCE TO THE MAIN CHARACTER OF THE MARTIAL ARTS MANGA FIST OF THE NORTH STAR. THE BULLET HOLES IN THE SHIRT RESEMBLE THE CONSTELLATION-SHAPED SCARS ON KENSHIRO'S CHEST.

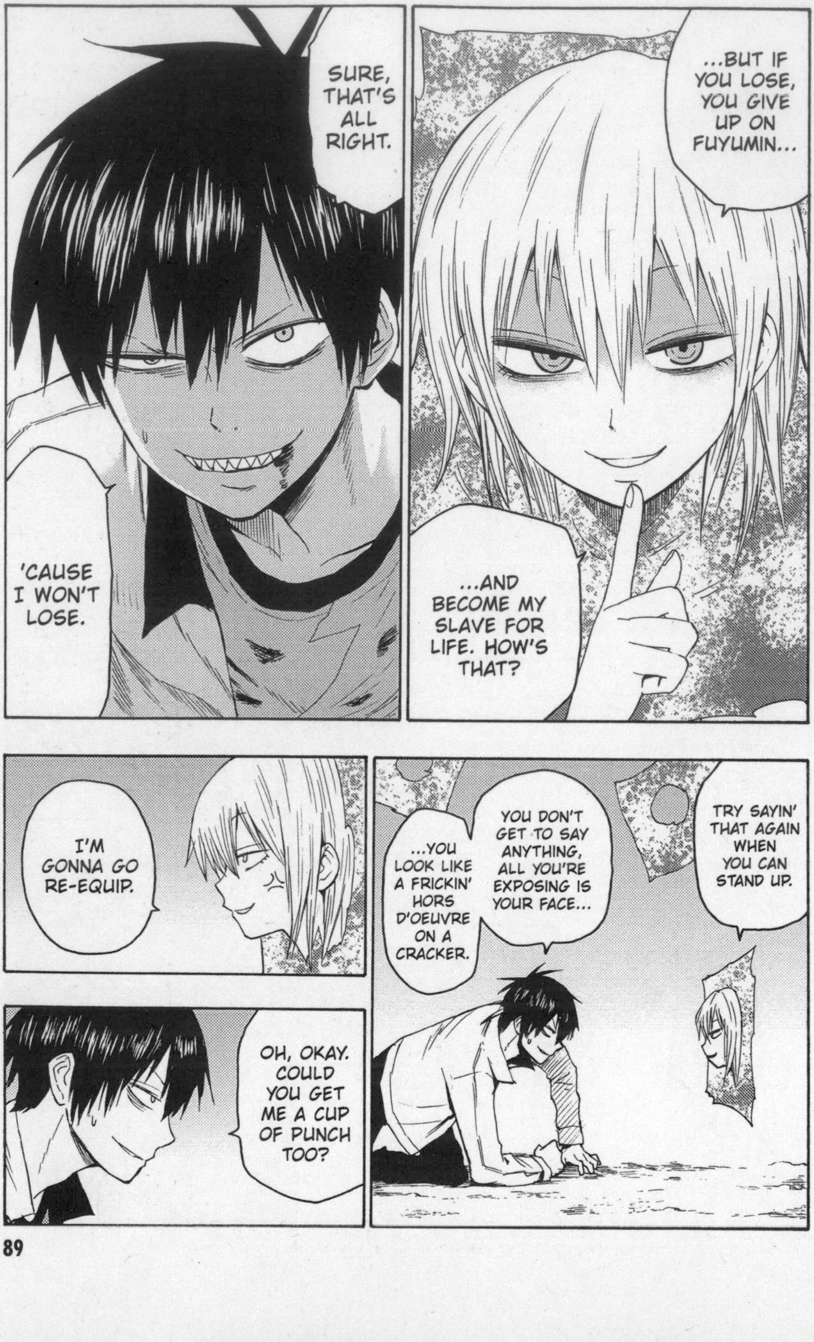
...BUT IF YOU LOSE, YOU GIVE UP ON FUYUMIN...
...AND BECOME MY SLAVE FOR LIFE. HOW'S THAT?
SURE, THAT'S ALL RIGHT.
'CAUSE I WON'T LOSE.
TRY SAYIN' THAT AGAIN WHEN YOU CAN STAND UP.
YOU DON'T GET TO SAY ANYTHING, ALL YOU'RE EXPOSING IS YOUR FACE...
...YOU LOOK LIKE A FRICKIN' HORS D'OEUVRE ON A CRACKER.
I'M GONNA GO RE-EQUIP.
OH, OKAY. COULD YOU GET ME A CUP OF PUNCH TOO?

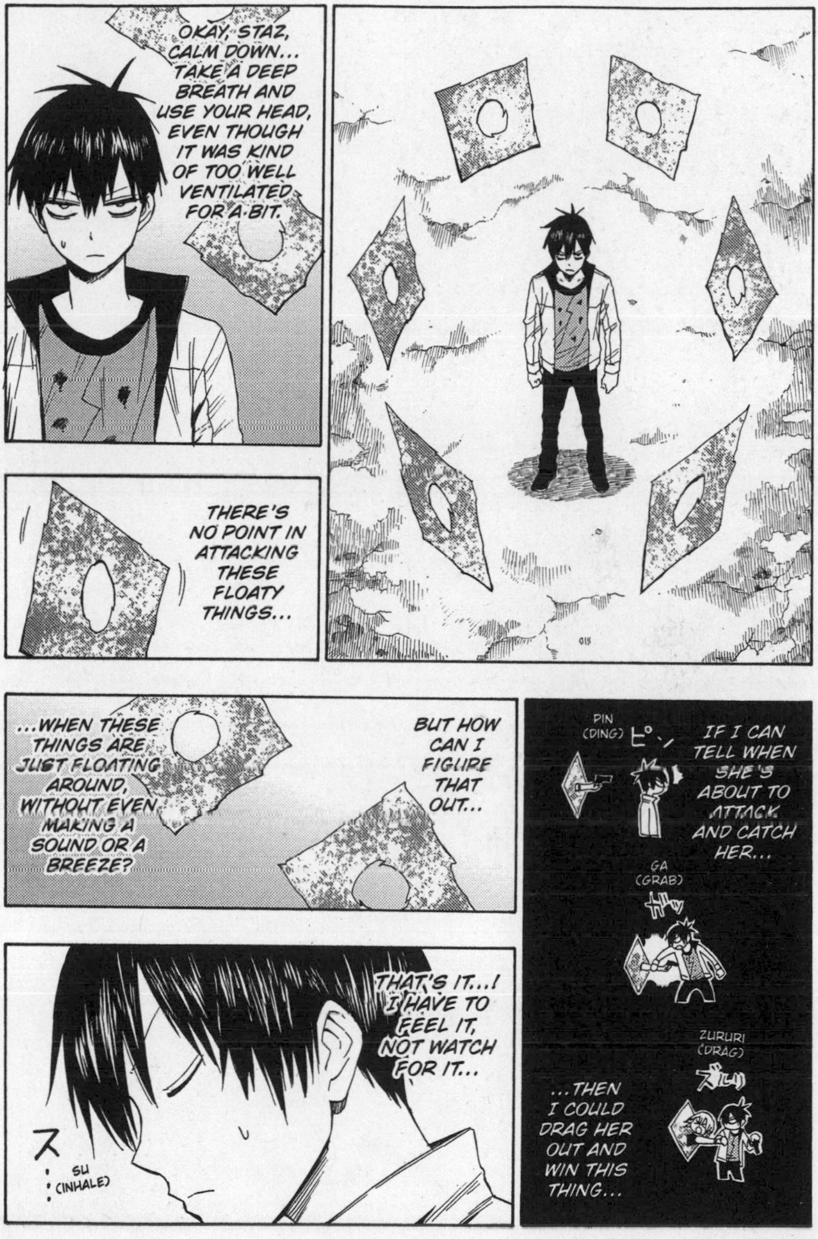
OKAY, STAZ, CALM DOWN... TAKE A DEEP BREATH AND USE YOUR HEAD, EVEN THOUGH IT WAS KIND OF TOO WELL VENTILATED FOR A BIT.
THERE'S NO POINT IN ATTACKING THESE FLOATY THINGS...
IF I CAN TELL WHEN SHE'S ABOUT TO ATTACK AND CATCH HER...
ピ、
PIN (DING)
ガッ
GA (GRAB)
ズルリ
ZURURI (DRAG)
...THEN I COULD DRAG HER OUT AND WIN THIS THING...
BUT HOW CAN I FIGURE THAT OUT...
...WHEN THESE THINGS ARE JUST FLOATING AROUND, WITHOUT EVEN MAKING A SOUND OR A BREEZE?
THAT'S IT...! I HAVE TO FEEL IT, NOT WATCH FOR IT...
ス
SU (INHALE)

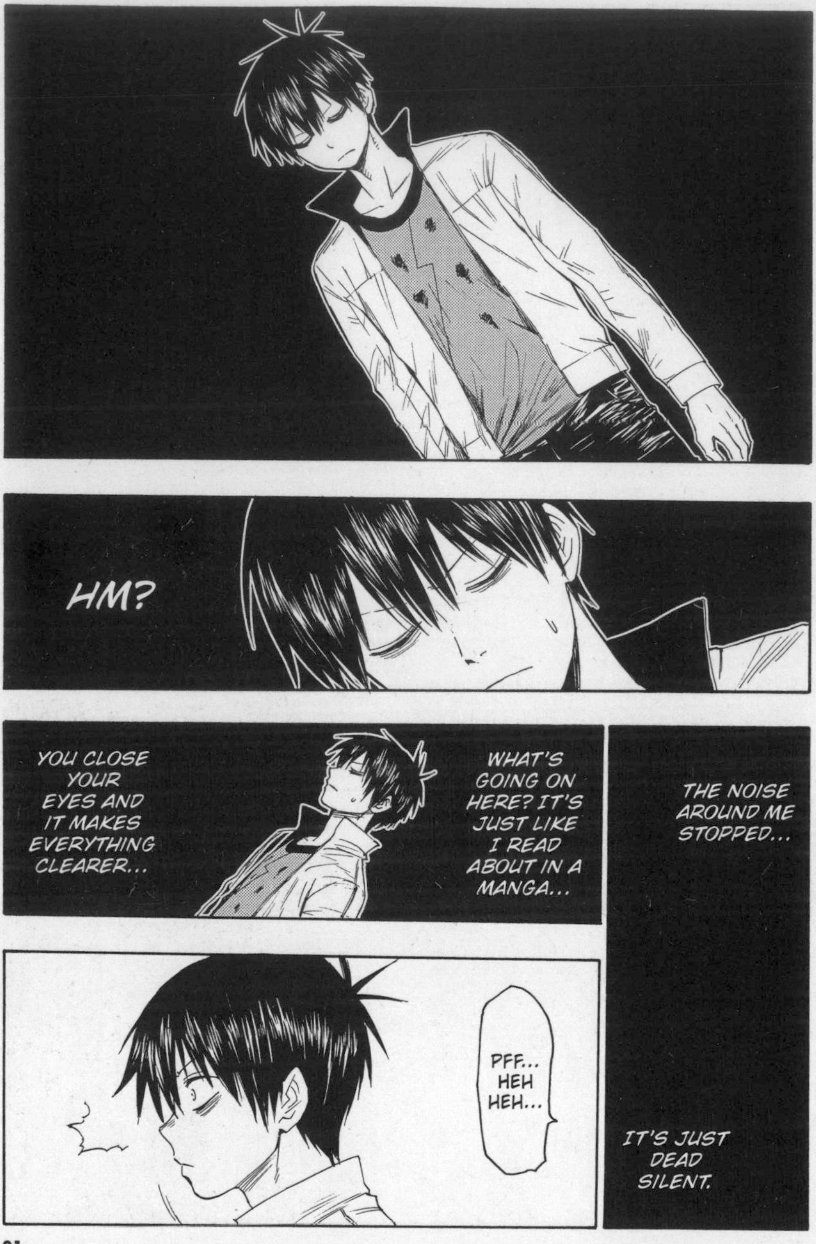
HM?
THE NOISE AROUND ME STOPPED...
IT'S JUST DEAD SILENT.
WHAT'S GOING ON HERE? IT'S JUST LIKE I READ ABOUT IN A MANGA...
YOU CLOSE YOUR EYES AND IT MAKES EVERYTHING CLEARER...
PFF... HEH HEH...

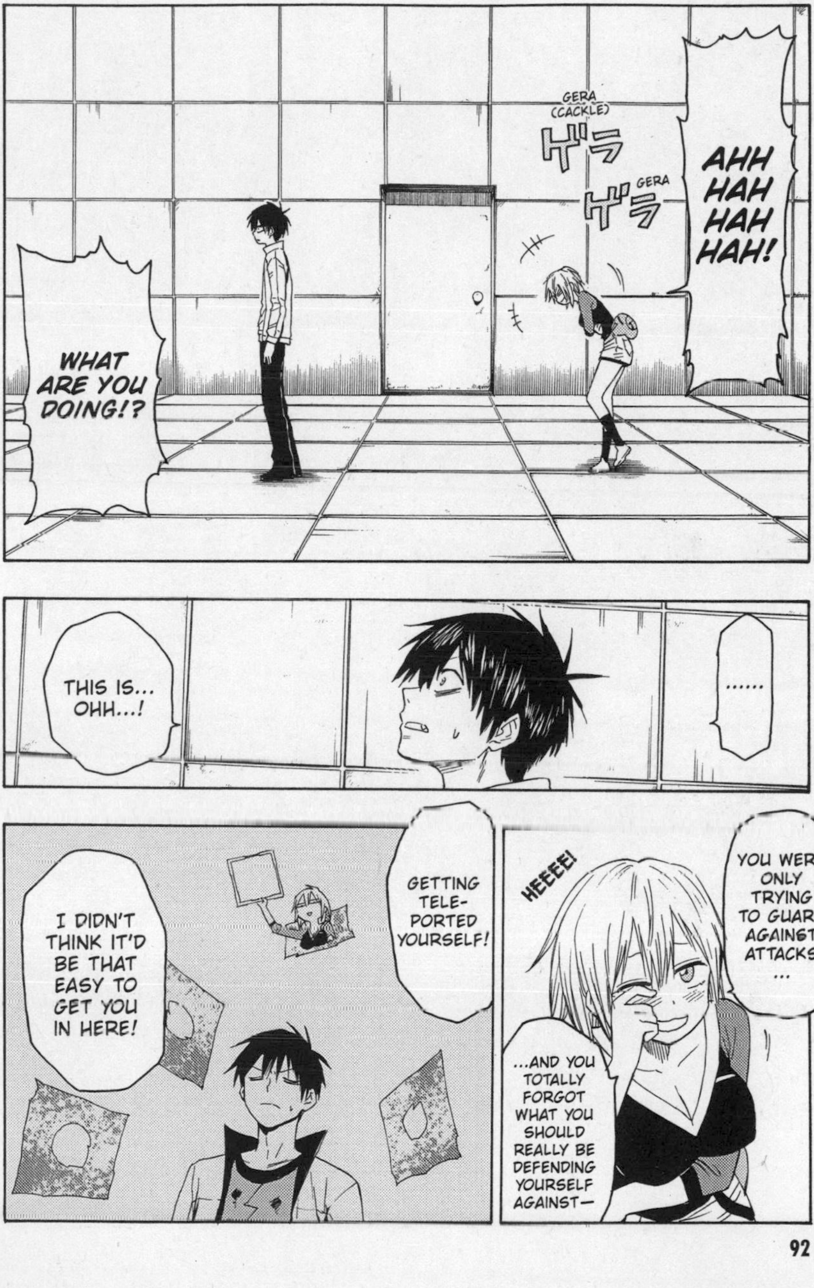
AHH HAH HAH HAH!
GERA (CACKLE)
ゲラ
GERA
ゲラ
WHAT ARE YOU DOING!?
......
THIS IS... OHH...!
YOU WERE ONLY TRYING TO GUARD AGAINST ATTACKS ...
HEEEE!
...AND YOU TOTALLY FORGOT WHAT YOU SHOULD REALLY BE DEFENDING YOURSELF AGAINST—
GETTING TELE-PORTED YOURSELF!
I DIDN'T THINK IT'D BE THAT EASY TO GET YOU IN HERE!

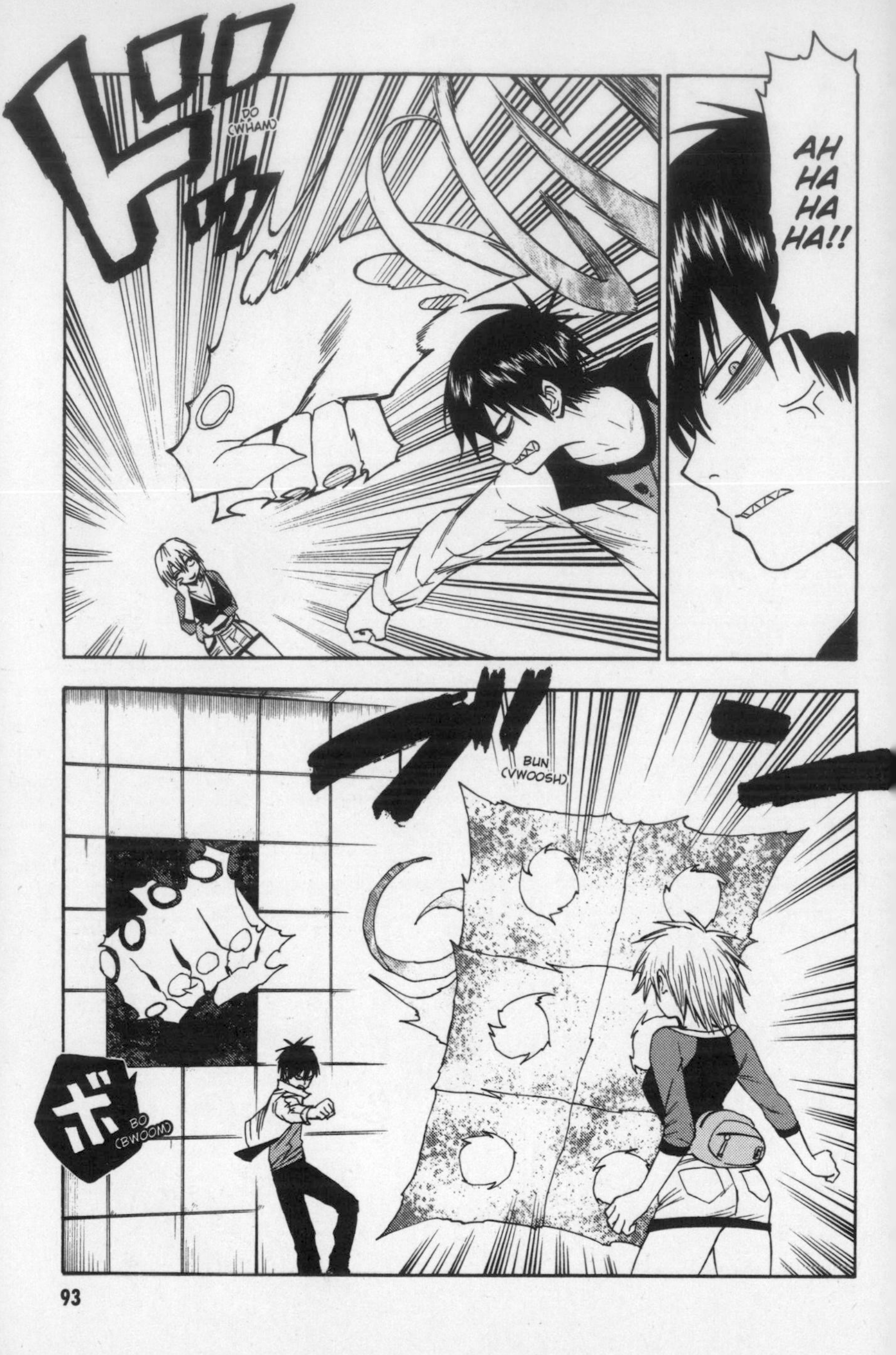
AH HA HA HA!!
DO (WHAM)
BUN (VWOOSH)
ボ
BO (BWOOM)

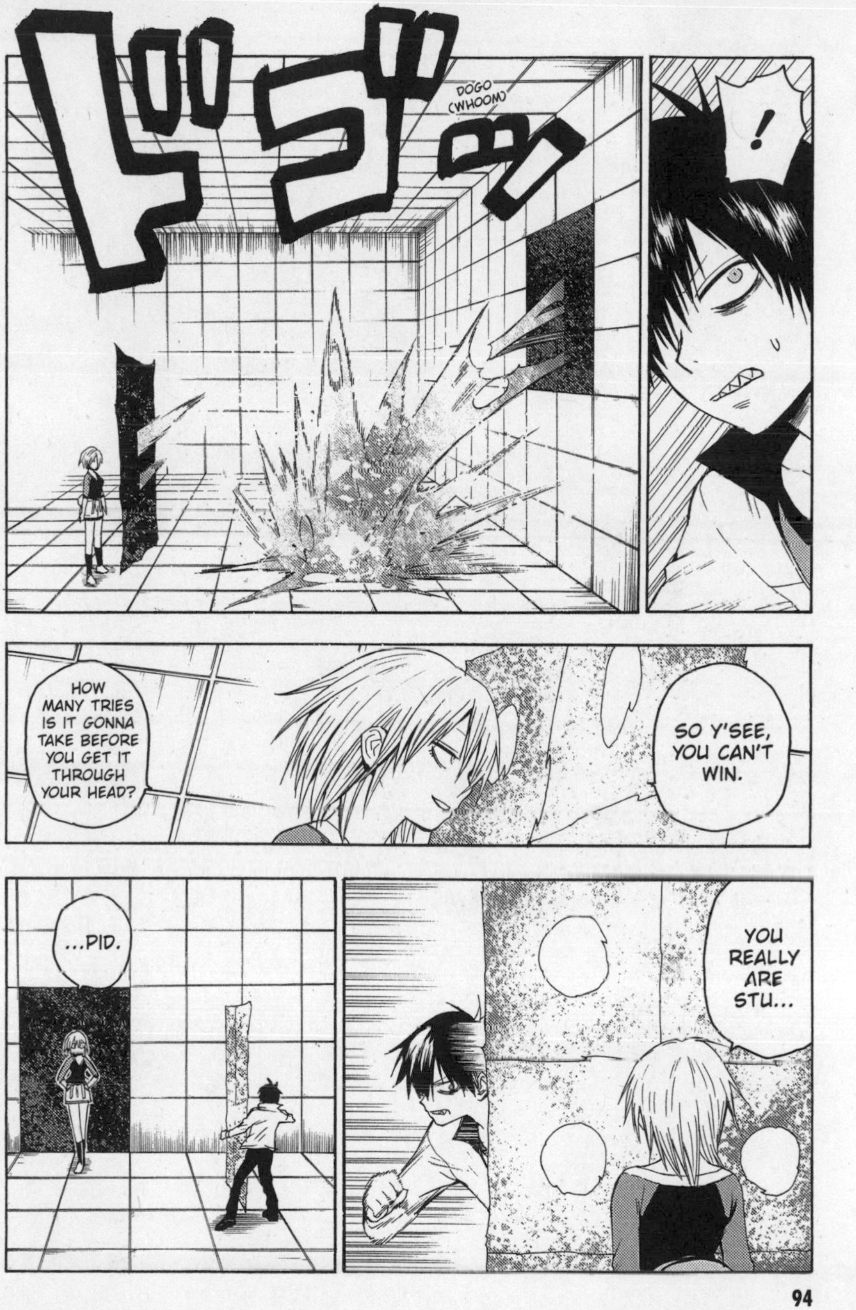
!
DOGO (WHOOM)
SO Y'SEE, YOU CAN'T WIN.
HOW MANY TRIES IS IT GONNA TAKE BEFORE YOU GET IT THROUGH YOUR HEAD?
YOU REALLY ARE STU...
...PID.

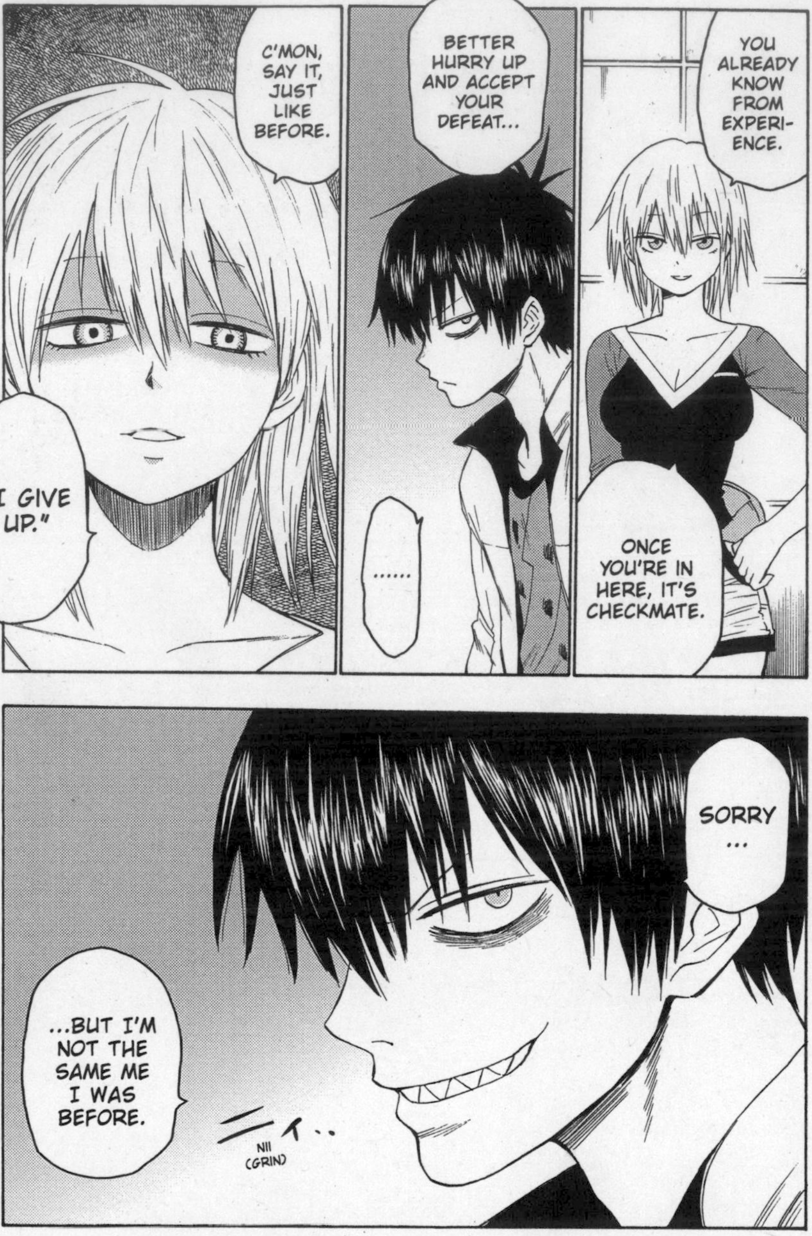
YOU ALREADY KNOW FROM EXPERIENCE.
ONCE YOU'RE IN HERE, IT'S CHECKMATE.
BETTER HURRY UP AND ACCEPT YOUR DEFEAT...
......
C'MON, SAY IT, JUST LIKE BEFORE.
"I GIVE UP."
SORRY...
...BUT I'M NOT THE SAME ME I WAS BEFORE.
NII (GRIN)

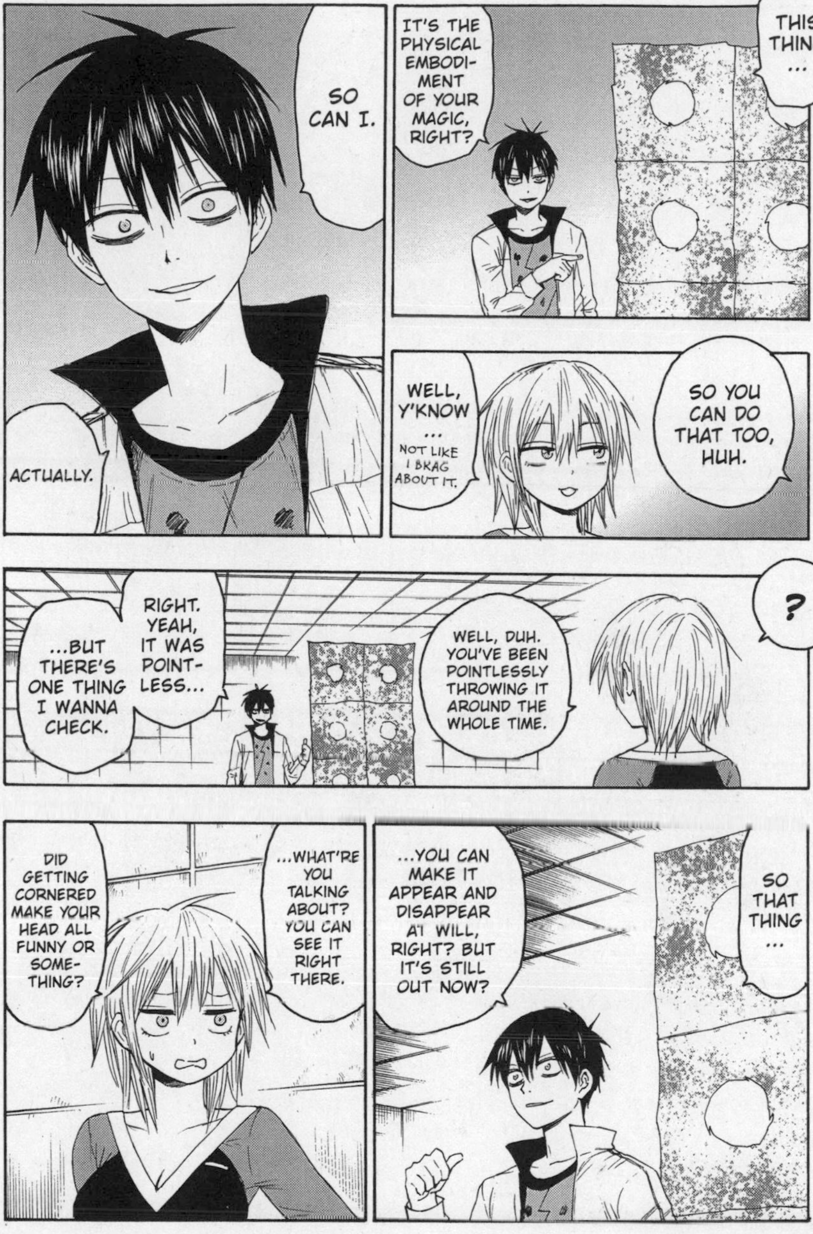
THIS THING ...
IT'S THE PHYSICAL EMBODIMENT OF YOUR MAGIC, RIGHT?
SO YOU CAN DO THAT TOO, HUH.
WELL, Y'KNOW ... NOT LIKE I BRAG ABOUT IT.
SO CAN I.
ACTUALLY.
?
WELL, DUH. YOU'VE BEEN POINTLESSLY THROWING IT AROUND THE WHOLE TIME.
RIGHT. YEAH, IT WAS POINTLESS...
...BUT THERE'S ONE THING I WANNA CHECK.
SO THAT THING ...
...YOU CAN MAKE IT APPEAR AND DISAPPEAR AT WILL, RIGHT? BUT IT'S STILL OUT NOW?
...WHAT'RE YOU TALKING ABOUT? YOU CAN SEE IT RIGHT THERE.
DID GETTING CORNERED MAKE YOUR HEAD ALL FUNNY OR SOMETHING?

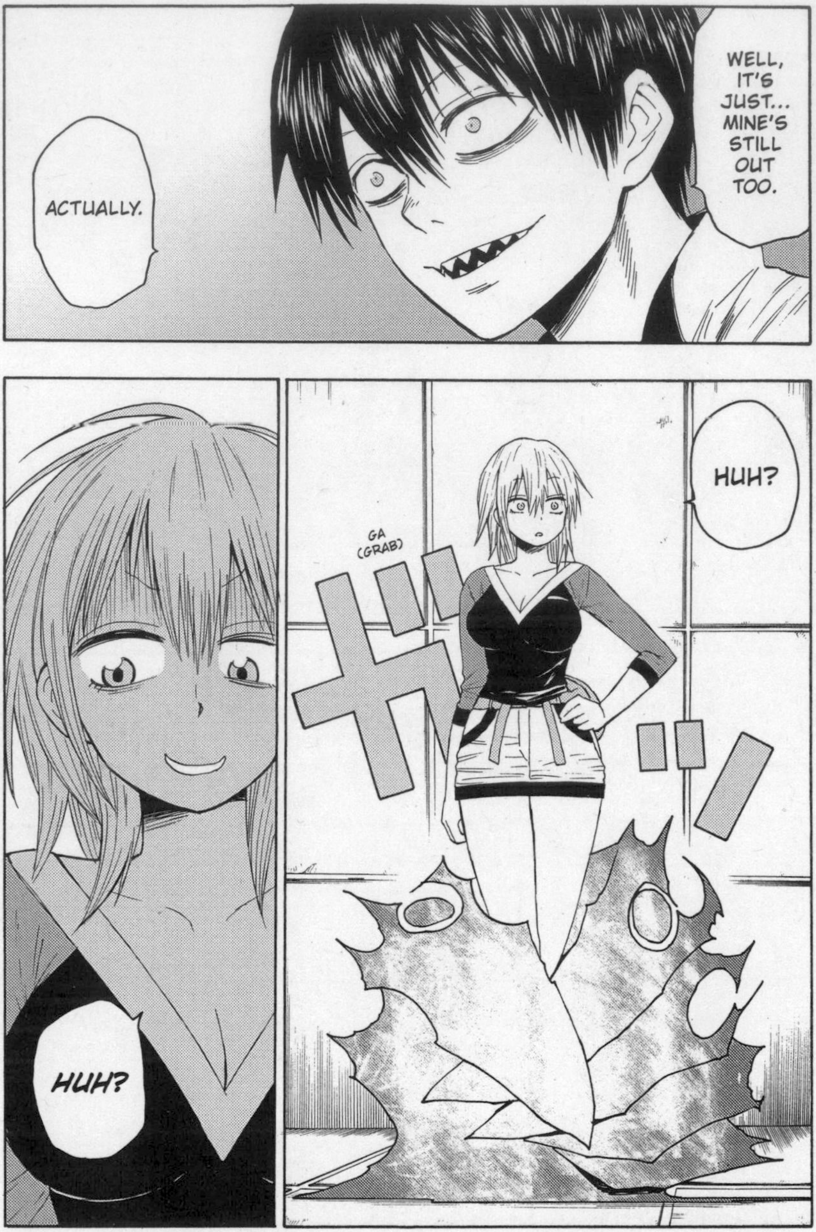
WELL, IT'S JUST... MINE'S STILL OUT TOO.
ACTUALLY.
HUH?
GA (GRAB)
HUH?

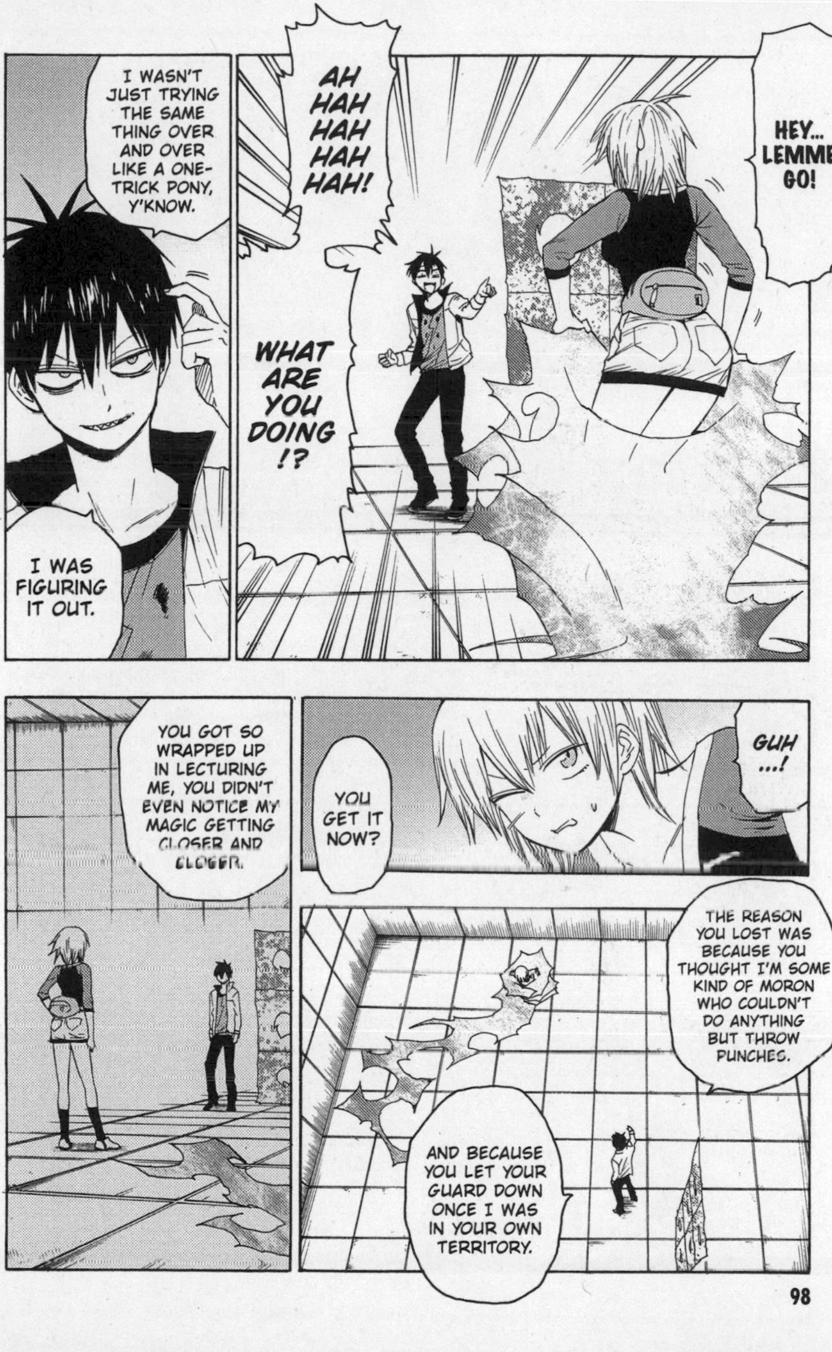
HEY... LEMME GO!
AH HAH HAH HAH HAH!
WHAT ARE YOU DOING!?
I WASN'T JUST TRYING THE SAME THING OVER AND OVER LIKE A ONE-TRICK PONY, Y'KNOW.
I WAS FIGURING IT OUT.
GUH...!
YOU GET IT NOW?
THE REASON YOU LOST WAS BECAUSE YOU THOUGHT I'M SOME KIND OF MORON WHO COULDN'T DO ANYTHING BUT THROW PUNCHES.
AND BECAUSE YOU LET YOUR GUARD DOWN ONCE I WAS IN YOUR OWN TERRITORY.
YOU GOT SO WRAPPED UP IN LECTURING ME, YOU DIDN'T EVEN NOTICE MY MAGIC GETTING CLOSER AND CLOSER.

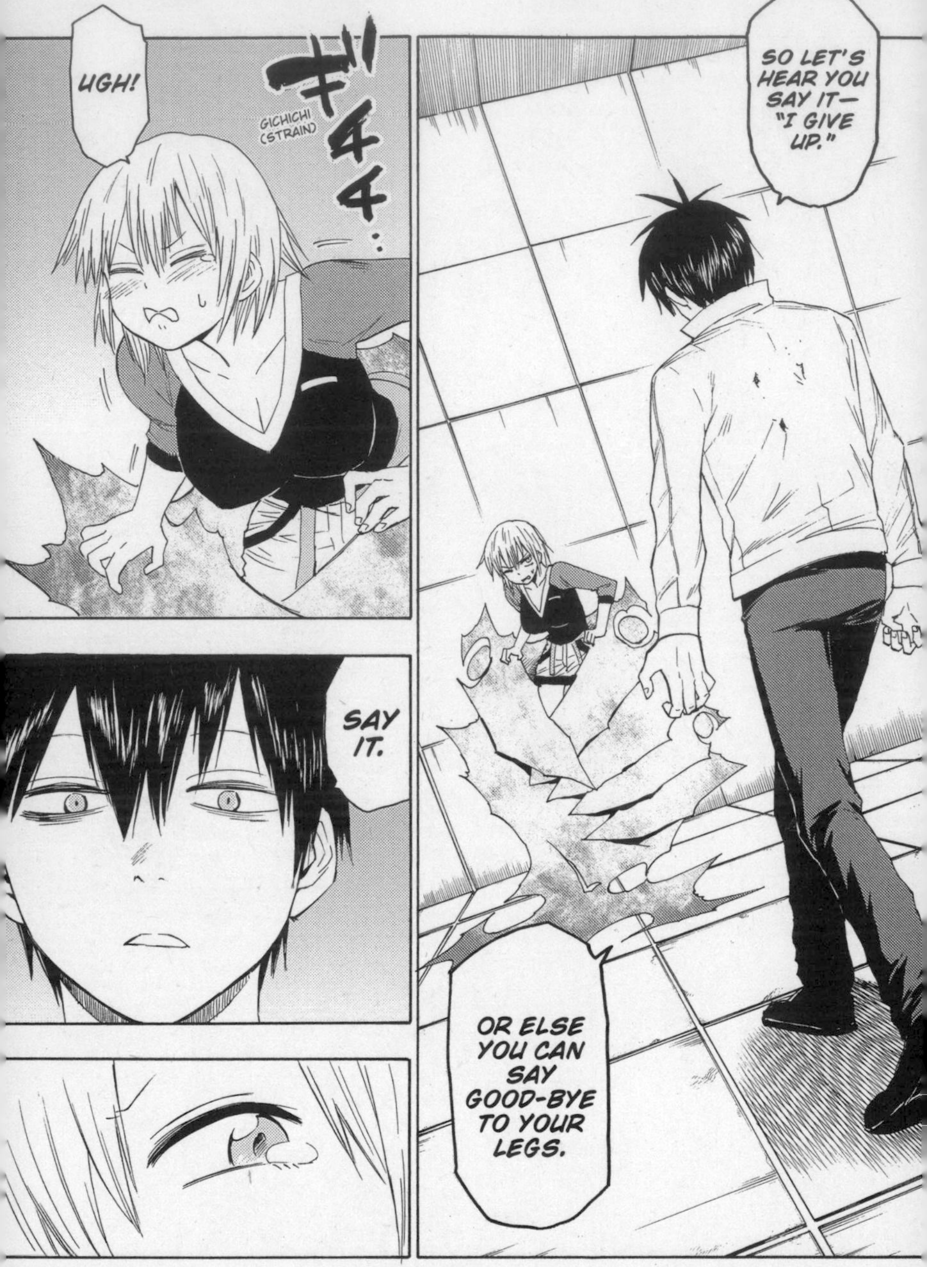
SO LET'S HEAR YOU SAY IT—"I GIVE UP."
OR ELSE YOU CAN SAY GOOD-BYE TO YOUR LEGS.
UGH!
GICHICHI (STRAIN)
SAY IT.

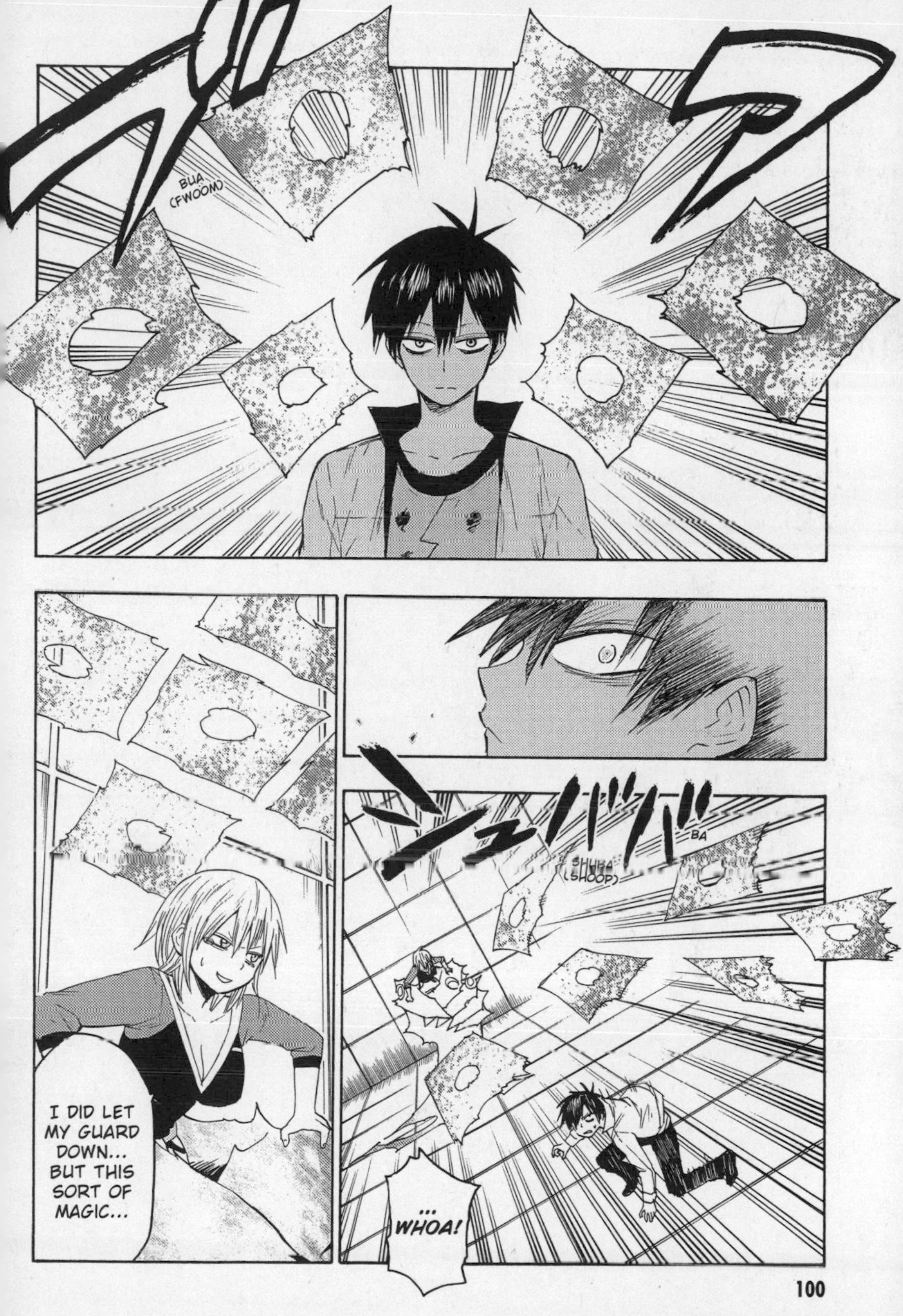
BUA
(FWOOM)
BA
SHUBA
(SHOOP)
... WHOA!
I DID LET MY GUARD DOWN... BUT THIS SORT OF MAGIC...

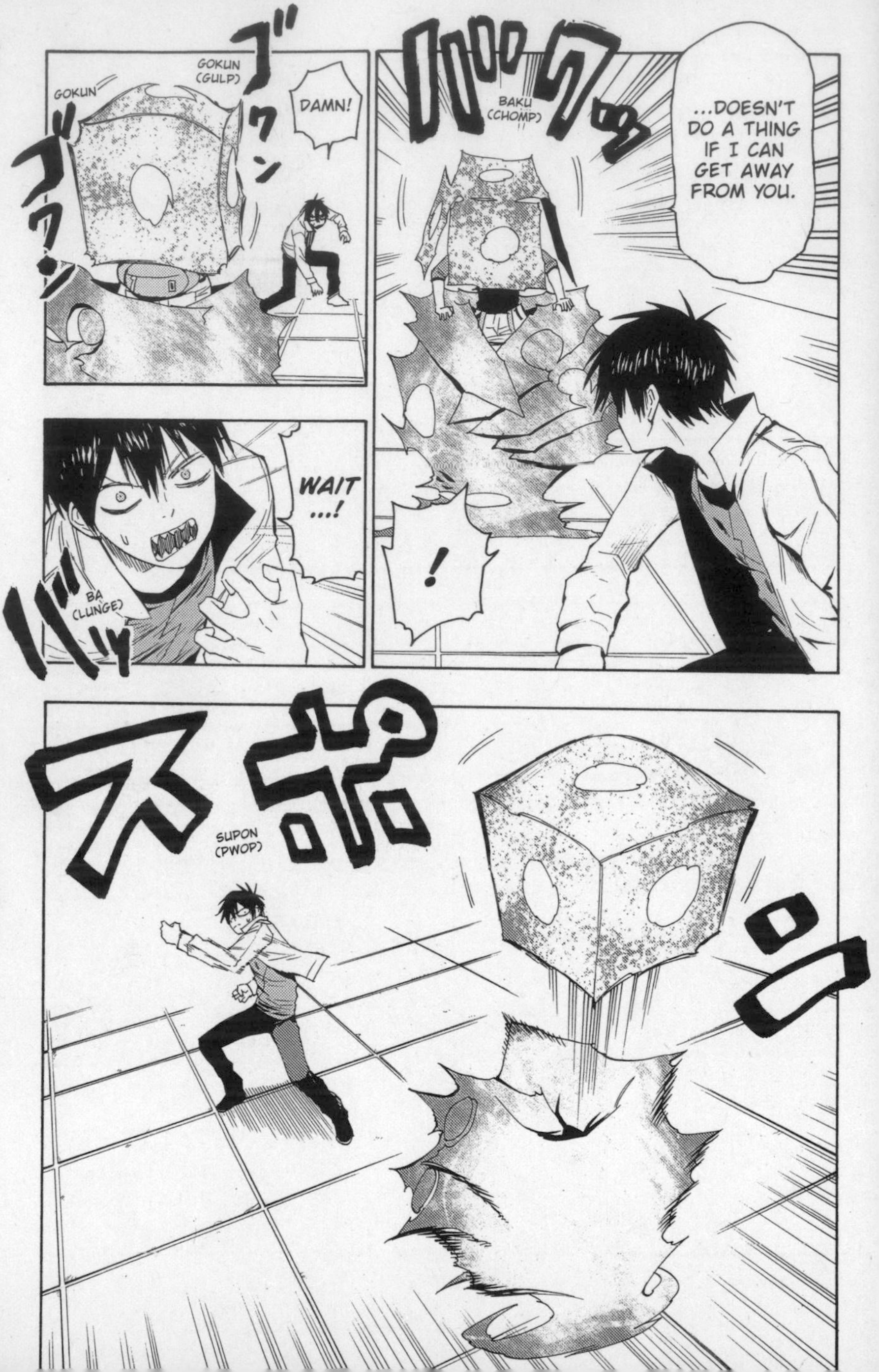
BAKU (CHOMP)
...DOESN'T DO A THING IF I CAN GET AWAY FROM YOU.
!
DAMN!
GOKUN (GULP)
GOKUN
WAIT ...!
BA (LUNGE)
SUPON (PWOP)

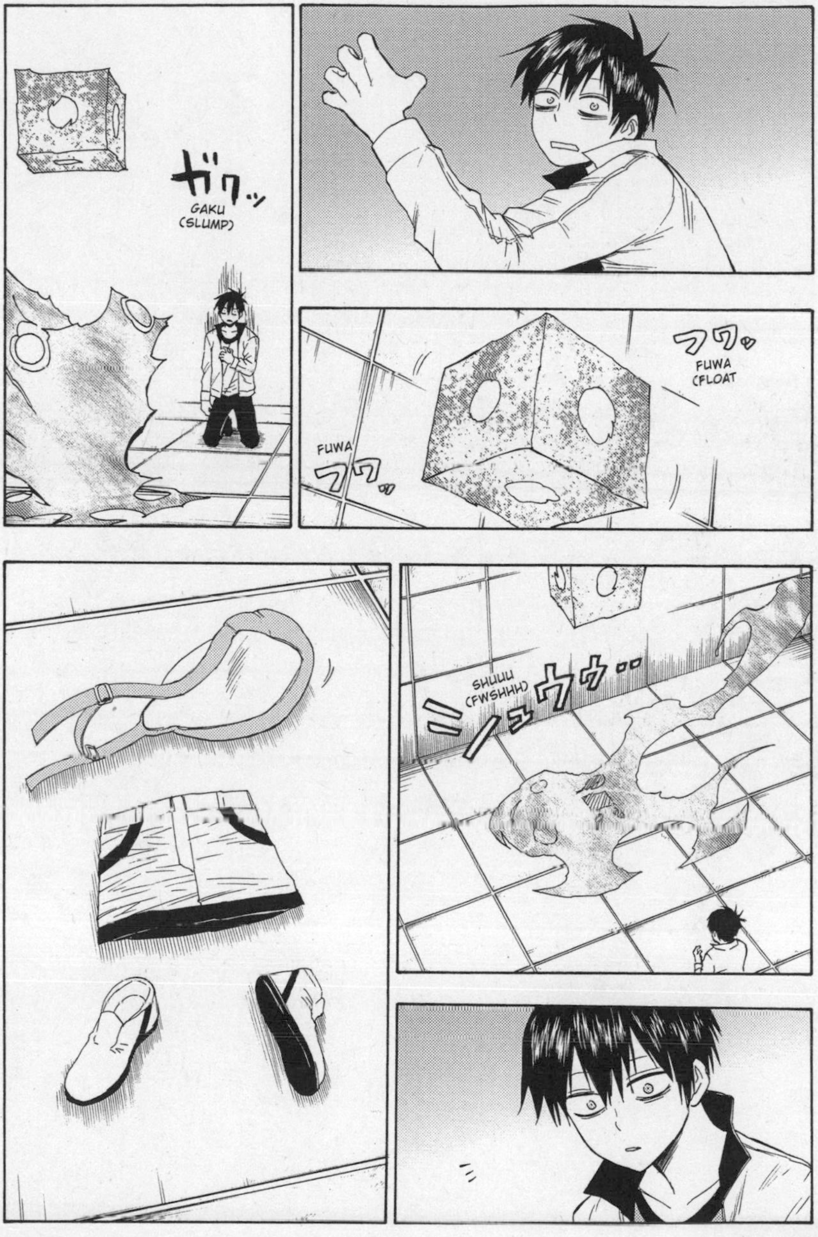
フワッ
FUWA
(FLOAT
FUWA
フワッ
ガクッ
GAKU
(SLUMP)
SHUUU
(FWSHHH)
シュウウ‥

......
WHAT HAP-PENED HERE...
スッ
SU (LIFT)
POTO (PLOP)
ポト

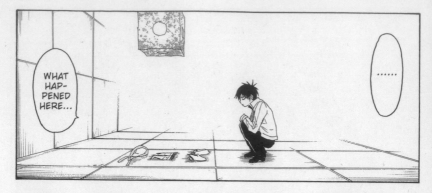

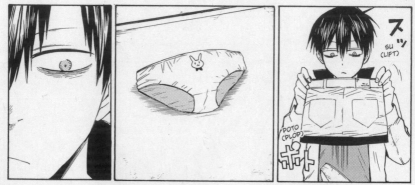

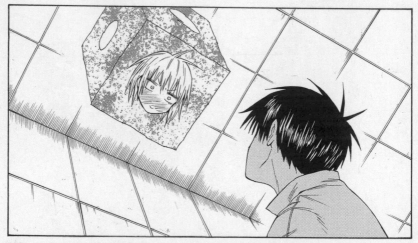

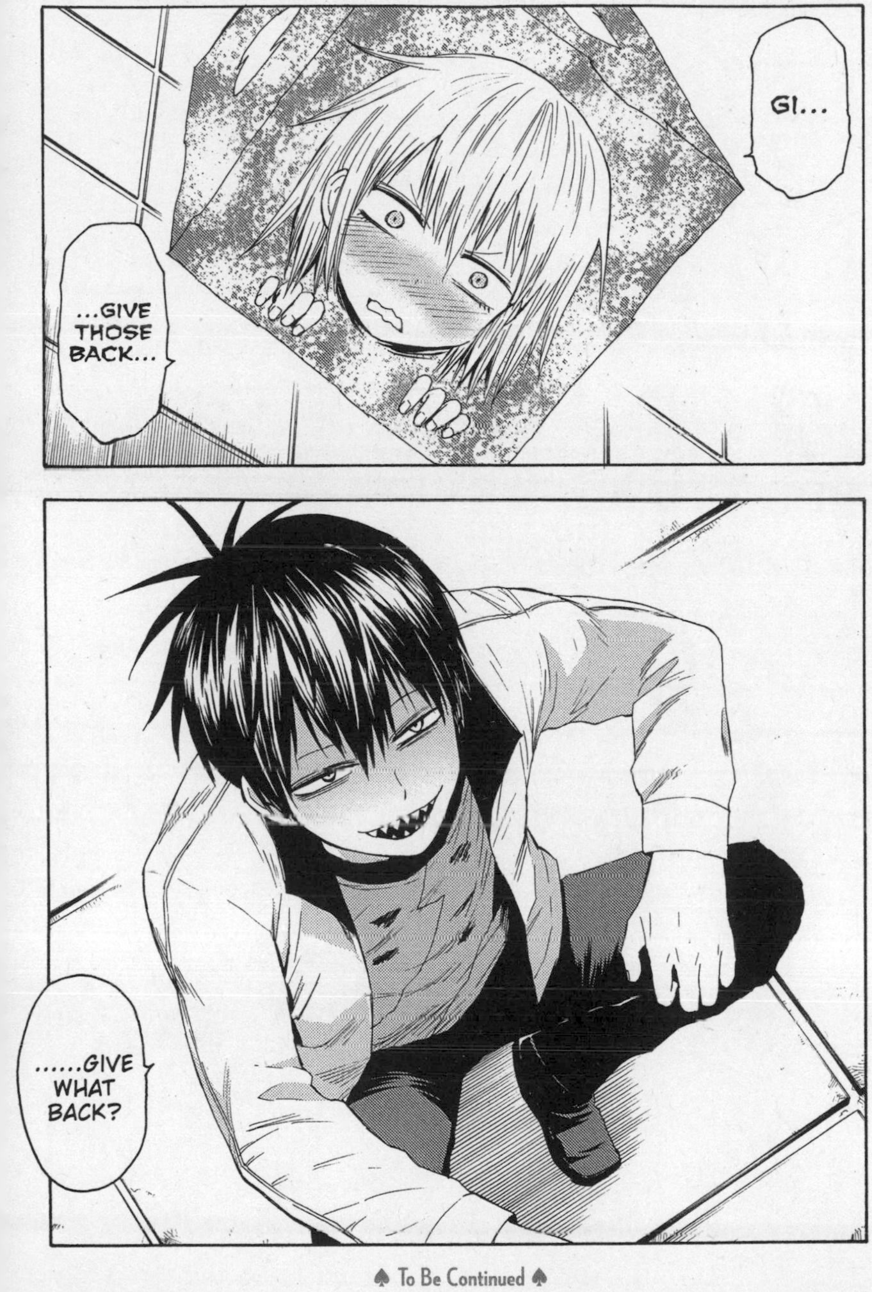
GI...
...GIVE THOSE BACK...
......GIVE WHAT BACK?

♠ To Be Continued ♠

OVER HERE! COME CLOSER!
OVER THERE...? BUT THERE'S NOTHING THERE...?
IT'S FINE, C'MON.
ARE...ARE YOU GOING TO PUSH ME OFF...? ARE YOU GOING TO PUSH ME OFF THE EDGE...?

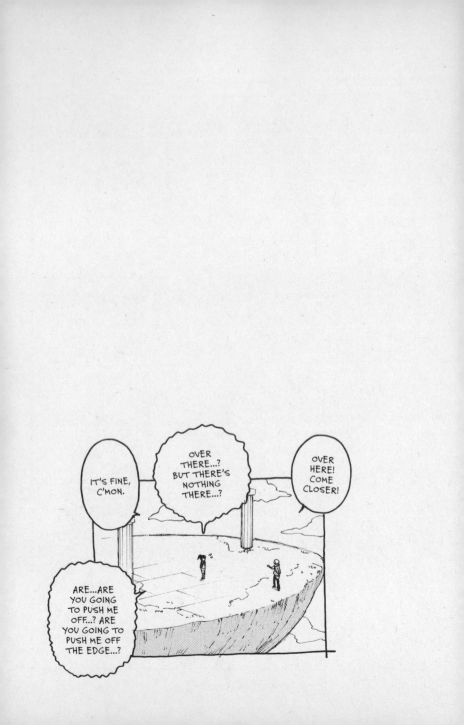

BLOOD LAD

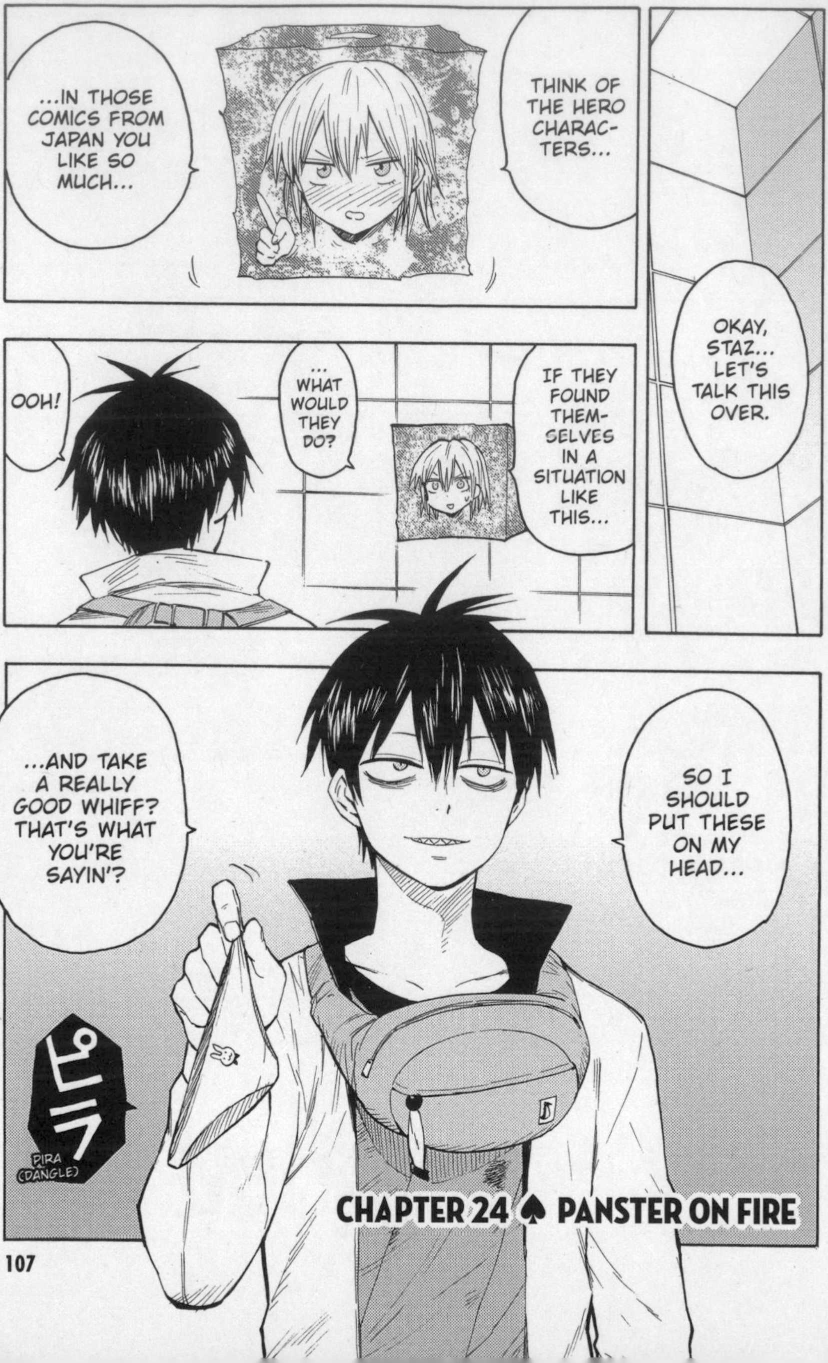
OKAY, STAZ... LET'S TALK THIS OVER.
THINK OF THE HERO CHARACTERS...
...IN THOSE COMICS FROM JAPAN YOU LIKE SO MUCH...
IF THEY FOUND THEMSELVES IN A SITUATION LIKE THIS...
...WHAT WOULD THEY DO?
OOH!
SO I SHOULD PUT THESE ON MY HEAD...
...AND TAKE A REALLY GOOD WHIFF? THAT'S WHAT YOU'RE SAYIN'?
ピラ
PIRA (DANGLE)
CHAPTER 24 ♠ PANSTER ON FIRE

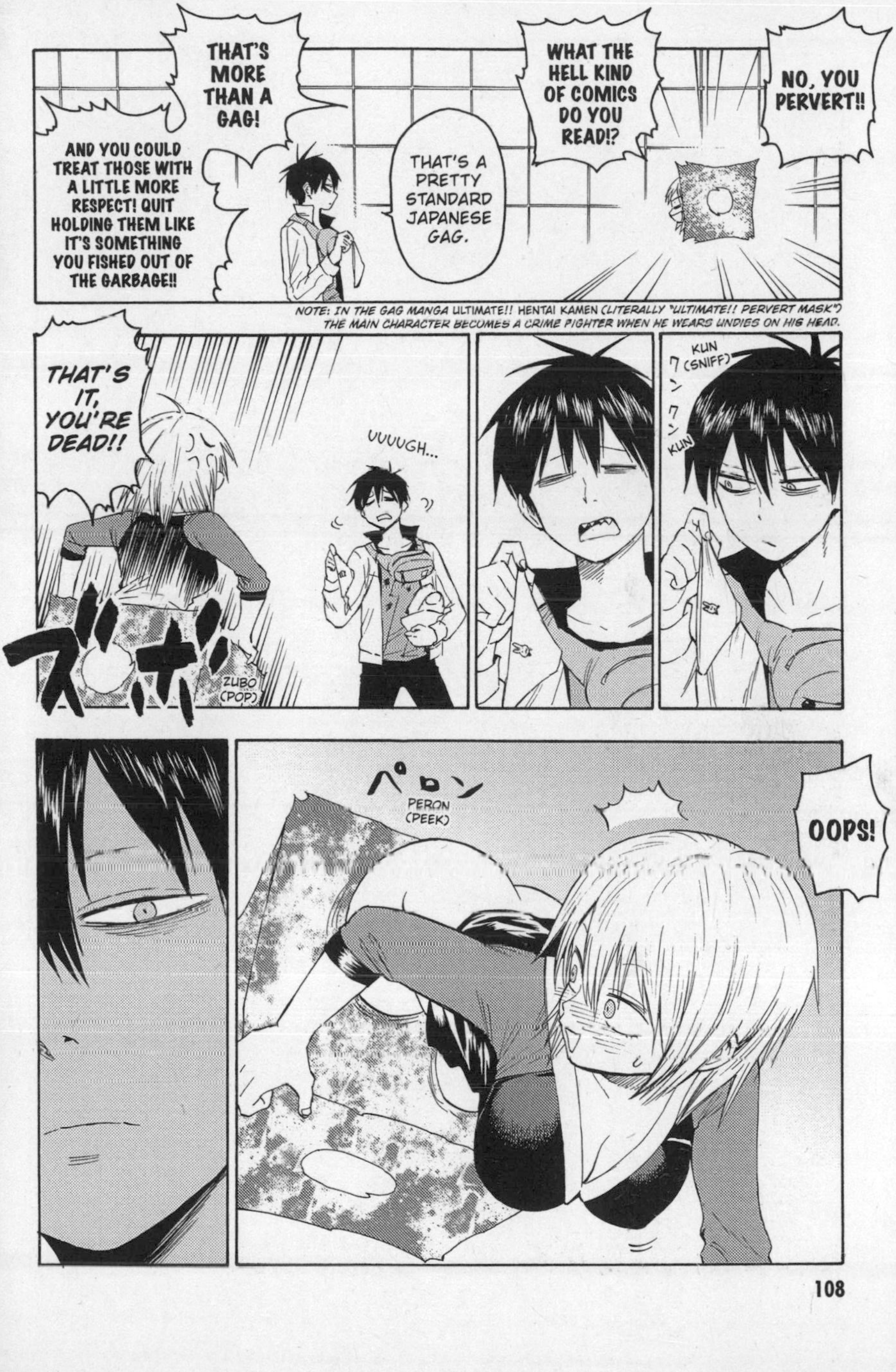
NO, YOU PERVERT!!
WHAT THE HELL KIND OF COMICS DO YOU READ!?
THAT'S A PRETTY STANDARD JAPANESE GAG.
THAT'S MORE THAN A GAG!
AND YOU COULD TREAT THOSE WITH A LITTLE MORE RESPECT! QUIT HOLDING THEM LIKE IT'S SOMETHING YOU FISHED OUT OF THE GARBAGE!!
NOTE: IN THE GAG MANGA ULTIMATE!! HENTAI KAMEN (LITERALLY "ULTIMATE!! PERVERT MASK") THE MAIN CHARACTER BECOMES A CRIME FIGHTER WHEN HE WEARS UNDIES ON HIS HEAD.
クンクン
KUN (SNIFF) KUN
UUUUGH...
THAT'S IT, YOU'RE DEAD!!
ズボ
ZUBO (POP)
OOPS!
ペロン
PERON (PEEK)

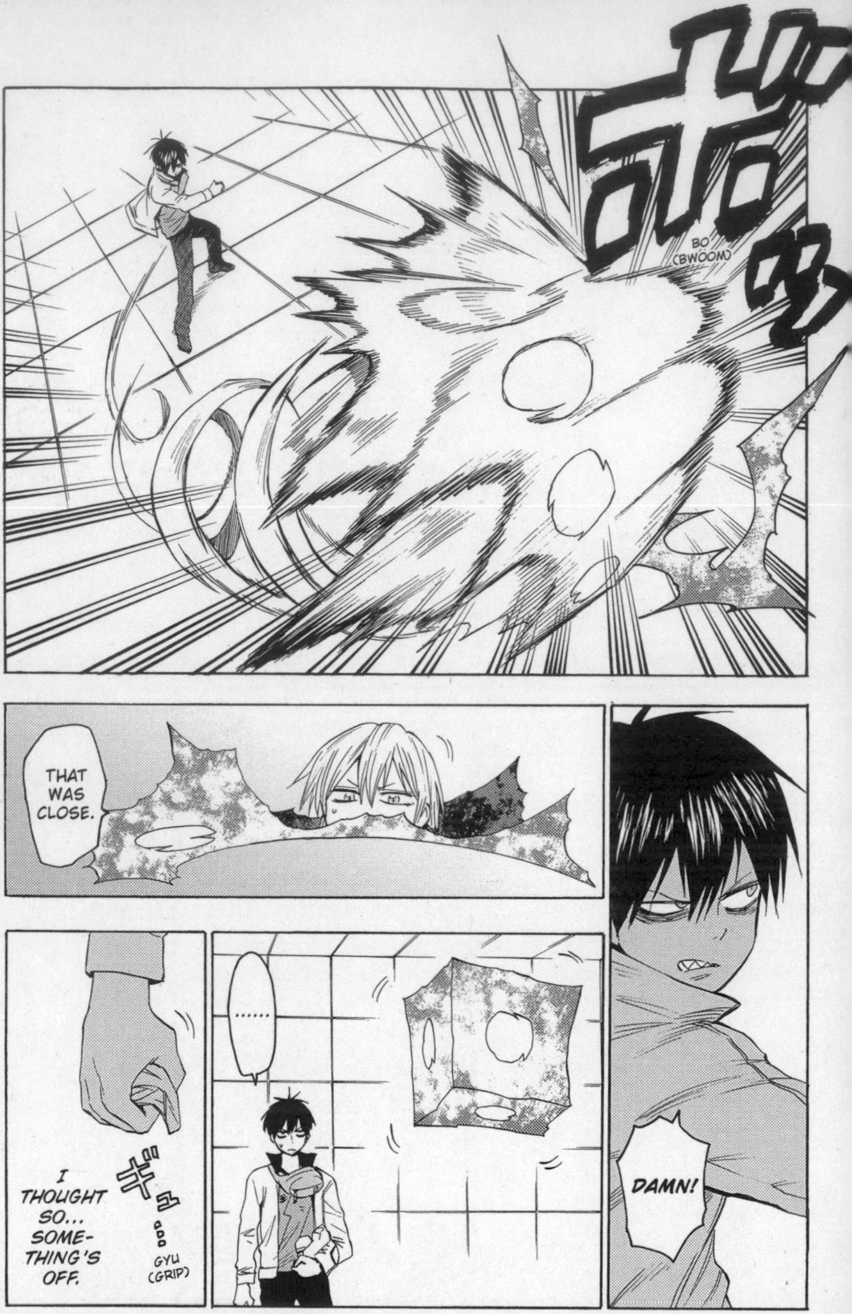
BO
(BWOOM)
DAMN!
THAT WAS CLOSE.
......
GYU
(GRIP)
I THOUGHT SO... SOME-THING'S OFF.

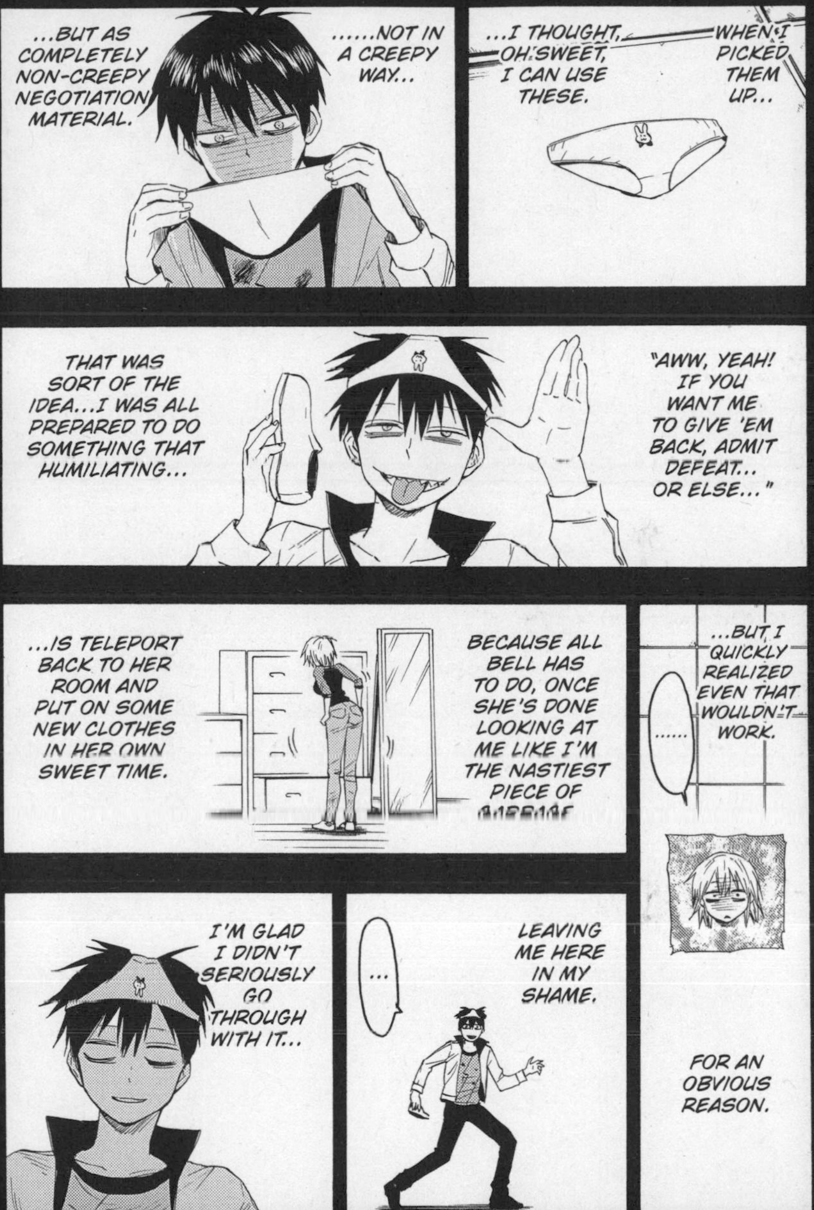
WHEN I PICKED THEM UP...
...I THOUGHT, OH SWEET, I CAN USE THESE.
......NOT IN A CREEPY WAY...
...BUT AS COMPLETELY NON-CREEPY NEGOTIATION MATERIAL.
"AWW, YEAH! IF YOU WANT ME TO GIVE 'EM BACK, ADMIT DEFEAT... OR ELSE..."
THAT WAS SORT OF THE IDEA...I WAS ALL PREPARED TO DO SOMETHING THAT HUMILIATING...
...BUT I QUICKLY REALIZED EVEN THAT WOULDN'T WORK.
......
FOR AN OBVIOUS REASON.
BECAUSE ALL BELL HAS TO DO, ONCE SHE'S DONE LOOKING AT ME LIKE I'M THE NASTIEST PIECE OF
...IS TELEPORT BACK TO HER ROOM AND PUT ON SOME NEW CLOTHES IN HER OWN SWEET TIME.
...
LEAVING ME HERE IN MY SHAME.
I'M GLAD I DIDN'T SERIOUSLY GO THROUGH WITH IT...

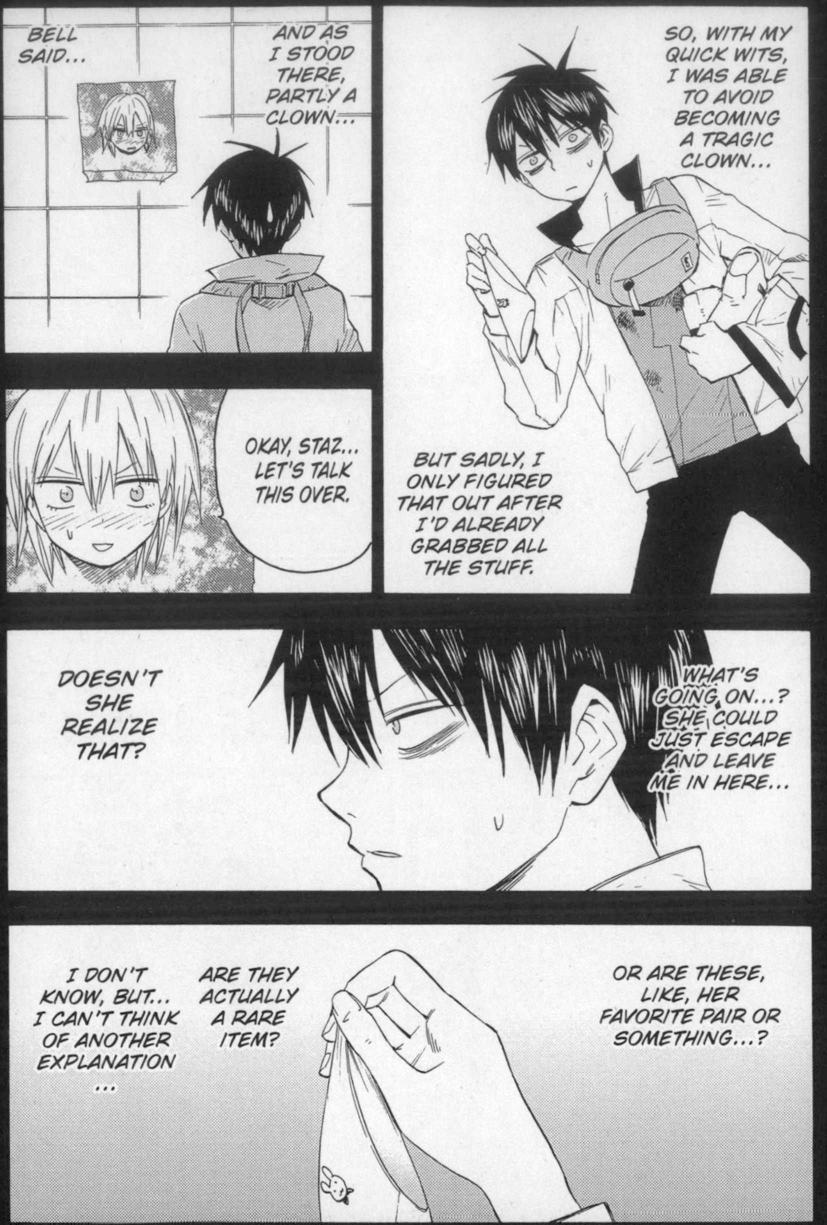
SO, WITH MY QUICK WITS, I WAS ABLE TO AVOID BECOMING A TRAGIC CLOWN...
BUT SADLY, I ONLY FIGURED THAT OUT AFTER I'D ALREADY GRABBED ALL THE STUFF.
AND AS I STOOD THERE, PARTLY A CLOWN...
BELL SAID...
OKAY, STAZ... LET'S TALK THIS OVER.
WHAT'S GOING ON...? SHE COULD JUST ESCAPE AND LEAVE ME IN HERE...
DOESN'T SHE REALIZE THAT?
OR ARE THESE, LIKE, HER FAVORITE PAIR OR SOMETHING...?
ARE THEY ACTUALLY A RARE ITEM?
I DON'T KNOW, BUT... I CAN'T THINK OF ANOTHER EXPLANATION ...

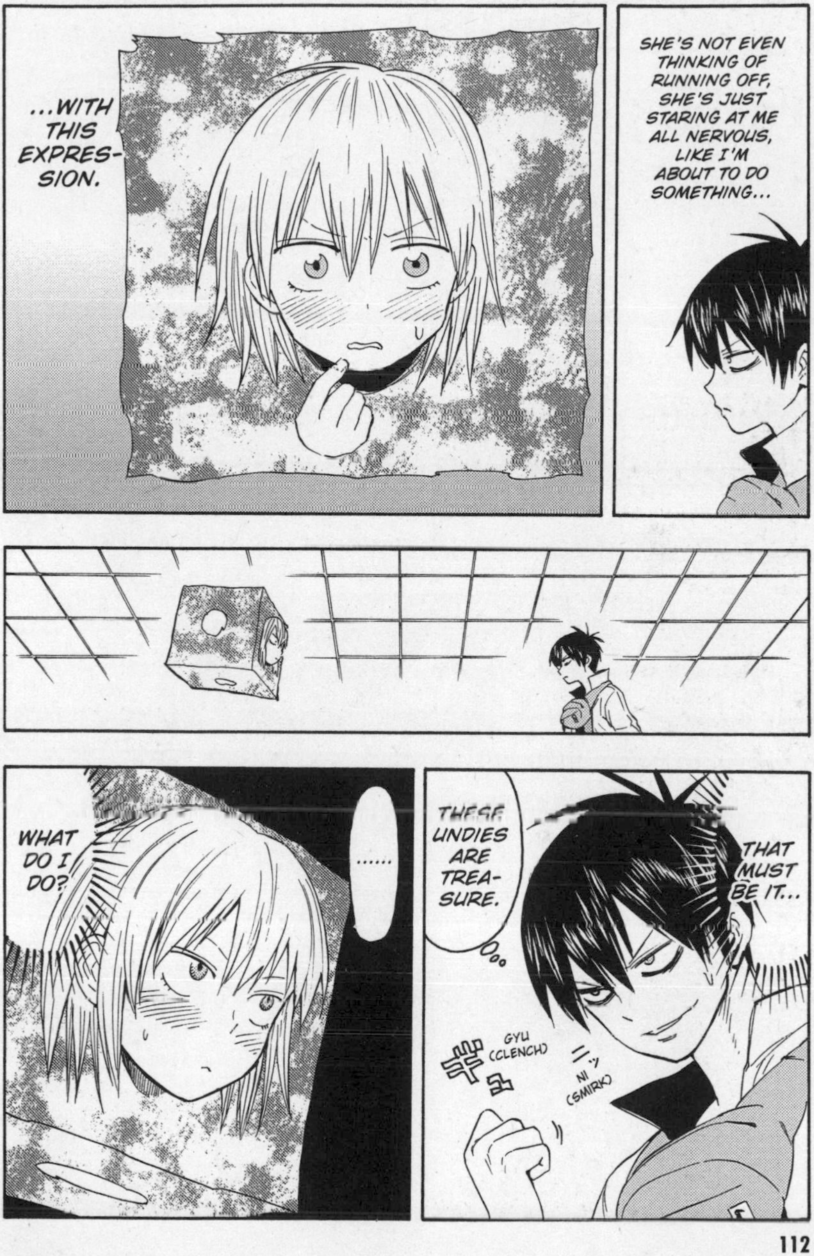
SHE'S NOT EVEN THINKING OF RUNNING OFF, SHE'S JUST STARING AT ME ALL NERVOUS, LIKE I'M ABOUT TO DO SOMETHING...
...WITH THIS EXPRES-SION.
THAT MUST BE IT...
THESE UNDIES ARE TREA-SURE.
GYU (CLENCH)
NI (SMIRK)
......
WHAT DO I DO?

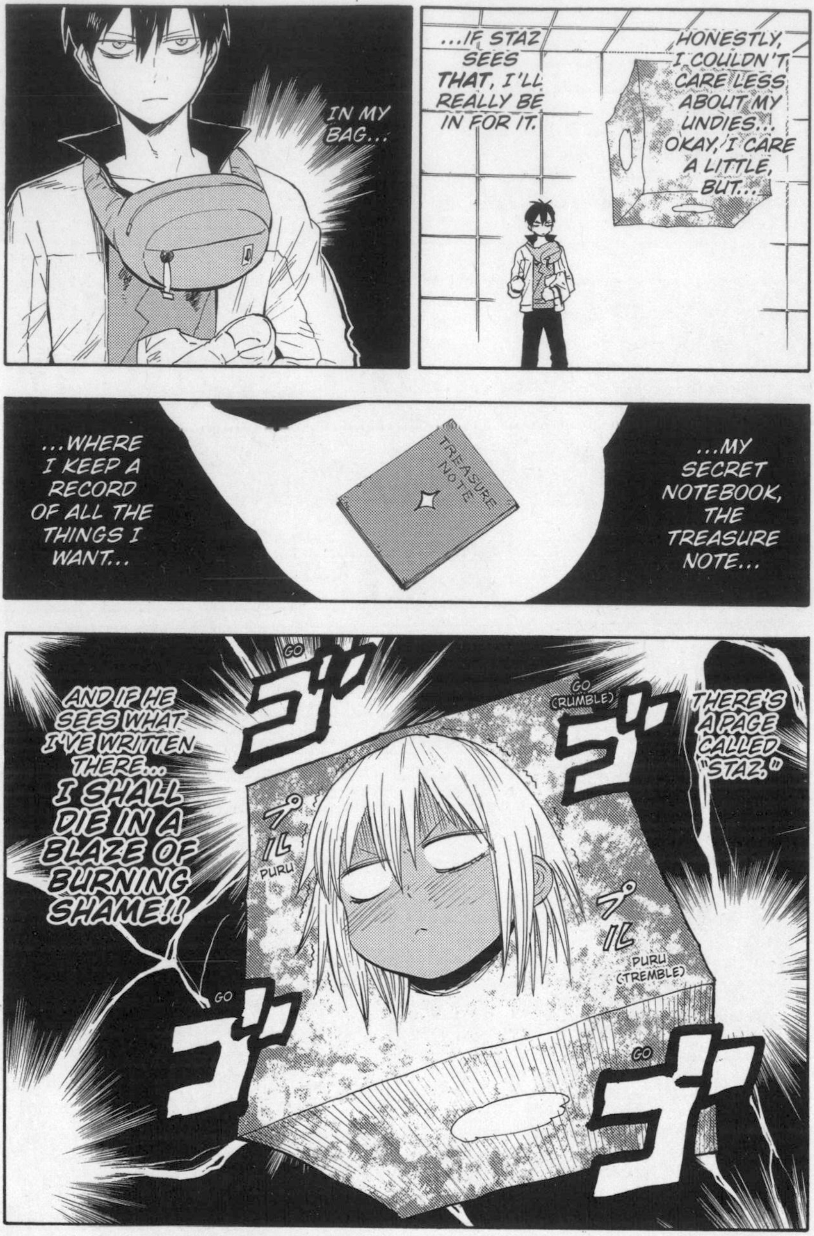
HONESTLY, I COULDN'T CARE LESS ABOUT MY UNDIES... OKAY, I CARE A LITTLE, BUT...
...IF STAZ SEES THAT, I'LL REALLY BE IN FOR IT.
IN MY BAG...
...MY SECRET NOTEBOOK, THE TREASURE NOTE...
TREASURE NOTE
...WHERE I KEEP A RECORD OF ALL THE THINGS I WANT...
THERE'S A PAGE CALLED "STAZ."
GO (RUMBLE)
GO
AND IF HE SEES WHAT I'VE WRITTEN THERE... I SHALL DIE IN A BLAZE OF BURNING SHAME!!
PURU
PURU (TREMBLE)
GO
GO

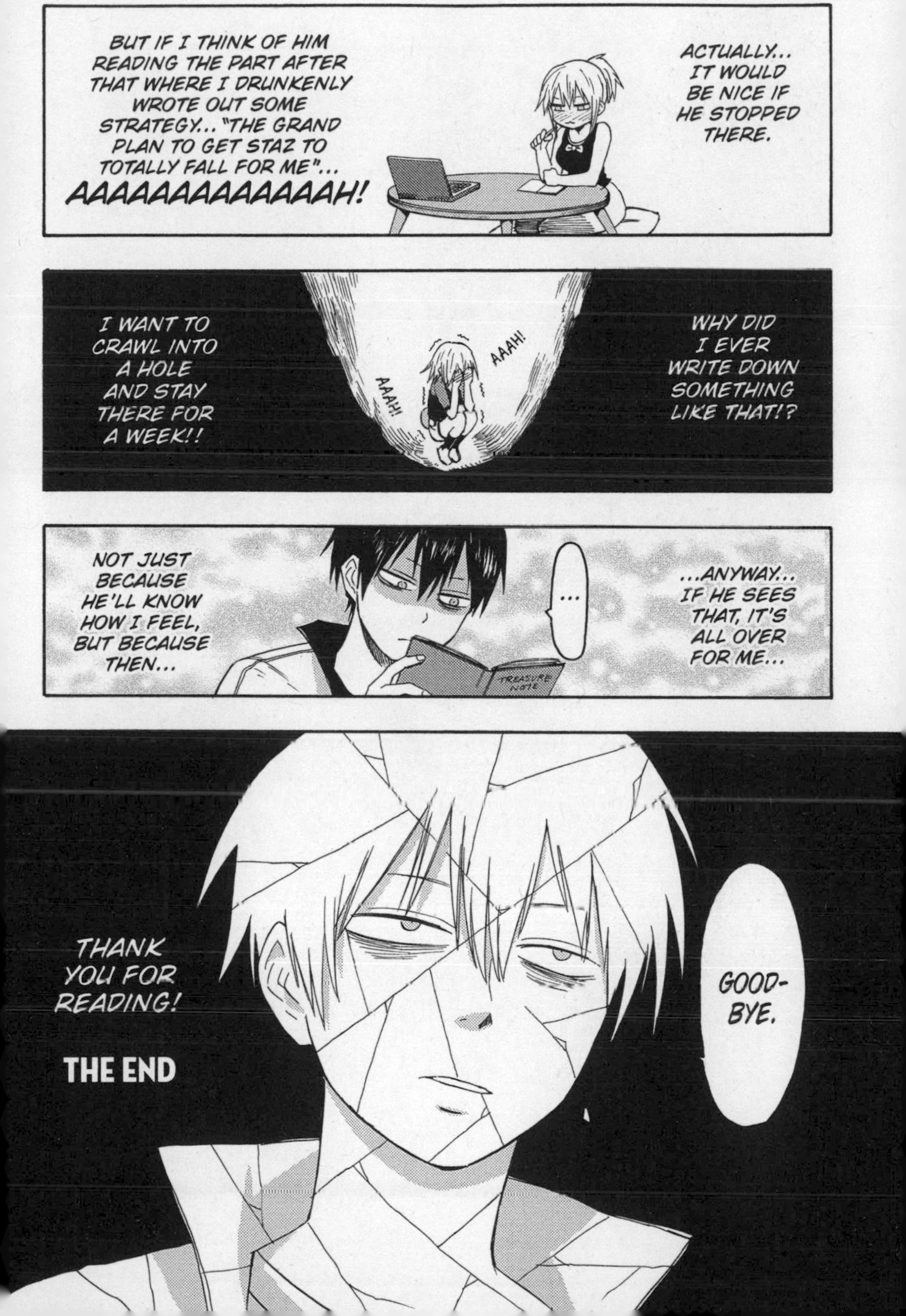
ACTUALLY... IT WOULD BE NICE IF HE STOPPED THERE.
BUT IF I THINK OF HIM READING THE PART AFTER THAT WHERE I DRUNKENLY WROTE OUT SOME STRATEGY... "THE GRAND PLAN TO GET STAZ TO TOTALLY FALL FOR ME"...
AAAAAAAAAAAAAH!
WHY DID I EVER WRITE DOWN SOMETHING LIKE THAT!?
AAAH!
AAAH!
I WANT TO CRAWL INTO A HOLE AND STAY THERE FOR A WEEK!!
...ANYWAY... IF HE SEES THAT, IT'S ALL OVER FOR ME...
...
TREASURE NOTE
NOT JUST BECAUSE HE'LL KNOW HOW I FEEL, BUT BECAUSE THEN...
GOOD-BYE.
THANK YOU FOR READING!
THE END

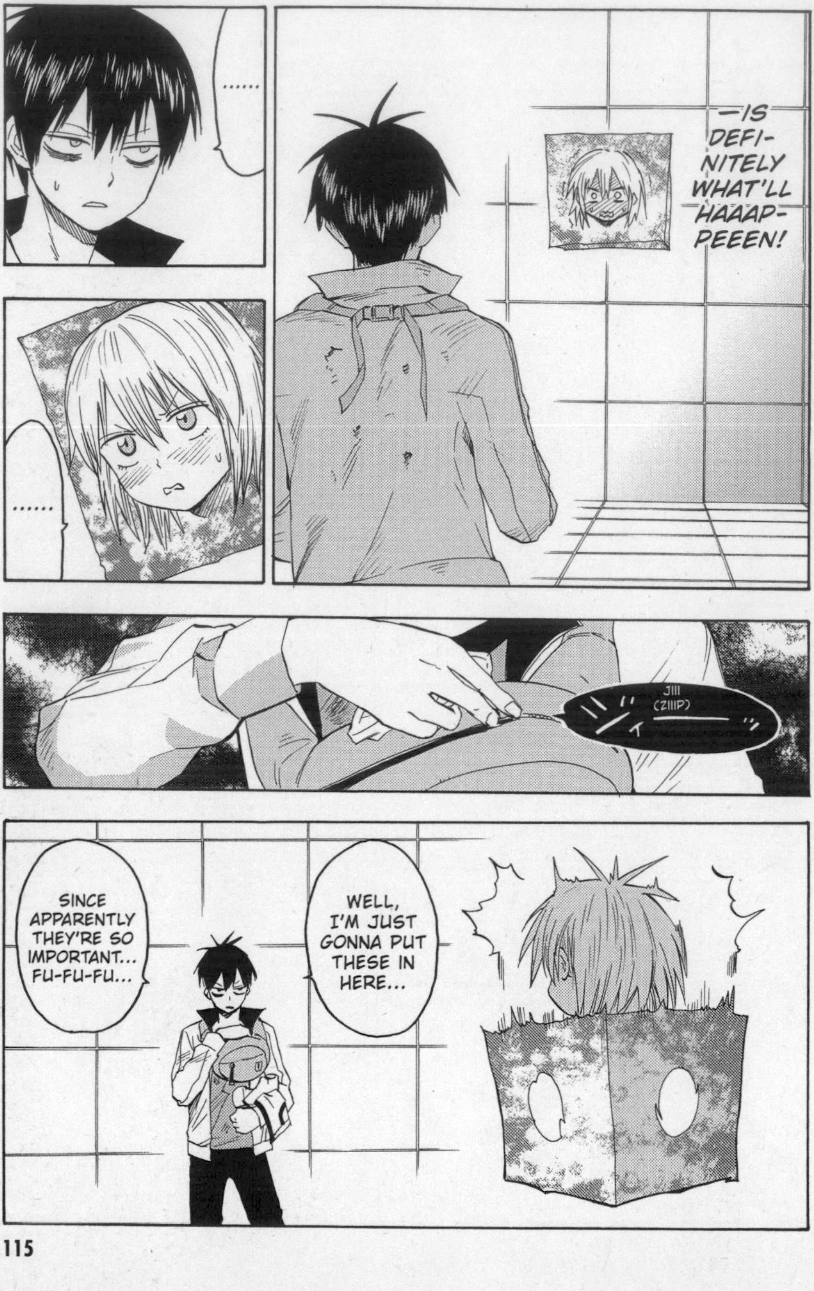
—IS DEFINITELY WHAT'LL HAAAPPEEEN!
......
......
JIII (ZIIIP)
WELL, I'M JUST GONNA PUT THESE IN HERE...
SINCE APPARENTLY THEY'RE SO IMPORTANT... FU-FU-FU...

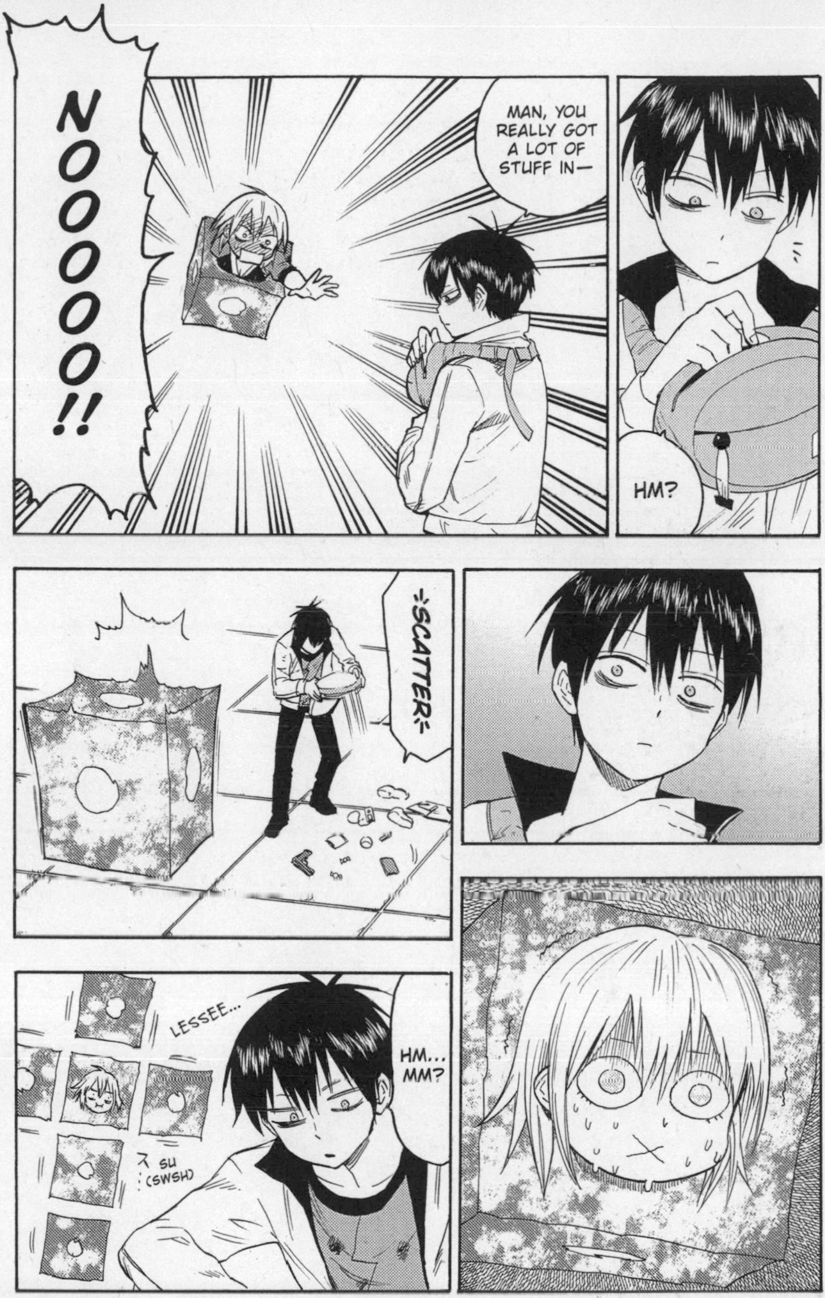
HM?
MAN, YOU REALLY GOT A LOT OF STUFF IN—
NOOOOOOO!!
SCATTER
HM... MM?
LESSEE...
ス SU (SWSH)

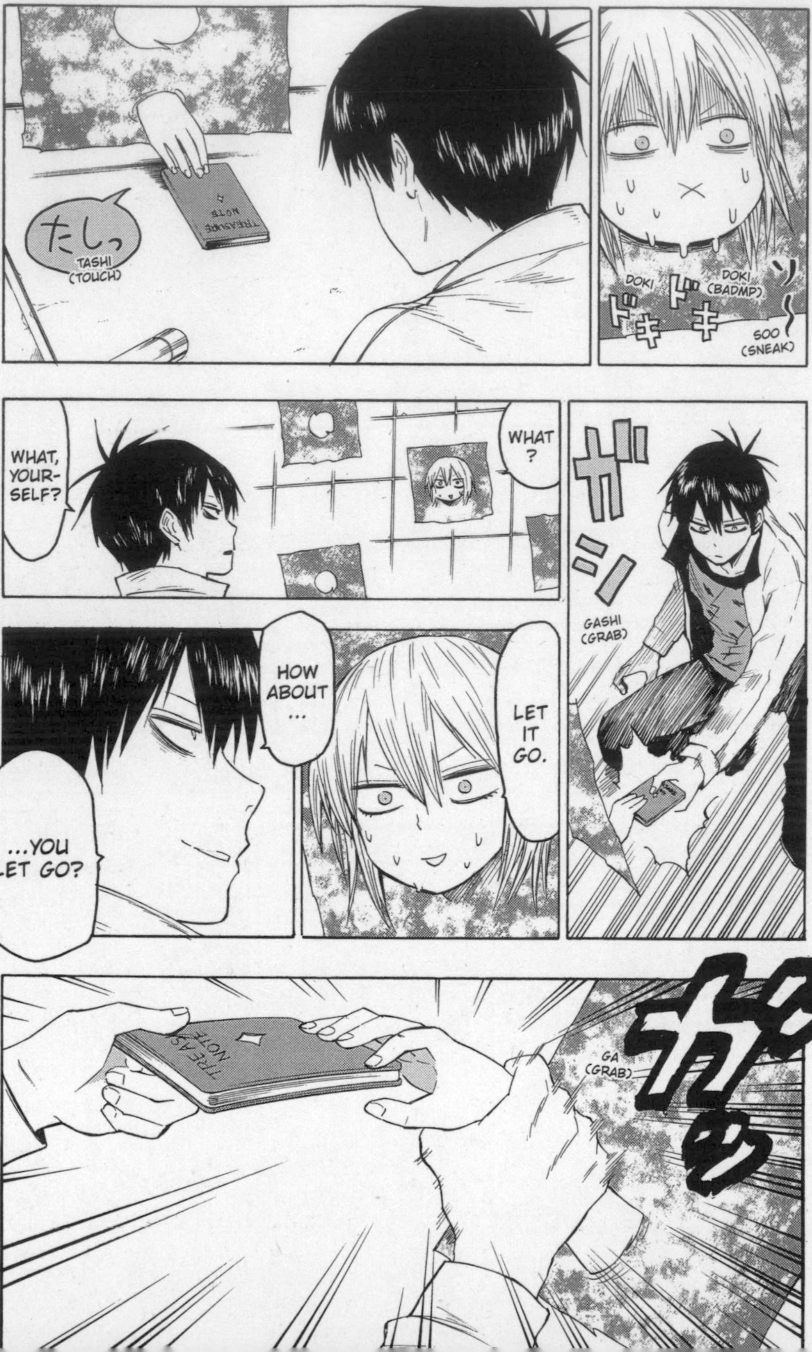
ソ～
SOO (SNEAK)
ドキ
DOKI (BADMP)
ドキ
DOKI
TREASURE NOTE
たしっ
TASHI (TOUCH)
ガシ
GASHI (GRAB)
WHAT?
WHAT, YOURSELF?
LET IT GO.
HOW ABOUT ...
...YOU LET GO?
TREASURE NOTE
ガッ
GA (GRAB)

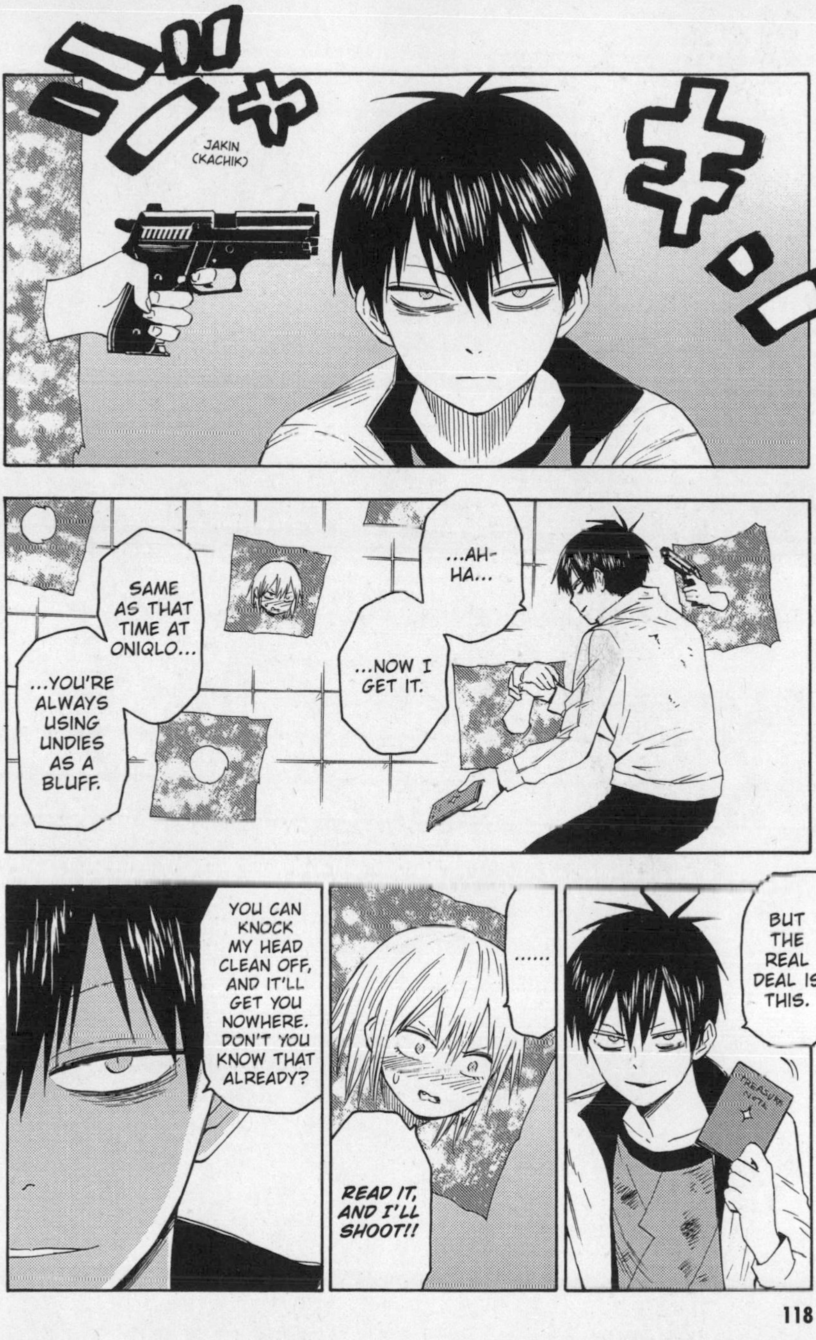
JAKIN (KACHIK)
...AH-HA...
...NOW I GET IT.
SAME AS THAT TIME AT ONIQLO...
...YOU'RE ALWAYS USING UNDIES AS A BLUFF.
BUT THE REAL DEAL IS THIS.
......
READ IT, AND I'LL SHOOT!!
YOU CAN KNOCK MY HEAD CLEAN OFF, AND IT'LL GET YOU NOWHERE. DON'T YOU KNOW THAT ALREADY?

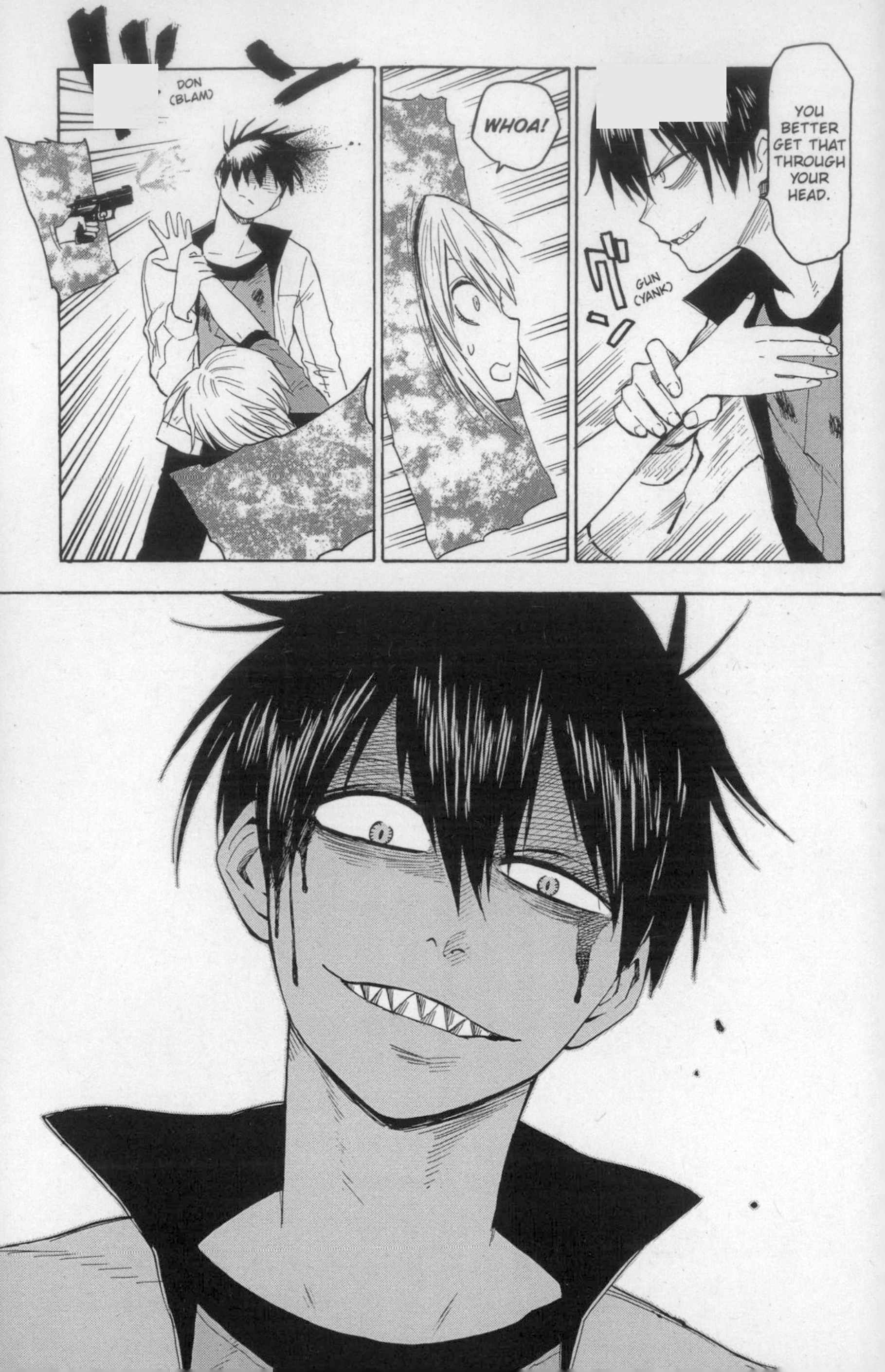
YOU BETTER GET THAT THROUGH YOUR HEAD.
GUN (YANK)
WHOA!
DON (BLAM)

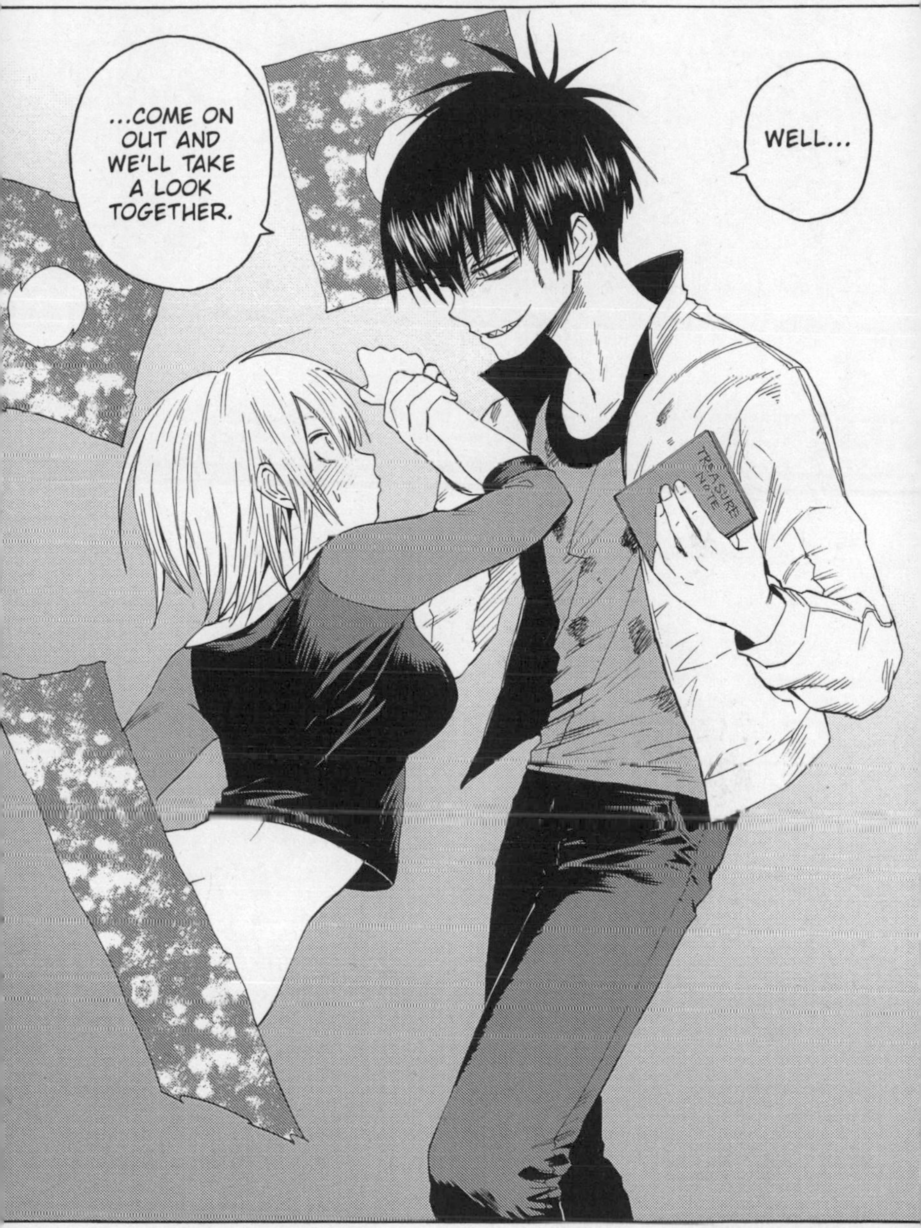
WELL...
...COME ON OUT AND WE'LL TAKE A LOOK TOGETHER.
TREASURE NOTE

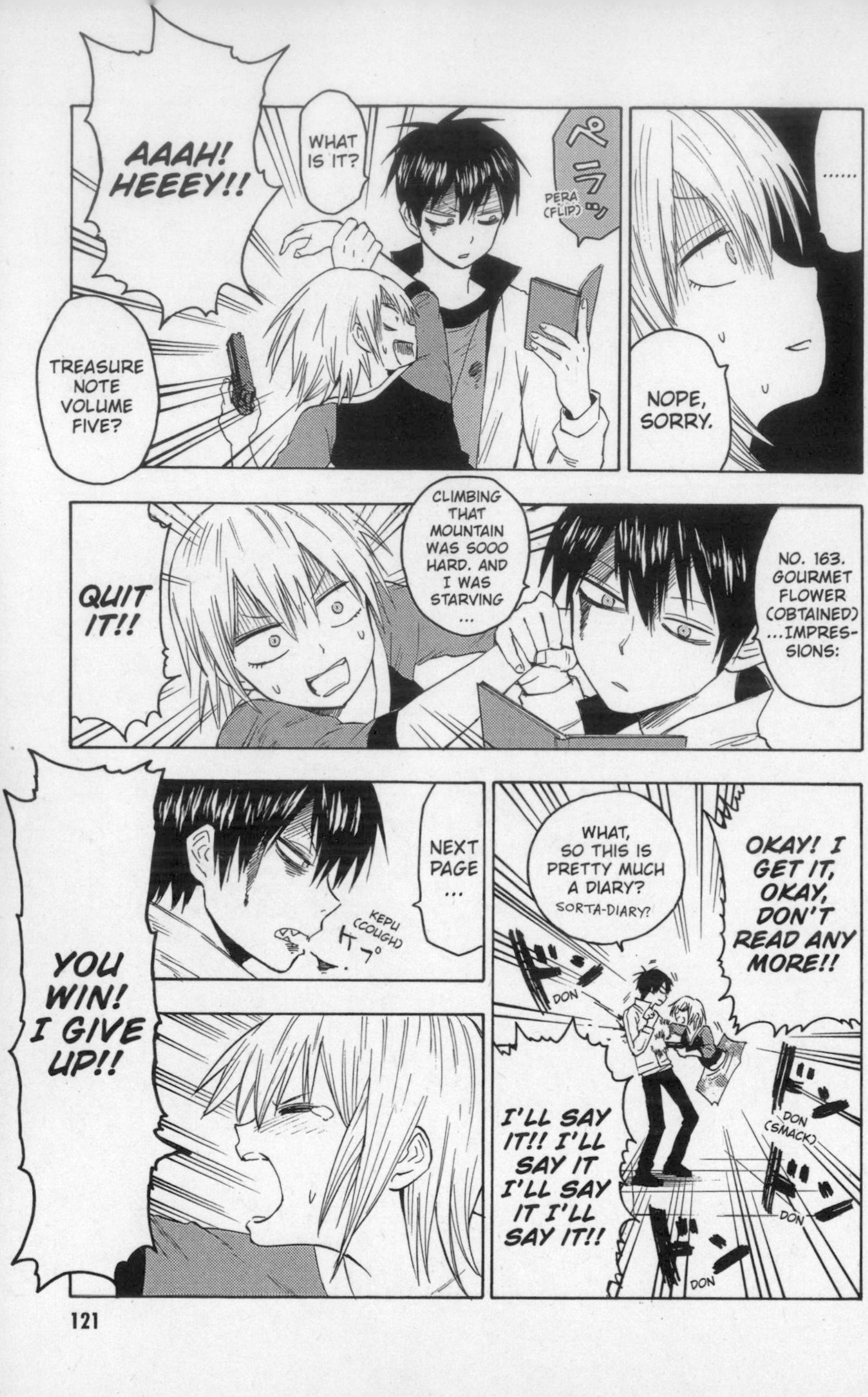
......
NOPE, SORRY.
ペラッ
PERA (FLIP)
WHAT IS IT?
AAAH! HEEEY!!
TREASURE NOTE VOLUME FIVE?
NO. 163. GOURMET FLOWER (OBTAINED) ...IMPRESSIONS:
CLIMBING THAT MOUNTAIN WAS SOOO HARD. AND I WAS STARVING ...
QUIT IT!!
WHAT, SO THIS IS PRETTY MUCH A DIARY?
SORTA-DIARY?
OKAY! I GET IT, OKAY, DON'T READ ANY MORE!!
DON
I'LL SAY IT!! I'LL SAY IT I'LL SAY IT I'LL SAY IT!!
DON (SMACK)
DON
DON
NEXT PAGE ...
KEPU (COUGH)
YOU WIN! I GIVE UP!!

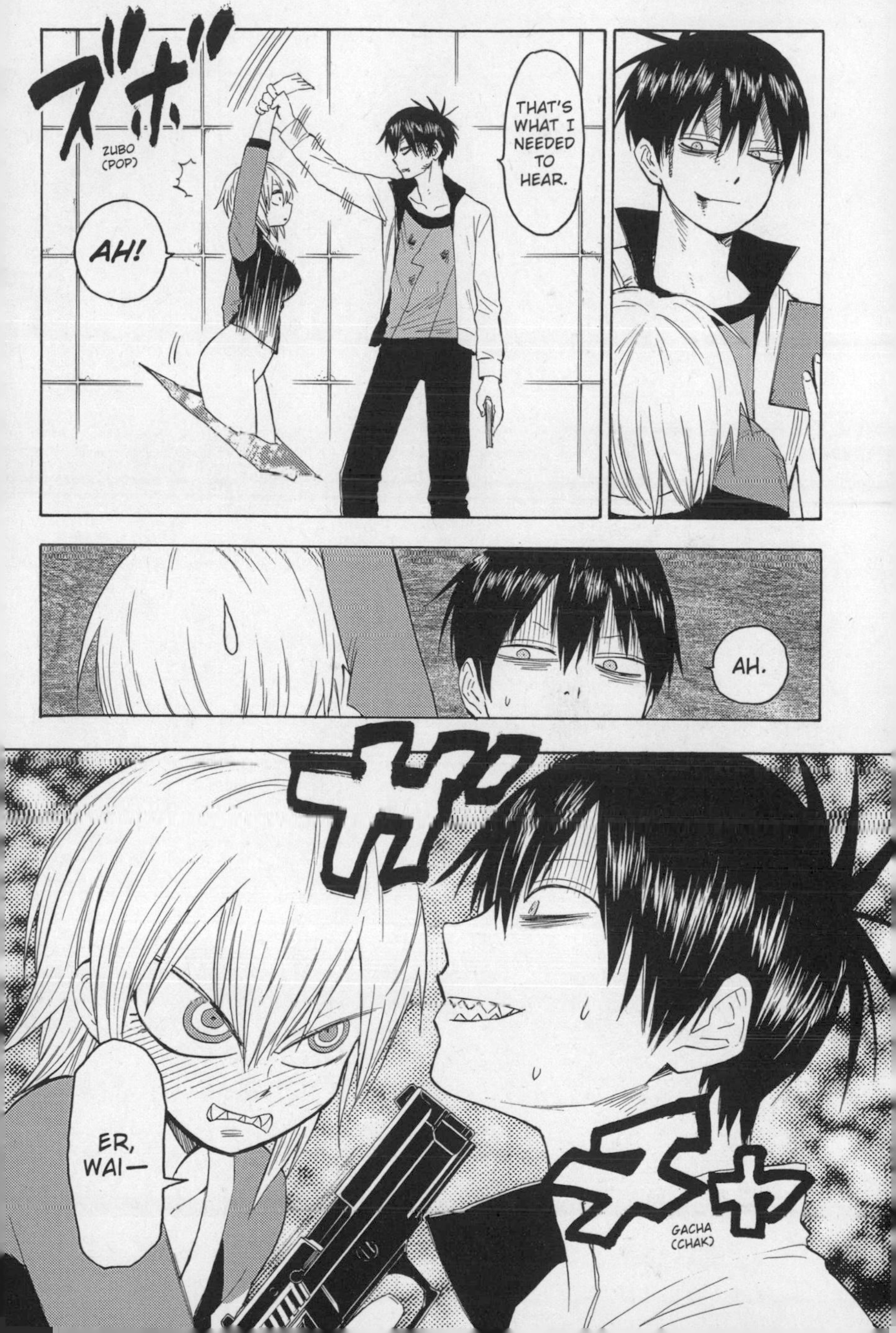
THAT'S WHAT I NEEDED TO HEAR.
ZUBO (POP)
AH!
AH.
GACHA (CHAK)
ER, WAI—

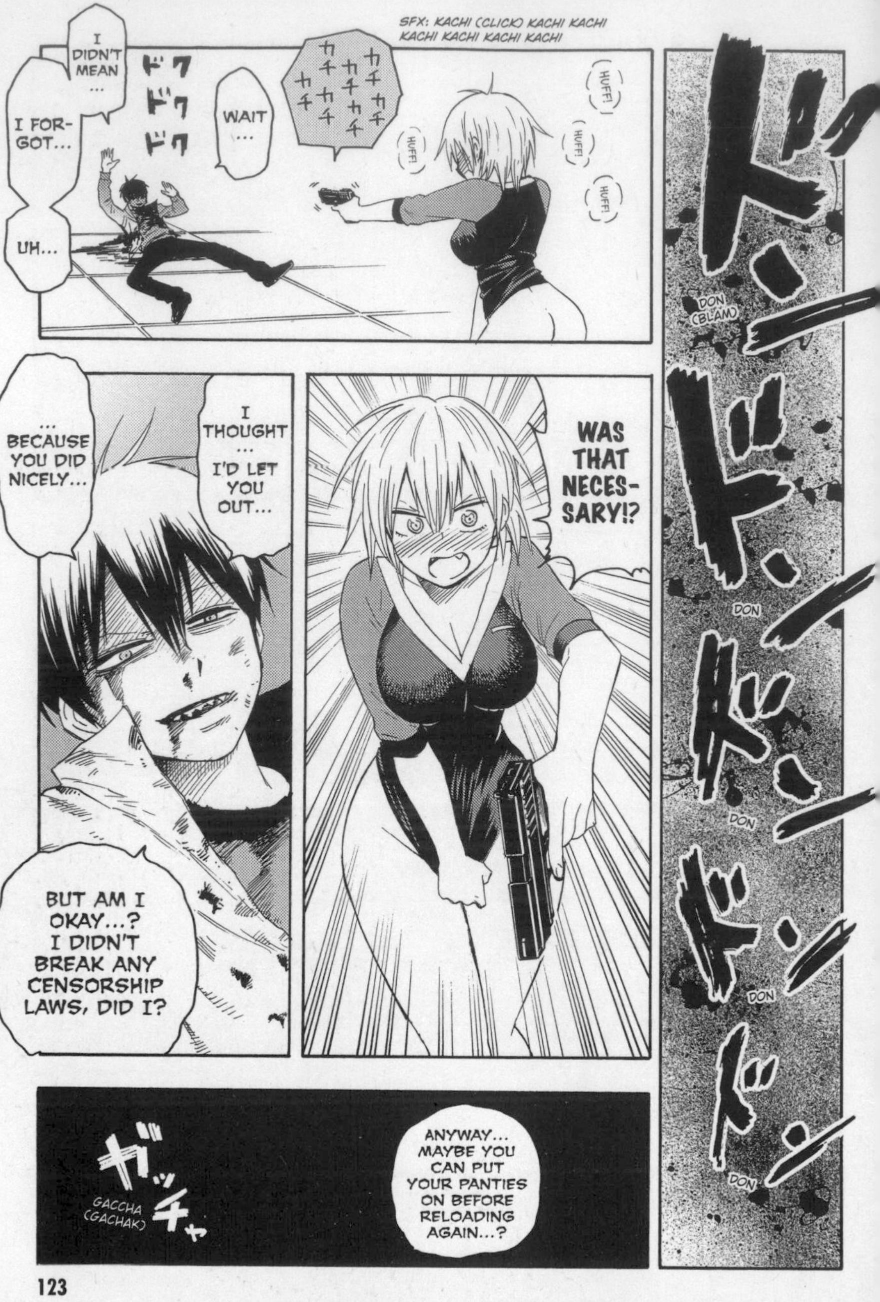
DON (BLAM)
DON
DON
DON
DON
SFX: KACHI (CLICK) KACHI KACHI KACHI KACHI KACHI KACHI
HUFF!
HUFF!
HUFF!
HUFF!
WAIT...
I DIDN'T MEAN...
I FOR-GOT...
UH...
WAS THAT NECES-SARY!?
I THOUGHT... I'D LET YOU OUT...
... BECAUSE YOU DID NICELY...
BUT AM I OKAY...? I DIDN'T BREAK ANY CENSORSHIP LAWS, DID I?
ANYWAY... MAYBE YOU CAN PUT YOUR PANTIES ON BEFORE RELOADING AGAIN...?
GACCHA (GACHAK)

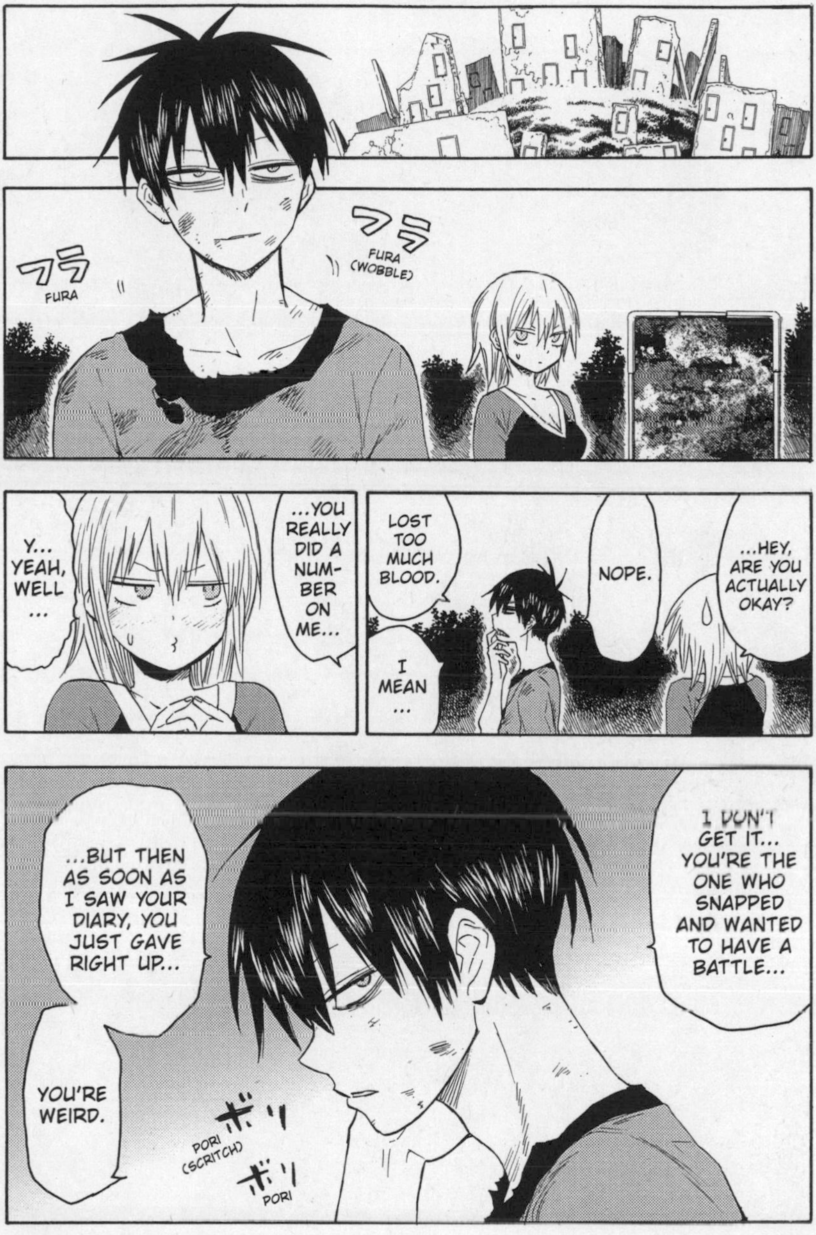

フラ
FURA (WOBBLE)
フラ
FURA
...HEY, ARE YOU ACTUALLY OKAY?
NOPE.
LOST TOO MUCH BLOOD.
I MEAN ...
...YOU REALLY DID A NUM-BER ON ME...
Y... YEAH, WELL ...
I DON'T GET IT... YOU'RE THE ONE WHO SNAPPED AND WANTED TO HAVE A BATTLE...
...BUT THEN AS SOON AS I SAW YOUR DIARY, YOU JUST GAVE RIGHT UP...
YOU'RE WEIRD.
ボリ
PORI (SCRITCH)
ボリ
PORI

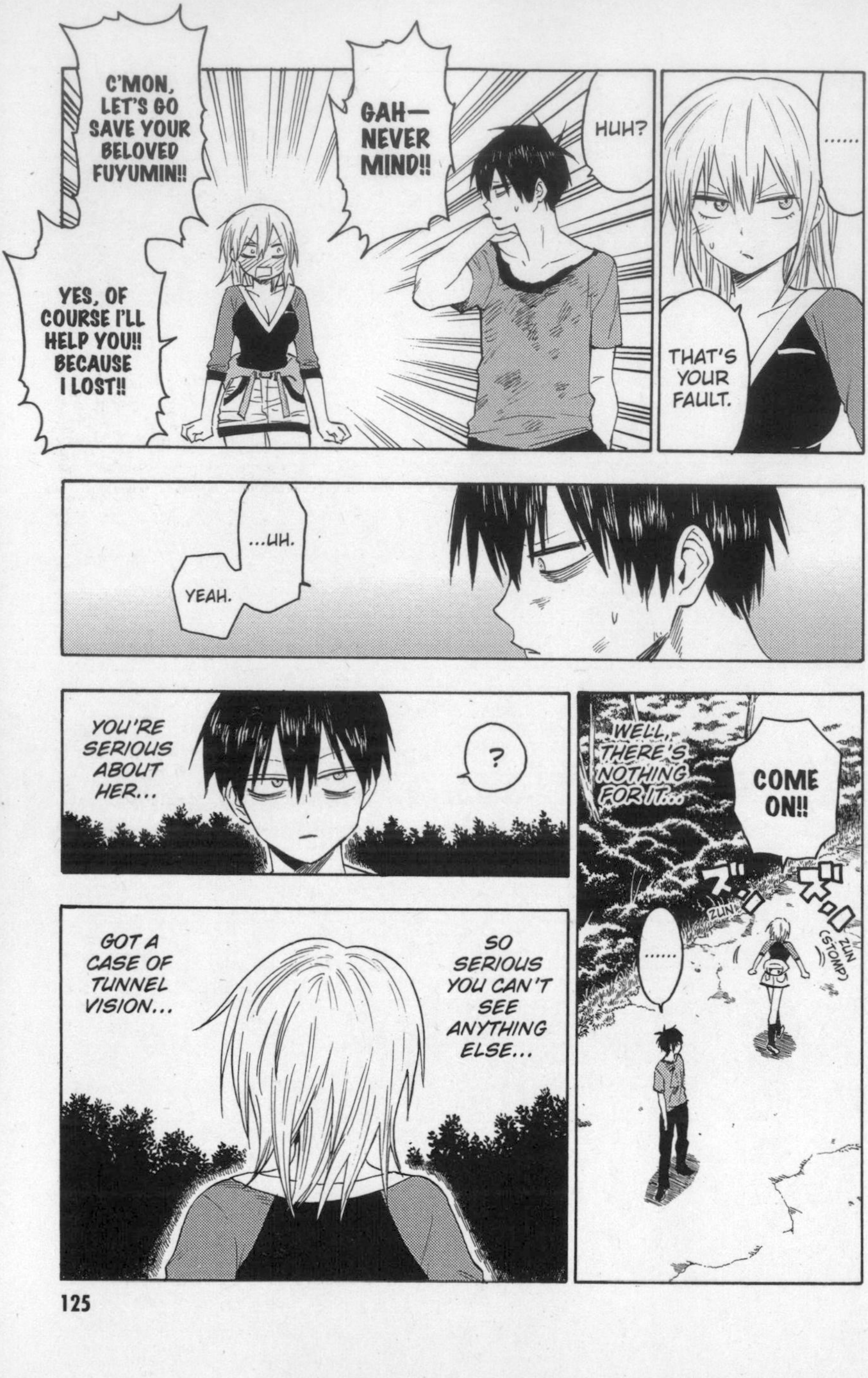
......
THAT'S YOUR FAULT.
HUH?
GAH— NEVER MIND!!
C'MON, LET'S GO SAVE YOUR BELOVED FUYUMIN!!
YES, OF COURSE I'LL HELP YOU!! BECAUSE I LOST!!
...UH.
YEAH.
WELL, THERE'S NOTHING FOR IT...
COME ON!!
ZUN (STOMP)
ZUN
......
?
YOU'RE SERIOUS ABOUT HER...
SO SERIOUS YOU CAN'T SEE ANYTHING ELSE...
GOT A CASE OF TUNNEL VISION...

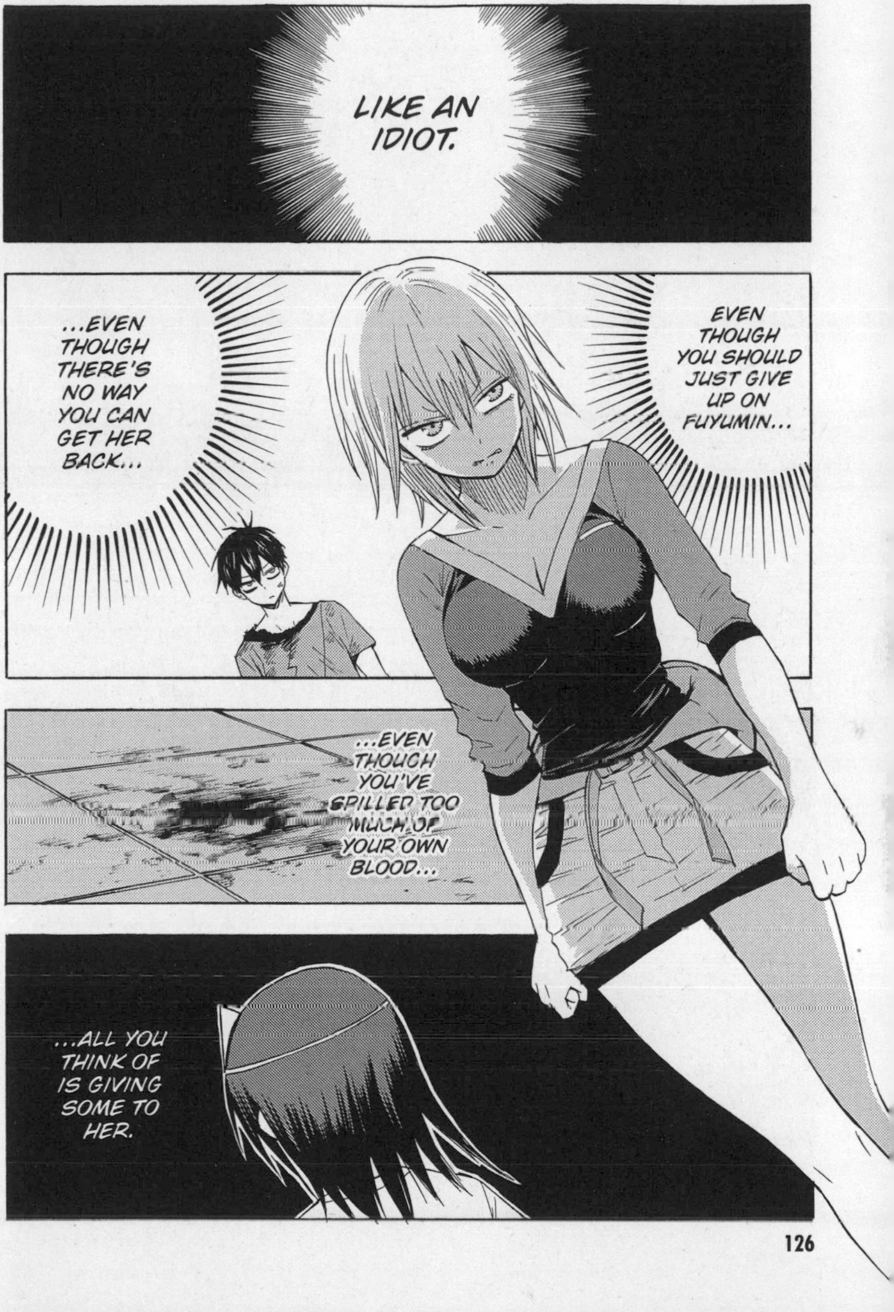
LIKE AN IDIOT.
EVEN THOUGH YOU SHOULD JUST GIVE UP ON FUYUMIN...
...EVEN THOUGH THERE'S NO WAY YOU CAN GET HER BACK...
...EVEN THOUGH YOU'VE SPILLED TOO MUCH OF YOUR OWN BLOOD...
...ALL YOU THINK OF IS GIVING SOME TO HER.

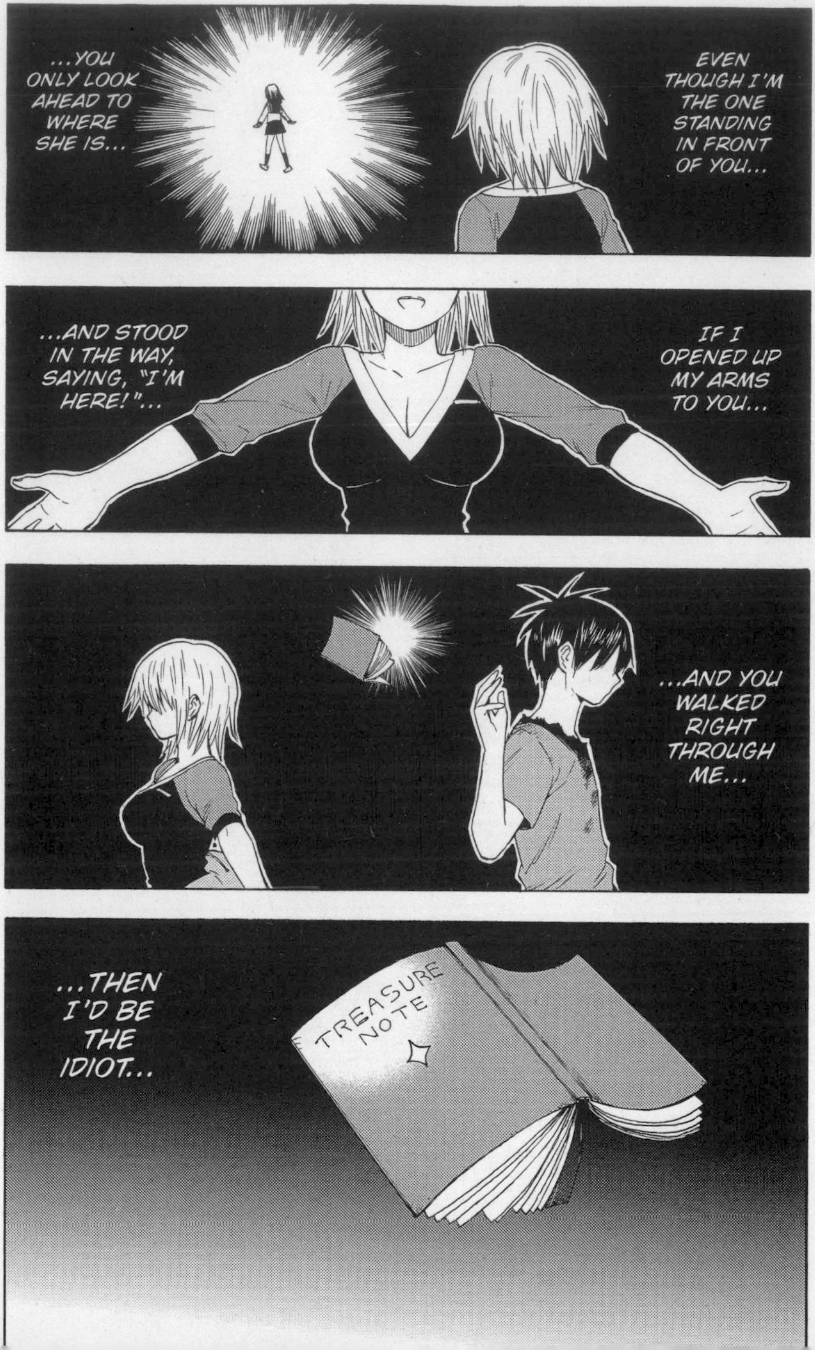
EVEN THOUGH I'M THE ONE STANDING IN FRONT OF YOU...
...YOU ONLY LOOK AHEAD TO WHERE SHE IS...
IF I OPENED UP MY ARMS TO YOU...
...AND STOOD IN THE WAY, SAYING, "I'M HERE!"...
...AND YOU WALKED RIGHT THROUGH ME...
...THEN I'D BE THE IDIOT...
TREASURE NOTE

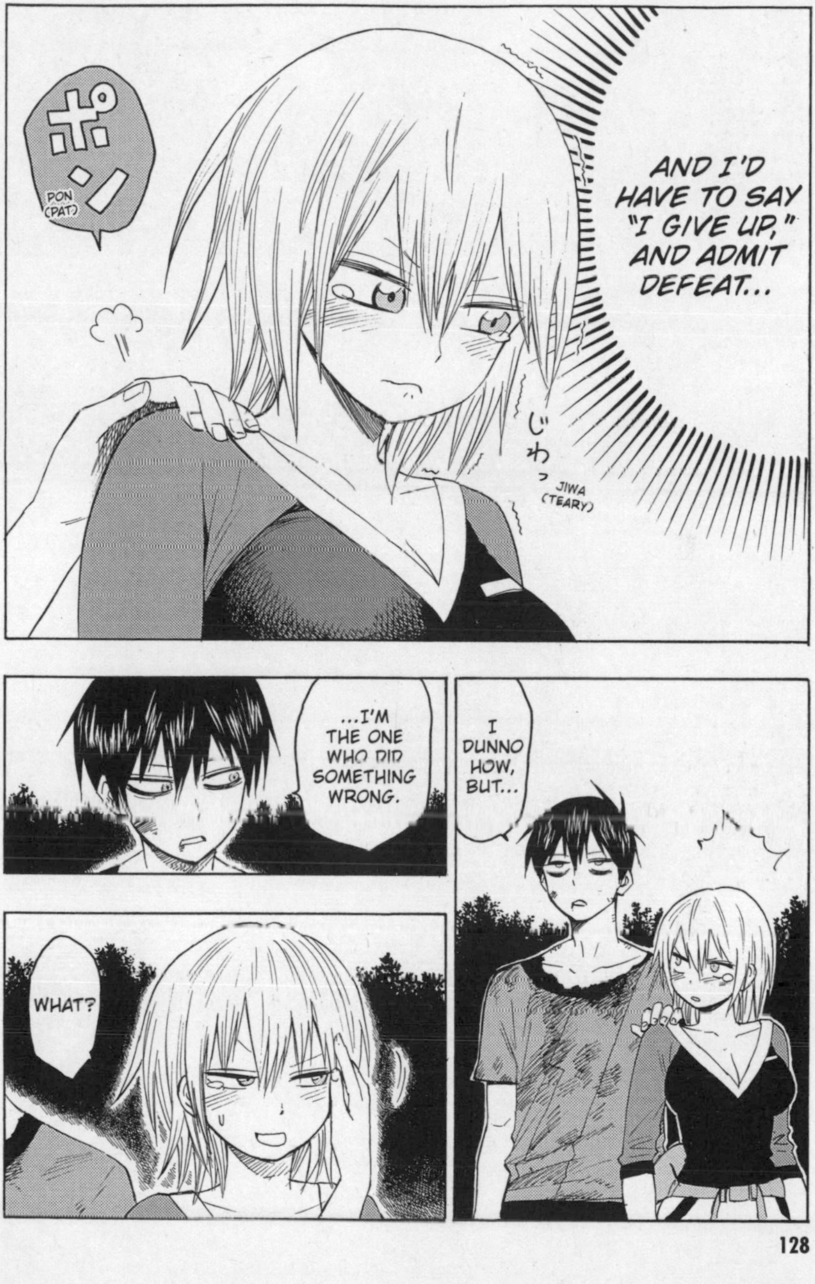
AND I'D HAVE TO SAY "I GIVE UP," AND ADMIT DEFEAT...
じわっ
JIWA (TEARY)
ポン
PON (PAT)
I DUNNO HOW, BUT...
...I'M THE ONE WHO DID SOMETHING WRONG.
WHAT?

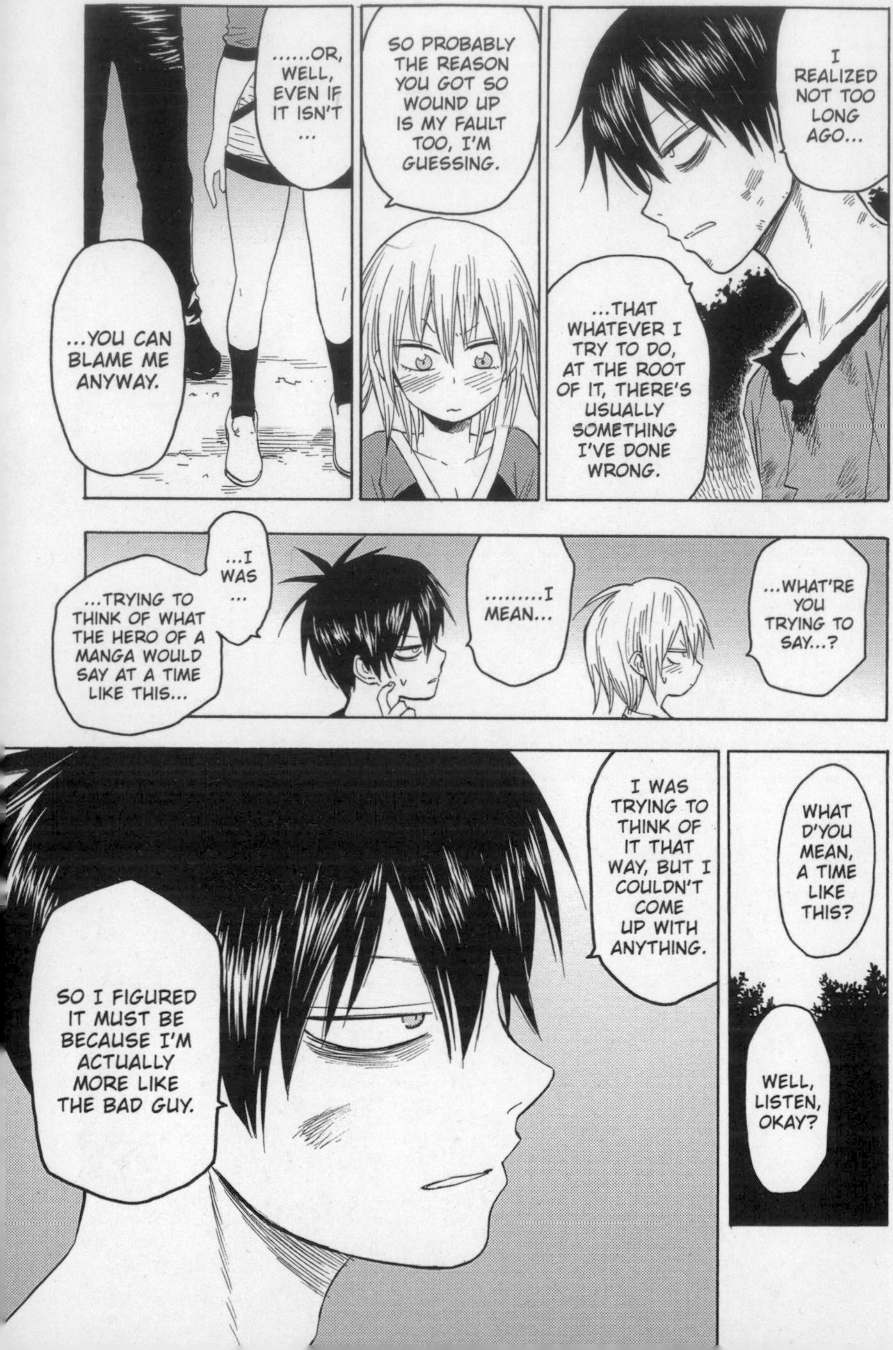
I REALIZED NOT TOO LONG AGO...
...THAT WHATEVER I TRY TO DO, AT THE ROOT OF IT, THERE'S USUALLY SOMETHING I'VE DONE WRONG.
SO PROBABLY THE REASON YOU GOT SO WOUND UP IS MY FAULT TOO, I'M GUESSING.
......OR, WELL, EVEN IF IT ISN'T ...
...YOU CAN BLAME ME ANYWAY.
...WHAT'RE YOU TRYING TO SAY...?
.........I MEAN...
...I WAS ...
...TRYING TO THINK OF WHAT THE HERO OF A MANGA WOULD SAY AT A TIME LIKE THIS...
WHAT D'YOU MEAN, A TIME LIKE THIS?
WELL, LISTEN, OKAY?
I WAS TRYING TO THINK OF IT THAT WAY, BUT I COULDN'T COME UP WITH ANYTHING.
SO I FIGURED IT MUST BE BECAUSE I'M ACTUALLY MORE LIKE THE BAD GUY.

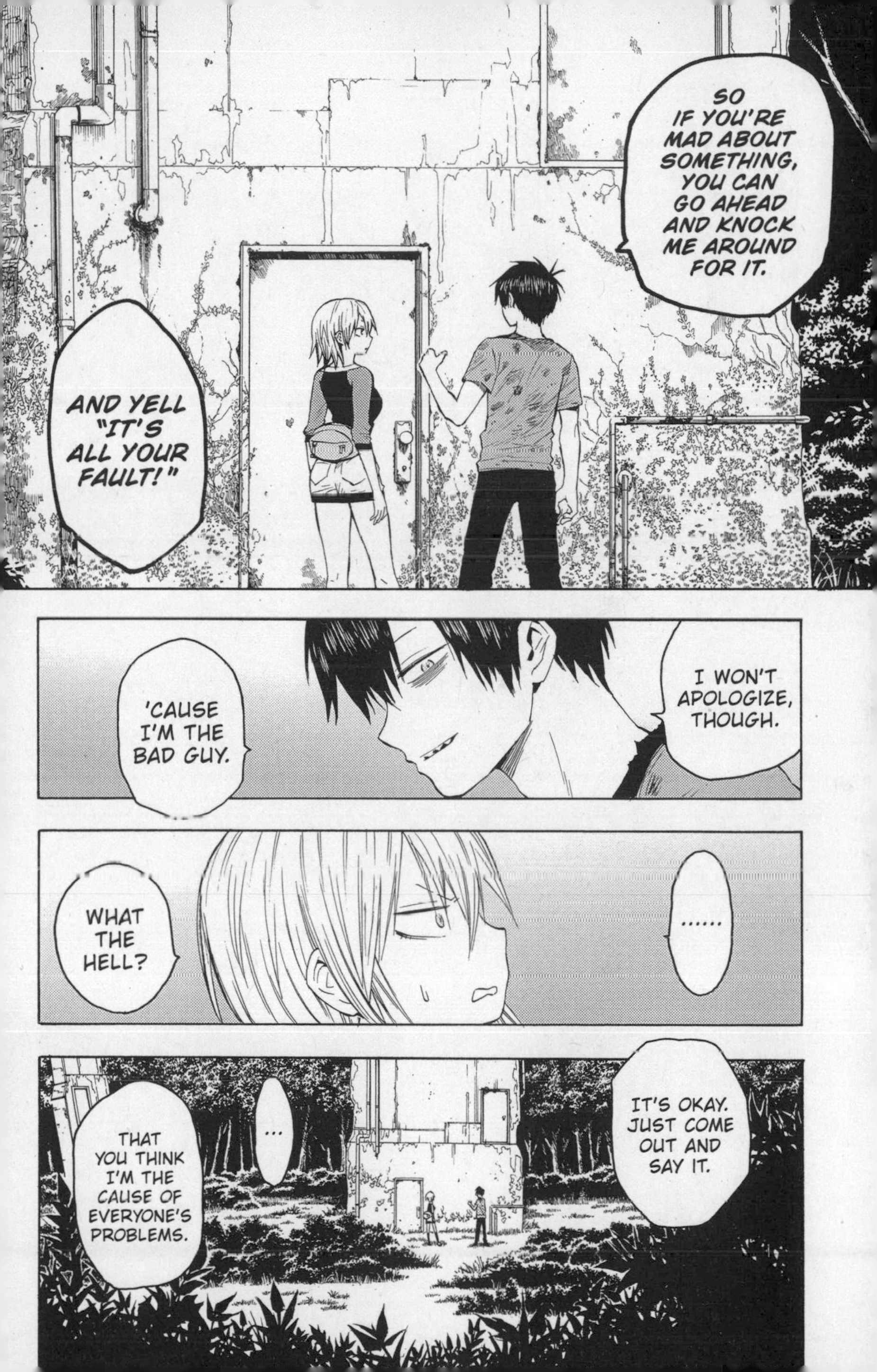
SO IF YOU'RE MAD ABOUT SOMETHING, YOU CAN GO AHEAD AND KNOCK ME AROUND FOR IT.
AND YELL "IT'S ALL YOUR FAULT!"
I WON'T APOLOGIZE, THOUGH.
'CAUSE I'M THE BAD GUY.
......
WHAT THE HELL?
IT'S OKAY. JUST COME OUT AND SAY IT.
...
THAT YOU THINK I'M THE CAUSE OF EVERYONE'S PROBLEMS.

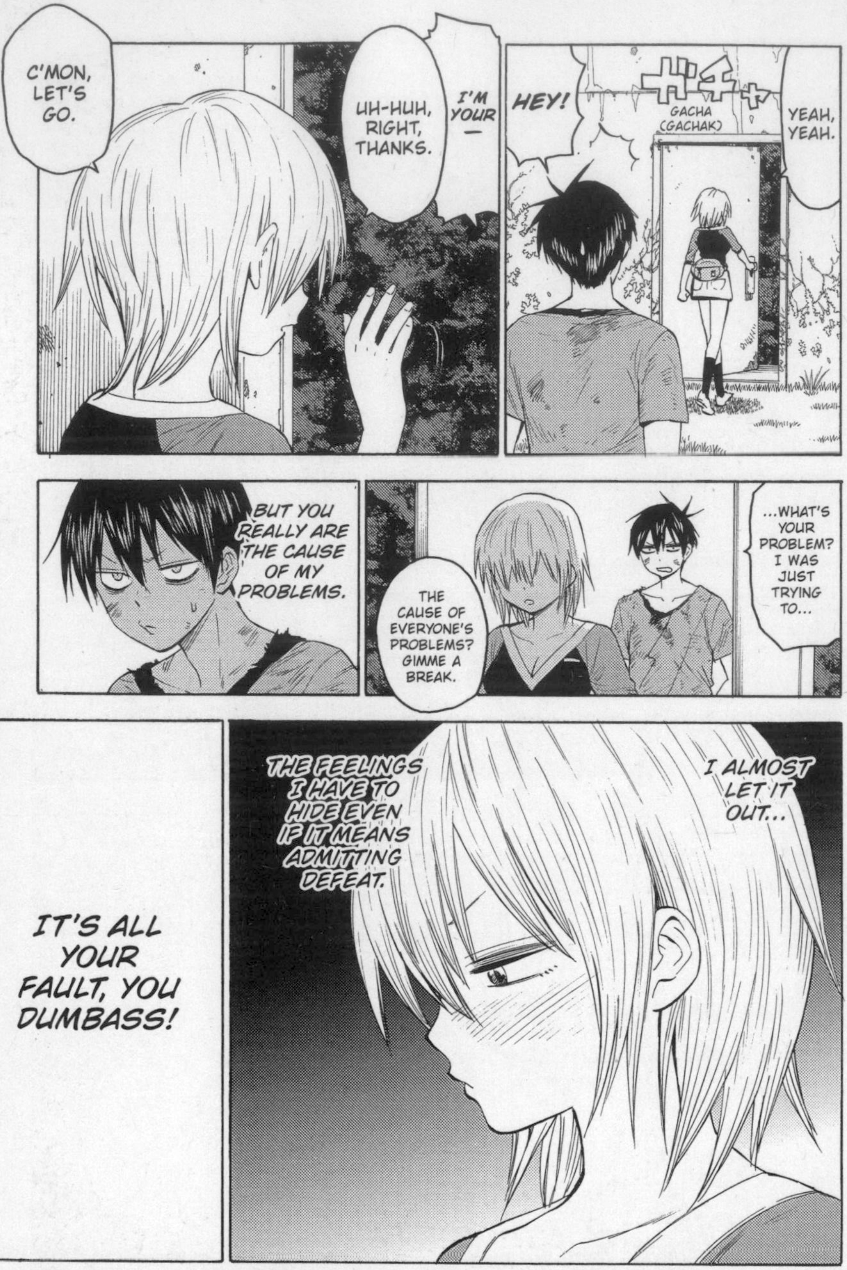
YEAH, YEAH.
ガチャ
GACHA (GACHAK)
HEY!
I'M YOUR —
UH-HUH, RIGHT, THANKS.
C'MON, LET'S GO.
...WHAT'S YOUR PROBLEM? I WAS JUST TRYING TO...
THE CAUSE OF EVERYONE'S PROBLEMS? GIMME A BREAK.
BUT YOU REALLY ARE THE CAUSE OF MY PROBLEMS.
I ALMOST LET IT OUT...
THE FEELINGS I HAVE TO HIDE EVEN IF IT MEANS ADMITTING DEFEAT.
IT'S ALL YOUR FAULT, YOU DUMBASS!

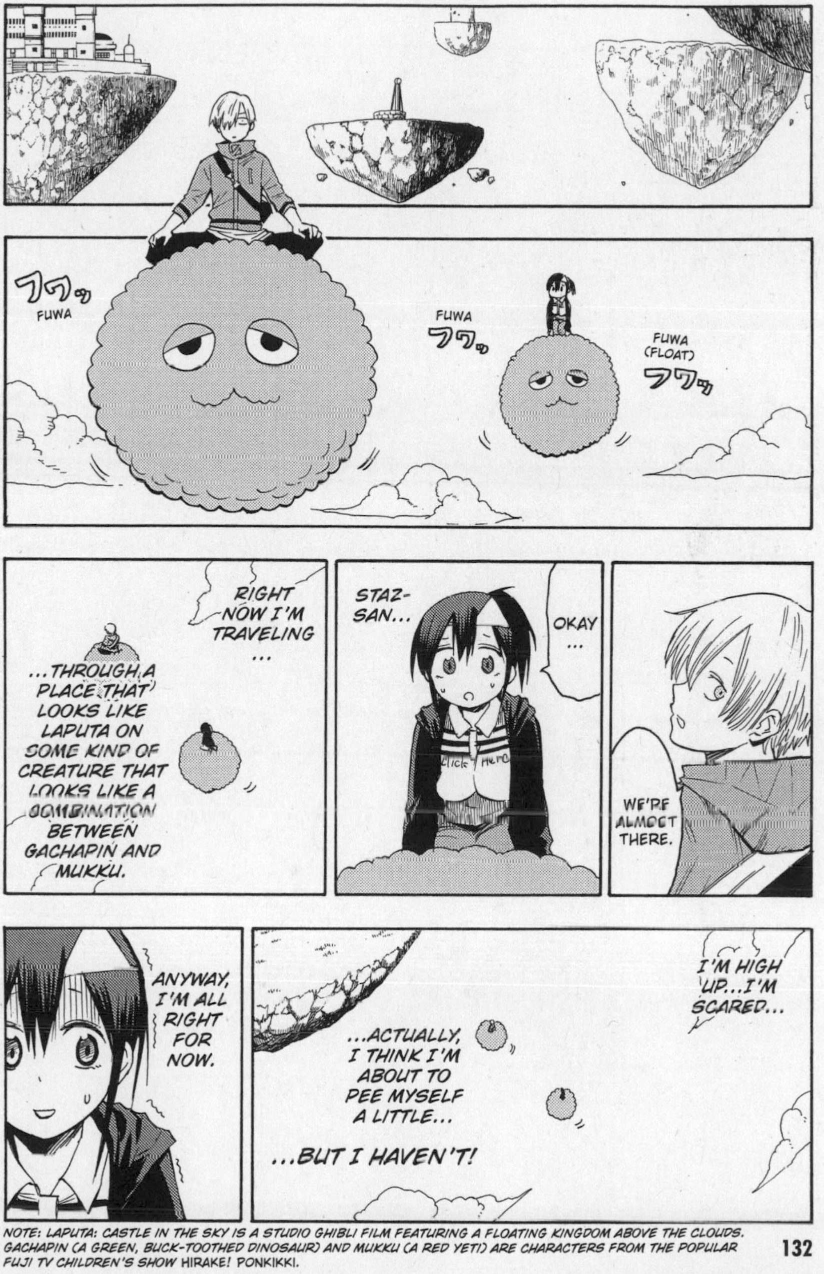
FUWA (FLOAT)
フワッ
FUWA
フワッ
FUWA
フワッ
WE'RE ALMOST THERE.
OKAY...
STAZ-SAN...
RIGHT NOW I'M TRAVELING...
...THROUGH A PLACE THAT LOOKS LIKE LAPUTA ON SOME KIND OF CREATURE THAT LOOKS LIKE A COMBINATION BETWEEN GACHAPIN AND MUKKU.
I'M HIGH UP...I'M SCARED...
...ACTUALLY, I THINK I'M ABOUT TO PEE MYSELF A LITTLE...
...BUT I HAVEN'T!
ANYWAY, I'M ALL RIGHT FOR NOW.

NOTE: LAPUTA: CASTLE IN THE SKY IS A STUDIO GHIBLI FILM FEATURING A FLOATING KINGDOM ABOVE THE CLOUDS. GACHAPIN (A GREEN, BUCK-TOOTHED DINOSAUR) AND MUKKU (A RED YETI) ARE CHARACTERS FROM THE POPULAR FUJI TV CHILDREN'S SHOW HIRAKE! PONKIKKI.

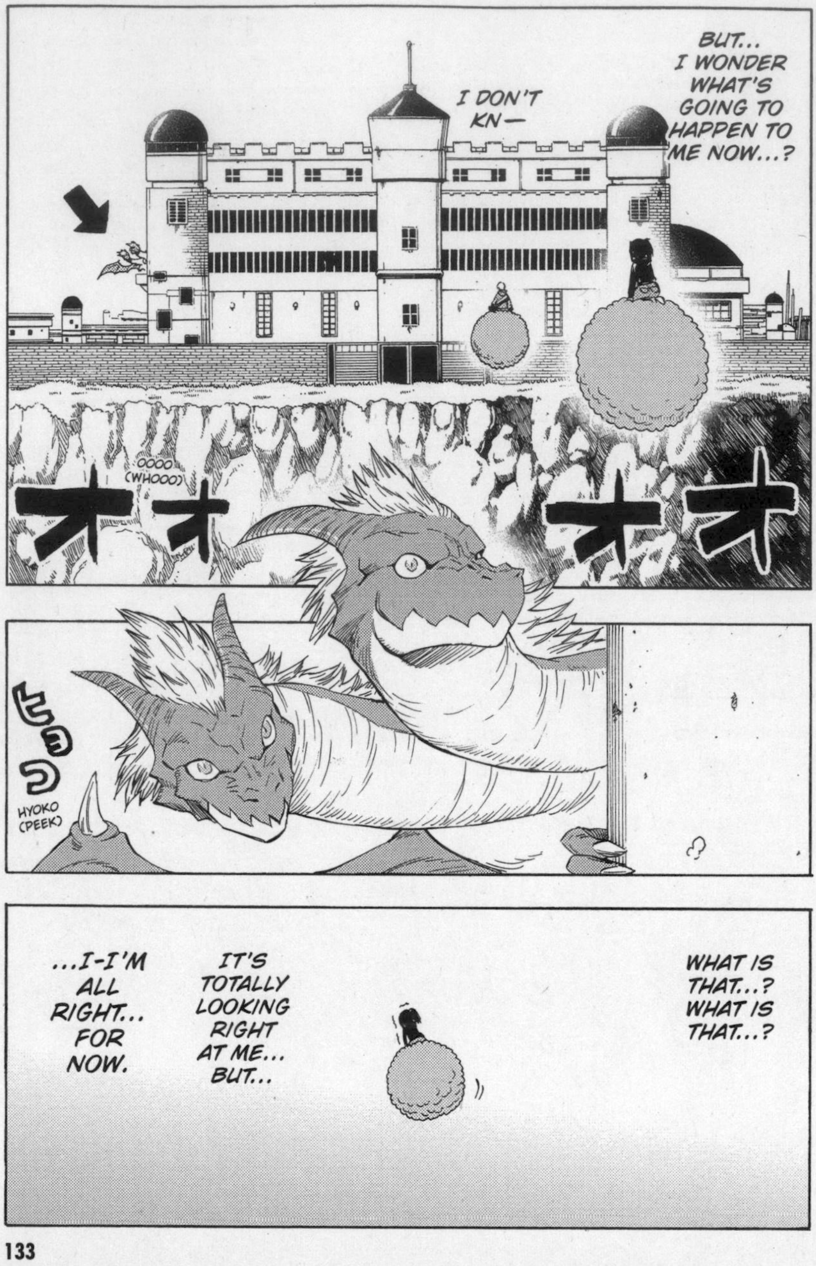
BUT... I WONDER WHAT'S GOING TO HAPPEN TO ME NOW...?
I DON'T KN—
オオ
OOOO (WHOOO)
オオ
ヒョっ
HYOKO (PEEK)
WHAT IS THAT...? WHAT IS THAT...?
IT'S TOTALLY LOOKING RIGHT AT ME... BUT...
...I-I'M ALL RIGHT... FOR NOW.

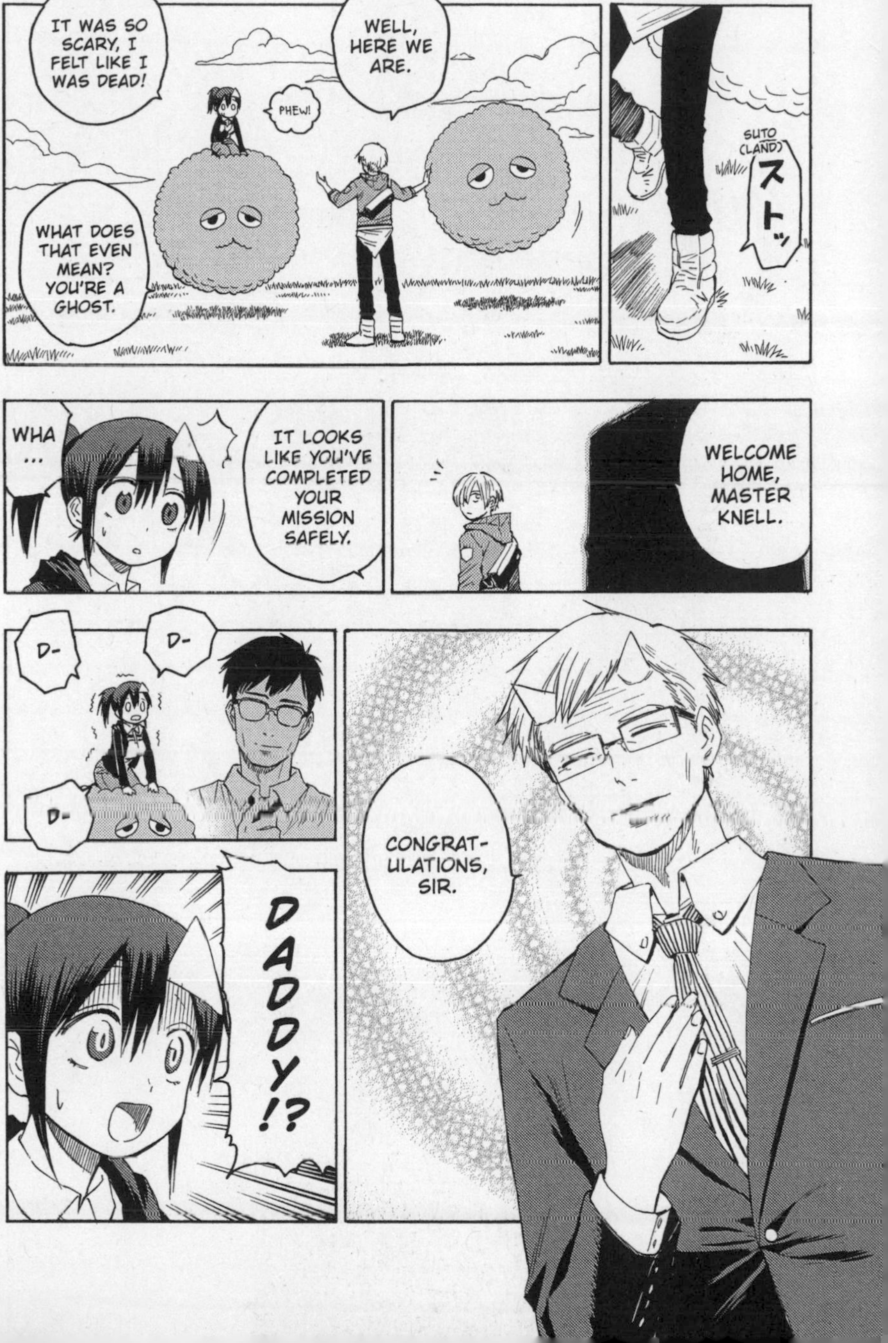
SUTO (LAND)
ストッ
WELL, HERE WE ARE.
PHEW!
IT WAS SO SCARY, I FELT LIKE I WAS DEAD!
WHAT DOES THAT EVEN MEAN? YOU'RE A GHOST.
WELCOME HOME, MASTER KNELL.
IT LOOKS LIKE YOU'VE COMPLETED YOUR MISSION SAFELY.
WHA ...
CONGRAT-ULATIONS, SIR.
D-
D-
D-
DADDY!?

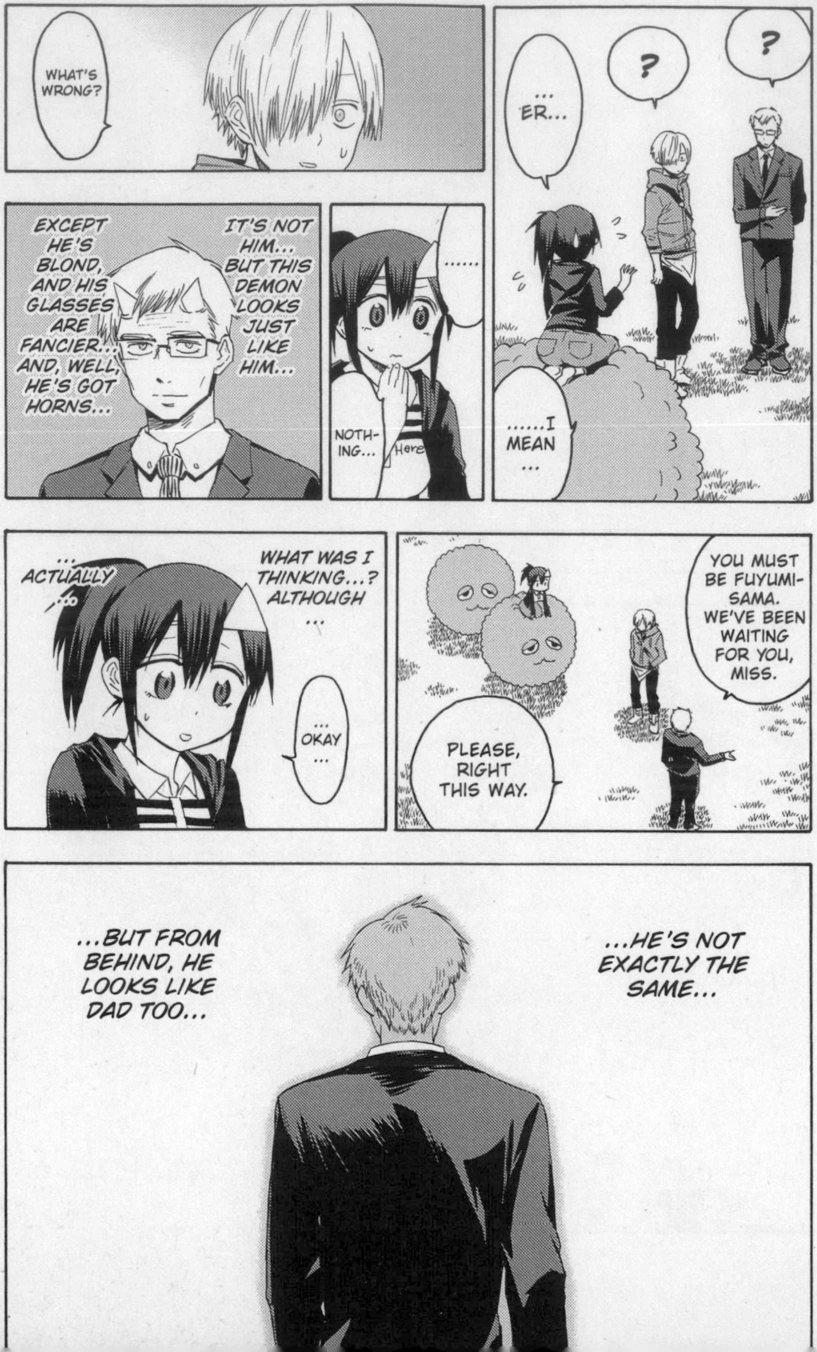
?
?
... ER...
......I MEAN ...
WHAT'S WRONG?
......
NOTH-ING...
Here
IT'S NOT HIM... BUT THIS DEMON LOOKS JUST LIKE HIM...
EXCEPT HE'S BLOND, AND HIS GLASSES ARE FANCIER... AND, WELL, HE'S GOT HORNS...
YOU MUST BE FUYUMI-SAMA. WE'VE BEEN WAITING FOR YOU, MISS.
PLEASE, RIGHT THIS WAY.
WHAT WAS I THINKING...? ALTHOUGH ...
... ACTUALLY ...
... OKAY ...
...HE'S NOT EXACTLY THE SAME...
...BUT FROM BEHIND, HE LOOKS LIKE DAD TOO...

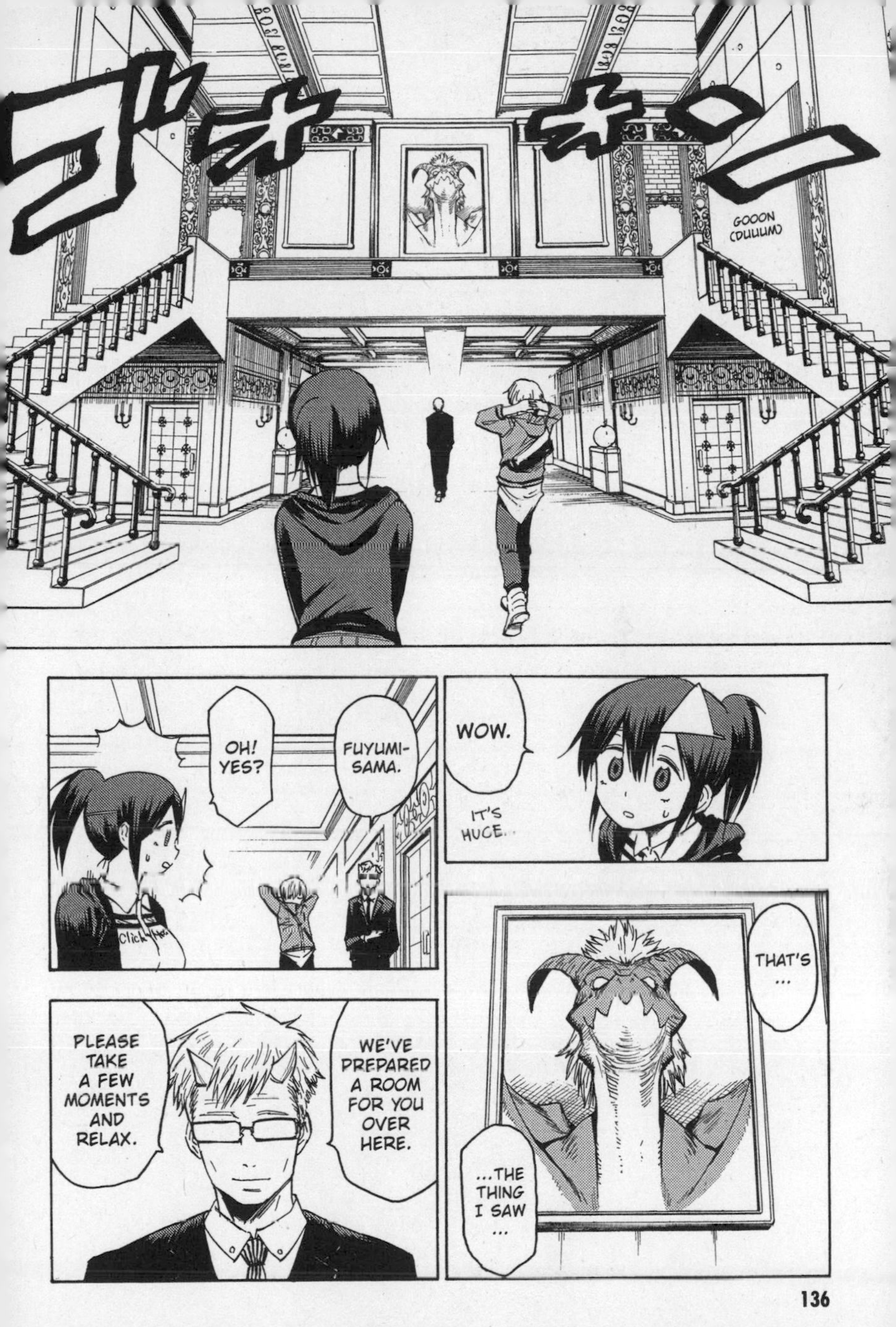
GOOON
(DUUUM)
WOW.
IT'S HUGE...
FUYUMI-SAMA.
OH! YES?
THAT'S ...
...THE THING I SAW ...
WE'VE PREPARED A ROOM FOR YOU OVER HERE.
PLEASE TAKE A FEW MOMENTS AND RELAX.

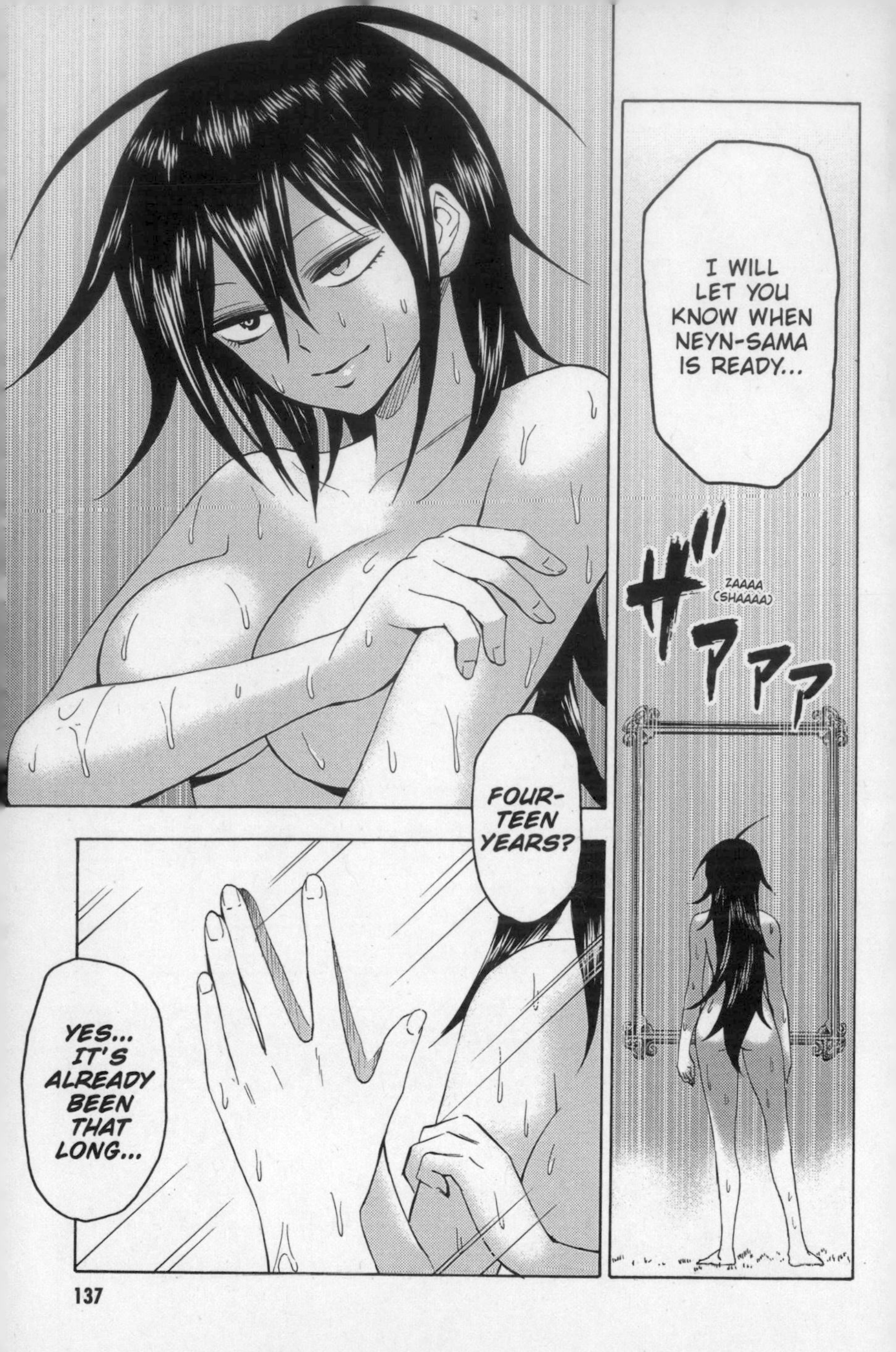
I WILL LET YOU KNOW WHEN NEYN-SAMA IS READY...
ZAAAA (SHAAAA)
FOUR-TEEN YEARS?
YES... IT'S ALREADY BEEN THAT LONG...

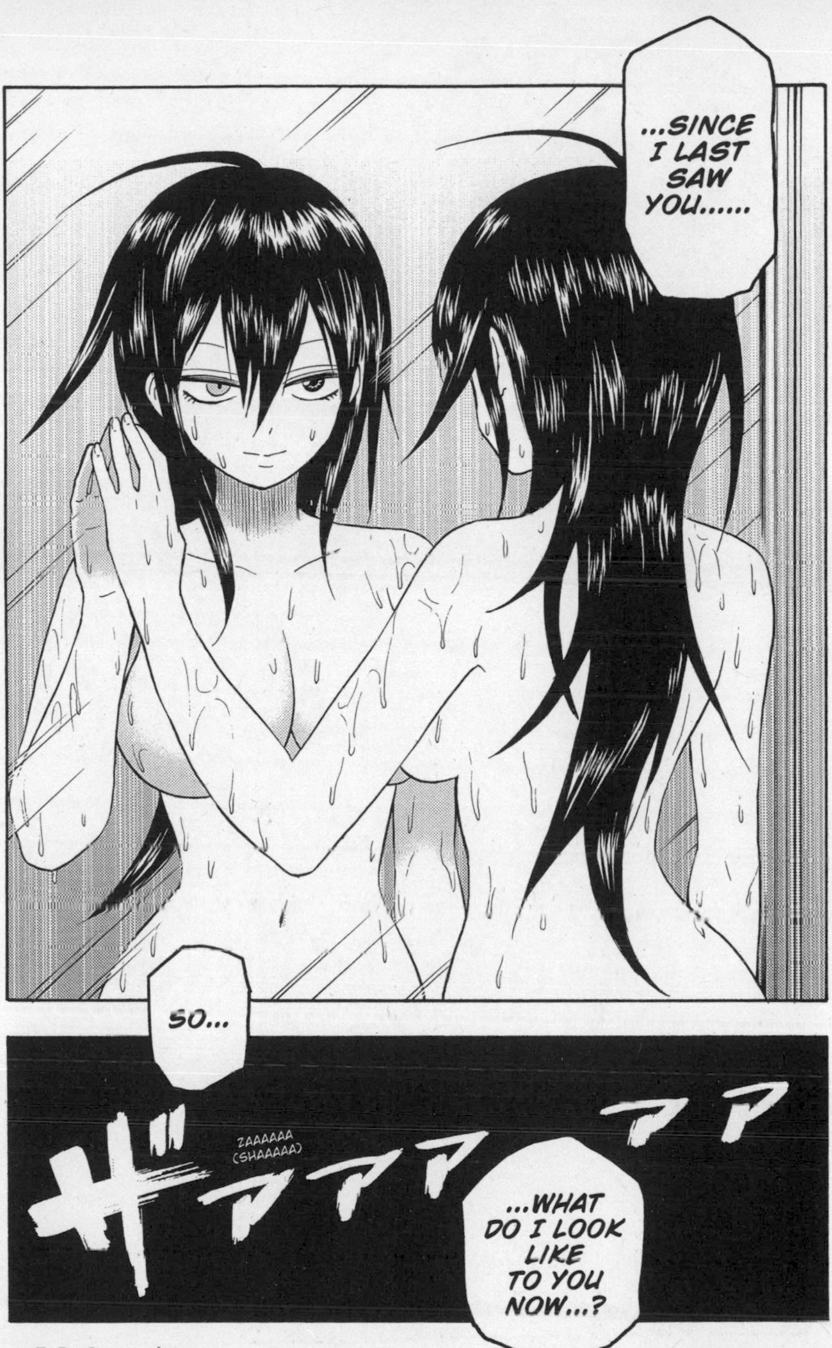
...SINCE I LAST SAW YOU......
SO...
ザアアア アア
ZAAAAAA (SHAAAAA)
...WHAT DO I LOOK LIKE TO YOU NOW...?

♠ To Be Continued ♠

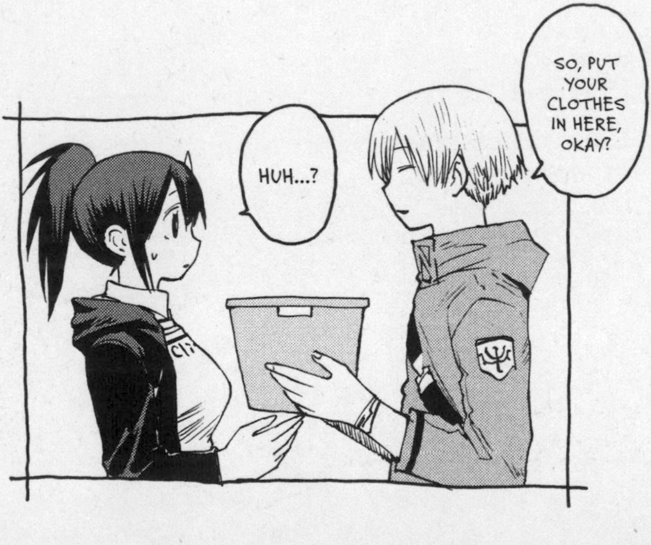
SO, PUT YOUR CLOTHES IN HERE, OKAY?
HUH...?

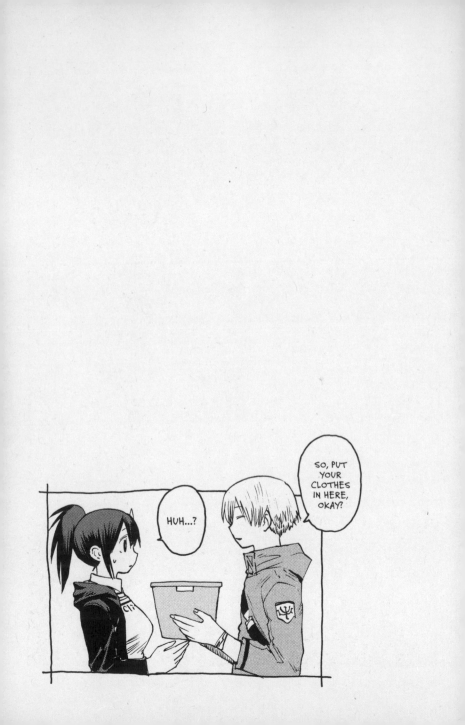

BLOOD LAD

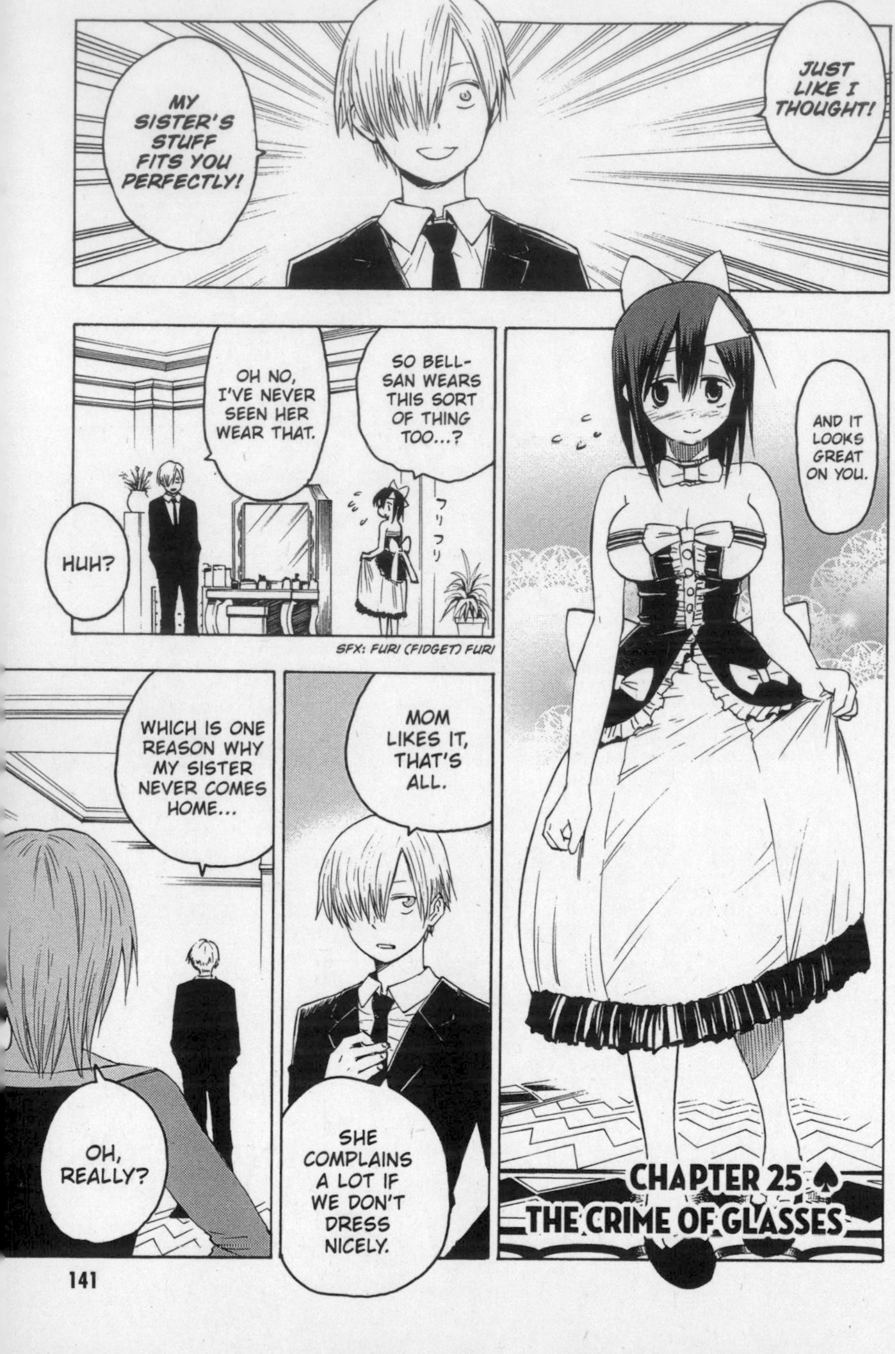
JUST LIKE I THOUGHT!
MY SISTER'S STUFF FITS YOU PERFECTLY!
AND IT LOOKS GREAT ON YOU.
CHAPTER 25
THE CRIME OF GLASSES
SO BELL-SAN WEARS THIS SORT OF THING TOO...?
OH NO, I'VE NEVER SEEN HER WEAR THAT.
フリフリ
HUH?
SFX: FURI (FIDGET) FURI
MOM LIKES IT, THAT'S ALL.
SHE COMPLAINS A LOT IF WE DON'T DRESS NICELY.
WHICH IS ONE REASON WHY MY SISTER NEVER COMES HOME...
OH, REALLY?

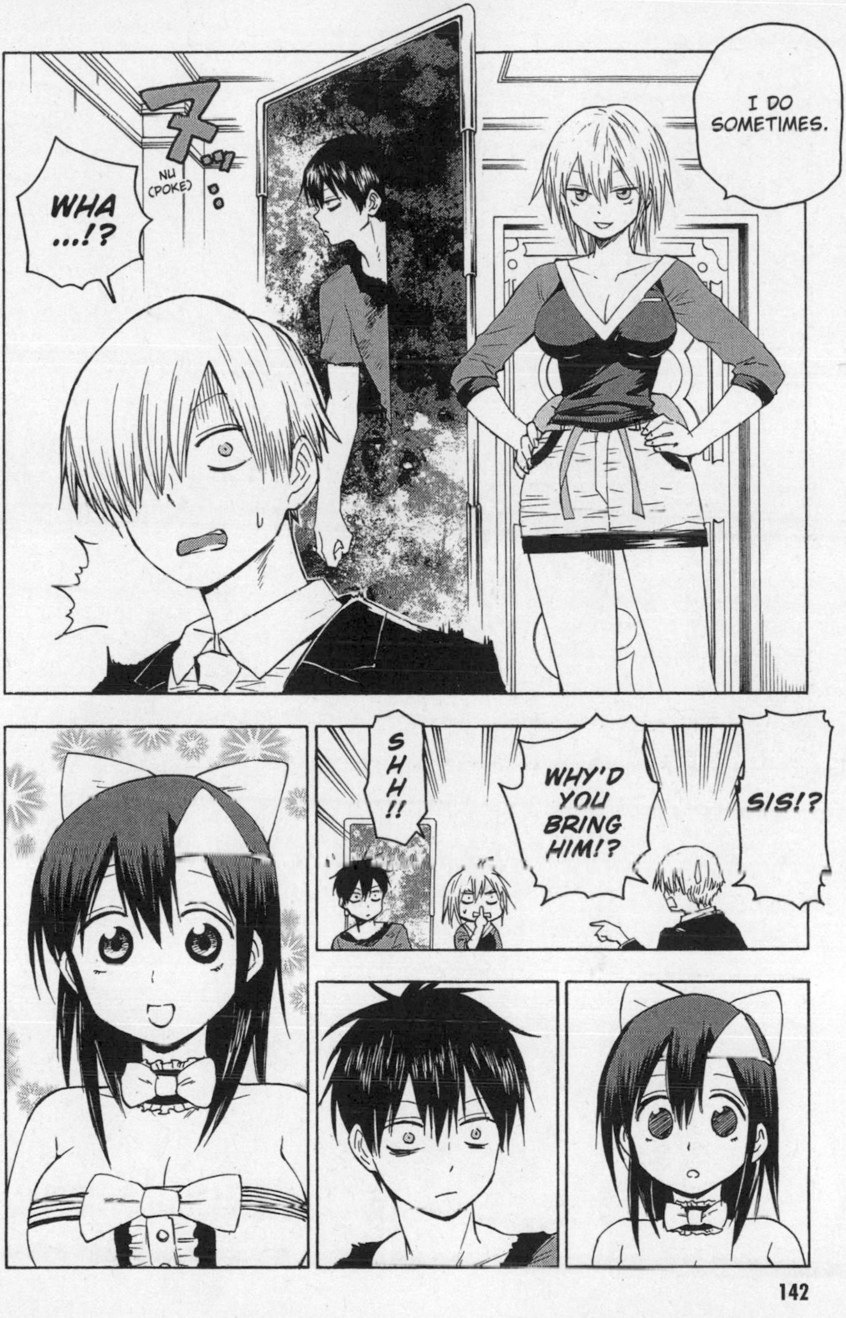
I DO SOMETIMES.
NU (POKE)
WHA ...!?
SIS!?
WHY'D YOU BRING HIM!?
SHH!!

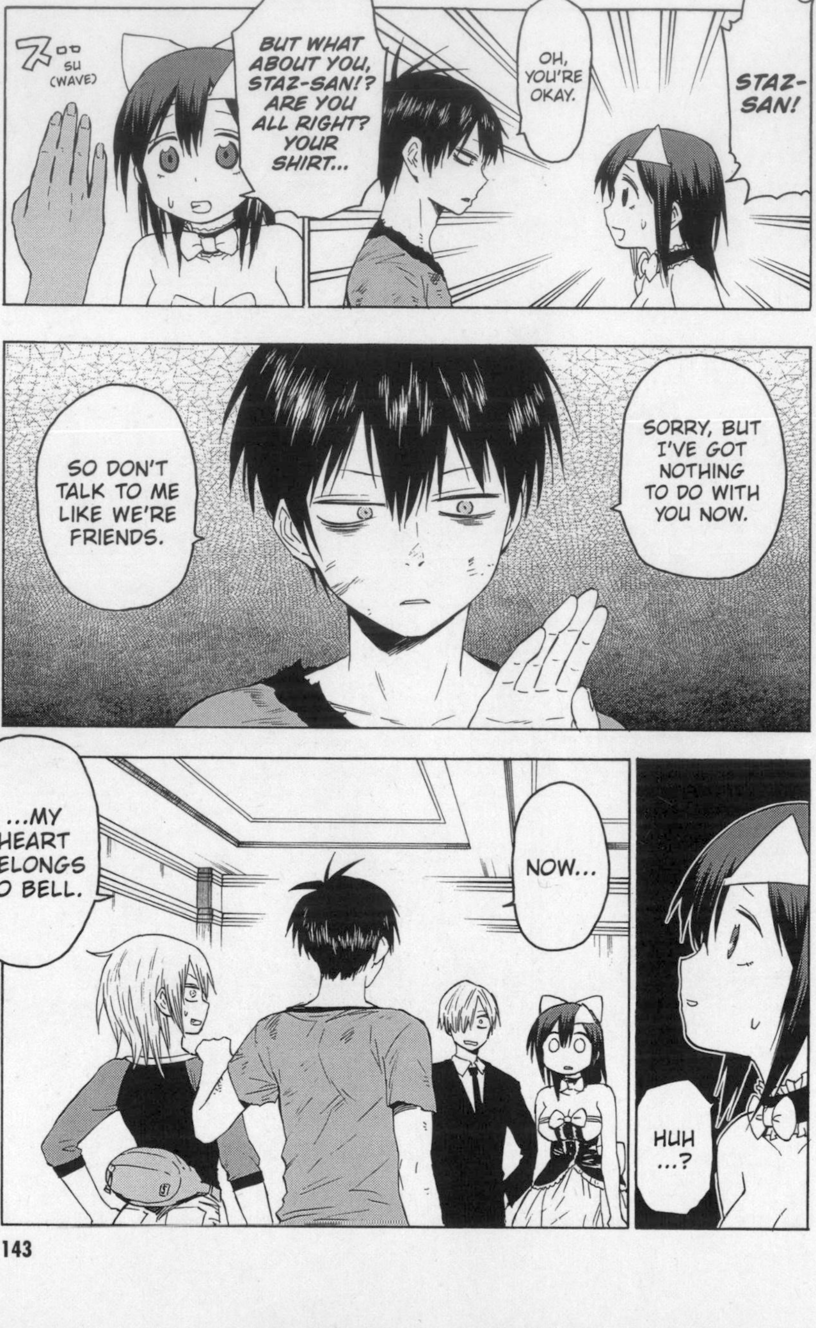
STAZ-SAN!
OH, YOU'RE OKAY.
BUT WHAT ABOUT YOU, STAZ-SAN!? ARE YOU ALL RIGHT? YOUR SHIRT...
SU (WAVE)
SORRY, BUT I'VE GOT NOTHING TO DO WITH YOU NOW.
SO DON'T TALK TO ME LIKE WE'RE FRIENDS.
HUH ...?
NOW...
...MY HEART BELONGS TO BELL.

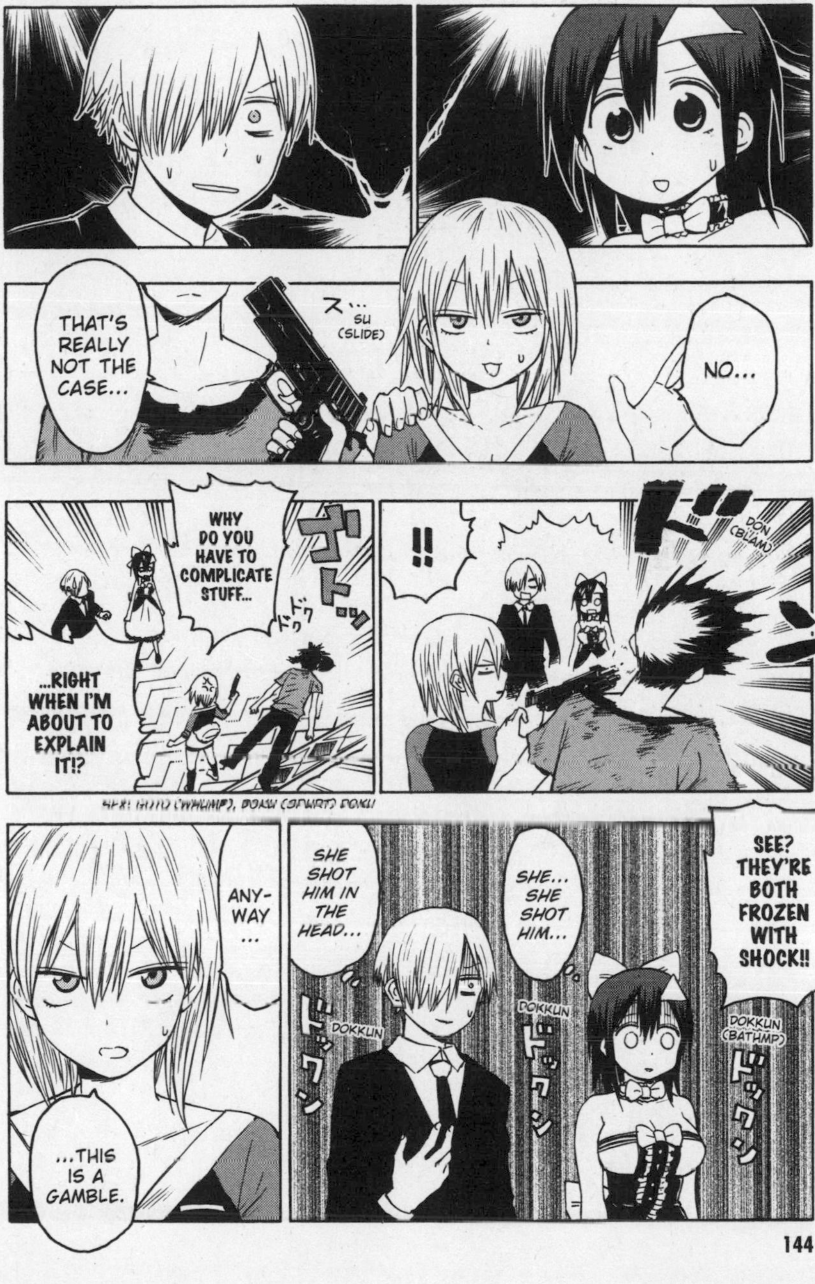
NO...
ス...
SU (SLIDE)
THAT'S REALLY NOT THE CASE...
ド
DON (BLAM)
!!
WHY DO YOU HAVE TO COMPLICATE STUFF...
ゴト
ドクドク
...RIGHT WHEN I'M ABOUT TO EXPLAIN IT!?
SFX: GOTO (WHUMP), DOKU (SQUIRT) DOKU
SEE? THEY'RE BOTH FROZEN WITH SHOCK!!
DOKKUN (BATHMP)
ドックン
SHE... SHE SHOT HIM...
DOKKUN
ドックン
SHE SHOT HIM IN THE HEAD...
DOKKUN
ドックン
ANY-WAY...
...THIS IS A GAMBLE.

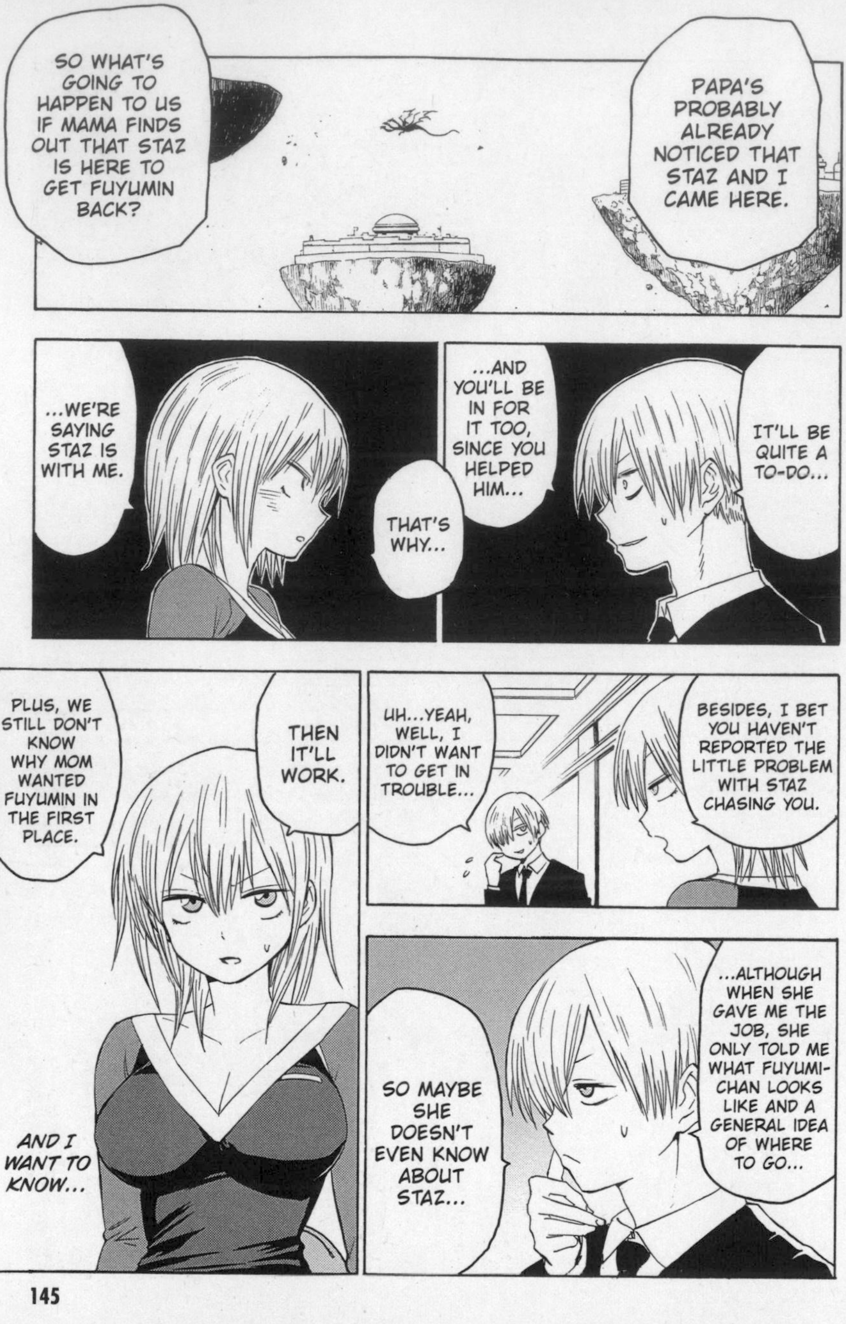
PAPA'S PROBABLY ALREADY NOTICED THAT STAZ AND I CAME HERE.
SO WHAT'S GOING TO HAPPEN TO US IF MAMA FINDS OUT THAT STAZ IS HERE TO GET FUYUMIN BACK?
IT'LL BE QUITE A TO-DO...
...AND YOU'LL BE IN FOR IT TOO, SINCE YOU HELPED HIM...
THAT'S WHY...
...WE'RE SAYING STAZ IS WITH ME.
BESIDES, I BET YOU HAVEN'T REPORTED THE LITTLE PROBLEM WITH STAZ CHASING YOU.
UH...YEAH, WELL, I DIDN'T WANT TO GET IN TROUBLE...
...ALTHOUGH WHEN SHE GAVE ME THE JOB, SHE ONLY TOLD ME WHAT FUYUMI-CHAN LOOKS LIKE AND A GENERAL IDEA OF WHERE TO GO...
SO MAYBE SHE DOESN'T EVEN KNOW ABOUT STAZ...
THEN IT'LL WORK.
PLUS, WE STILL DON'T KNOW WHY MOM WANTED FUYUMIN IN THE FIRST PLACE.
AND I WANT TO KNOW...

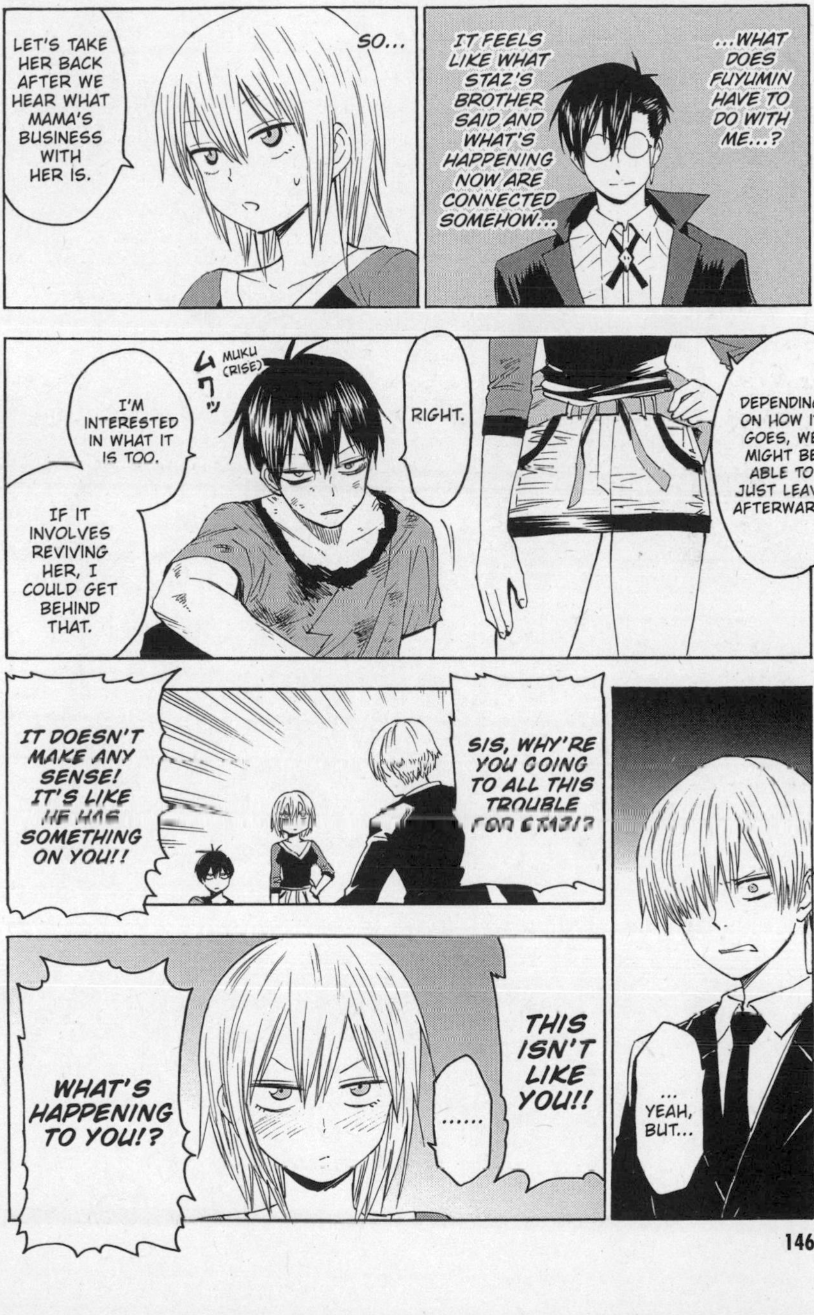
...WHAT DOES FUYUMIN HAVE TO DO WITH ME...?
IT FEELS LIKE WHAT STAZ'S BROTHER SAID AND WHAT'S HAPPENING NOW ARE CONNECTED SOMEHOW...
SO...
LET'S TAKE HER BACK AFTER WE HEAR WHAT MAMA'S BUSINESS WITH HER IS.
DEPENDING ON HOW IT GOES, WE MIGHT BE ABLE TO JUST LEAVE AFTERWARD.
RIGHT.
ムクッ
MUKU (RISE)
I'M INTERESTED IN WHAT IT IS TOO.
IF IT INVOLVES REVIVING HER, I COULD GET BEHIND THAT.
... YEAH, BUT...
SIS, WHY'RE YOU GOING TO ALL THIS TROUBLE FOR STAZ!?
IT DOESN'T MAKE ANY SENSE! IT'S LIKE HE HAS SOMETHING ON YOU!!
THIS ISN'T LIKE YOU!!
......
WHAT'S HAPPENING TO YOU!?

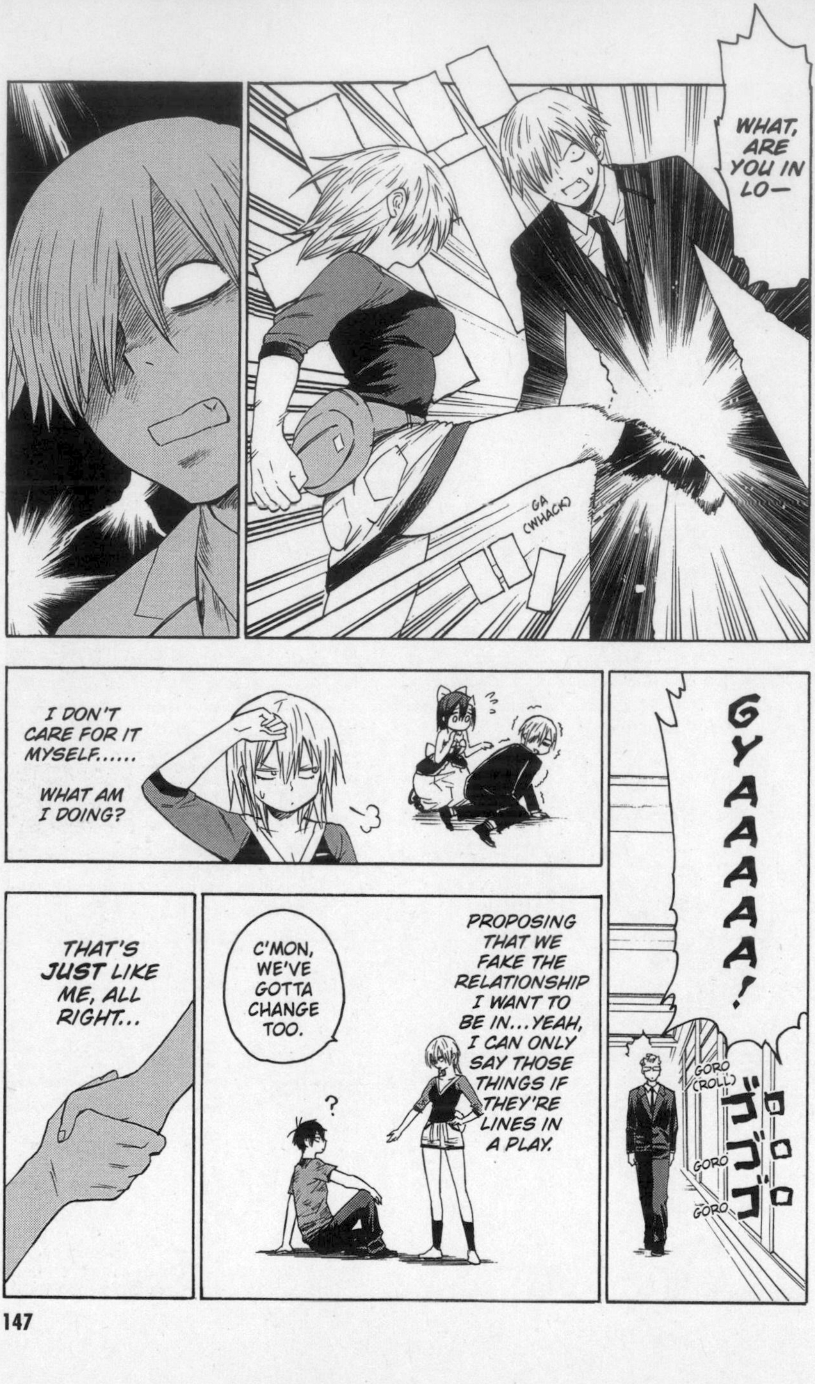
WHAT, ARE YOU IN LO—
GA (WHACK)
GYAAAAAA!
GORO (ROLL)
GORO
GORO
I DON'T CARE FOR IT MYSELF......
WHAT AM I DOING?
PROPOSING THAT WE FAKE THE RELATIONSHIP I WANT TO BE IN…YEAH, I CAN ONLY SAY THOSE THINGS IF THEY'RE LINES IN A PLAY.
C'MON, WE'VE GOTTA CHANGE TOO.
THAT'S JUST LIKE ME, ALL RIGHT…

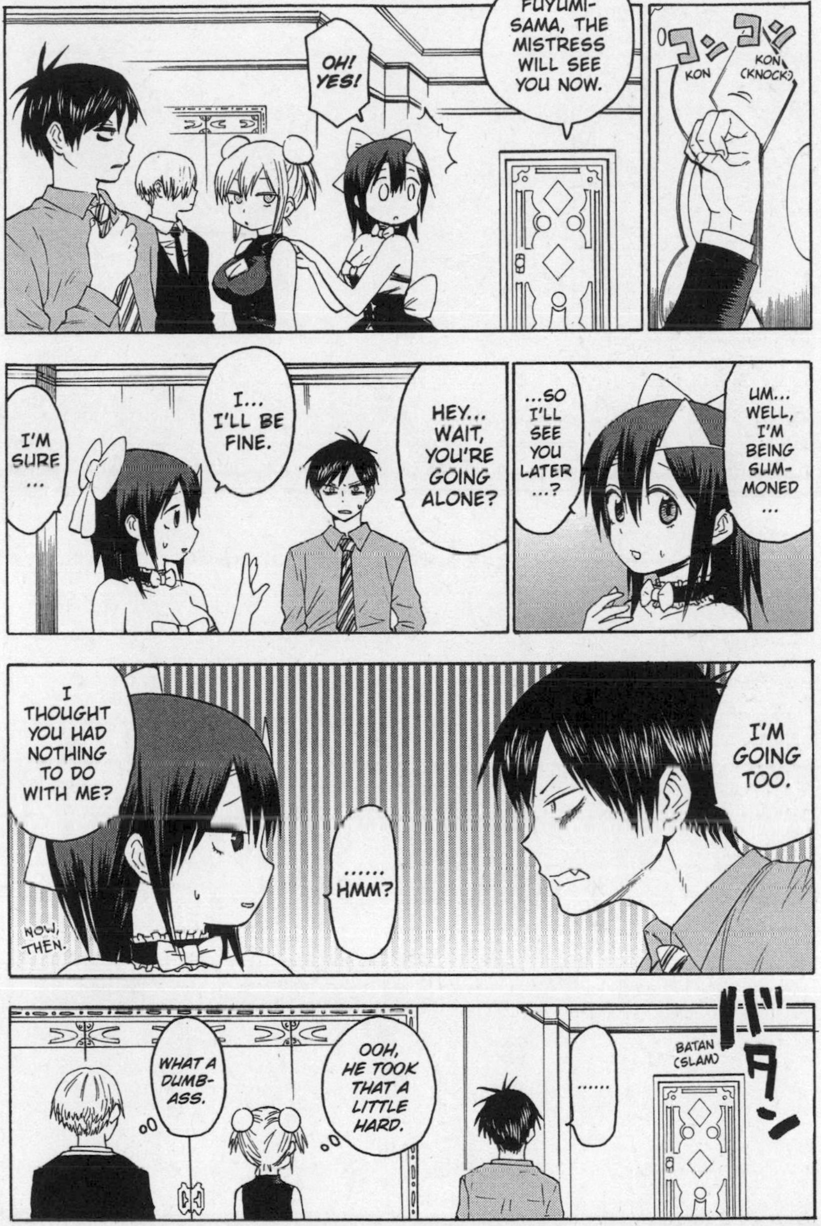
コンコン
KON KON (KNOCK)
FUYUMI-SAMA, THE MISTRESS WILL SEE YOU NOW.
OH! YES!
UM... WELL, I'M BEING SUMMONED...
...SO I'LL SEE YOU LATER...?
HEY... WAIT, YOU'RE GOING ALONE?
I... I'LL BE FINE.
I'M SURE...
I'M GOING TOO.
......HMM?
I THOUGHT YOU HAD NOTHING TO DO WITH ME?
NOW, THEN.
バタン
BATAN (SLAM)
......
OOH, HE TOOK THAT A LITTLE HARD.
WHAT A DUMBASS.

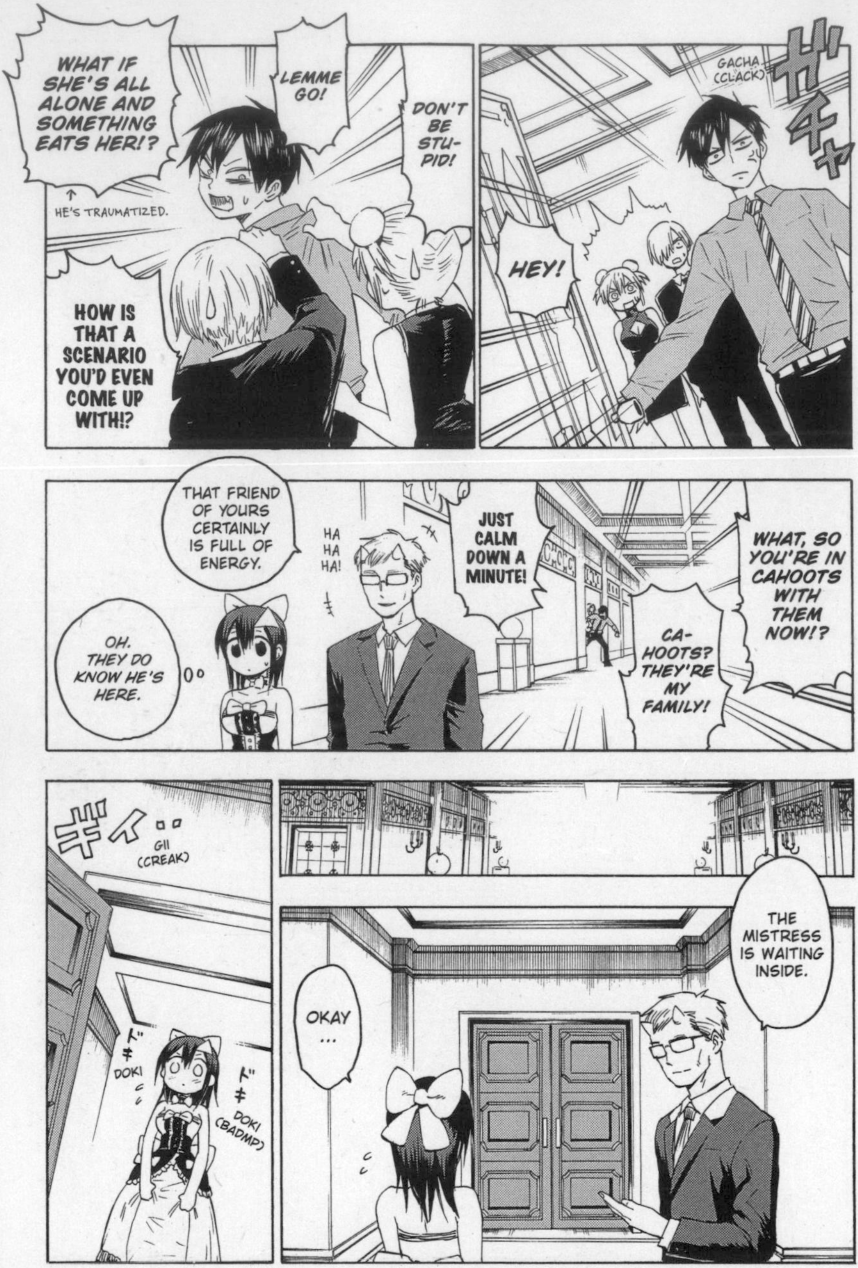
ガチャ
GACHA (CLACK)
HEY!
LEMME GO!
DON'T BE STU-PID!
WHAT IF SHE'S ALL ALONE AND SOMETHING EATS HER!?
↑ HE'S TRAUMATIZED.
HOW IS THAT A SCENARIO YOU'D EVEN COME UP WITH!?
WHAT, SO YOU'RE IN CAHOOTS WITH THEM NOW!?
CA-HOOTS? THEY'RE MY FAMILY!
JUST CALM DOWN A MINUTE!
THAT FRIEND OF YOURS CERTAINLY IS FULL OF ENERGY.
HA HA HA!
OH. THEY DO KNOW HE'S HERE.
THE MISTRESS IS WAITING INSIDE.
OKAY ...
ギィ
GII (CREAK)
ドキ
DOKI
ドキ
DOKI (BADMP)

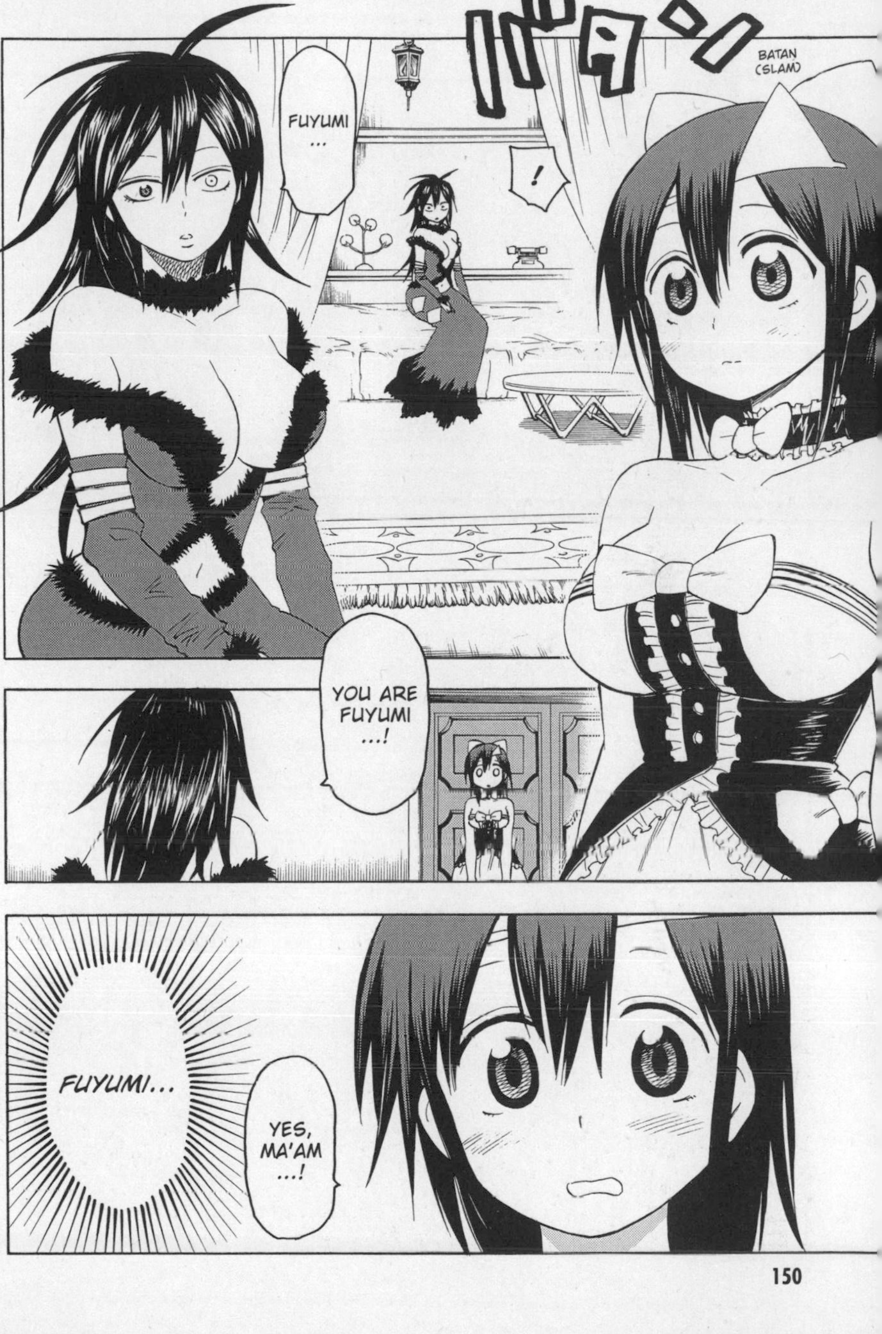
BATAN
(SLAM)
!
FUYUMI ...
YOU ARE FUYUMI ...!
FUYUMI...
YES, MA'AM ...!

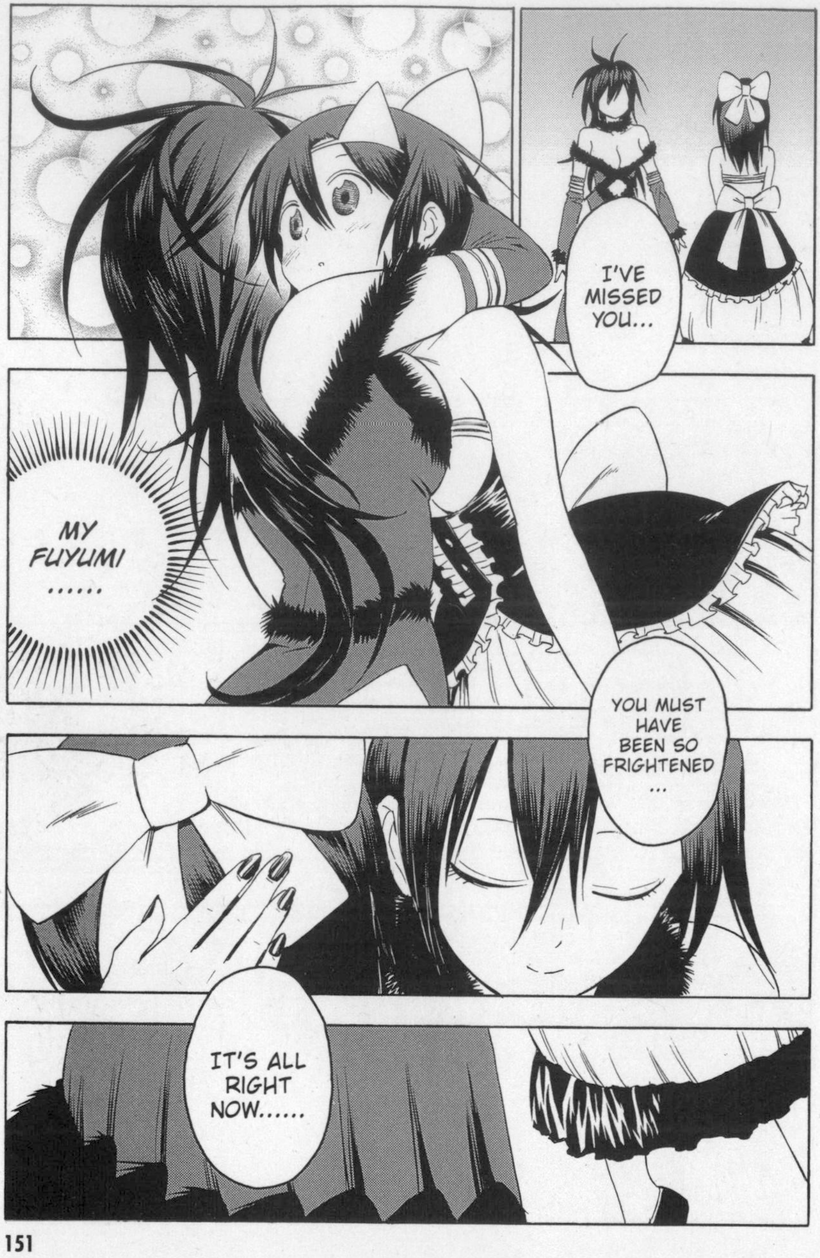
I'VE MISSED YOU...
MY FUYUMI ......
YOU MUST HAVE BEEN SO FRIGHTENED ...
IT'S ALL RIGHT NOW......

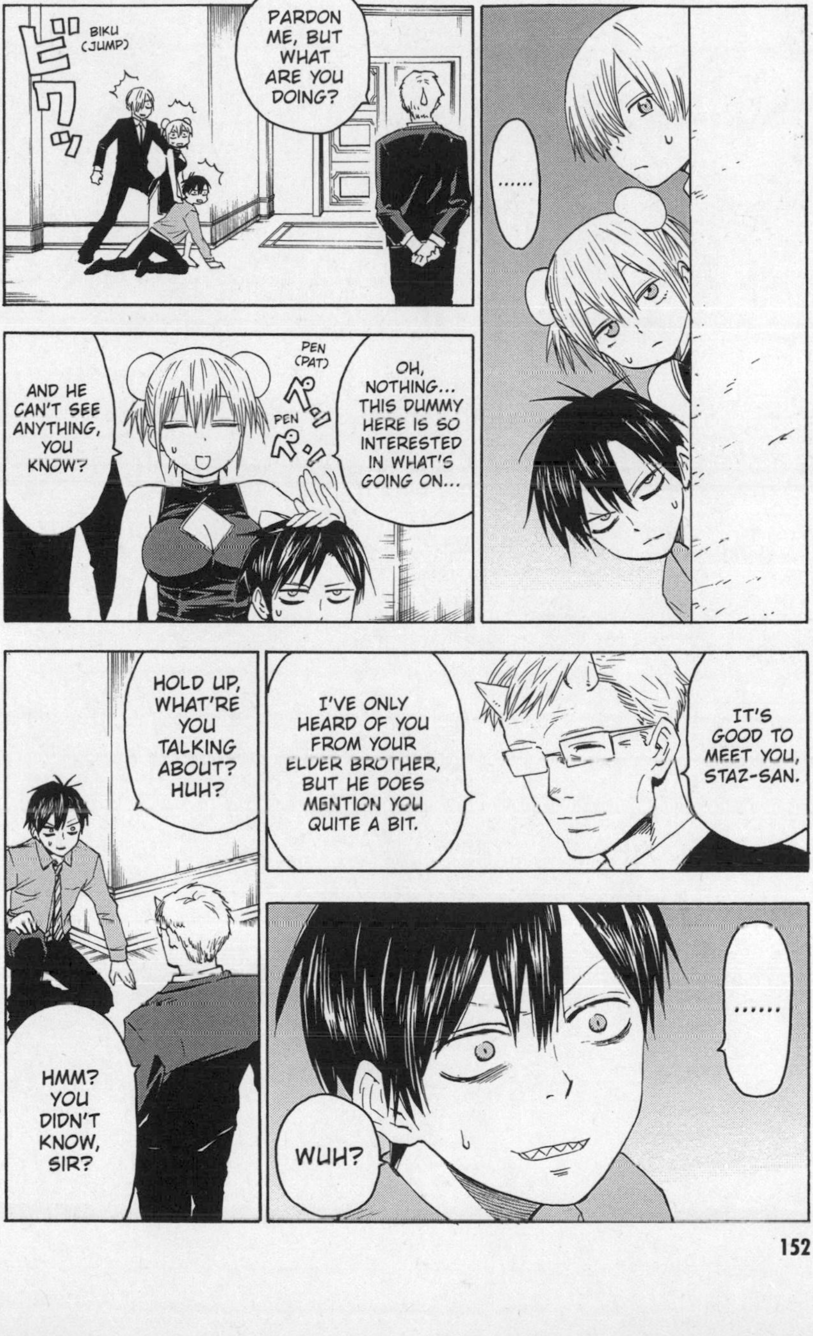
......
PARDON ME, BUT WHAT ARE YOU DOING?
BIKU (JUMP)
OH, NOTHING... THIS DUMMY HERE IS SO INTERESTED IN WHAT'S GOING ON...
PEN (PAT)
PEN
AND HE CAN'T SEE ANYTHING, YOU KNOW?
IT'S GOOD TO MEET YOU, STAZ-SAN.
I'VE ONLY HEARD OF YOU FROM YOUR ELDER BROTHER, BUT HE DOES MENTION YOU QUITE A BIT.
......
WUH?
HOLD UP, WHAT'RE YOU TALKING ABOUT? HUH?
HMM? YOU DIDN'T KNOW, SIR?

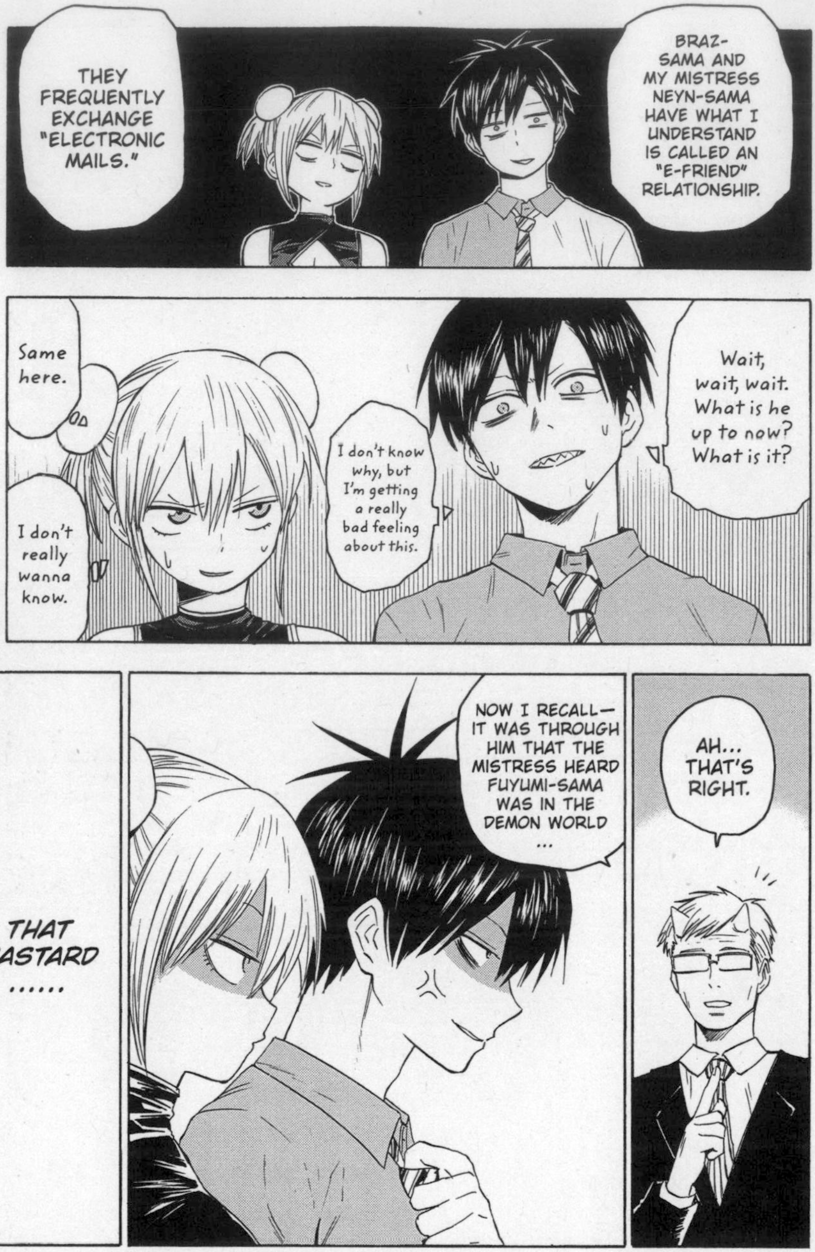
BRAZ-SAMA AND MY MISTRESS NEYN-SAMA HAVE WHAT I UNDERSTAND IS CALLED AN "E-FRIEND" RELATIONSHIP.
THEY FREQUENTLY EXCHANGE "ELECTRONIC MAILS."
Wait, wait, wait. What is he up to now? What is it?
I don't know why, but I'm getting a really bad feeling about this.
Same here.
I don't really wanna know.
AH... THAT'S RIGHT.
NOW I RECALL—IT WAS THROUGH HIM THAT THE MISTRESS HEARD FUYUMI-SAMA WAS IN THE DEMON WORLD ...
THAT BASTARD ......

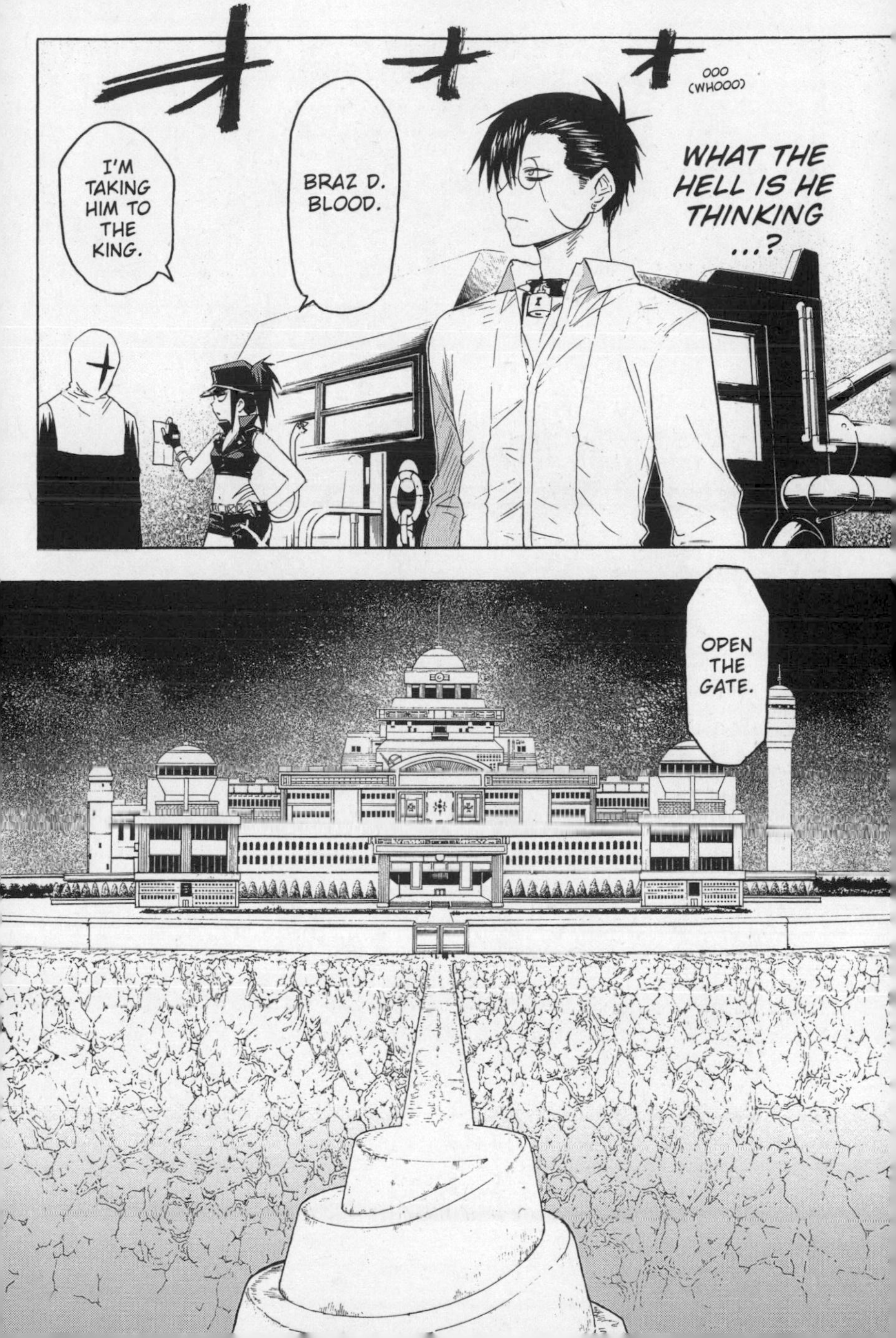

オオオ
OOO
(WHOOO)
WHAT THE HELL IS HE THINKING ...?
BRAZ D. BLOOD.
I'M TAKING HIM TO THE KING.
OPEN THE GATE.

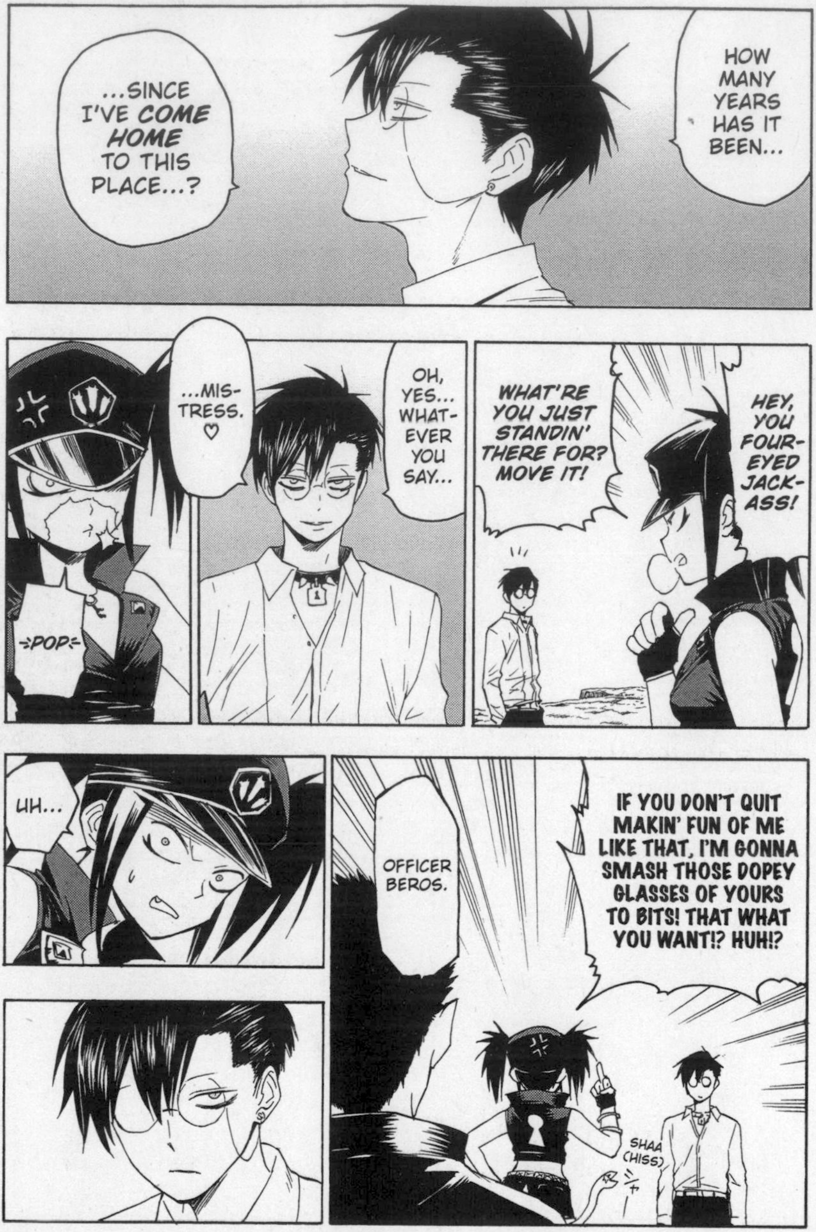
HOW MANY YEARS HAS IT BEEN...
...SINCE I'VE *COME HOME* TO THIS PLACE...?
HEY, YOU FOUR-EYED JACK-ASS!
WHAT'RE YOU JUST STANDIN' THERE FOR? MOVE IT!
OH, YES... WHAT-EVER YOU SAY...
...MIS-TRESS. ♡
POP
IF YOU DON'T QUIT MAKIN' FUN OF ME LIKE THAT, I'M GONNA SMASH THOSE DOPEY GLASSES OF YOURS TO BITS! THAT WHAT YOU WANT!? HUH!?
OFFICER BEROS.
SHAA (HISS)
UH...

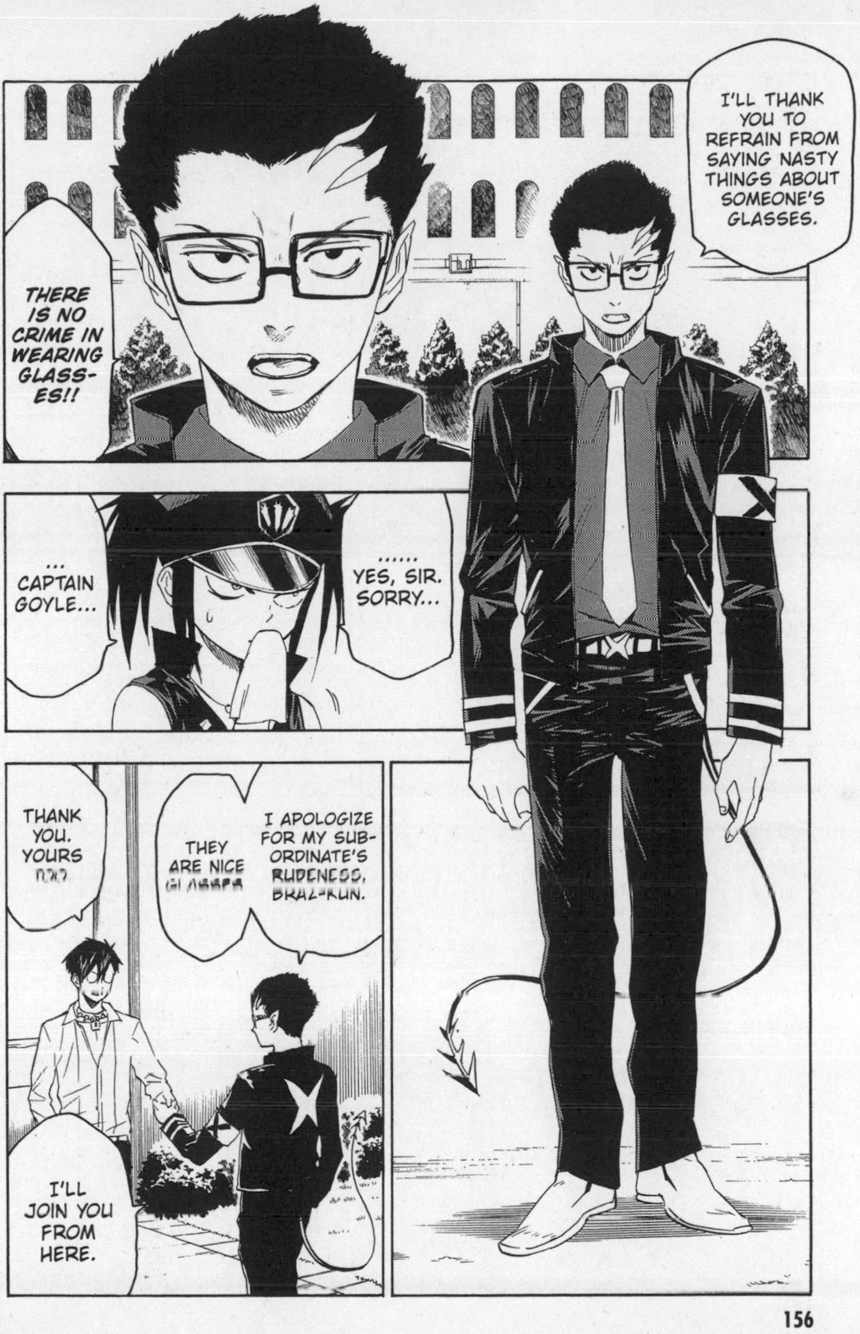

I'LL THANK YOU TO REFRAIN FROM SAYING NASTY THINGS ABOUT SOMEONE'S GLASSES.
THERE IS NO CRIME IN WEARING GLASS-ES!!
...... YES, SIR. SORRY...
... CAPTAIN GOYLE...
I APOLOGIZE FOR MY SUB-ORDINATE'S RUDENESS, BRAZ-KUN.
THEY ARE NICE GLASSES
THANK YOU. YOURS TOO.
I'LL JOIN YOU FROM HERE.

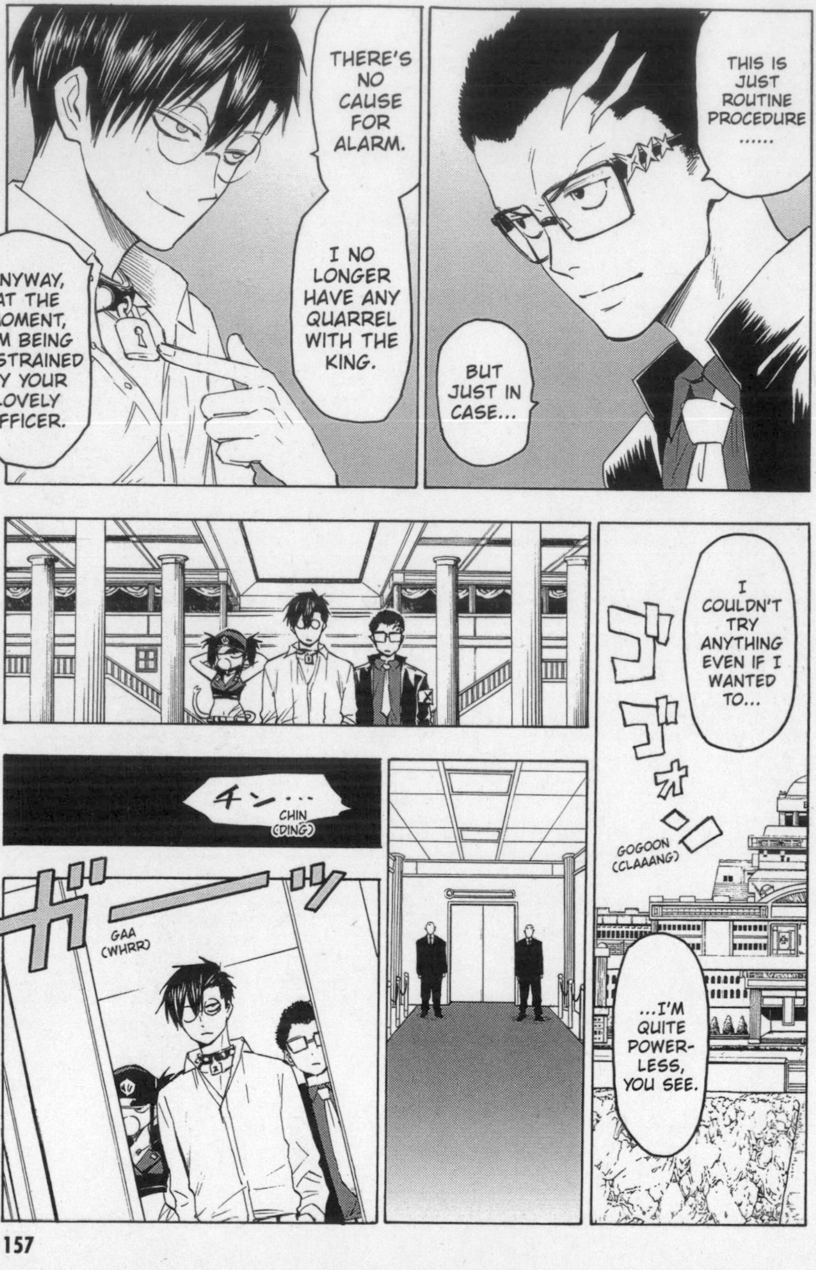
THIS IS JUST ROUTINE PROCEDURE ......
BUT JUST IN CASE...
THERE'S NO CAUSE FOR ALARM.
I NO LONGER HAVE ANY QUARREL WITH THE KING.
ANYWAY, AT THE MOMENT, I'M BEING RESTRAINED BY YOUR LOVELY OFFICER.
I COULDN'T TRY ANYTHING EVEN IF I WANTED TO...
ゴゴォン
GOGOON (CLAAANG)
...I'M QUITE POWER-LESS, YOU SEE.
チン...
CHIN (DING)
ガーッ
GAA (WHRR)

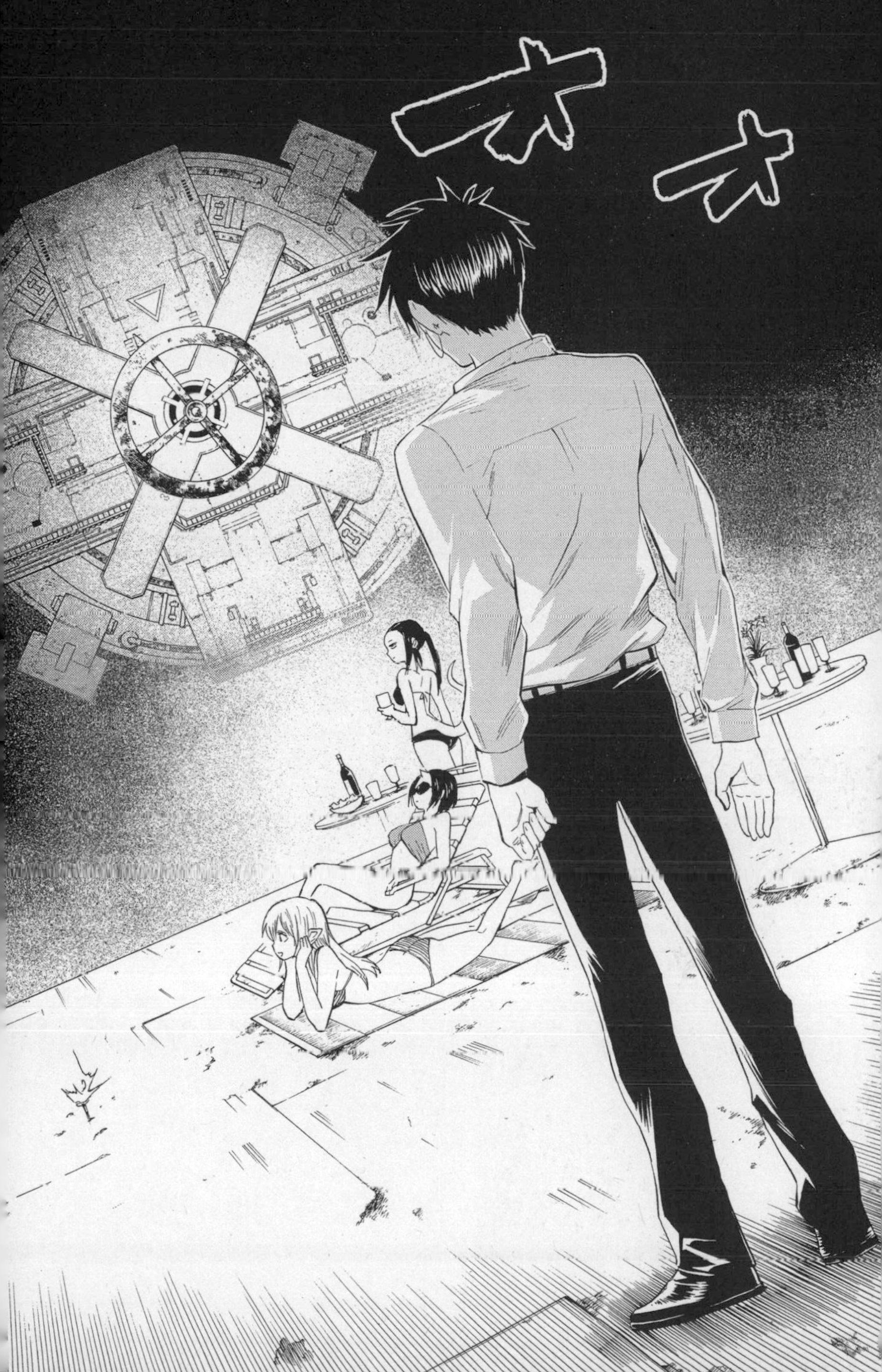
オオ

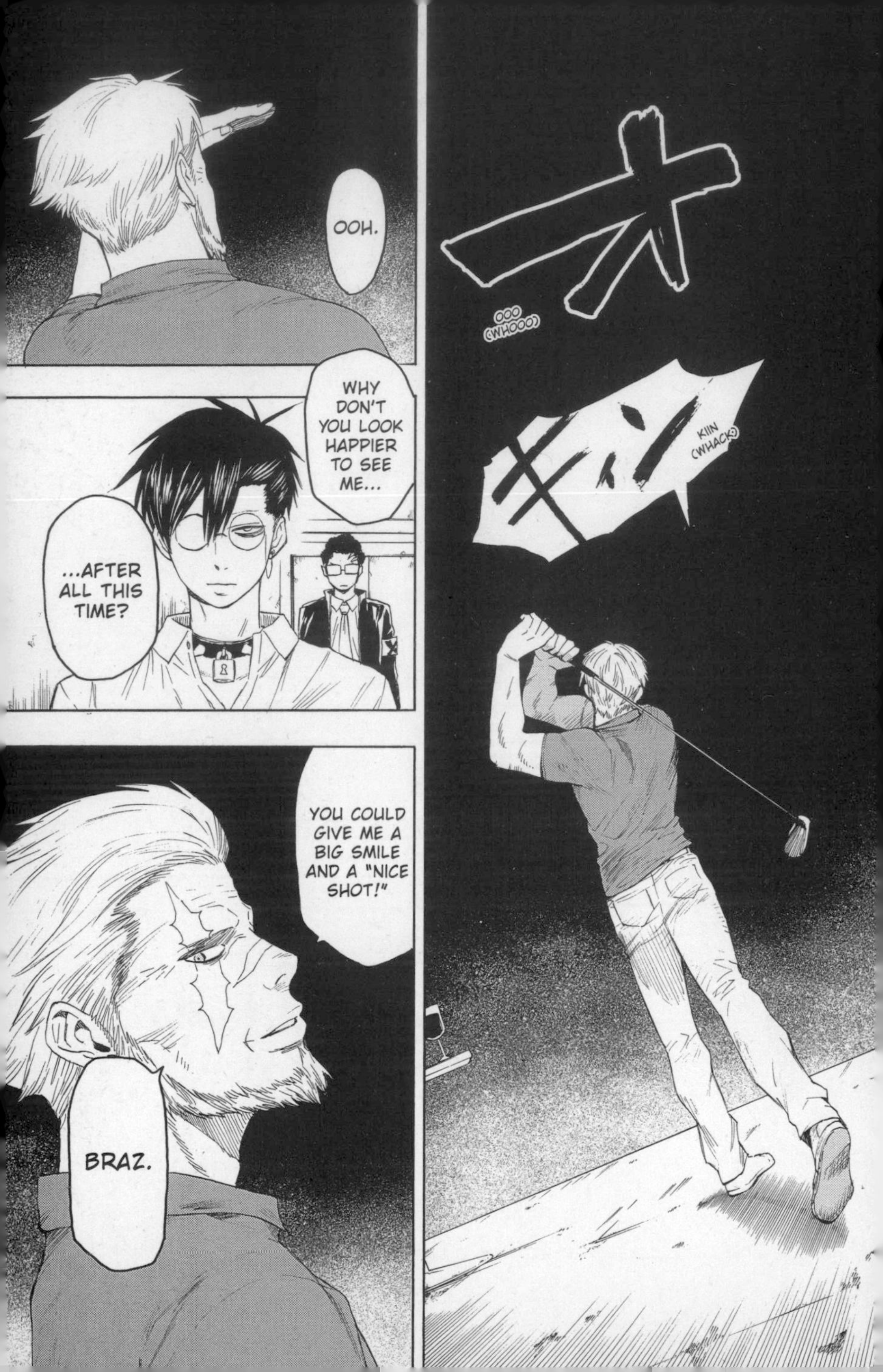
OOO (WHOOO)
KIIN (WHACK)
OOH.
WHY DON'T YOU LOOK HAPPIER TO SEE ME...
...AFTER ALL THIS TIME?
YOU COULD GIVE ME A BIG SMILE AND A "NICE SHOT!"
BRAZ.

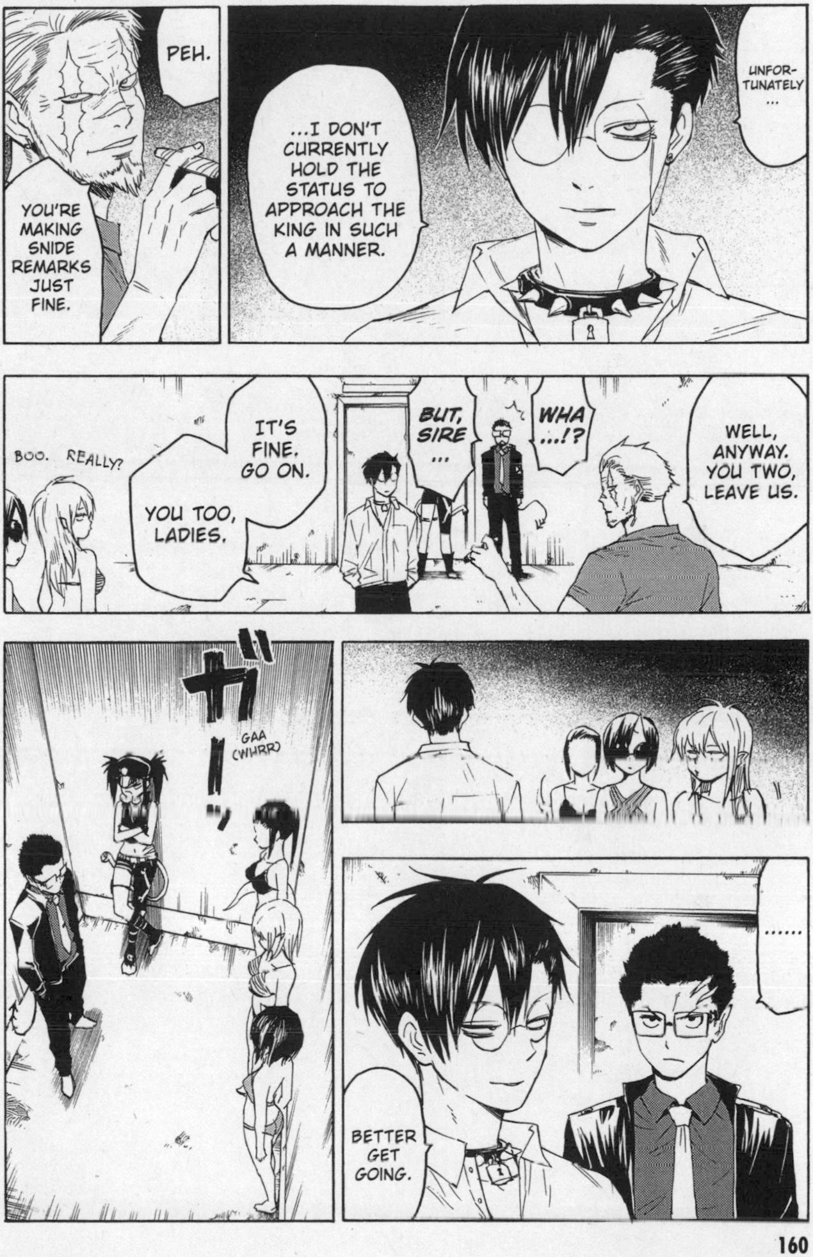
UNFOR-TUNATELY...
...I DON'T CURRENTLY HOLD THE STATUS TO APPROACH THE KING IN SUCH A MANNER.
PEH.
YOU'RE MAKING SNIDE REMARKS JUST FINE.
WELL, ANYWAY. YOU TWO, LEAVE US.
WHA...!?
BUT, SIRE...
IT'S FINE. GO ON.
YOU TOO, LADIES.
REALLY?
BOO.
......
BETTER GET GOING.
ガ!!
GAA (WHRR)

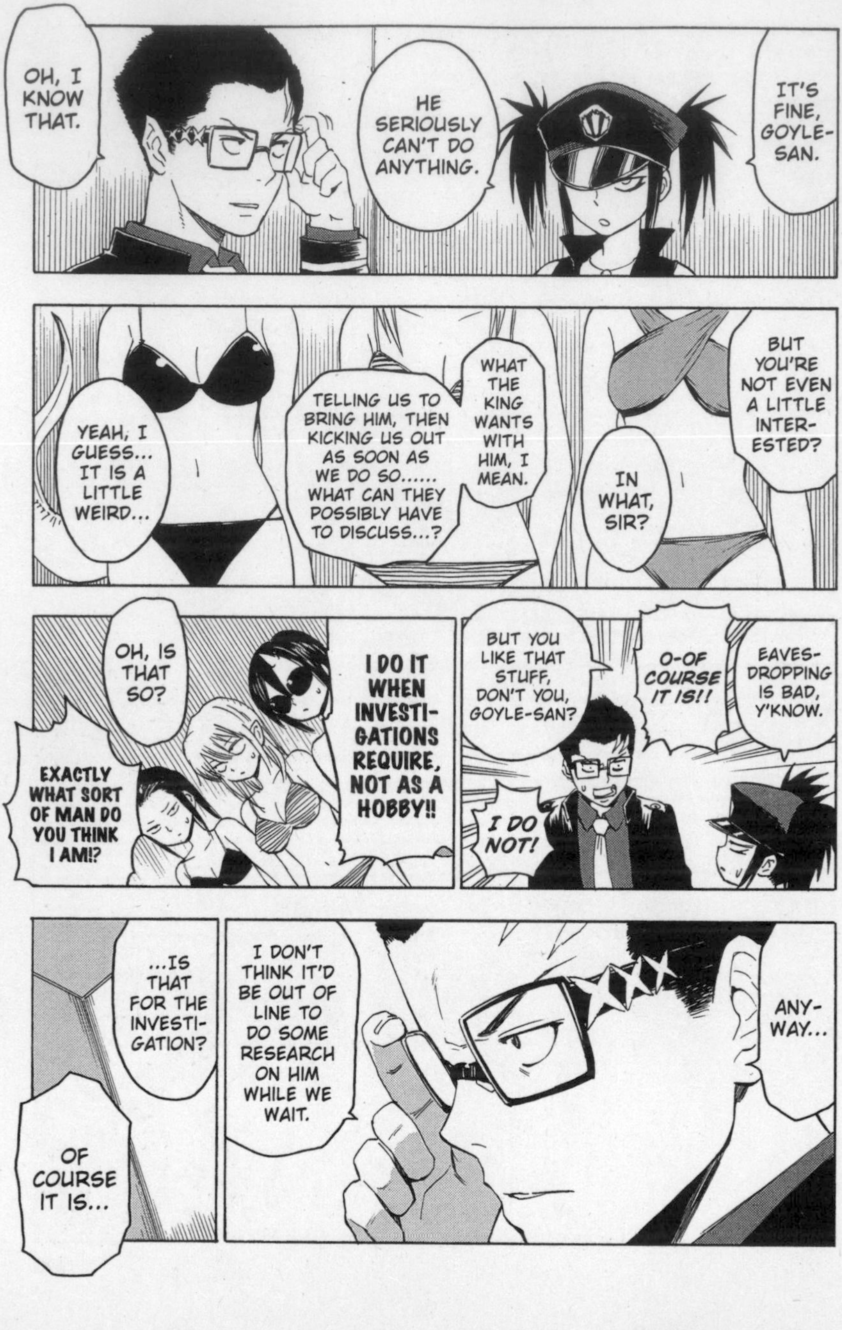
IT'S FINE, GOYLE-SAN.
HE SERIOUSLY CAN'T DO ANYTHING.
OH, I KNOW THAT.
BUT YOU'RE NOT EVEN A LITTLE INTERESTED?
IN WHAT, SIR?
WHAT THE KING WANTS WITH HIM, I MEAN.
TELLING US TO BRING HIM, THEN KICKING US OUT AS SOON AS WE DO SO...... WHAT CAN THEY POSSIBLY HAVE TO DISCUSS...?
YEAH, I GUESS... IT IS A LITTLE WEIRD...
EAVESDROPPING IS BAD, Y'KNOW.
O-OF COURSE IT IS!!
BUT YOU LIKE THAT STUFF, DON'T YOU, GOYLE-SAN?
I DO NOT!
I DO IT WHEN INVESTIGATIONS REQUIRE, NOT AS A HOBBY!!
OH, IS THAT SO?
EXACTLY WHAT SORT OF MAN DO YOU THINK I AM!?
ANYWAY...
I DON'T THINK IT'D BE OUT OF LINE TO DO SOME RESEARCH ON HIM WHILE WE WAIT.
...IS THAT FOR THE INVESTIGATION?
OF COURSE IT IS...

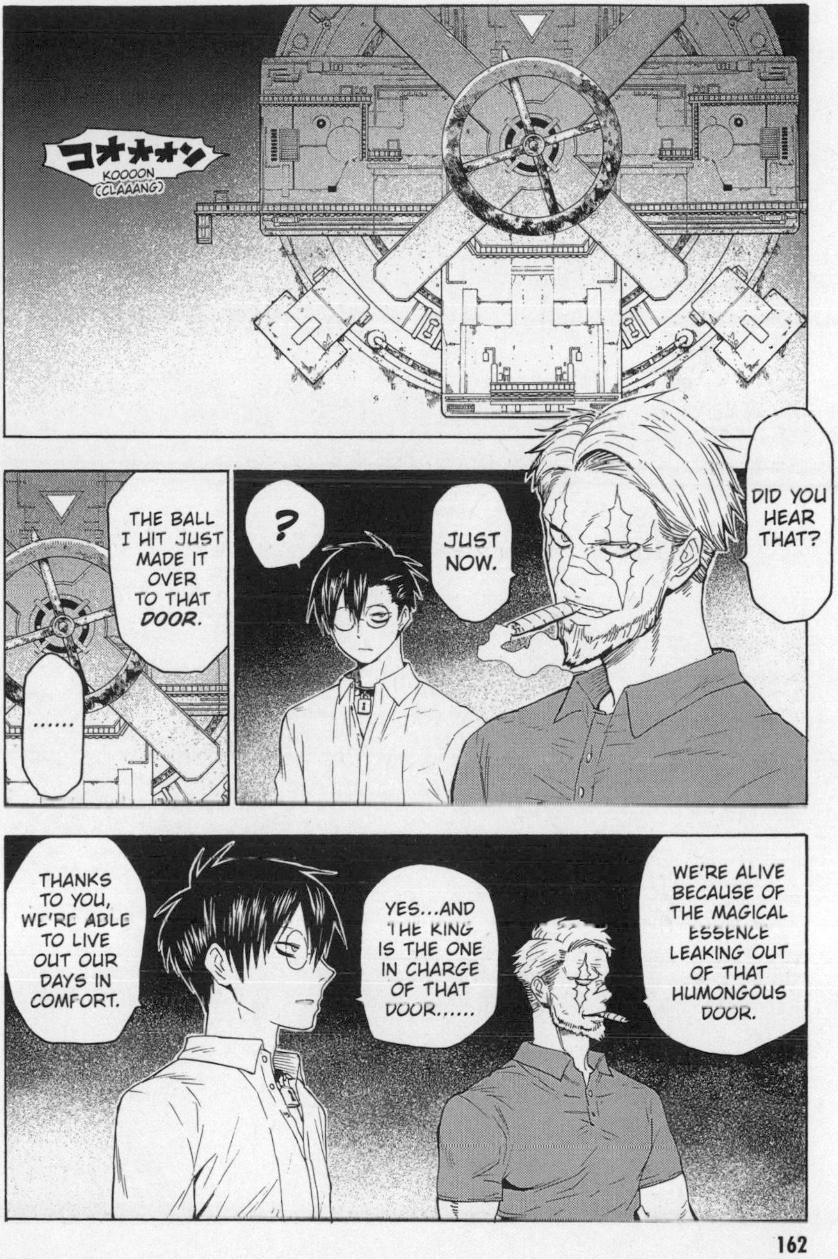
コオォォン
KOOOON
(CLAAANG)
DID YOU HEAR THAT?
JUST NOW.
?
THE BALL I HIT JUST MADE IT OVER TO THAT DOOR.
......
WE'RE ALIVE BECAUSE OF THE MAGICAL ESSENCE LEAKING OUT OF THAT HUMONGOUS DOOR.
YES...AND THE KING IS THE ONE IN CHARGE OF THAT DOOR......
THANKS TO YOU, WE'RE ABLE TO LIVE OUT OUR DAYS IN COMFORT.

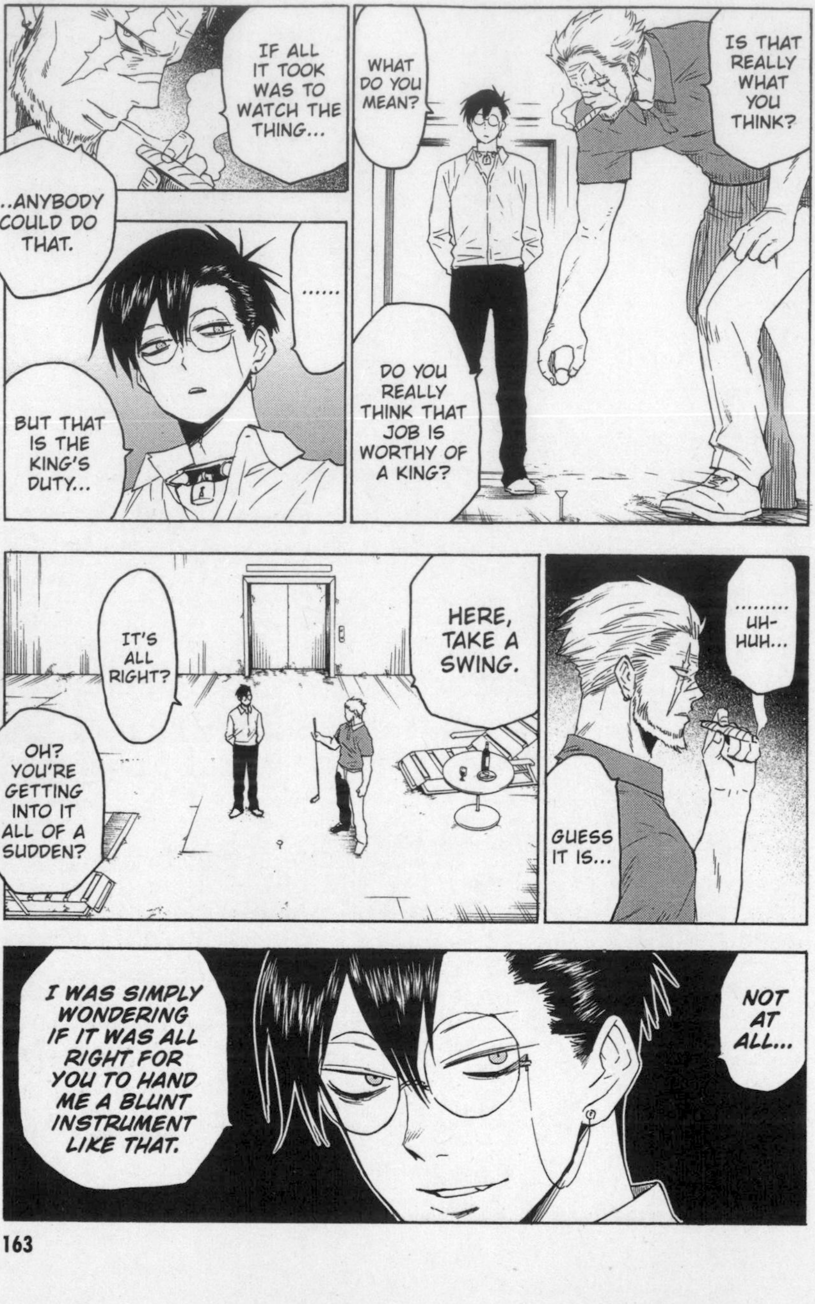
IS THAT REALLY WHAT YOU THINK?
WHAT DO YOU MEAN?
DO YOU REALLY THINK THAT JOB IS WORTHY OF A KING?
IF ALL IT TOOK WAS TO WATCH THE THING...
...ANYBODY COULD DO THAT.
......
BUT THAT IS THE KING'S DUTY...
.... UH-HUH...
GUESS IT IS...
HERE, TAKE A SWING.
IT'S ALL RIGHT?
OH? YOU'RE GETTING INTO IT ALL OF A SUDDEN?
NOT AT ALL...
I WAS SIMPLY WONDERING IF IT WAS ALL RIGHT FOR YOU TO HAND ME A BLUNT INSTRUMENT LIKE THAT.

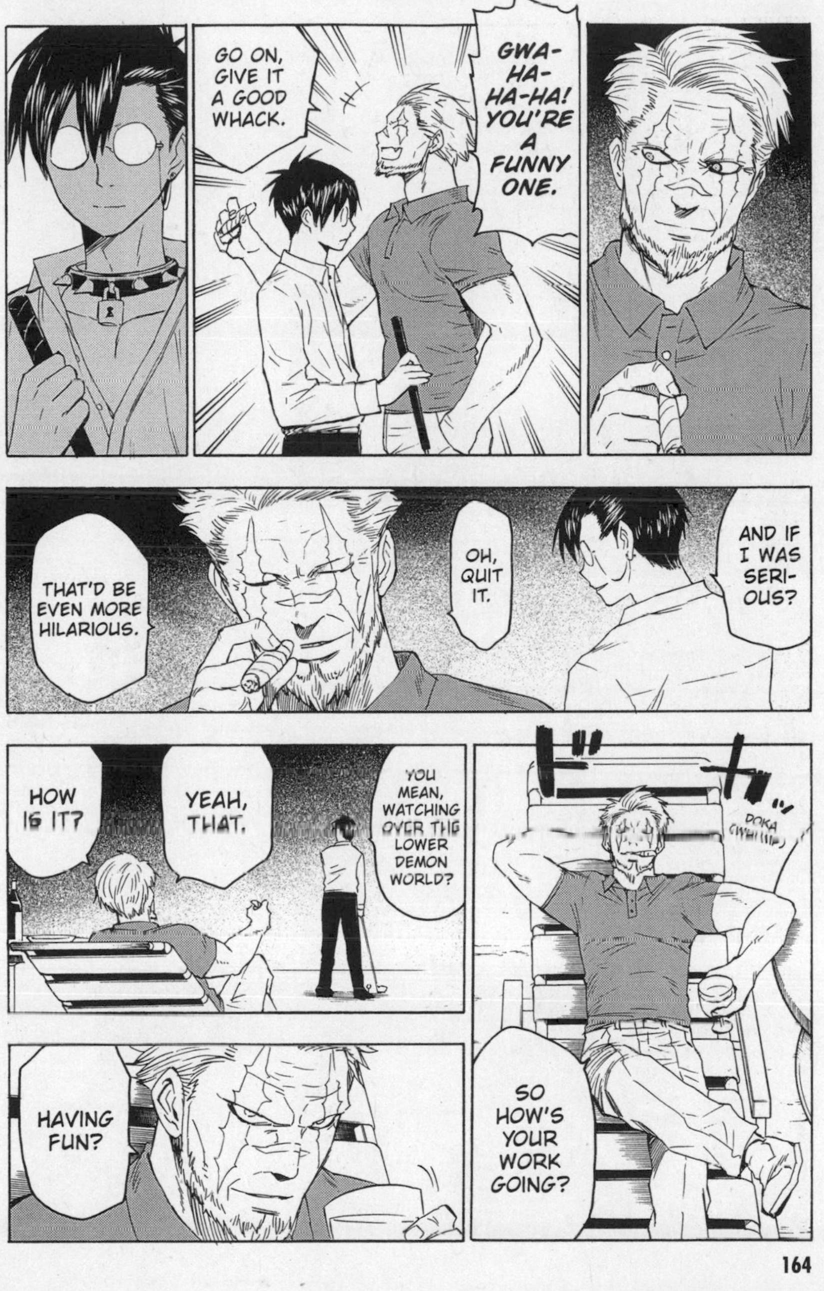
GWA-HA-HA-HA! YOU'RE A FUNNY ONE.
GO ON, GIVE IT A GOOD WHACK.
AND IF I WAS SERIOUS?
OH, QUIT IT.
THAT'D BE EVEN MORE HILARIOUS.
DOKA
SO HOW'S YOUR WORK GOING?
YOU MEAN, WATCHING OVER THE LOWER DEMON WORLD?
YEAH, THAT.
HOW IS IT?
HAVING FUN?

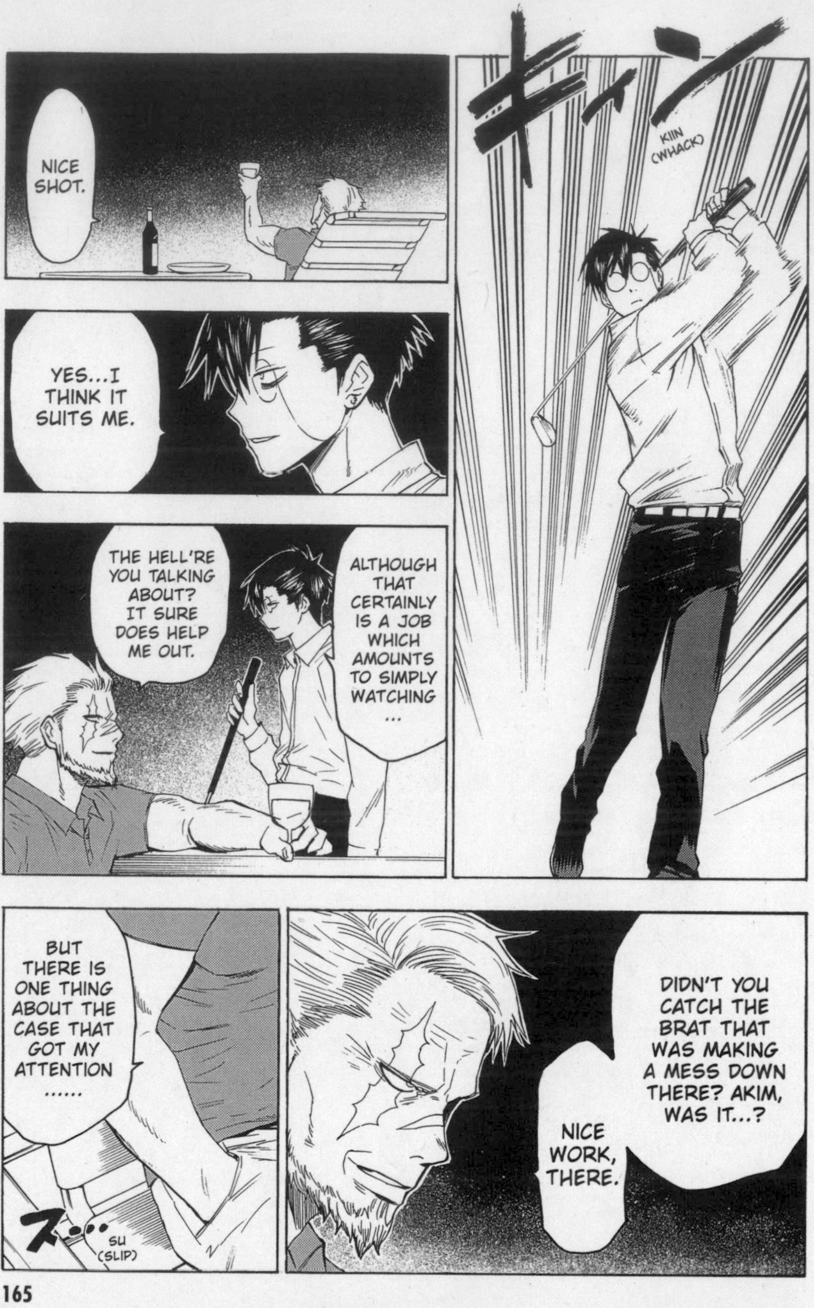
キィン
KIIN (WHACK)
NICE SHOT.
YES...I THINK IT SUITS ME.
ALTHOUGH THAT CERTAINLY IS A JOB WHICH AMOUNTS TO SIMPLY WATCHING ...
THE HELL'RE YOU TALKING ABOUT? IT SURE DOES HELP ME OUT.
DIDN'T YOU CATCH THE BRAT THAT WAS MAKING A MESS DOWN THERE? AKIM, WAS IT...?
NICE WORK, THERE.
BUT THERE IS ONE THING ABOUT THE CASE THAT GOT MY ATTENTION ......
ス...
SU (SLIP)

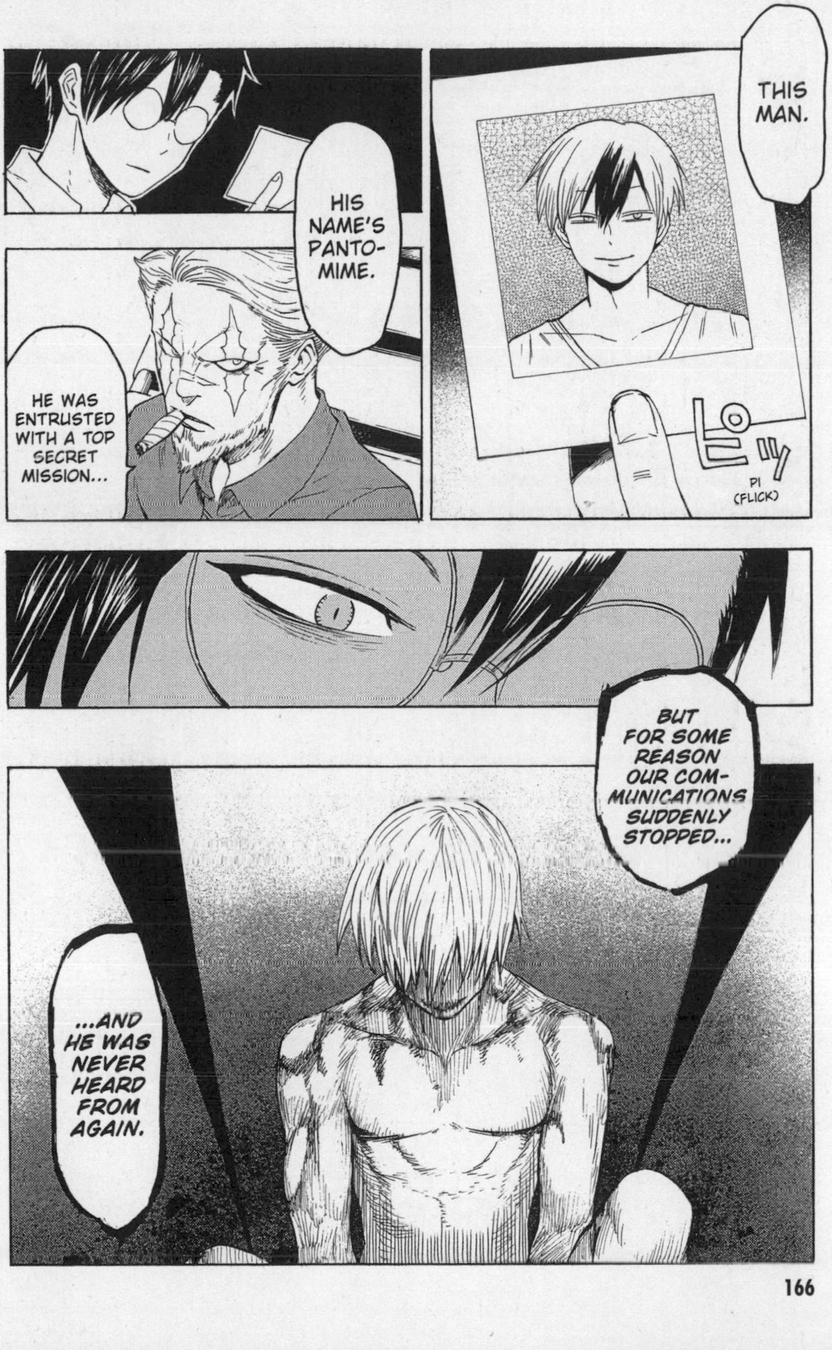
THIS MAN.
ピッ
PI (FLICK)
HIS NAME'S PANTO-MIME.
HE WAS ENTRUSTED WITH A TOP SECRET MISSION...
BUT FOR SOME REASON OUR COM-MUNICATIONS SUDDENLY STOPPED...
...AND HE WAS NEVER HEARD FROM AGAIN.

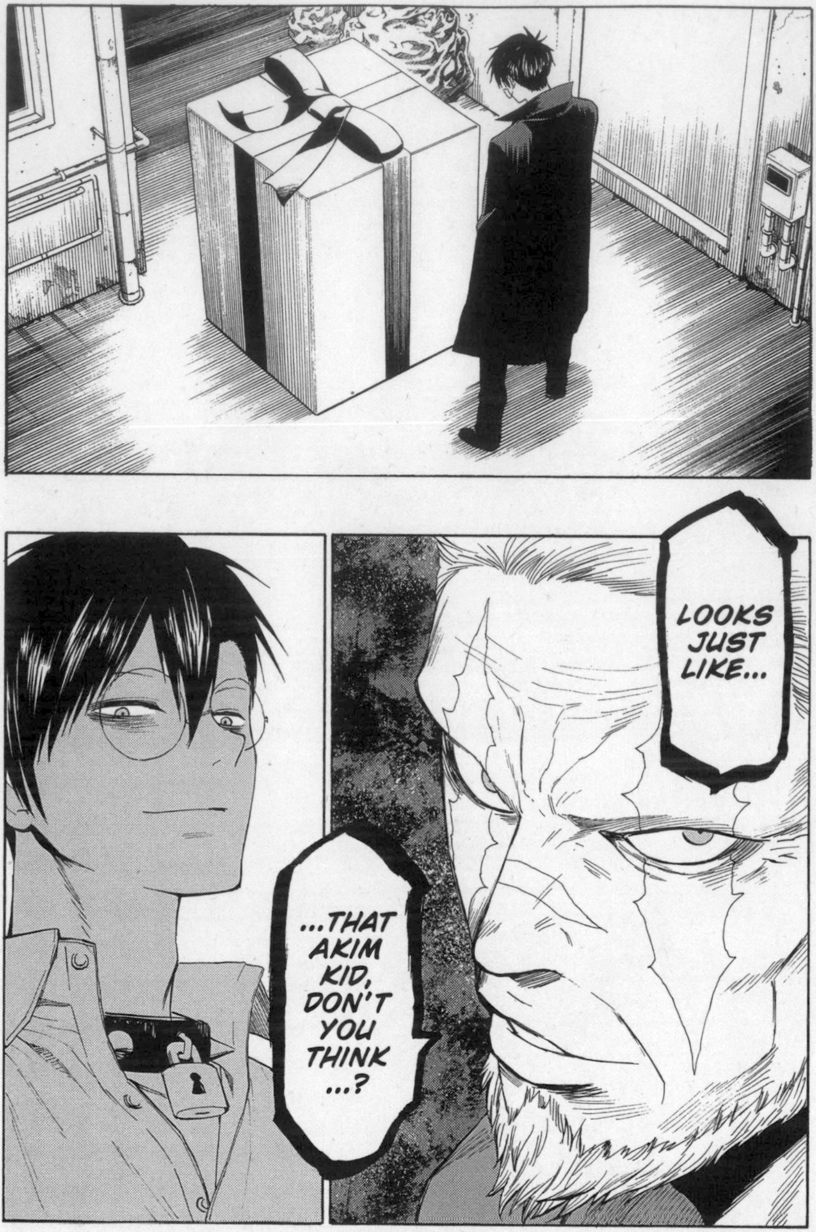
LOOKS JUST LIKE...
...THAT AKIM KID, DON'T YOU THINK ...?

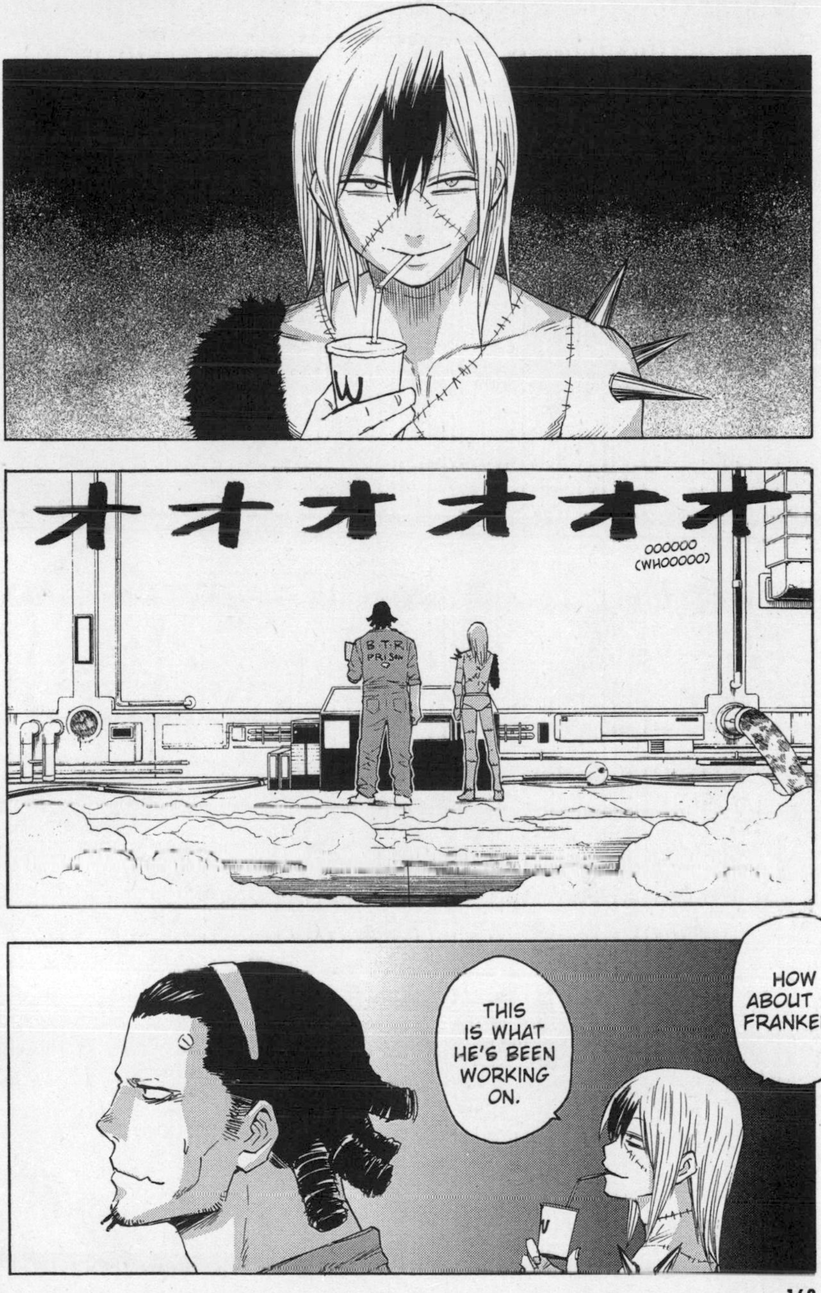
オオオオオオ
OOOOOO (WHOOOOO)
HOW ABOUT IT, FRANKEN?
THIS IS WHAT HE'S BEEN WORKING ON.

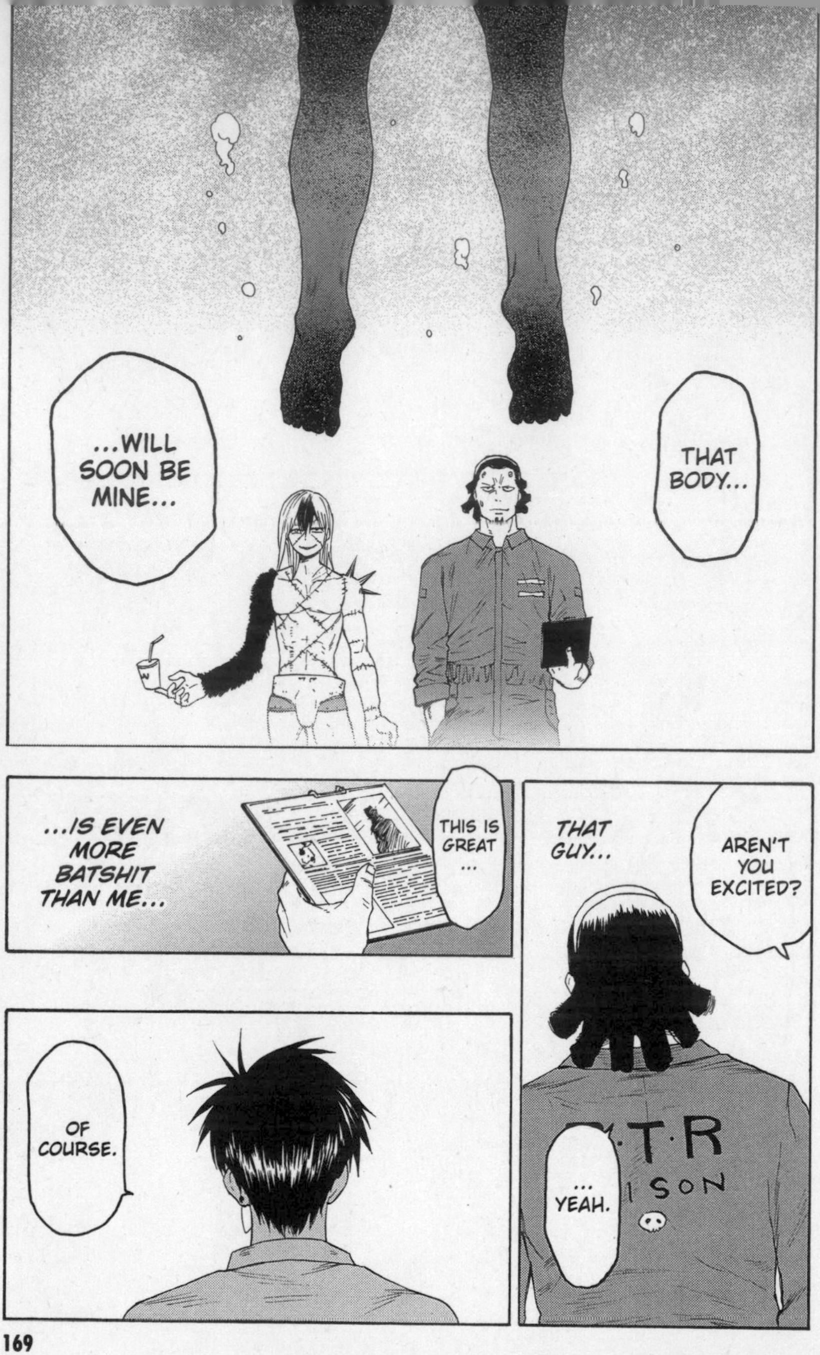
THAT BODY...
...WILL SOON BE MINE...
AREN'T YOU EXCITED?
THAT GUY...
...YEAH.
THIS IS GREAT ...
...IS EVEN MORE BATSHIT THAN ME...
OF COURSE.

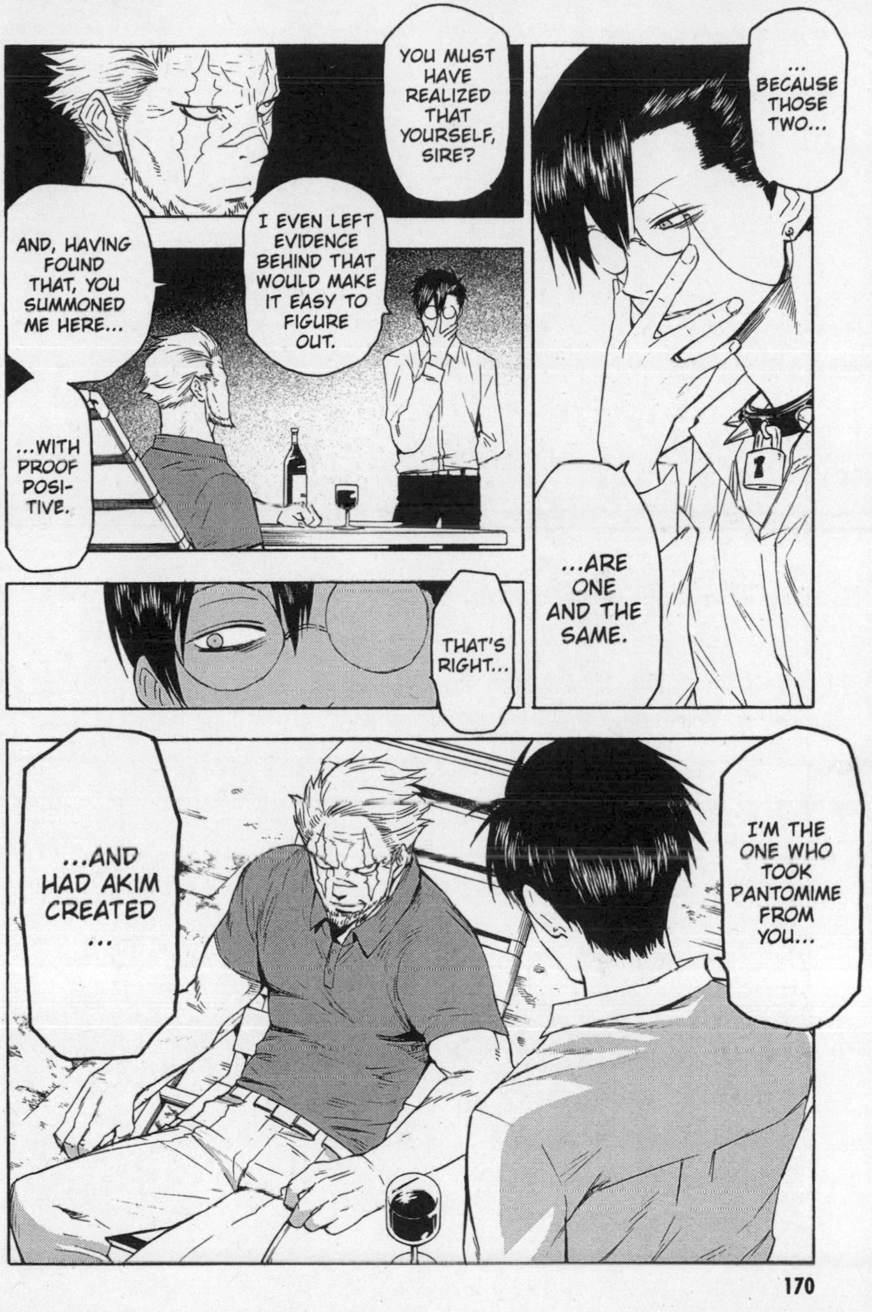

... BECAUSE THOSE TWO...
...ARE ONE AND THE SAME.
YOU MUST HAVE REALIZED THAT YOURSELF, SIRE?
I EVEN LEFT EVIDENCE BEHIND THAT WOULD MAKE IT EASY TO FIGURE OUT.
AND, HAVING FOUND THAT, YOU SUMMONED ME HERE...
...WITH PROOF POSI-TIVE.
THAT'S RIGHT...
I'M THE ONE WHO TOOK PANTOMIME FROM YOU...
...AND HAD AKIM CREATED ...

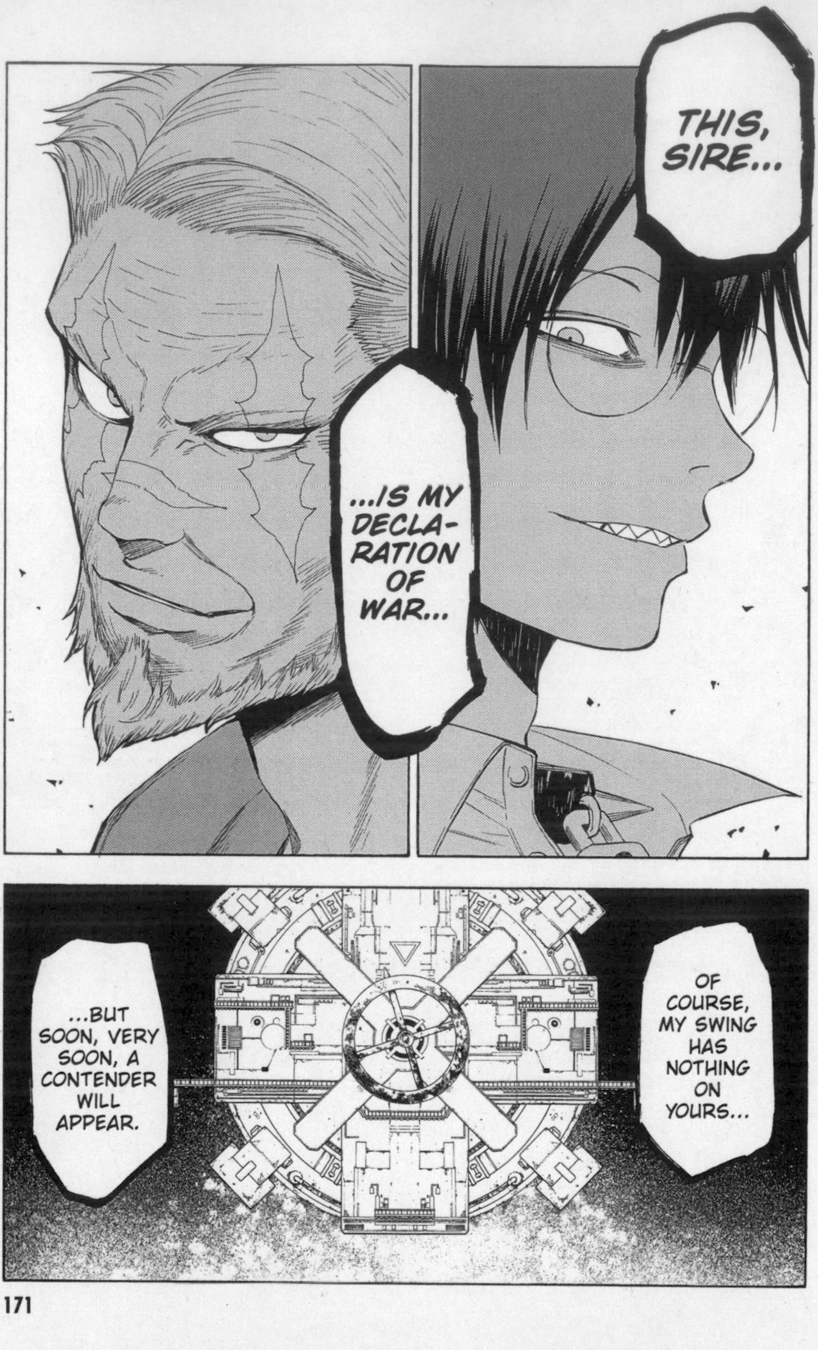
THIS, SIRE...
...IS MY DECLA-RATION OF WAR...
OF COURSE, MY SWING HAS NOTHING ON YOURS...
...BUT SOON, VERY SOON, A CONTENDER WILL APPEAR.

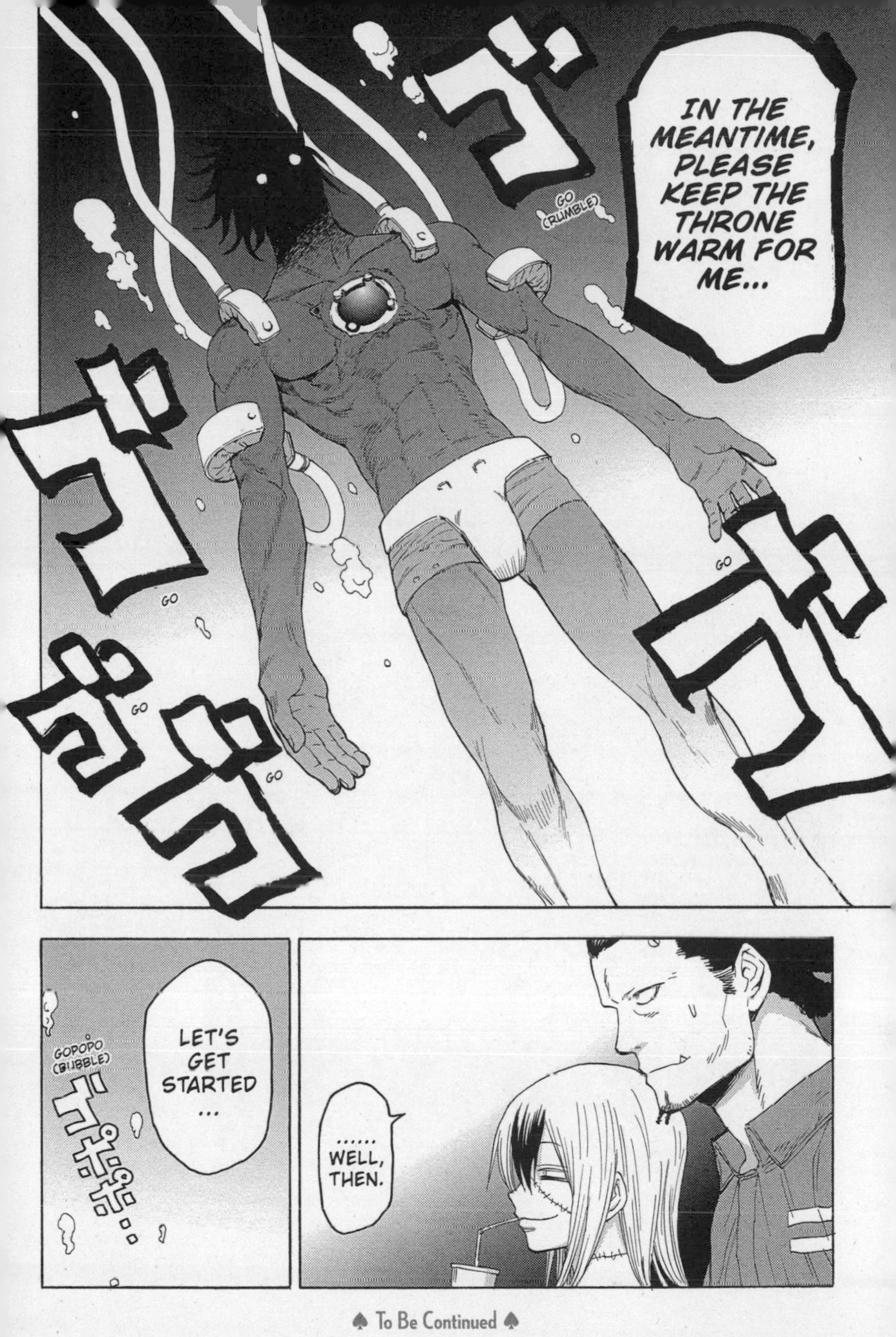
IN THE MEANTIME, PLEASE KEEP THE THRONE WARM FOR ME...
GO (RUMBLE)
GO
GO
GO
GO
...... WELL, THEN.
LET'S GET STARTED ...
GOPOPO (BUBBLE)

♠ To Be Continued ♠

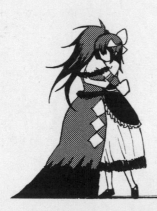

TO BE

continued...

BLOOD LAD

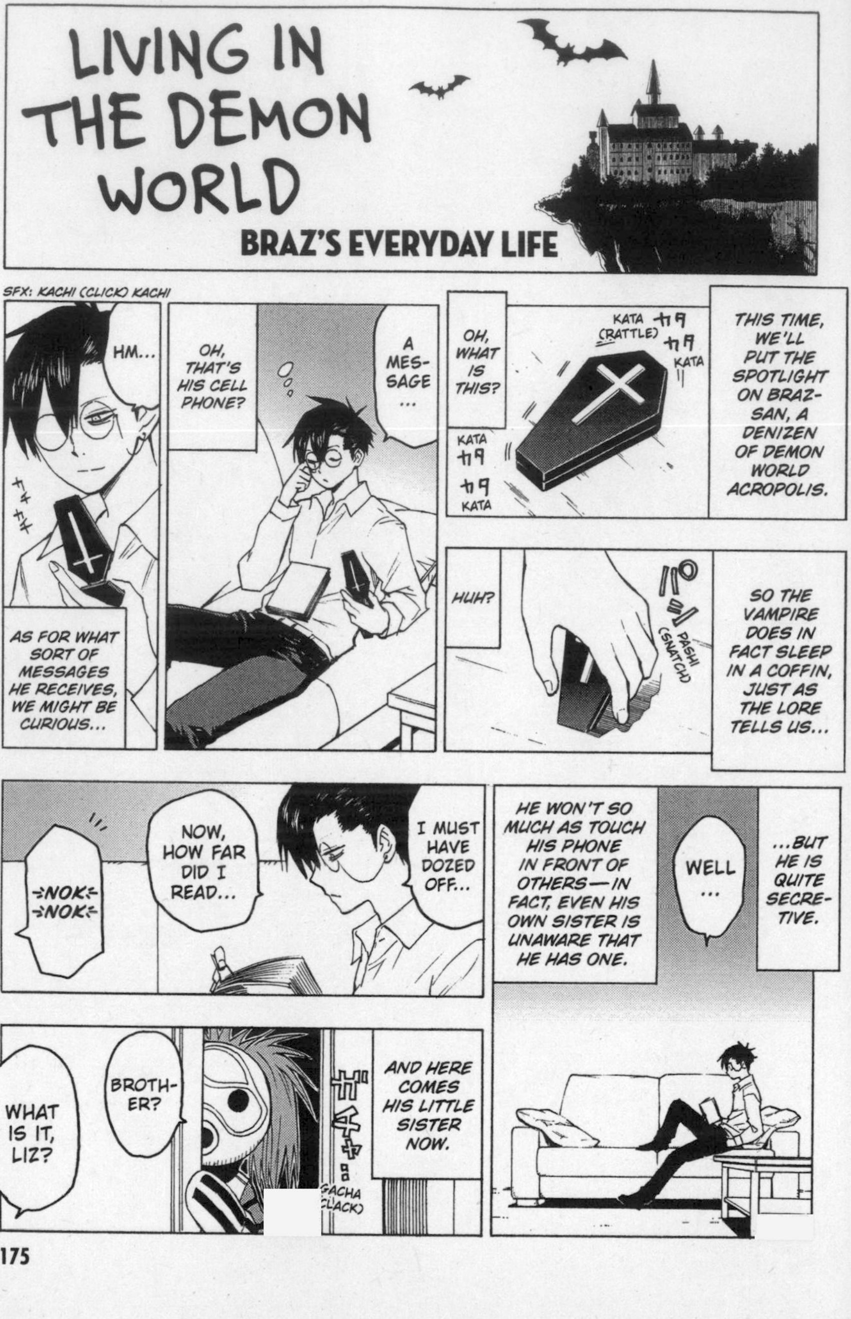
LIVING IN THE DEMON WORLD
BRAZ'S EVERYDAY LIFE
SFX: KACHI (CLICK) KACHI
THIS TIME, WE'LL PUT THE SPOTLIGHT ON BRAZ-SAN, A DENIZEN OF DEMON WORLD ACROPOLIS.
KATA (RATTLE) KATA
OH, WHAT IS THIS?
KATA KATA
SO THE VAMPIRE DOES IN FACT SLEEP IN A COFFIN, JUST AS THE LORE TELLS US...
PASHI (SNATCH)
HUH?
A MES-SAGE...
OH, THAT'S HIS CELL PHONE?
HM...
AS FOR WHAT SORT OF MESSAGES HE RECEIVES, WE MIGHT BE CURIOUS...
...BUT HE IS QUITE SECRE-TIVE.
WELL...
HE WON'T SO MUCH AS TOUCH HIS PHONE IN FRONT OF OTHERS—IN FACT, EVEN HIS OWN SISTER IS UNAWARE THAT HE HAS ONE.
I MUST HAVE DOZED OFF...
NOW, HOW FAR DID I READ...
NOK NOK
AND HERE COMES HIS LITTLE SISTER NOW.
GACHA (CLACK)
BROTH-ER?
WHAT IS IT, LIZ?

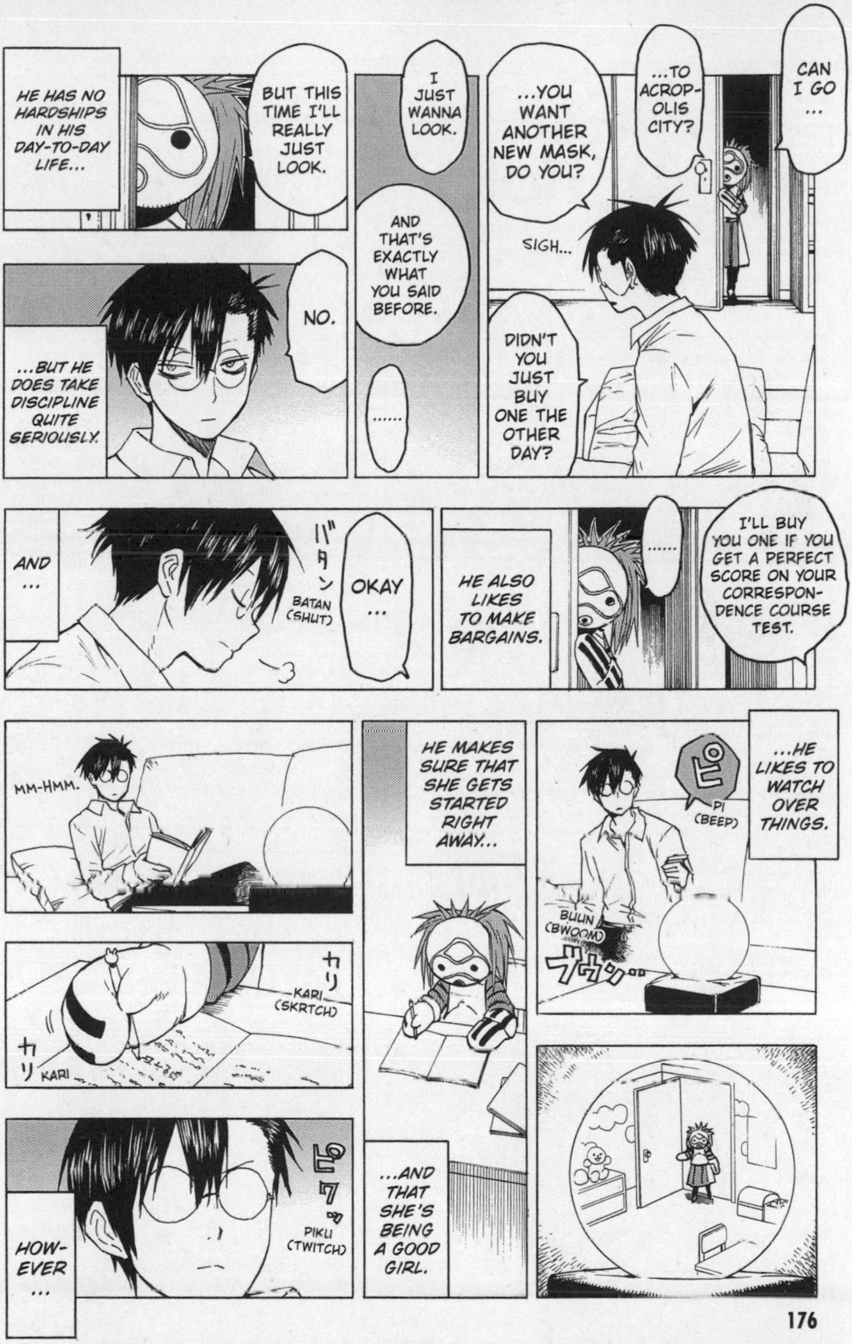
CAN I GO ...
...TO ACROPOLIS CITY?
...YOU WANT ANOTHER NEW MASK, DO YOU?
SIGH...
DIDN'T YOU JUST BUY ONE THE OTHER DAY?
I JUST WANNA LOOK.
AND THAT'S EXACTLY WHAT YOU SAID BEFORE.
......
BUT THIS TIME I'LL REALLY JUST LOOK.
HE HAS NO HARDSHIPS IN HIS DAY-TO-DAY LIFE...
NO.
...BUT HE DOES TAKE DISCIPLINE QUITE SERIOUSLY.
I'LL BUY YOU ONE IF YOU GET A PERFECT SCORE ON YOUR CORRESPONDENCE COURSE TEST.
......
HE ALSO LIKES TO MAKE BARGAINS.
OKAY ...
バタン
BATAN (SHUT)
AND ...
...HE LIKES TO WATCH OVER THINGS.
ピ
PI (BEEP)
BUUN (BWOOM)
HE MAKES SURE THAT SHE GETS STARTED RIGHT AWAY...
...AND THAT SHE'S BEING A GOOD GIRL.
MM-HMM.
カリ
KARI (SKRTCH)
カリ
KARI
ピクッ
PIKU (TWITCH)
HOW-EVER ...

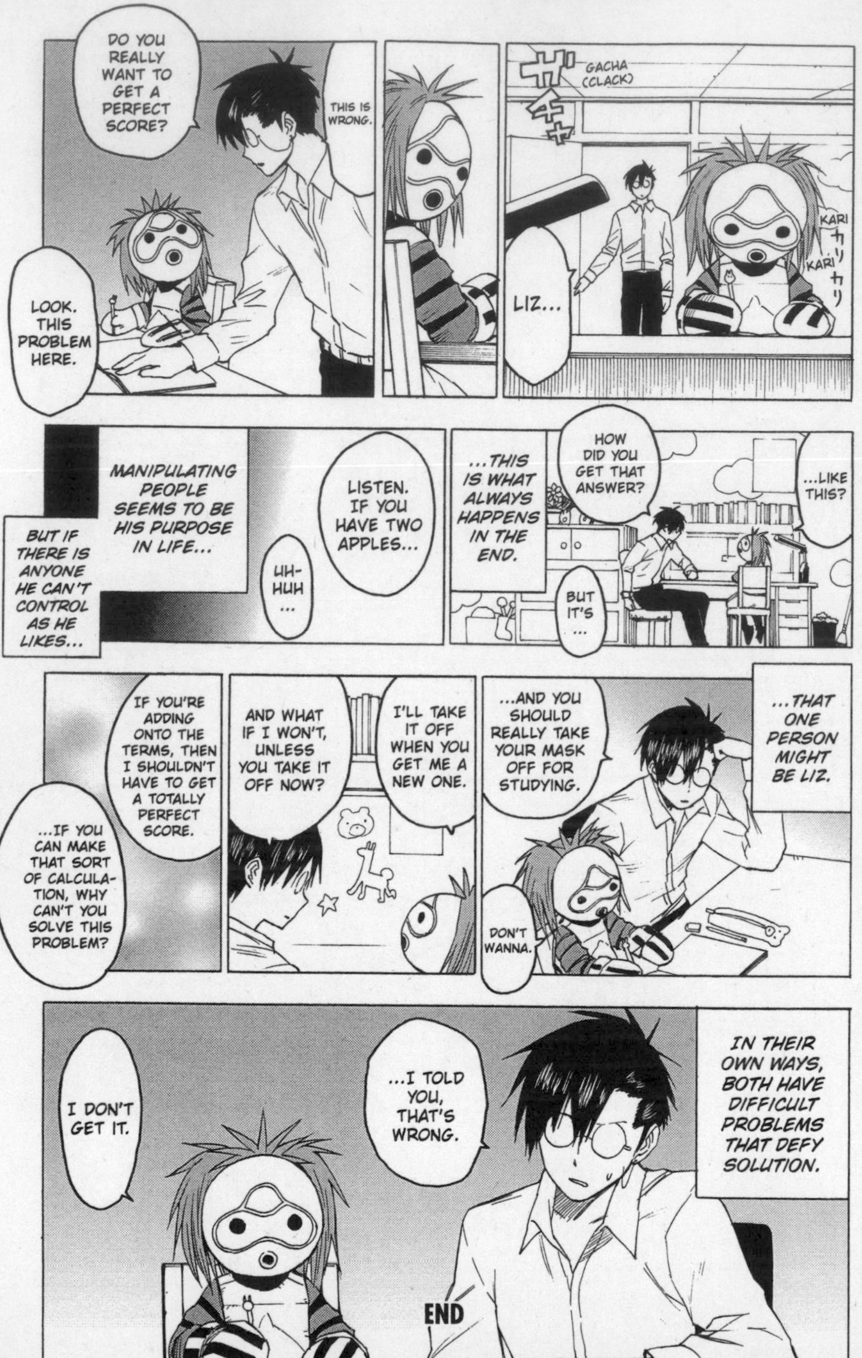
GACHA (CLACK)
KARI カリ
KARI カリ
LIZ...
THIS IS WRONG.
DO YOU REALLY WANT TO GET A PERFECT SCORE?
LOOK. THIS PROBLEM HERE.
...LIKE THIS?
HOW DID YOU GET THAT ANSWER?
...THIS IS WHAT ALWAYS HAPPENS IN THE END.
BUT IT'S ...
LISTEN. IF YOU HAVE TWO APPLES...
UH-HUH ...
MANIPULATING PEOPLE SEEMS TO BE HIS PURPOSE IN LIFE...
BUT IF THERE IS ANYONE HE CAN'T CONTROL AS HE LIKES...
...THAT ONE PERSON MIGHT BE LIZ.
...AND YOU SHOULD REALLY TAKE YOUR MASK OFF FOR STUDYING.
DON'T WANNA.
I'LL TAKE IT OFF WHEN YOU GET ME A NEW ONE.
AND WHAT IF I WON'T, UNLESS YOU TAKE IT OFF NOW?
IF YOU'RE ADDING ONTO THE TERMS, THEN I SHOULDN'T HAVE TO GET A TOTALLY PERFECT SCORE.
...IF YOU CAN MAKE THAT SORT OF CALCULATION, WHY CAN'T YOU SOLVE THIS PROBLEM?
IN THEIR OWN WAYS, BOTH HAVE DIFFICULT PROBLEMS THAT DEFY SOLUTION.
...I TOLD YOU, THAT'S WRONG.
I DON'T GET IT.
END

BLOOD LAD 5

These images appeared under the jacket of the original edition of *Blood Lad*!

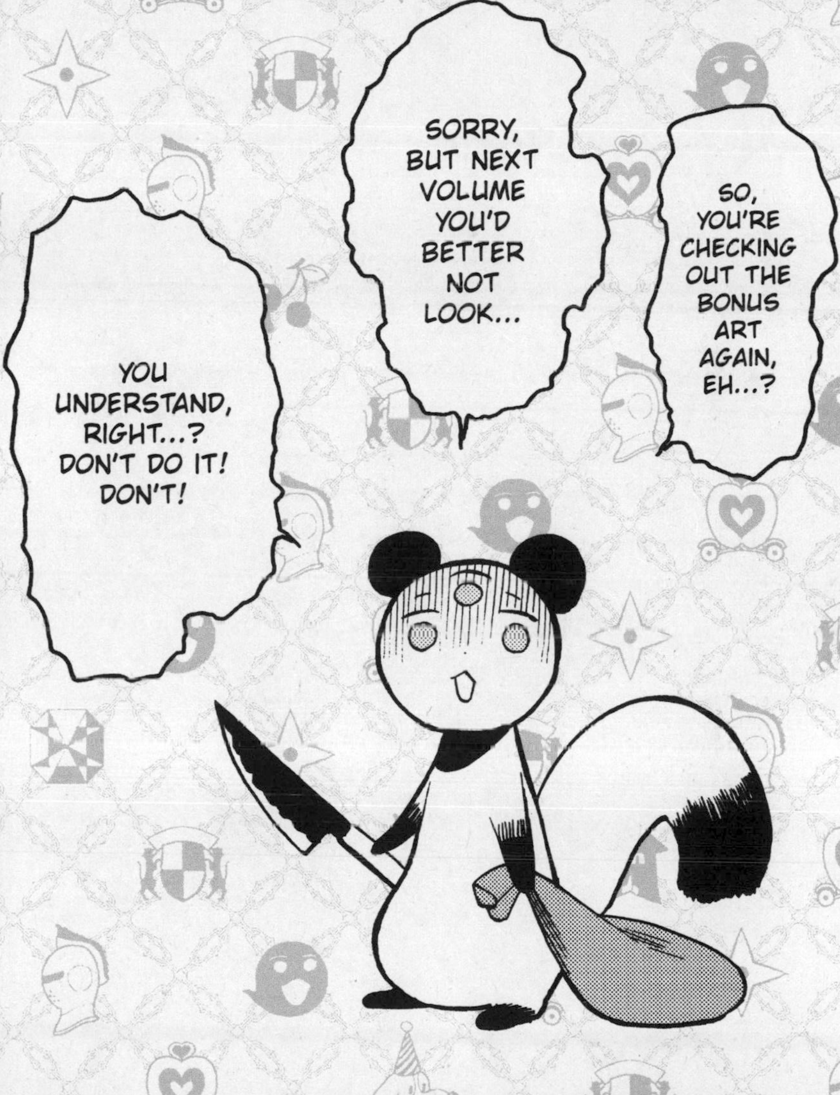

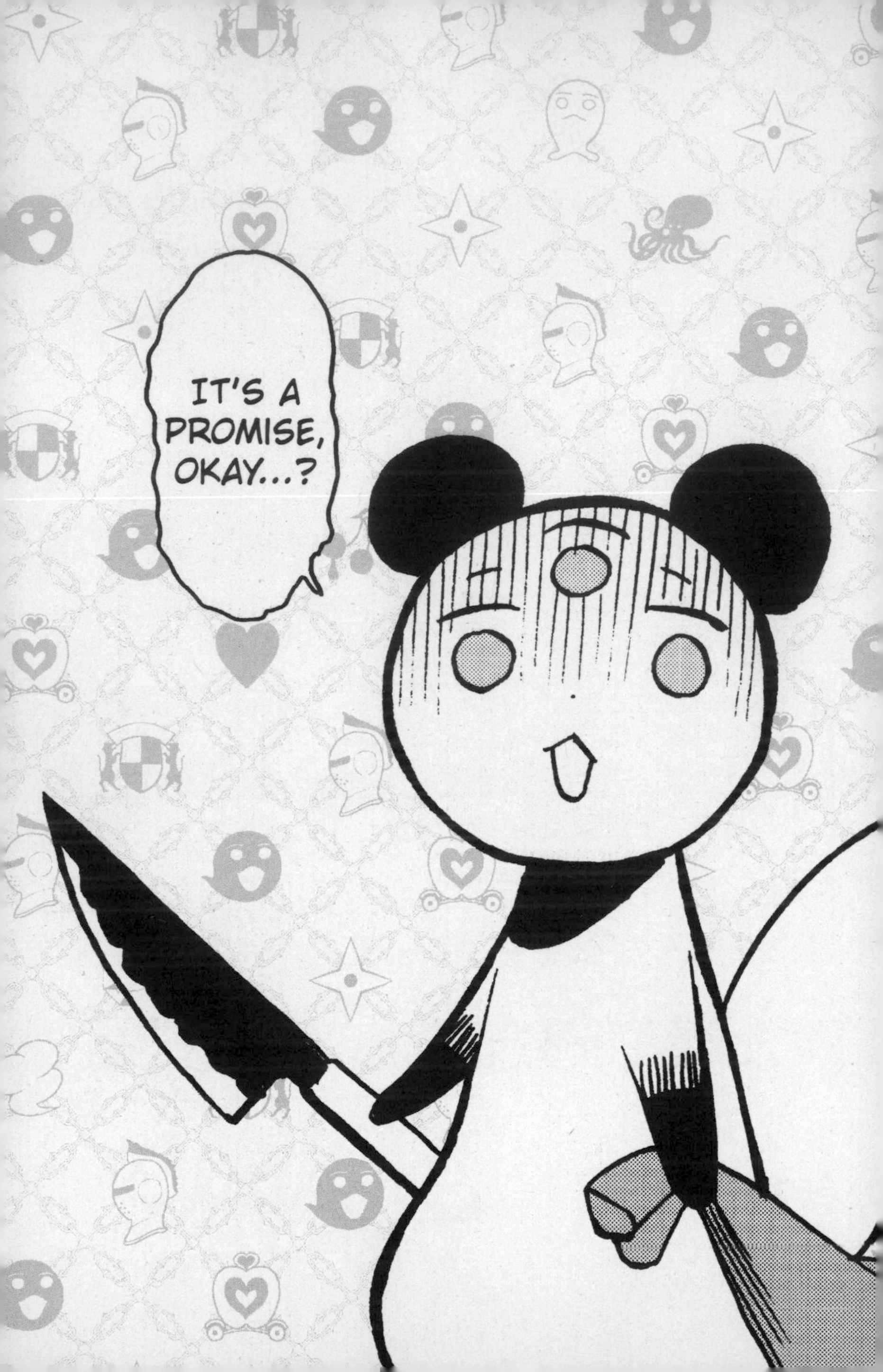
IT'S A PROMISE, OKAY...?

BLOOD LAD

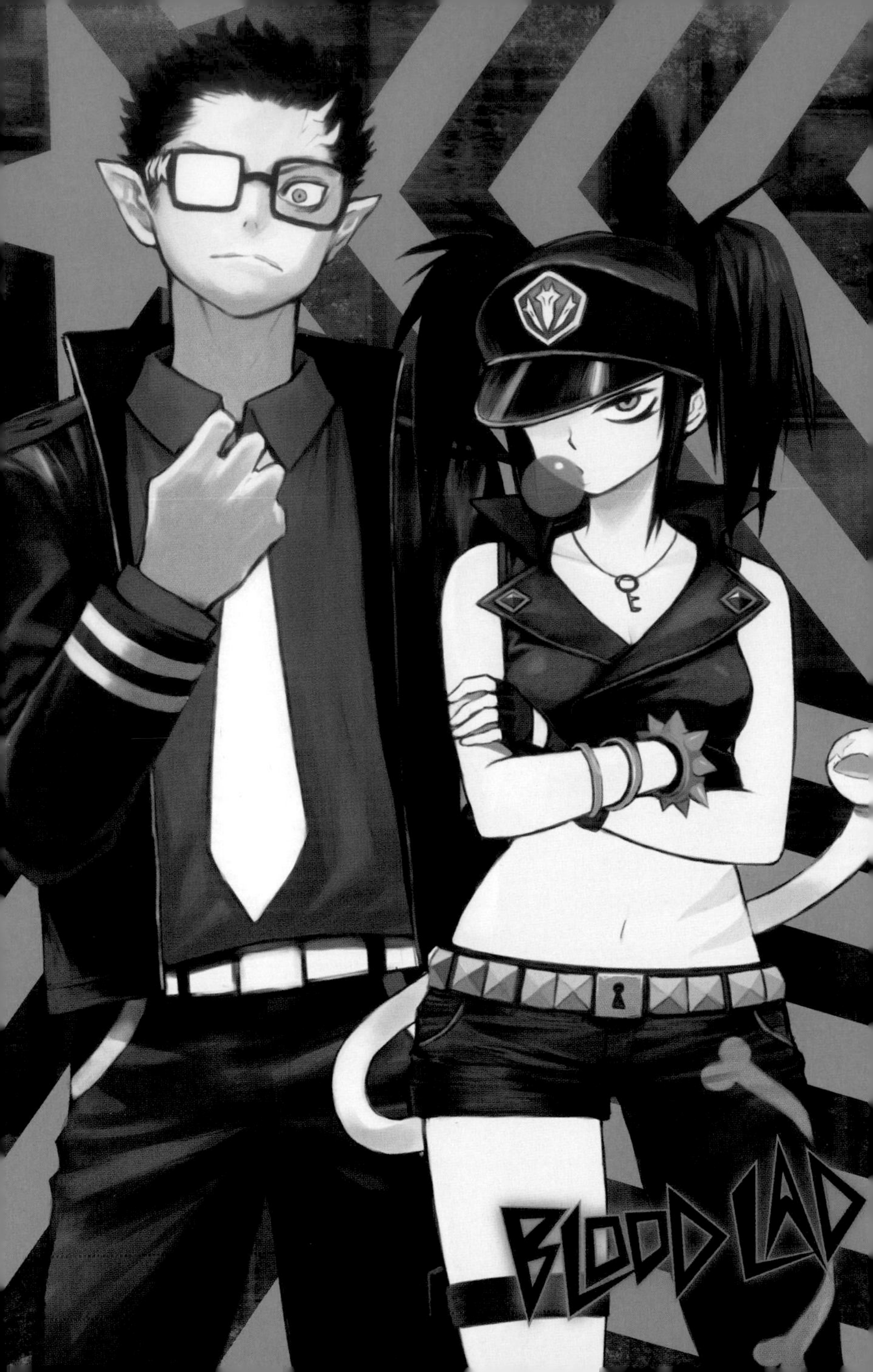
BLOOD LAD

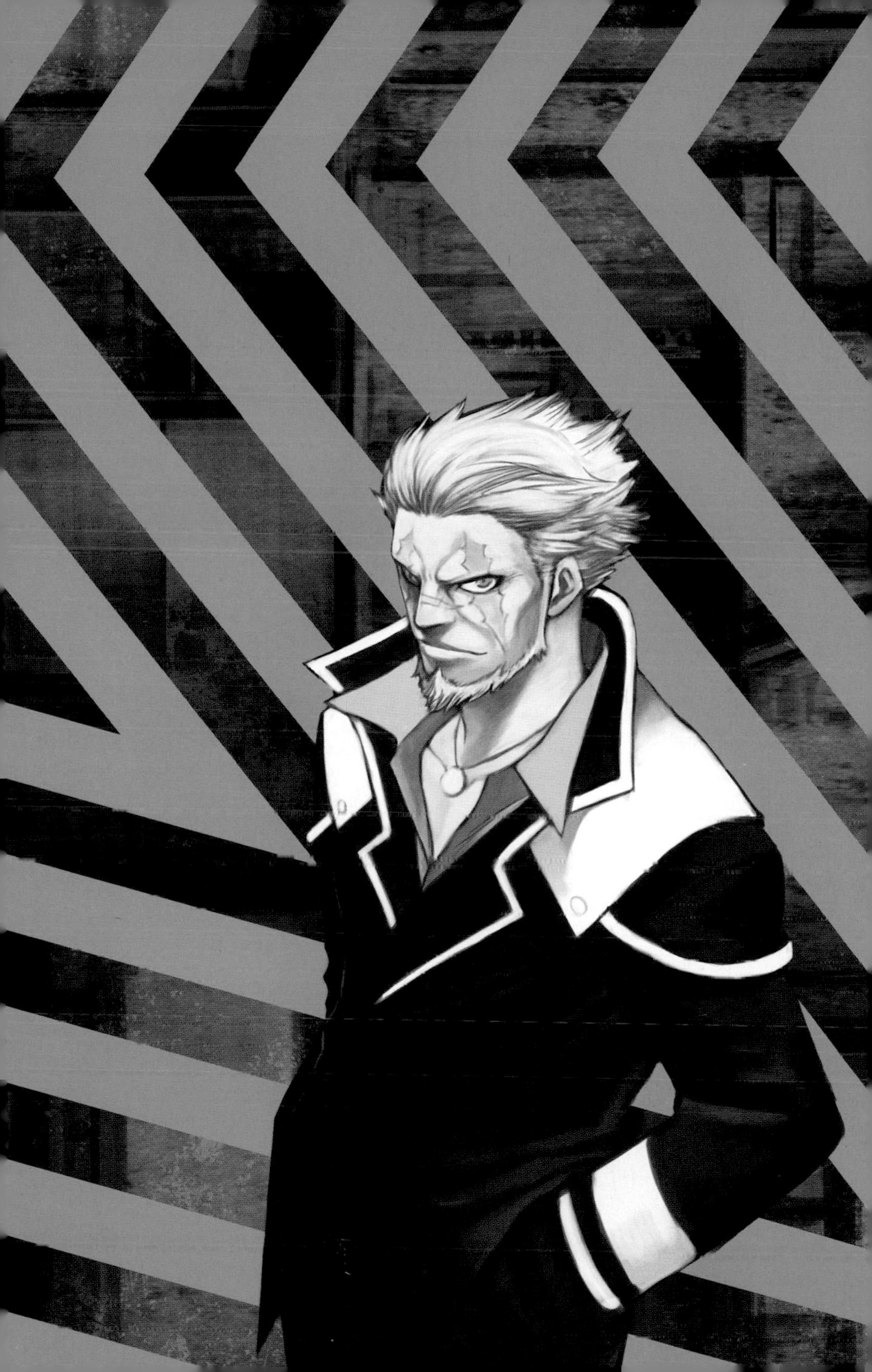

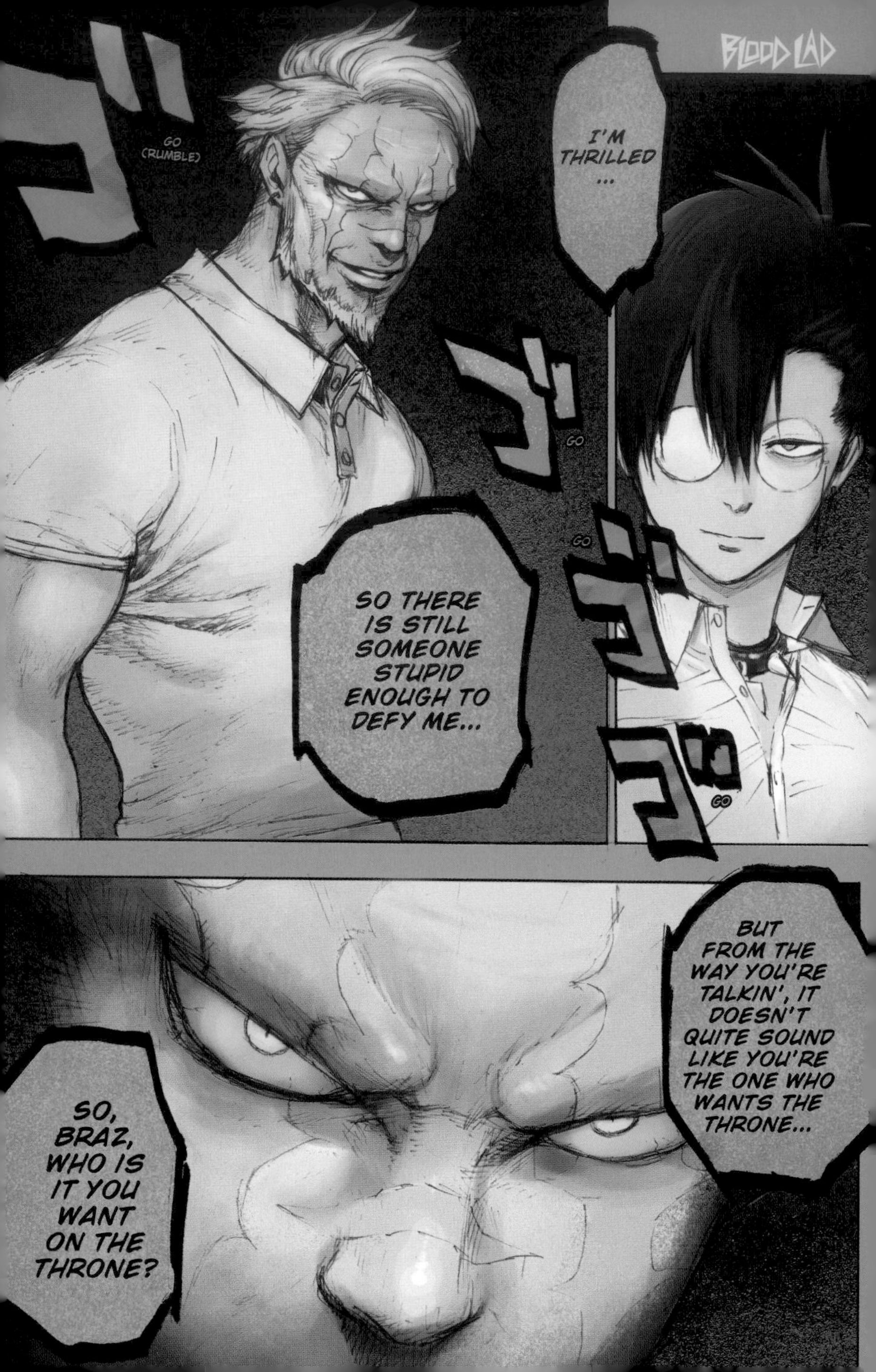
BLOOD LAD
I'M THRILLED ...
GO
GO
GO
GO (RUMBLE)
SO THERE IS STILL SOMEONE STUPID ENOUGH TO DEFY ME...
BUT FROM THE WAY YOU'RE TALKIN', IT DOESN'T QUITE SOUND LIKE YOU'RE THE ONE WHO WANTS THE THRONE...
SO, BRAZ, WHO IS IT YOU WANT ON THE THRONE?

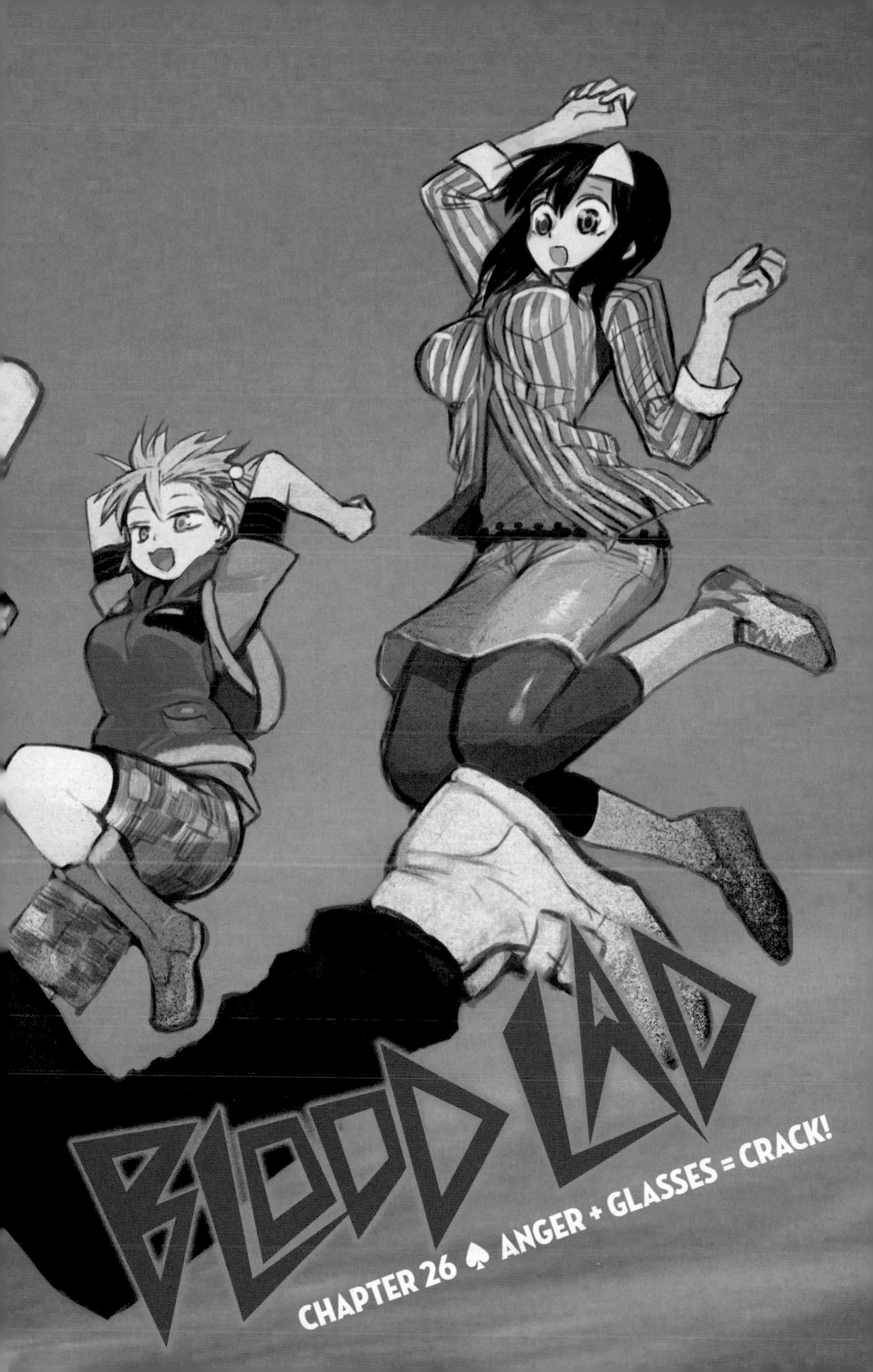
BLOOD LAD
CHAPTER 26 ♠ ANGER + GLASSES = CRACK!

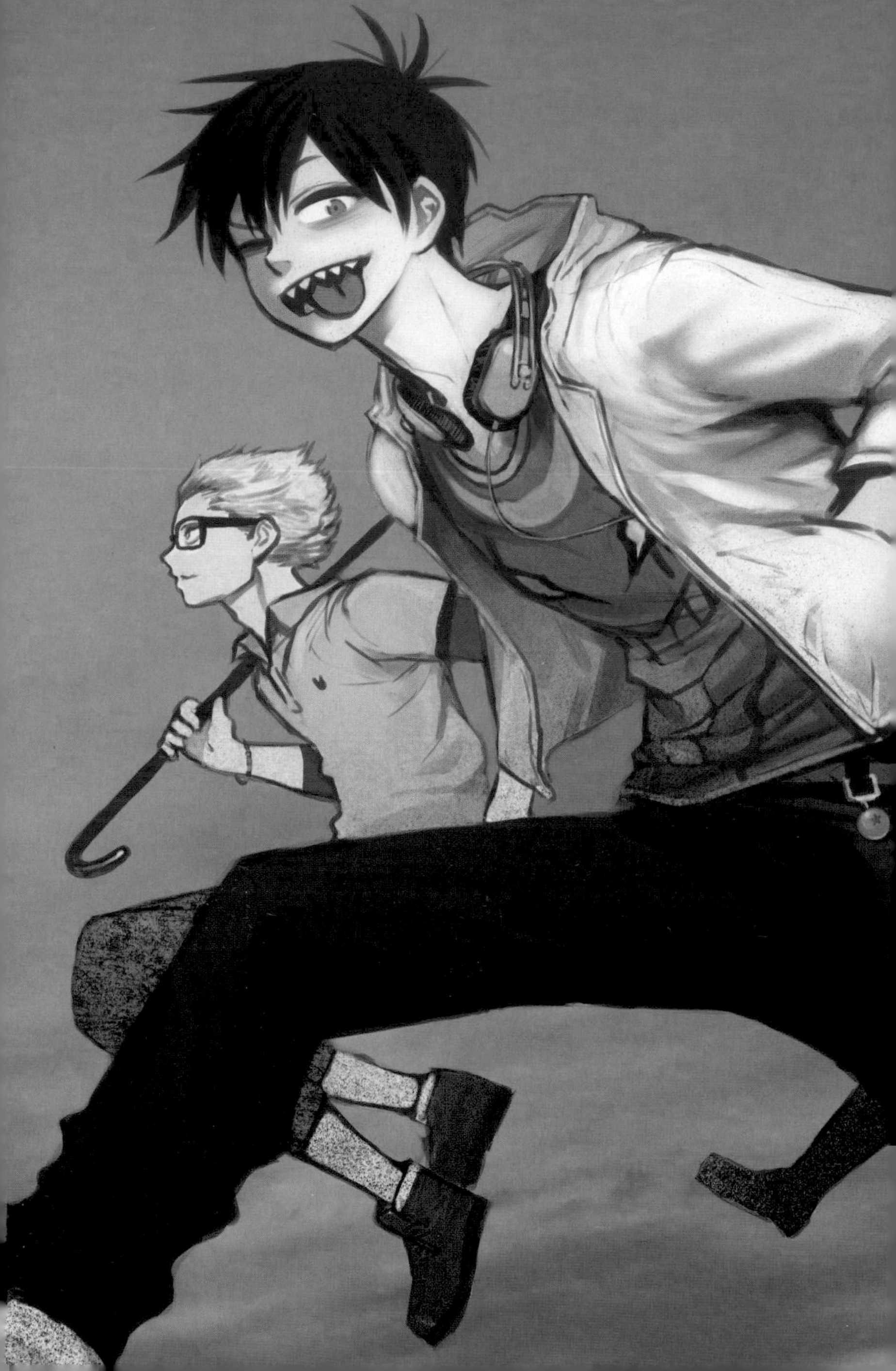

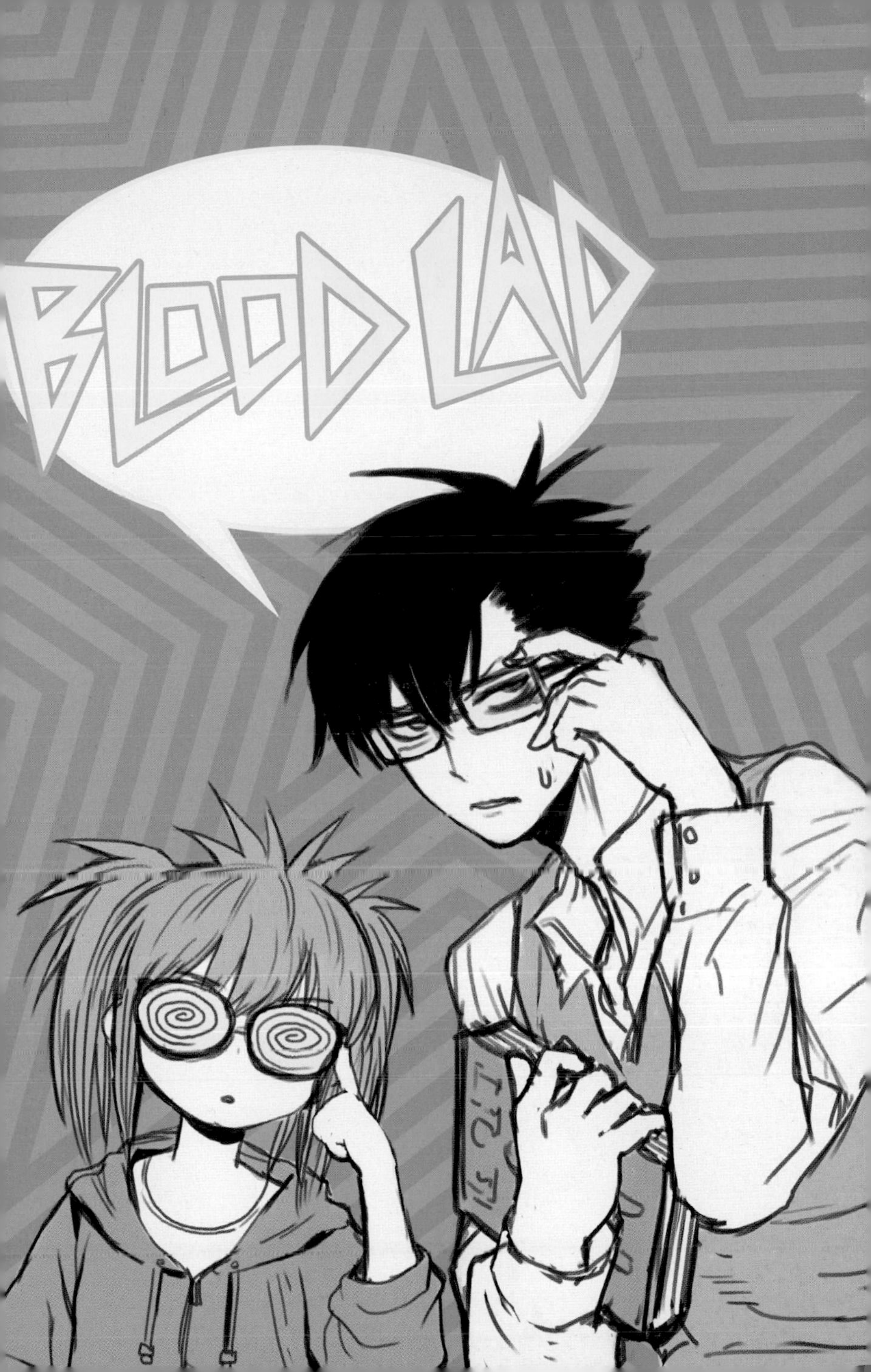
BLOOD LAD

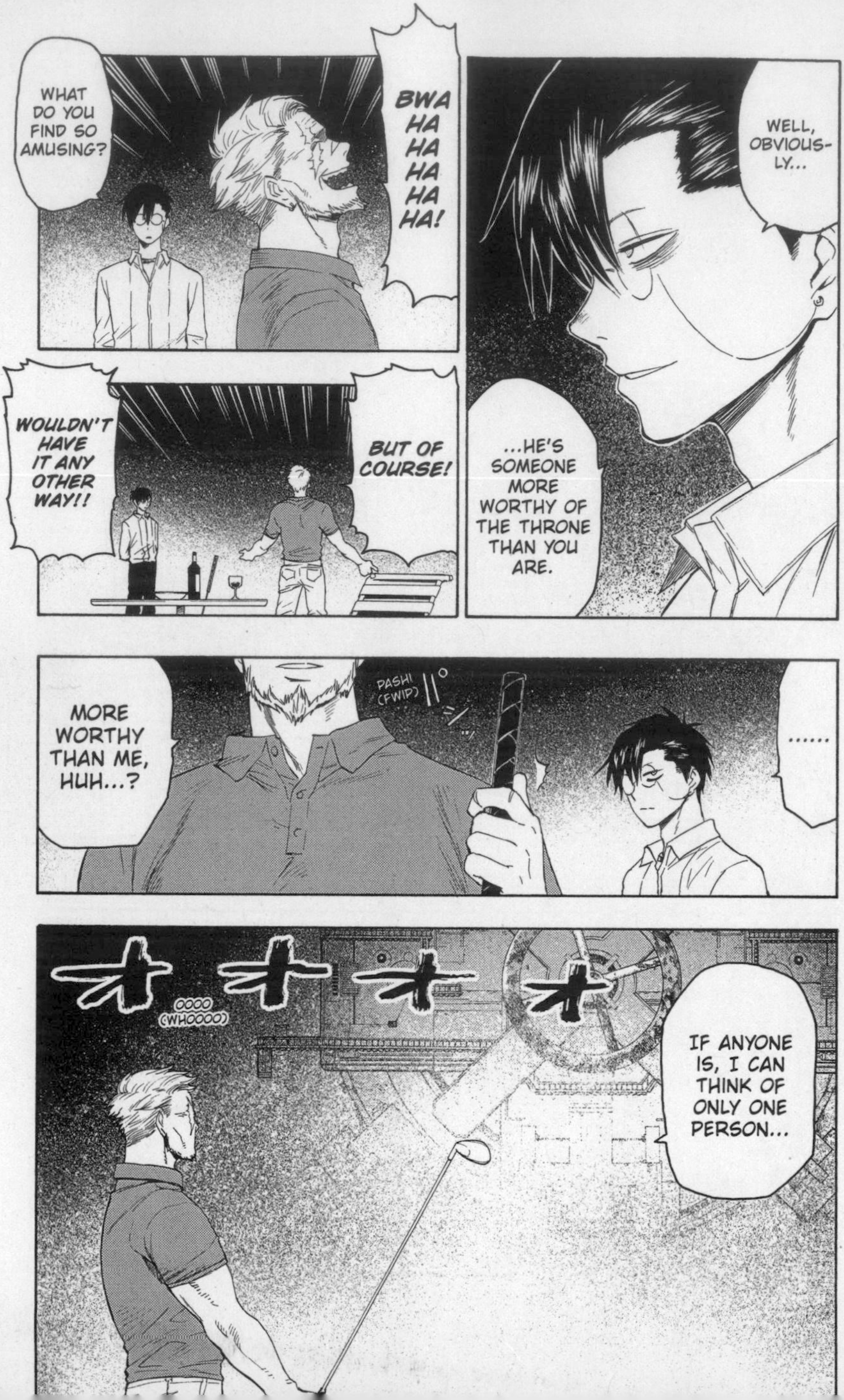
WELL, OBVIOUS-LY...
...HE'S SOMEONE MORE WORTHY OF THE THRONE THAN YOU ARE.
BWA HA HA HA HA HA!
WHAT DO YOU FIND SO AMUSING?
BUT OF COURSE!
WOULDN'T HAVE IT ANY OTHER WAY!!
......
PASHI (FWIP)
MORE WORTHY THAN ME, HUH...?
IF ANYONE IS, I CAN THINK OF ONLY ONE PERSON...
オオオオ
OOOO (WHOOOO)

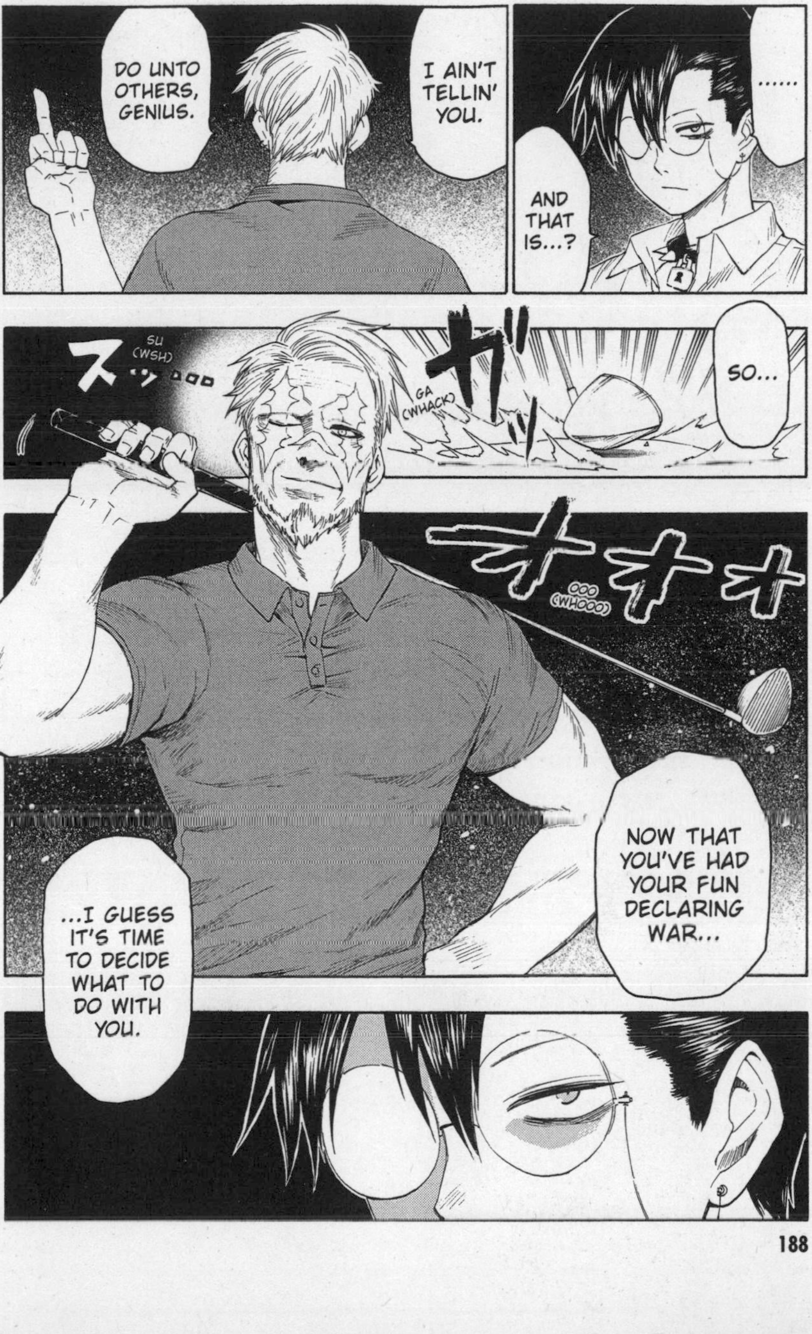
......
AND THAT IS...?
I AIN'T TELLIN' YOU.
DO UNTO OTHERS, GENIUS.
SO...
GA (WHACK)
SU (WSH)
OOO (WHOOO)
NOW THAT YOU'VE HAD YOUR FUN DECLARING WAR...
...I GUESS IT'S TIME TO DECIDE WHAT TO DO WITH YOU.

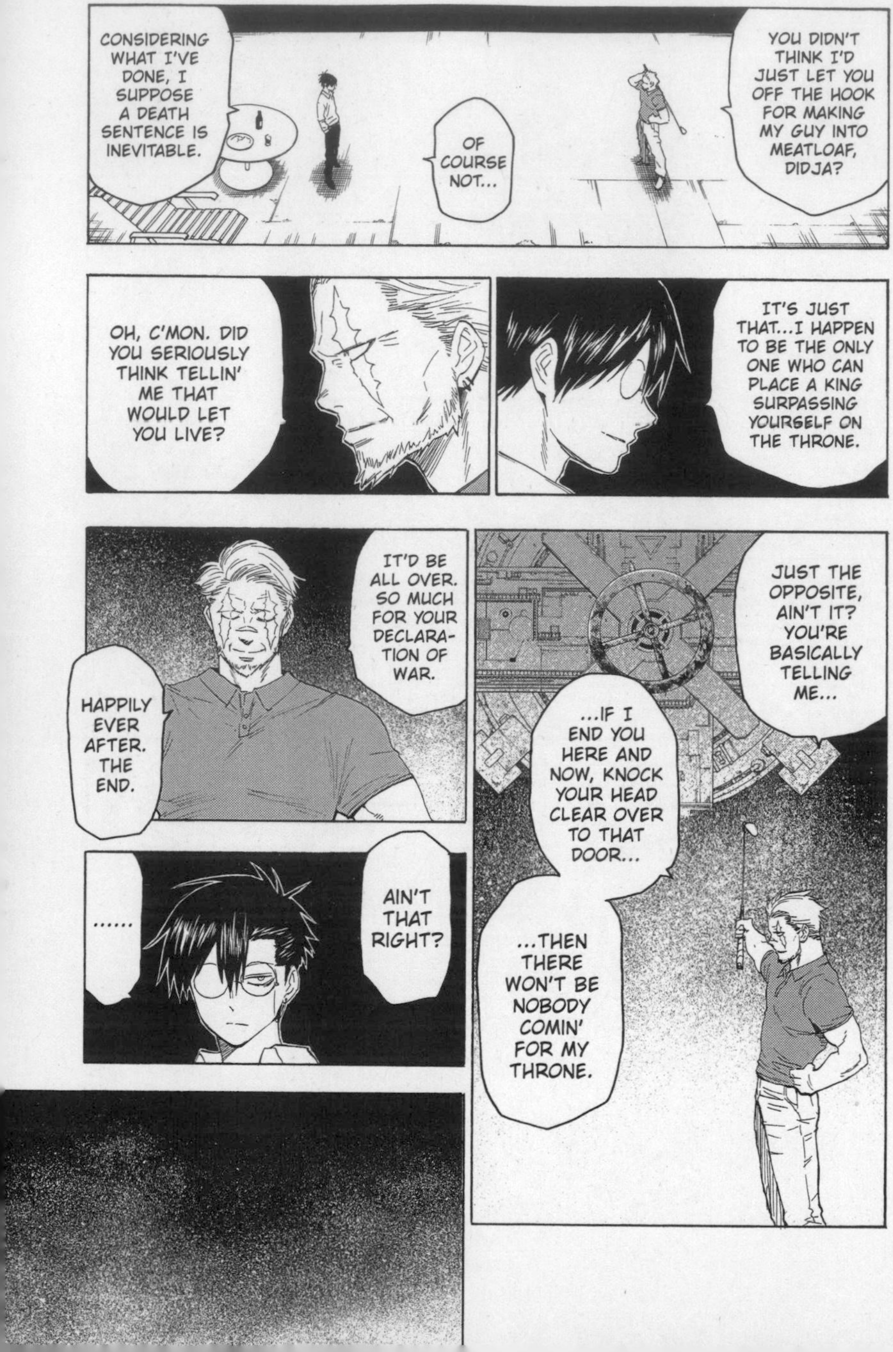
YOU DIDN'T THINK I'D JUST LET YOU OFF THE HOOK FOR MAKING MY GUY INTO MEATLOAF, DIDJA?
OF COURSE NOT...
CONSIDERING WHAT I'VE DONE, I SUPPOSE A DEATH SENTENCE IS INEVITABLE.
IT'S JUST THAT...I HAPPEN TO BE THE ONLY ONE WHO CAN PLACE A KING SURPASSING YOURSELF ON THE THRONE.
OH, C'MON. DID YOU SERIOUSLY THINK TELLIN' ME THAT WOULD LET YOU LIVE?
JUST THE OPPOSITE, AIN'T IT? YOU'RE BASICALLY TELLING ME...
...IF I END YOU HERE AND NOW, KNOCK YOUR HEAD CLEAR OVER TO THAT DOOR...
...THEN THERE WON'T BE NOBODY COMIN' FOR MY THRONE.
IT'D BE ALL OVER. SO MUCH FOR YOUR DECLARATION OF WAR.
HAPPILY EVER AFTER. THE END.
AIN'T THAT RIGHT?
......

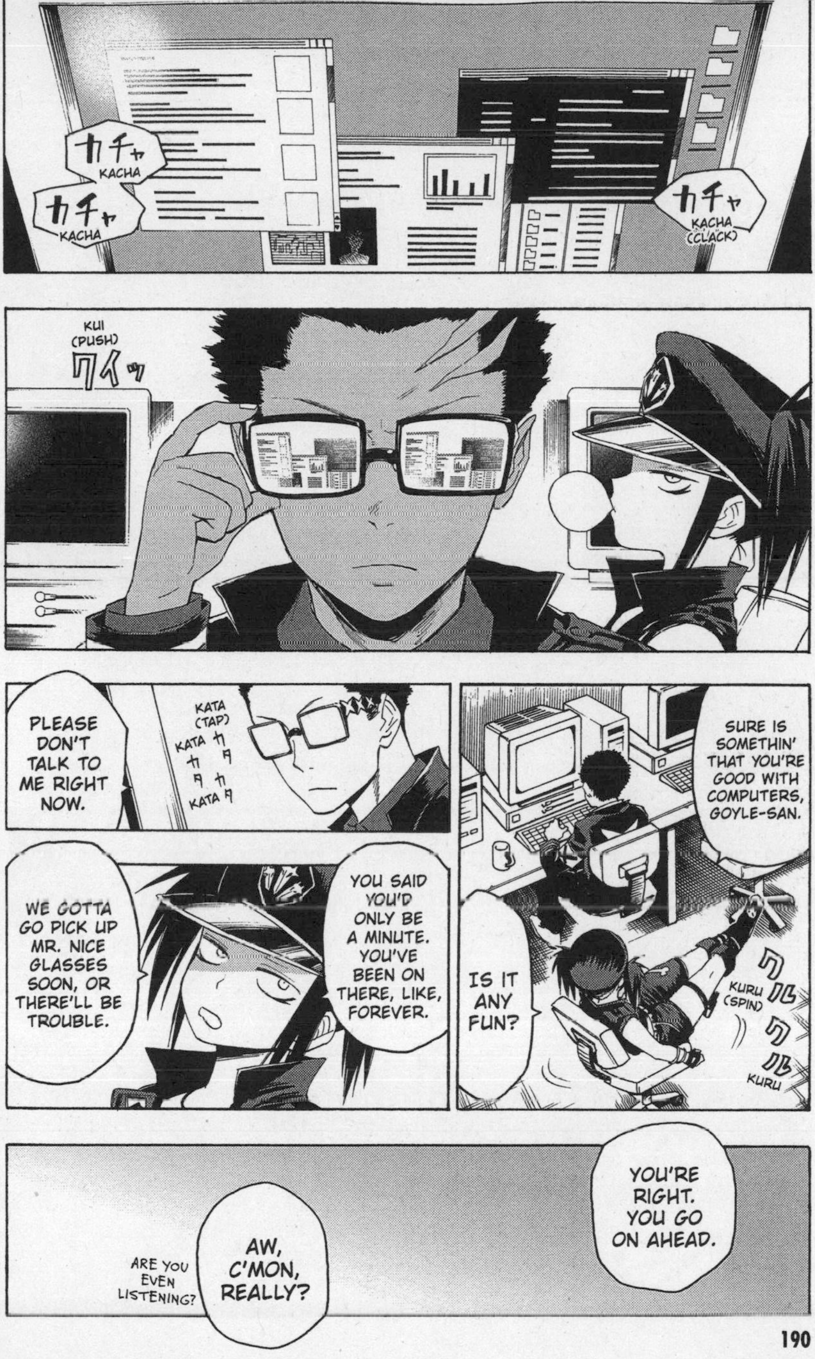
カチャ
KACHA (CLACK)
カチャ
KACHA
カチャ
KACHA
KUI (PUSH)
クイッ
SURE IS SOMETHIN' THAT YOU'RE GOOD WITH COMPUTERS, GOYLE-SAN.
IS IT ANY FUN?
クル
KURU (SPIN)
クル
KURU
PLEASE DON'T TALK TO ME RIGHT NOW.
KATA (TAP)
KATA カタ
カタ
KATA タ
YOU SAID YOU'D ONLY BE A MINUTE. YOU'VE BEEN ON THERE, LIKE, FOREVER.
WE GOTTA GO PICK UP MR. NICE GLASSES SOON, OR THERE'LL BE TROUBLE.
YOU'RE RIGHT. YOU GO ON AHEAD.
AW, C'MON, REALLY?
ARE YOU EVEN LISTENING?

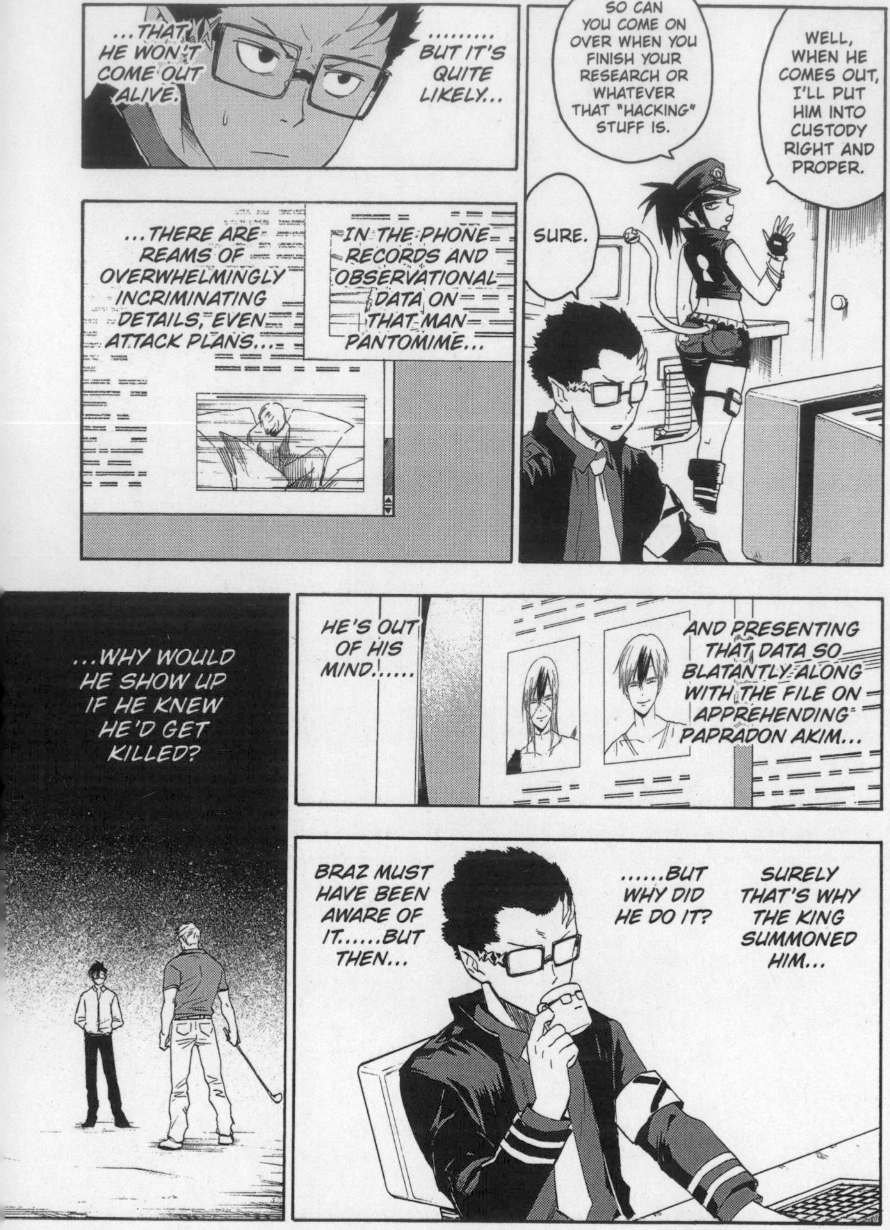
WELL, WHEN HE COMES OUT, I'LL PUT HIM INTO CUSTODY RIGHT AND PROPER.
SO CAN YOU COME ON OVER WHEN YOU FINISH YOUR RESEARCH OR WHATEVER THAT "HACKING" STUFF IS.
SURE.
.........BUT IT'S QUITE LIKELY...
...THAT HE WON'T COME OUT ALIVE.
IN THE PHONE RECORDS AND OBSERVATIONAL DATA ON THAT MAN PANTOMIME...
...THERE ARE REAMS OF OVERWHELMINGLY INCRIMINATING DETAILS, EVEN ATTACK PLANS...
AND PRESENTING THAT DATA SO BLATANTLY ALONG WITH THE FILE ON APPREHENDING PAPRADON AKIM...
HE'S OUT OF HIS MIND......
SURELY THAT'S WHY THE KING SUMMONED HIM...
......BUT WHY DID HE DO IT?
BRAZ MUST HAVE BEEN AWARE OF IT......BUT THEN...
...WHY WOULD HE SHOW UP IF HE KNEW HE'D GET KILLED?

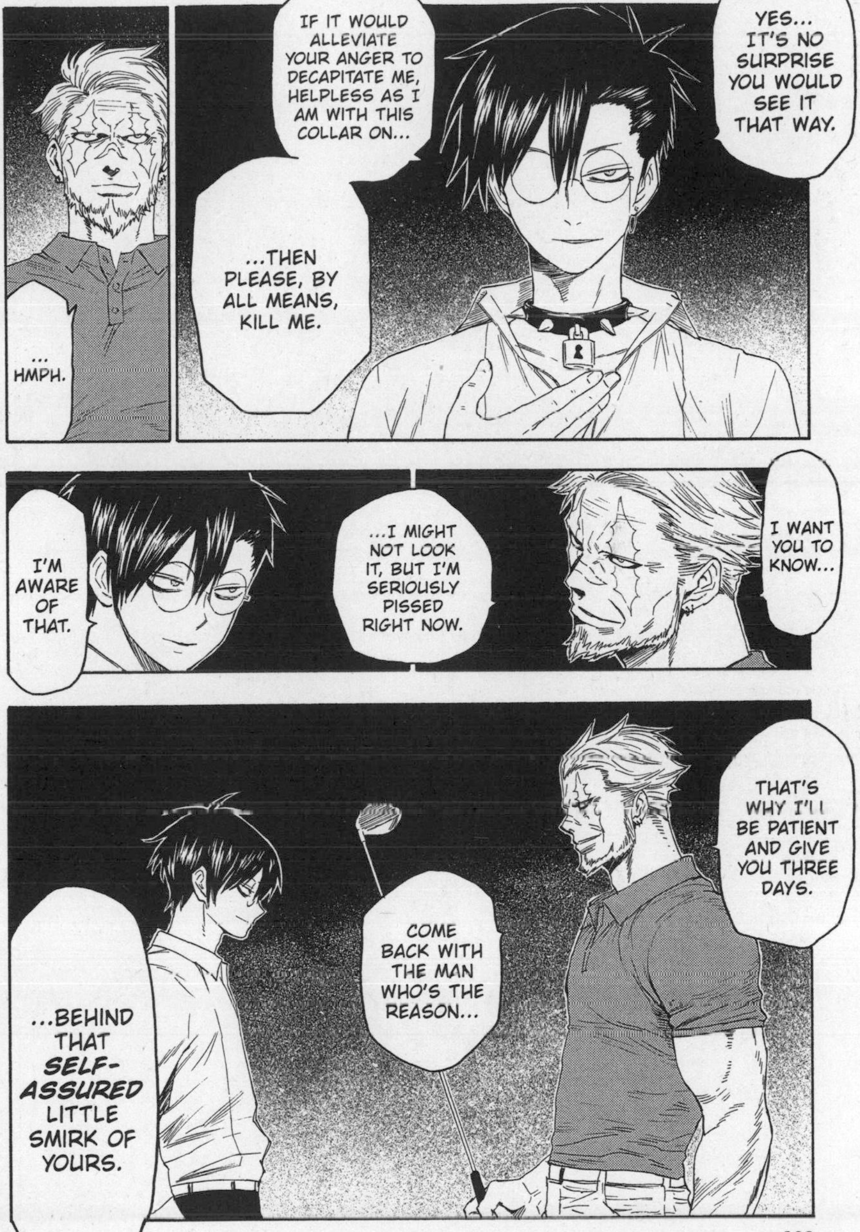
YES... IT'S NO SURPRISE YOU WOULD SEE IT THAT WAY.
IF IT WOULD ALLEVIATE YOUR ANGER TO DECAPITATE ME, HELPLESS AS I AM WITH THIS COLLAR ON...
...THEN PLEASE, BY ALL MEANS, KILL ME.
... HMPH.
I WANT YOU TO KNOW...
...I MIGHT NOT LOOK IT, BUT I'M SERIOUSLY PISSED RIGHT NOW.
I'M AWARE OF THAT.
THAT'S WHY I'LL BE PATIENT AND GIVE YOU THREE DAYS.
COME BACK WITH THE MAN WHO'S THE REASON...
...BEHIND THAT ***SELF-ASSURED*** LITTLE SMIRK OF YOURS.

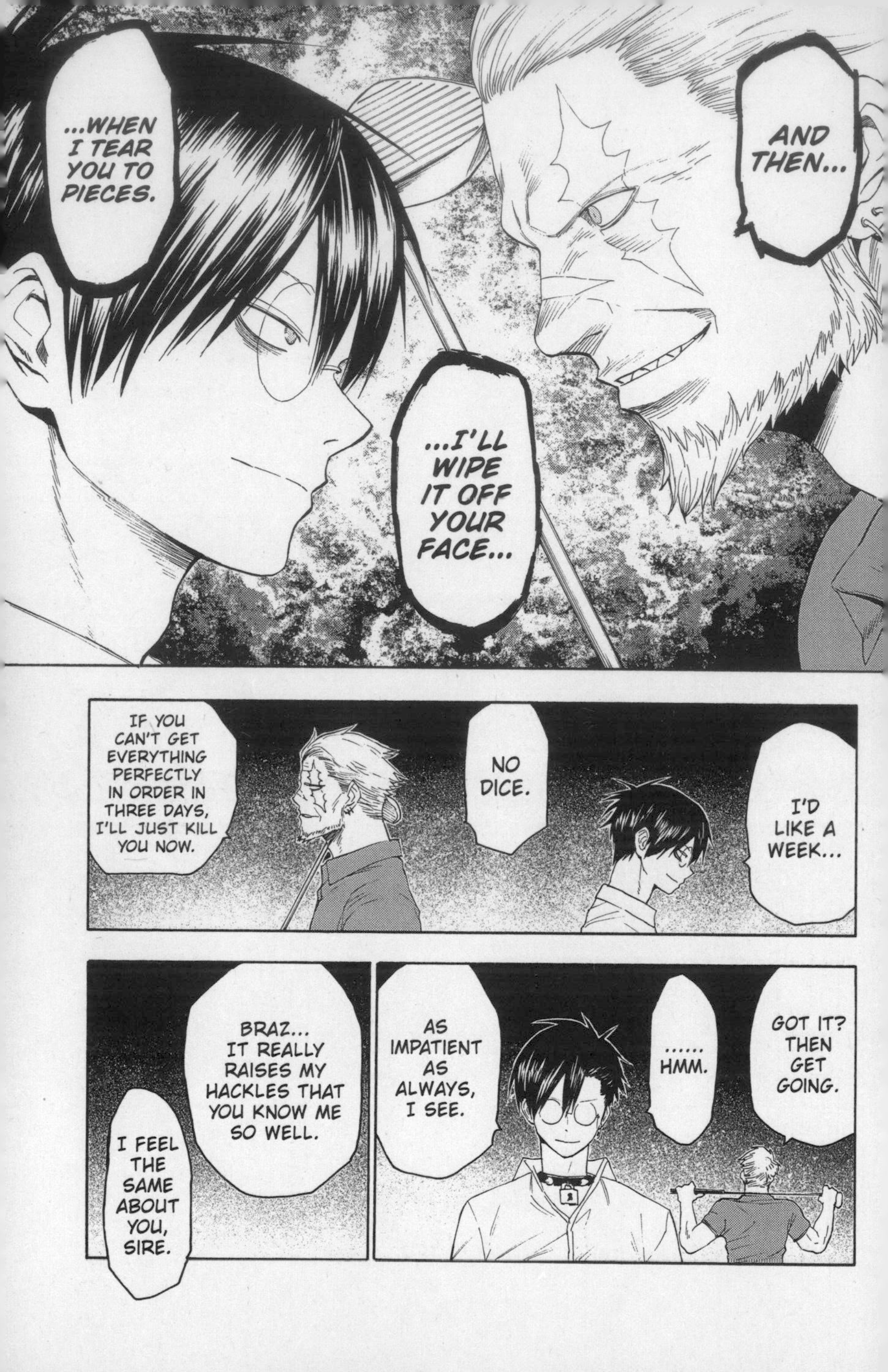
AND THEN...
...I'LL WIPE IT OFF YOUR FACE...
...WHEN I TEAR YOU TO PIECES.
I'D LIKE A WEEK...
NO DICE.
IF YOU CAN'T GET EVERYTHING PERFECTLY IN ORDER IN THREE DAYS, I'LL JUST KILL YOU NOW.
GOT IT? THEN GET GOING.
......HMM.
AS IMPATIENT AS ALWAYS, I SEE.
BRAZ... IT REALLY RAISES MY HACKLES THAT YOU KNOW ME SO WELL.
I FEEL THE SAME ABOUT YOU, SIRE.

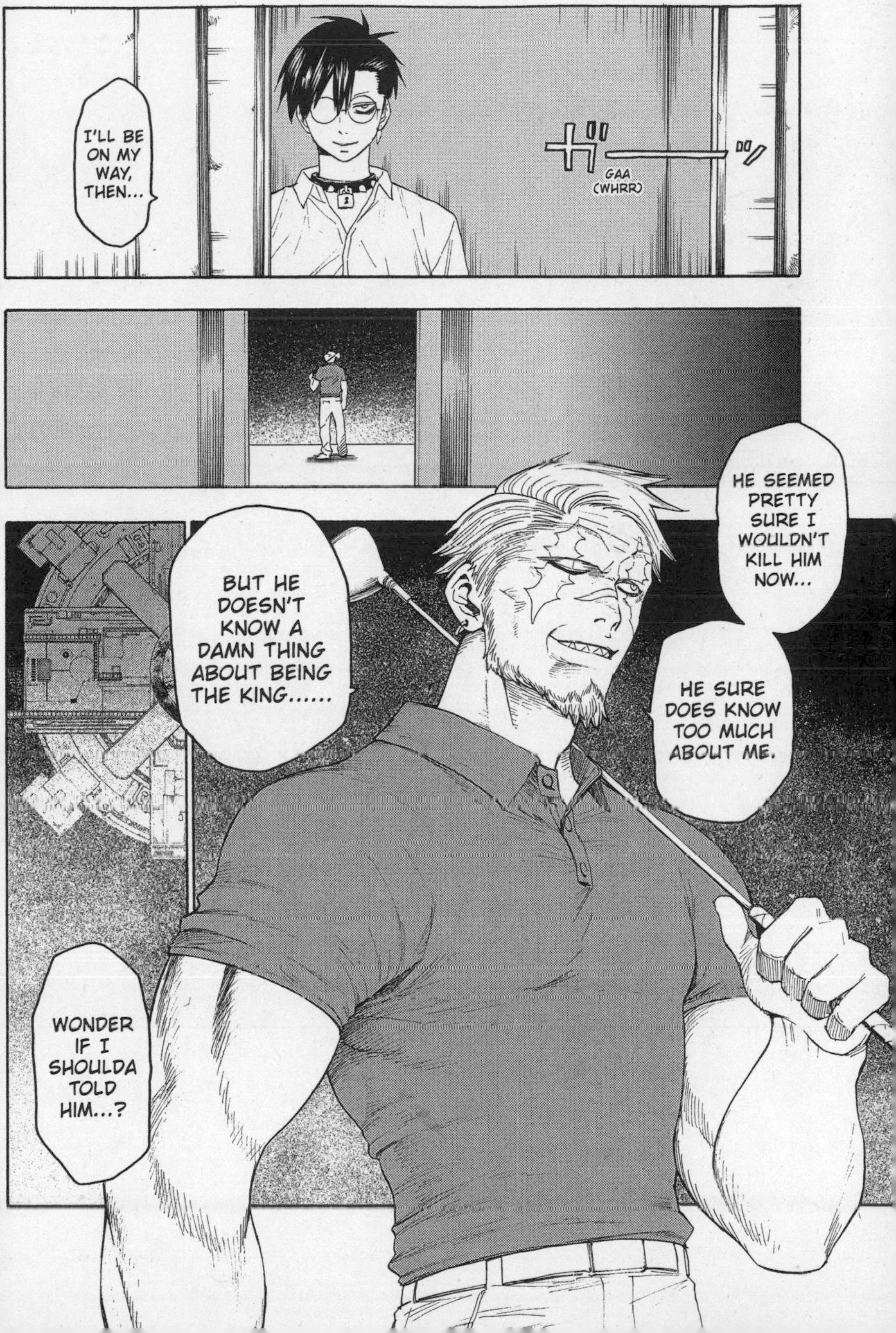
GAA (WHRR)
I'LL BE ON MY WAY, THEN...
HE SEEMED PRETTY SURE I WOULDN'T KILL HIM NOW...
HE SURE DOES KNOW TOO MUCH ABOUT ME.
BUT HE DOESN'T KNOW A DAMN THING ABOUT BEING THE KING......
WONDER IF I SHOULDA TOLD HIM...?

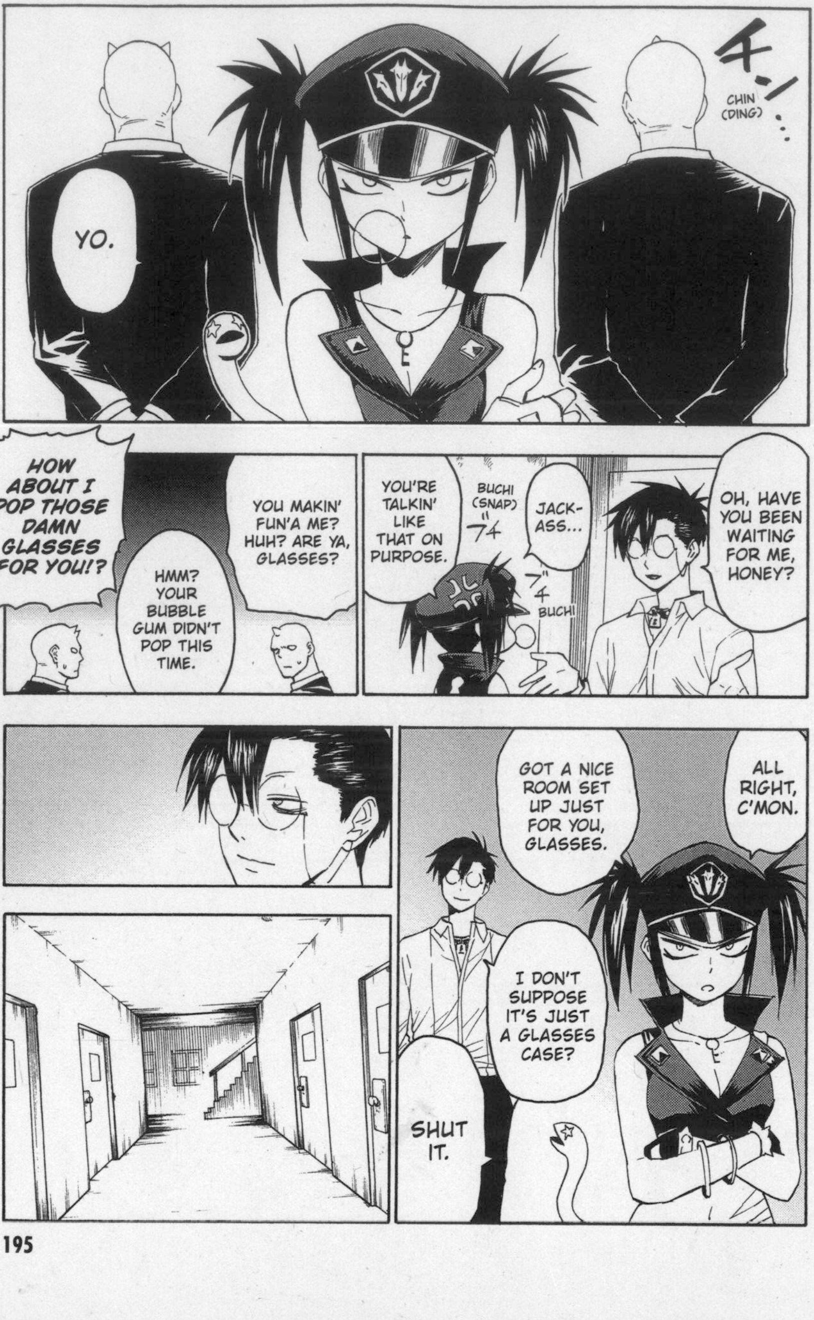

チン
CHIN (DING)...
YO.
OH, HAVE YOU BEEN WAITING FOR ME, HONEY?
JACK-ASS...
BUCHI (SNAP)
BUCHI
YOU'RE TALKIN' LIKE THAT ON PURPOSE.
YOU MAKIN' FUN'A ME? HUH? ARE YA, GLASSES?
HMM? YOUR BUBBLE GUM DIDN'T POP THIS TIME.
HOW ABOUT I POP THOSE DAMN GLASSES FOR YOU!?
ALL RIGHT, C'MON.
GOT A NICE ROOM SET UP JUST FOR YOU, GLASSES.
I DON'T SUPPOSE IT'S JUST A GLASSES CASE?
SHUT IT.

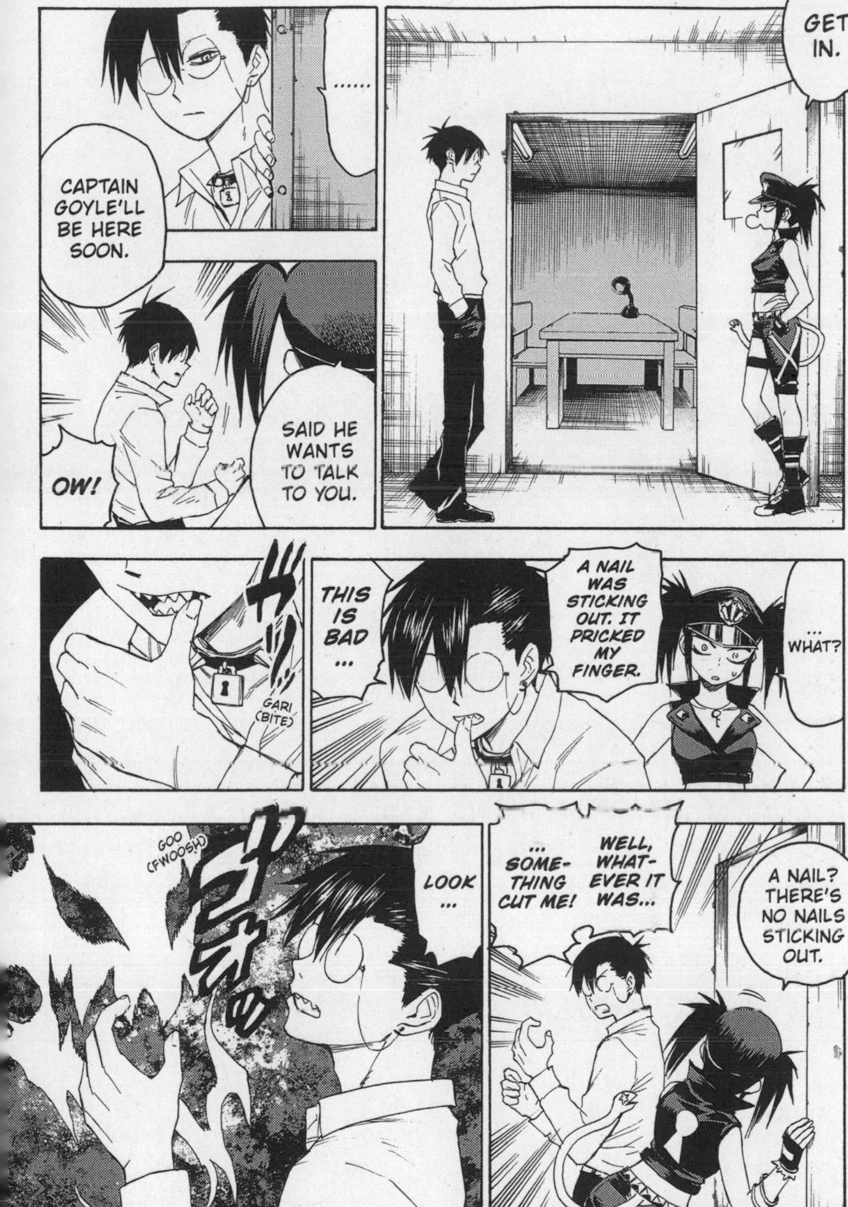
GET IN.
......
CAPTAIN GOYLE'LL BE HERE SOON.
SAID HE WANTS TO TALK TO YOU.
OW!
... WHAT?
A NAIL WAS STICKING OUT. IT PRICKED MY FINGER.
THIS IS BAD ...
GARI (BITE)
A NAIL? THERE'S NO NAILS STICKING OUT.
WELL, WHAT-EVER IT WAS...
... SOME-THING CUT ME!
LOOK ...
GOO (FWOOSH)

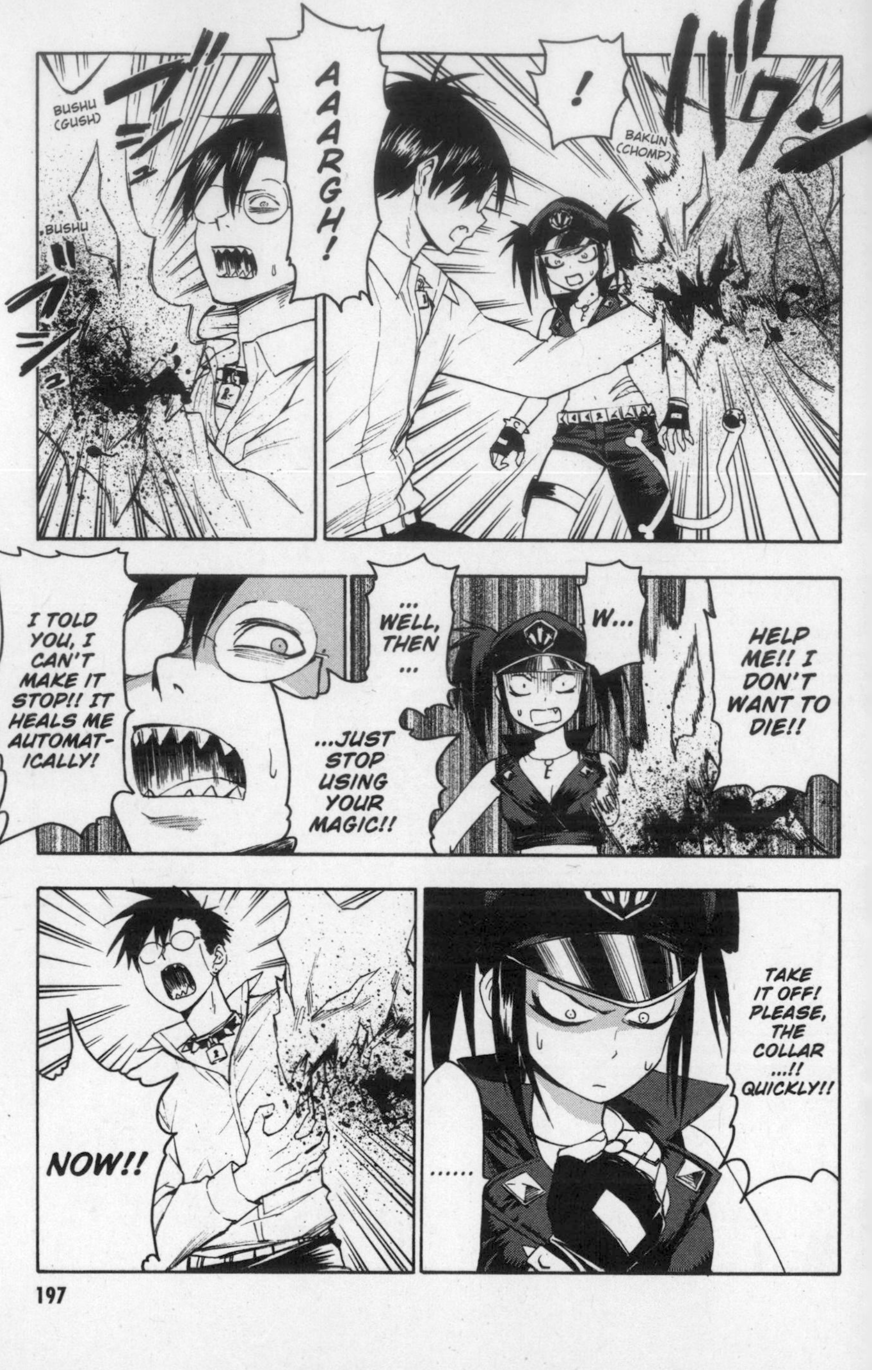

!
BAKUN (CHOMP)
AAAARGH!
BUSHU (GUSH)
BUSHU
HELP ME!! I DON'T WANT TO DIE!!
W...
... WELL, THEN ...
...JUST STOP USING YOUR MAGIC!!
I TOLD YOU, I CAN'T MAKE IT STOP!! IT HEALS ME AUTOMATICALLY!
TAKE IT OFF! PLEASE, THE COLLAR ...!! QUICKLY!!
......
NOW!!

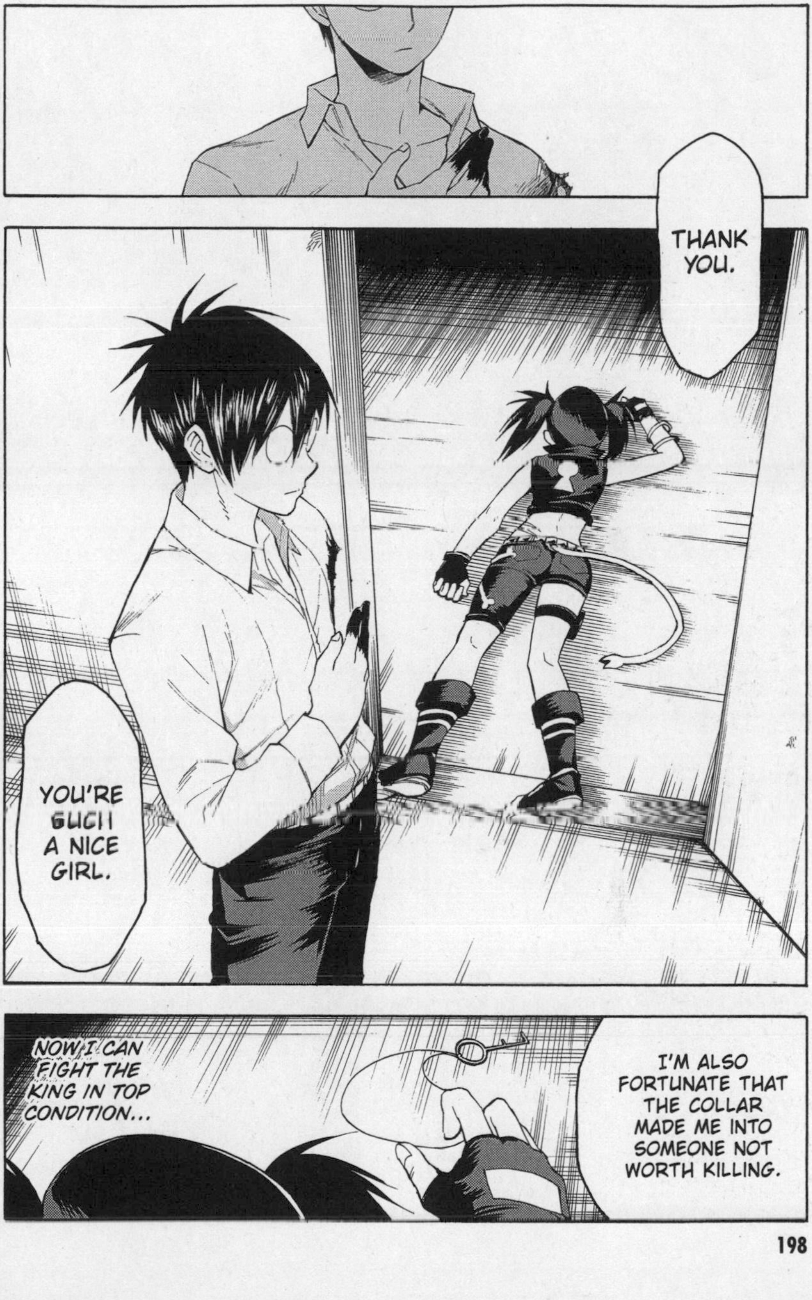
THANK YOU.
YOU'RE SUCH A NICE GIRL.
I'M ALSO FORTUNATE THAT THE COLLAR MADE ME INTO SOMEONE NOT WORTH KILLING.
NOW I CAN FIGHT THE KING IN TOP CONDITION...

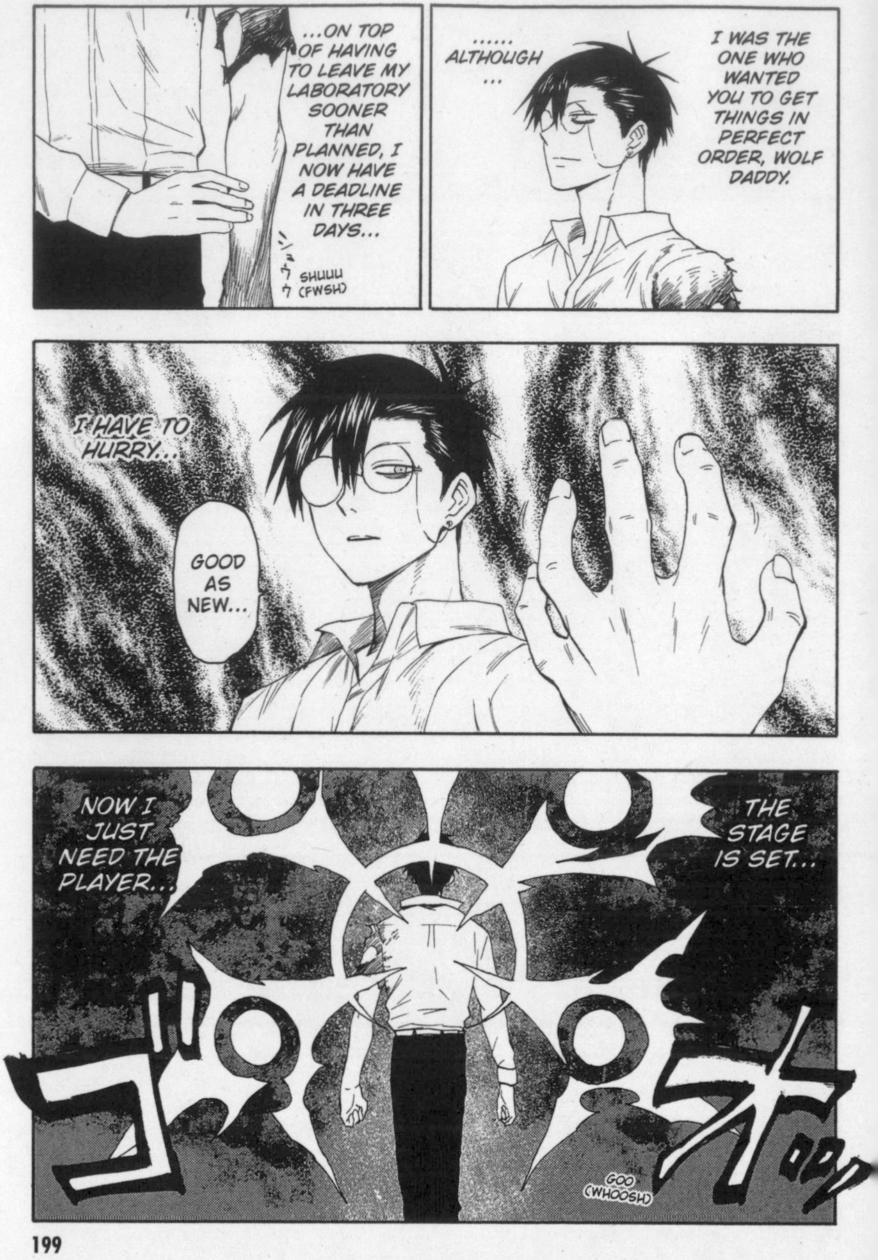
I WAS THE ONE WHO WANTED YOU TO GET THINGS IN PERFECT ORDER, WOLF DADDY.
...... ALTHOUGH ...
...ON TOP OF HAVING TO LEAVE MY LABORATORY SOONER THAN PLANNED, I NOW HAVE A DEADLINE IN THREE DAYS...
シュウウ
SHUUU (FWSH)
GOOD AS NEW...
I HAVE TO HURRY...
THE STAGE IS SET...
NOW I JUST NEED THE PLAYER...
GOO (WHOOSH)

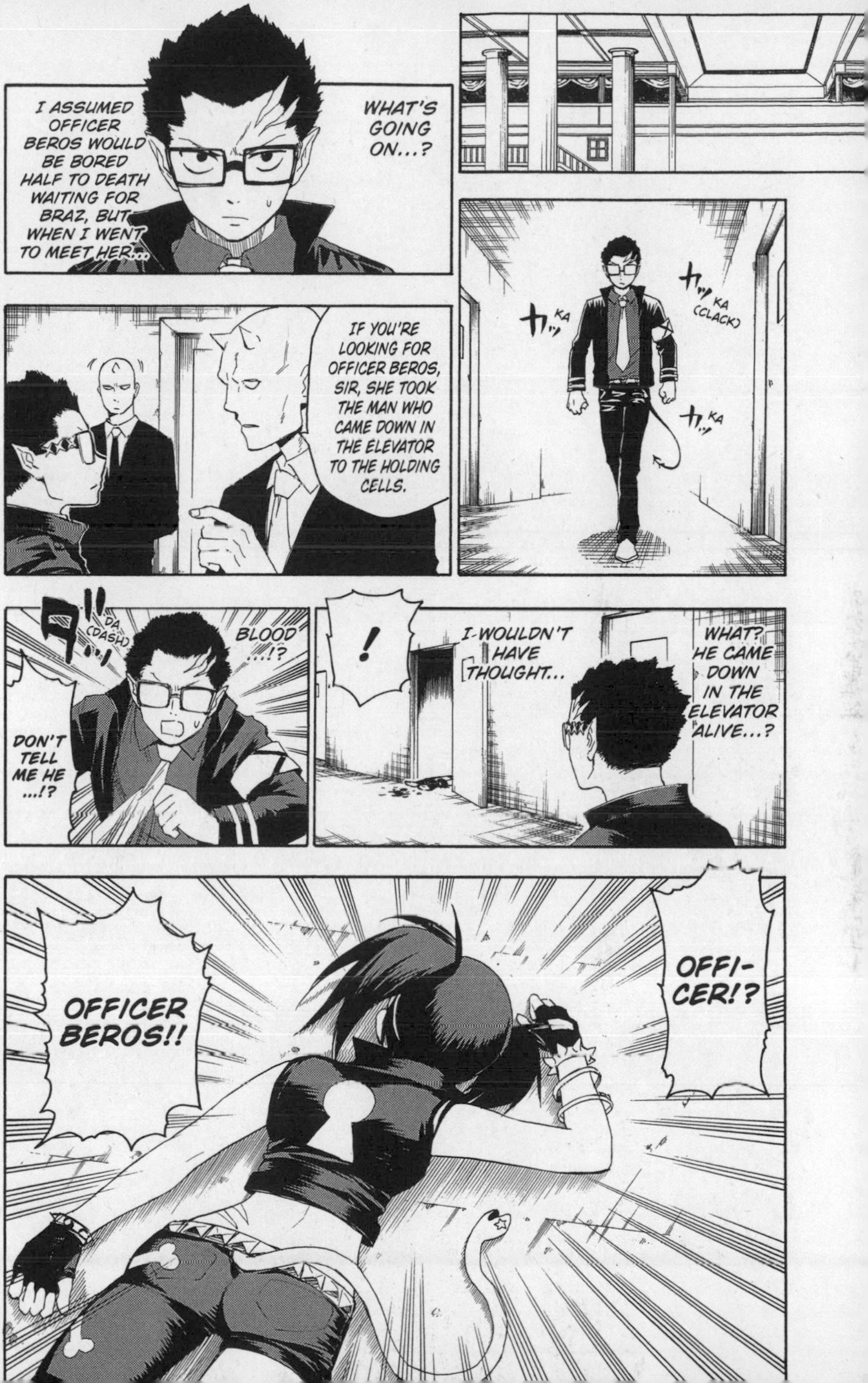
WHAT'S GOING ON...?
I ASSUMED OFFICER BEROS WOULD BE BORED HALF TO DEATH WAITING FOR BRAZ, BUT WHEN I WENT TO MEET HER...
KA (CLACK)
KA
KA
IF YOU'RE LOOKING FOR OFFICER BEROS, SIR, SHE TOOK THE MAN WHO CAME DOWN IN THE ELEVATOR TO THE HOLDING CELLS.
WHAT? HE CAME DOWN IN THE ELEVATOR ALIVE...?
I-WOULDN'T HAVE THOUGHT...
!
BLOOD ...!?
DA (DASH)
DON'T TELL ME HE ...!?
OFFI- CER!?
OFFICER BEROS!!

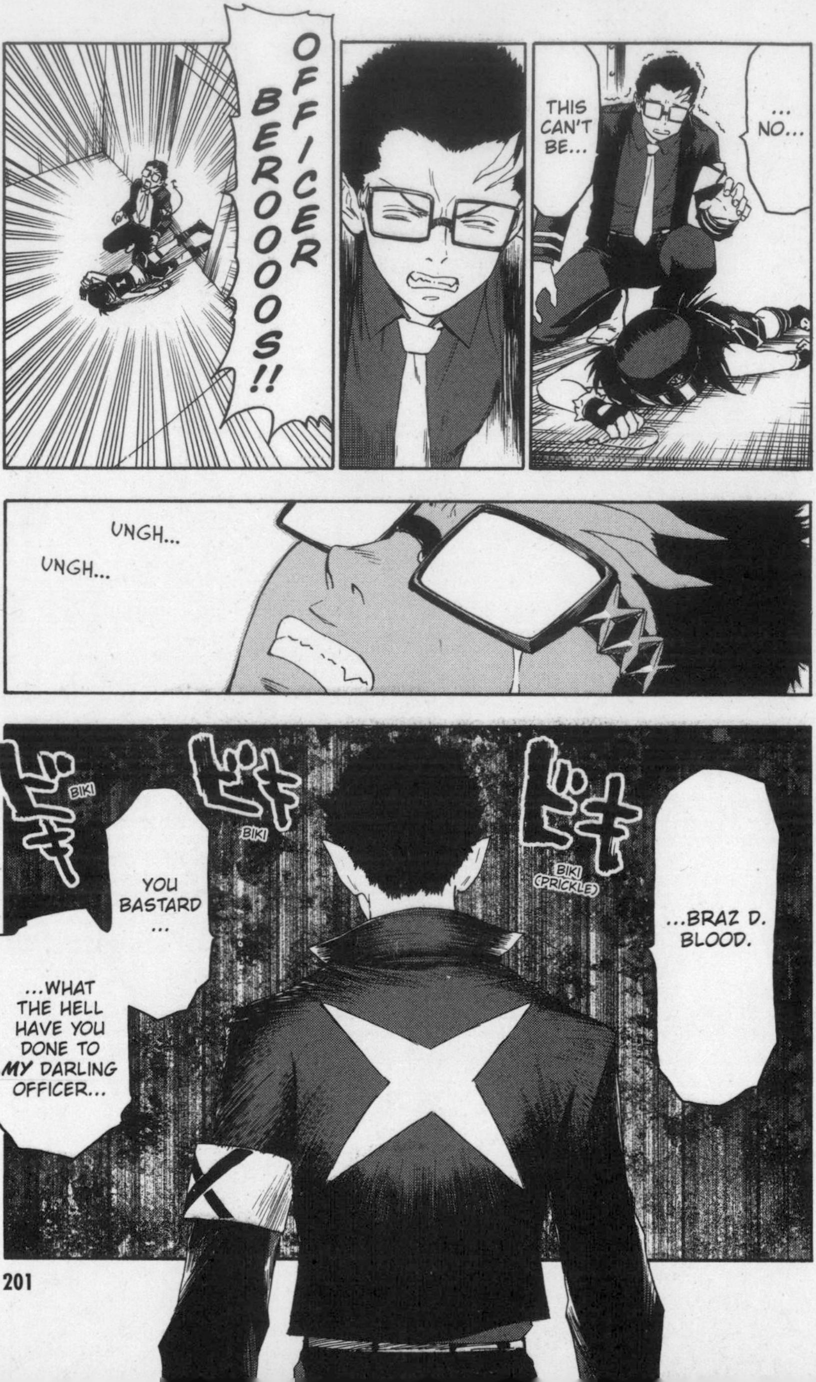
...NO...
THIS CAN'T BE...
OFFICER BEROOOOOS!!
UNGH...
UNGH...
...BRAZ D. BLOOD.
ビキ
BIKI (PRICKLE)
ビキ
BIKI
ビキ
BIKI
YOU BASTARD ...
...WHAT THE HELL HAVE YOU DONE TO *MY* DARLING OFFICER...

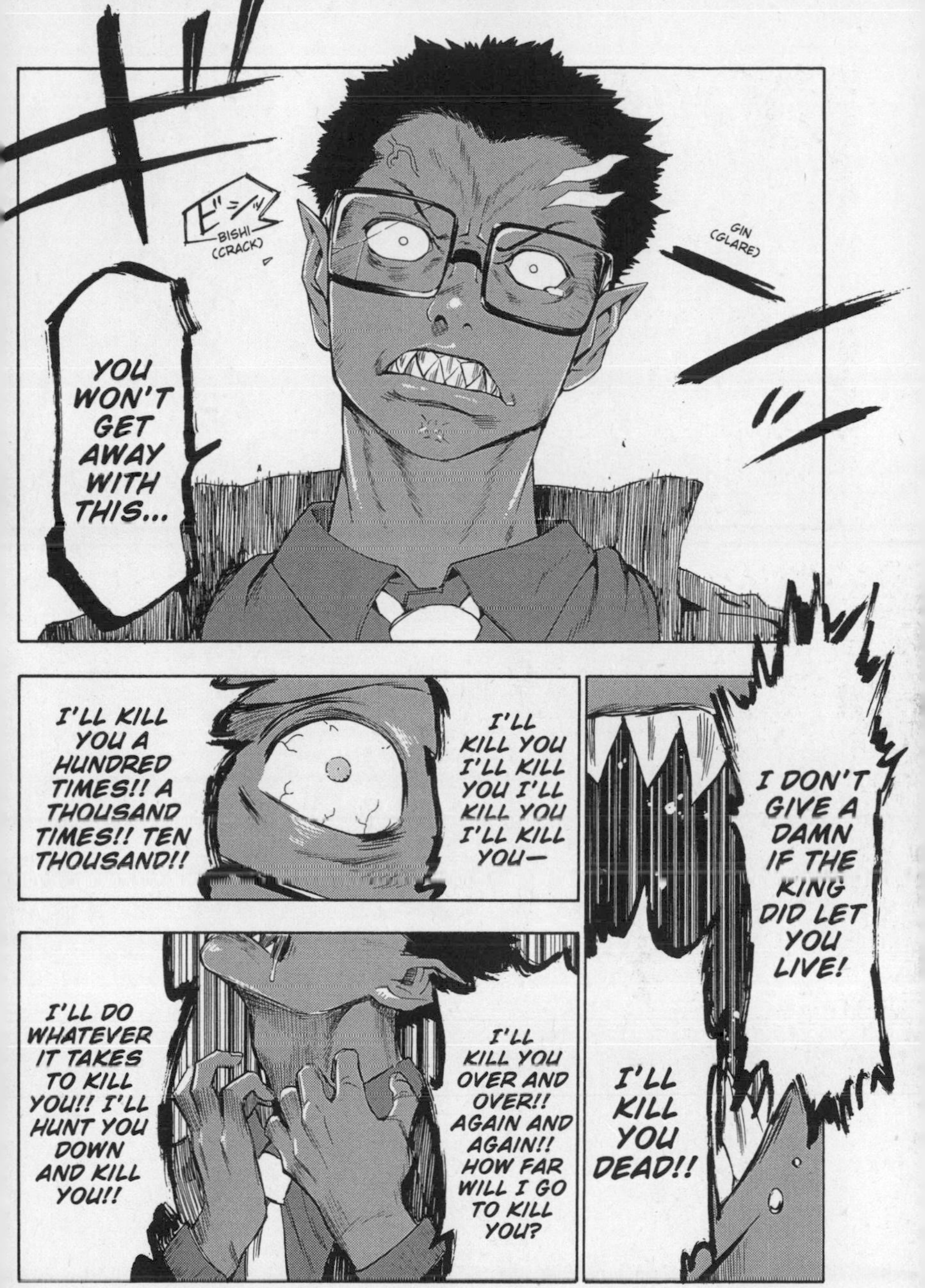
GIN (GLARE)
BISHI (CRACK)
YOU WON'T GET AWAY WITH THIS...
I DON'T GIVE A DAMN IF THE KING DID LET YOU LIVE!
I'LL KILL YOU DEAD!!
I'LL KILL YOU I'LL KILL YOU I'LL KILL YOU I'LL KILL YOU—
I'LL KILL YOU A HUNDRED TIMES!! A THOUSAND TIMES!! TEN THOUSAND!!
I'LL KILL YOU OVER AND OVER!! AGAIN AND AGAIN!! HOW FAR WILL I GO TO KILL YOU?
I'LL DO WHATEVER IT TAKES TO KILL YOU!! I'LL HUNT YOU DOWN AND KILL YOU!!

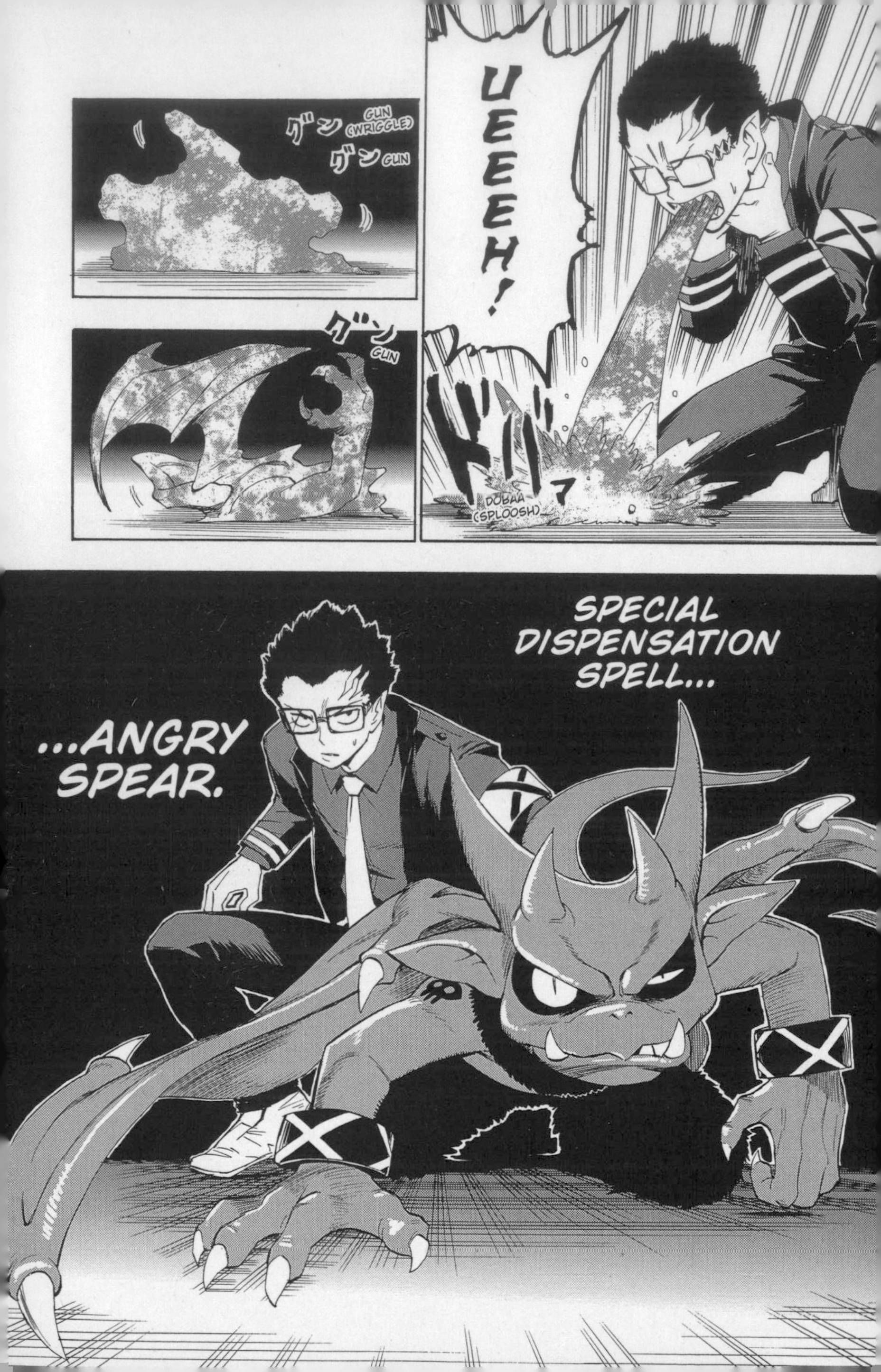
UEEEH!
ドバァ
DOBAA (SPLOOSH)
グン GUN (WRIGGLE)
グン GUN
グン GUN
SPECIAL DISPENSATION SPELL...
...ANGRY SPEAR.

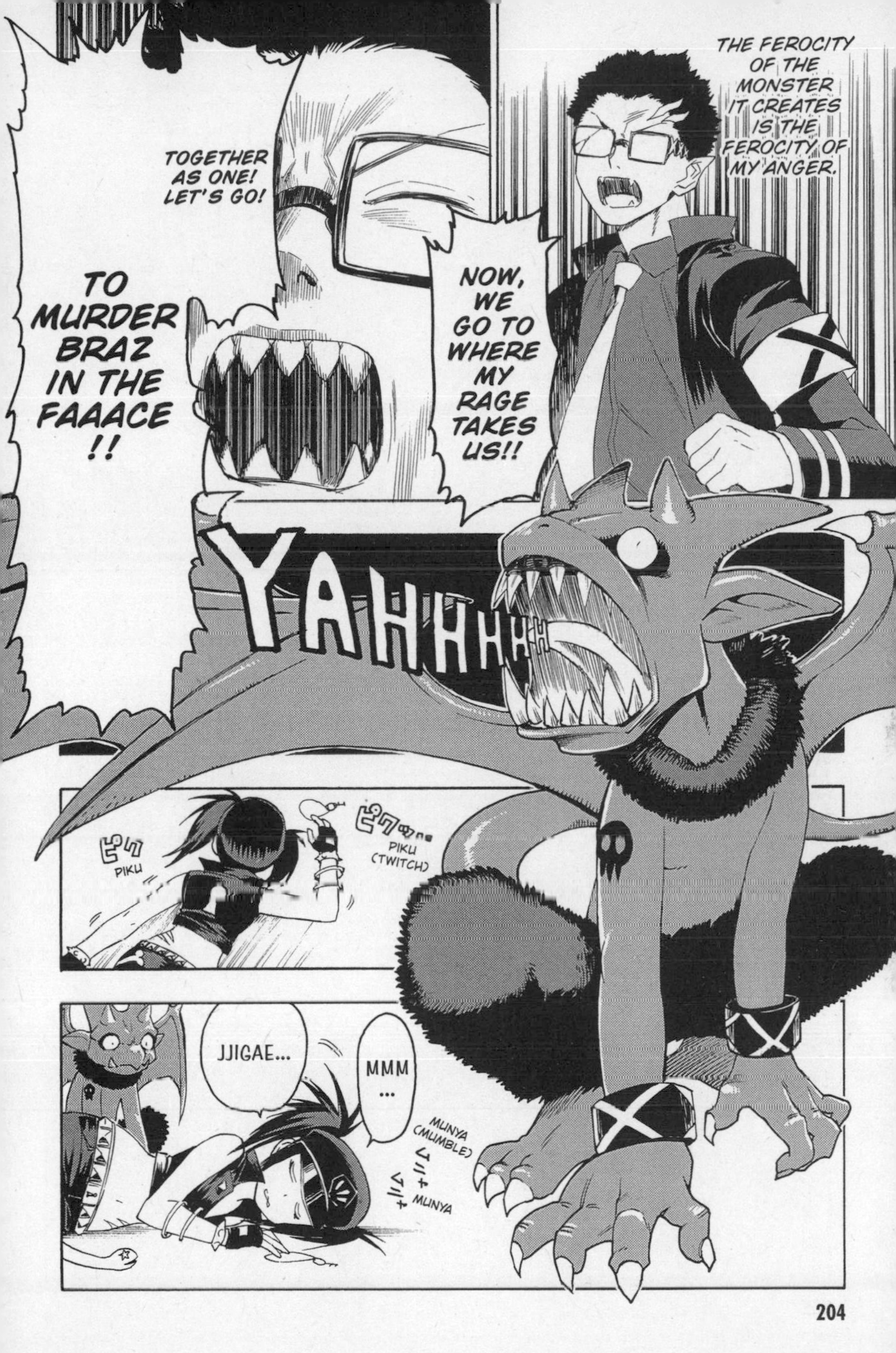
THE FEROCITY OF THE MONSTER IT CREATES IS THE FEROCITY OF MY ANGER.
NOW, WE GO TO WHERE MY RAGE TAKES US!!
TOGETHER AS ONE! LET'S GO!
TO MURDER BRAZ IN THE FAAACE!!
YAHHHHHH
PIKU (TWITCH)
PIKU
MMM...
JJIGAE...
MUNYA (MUMBLE)
MUNYA

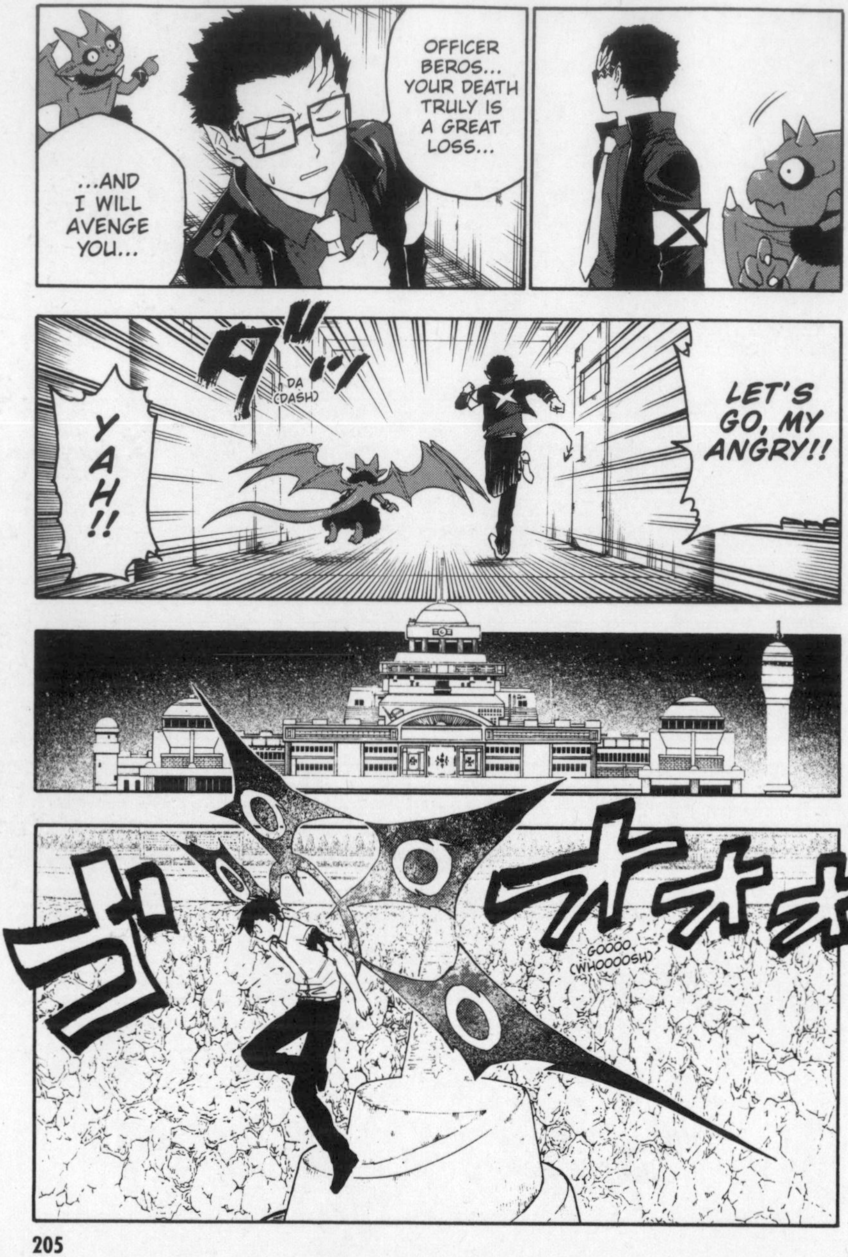
OFFICER BEROS... YOUR DEATH TRULY IS A GREAT LOSS...
...AND I WILL AVENGE YOU...
LET'S GO, MY ANGRY!!
ダッ
DA (DASH)
YAH!!
ゴオオオ
GOOOO, (WHOOOOSH)

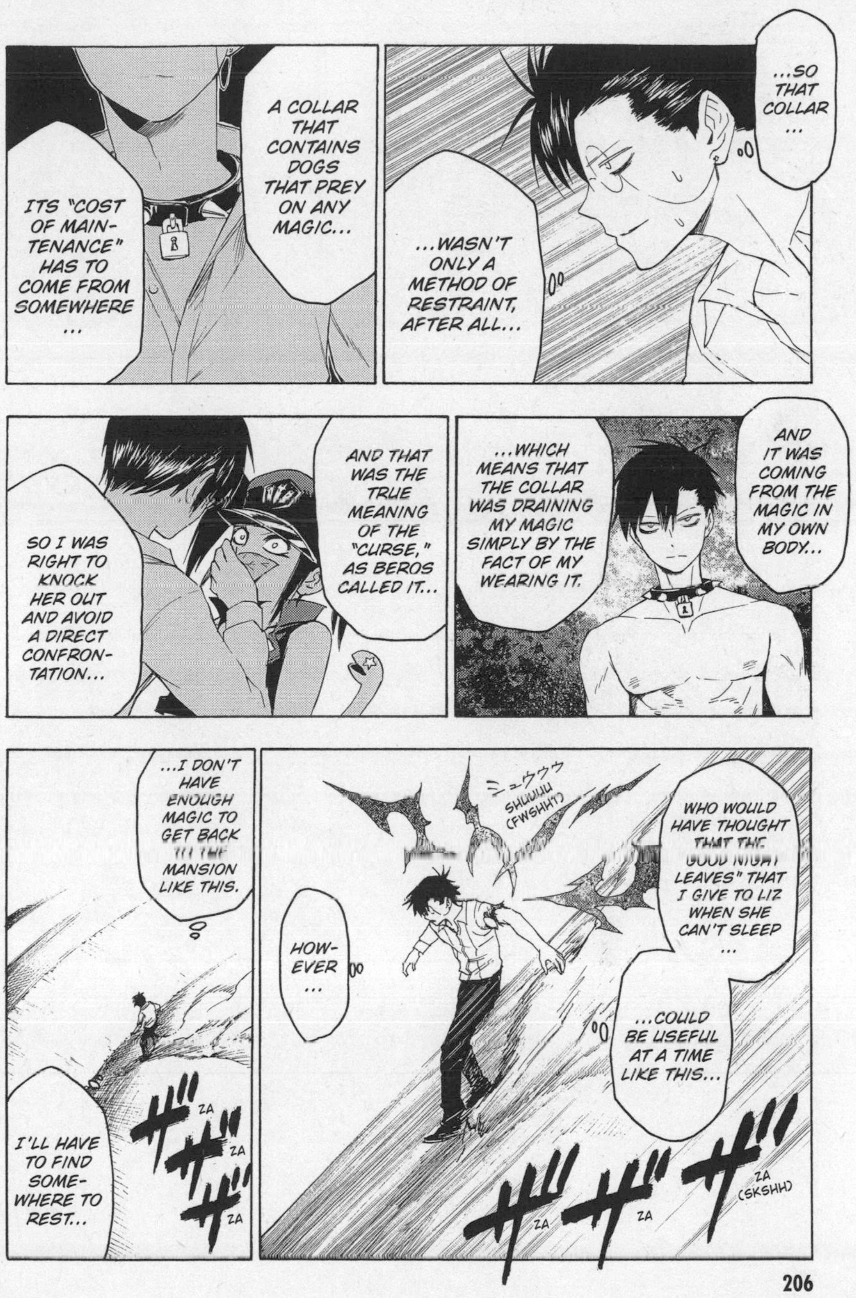
...SO THAT COLLAR ...
...WASN'T ONLY A METHOD OF RESTRAINT, AFTER ALL...
A COLLAR THAT CONTAINS DOGS THAT PREY ON ANY MAGIC...
ITS "COST OF MAIN-TENANCE" HAS TO COME FROM SOMEWHERE ...
AND IT WAS COMING FROM THE MAGIC IN MY OWN BODY...
...WHICH MEANS THAT THE COLLAR WAS DRAINING MY MAGIC SIMPLY BY THE FACT OF MY WEARING IT.
AND THAT WAS THE TRUE MEANING OF THE "CURSE," AS BEROS CALLED IT...
SO I WAS RIGHT TO KNOCK HER OUT AND AVOID A DIRECT CONFRON-TATION...
シュウウウ SHUUUU (FWSHHH)
WHO WOULD HAVE THOUGHT THAT THE GOOD NIGHT LEAVES" THAT I GIVE TO LIZ WHEN SHE CAN'T SLEEP ...
HOW-EVER ...
...COULD BE USEFUL AT A TIME LIKE THIS...
ザ ZA (SKSHH)
ザ ZA
ザ ZA
...I DON'T HAVE ENOUGH MAGIC TO GET BACK TO THE MANSION LIKE THIS.
I'LL HAVE TO FIND SOME-WHERE TO REST...
ザ ZA
ザ ZA
ザ ZA

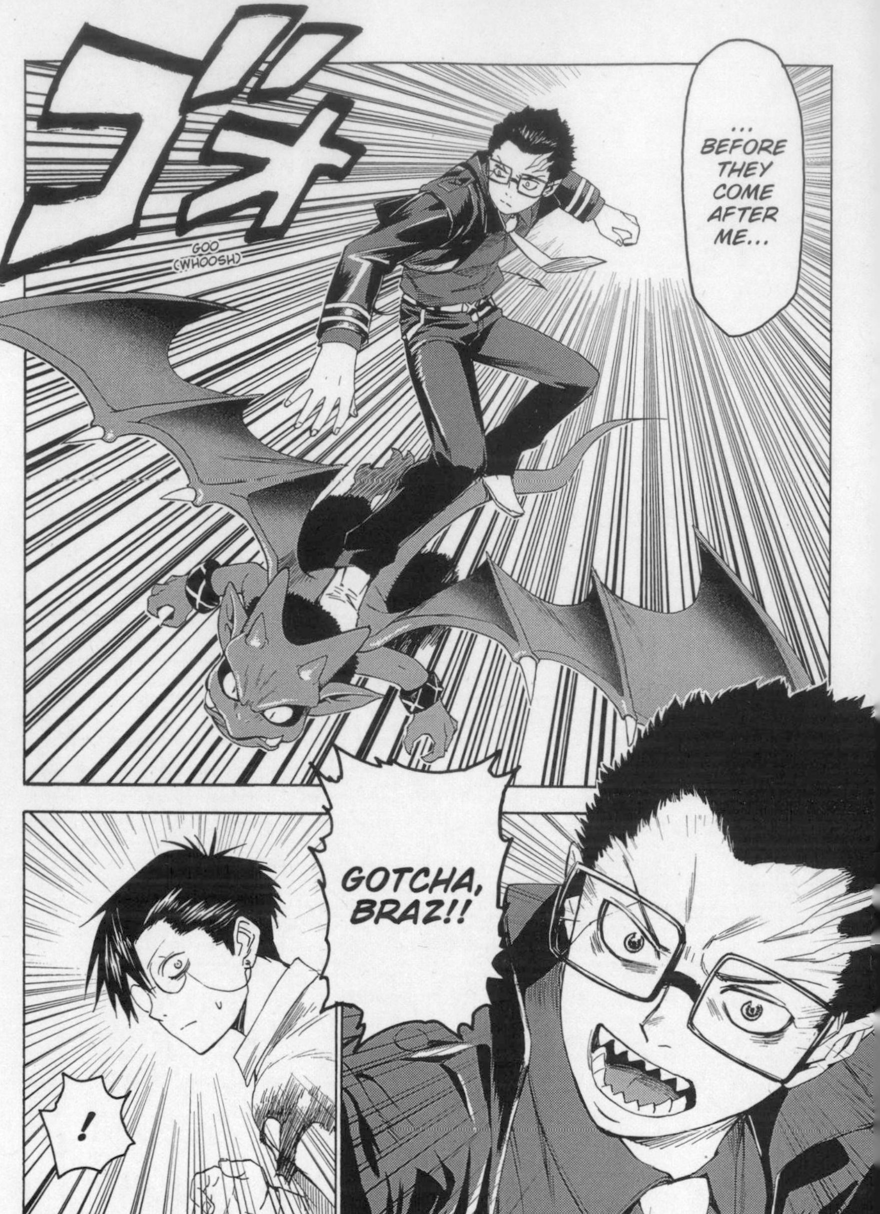
...BEFORE THEY COME AFTER ME...
GOO (WHOOSH)
GOTCHA, BRAZ!!
!

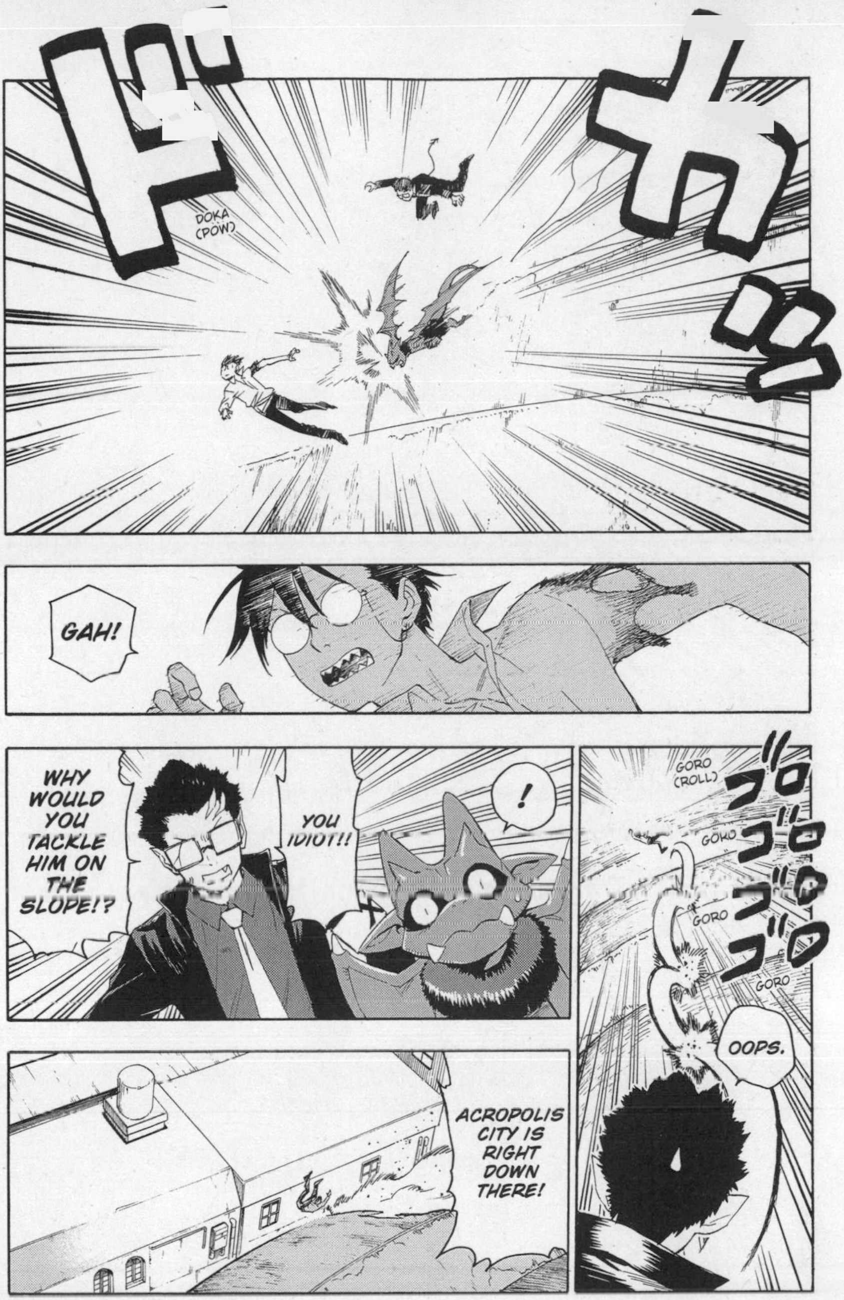
DOKA (POW)
GAH!
GORO (ROLL)
GORO
GORO
GORO
OOPS.
!
YOU IDIOT!!
WHY WOULD YOU TACKLE HIM ON THE SLOPE!?
ACROPOLIS CITY IS RIGHT DOWN THERE!

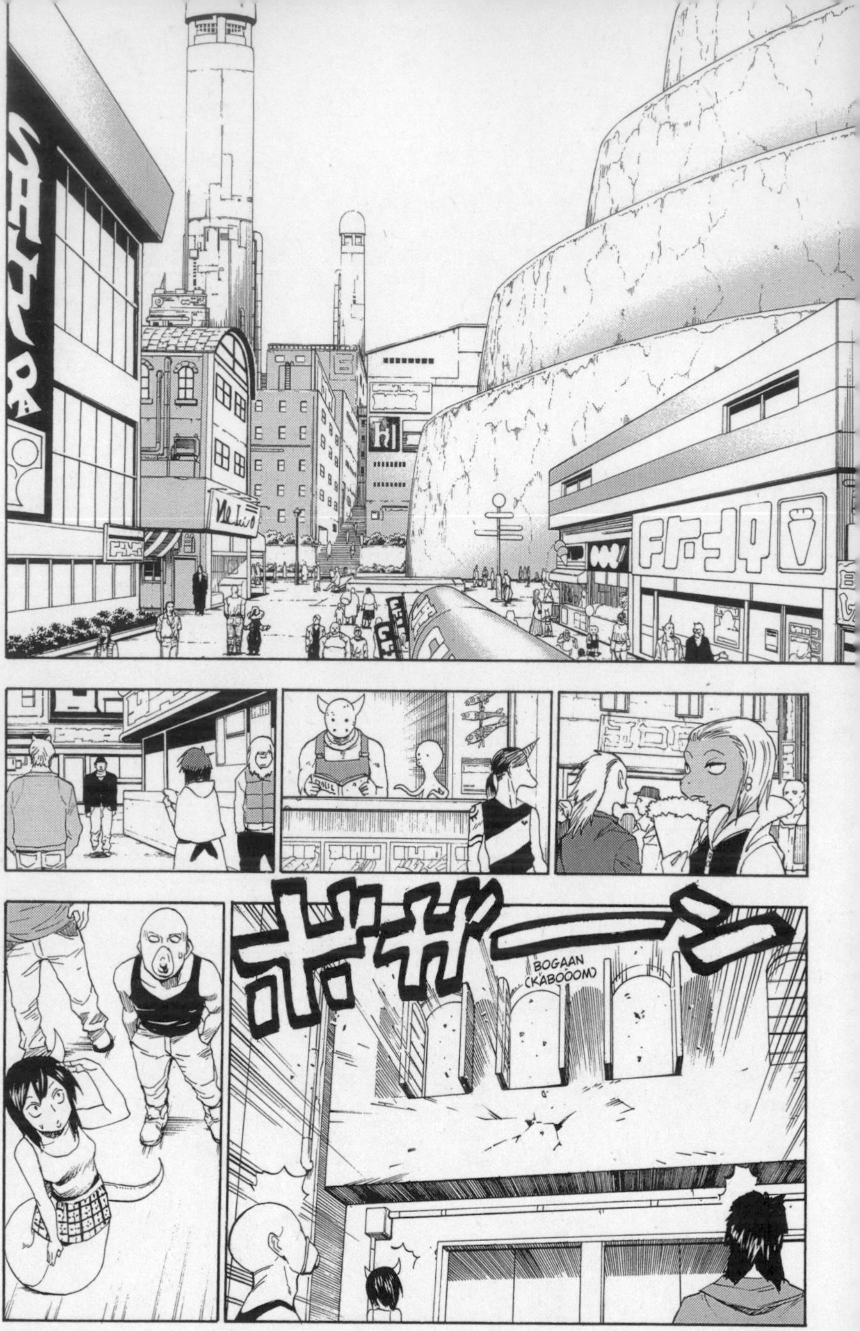
ボガーン
BOGAAN
(KABOOOM)

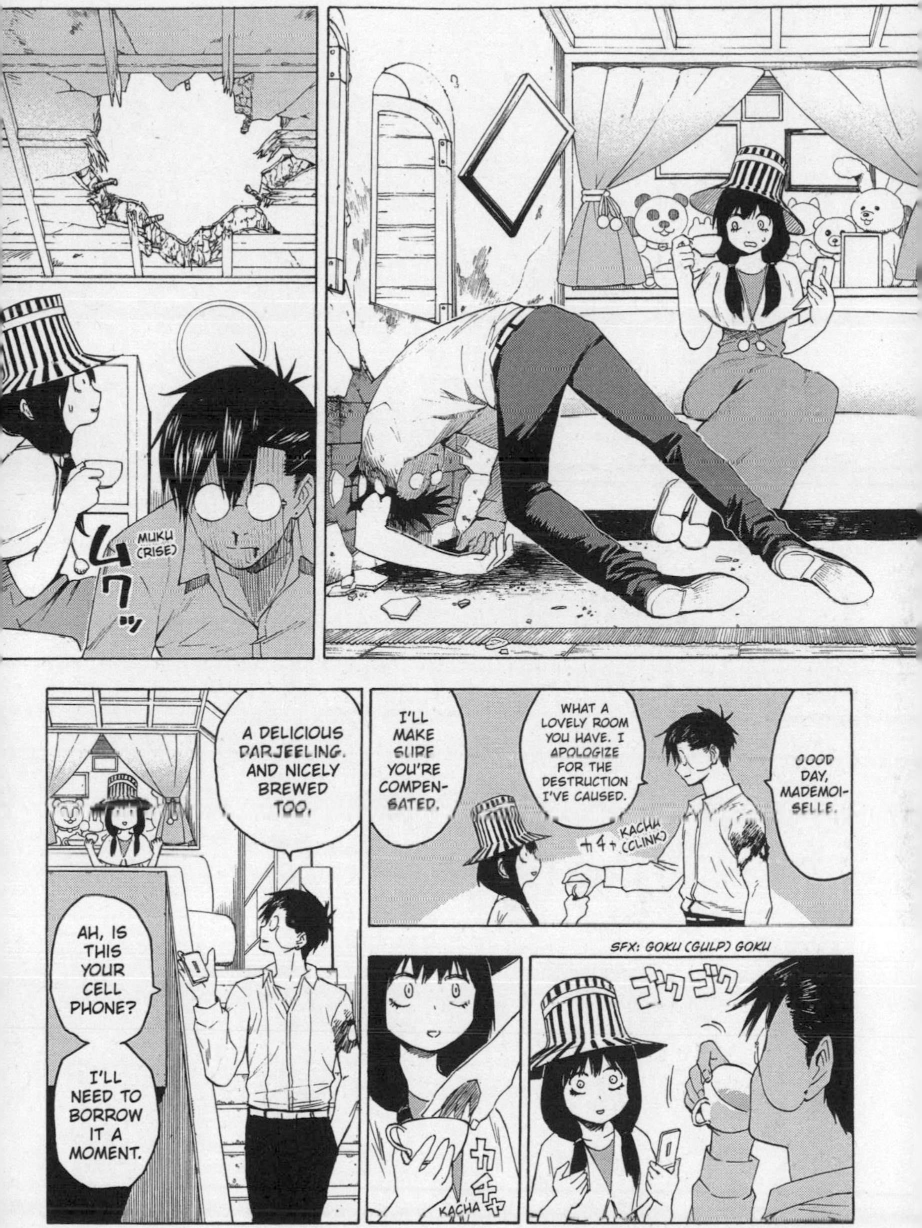
ムクッ
MUKU (RISE)
GOOD DAY, MADEMOISELLE.
WHAT A LOVELY ROOM YOU HAVE. I APOLOGIZE FOR THE DESTRUCTION I'VE CAUSED.
カチャ
KACHA (CLINK)
I'LL MAKE SURE YOU'RE COMPENSATED.
SFX: GOKU (GULP) GOKU
ゴクゴク
カチャ
KACHA
A DELICIOUS DARJEELING. AND NICELY BREWED TOO.
AH, IS THIS YOUR CELL PHONE?
I'LL NEED TO BORROW IT A MOMENT.

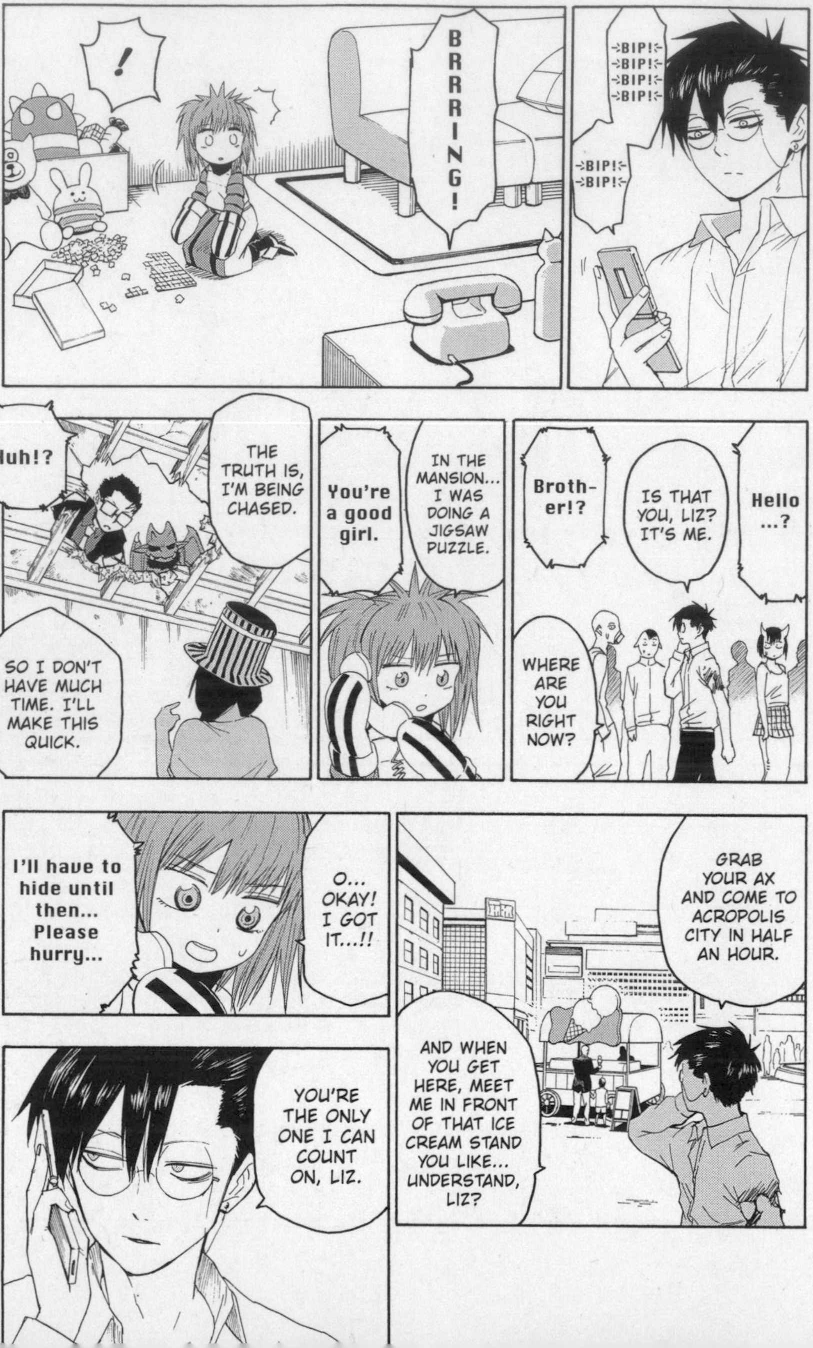

BIP! BIP! BIP! BIP!
BIP! BIP!
BRRRING!
!
Hello...?
IS THAT YOU, LIZ? IT'S ME.
Broth-er!?
WHERE ARE YOU RIGHT NOW?
IN THE MANSION... I WAS DOING A JIGSAW PUZZLE.
You're a good girl.
THE TRUTH IS, I'M BEING CHASED.
Huh!?
SO I DON'T HAVE MUCH TIME. I'LL MAKE THIS QUICK.
GRAB YOUR AX AND COME TO ACROPOLIS CITY IN HALF AN HOUR.
AND WHEN YOU GET HERE, MEET ME IN FRONT OF THAT ICE CREAM STAND YOU LIKE... UNDERSTAND, LIZ?
O... OKAY! I GOT IT...!!
I'll have to hide until then... Please hurry...
YOU'RE THE ONLY ONE I CAN COUNT ON, LIZ.

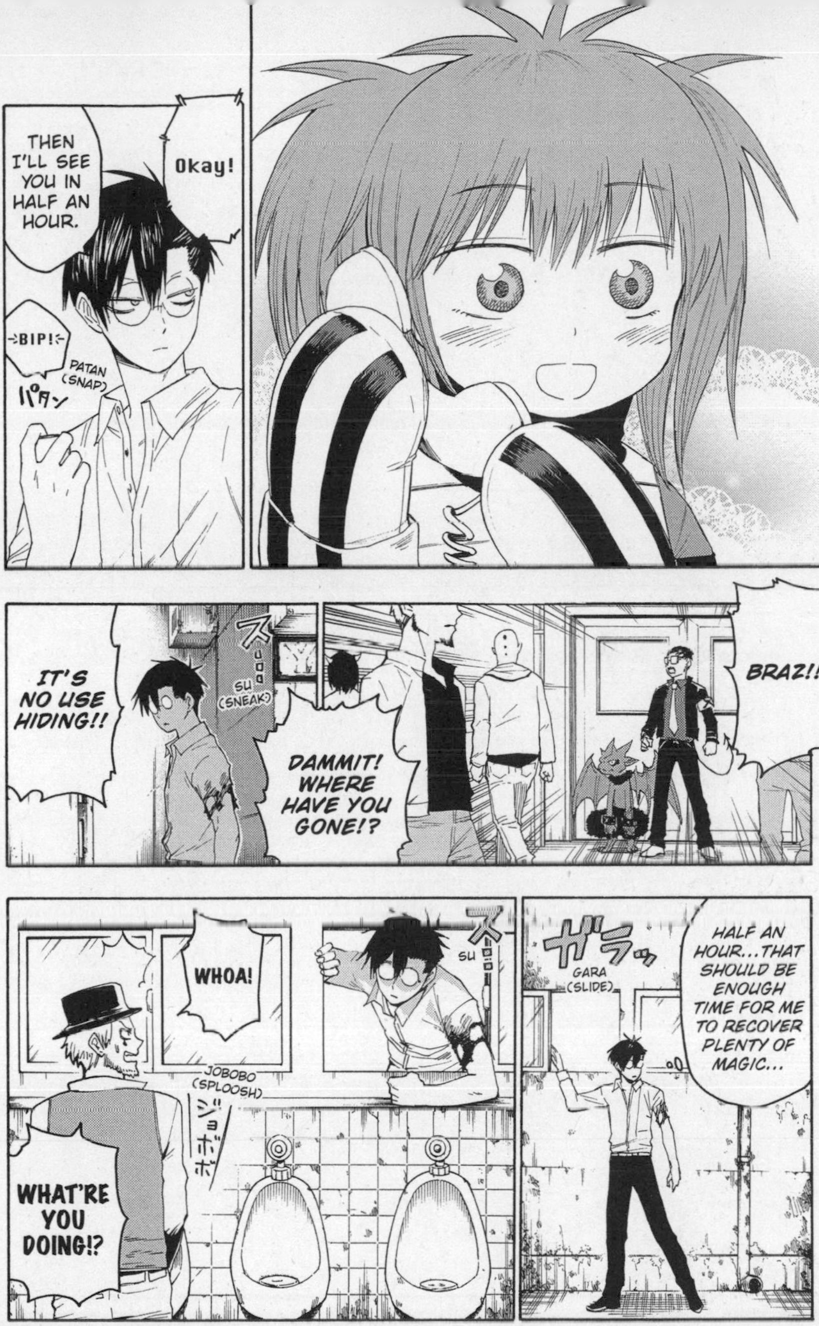
Okay!
THEN I'LL SEE YOU IN HALF AN HOUR.
BIP!
PATAN (SNAP)
パタン
BRAZ!!
DAMMIT! WHERE HAVE YOU GONE!?
ス
SU (SNEAK)
IT'S NO USE HIDING!!
HALF AN HOUR...THAT SHOULD BE ENOUGH TIME FOR ME TO RECOVER PLENTY OF MAGIC...
ガラッ
GARA (SLIDE)
ス
SU
JOBOBO (SPLOOSH)
ジョボボ
WHOA!
WHAT'RE YOU DOING!?

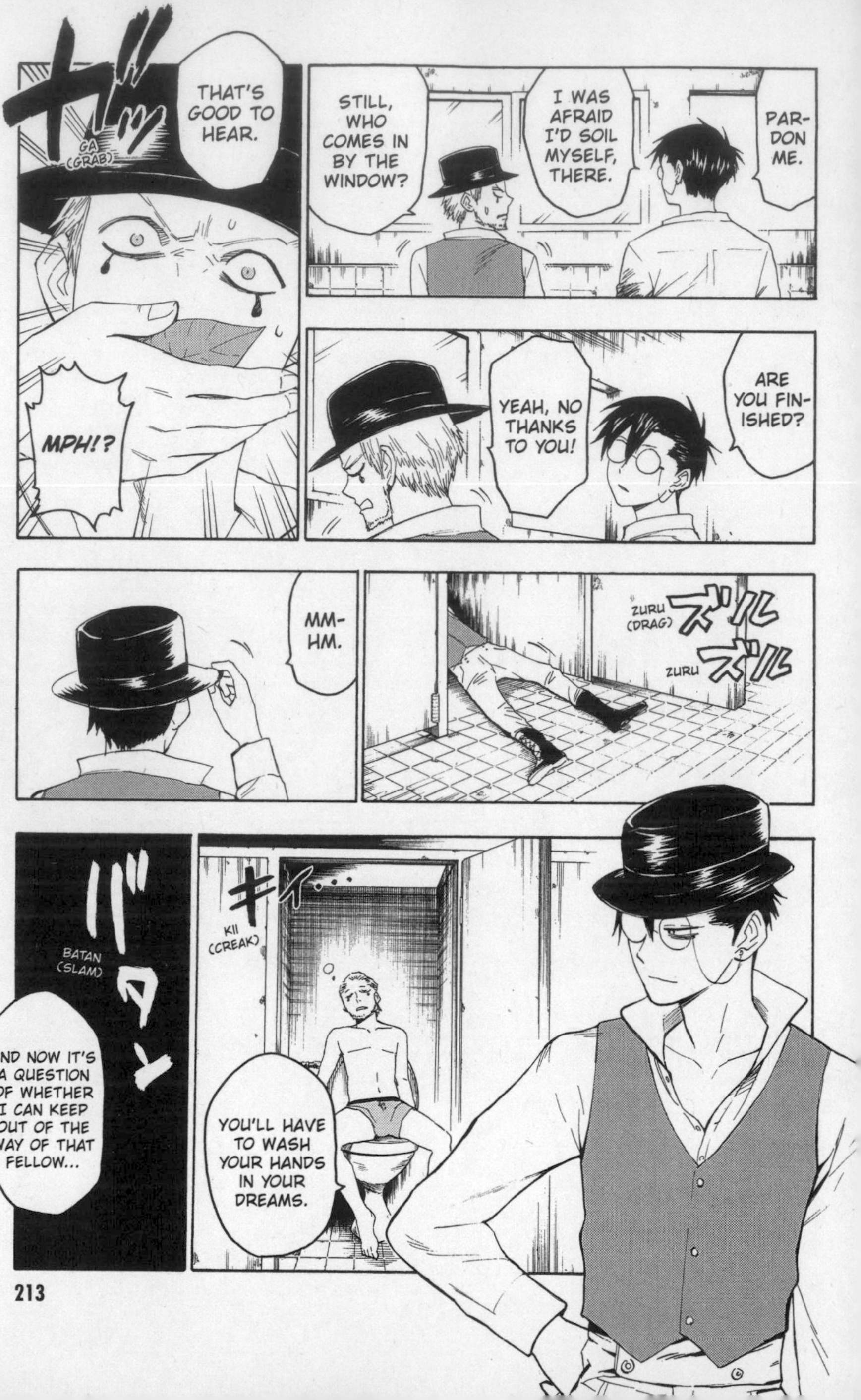
PARDON ME.
I WAS AFRAID I'D SOIL MYSELF, THERE.
STILL, WHO COMES IN BY THE WINDOW?
ARE YOU FINISHED?
YEAH, NO THANKS TO YOU!
THAT'S GOOD TO HEAR.
GA (GRAB)
MPH!?
ZURU (DRAG)
ZURU
MM-HM.
KII (CREAK)
YOU'LL HAVE TO WASH YOUR HANDS IN YOUR DREAMS.
BATAN (SLAM)
AND NOW IT'S A QUESTION OF WHETHER I CAN KEEP OUT OF THE WAY OF THAT FELLOW...

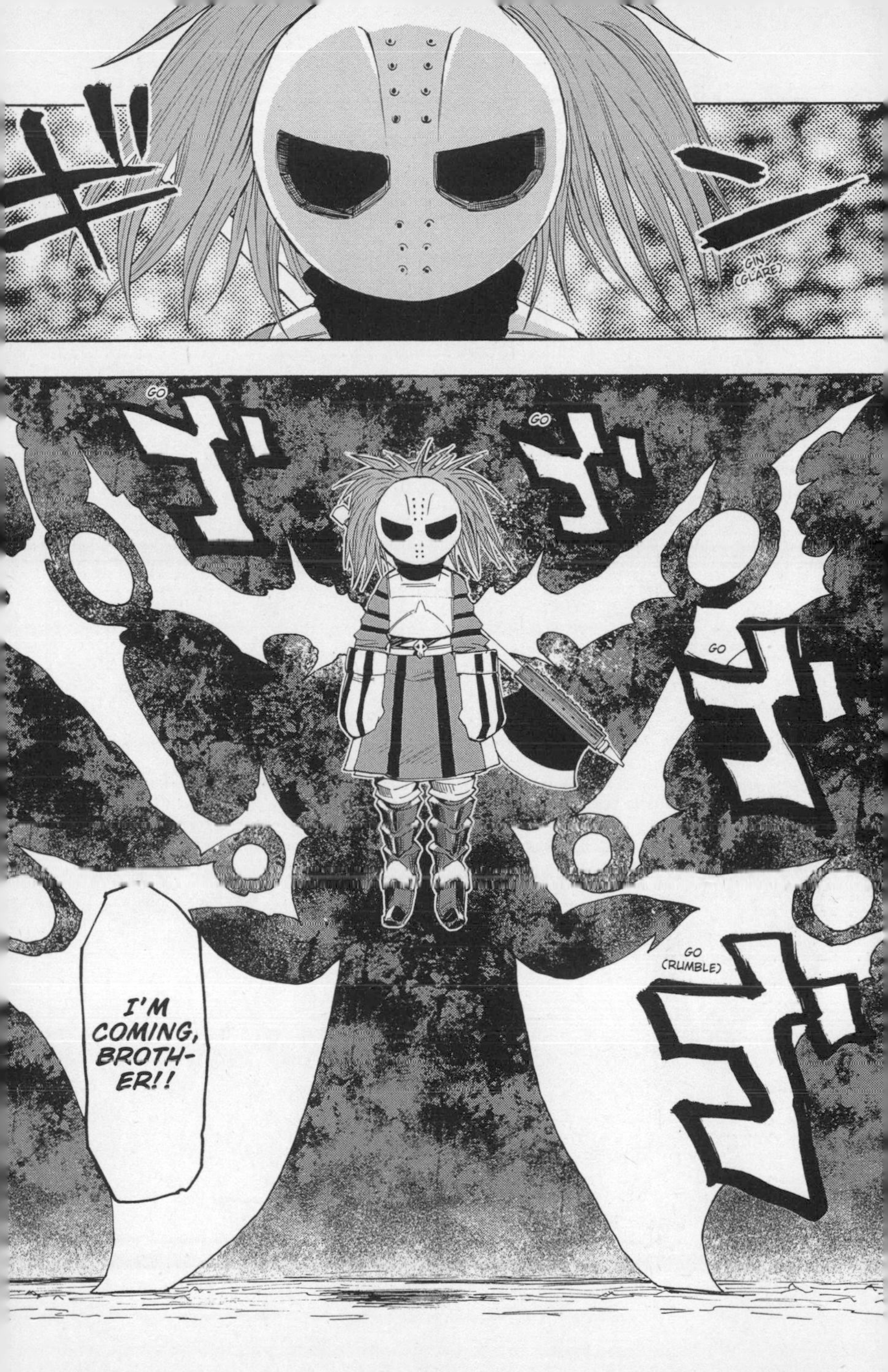
GIN (GLARE)
GO
GO
GO
GO (RUMBLE)
I'M COMING, BROTHER!!

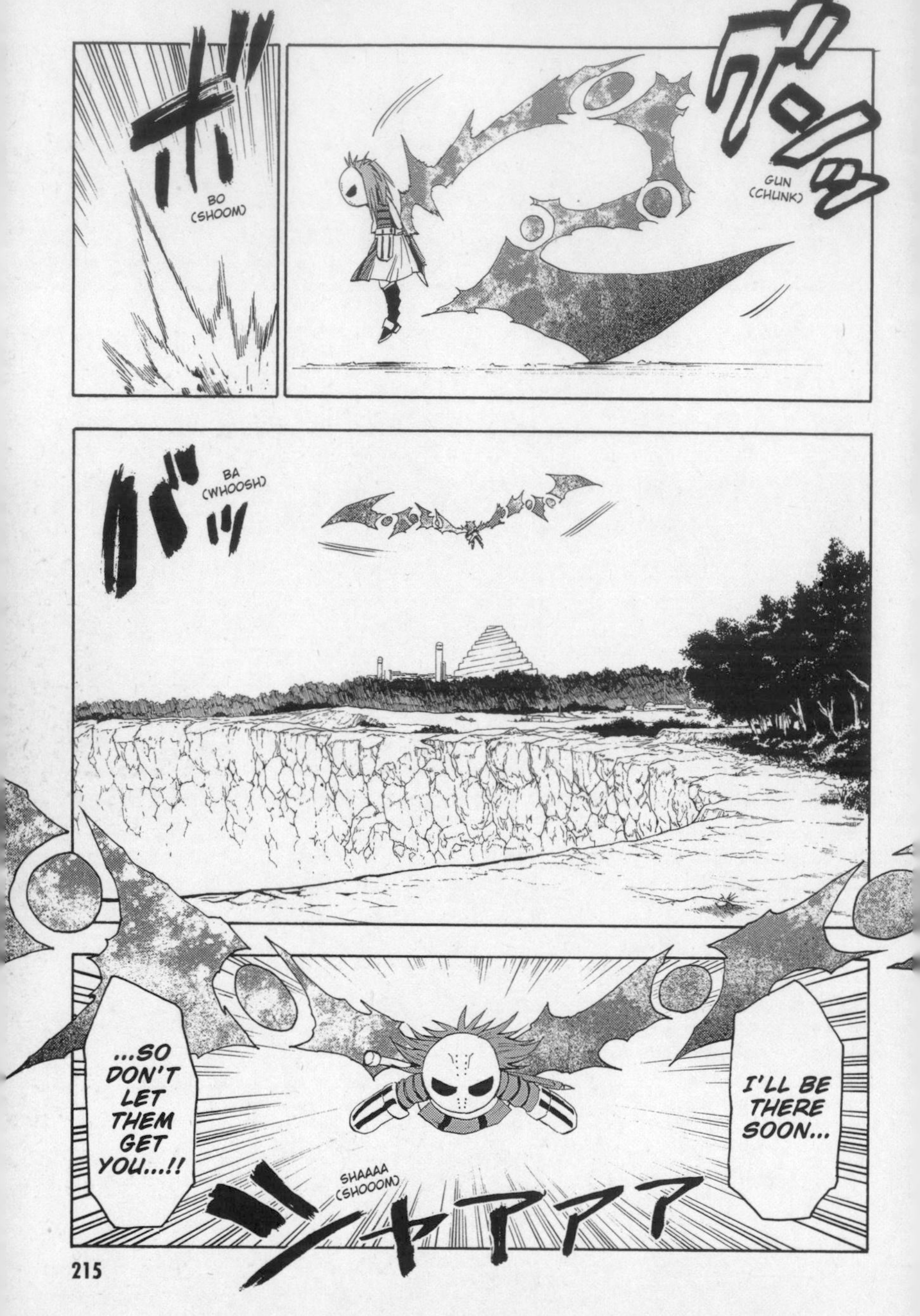
GUN (CHUNK)
BO (SHOOM)
BA (WHOOSH)
I'LL BE THERE SOON...
...SO DON'T LET THEM GET YOU...!!
SHAAA (SHOOOM)

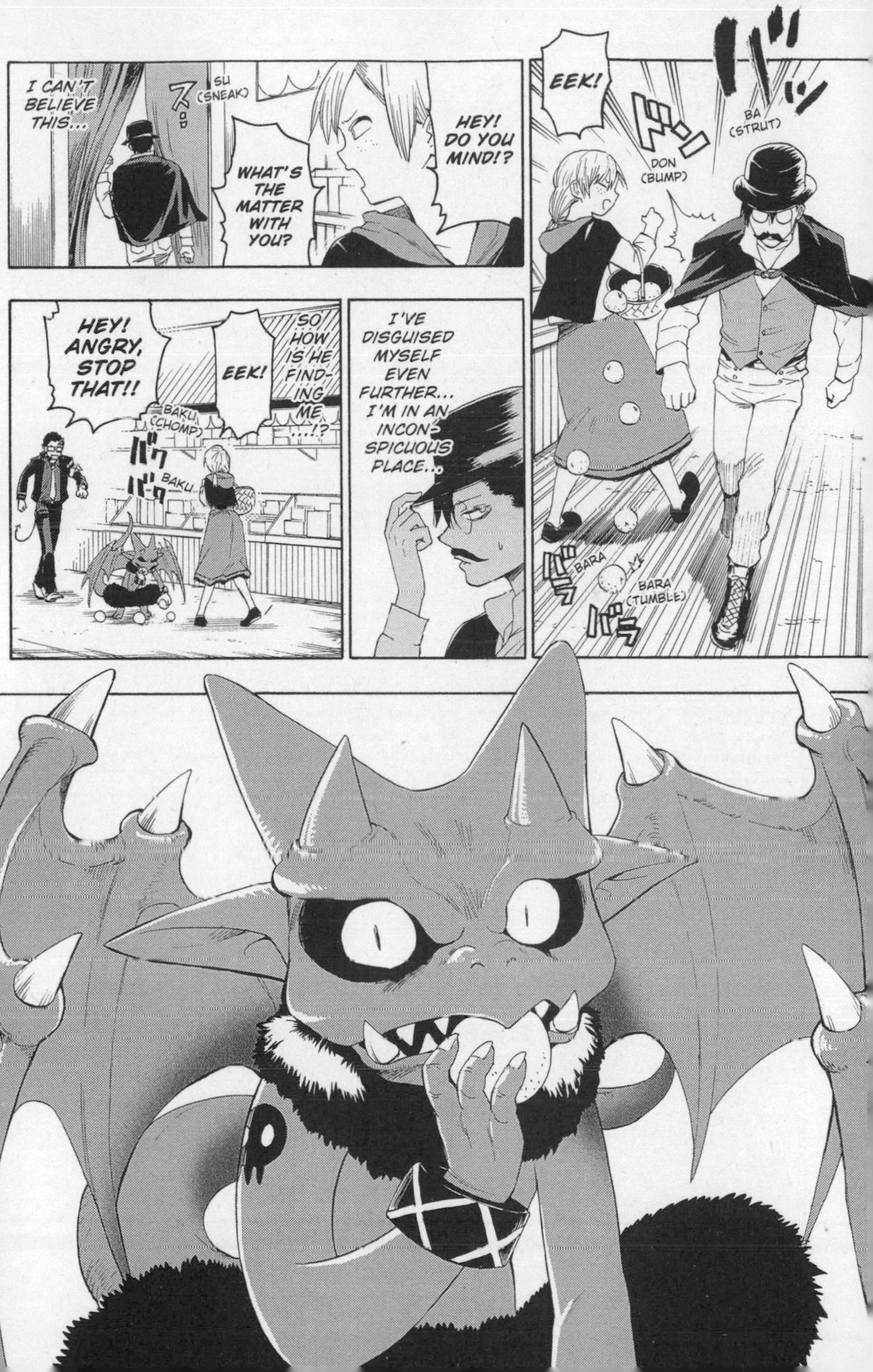

EEK!
BA (STRUT)
DON (BUMP)
BARA
BARA (TUMBLE)
HEY! DO YOU MIND!?
WHAT'S THE MATTER WITH YOU?
SU (SNEAK)
I CAN'T BELIEVE THIS...
I'VE DISGUISED MYSELF EVEN FURTHER... I'M IN AN INCONSPICUOUS PLACE...
SO HOW IS HE FINDING ME...!?
EEK!
HEY! ANGRY, STOP THAT!!
BAKU (CHOMP)
BAKU

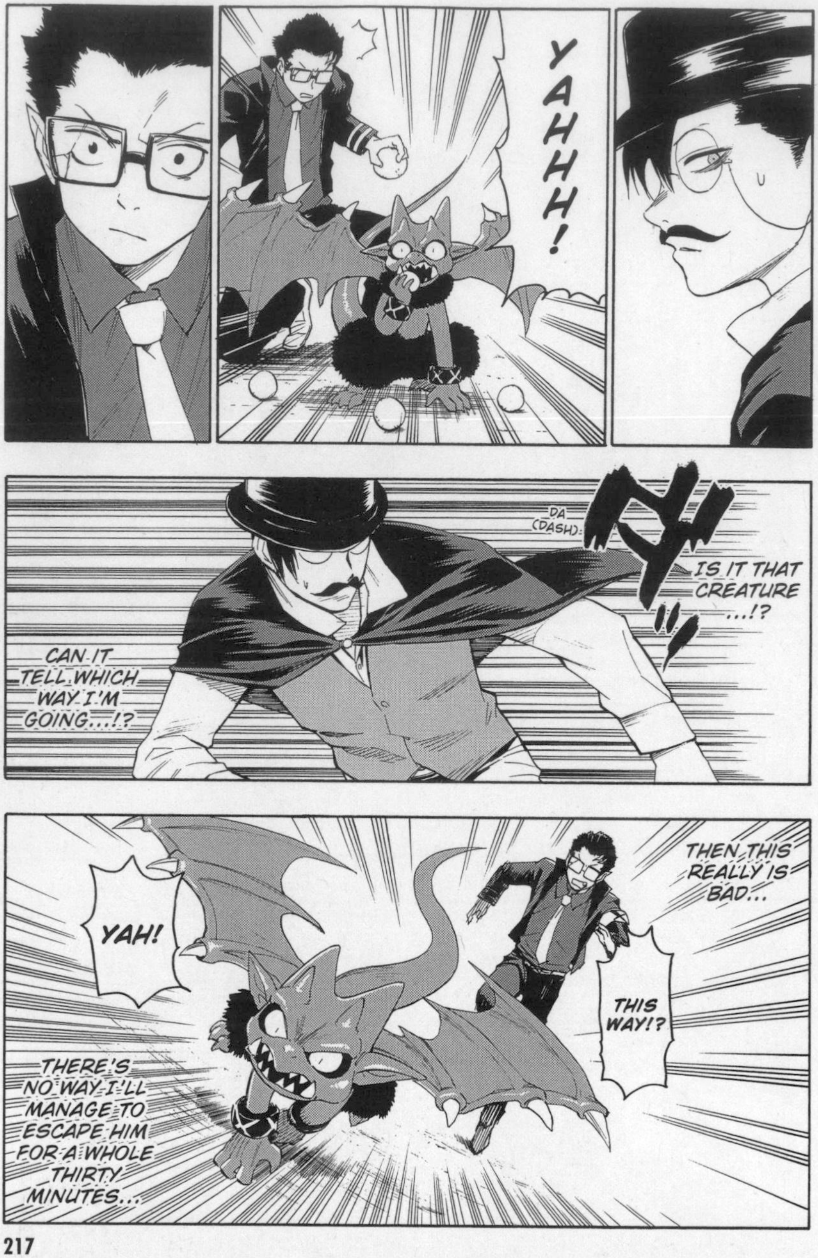
YAHHH!
DA (DASH)
IS IT THAT CREATURE ...!?
CAN IT TELL WHICH WAY I'M GOING...!?
THEN THIS REALLY IS BAD...
THIS WAY!?
YAH!
THERE'S NO WAY I'LL MANAGE TO ESCAPE HIM FOR A WHOLE THIRTY MINUTES...

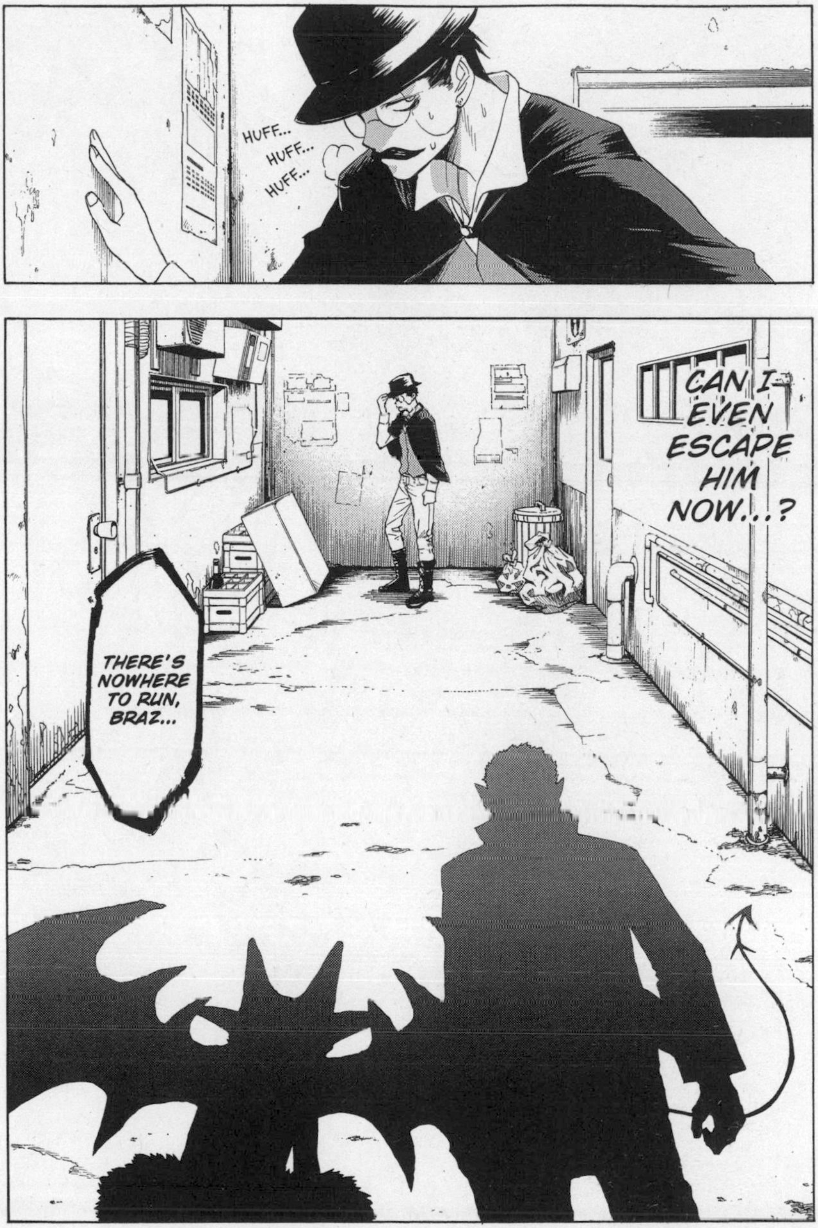
HUFF... HUFF... HUFF...
CAN I EVEN ESCAPE HIM NOW...?
THERE'S NOWHERE TO RUN, BRAZ...

♠ To Be Continued ♠

GOOD NIGHT LEAF

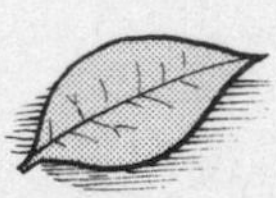

RARITY: ☆☆

JUST A HINT OF THIS LEAF'S SCENT IS VERY RELAXING, BUT GET TOO MUCH OF A WHIFF, AND YOU'LL CONK RIGHT OUT. IT'S SAID TO MAKE A LOVELY ADDITION TO HERBAL TEA.

BLOOD LAD

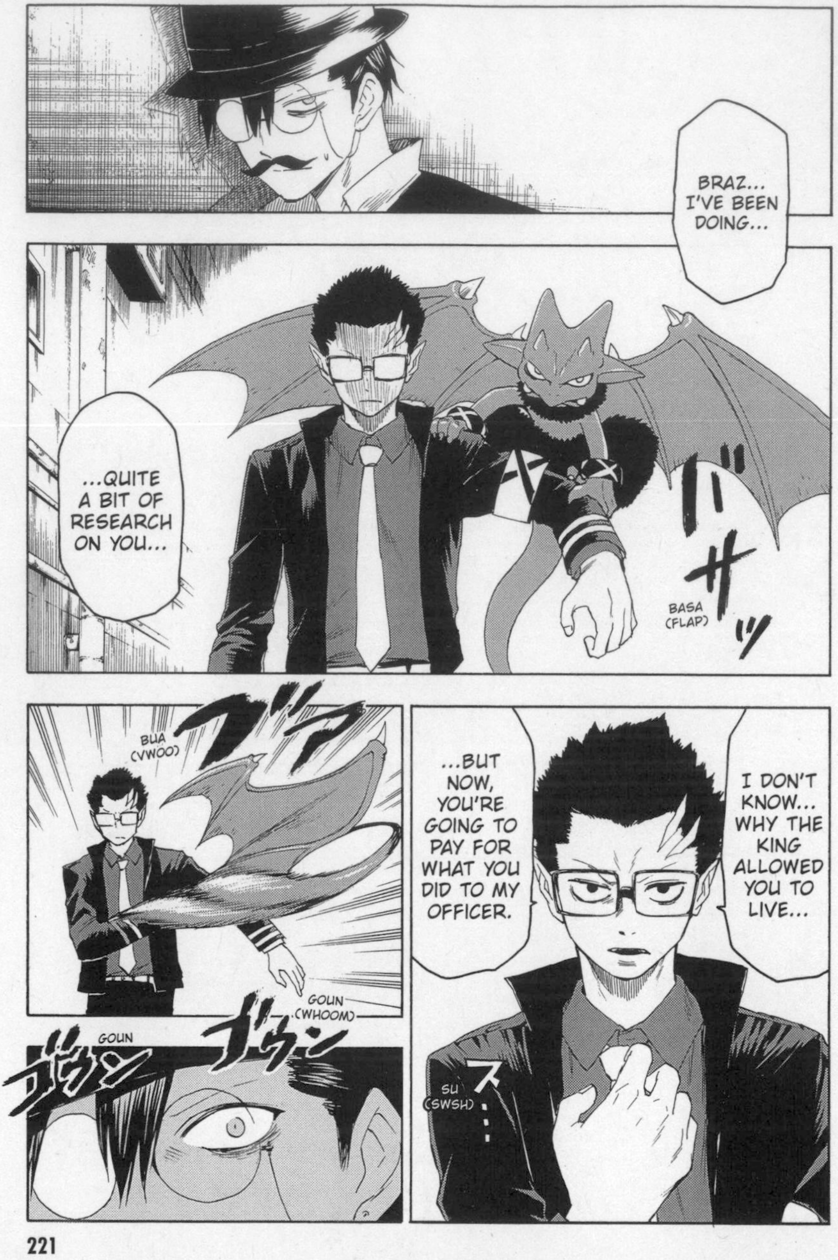
BRAZ... I'VE BEEN DOING...
...QUITE A BIT OF RESEARCH ON YOU...
BASA (FLAP)
I DON'T KNOW... WHY THE KING ALLOWED YOU TO LIVE...
...BUT NOW, YOU'RE GOING TO PAY FOR WHAT YOU DID TO MY OFFICER.
SU (SWSH)
BUA (VWOO)
GOUN (WHOOM)
GOUN

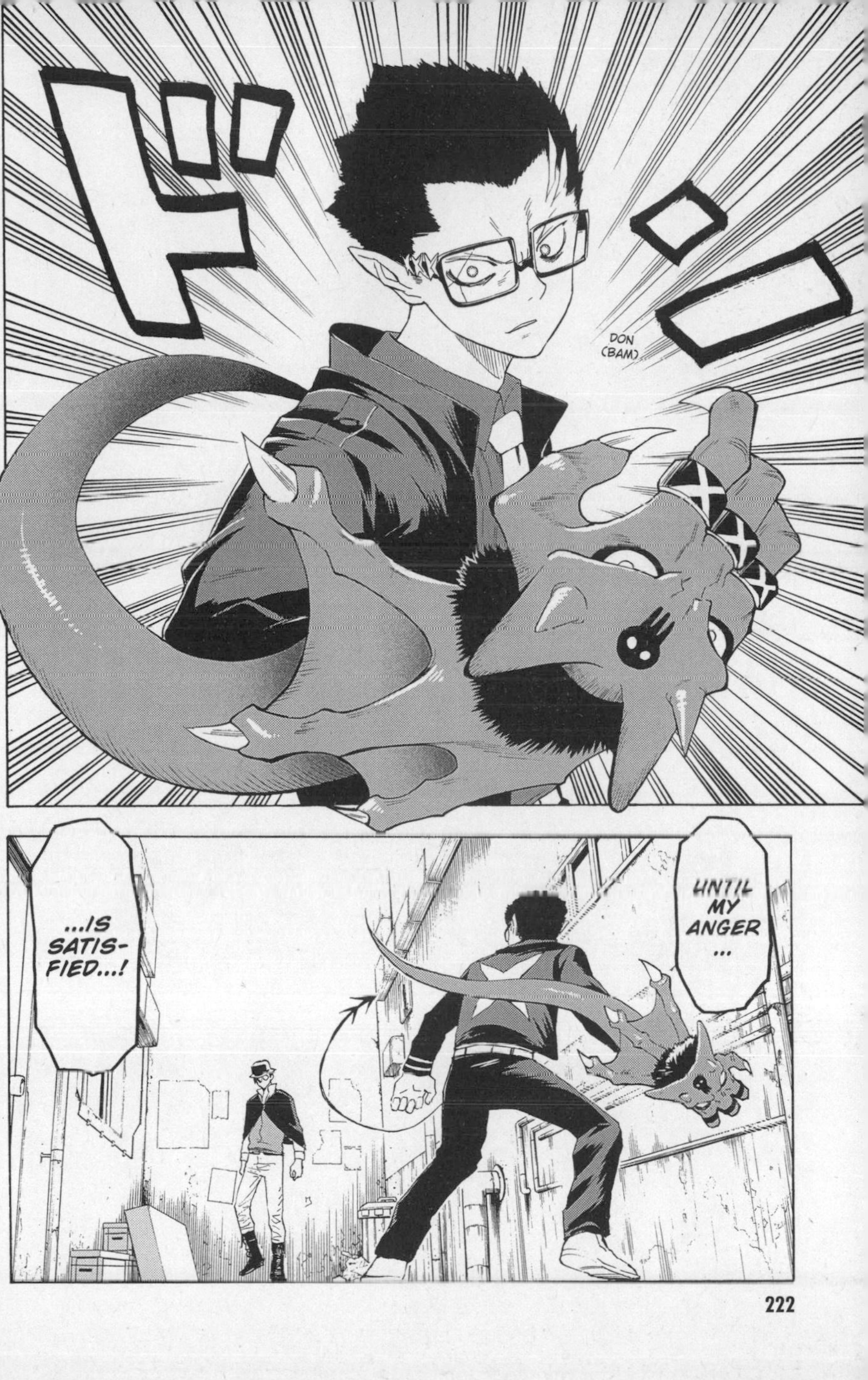
DON (BAM)
UNTIL MY ANGER ...
...IS SATIS-FIED...!

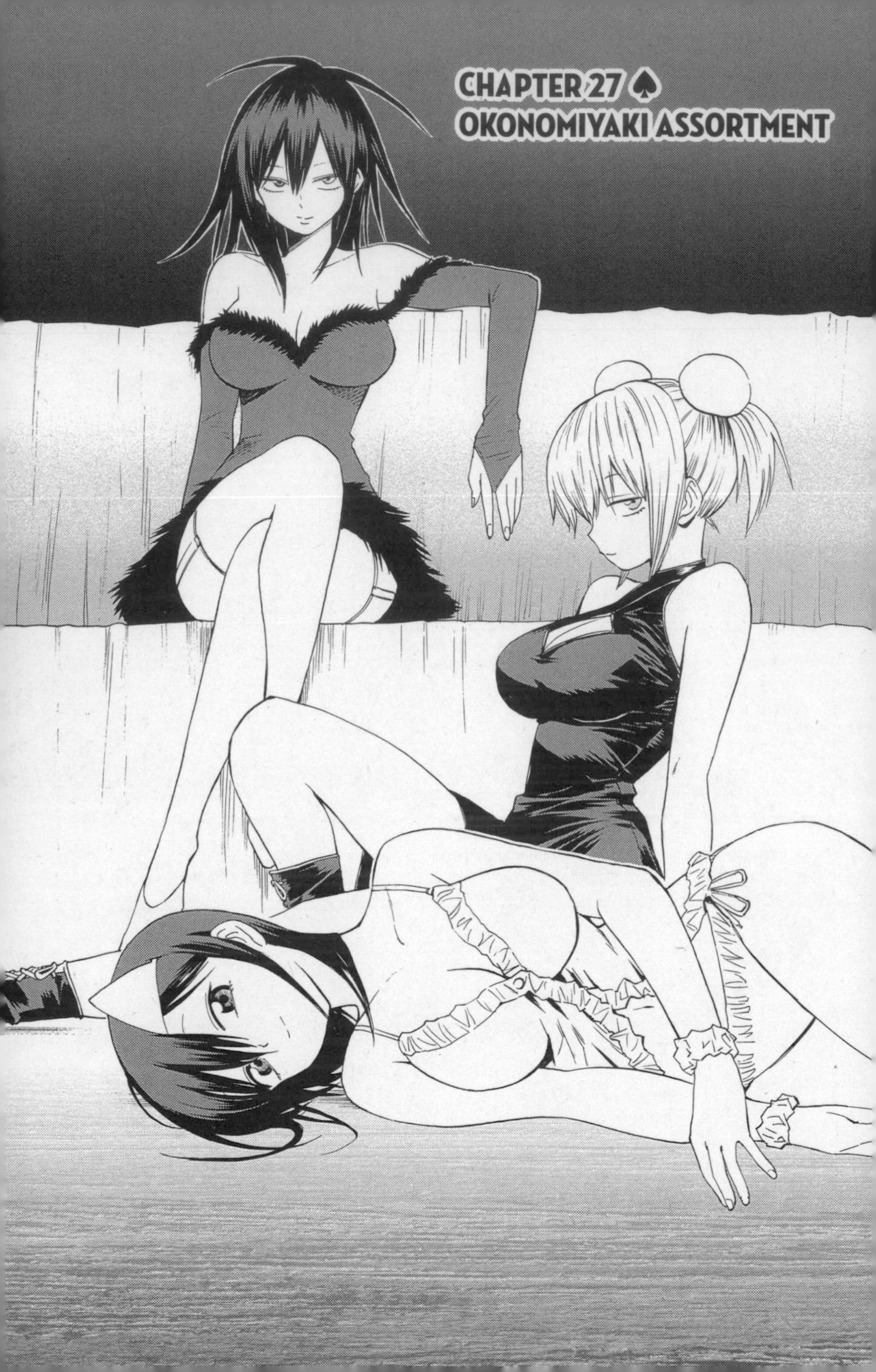
CHAPTER 27 ♠
OKONOMIYAKI ASSORTMENT

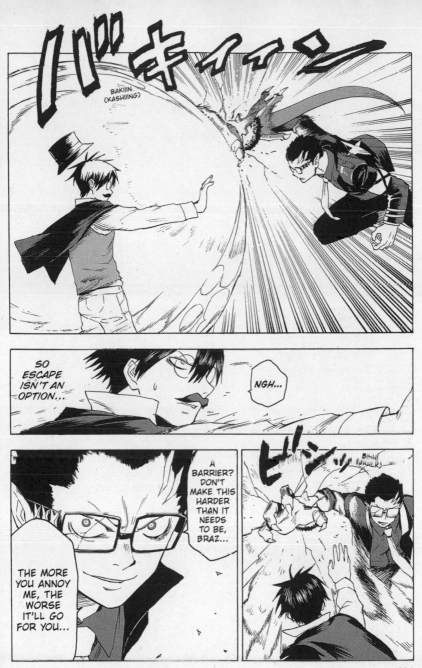

BAKIIIN
(KASHIIING)

SO ESCAPE ISN'T AN OPTION...

NGH...

A BARRIER? DON'T MAKE THIS HARDER THAN IT NEEDS TO BE, BRAZ...

THE MORE YOU ANNOY ME, THE WORSE IT'LL GO FOR YOU...

BISHI
(WHACK)

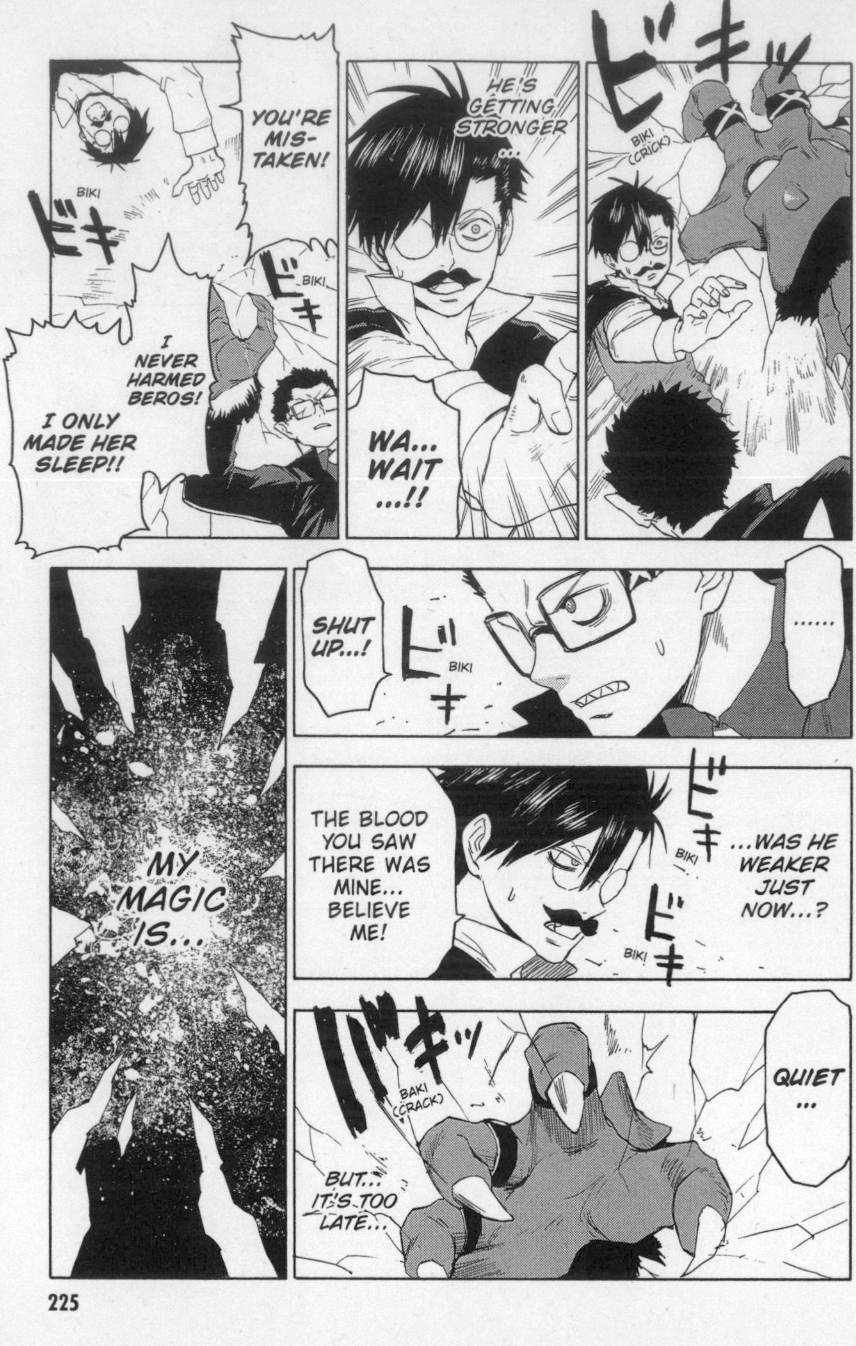
ビキッ
BIKI (CRICK)
HE'S GETTING STRONGER ...
WA... WAIT ...!!
YOU'RE MIS-TAKEN!
ビキ
BIKI
ビキ
BIKI
I NEVER HARMED BEROS!
I ONLY MADE HER SLEEP!!
......
SHUT UP...!
ビキ
BIKI
...WAS HE WEAKER JUST NOW...?
ビキ
BIKI
ビキ
BIKI
THE BLOOD YOU SAW THERE WAS MINE... BELIEVE ME!
QUIET ...
バキッ
BAKI (CRACK)
BUT... IT'S TOO LATE...
MY MAGIC IS...

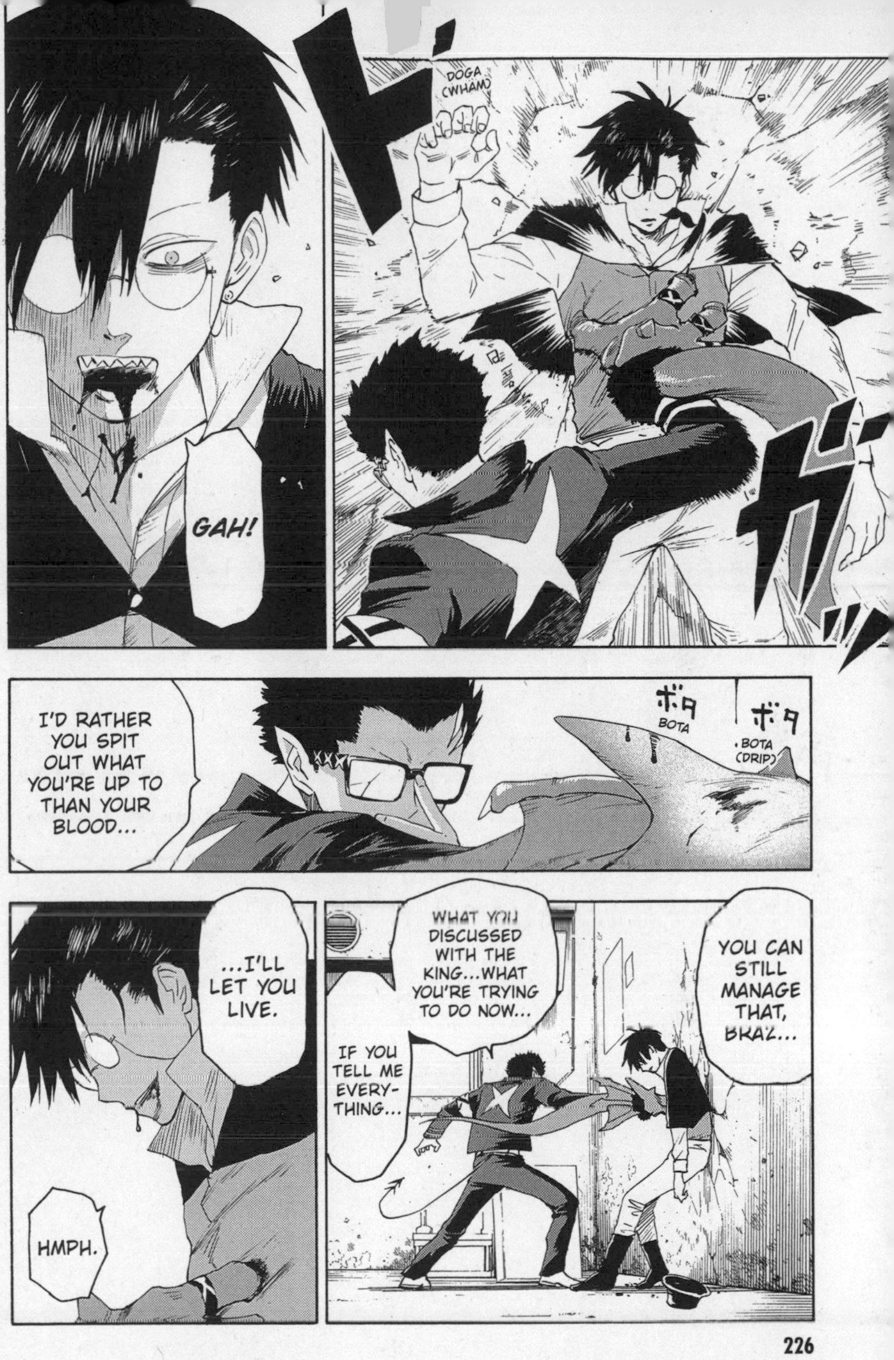
DOGA (WHAM)
GAH!
ボタ
BOTA (DRIP)
ボタ
BOTA
I'D RATHER YOU SPIT OUT WHAT YOU'RE UP TO THAN YOUR BLOOD...
YOU CAN STILL MANAGE THAT, BRAZ...
WHAT YOU DISCUSSED WITH THE KING...WHAT YOU'RE TRYING TO DO NOW...
IF YOU TELL ME EVERYTHING...
...I'LL LET YOU LIVE.
HMPH.

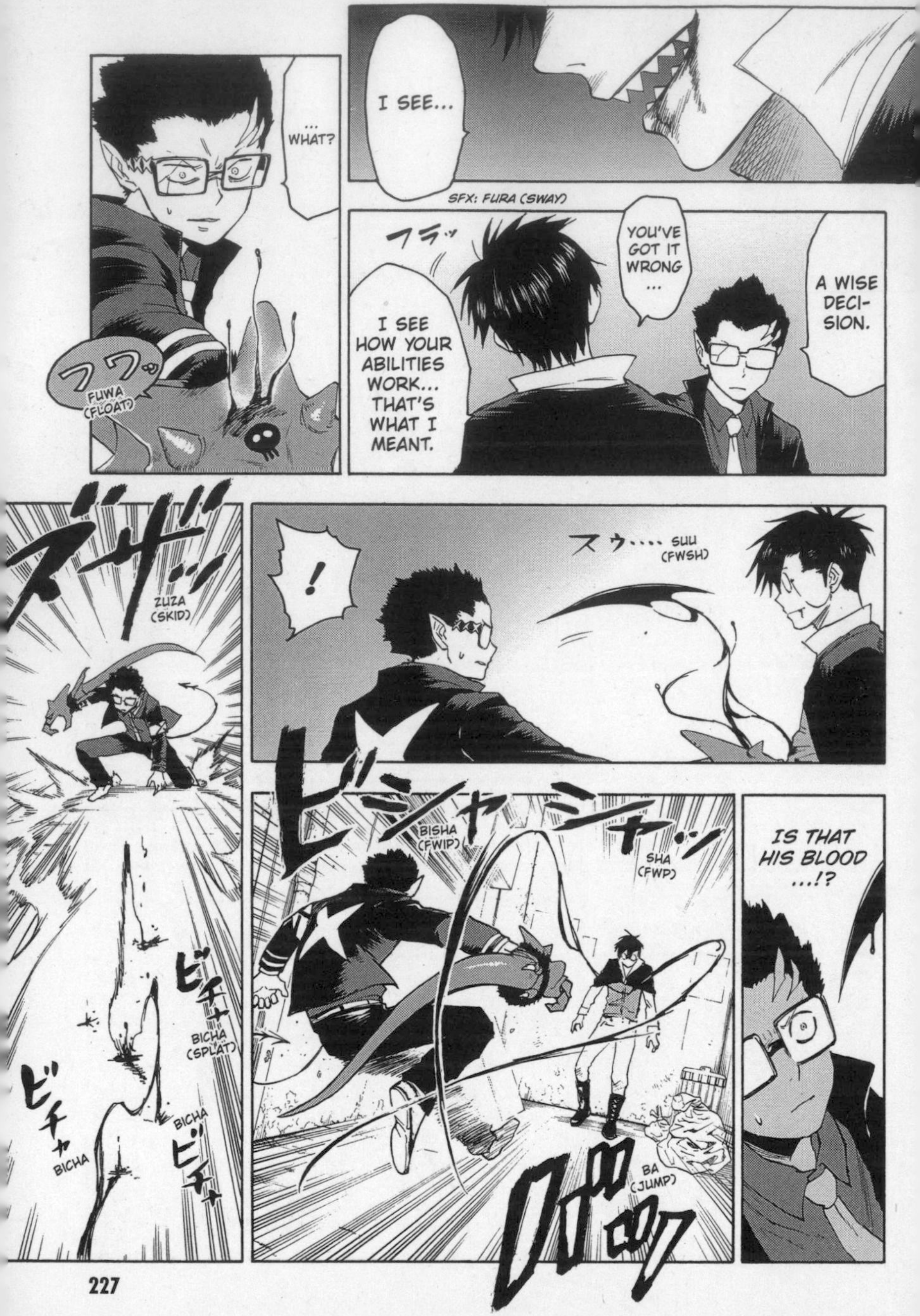
I SEE...
SFX: FURA (SWAY)
A WISE DECISION.
YOU'VE GOT IT WRONG...
フラッ
I SEE HOW YOUR ABILITIES WORK... THAT'S WHAT I MEANT.
... WHAT?
フワッ
FUWA (FLOAT)
スウ…
SUU (FWSH)
!
IS THAT HIS BLOOD ...!?
ビシャシャッ
BISHA (FWIP)
SHA (FWP)
バッ
BA (JUMP)
ズザッ
ZUZA (SKID)
ビチャ
BICHA (SPLAT)
ビチャ
BICHA
ビチャ
BICHA

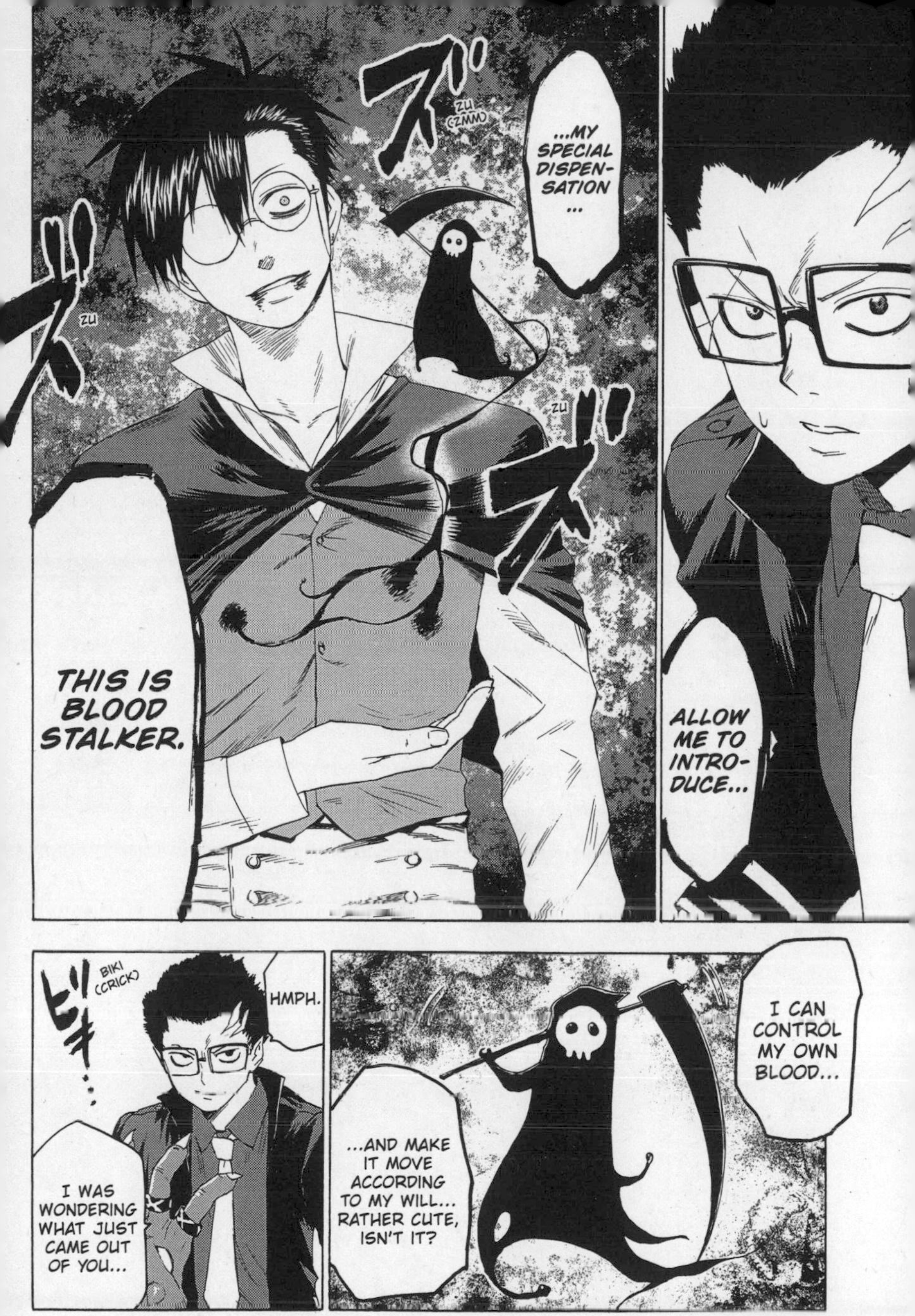
ALLOW ME TO INTRODUCE...
...MY SPECIAL DISPENSATION...
ZU (ZMM)
ZU
ZU
THIS IS BLOOD STALKER.
I CAN CONTROL MY OWN BLOOD...
...AND MAKE IT MOVE ACCORDING TO MY WILL... RATHER CUTE, ISN'T IT?
BIKI (CRICK)
HMPH.
I WAS WONDERING WHAT JUST CAME OUT OF YOU...

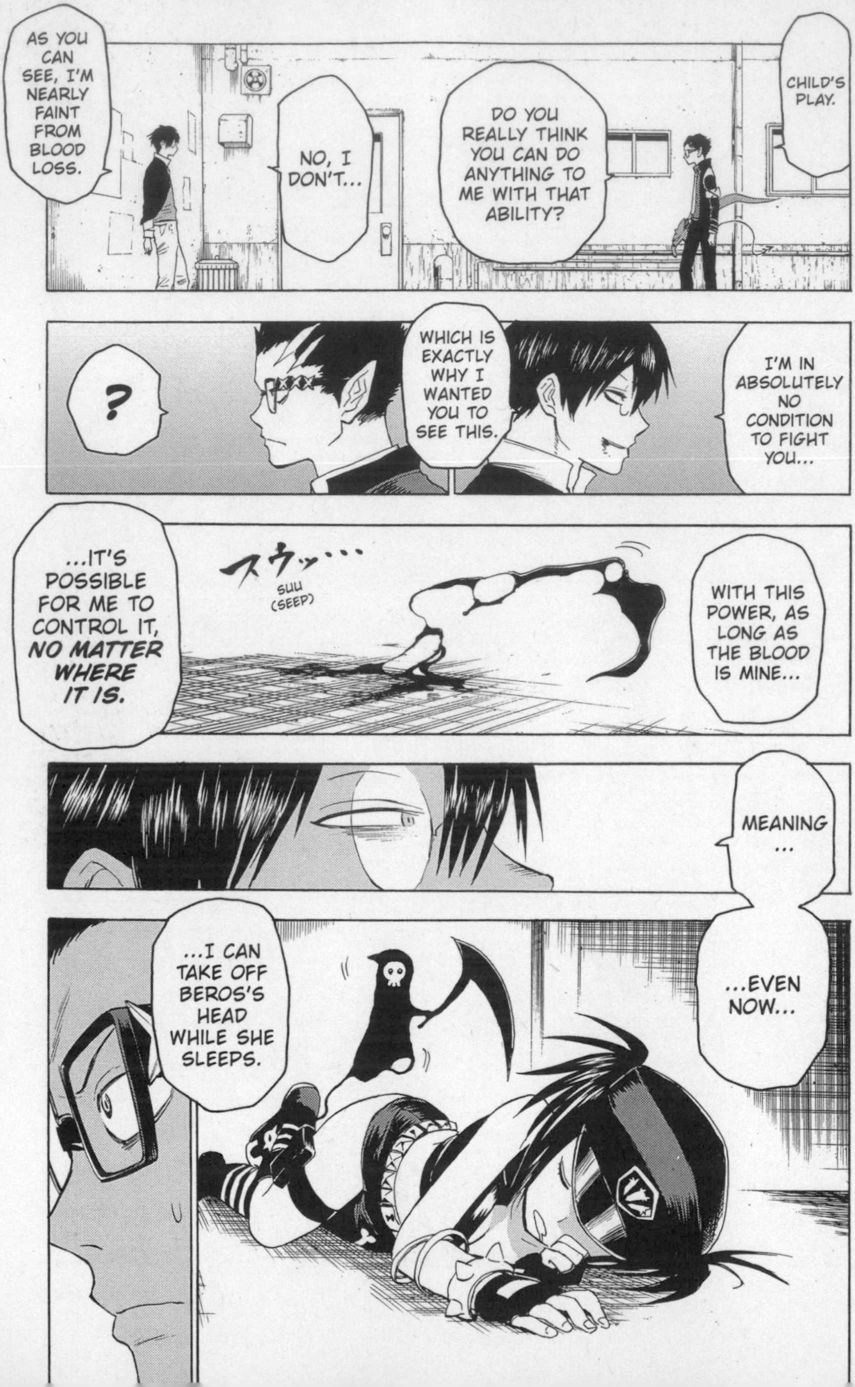
CHILD'S PLAY.
DO YOU REALLY THINK YOU CAN DO ANYTHING TO ME WITH THAT ABILITY?
NO, I DON'T...
AS YOU CAN SEE, I'M NEARLY FAINT FROM BLOOD LOSS.
I'M IN ABSOLUTELY NO CONDITION TO FIGHT YOU...
WHICH IS EXACTLY WHY I WANTED YOU TO SEE THIS.
?
WITH THIS POWER, AS LONG AS THE BLOOD IS MINE...
スウッ・・・
SUU (SEEP)
...IT'S POSSIBLE FOR ME TO CONTROL IT, ***NO MATTER WHERE IT IS.***
MEANING ...
...EVEN NOW...
...I CAN TAKE OFF BEROS'S HEAD WHILE SHE SLEEPS.

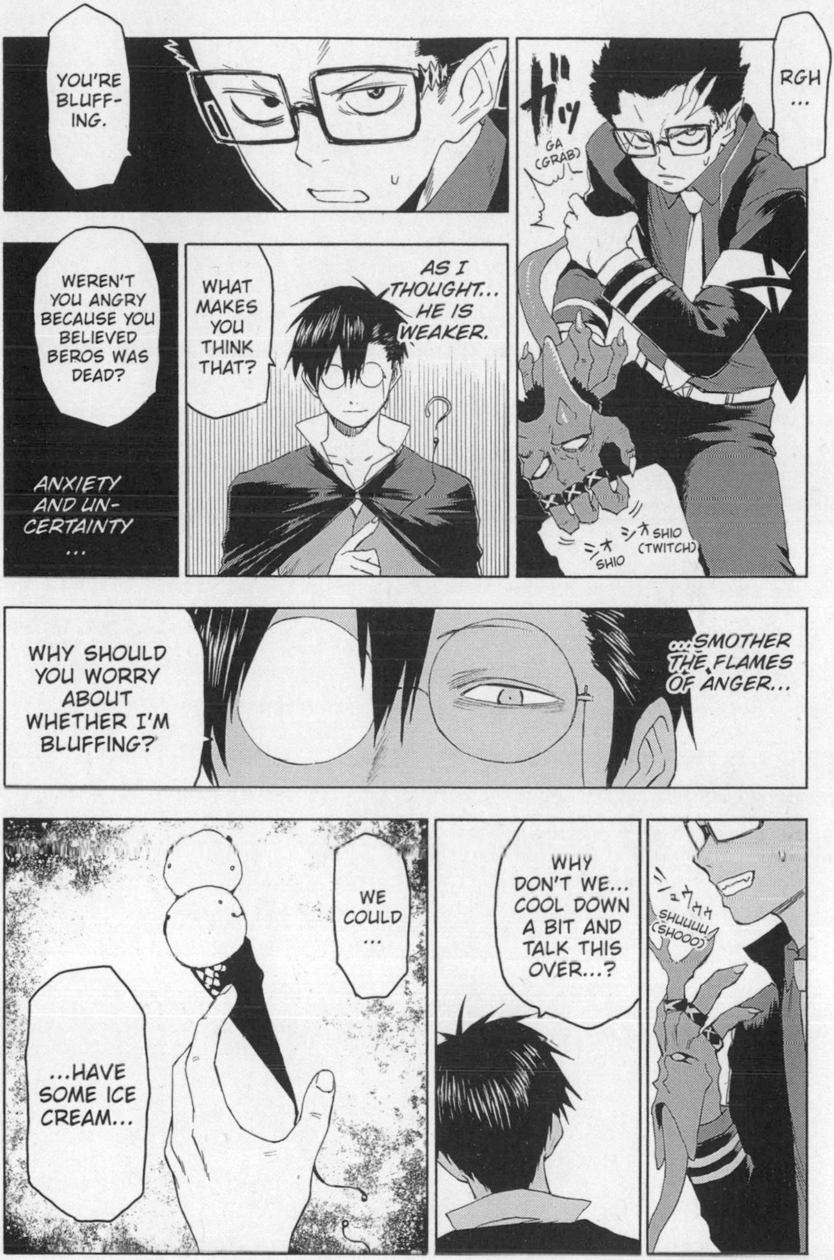
RGH ...
GA (GRAB)
SHIO SHIO (TWITCH)
YOU'RE BLUFF-ING.
WHAT MAKES YOU THINK THAT?
AS I THOUGHT... HE IS WEAKER.
WEREN'T YOU ANGRY BECAUSE YOU BELIEVED BEROS WAS DEAD?
ANXIETY AND UN-CERTAINTY ...
...SMOTHER THE FLAMES OF ANGER...
WHY SHOULD YOU WORRY ABOUT WHETHER I'M BLUFFING?
SHUUUU (SHOOO)
WHY DON'T WE... COOL DOWN A BIT AND TALK THIS OVER...?
WE COULD ...
...HAVE SOME ICE CREAM...

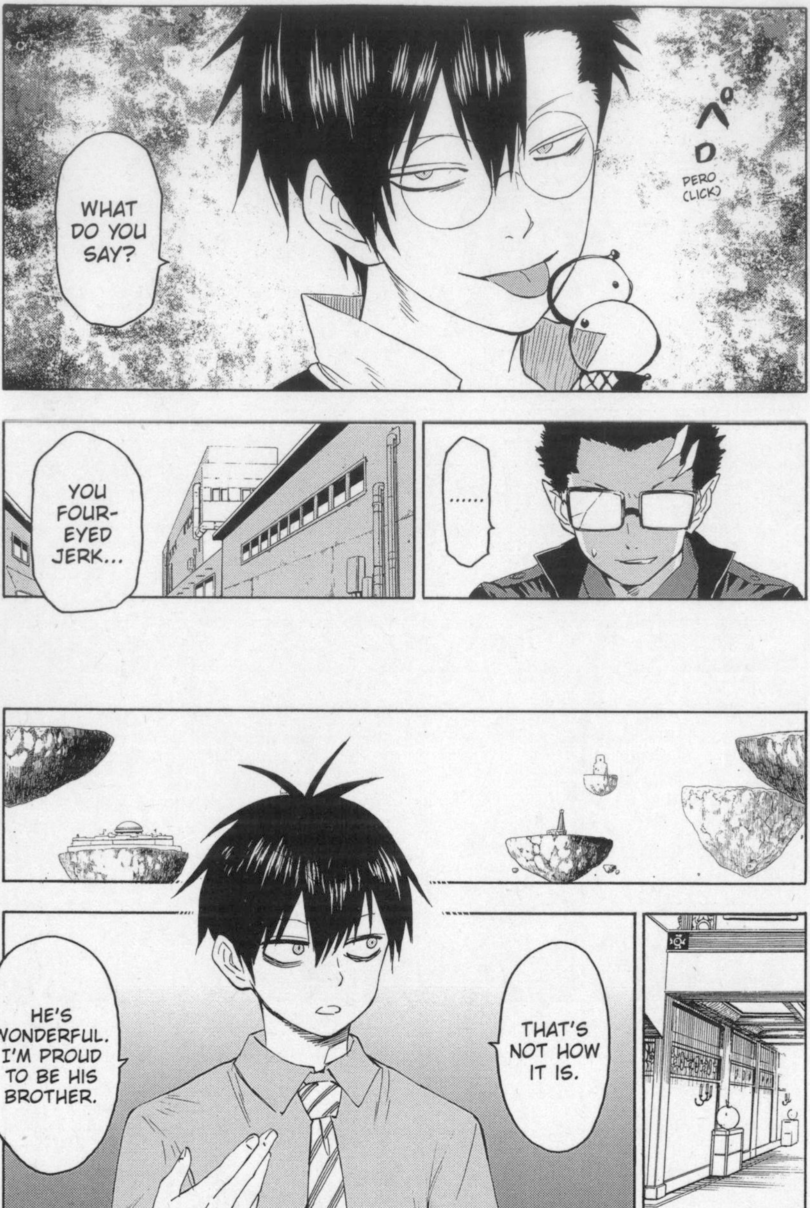
PERO (CLICK)
WHAT DO YOU SAY?
......
YOU FOUR-EYED JERK...
THAT'S NOT HOW IT IS.
HE'S WONDERFUL. I'M PROUD TO BE HIS BROTHER.

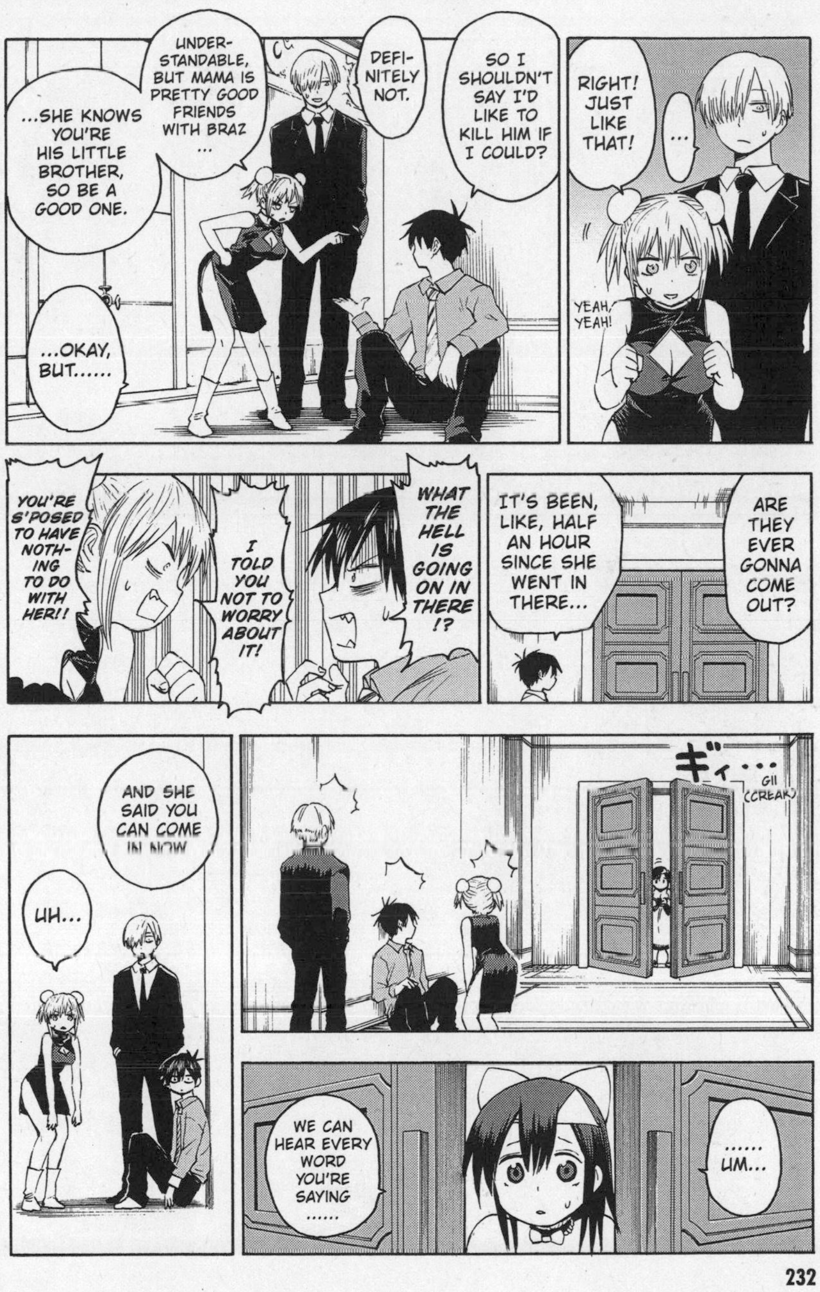
…
RIGHT! JUST LIKE THAT!
YEAH, YEAH!
SO I SHOULDN'T SAY I'D LIKE TO KILL HIM IF I COULD?
DEFI-NITELY NOT.
UNDER-STANDABLE, BUT MAMA IS PRETTY GOOD FRIENDS WITH BRAZ …
…SHE KNOWS YOU'RE HIS LITTLE BROTHER, SO BE A GOOD ONE.
…OKAY, BUT……
ARE THEY EVER GONNA COME OUT?
IT'S BEEN, LIKE, HALF AN HOUR SINCE SHE WENT IN THERE…
WHAT THE HELL IS GOING ON IN THERE!?
I TOLD YOU NOT TO WORRY ABOUT IT!
YOU'RE S'POSED TO HAVE NOTH-ING TO DO WITH HER!!
ギィ…
GII (CREAK)
……UM…
WE CAN HEAR EVERY WORD YOU'RE SAYING ……
AND SHE SAID YOU CAN COME IN NOW
UH…

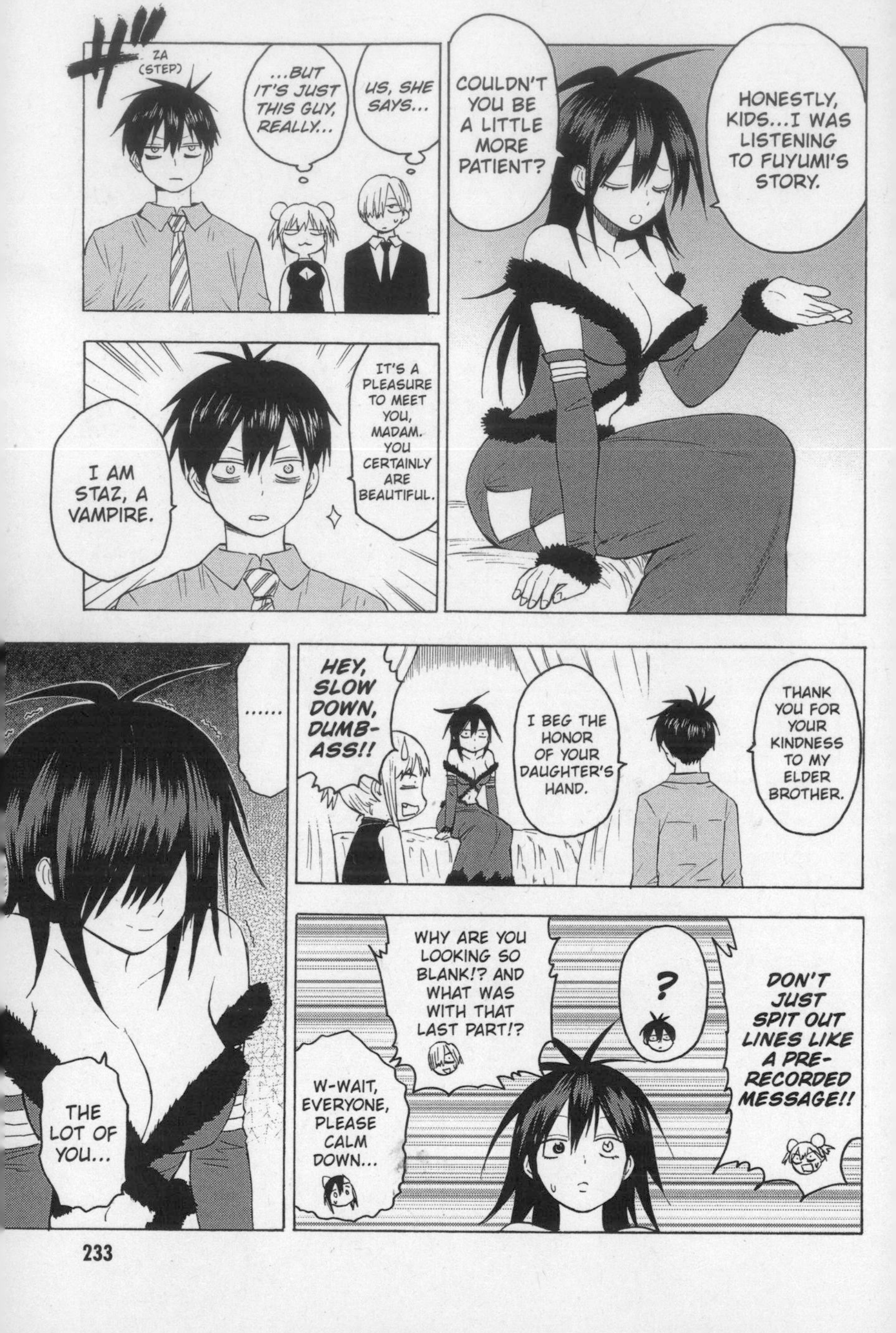
HONESTLY, KIDS...I WAS LISTENING TO FUYUMI'S STORY.
COULDN'T YOU BE A LITTLE MORE PATIENT?
US, SHE SAYS...
...BUT IT'S JUST THIS GUY, REALLY...
ZA (STEP)
IT'S A PLEASURE TO MEET YOU, MADAM. YOU CERTAINLY ARE BEAUTIFUL.
I AM STAZ, A VAMPIRE.
THANK YOU FOR YOUR KINDNESS TO MY ELDER BROTHER.
I BEG THE HONOR OF YOUR DAUGHTER'S HAND.
HEY, SLOW DOWN, DUMB-ASS!!
DON'T JUST SPIT OUT LINES LIKE A PRE-RECORDED MESSAGE!!
?
WHY ARE YOU LOOKING SO BLANK!? AND WHAT WAS WITH THAT LAST PART!?
W-WAIT, EVERYONE, PLEASE CALM DOWN...
......
THE LOT OF YOU...

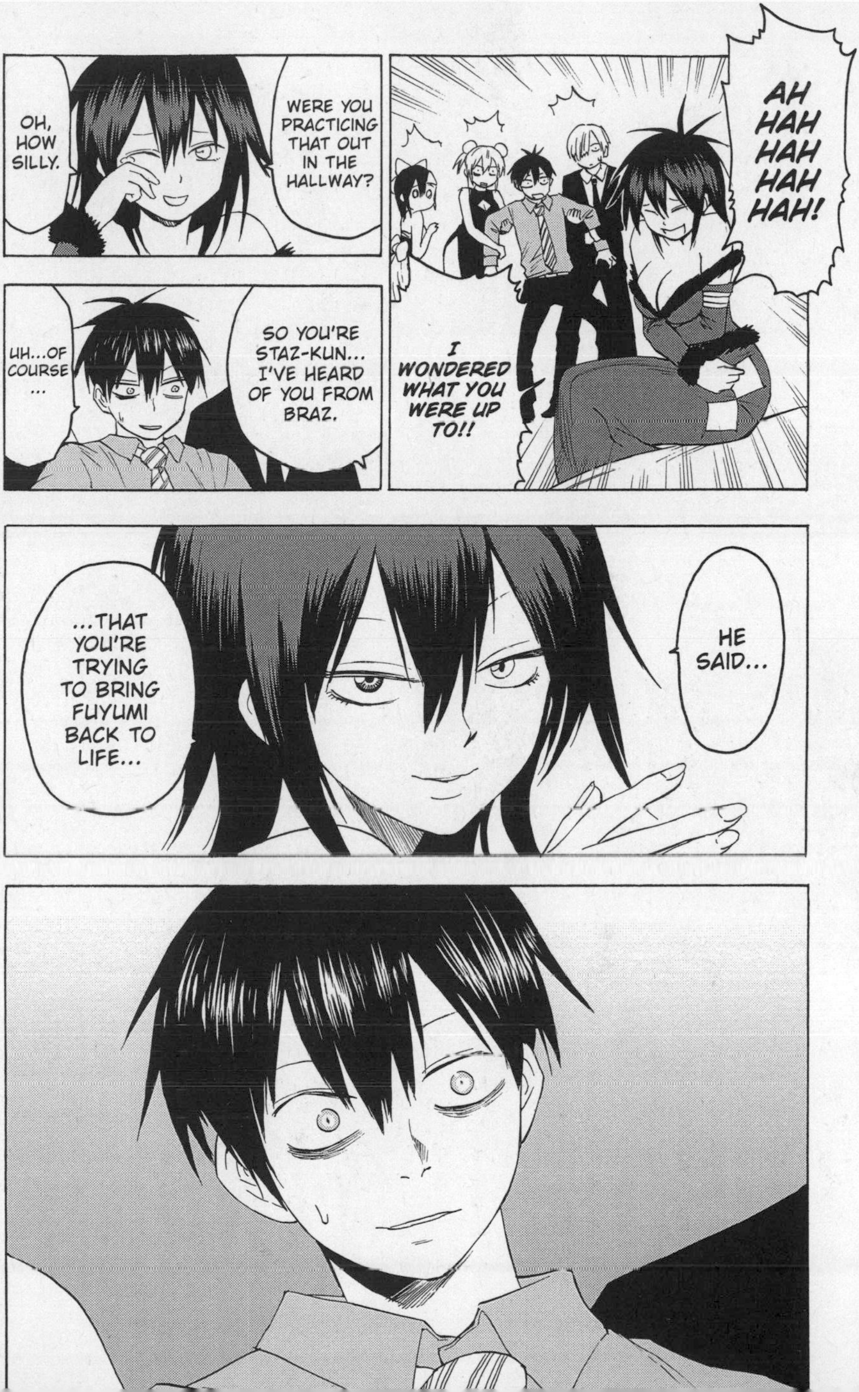
AH HAH HAH HAH HAH!
I WONDERED WHAT YOU WERE UP TO!!
WERE YOU PRACTICING THAT OUT IN THE HALLWAY?
OH, HOW SILLY.
SO YOU'RE STAZ-KUN... I'VE HEARD OF YOU FROM BRAZ.
UH...OF COURSE ...
HE SAID...
...THAT YOU'RE TRYING TO BRING FUYUMI BACK TO LIFE...

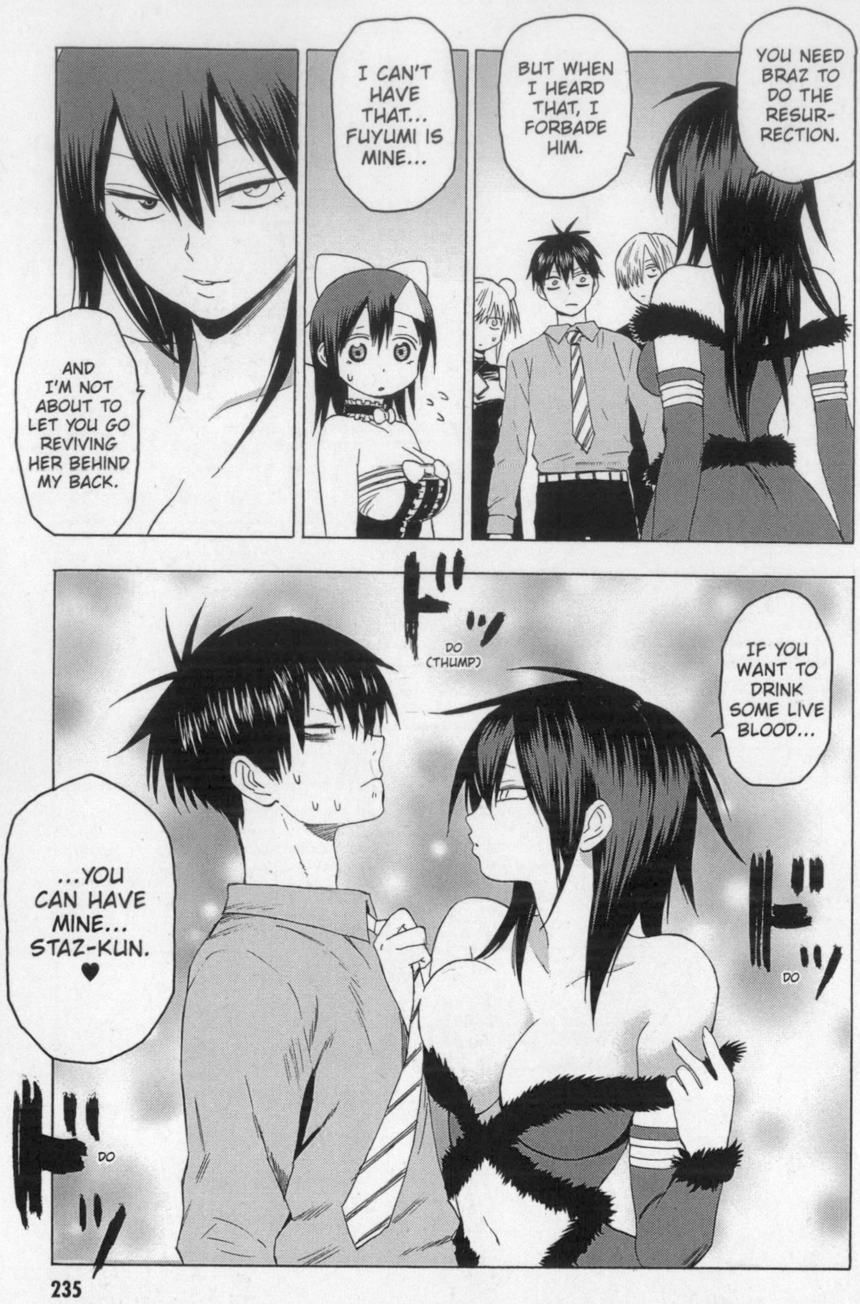
YOU NEED BRAZ TO DO THE RESURRECTION.
BUT WHEN I HEARD THAT, I FORBADE HIM.
I CAN'T HAVE THAT... FUYUMI IS MINE...
AND I'M NOT ABOUT TO LET YOU GO REVIVING HER BEHIND MY BACK.
IF YOU WANT TO DRINK SOME LIVE BLOOD...
DO (THUMP)
DO
...YOU CAN HAVE MINE... STAZ-KUN. ♥
DO

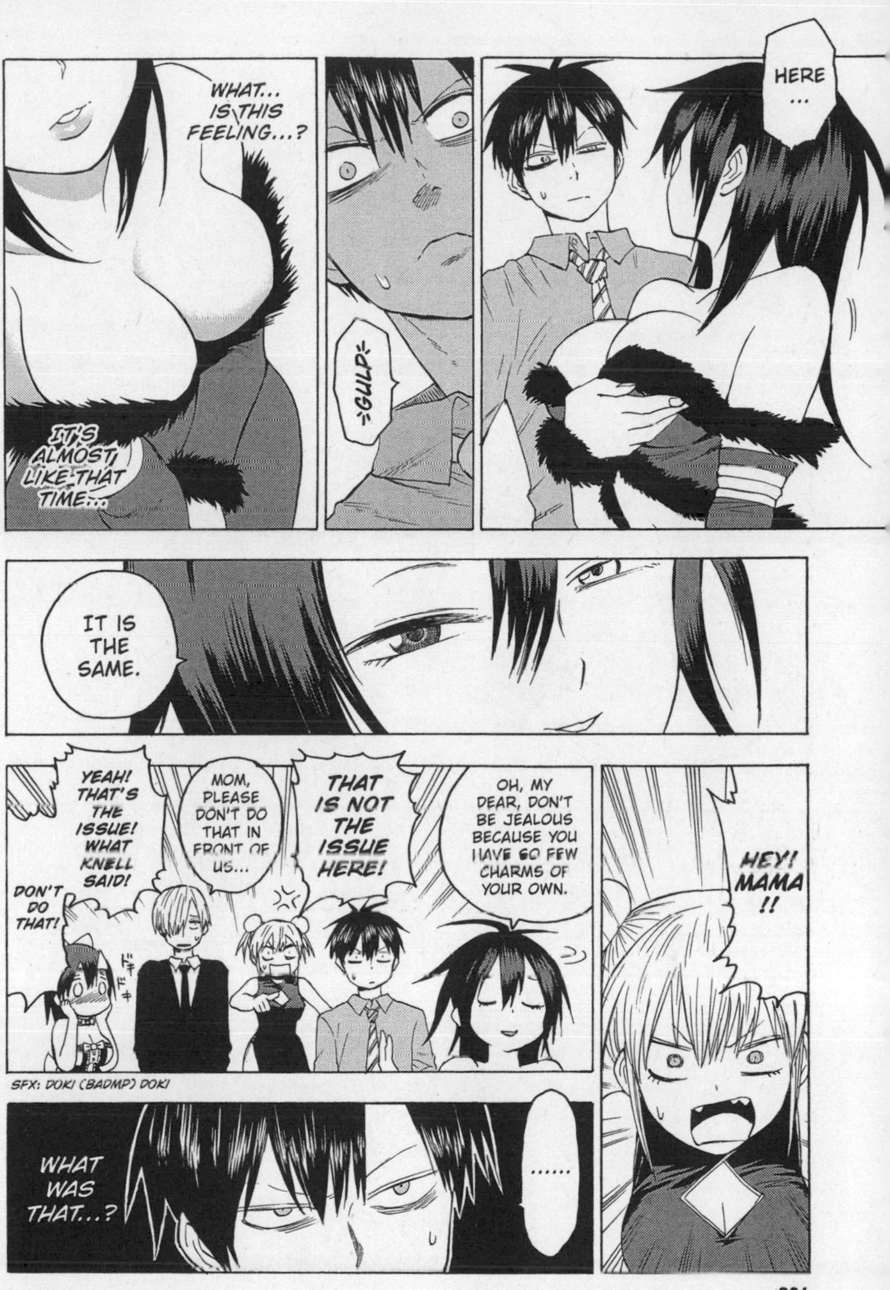
HERE...
GULP
WHAT... IS THIS FEELING...?
IT'S ALMOST LIKE THAT TIME...
IT IS THE SAME.
HEY! MAMA!!
OH, MY DEAR, DON'T BE JEALOUS BECAUSE YOU HAVE SO FEW CHARMS OF YOUR OWN.
THAT IS NOT THE ISSUE HERE!
MOM, PLEASE DON'T DO THAT IN FRONT OF US...
YEAH! THAT'S THE ISSUE! WHAT KNELL SAID!
DON'T DO THAT!
SFX: DOKI (BADMP) DOKI
......
WHAT WAS THAT...?

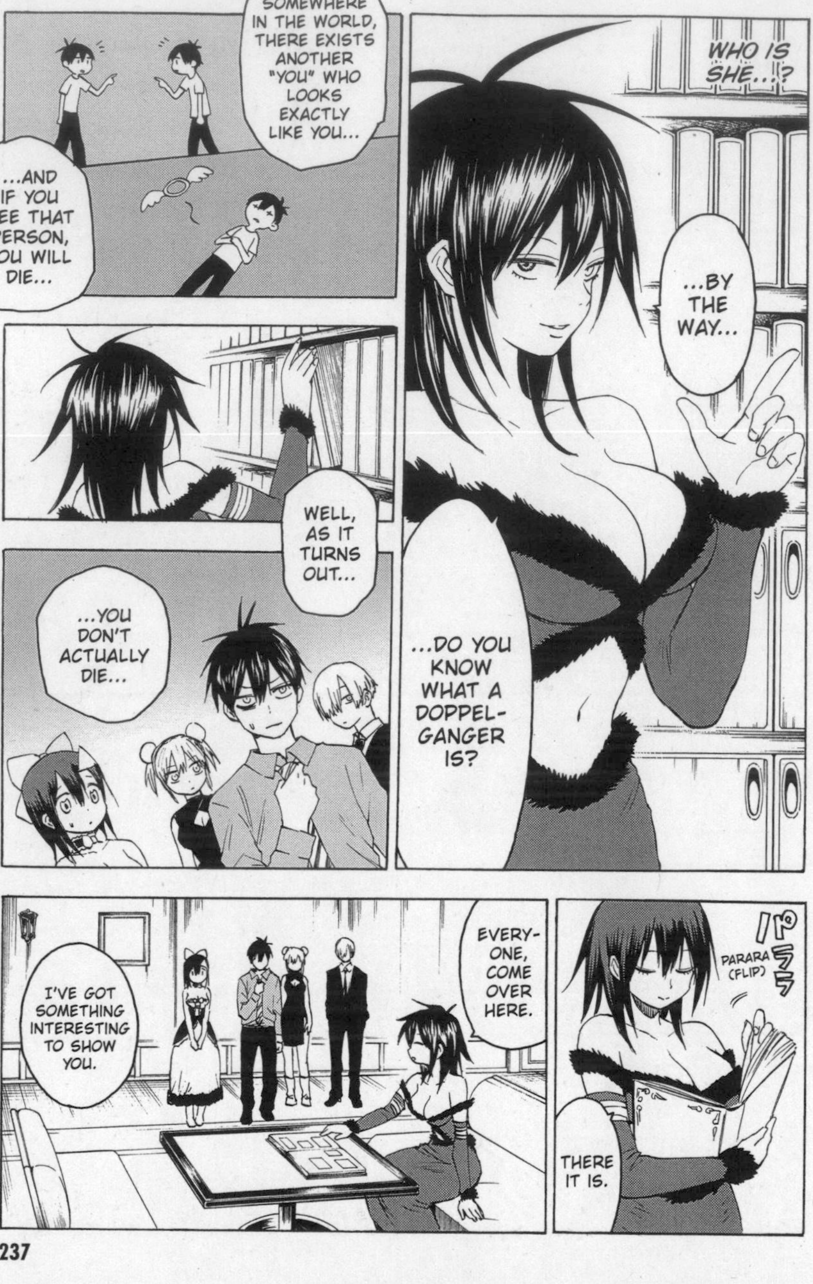
WHO IS SHE...?
...BY THE WAY...
...DO YOU KNOW WHAT A DOPPEL-GANGER IS?
SOMEWHERE IN THE WORLD, THERE EXISTS ANOTHER "YOU" WHO LOOKS EXACTLY LIKE YOU...
...AND IF YOU SEE THAT PERSON, YOU WILL DIE...
WELL, AS IT TURNS OUT...
...YOU DON'T ACTUALLY DIE...
PARARA (FLIP)
THERE IT IS.
EVERY-ONE, COME OVER HERE.
I'VE GOT SOMETHING INTERESTING TO SHOW YOU.

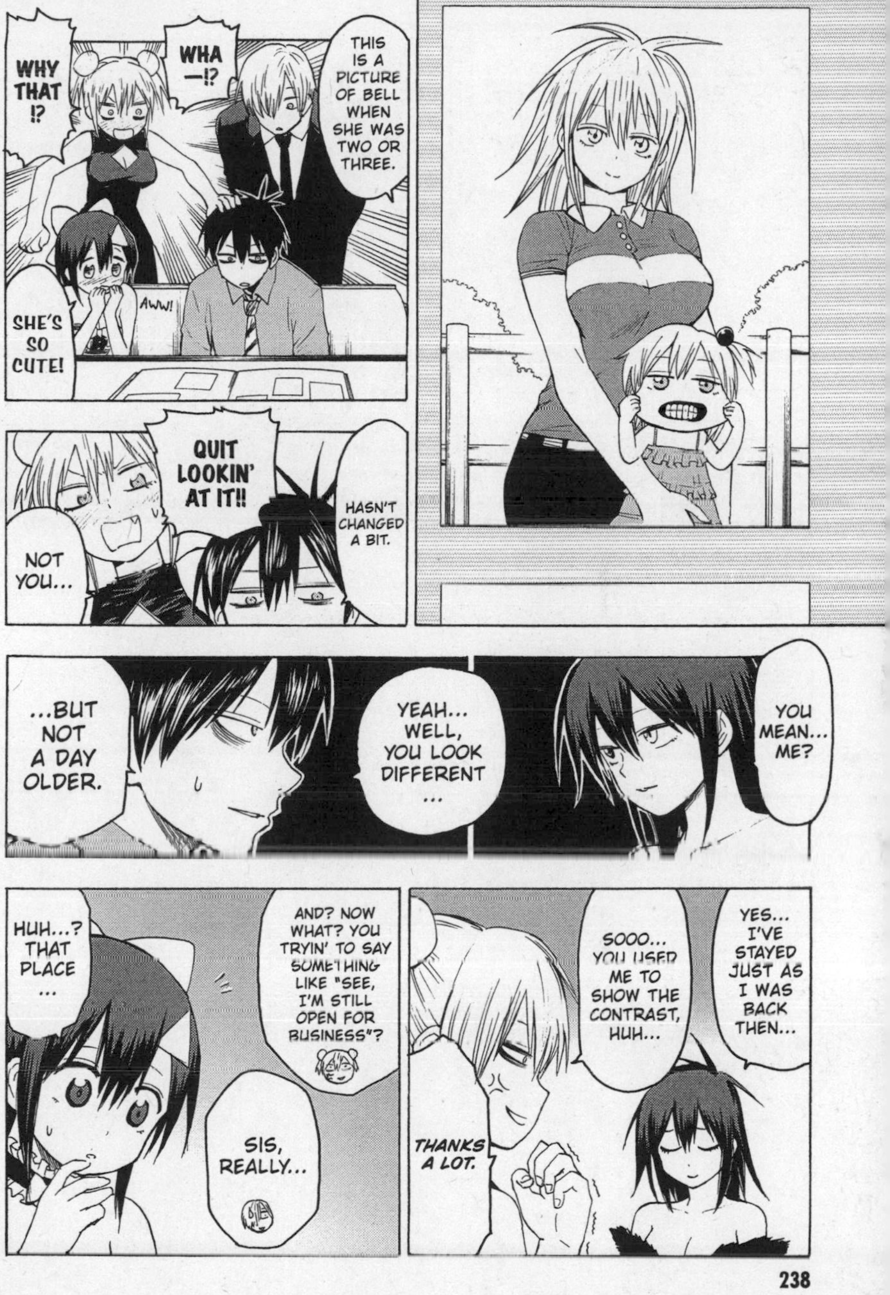
THIS IS A PICTURE OF BELL WHEN SHE WAS TWO OR THREE.
WHA—!?
WHY THAT!?
AWW!
SHE'S SO CUTE!
HASN'T CHANGED A BIT.
QUIT LOOKIN' AT IT!!
NOT YOU...
YOU MEAN... ME?
YEAH... WELL, YOU LOOK DIFFERENT...
...BUT NOT A DAY OLDER.
YES... I'VE STAYED JUST AS I WAS BACK THEN...
SOOO... YOU USED ME TO SHOW THE CONTRAST, HUH...
THANKS A LOT.
AND? NOW WHAT? YOU TRYIN' TO SAY SOMETHING LIKE "SEE, I'M STILL OPEN FOR BUSINESS"?
HUH...? THAT PLACE...
SIS, REALLY...

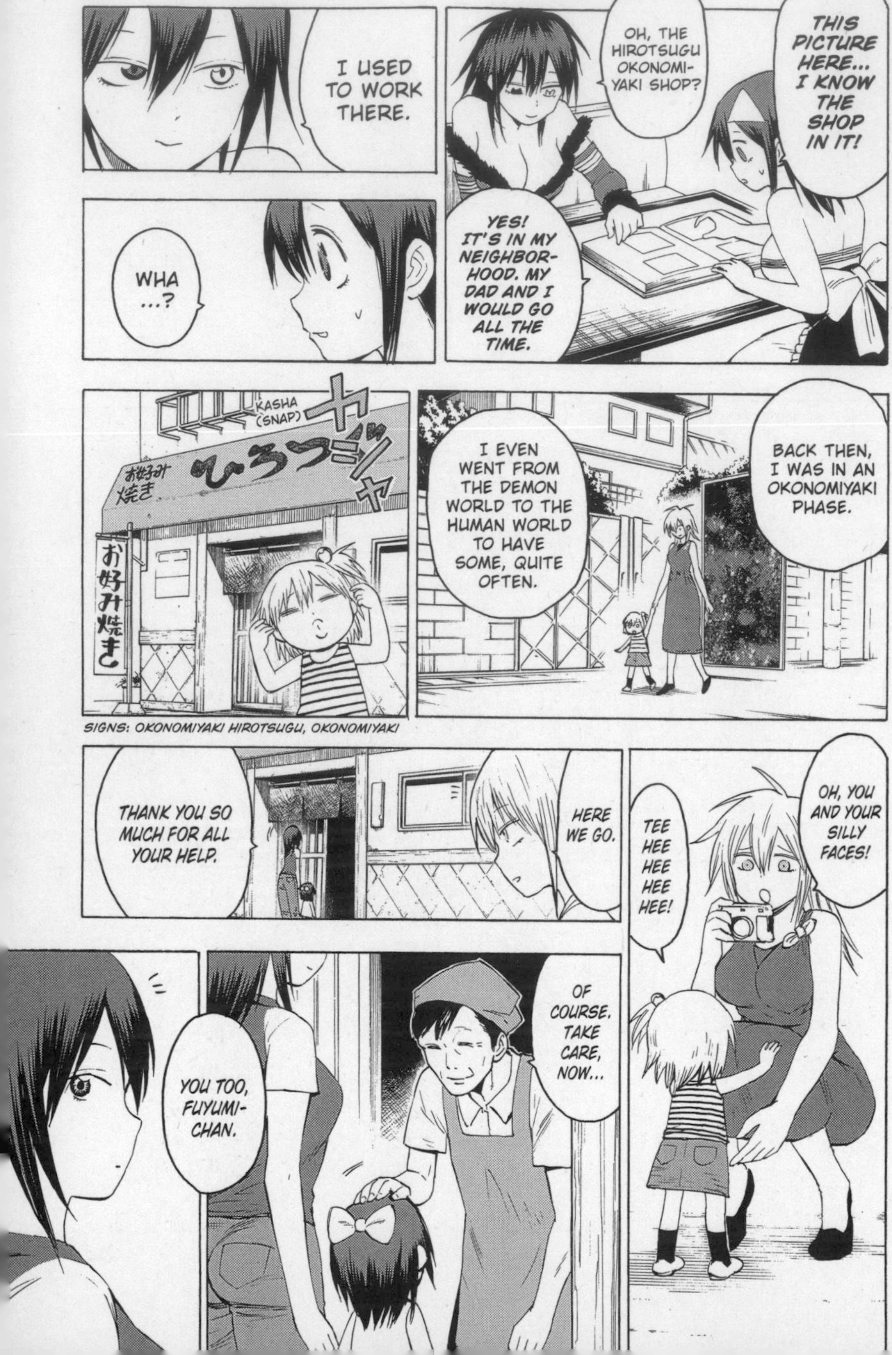
THIS PICTURE HERE... I KNOW THE SHOP IN IT!
OH, THE HIROTSUGU OKONOMIYAKI SHOP?
YES! IT'S IN MY NEIGHBORHOOD. MY DAD AND I WOULD GO ALL THE TIME.
I USED TO WORK THERE.
WHA ...?
BACK THEN, I WAS IN AN OKONOMIYAKI PHASE.
I EVEN WENT FROM THE DEMON WORLD TO THE HUMAN WORLD TO HAVE SOME, QUITE OFTEN.
KASHA (SNAP)
お好み焼き
お好み焼き
SIGNS: OKONOMIYAKI HIROTSUGU, OKONOMIYAKI
OH, YOU AND YOUR SILLY FACES!
TEE HEE HEE HEE HEE!
HERE WE GO.
THANK YOU SO MUCH FOR ALL YOUR HELP.
OF COURSE. TAKE CARE, NOW...
YOU TOO, FUYUMI-CHAN.

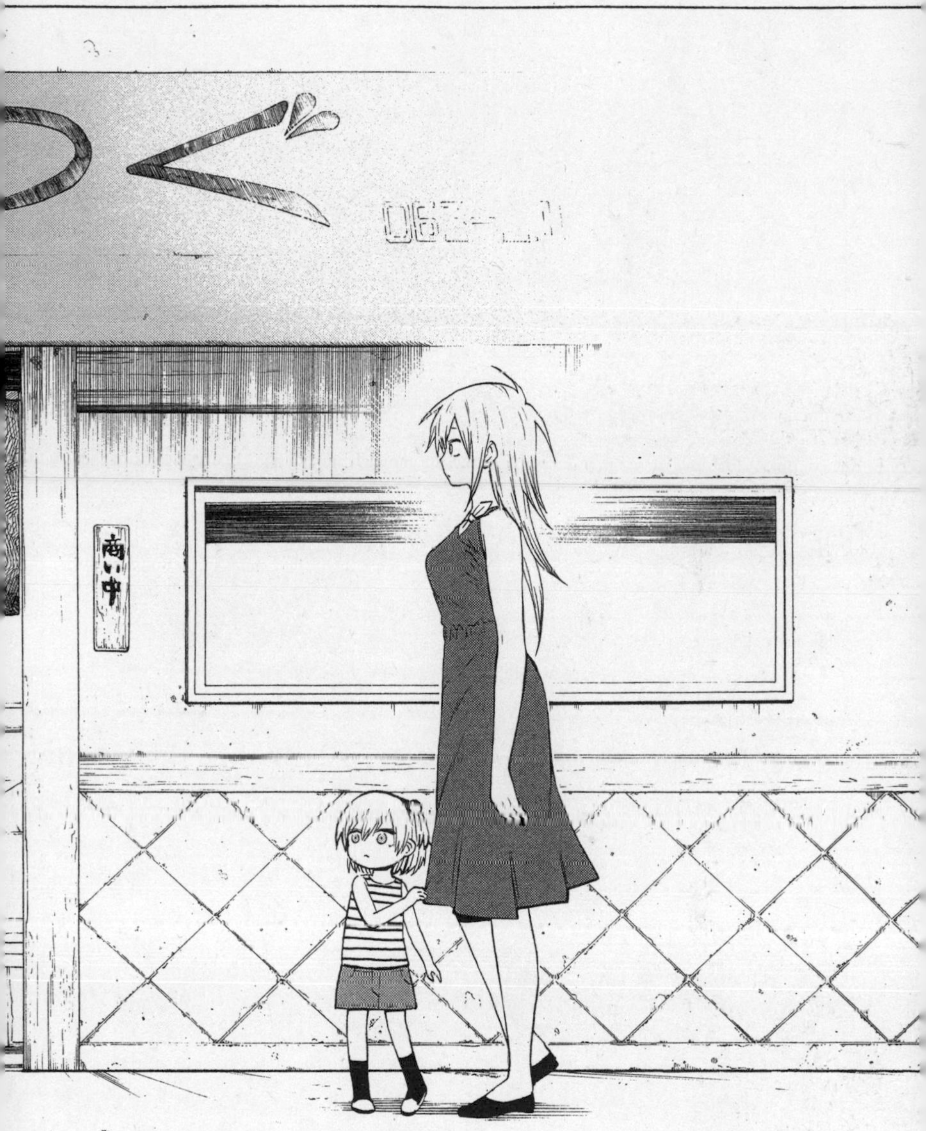
商い中
SIGN: OPEN

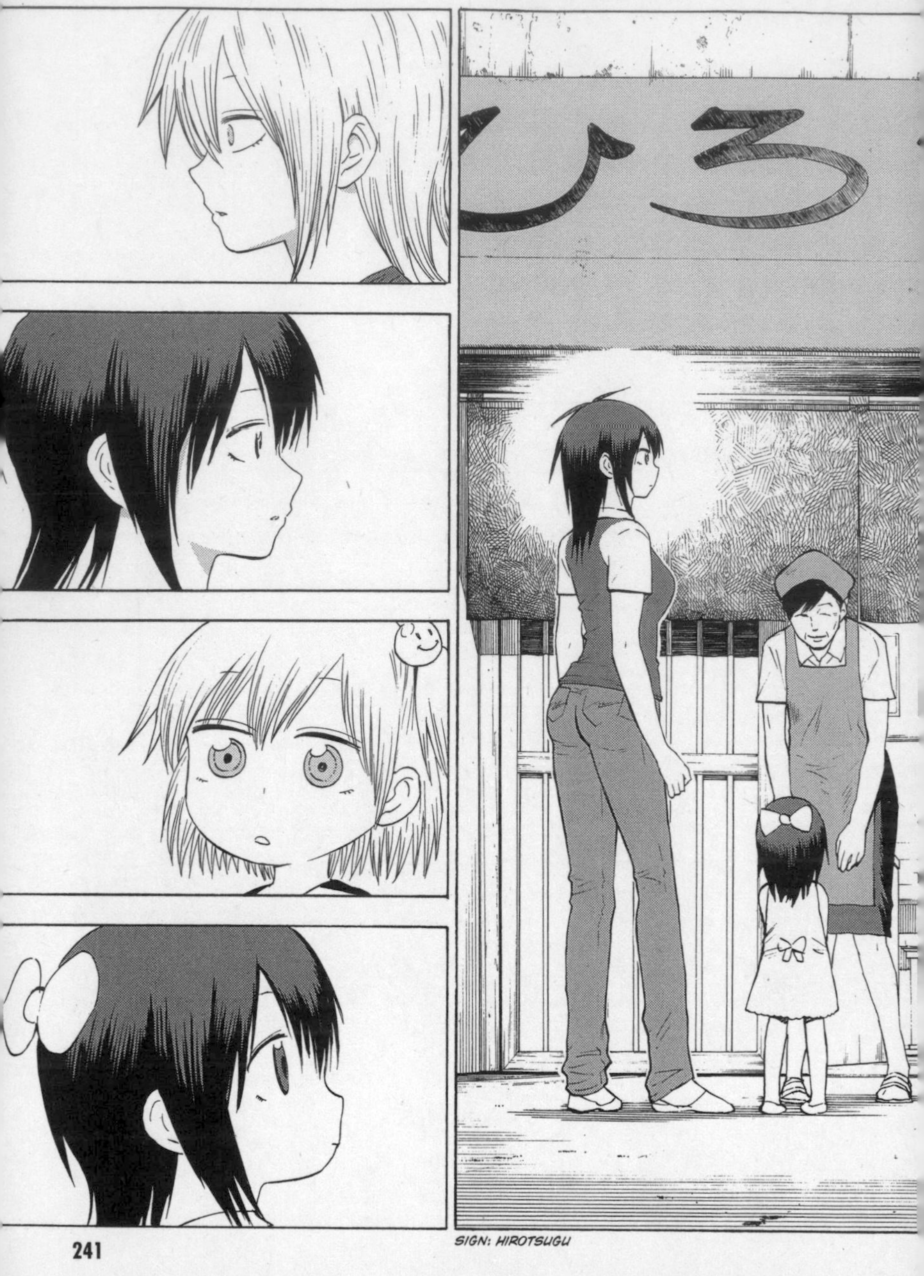
ひろ

SIGN: HIROTSUGU

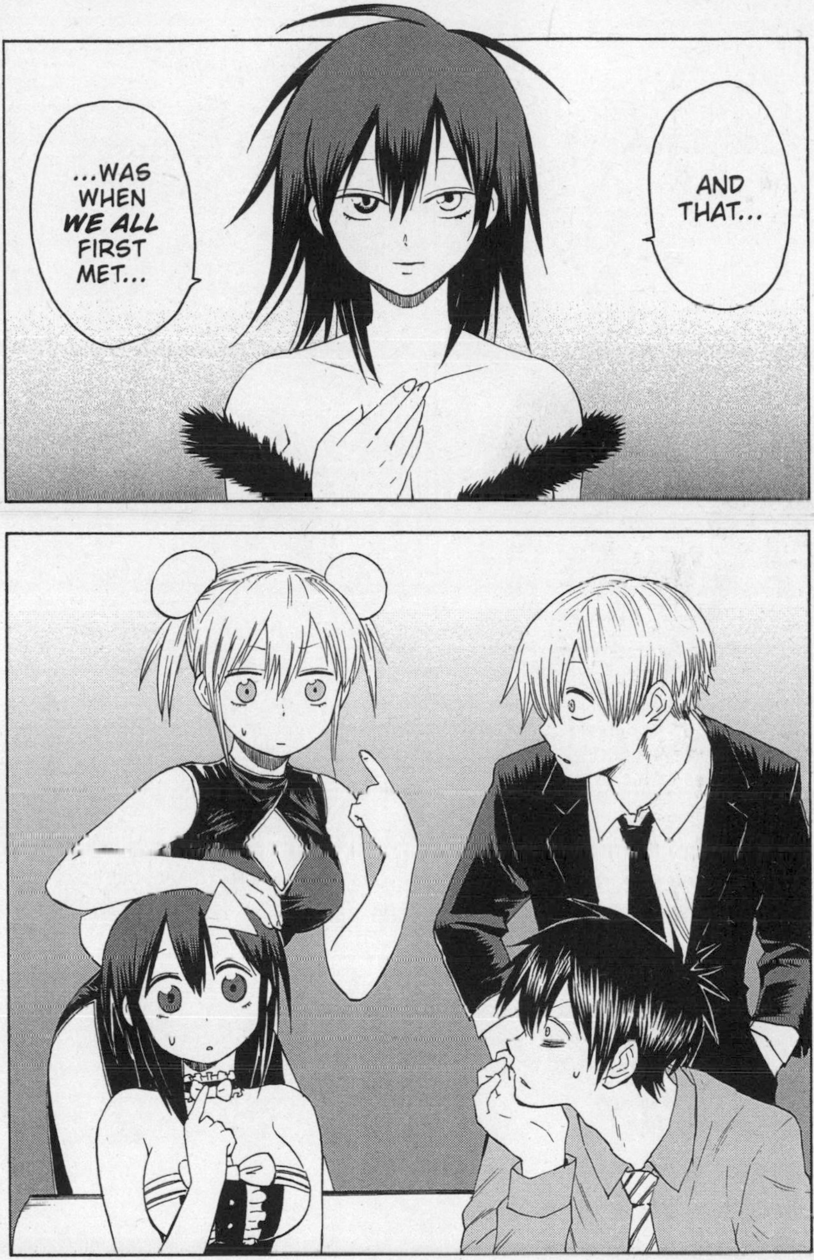
AND THAT...
...WAS WHEN ***WE ALL*** FIRST MET...

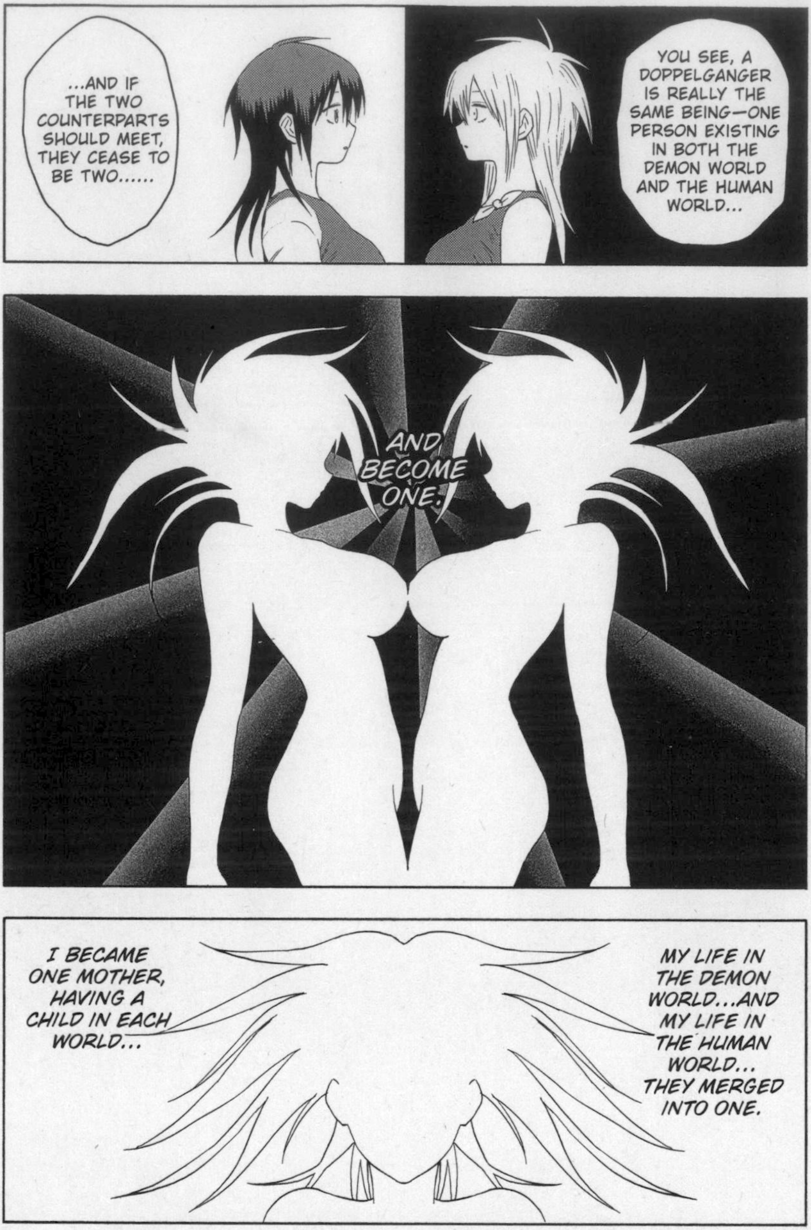
YOU SEE, A DOPPELGANGER IS REALLY THE SAME BEING—ONE PERSON EXISTING IN BOTH THE DEMON WORLD AND THE HUMAN WORLD...
...AND IF THE TWO COUNTERPARTS SHOULD MEET, THEY CEASE TO BE TWO......
AND BECOME ONE.
MY LIFE IN THE DEMON WORLD...AND MY LIFE IN THE HUMAN WORLD... THEY MERGED INTO ONE.
I BECAME ONE MOTHER, HAVING A CHILD IN EACH WORLD...

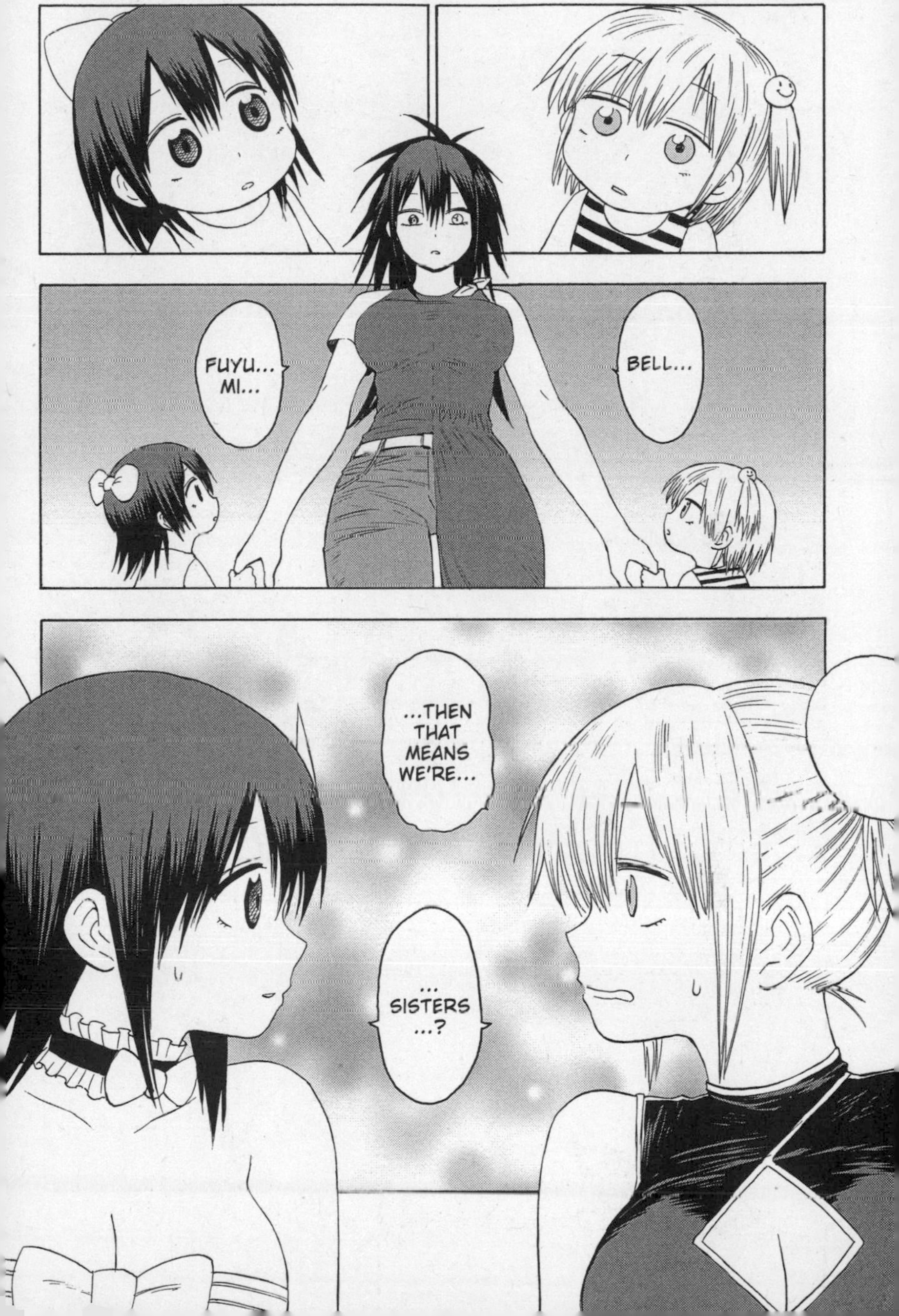
BELL...
FUYU... MI...
...THEN THAT MEANS WE'RE...
... SISTERS ...?

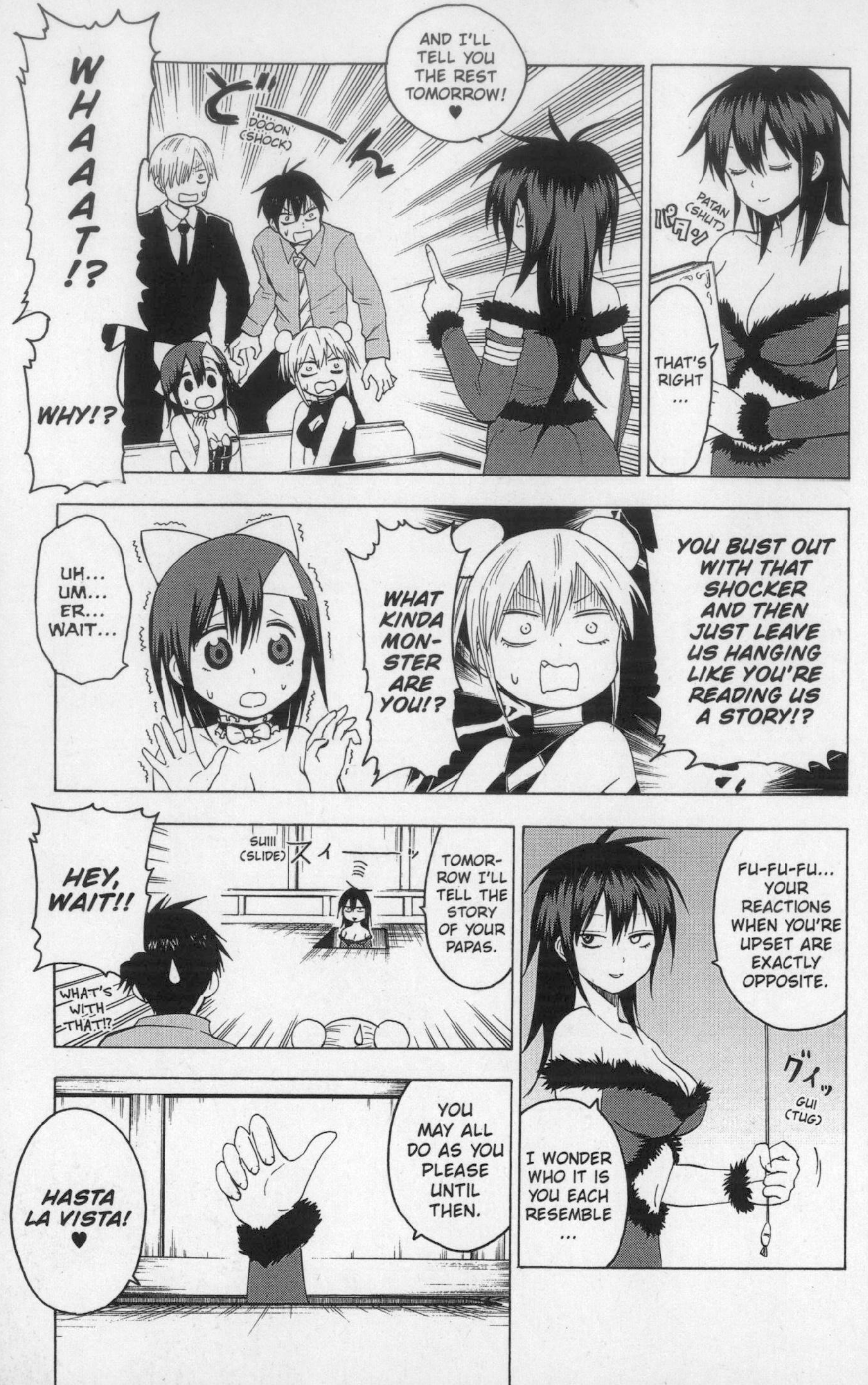
PATAN (SHUT) パタッ
THAT'S RIGHT ...
AND I'LL TELL YOU THE REST TOMORROW! ♥
DOOON (SHOCK)
WHAAAAT!?
WHY!?
YOU BUST OUT WITH THAT SHOCKER AND THEN JUST LEAVE US HANGING LIKE YOU'RE READING US A STORY!?
WHAT KINDA MON-STER ARE YOU!?
UH... UM... ER... WAIT...
FU-FU-FU... YOUR REACTIONS WHEN YOU'RE UPSET ARE EXACTLY OPPOSITE.
グイッ GUI (TUG)
I WONDER WHO IT IS YOU EACH RESEMBLE ...
TOMOR-ROW I'LL TELL THE STORY OF YOUR PAPAS.
SUIII (SLIDE) スィーーッ
HEY, WAIT!!
WHAT'S WITH THAT!?
YOU MAY ALL DO AS YOU PLEASE UNTIL THEN.
HASTA LA VISTA! ♥

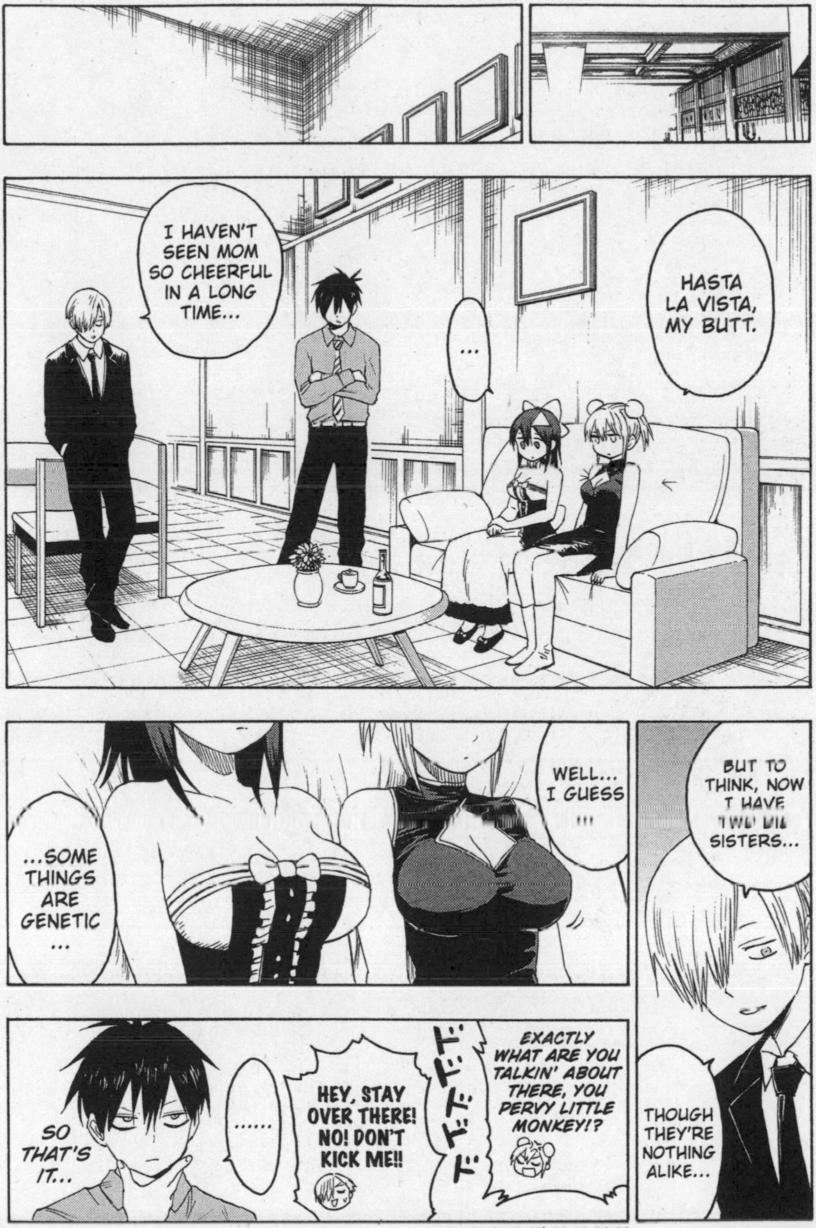
HASTA LA VISTA, MY BUTT.
...
I HAVEN'T SEEN MOM SO CHEERFUL IN A LONG TIME...
BUT TO THINK, NOW I HAVE TWO LIL SISTERS...
THOUGH THEY'RE NOTHING ALIKE...
WELL... I GUESS...
...SOME THINGS ARE GENETIC...
EXACTLY WHAT ARE YOU TALKIN' ABOUT THERE, YOU PERVY LITTLE MONKEY!?
ドドドドド
HEY, STAY OVER THERE! NO! DON'T KICK ME!!
......
SO THAT'S IT...

SFX: DO (STOMP) DO DO DO DO

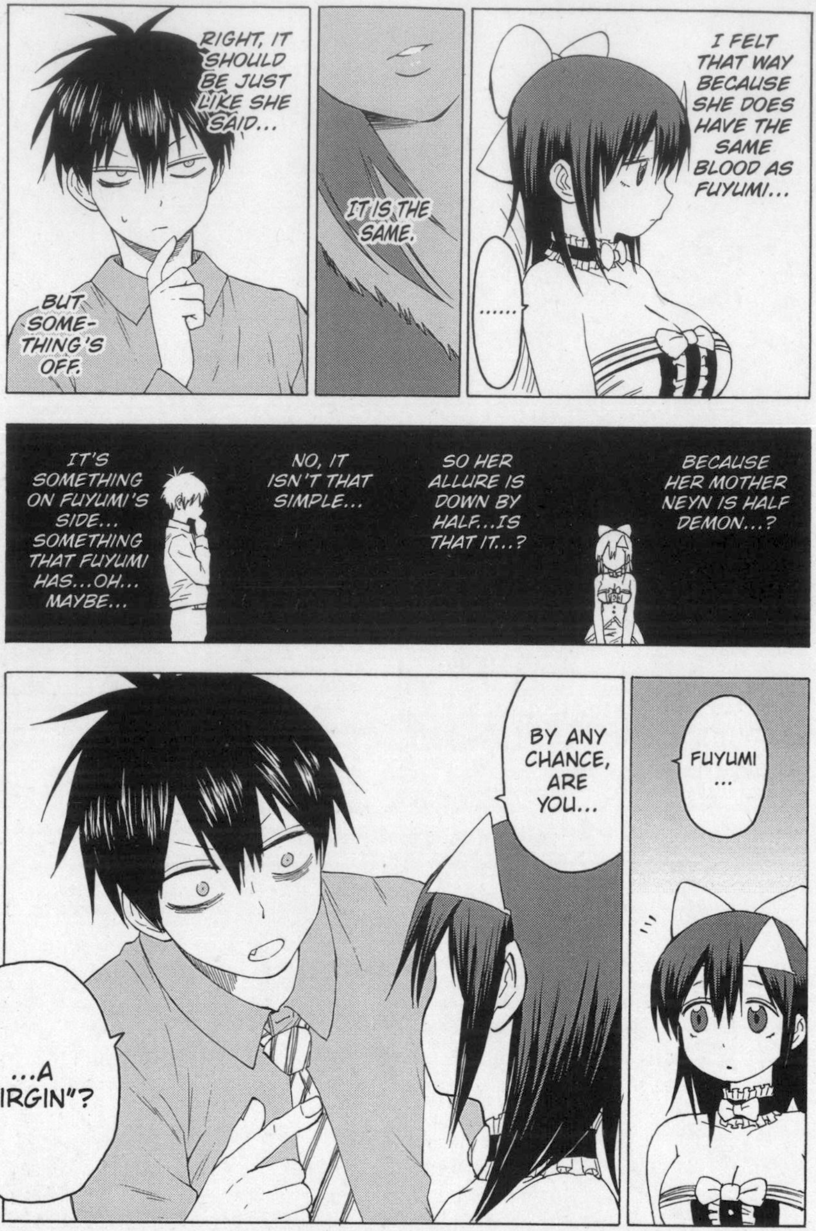

I FELT THAT WAY BECAUSE SHE DOES HAVE THE SAME BLOOD AS FUYUMI...
......
IT IS THE SAME.
RIGHT, IT SHOULD BE JUST LIKE SHE SAID...
BUT SOME-THING'S OFF.
BECAUSE HER MOTHER NEYN IS HALF DEMON...?
SO HER ALLURE IS DOWN BY HALF...IS THAT IT...?
NO, IT ISN'T THAT SIMPLE...
IT'S SOMETHING ON FUYUMI'S SIDE... SOMETHING THAT FUYUMI HAS...OH... MAYBE...
FUYUMI ...
BY ANY CHANCE, ARE YOU...
...A "VIRGIN"?

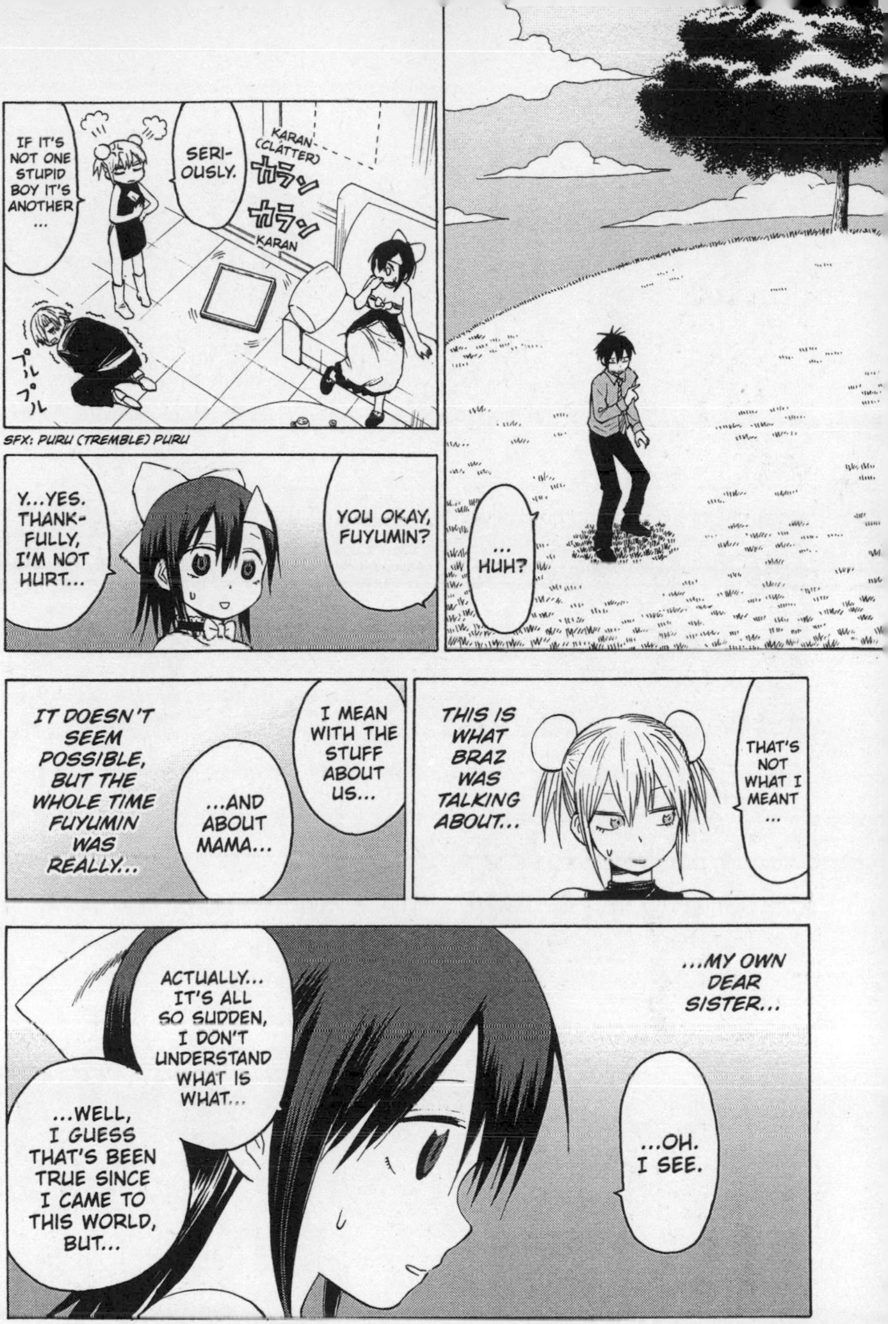
...
HUH?
KARAN (CLATTER)
カラッ
カラッ
KARAN
SERIOUSLY.
IF IT'S NOT ONE STUPID BOY IT'S ANOTHER...
プルプル
SFX: PURU (TREMBLE) PURU
YOU OKAY, FUYUMIN?
Y...YES. THANKFULLY, I'M NOT HURT...
THAT'S NOT WHAT I MEANT...
THIS IS WHAT BRAZ WAS TALKING ABOUT...
I MEAN WITH THE STUFF ABOUT US...
...AND ABOUT MAMA...
IT DOESN'T SEEM POSSIBLE, BUT THE WHOLE TIME FUYUMIN WAS REALLY...
...MY OWN DEAR SISTER...
...OH. I SEE.
ACTUALLY... IT'S ALL SO SUDDEN, I DON'T UNDERSTAND WHAT IS WHAT...
...WELL, I GUESS THAT'S BEEN TRUE SINCE I CAME TO THIS WORLD, BUT...

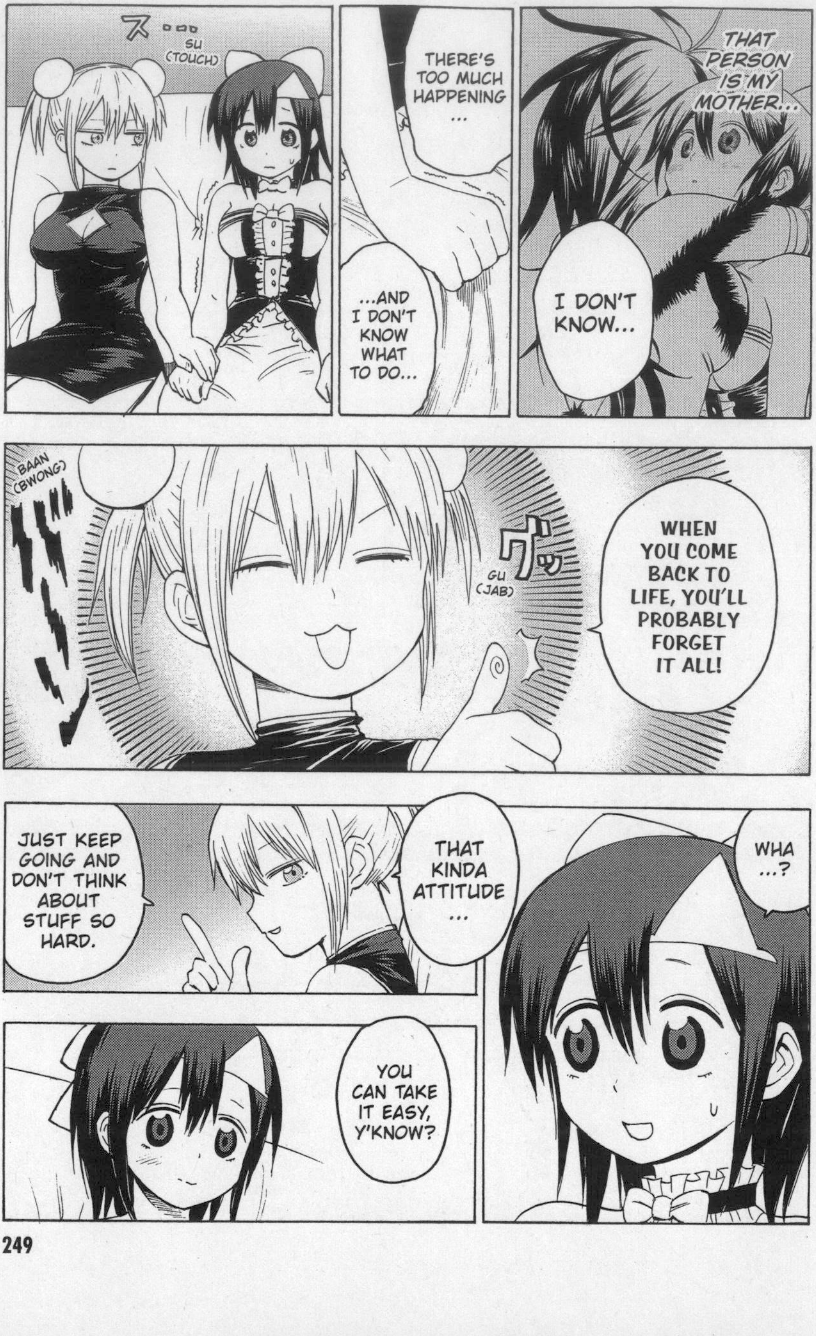
THAT PERSON IS MY MOTHER...
I DON'T KNOW...
THERE'S TOO MUCH HAPPENING ...
...AND I DON'T KNOW WHAT TO DO...
SU (TOUCH)
WHEN YOU COME BACK TO LIFE, YOU'LL PROBABLY FORGET IT ALL!
GU (JAB)
BAAN (BWONG)
WHA ...?
THAT KINDA ATTITUDE ...
JUST KEEP GOING AND DON'T THINK ABOUT STUFF SO HARD.
YOU CAN TAKE IT EASY, Y'KNOW?

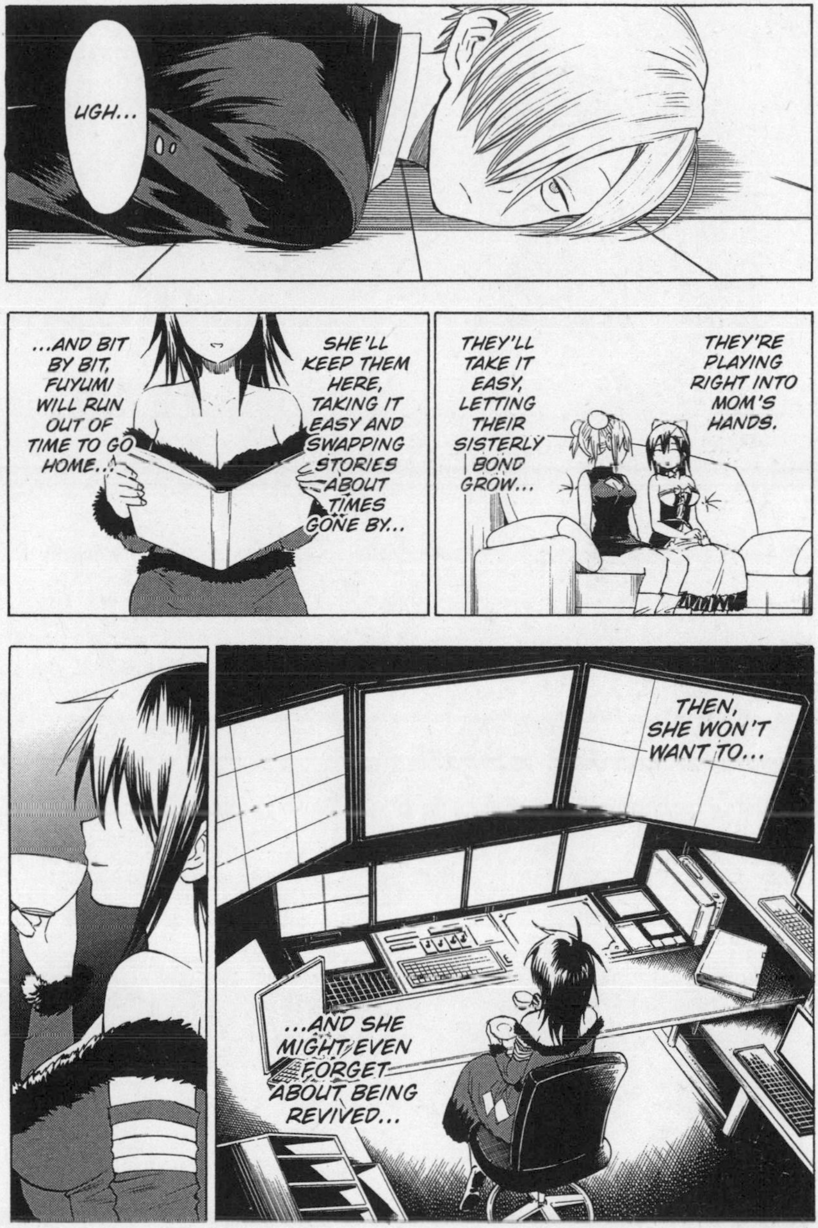
UGH...
THEY'RE PLAYING RIGHT INTO MOM'S HANDS.
THEY'LL TAKE IT EASY, LETTING THEIR SISTERLY BOND GROW...
SHE'LL KEEP THEM HERE, TAKING IT EASY AND SWAPPING STORIES ABOUT TIMES GONE BY...
...AND BIT BY BIT, FUYUMI WILL RUN OUT OF TIME TO GO HOME...
THEN, SHE WON'T WANT TO...
...AND SHE MIGHT EVEN FORGET ABOUT BEING REVIVED...

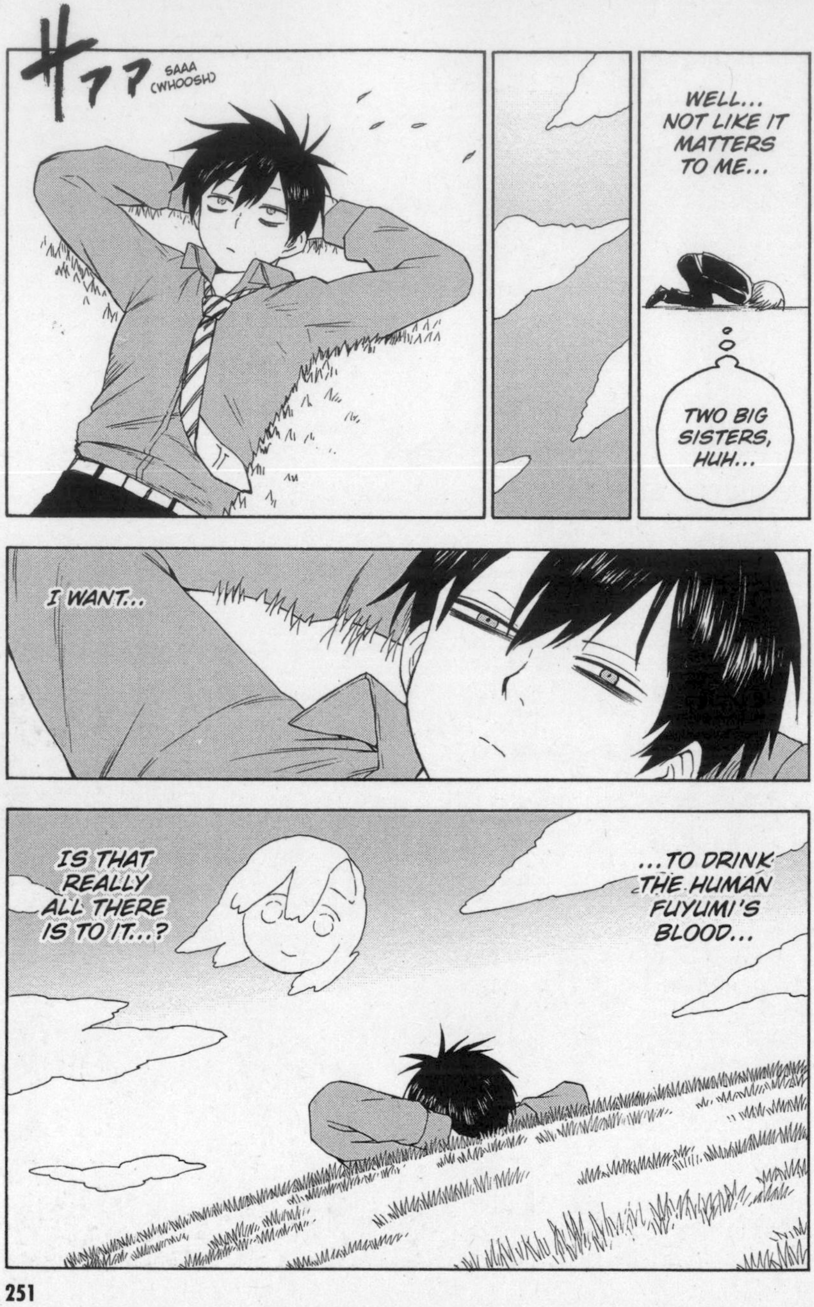
WELL... NOT LIKE IT MATTERS TO ME...
TWO BIG SISTERS, HUH...
サァァ
SAAA (WHOOSH)
I WANT...
...TO DRINK THE HUMAN FUYUMI'S BLOOD...
IS THAT REALLY ALL THERE IS TO IT...?

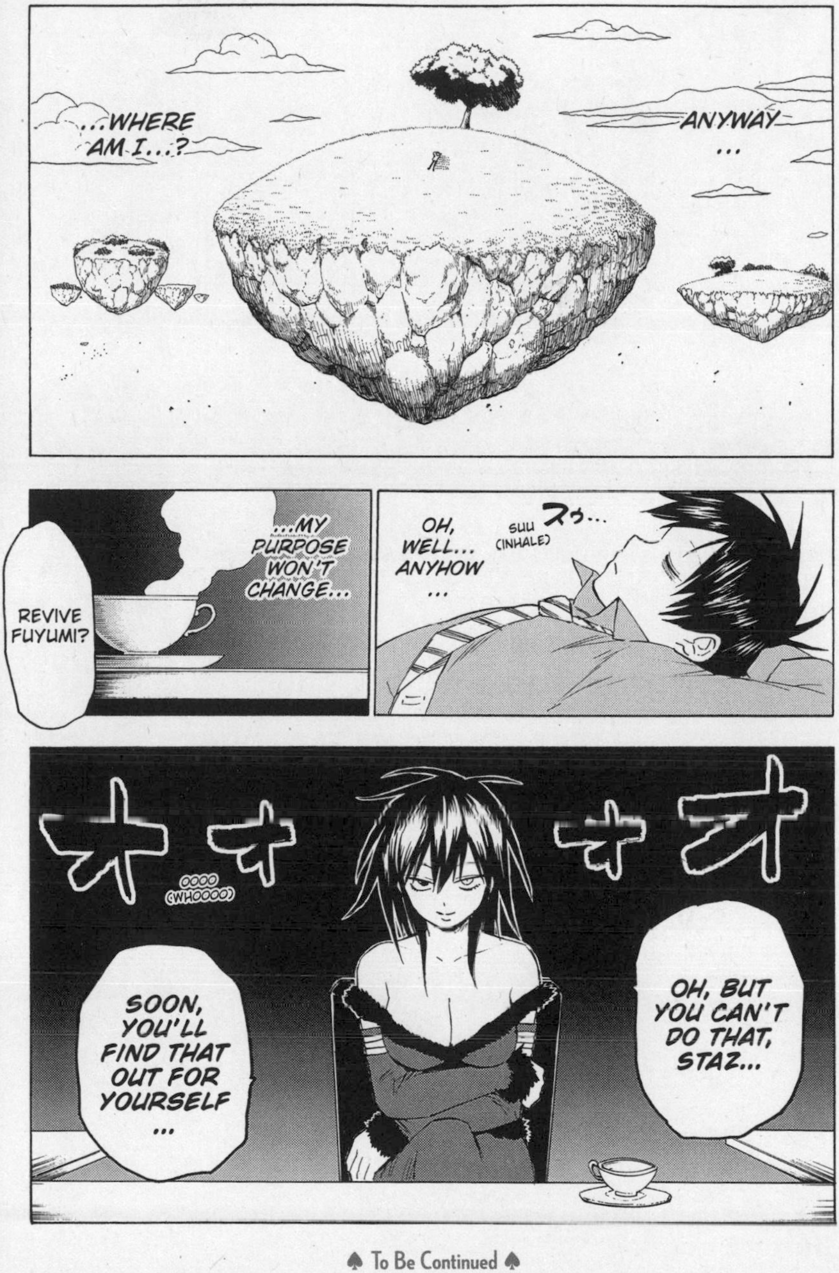
ANYWAY ...
...WHERE AM I...?
スゥ...
SUU (INHALE)
OH, WELL... ANYHOW ...
...MY PURPOSE WON'T CHANGE...
REVIVE FUYUMI?
OH, BUT YOU CAN'T DO THAT, STAZ...
OOOO (WHOOOO)
SOON, YOU'LL FIND THAT OUT FOR YOURSELF ...

♠ To Be Continued ♠

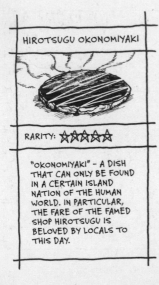

HIROTSUGU OKONOMIYAKI

RARITY: ☆☆☆☆☆

"OKONOMIYAKI" – A DISH
THAT CAN ONLY BE FOUND
IN A CERTAIN ISLAND
NATION OF THE HUMAN
WORLD. IN PARTICULAR,
THE FARE OF THE FAMED
SHOP HIROTSUGU IS
BELOVED BY LOCALS TO
THIS DAY.

BLOOD LAD

CHAPTER 28 ♠ SUPER YOUNG

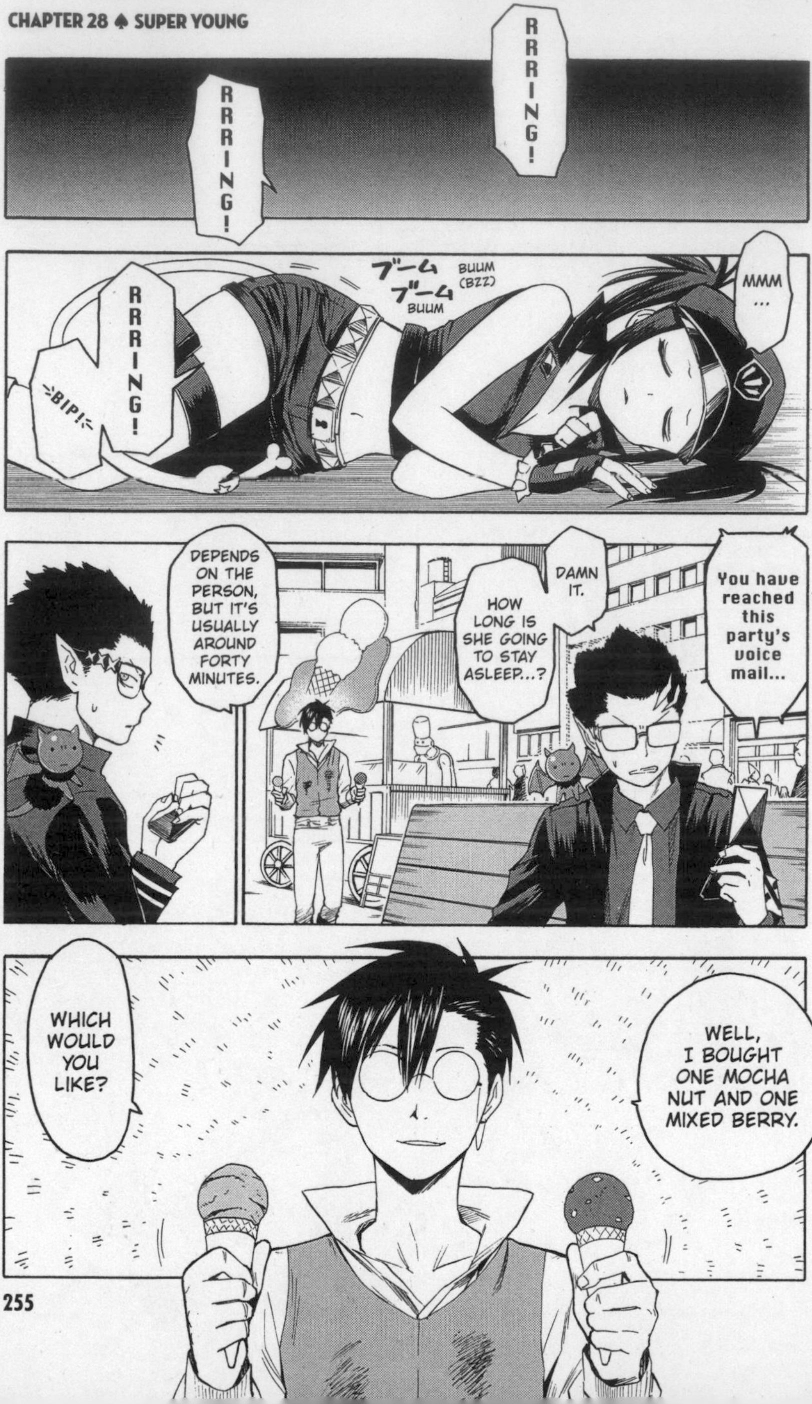
RRRING!
RRRING!
MMM...
ブーム ブーム
BUUM (BZZ) BUUM
RRRING!
BIP!
You have reached this party's voice mail...
DAMN IT.
HOW LONG IS SHE GOING TO STAY ASLEEP...?
DEPENDS ON THE PERSON, BUT IT'S USUALLY AROUND FORTY MINUTES.
WELL, I BOUGHT ONE MOCHA NUT AND ONE MIXED BERRY.
WHICH WOULD YOU LIKE?

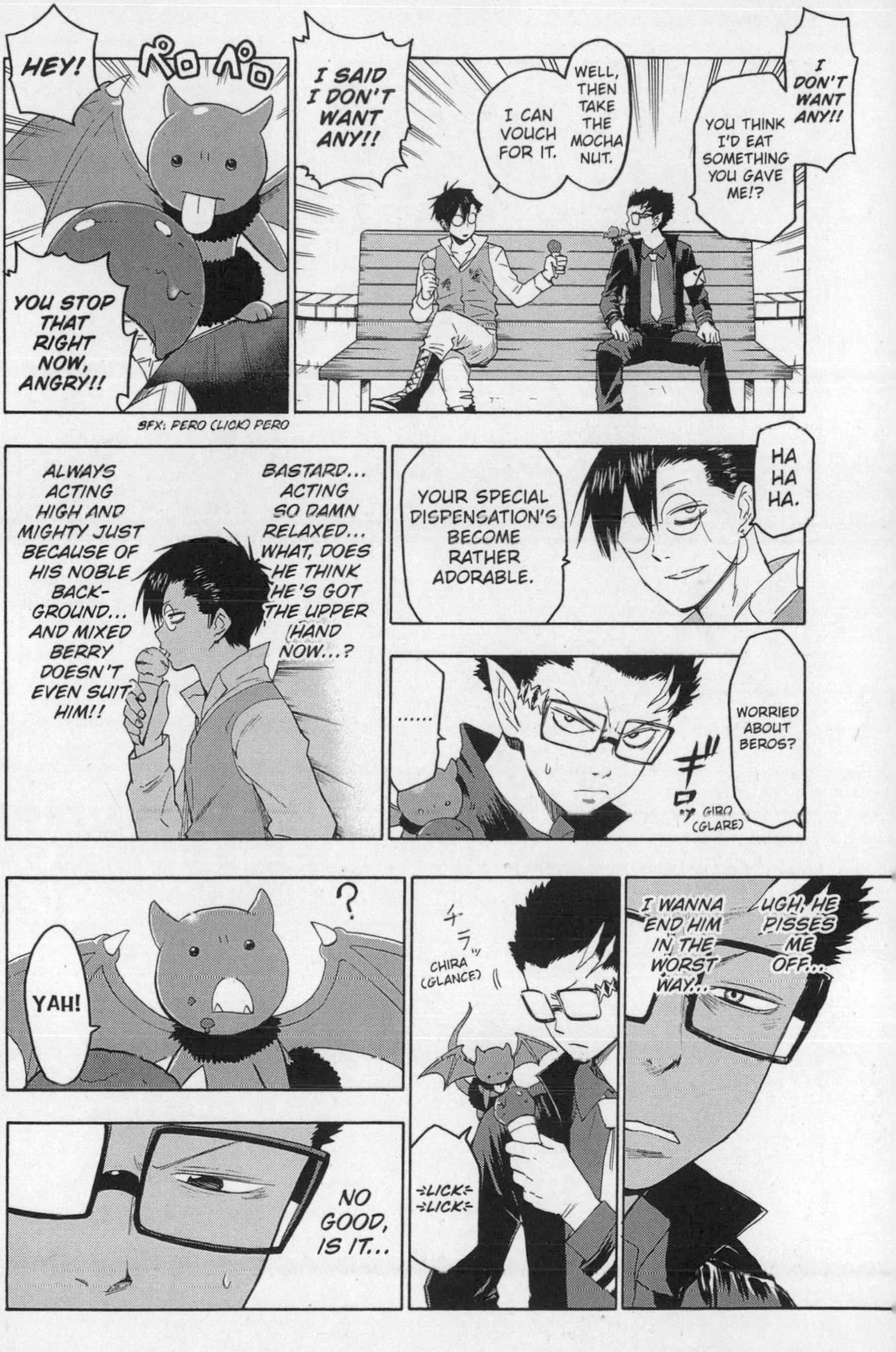
I DON'T WANT ANY!!
YOU THINK I'D EAT SOMETHING YOU GAVE ME!?
WELL, THEN TAKE THE MOCHA NUT.
I CAN VOUCH FOR IT.
I SAID I DON'T WANT ANY!!
HEY!
ペロペロ
YOU STOP THAT RIGHT NOW, ANGRY!!
SFX: PERO (LICK) PERO
HA HA HA.
YOUR SPECIAL DISPENSATION'S BECOME RATHER ADORABLE.
WORRIED ABOUT BEROS?
ギロッ
GIRO (GLARE)
......
BASTARD... ACTING SO DAMN RELAXED... WHAT, DOES HE THINK HE'S GOT THE UPPER HAND NOW...?
ALWAYS ACTING HIGH AND MIGHTY JUST BECAUSE OF HIS NOBLE BACKGROUND... AND MIXED BERRY DOESN'T EVEN SUIT HIM!!
UGH, HE PISSES ME OFF...
I WANNA END HIM IN THE WORST WAY...
チラッ
CHIRA (GLANCE)
LICK
LICK
?
YAH!
NO GOOD, IS IT...

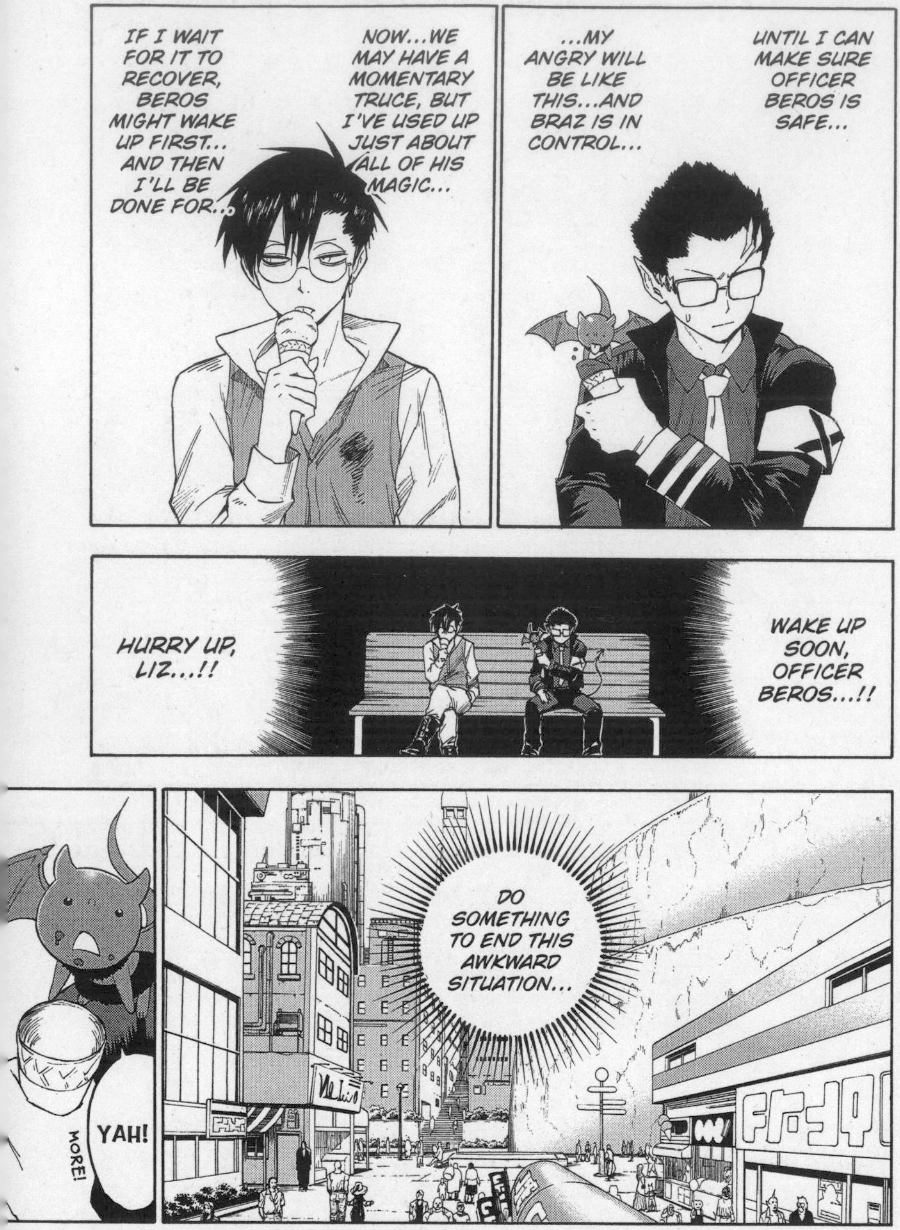
UNTIL I CAN MAKE SURE OFFICER BEROS IS SAFE...
...MY ANGRY WILL BE LIKE THIS...AND BRAZ IS IN CONTROL...
NOW...WE MAY HAVE A MOMENTARY TRUCE, BUT I'VE USED UP JUST ABOUT ALL OF HIS MAGIC...
IF I WAIT FOR IT TO RECOVER, BEROS MIGHT WAKE UP FIRST... AND THEN I'LL BE DONE FOR...
WAKE UP SOON, OFFICER BEROS...!!
HURRY UP, LIZ...!!
DO SOMETHING TO END THIS AWKWARD SITUATION...
YAH!
MORE!

CHAPTER 28 ♠ SUPER YOUNG

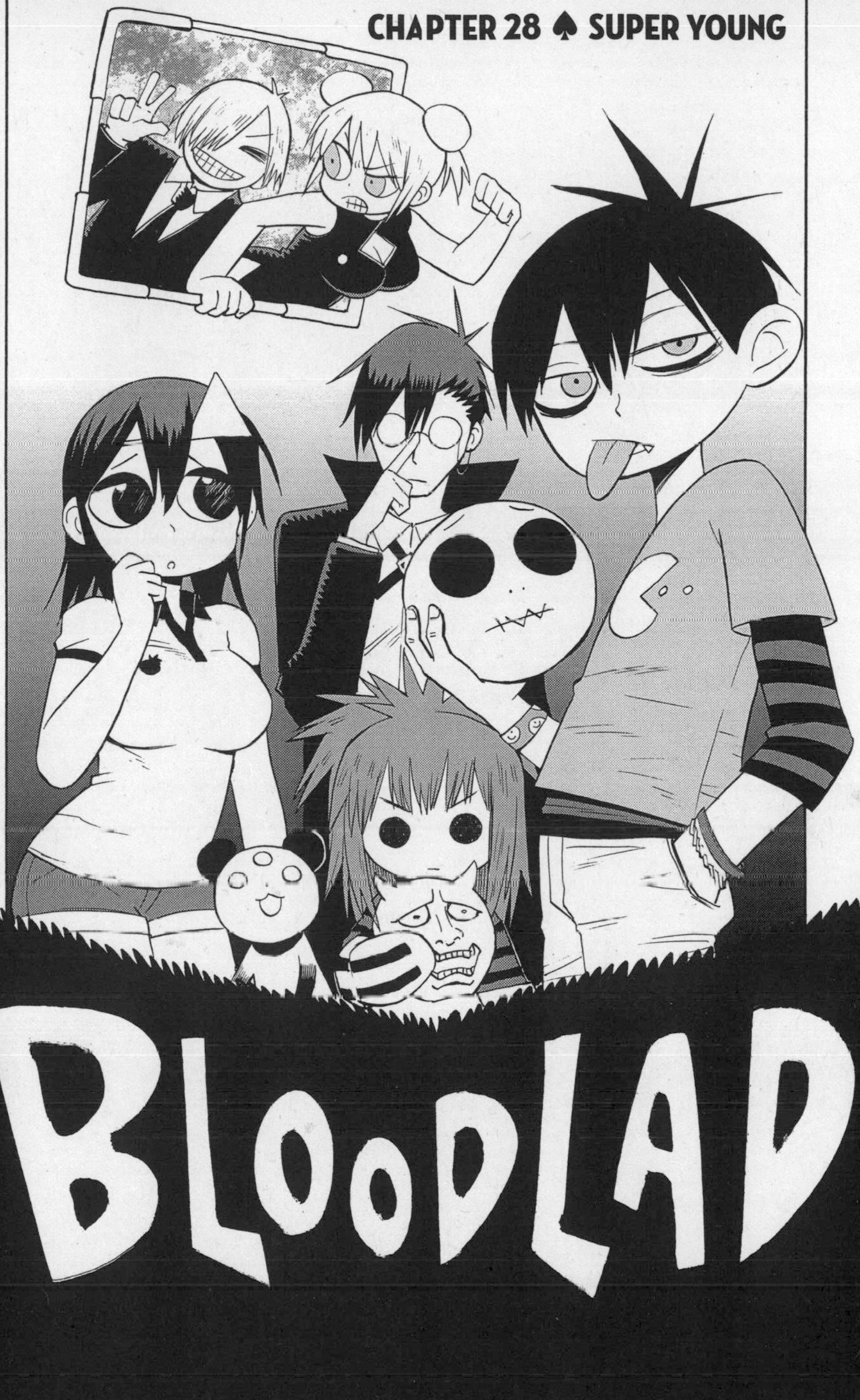
BLOODLAD

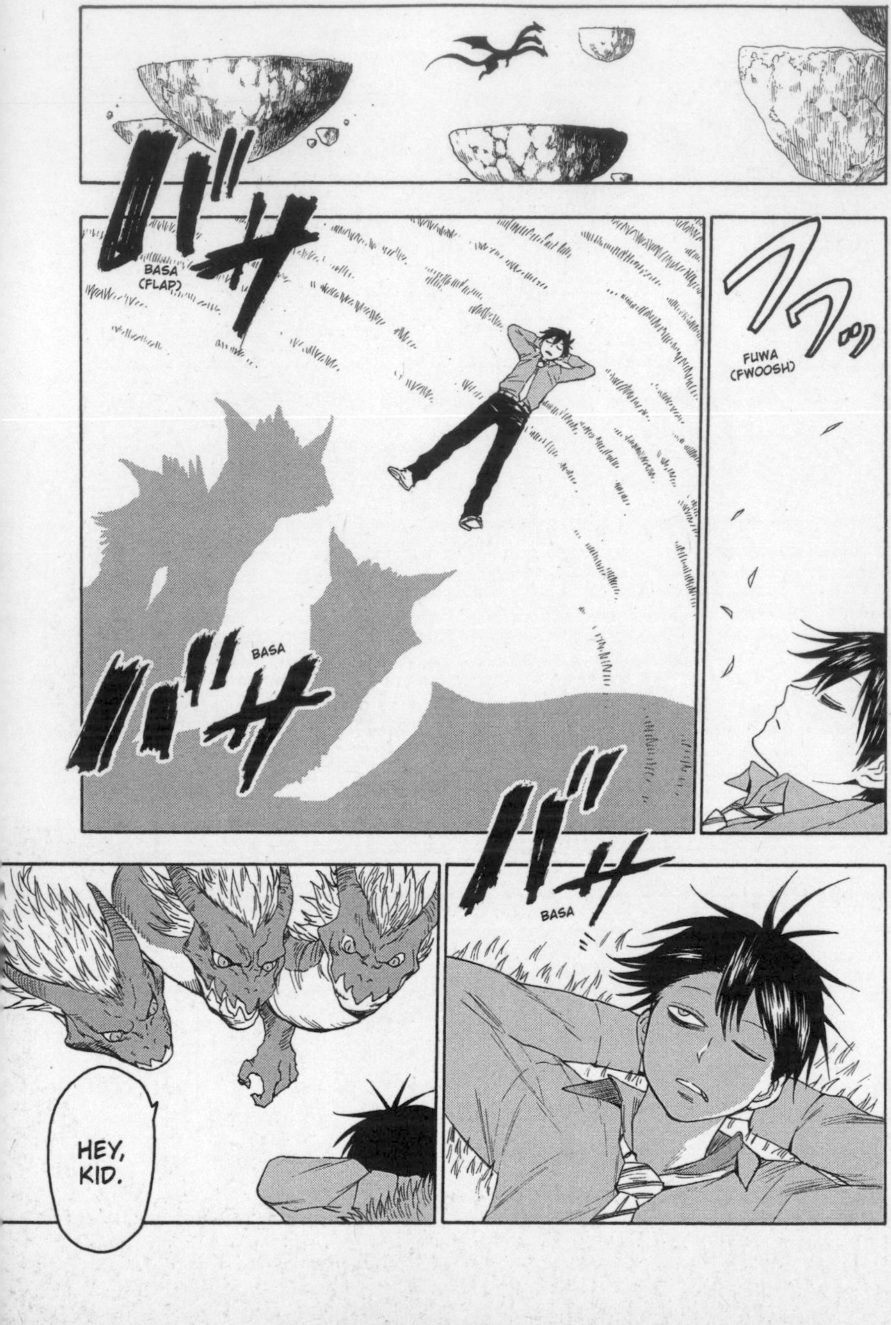
FUWA (FWOOSH)
BASA (FLAP)
BASA
BASA
HEY, KID.

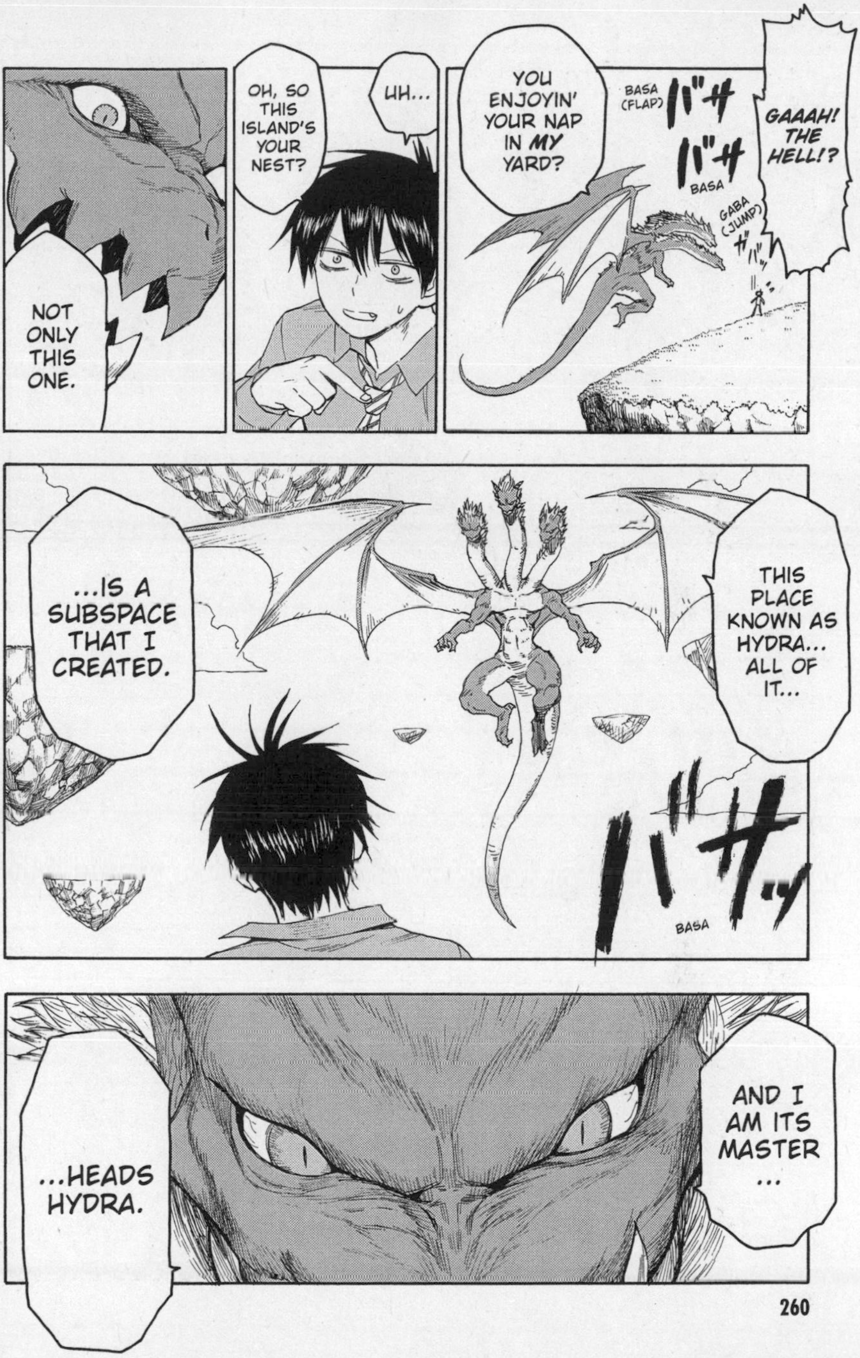
GAAAH! THE HELL!?
BASA (FLAP) バサ
バサ BASA
GABA (JUMP) ガバッ
YOU ENJOYIN' YOUR NAP IN MY YARD?
UH...
OH, SO THIS ISLAND'S YOUR NEST?
NOT ONLY THIS ONE.
THIS PLACE KNOWN AS HYDRA... ALL OF IT...
...IS A SUBSPACE THAT I CREATED.
バサッ BASA
AND I AM ITS MASTER ...
...HEADS HYDRA.

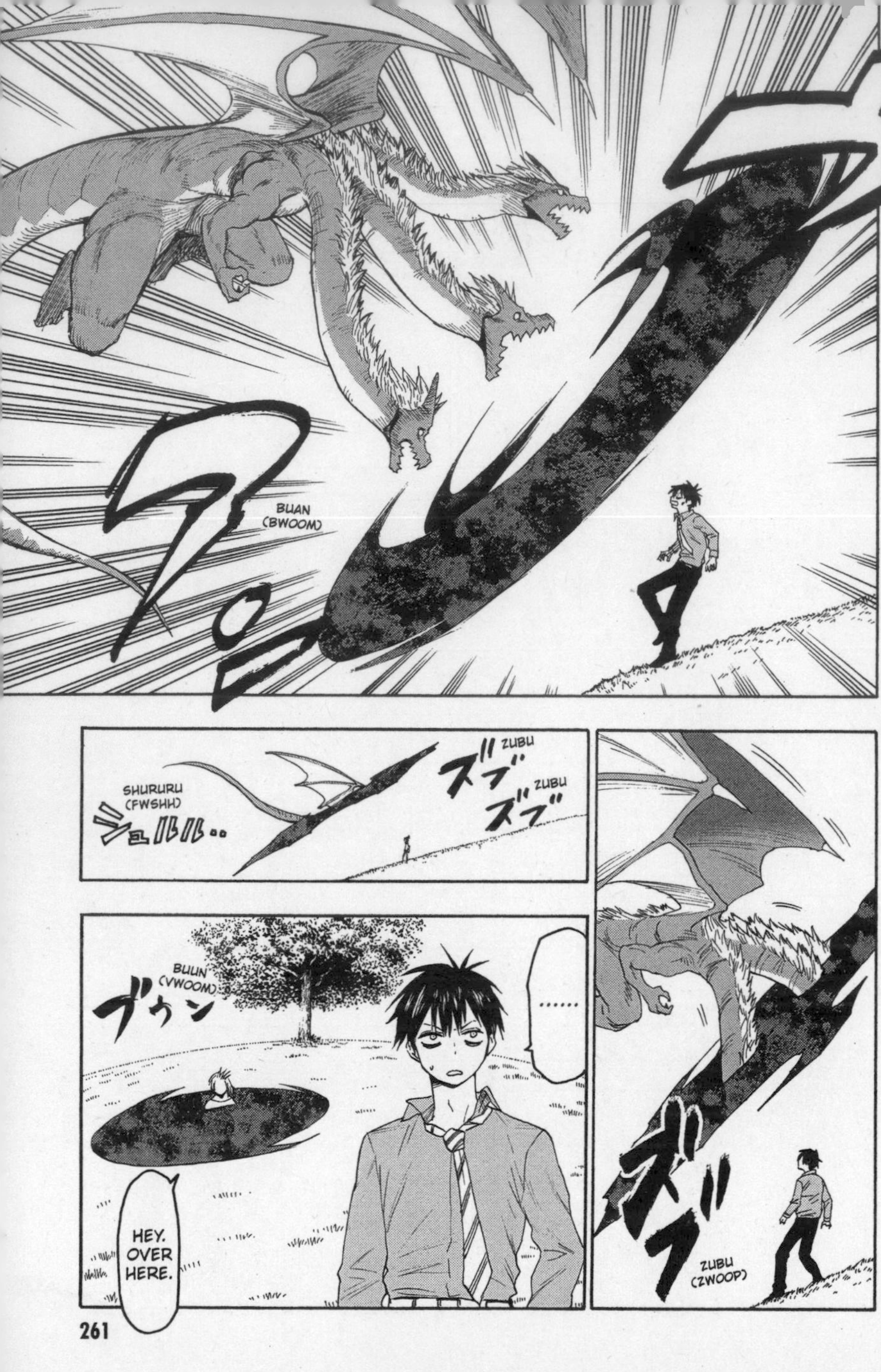
BUAN
(BWOOM)
ZUBU
(ZWOOP)
ZUBU
ズブ
ZUBU
ズブ
SHURURU
(FWSHH)
シュルル..
......
BUUN
(VWOOM)
ブウン
HEY. OVER HERE.

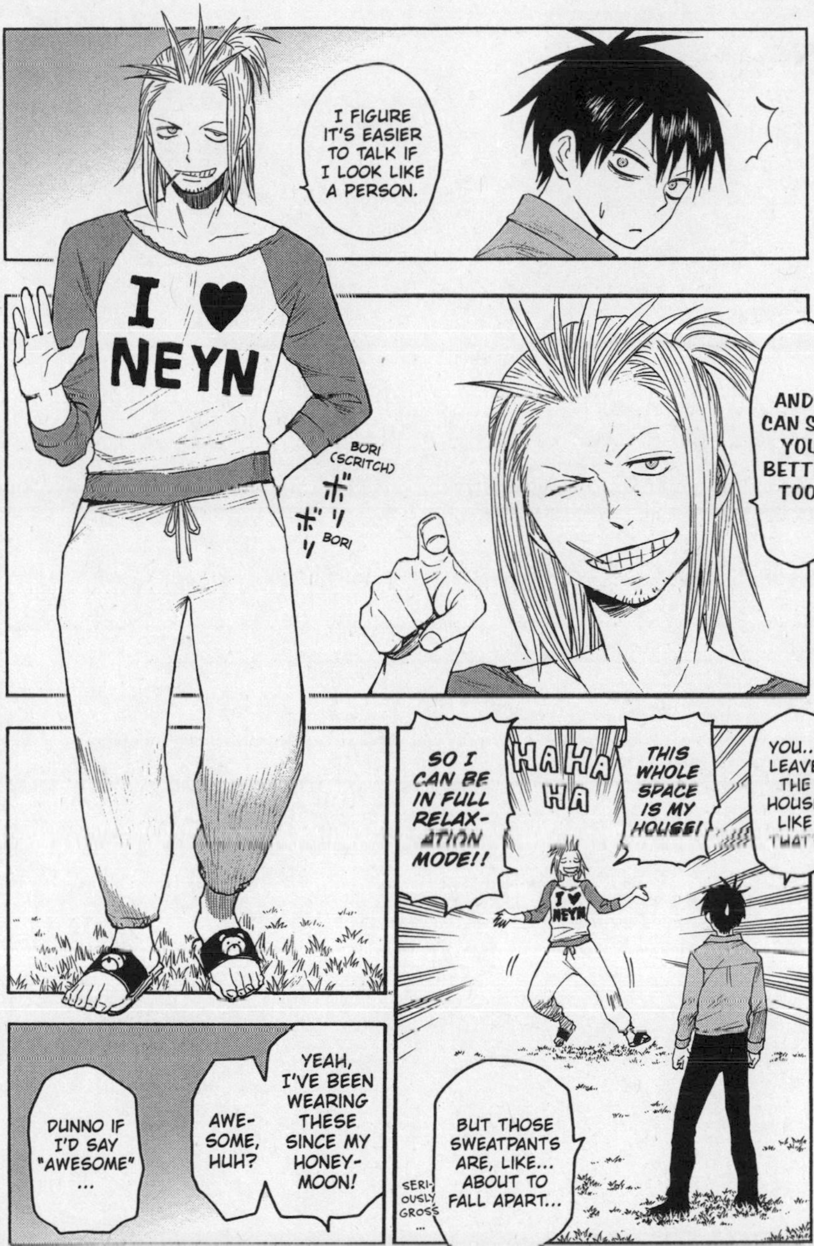
I FIGURE IT'S EASIER TO TALK IF I LOOK LIKE A PERSON.
I ♥ NEYN
AND I CAN SEE YOU BETTER TOO.
ボリ BORI (SCRITCH)
ボリ BORI
YOU... LEAVE THE HOUSE LIKE THAT?
THIS WHOLE SPACE IS MY HOUSE!
HAHA HA
SO I CAN BE IN FULL RELAX-ATION MODE!!
I ♥ NEYN
BUT THOSE SWEATPANTS ARE, LIKE... ABOUT TO FALL APART...
SERI-OUSLY GROSS ...
YEAH, I'VE BEEN WEARING THESE SINCE MY HONEY-MOON!
AWE-SOME, HUH?
DUNNO IF I'D SAY "AWESOME" ...

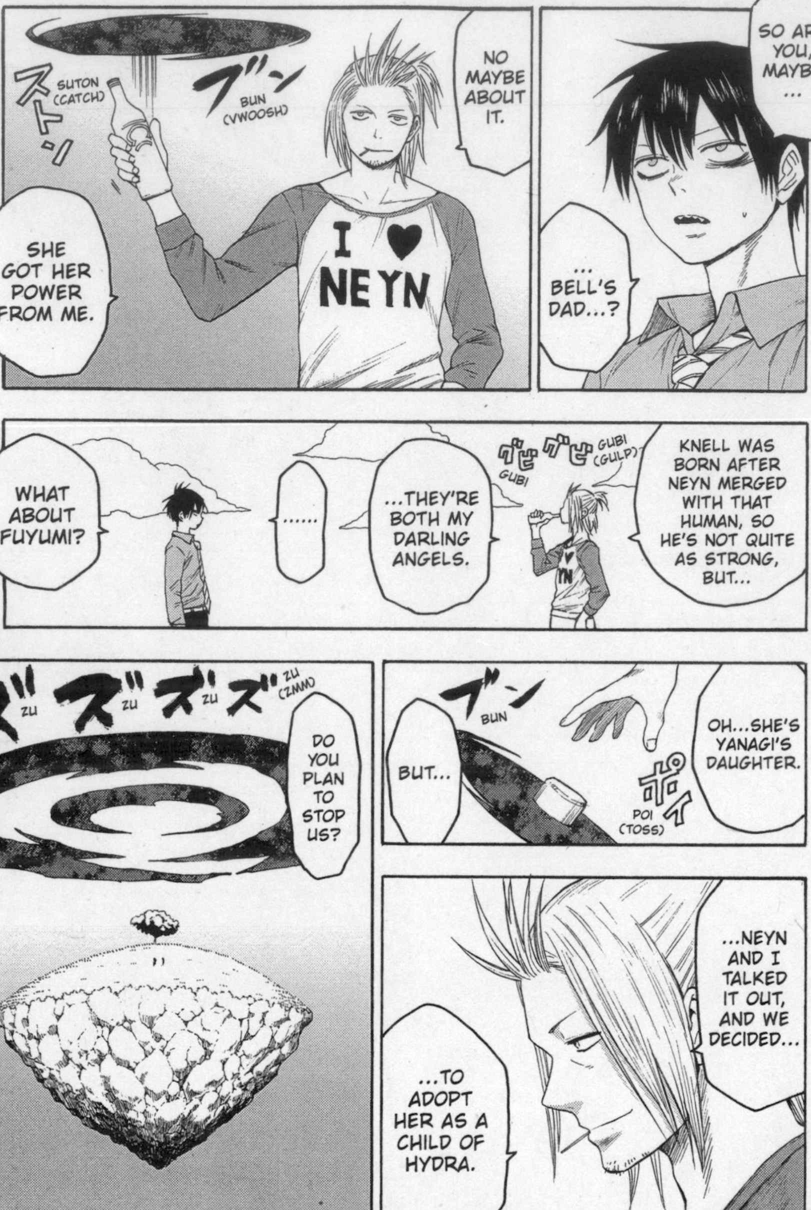
SO ARE YOU, MAYBE ...
... BELL'S DAD...?
NO MAYBE ABOUT IT.
BUN (VWOOSH)
SUTON (CATCH)
SHE GOT HER POWER FROM ME.
KNELL WAS BORN AFTER NEYN MERGED WITH THAT HUMAN, SO HE'S NOT QUITE AS STRONG, BUT...
GUBI GUBI (GULP)
...THEY'RE BOTH MY DARLING ANGELS.
......
WHAT ABOUT FUYUMI?
OH...SHE'S YANAGI'S DAUGHTER.
POI (TOSS)
BUN
BUT...
...NEYN AND I TALKED IT OUT, AND WE DECIDED...
...TO ADOPT HER AS A CHILD OF HYDRA.
ZU ZU ZU ZU (ZMM)
DO YOU PLAN TO STOP US?

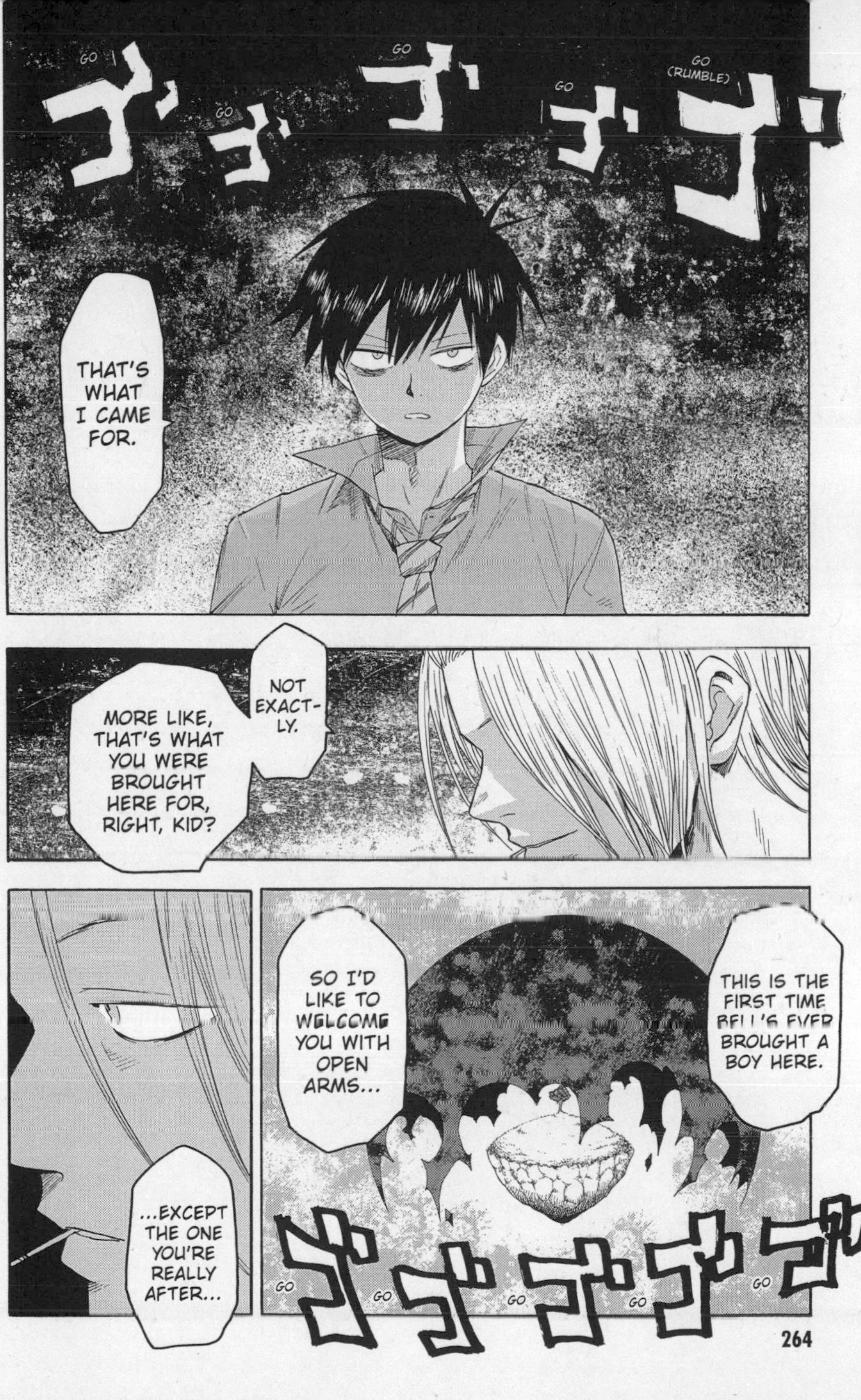
GO
GO
GO
GO
GO (RUMBLE)
THAT'S WHAT I CAME FOR.
NOT EXACT-LY.
MORE LIKE, THAT'S WHAT YOU WERE BROUGHT HERE FOR, RIGHT, KID?
THIS IS THE FIRST TIME BELL'S EVER BROUGHT A BOY HERE.
SO I'D LIKE TO WELCOME YOU WITH OPEN ARMS...
GO GO GO GO GO
...EXCEPT THE ONE YOU'RE REALLY AFTER...

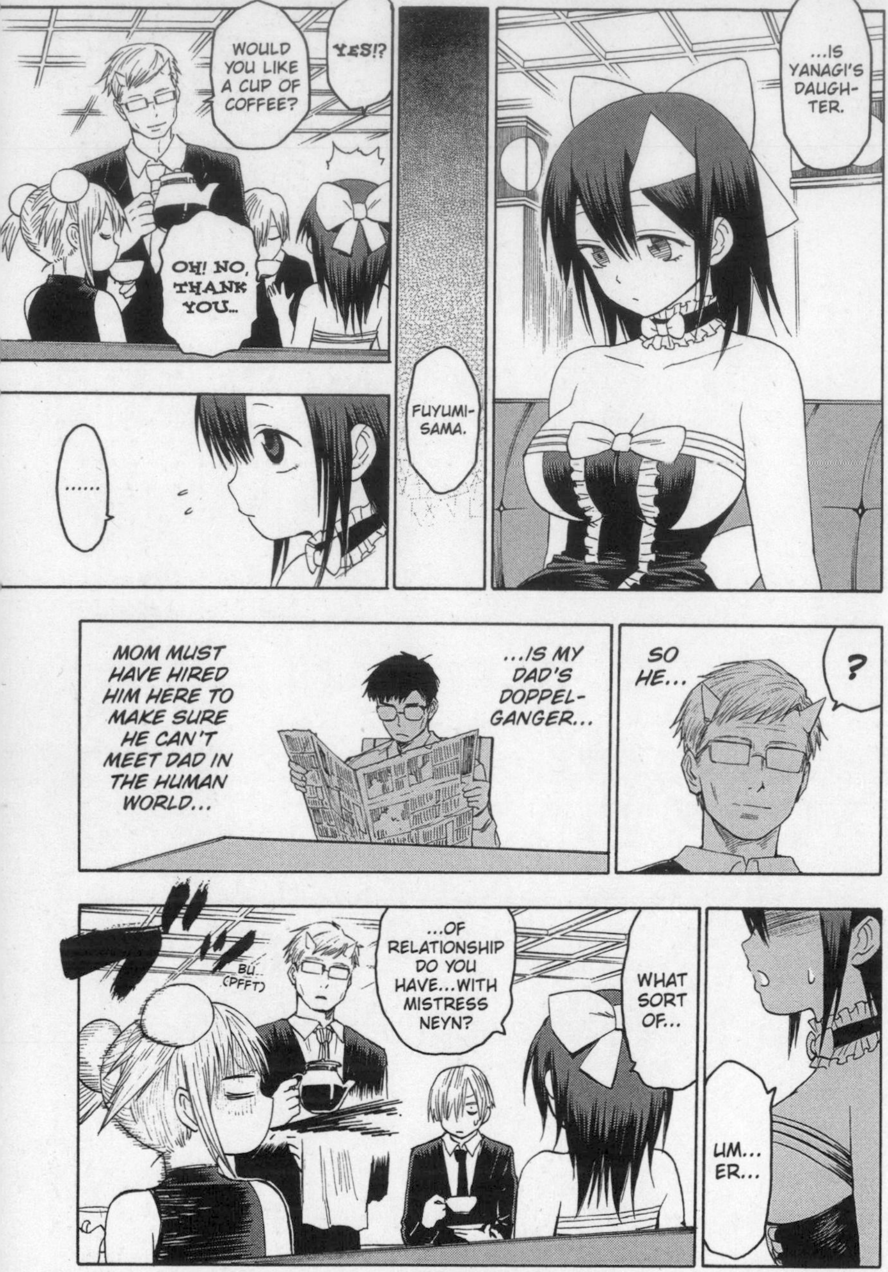
...IS YANAGI'S DAUGHTER.
FUYUMI-SAMA.
YES!?
WOULD YOU LIKE A CUP OF COFFEE?
OH! NO, THANK YOU...
......
?
SO HE...
...IS MY DAD'S DOPPEL-GANGER...
MOM MUST HAVE HIRED HIM HERE TO MAKE SURE HE CAN'T MEET DAD IN THE HUMAN WORLD...
UM... ER...
WHAT SORT OF...
...OF RELATIONSHIP DO YOU HAVE...WITH MISTRESS NEYN?
BU... (PFFT)

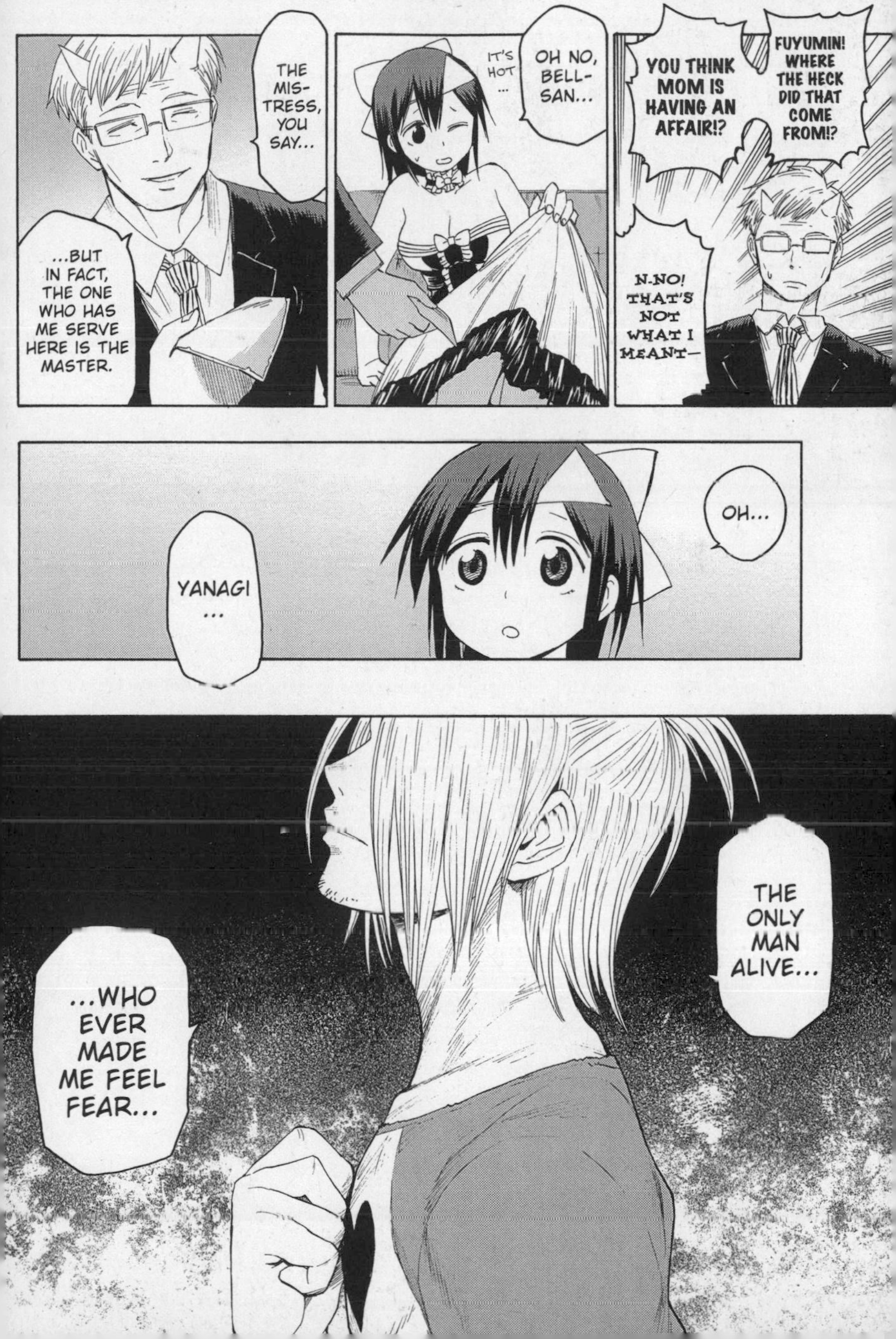
FUYUMIN! WHERE THE HECK DID THAT COME FROM!?
YOU THINK MOM IS HAVING AN AFFAIR!?
N-NO! THAT'S NOT WHAT I MEANT—
OH NO, BELL-SAN...
IT'S HOT ...
THE MIS-TRESS, YOU SAY...
...BUT IN FACT, THE ONE WHO HAS ME SERVE HERE IS THE MASTER.
OH...
YANAGI ...
THE ONLY MAN ALIVE...
...WHO EVER MADE ME FEEL FEAR...

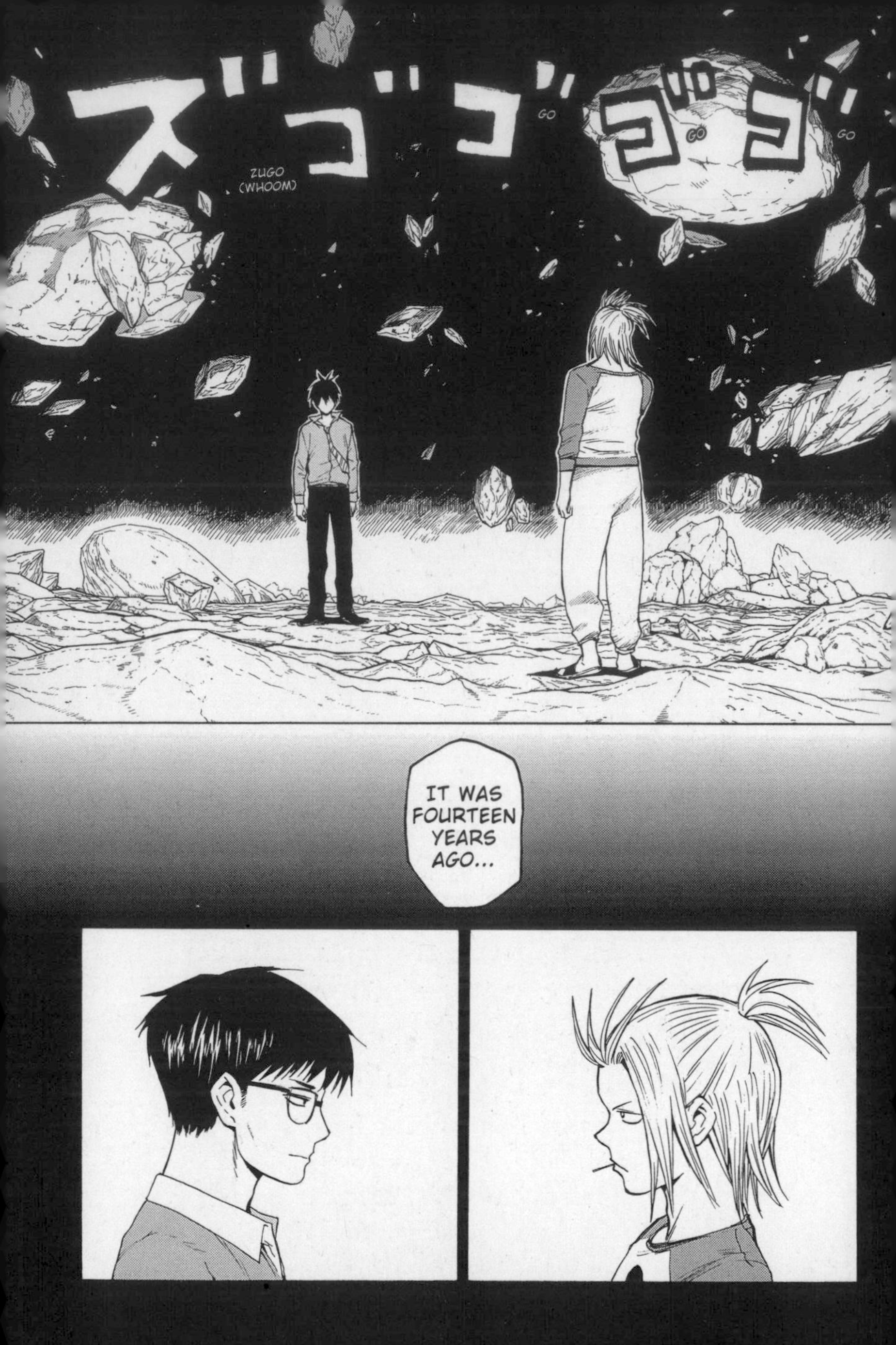
ZUGO (WHOOM)
GO
GO
GO
IT WAS FOURTEEN YEARS AGO...

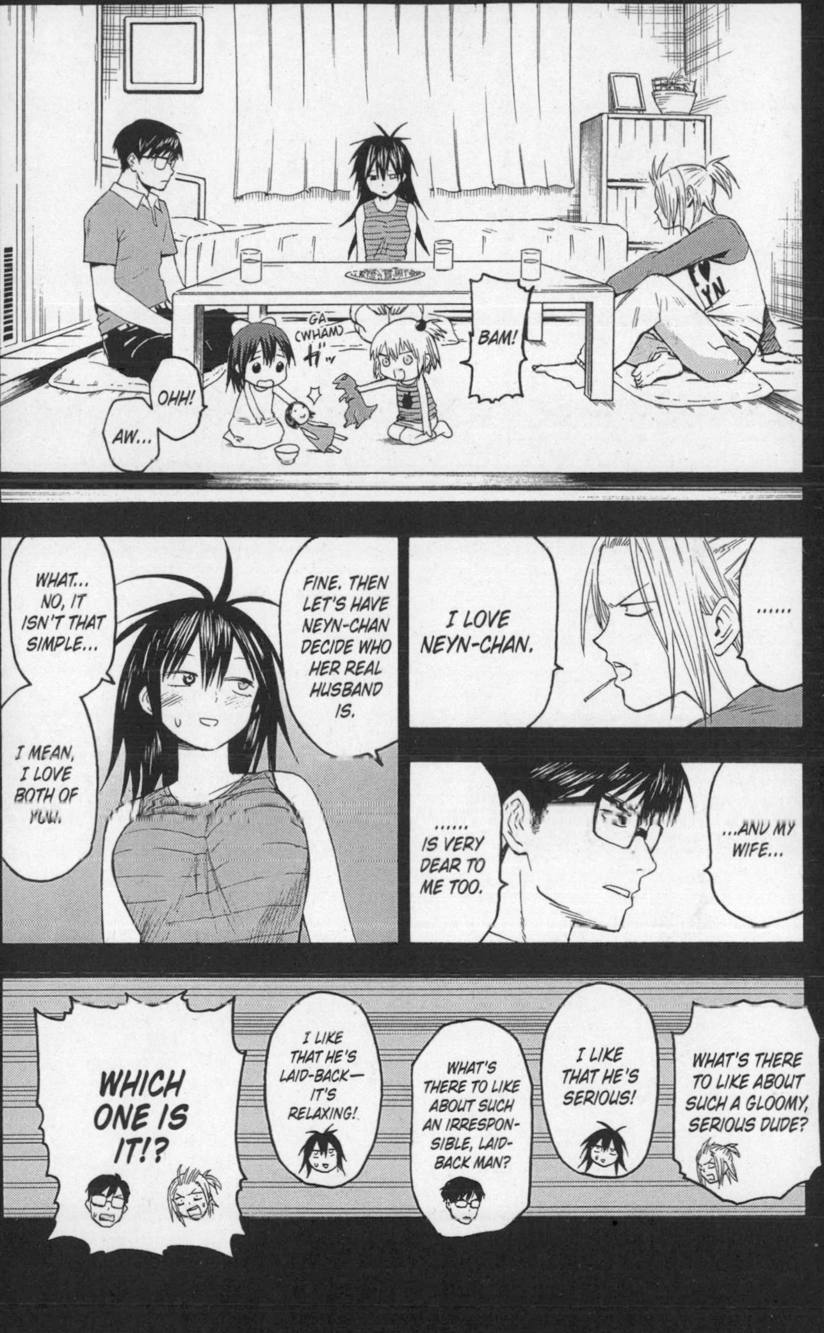
BAM!
GA (WHAM) ガッ
OHH!
AW...
......
I LOVE NEYN-CHAN.
...AND MY WIFE...
...... IS VERY DEAR TO ME TOO.
FINE. THEN LET'S HAVE NEYN-CHAN DECIDE WHO HER REAL HUSBAND IS.
WHAT... NO, IT ISN'T THAT SIMPLE...
I MEAN, I LOVE BOTH OF YOU.
WHAT'S THERE TO LIKE ABOUT SUCH A GLOOMY, SERIOUS DUDE?
I LIKE THAT HE'S SERIOUS!
WHAT'S THERE TO LIKE ABOUT SUCH AN IRRESPONSIBLE, LAID-BACK MAN?
I LIKE THAT HE'S LAID-BACK— IT'S RELAXING!
WHICH ONE IS IT!?

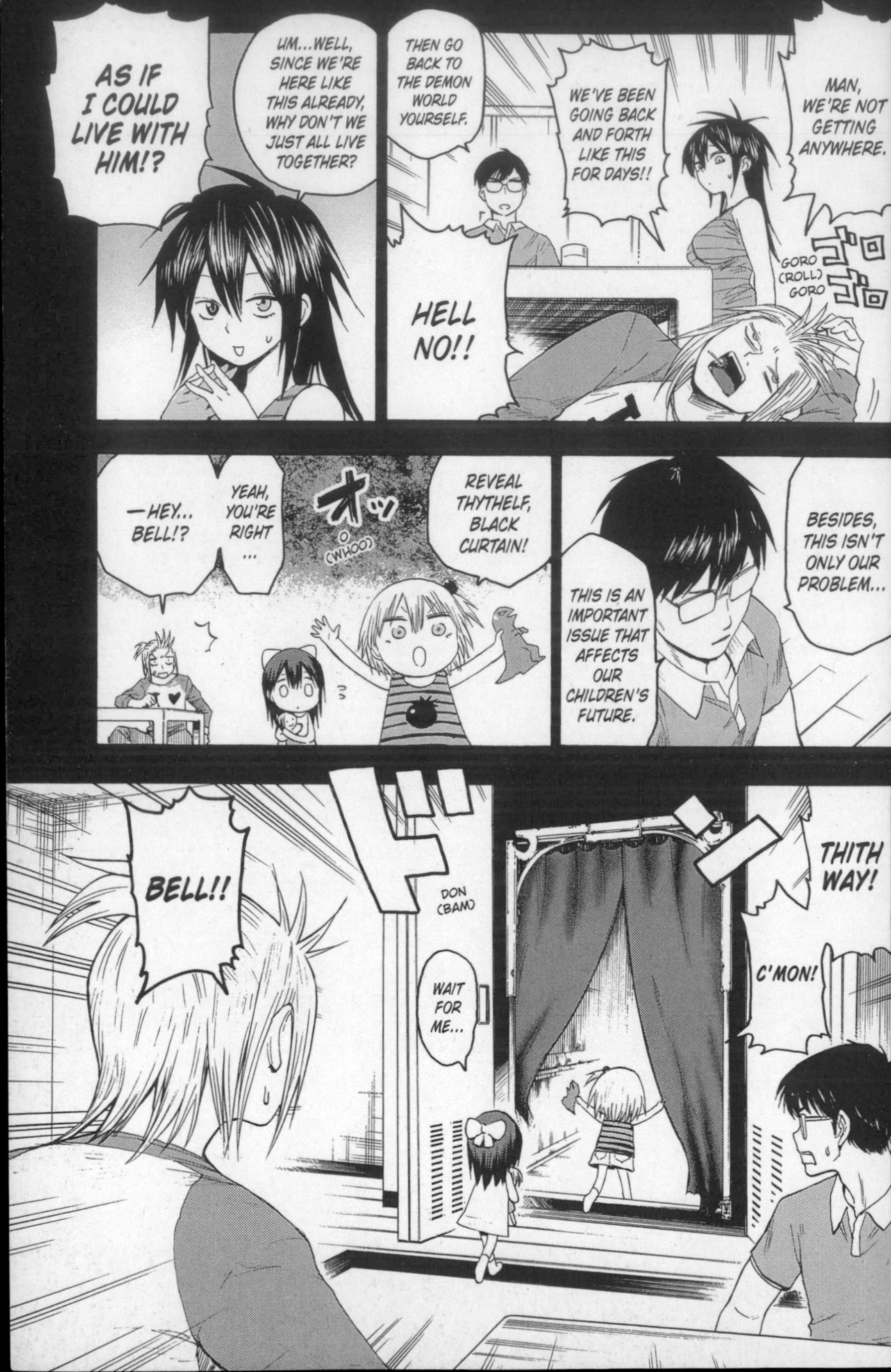
MAN, WE'RE NOT GETTING ANYWHERE.
GORO (ROLL) GORO
ゴロゴロ
WE'VE BEEN GOING BACK AND FORTH LIKE THIS FOR DAYS!!
THEN GO BACK TO THE DEMON WORLD YOURSELF.
HELL NO!!
UM...WELL, SINCE WE'RE HERE LIKE THIS ALREADY, WHY DON'T WE JUST ALL LIVE TOGETHER?
AS IF I COULD LIVE WITH HIM!?
BESIDES, THIS ISN'T ONLY OUR PROBLEM...
THIS IS AN IMPORTANT ISSUE THAT AFFECTS OUR CHILDREN'S FUTURE.
REVEAL THYTHELF, BLACK CURTAIN!
オッ
O (WHOO)
YEAH, YOU'RE RIGHT ...
—HEY... BELL!?
THITH WAY!
C'MON!
ド
DON (BAM)
WAIT FOR ME...
BELL!!

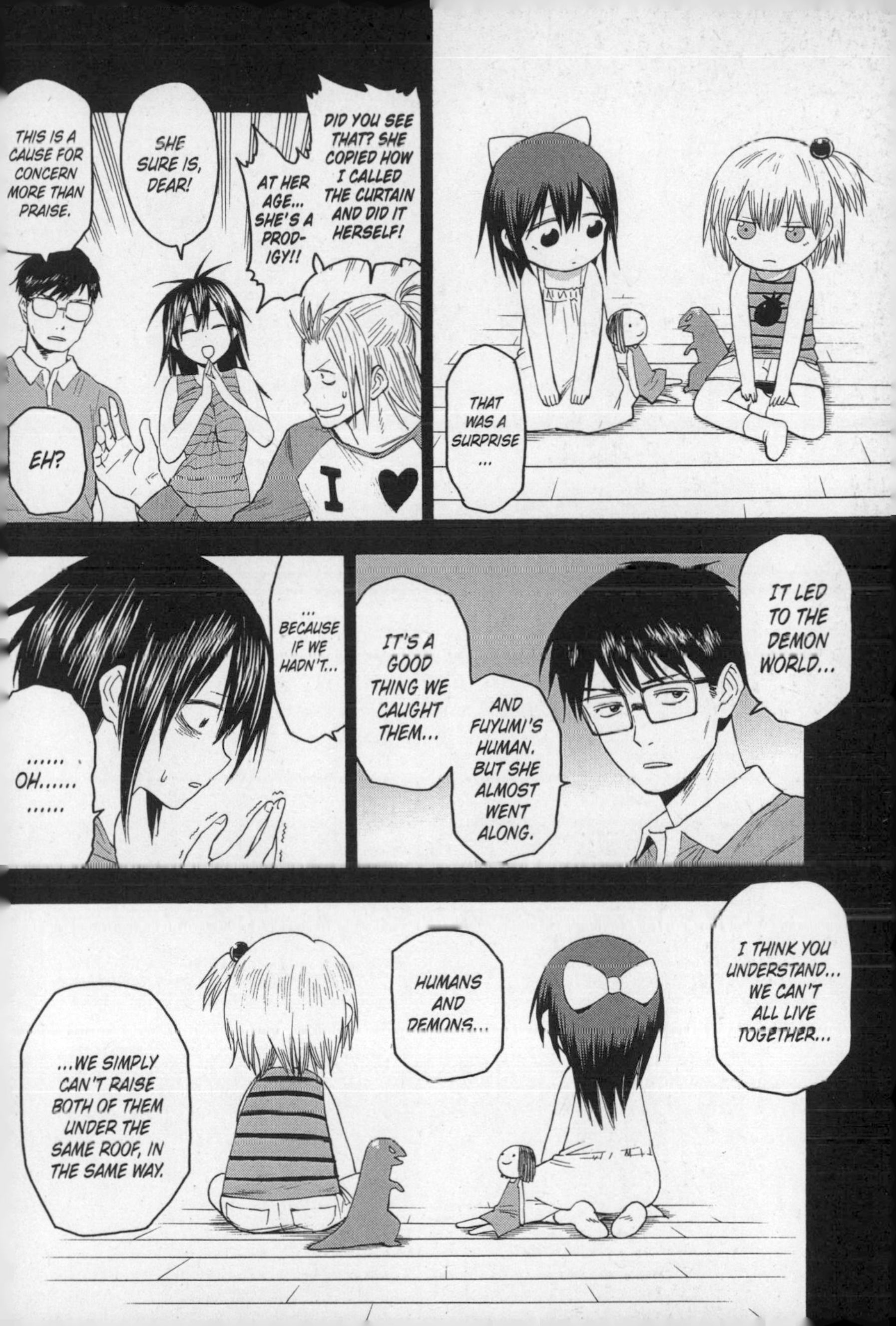
THAT WAS A SURPRISE...
DID YOU SEE THAT? SHE COPIED HOW I CALLED THE CURTAIN AND DID IT HERSELF!
AT HER AGE... SHE'S A PROD-IGY!!
SHE SURE IS, DEAR!
THIS IS A CAUSE FOR CONCERN MORE THAN PRAISE.
EH?
IT LED TO THE DEMON WORLD...
AND FUYUMI'S HUMAN. BUT SHE ALMOST WENT ALONG.
IT'S A GOOD THING WE CAUGHT THEM...
...BECAUSE IF WE HADN'T...
...... OH...... ......
I THINK YOU UNDERSTAND... WE CAN'T ALL LIVE TOGETHER...
HUMANS AND DEMONS...
...WE SIMPLY CAN'T RAISE BOTH OF THEM UNDER THE SAME ROOF, IN THE SAME WAY.

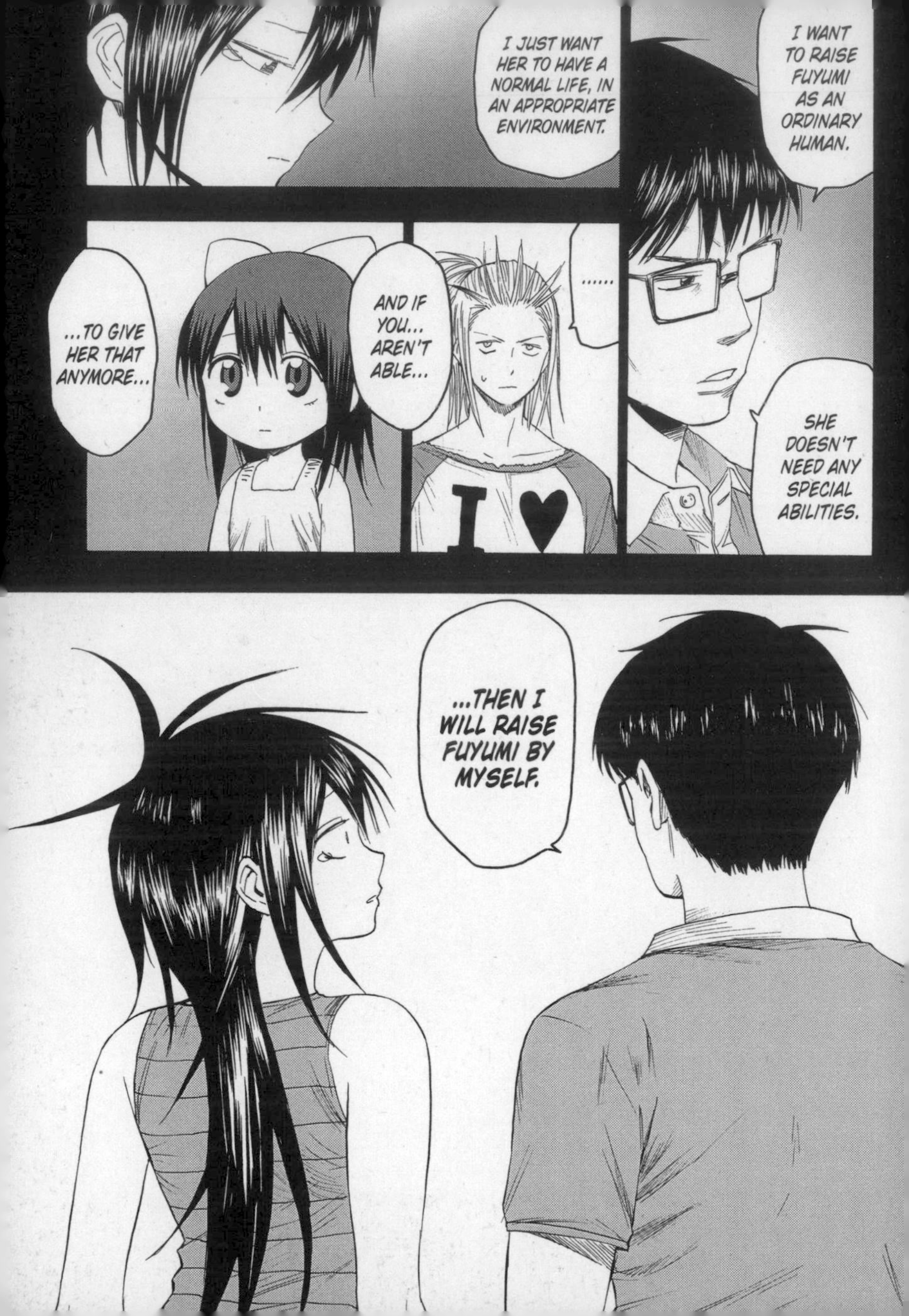
I WANT TO RAISE FUYUMI AS AN ORDINARY HUMAN.
SHE DOESN'T NEED ANY SPECIAL ABILITIES.
I JUST WANT HER TO HAVE A NORMAL LIFE, IN AN APPROPRIATE ENVIRONMENT.
......
AND IF YOU... AREN'T ABLE...
...TO GIVE HER THAT ANYMORE...
...THEN I WILL RAISE FUYUMI BY MYSELF.

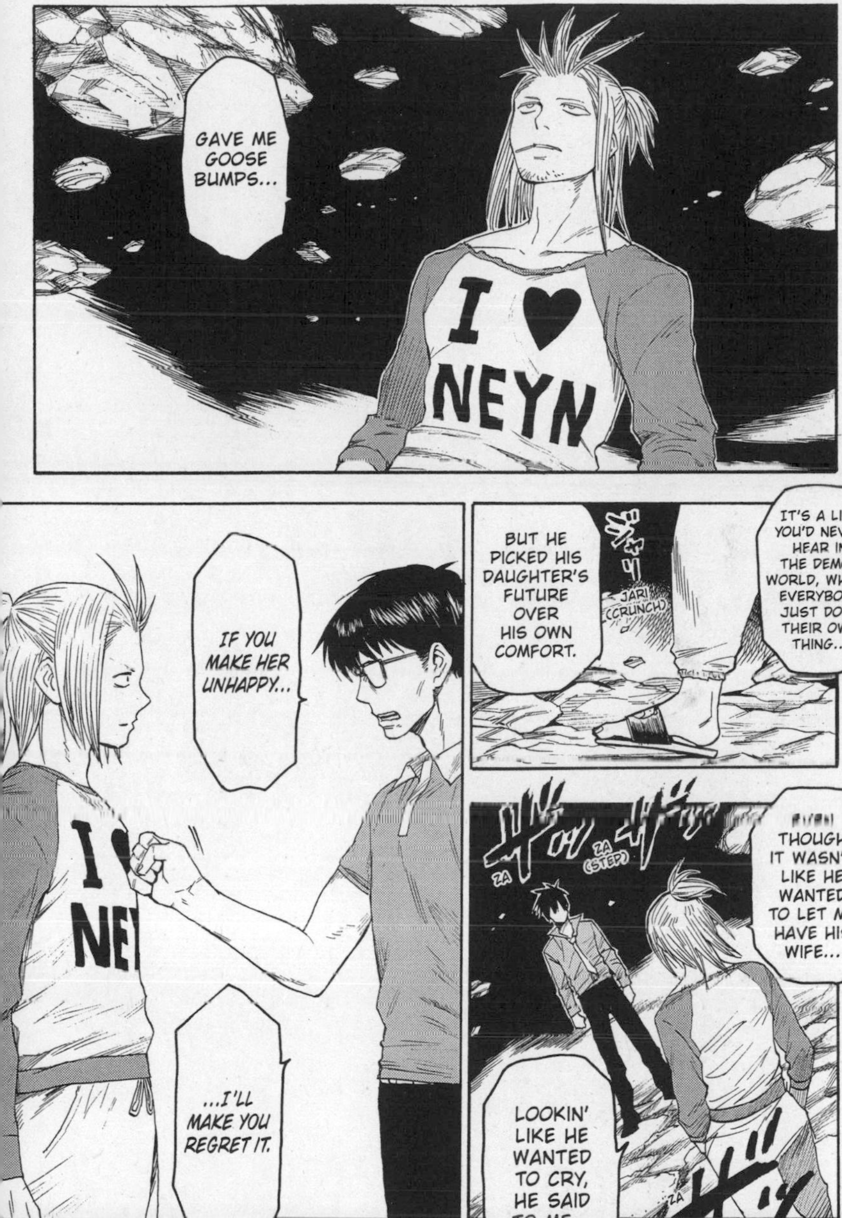
GAVE ME GOOSE BUMPS...
I ♥ NEYN
IT'S A LINE YOU'D NEVER HEAR IN THE DEMON WORLD, WHERE EVERYBODY JUST DOES THEIR OWN THING...
BUT HE PICKED HIS DAUGHTER'S FUTURE OVER HIS OWN COMFORT.
JARI (CRUNCH)
THOUGH IT WASN'T LIKE HE WANTED TO LET ME HAVE HIS WIFE...
ZA
ZA (STEP)
LOOKIN' LIKE HE WANTED TO CRY, HE SAID TO ME...
ZA
IF YOU MAKE HER UNHAPPY...
...I'LL MAKE YOU REGRET IT.

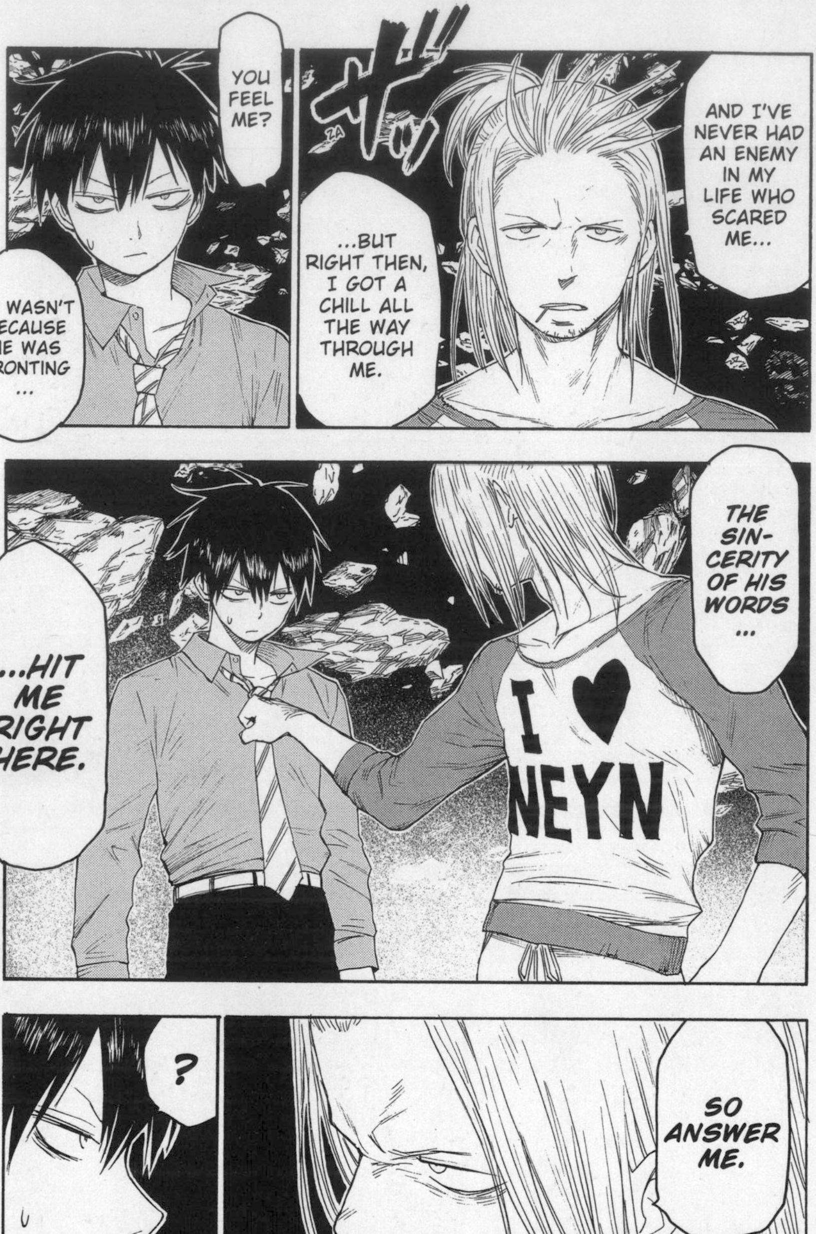
ZA
AND I'VE NEVER HAD AN ENEMY IN MY LIFE WHO SCARED ME...
...BUT RIGHT THEN, I GOT A CHILL ALL THE WAY THROUGH ME.
YOU FEEL ME?
IT WASN'T BECAUSE HE WAS FRONTING...
THE SIN-CERITY OF HIS WORDS...
I ♥ NEYN
...HIT ME RIGHT HERE.
SO ANSWER ME.
?

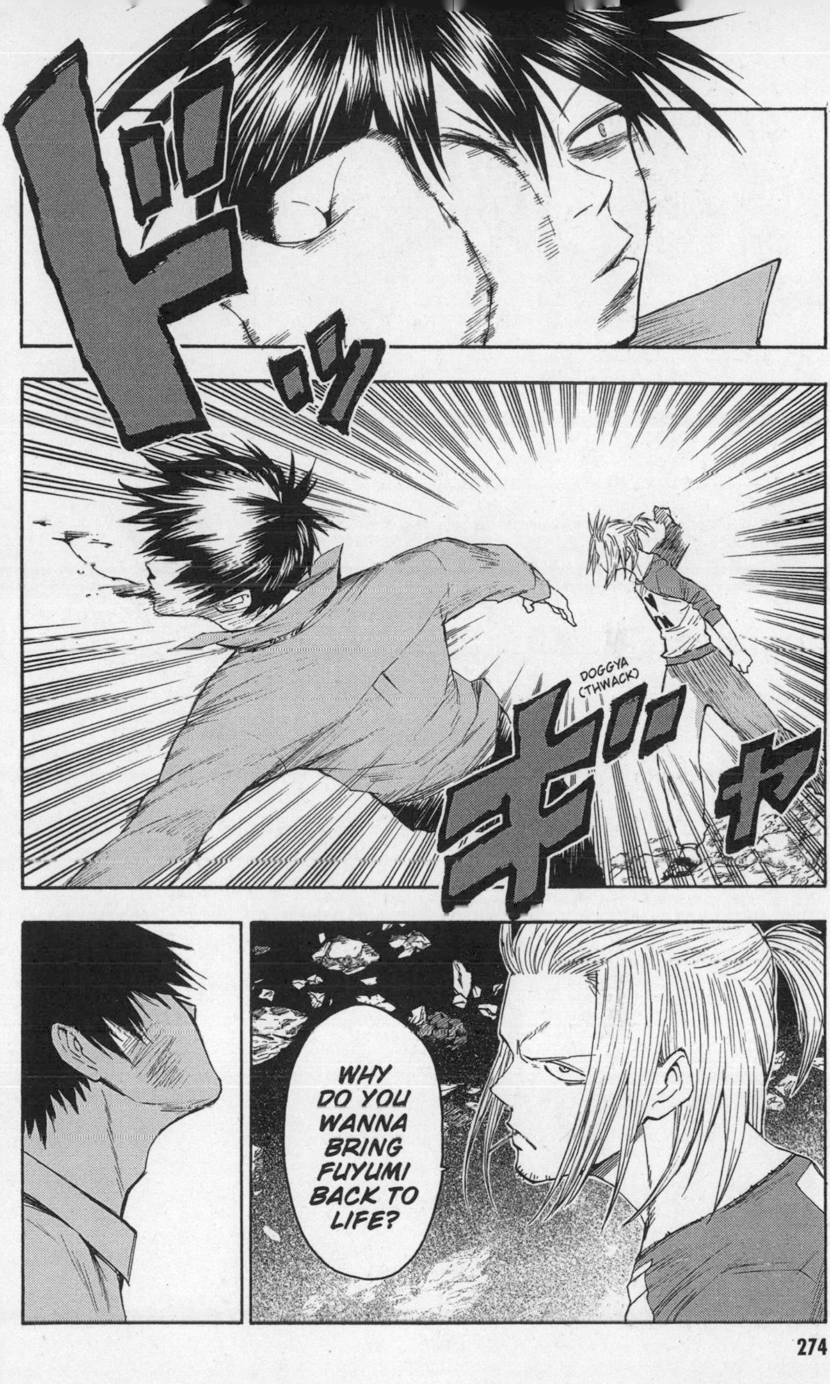
DOGGYA (THWACK)
WHY DO YOU WANNA BRING FUYUMI BACK TO LIFE?

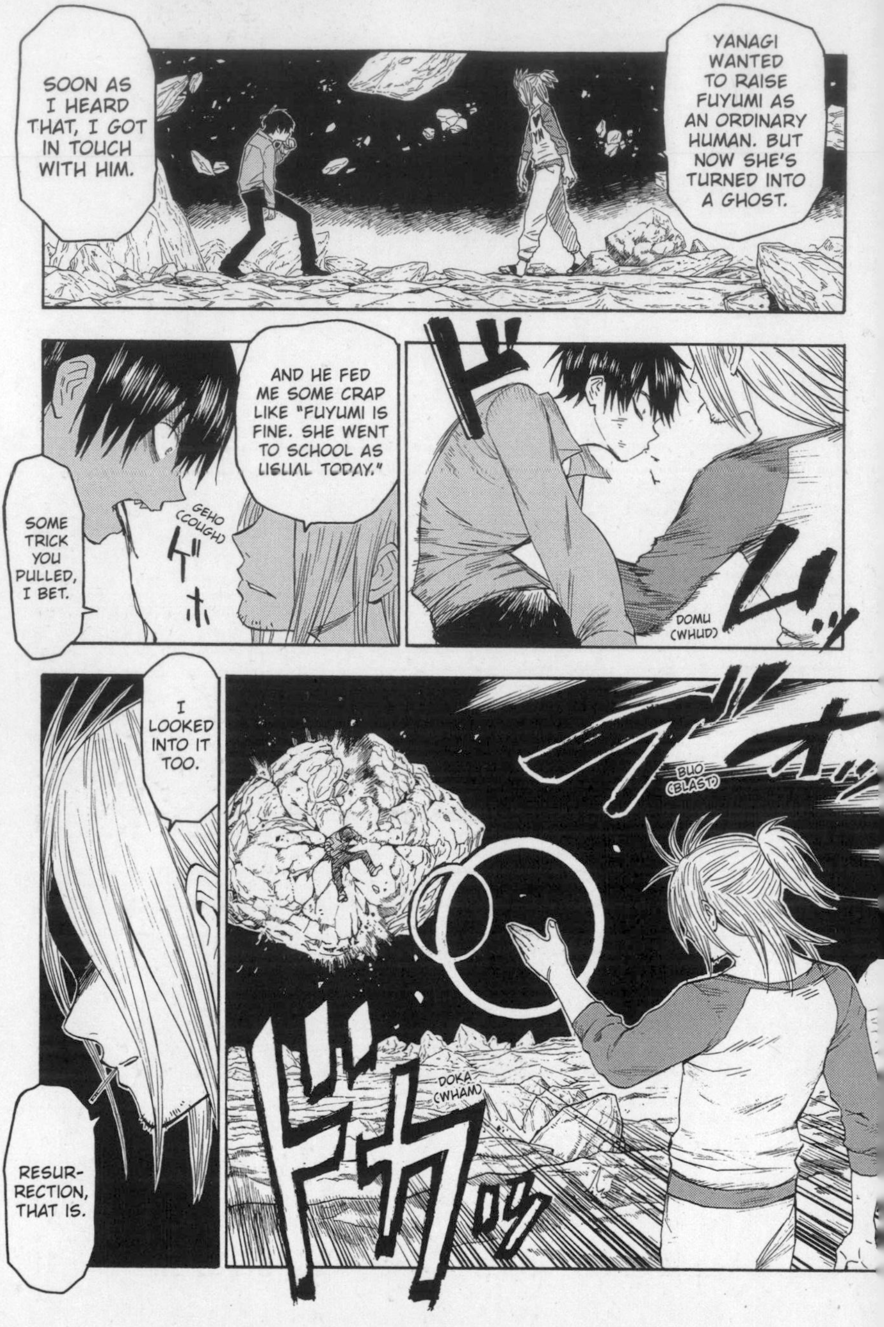
YANAGI WANTED TO RAISE FUYUMI AS AN ORDINARY HUMAN. BUT NOW SHE'S TURNED INTO A GHOST.
SOON AS I HEARD THAT, I GOT IN TOUCH WITH HIM.
DOMU (WHUD)
AND HE FED ME SOME CRAP LIKE "FUYUMI IS FINE. SHE WENT TO SCHOOL AS USUAL TODAY."
GEHO (COUGH)
SOME TRICK YOU PULLED, I BET.
BUO (BLAST)
DOKA (WHAM)
I LOOKED INTO IT TOO.
RESUR-RECTION, THAT IS.

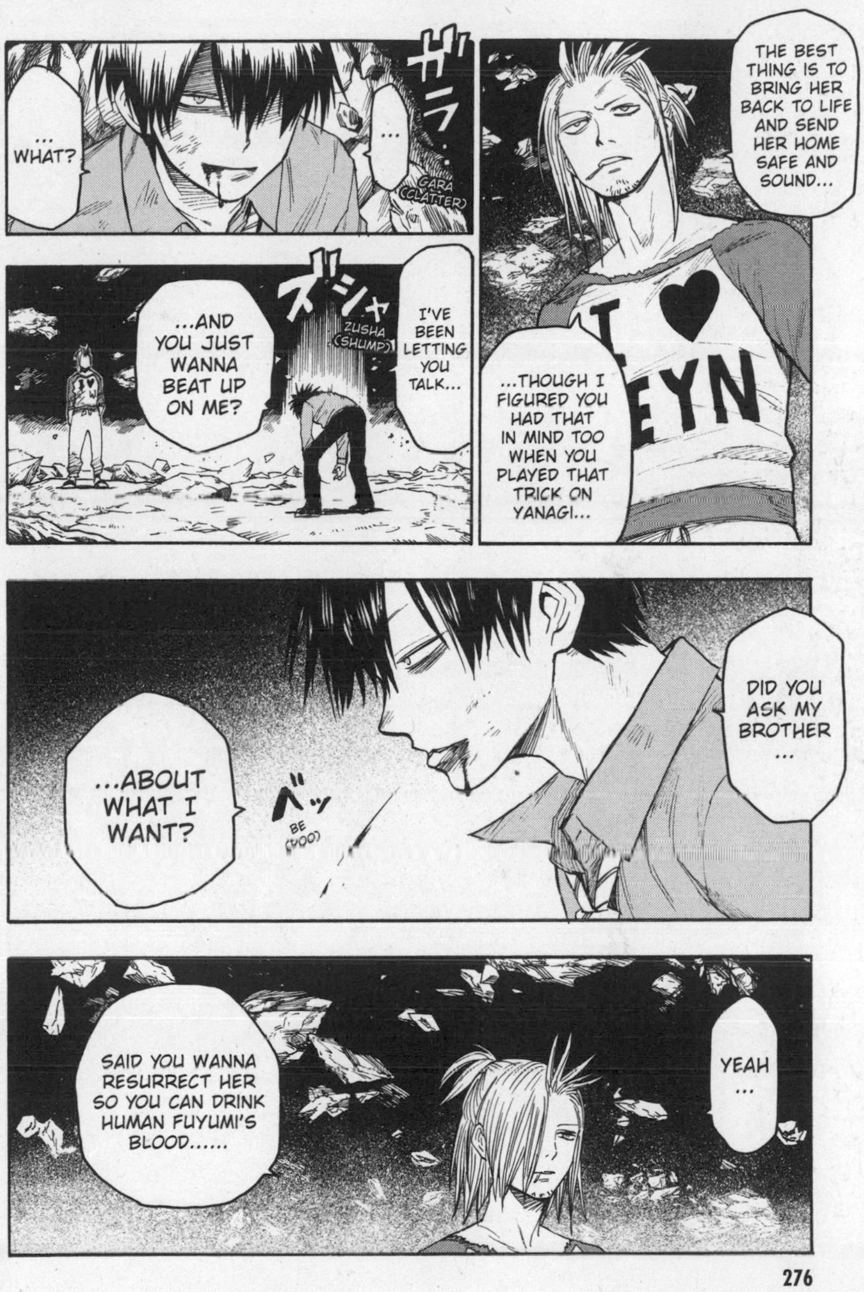

THE BEST THING IS TO BRING HER BACK TO LIFE AND SEND HER HOME SAFE AND SOUND...
...THOUGH I FIGURED YOU HAD THAT IN MIND TOO WHEN YOU PLAYED THAT TRICK ON YANAGI...
I ♥ EYN
...
ガラ
GARA (CLATTER)
... WHAT?
I'VE BEEN LETTING YOU TALK...
ズシャ
ZUSHA (SHUMP)
...AND YOU JUST WANNA BEAT UP ON ME?
DID YOU ASK MY BROTHER ...
ベッ
BE (PTOO)
...ABOUT WHAT I WANT?
YEAH ...
SAID YOU WANNA RESURRECT HER SO YOU CAN DRINK HUMAN FUYUMI'S BLOOD......

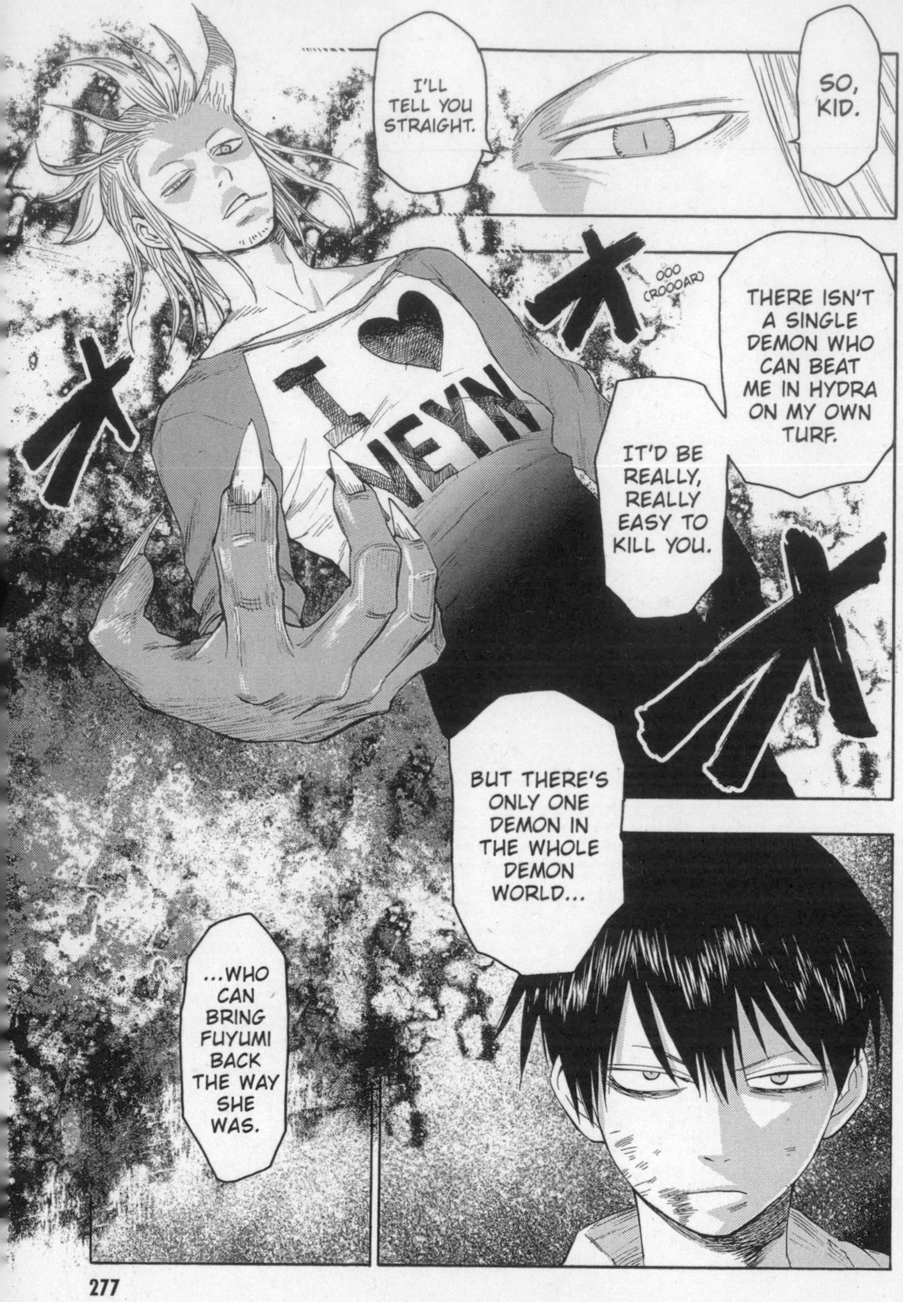
SO, KID.
I'LL TELL YOU STRAIGHT.
OOO (ROOOAR)
THERE ISN'T A SINGLE DEMON WHO CAN BEAT ME IN HYDRA ON MY OWN TURF.
IT'D BE REALLY, REALLY EASY TO KILL YOU.
BUT THERE'S ONLY ONE DEMON IN THE WHOLE DEMON WORLD...
...WHO CAN BRING FUYUMI BACK THE WAY SHE WAS.

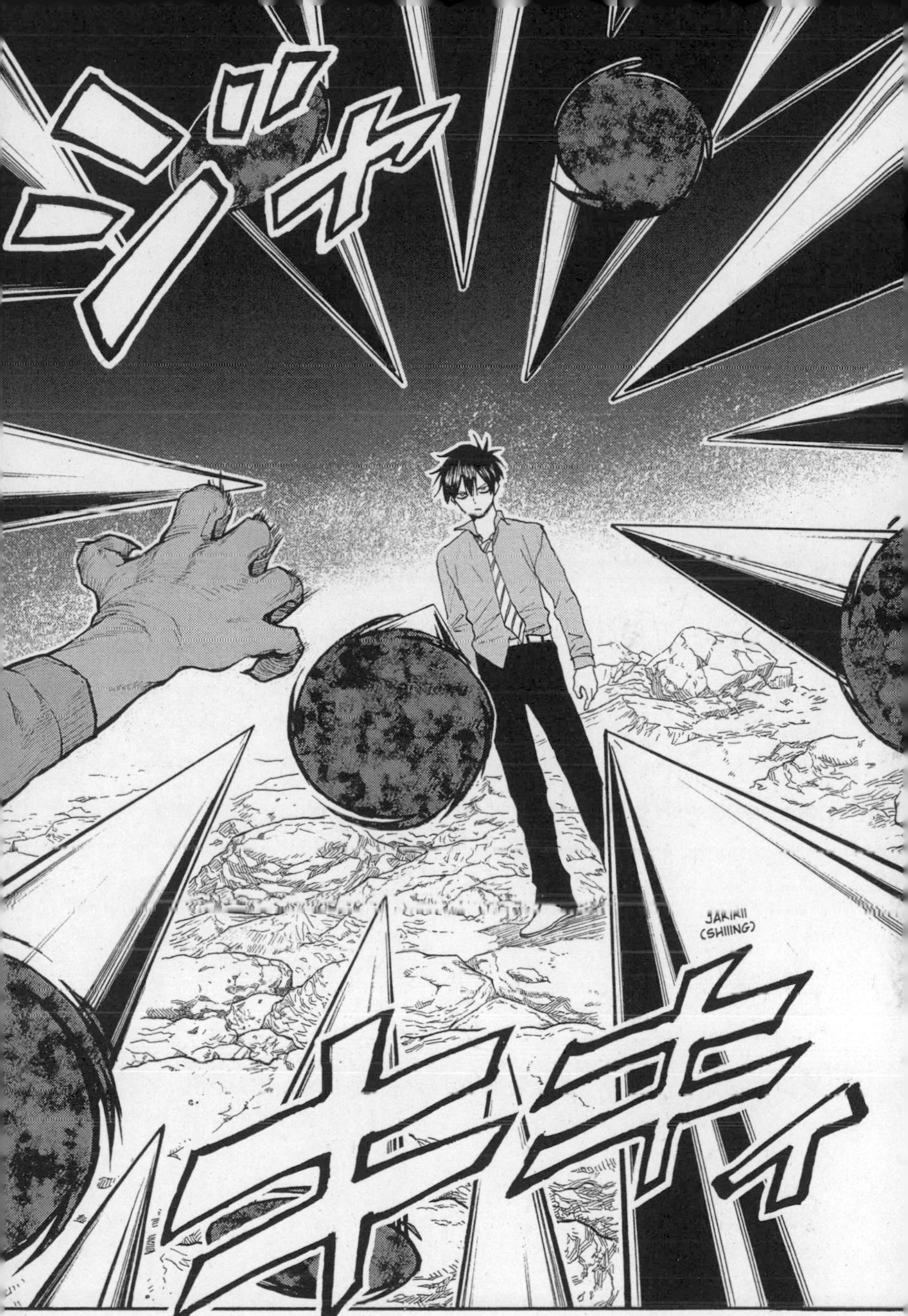
JAKIKII
(SHIIING)

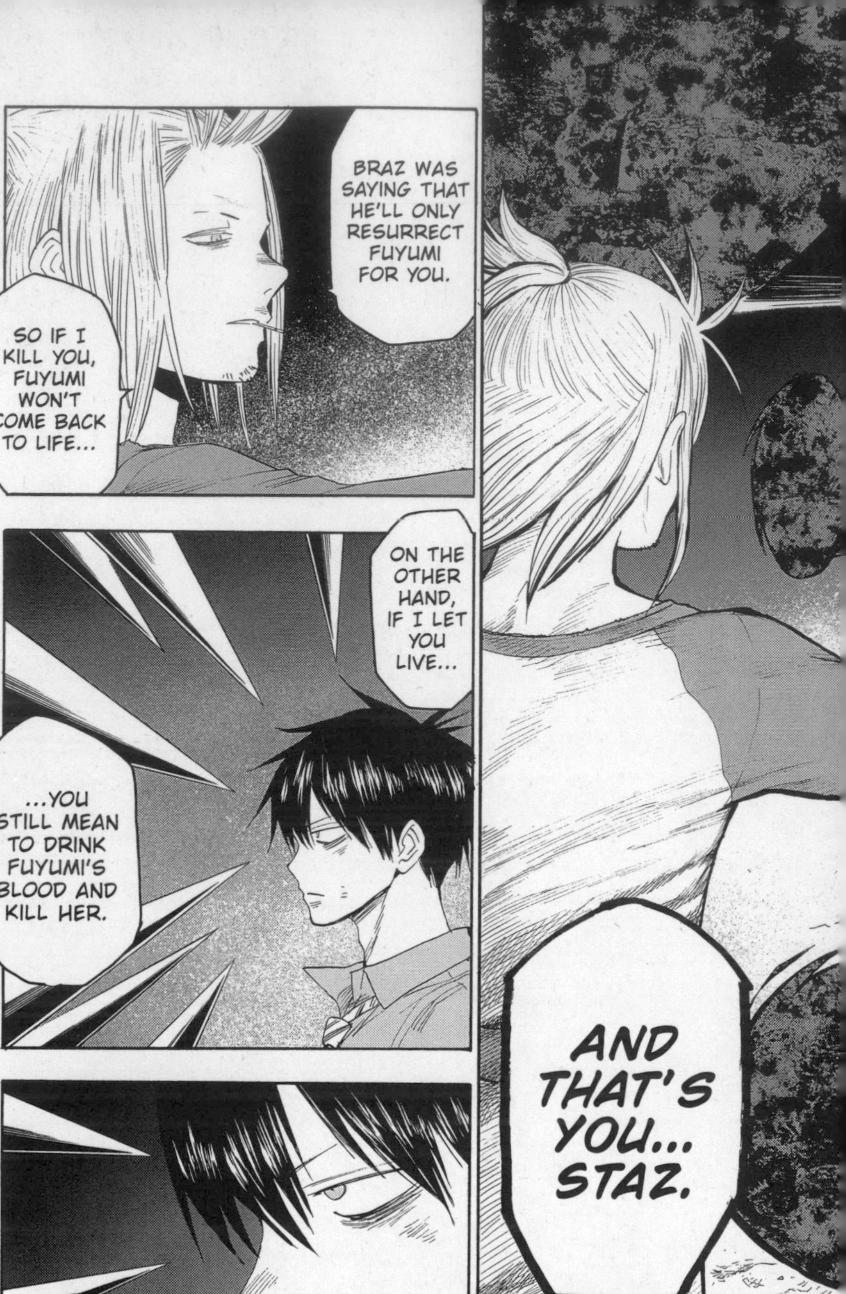
BRAZ WAS SAYING THAT HE'LL ONLY RESURRECT FUYUMI FOR YOU.
SO IF I KILL YOU, FUYUMI WON'T COME BACK TO LIFE...
ON THE OTHER HAND, IF I LET YOU LIVE...
...YOU STILL MEAN TO DRINK FUYUMI'S BLOOD AND KILL HER.
AND THAT'S YOU... STAZ.

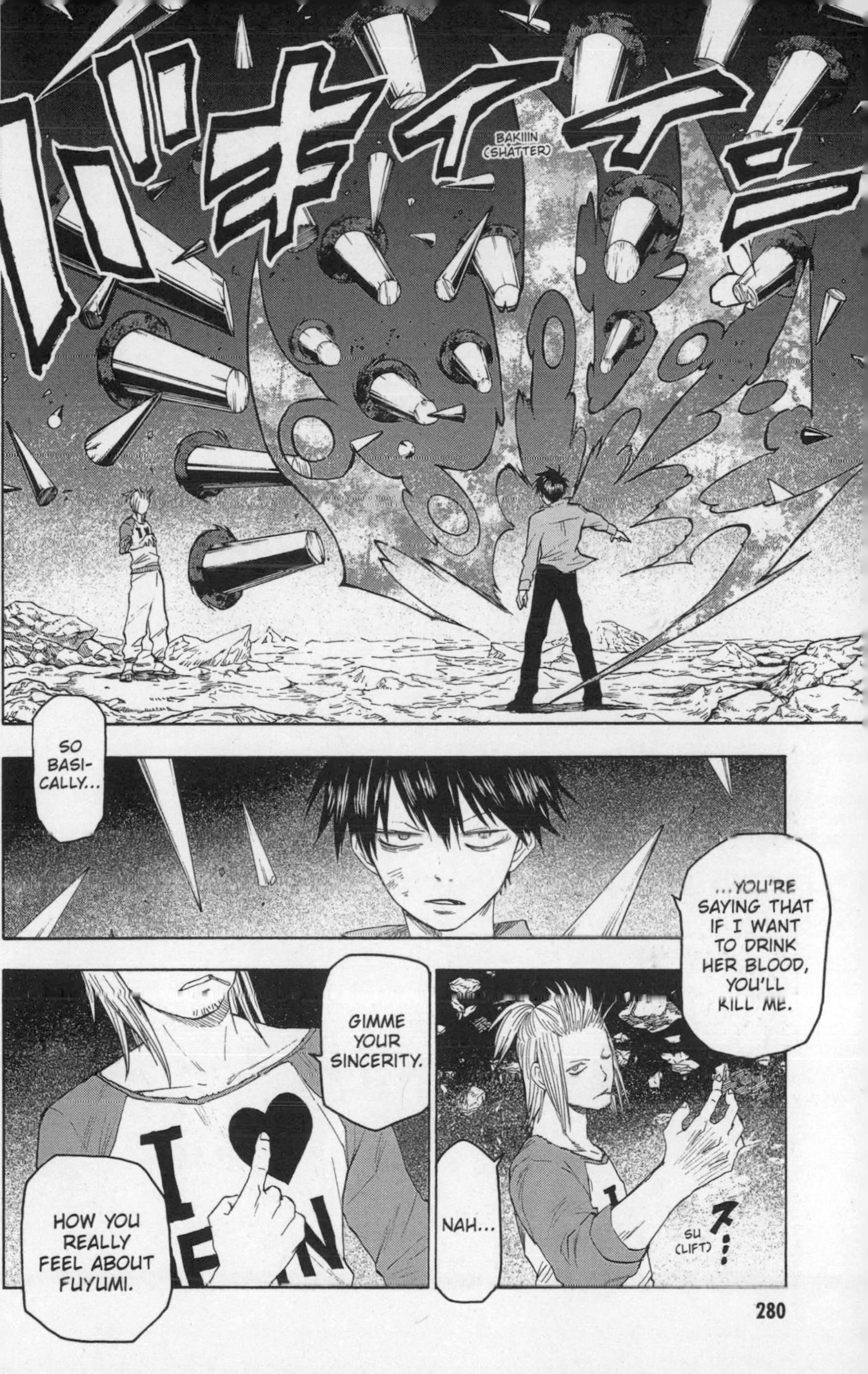
BAKIIIN (SHATTER)
SO BASI-CALLY...
...YOU'RE SAYING THAT IF I WANT TO DRINK HER BLOOD, YOU'LL KILL ME.
SU (LIFT)
NAH...
GIMME YOUR SINCERITY.
HOW YOU REALLY FEEL ABOUT FUYUMI.

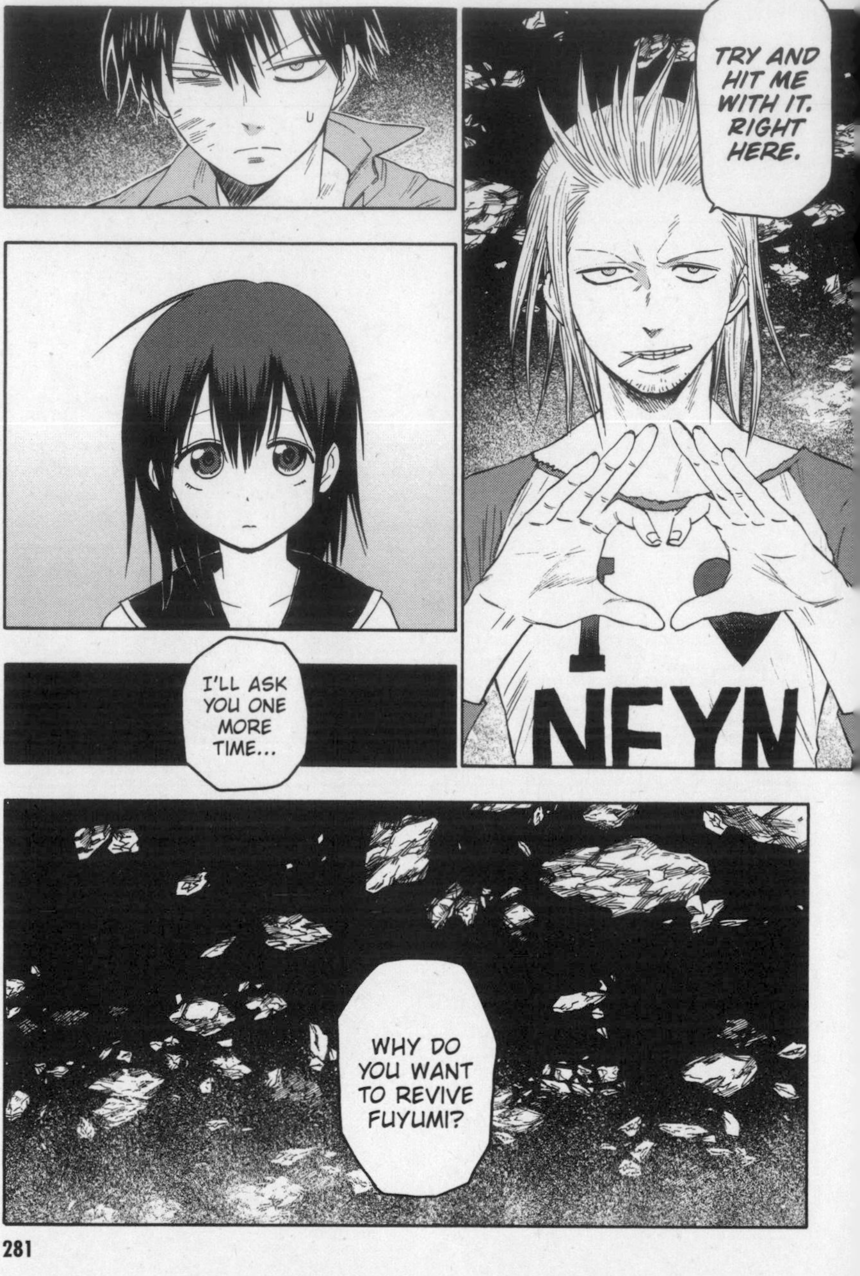
TRY AND HIT ME WITH IT. RIGHT HERE.
I'LL ASK YOU ONE MORE TIME...
WHY DO YOU WANT TO REVIVE FUYUMI?

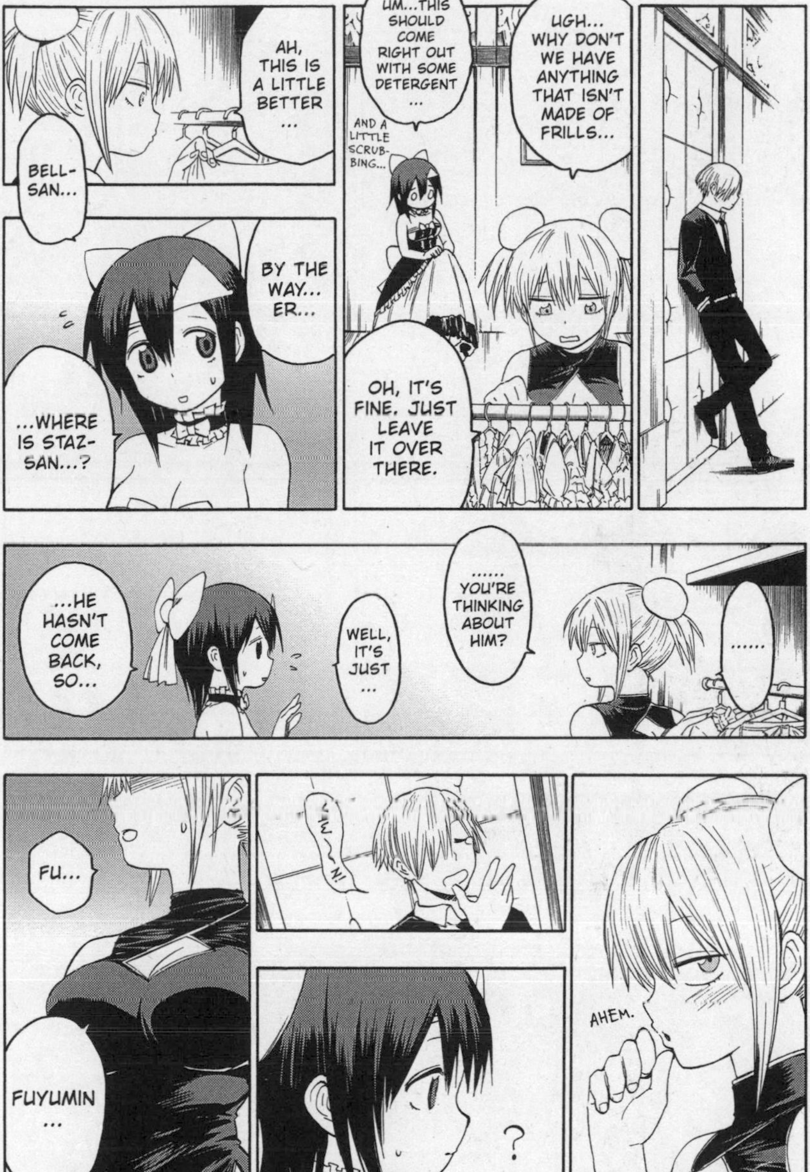
UGH... WHY DON'T WE HAVE ANYTHING THAT ISN'T MADE OF FRILLS...
UM...THIS SHOULD COME RIGHT OUT WITH SOME DETERGENT ...
AND A LITTLE SCRUB-BING...
OH, IT'S FINE. JUST LEAVE IT OVER THERE.
AH, THIS IS A LITTLE BETTER ...
BELL-SAN...
BY THE WAY... ER...
...WHERE IS STAZ-SAN...?
......
...... YOU'RE THINKING ABOUT HIM?
WELL, IT'S JUST ...
...HE HASN'T COME BACK, SO...
AHEM.
N~~N!
?
FU...
FUYUMIN ...

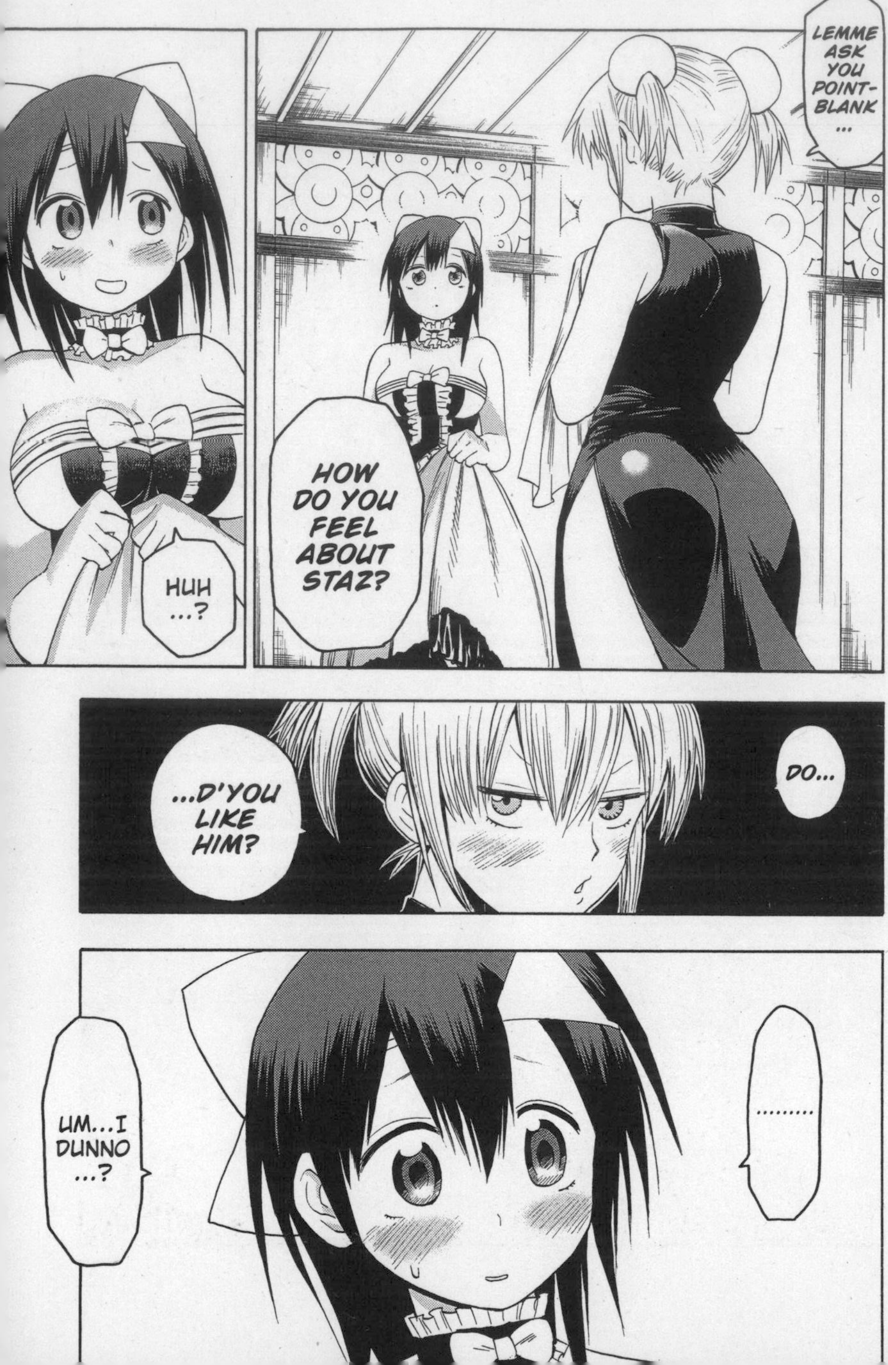
LEMME ASK YOU POINT-BLANK ...
HOW DO YOU FEEL ABOUT STAZ?
HUH ...?
DO...
...D'YOU LIKE HIM?
....
UM...I DUNNO ...?

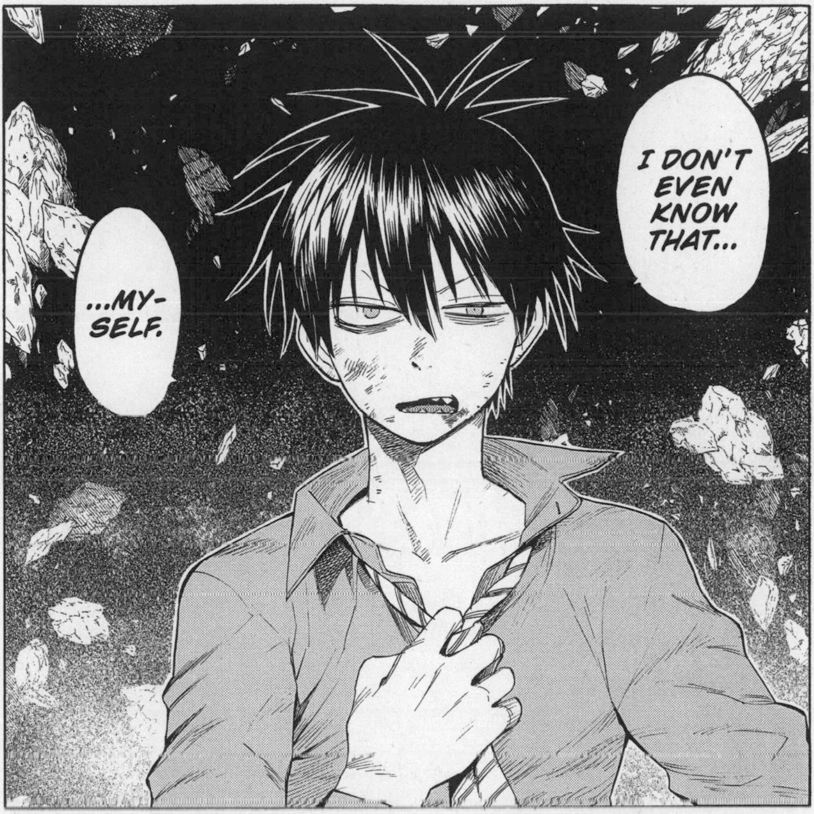
I DON'T EVEN KNOW THAT...
...MY-SELF.

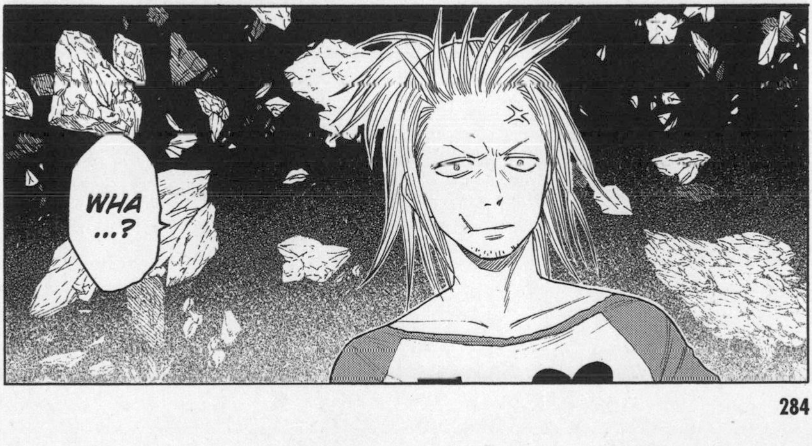
WHA ...?

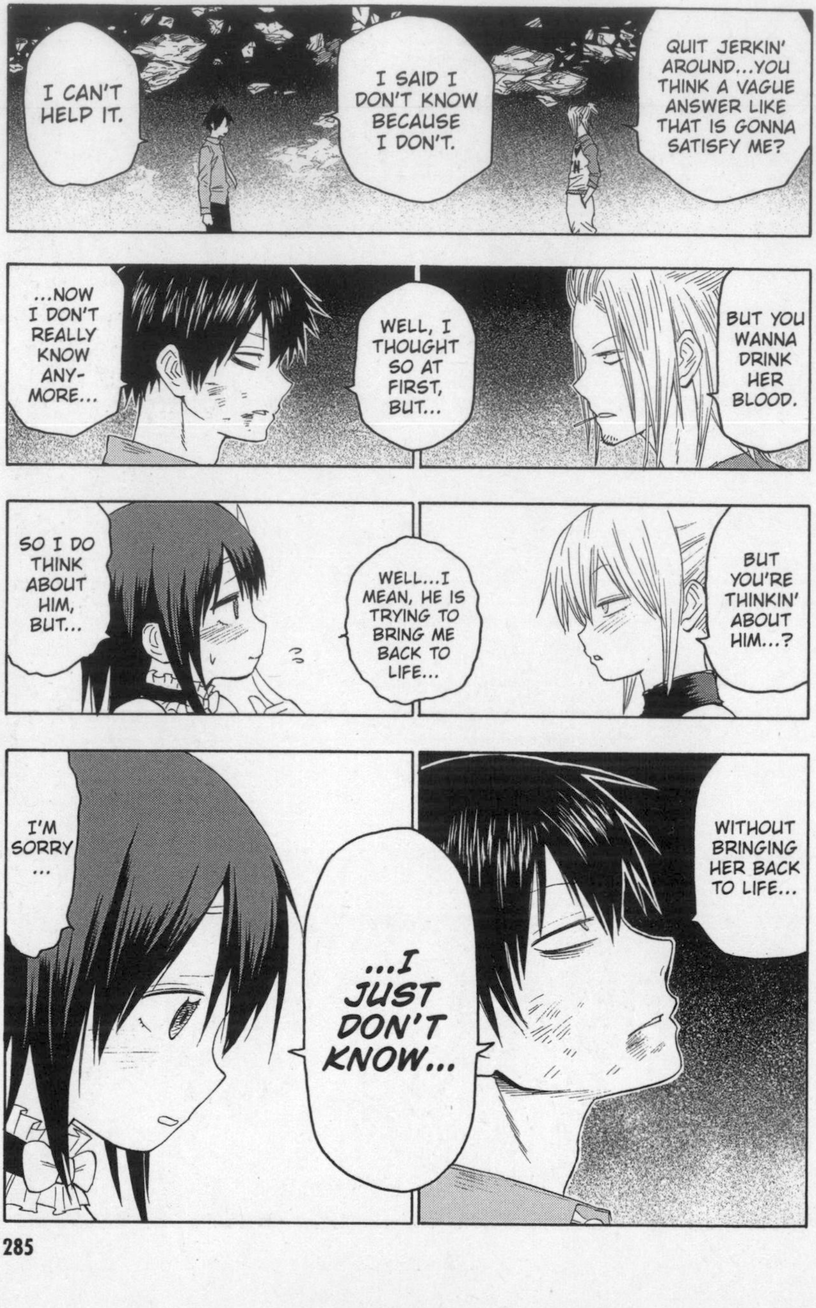
QUIT JERKIN' AROUND...YOU THINK A VAGUE ANSWER LIKE THAT IS GONNA SATISFY ME?
I SAID I DON'T KNOW BECAUSE I DON'T.
I CAN'T HELP IT.
BUT YOU WANNA DRINK HER BLOOD.
WELL, I THOUGHT SO AT FIRST, BUT...
...NOW I DON'T REALLY KNOW ANY-MORE...
BUT YOU'RE THINKIN' ABOUT HIM...?
WELL...I MEAN, HE IS TRYING TO BRING ME BACK TO LIFE...
SO I DO THINK ABOUT HIM, BUT...
WITHOUT BRINGING HER BACK TO LIFE...
...I JUST DON'T KNOW...
I'M SORRY...

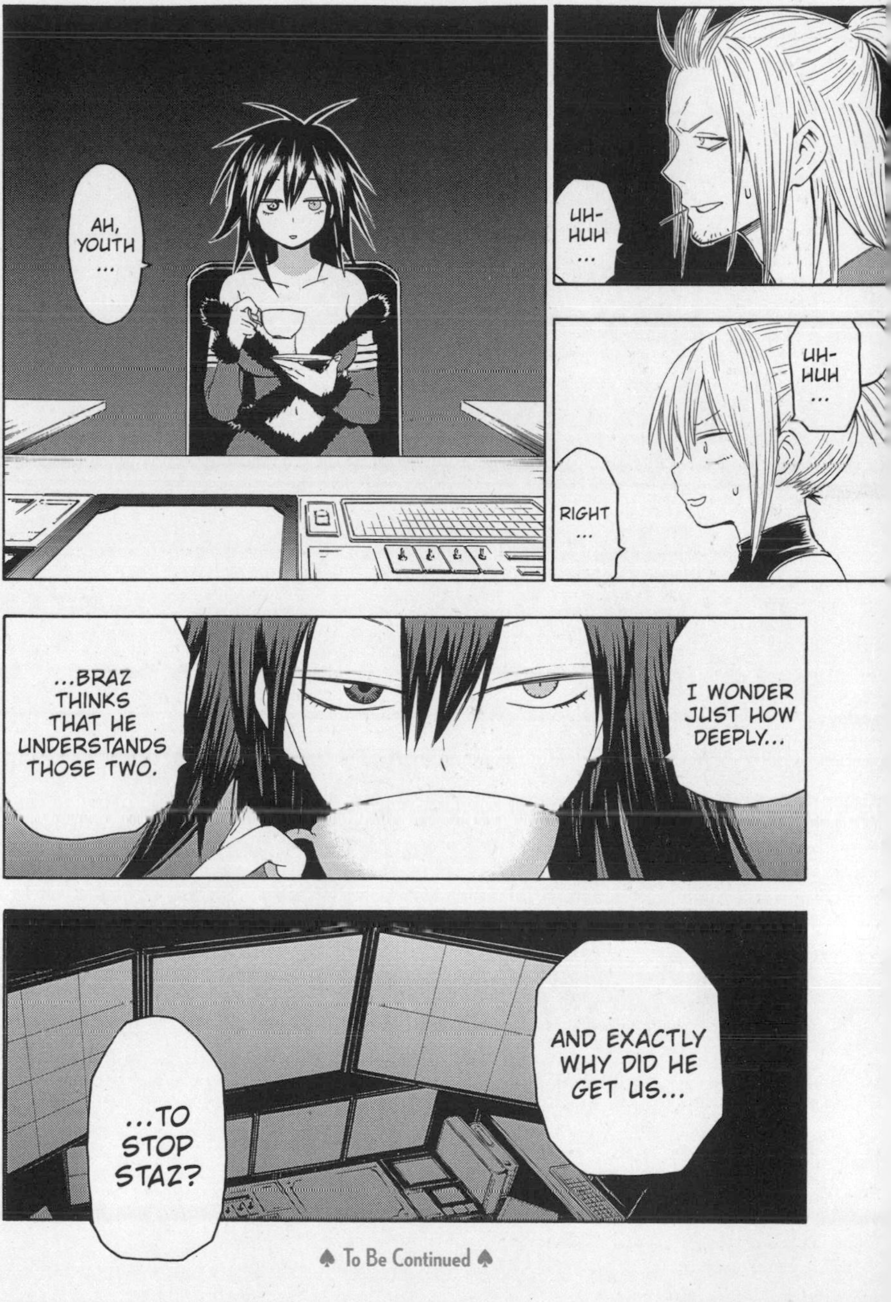
UH-HUH ...
UH-HUH ...
RIGHT ...
AH, YOUTH ...
I WONDER JUST HOW DEEPLY...
...BRAZ THINKS THAT HE UNDERSTANDS THOSE TWO.
AND EXACTLY WHY DID HE GET US...
...TO STOP STAZ?

♠ To Be Continued ♠

ACROPOLIS ICE CREAM

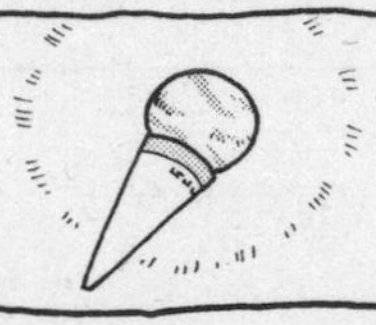

RARITY: ☆

IT SAYS "ACROPOLIS," BUT IT'S PERFECTLY ORDINARY ICE CREAM. CHOCOLATE CHIP AND MIXED BERRY ARE SAID TO BE POPULAR WITH CHILDREN.

BLOOD LAD

CHAPTER 29 ♠ A TINY ROOM OF CURSES AND OATHS

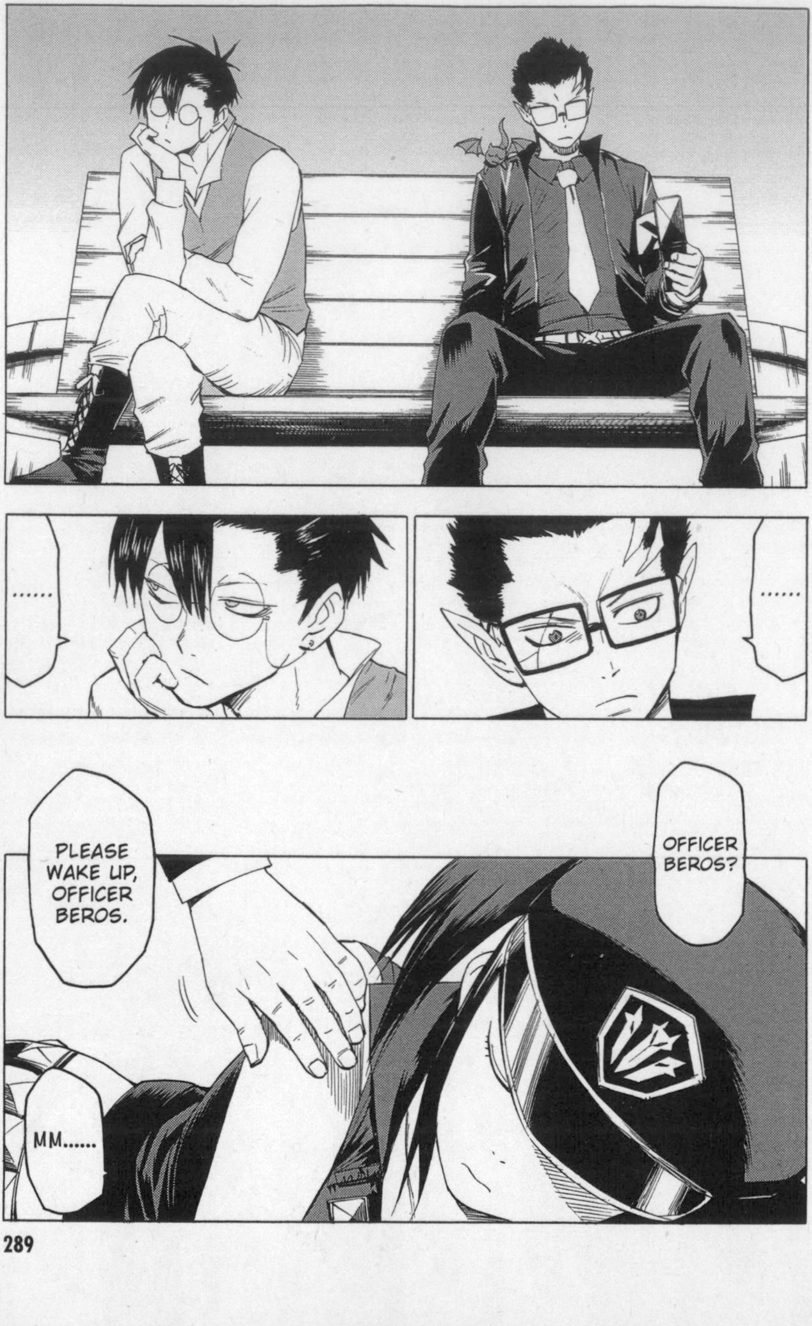
……
……
OFFICER BEROS?
PLEASE WAKE UP, OFFICER BEROS.
MM……

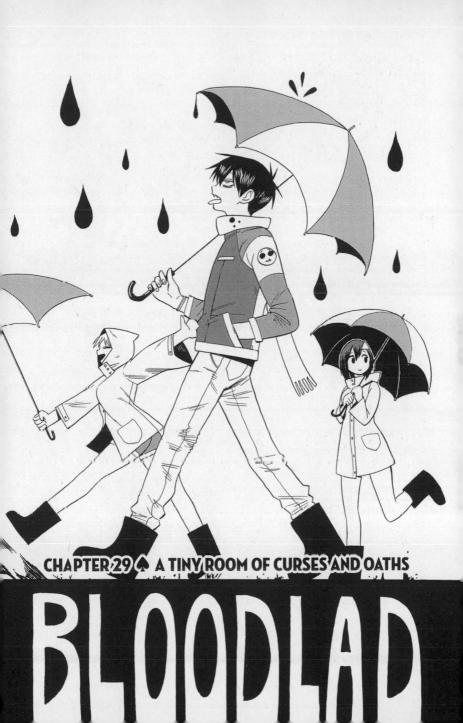

CHAPTER 29 ♠ A TINY ROOM OF CURSES AND OATHS

BLOODLAD

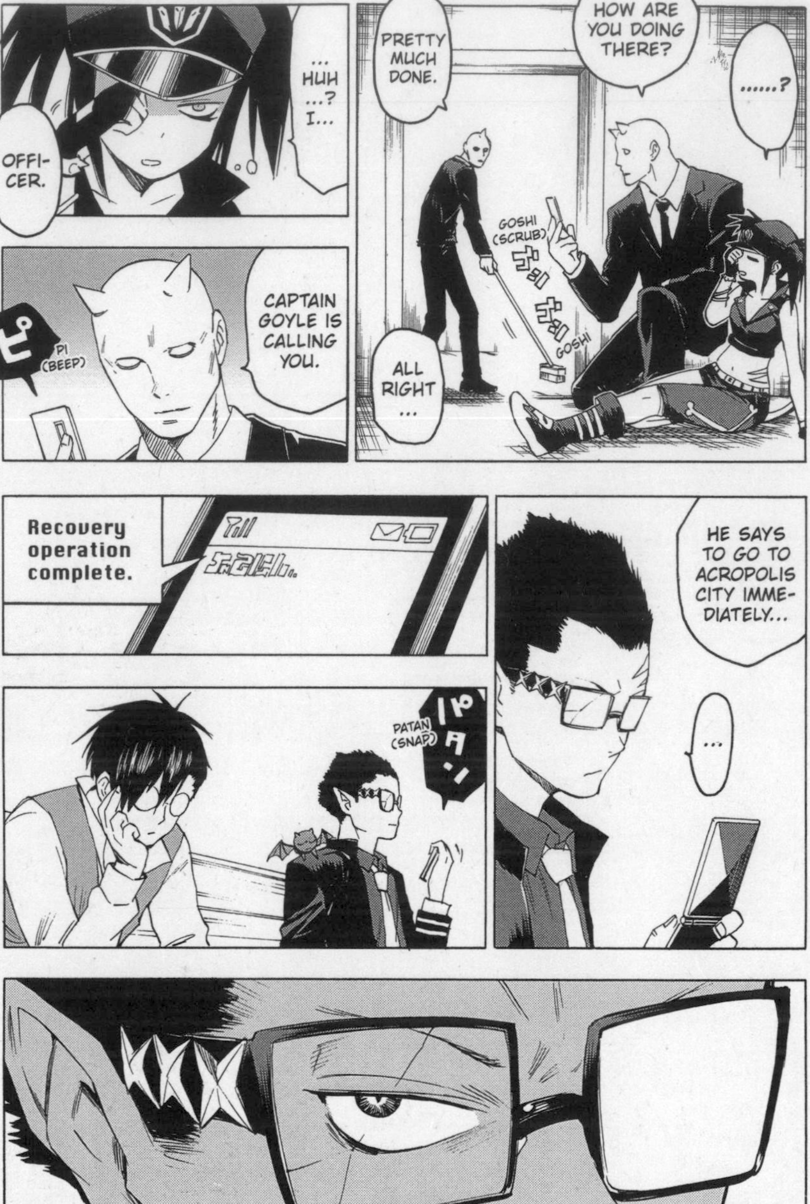
HOW ARE YOU DOING THERE?
......?
PRETTY MUCH DONE.
GOSHI (SCRUB)
GOSHI
ALL RIGHT ...
... HUH ...? I...
OFFICER.
CAPTAIN GOYLE IS CALLING YOU.
PI (BEEP)
HE SAYS TO GO TO ACROPOLIS CITY IMMEDIATELY...
...
Recovery operation complete.
PATAN (SNAP)

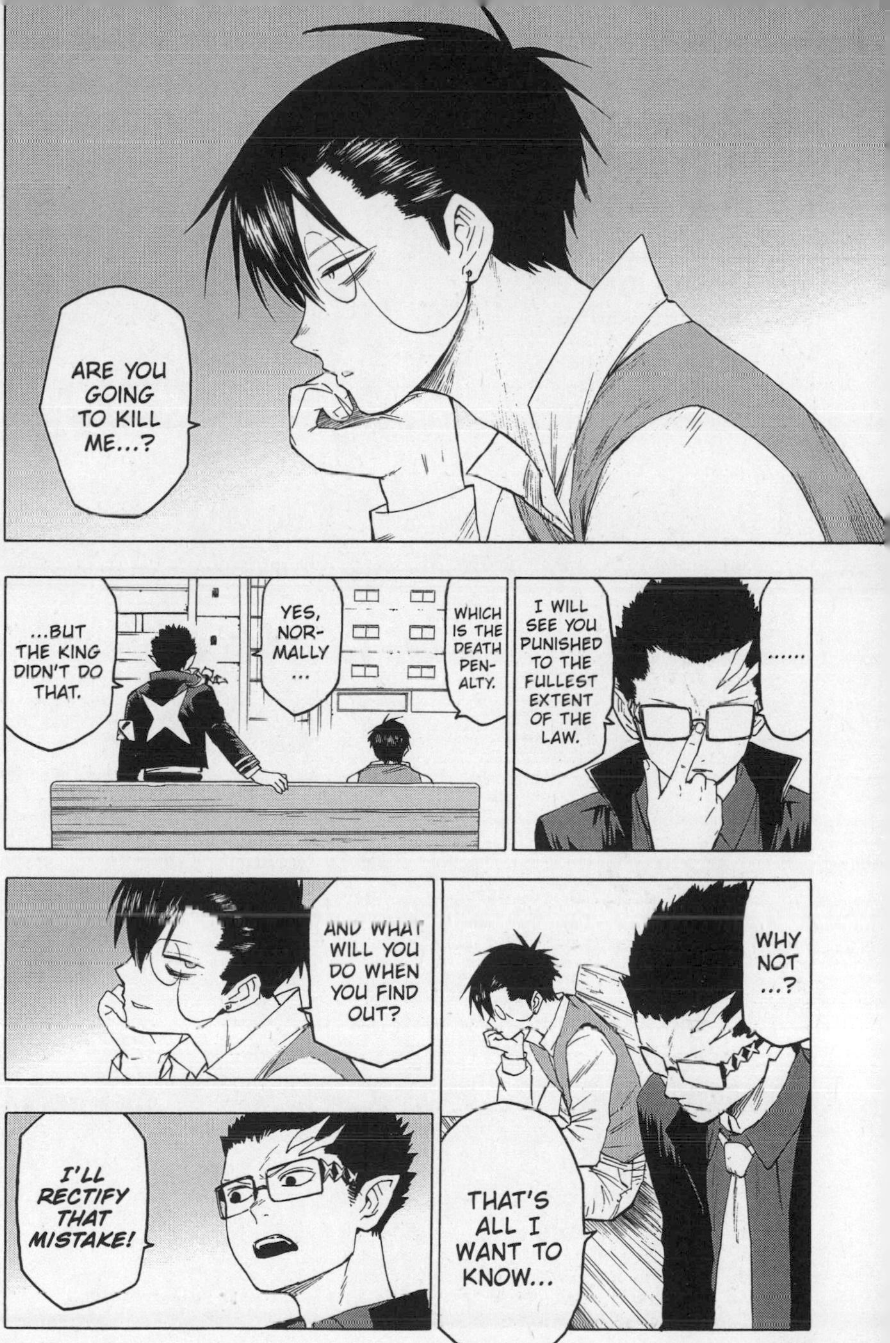
ARE YOU GOING TO KILL ME...?
......
I WILL SEE YOU PUNISHED TO THE FULLEST EXTENT OF THE LAW.
WHICH IS THE DEATH PENALTY.
YES, NORMALLY...
...BUT THE KING DIDN'T DO THAT.
WHY NOT...?
THAT'S ALL I WANT TO KNOW...
AND WHAT WILL YOU DO WHEN YOU FIND OUT?
I'LL RECTIFY THAT MISTAKE!

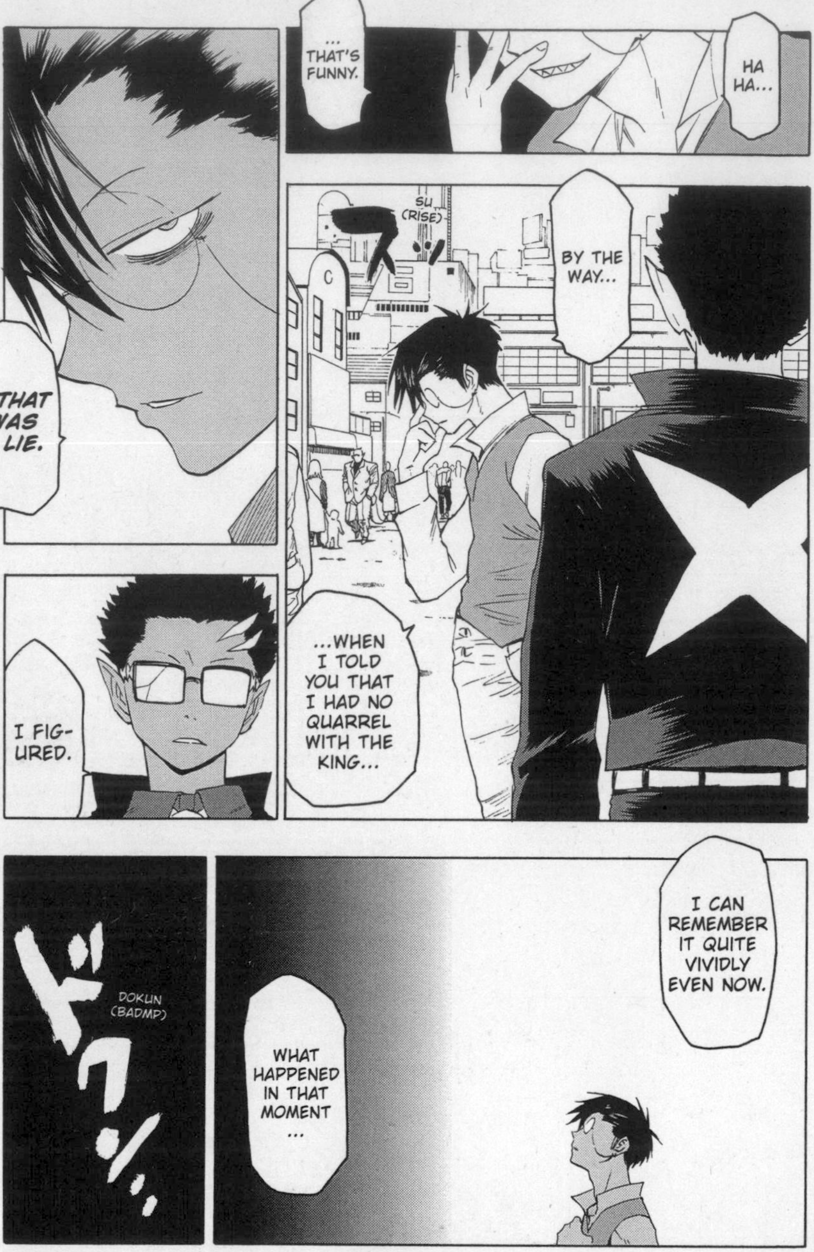
HA HA...
...THAT'S FUNNY.
SU (RISE)
BY THE WAY...
...WHEN I TOLD YOU THAT I HAD NO QUARREL WITH THE KING...
...THAT WAS A LIE.
I FIG-URED.
I CAN REMEMBER IT QUITE VIVIDLY EVEN NOW.
WHAT HAPPENED IN THAT MOMENT ...
DOKUN (BADMP)

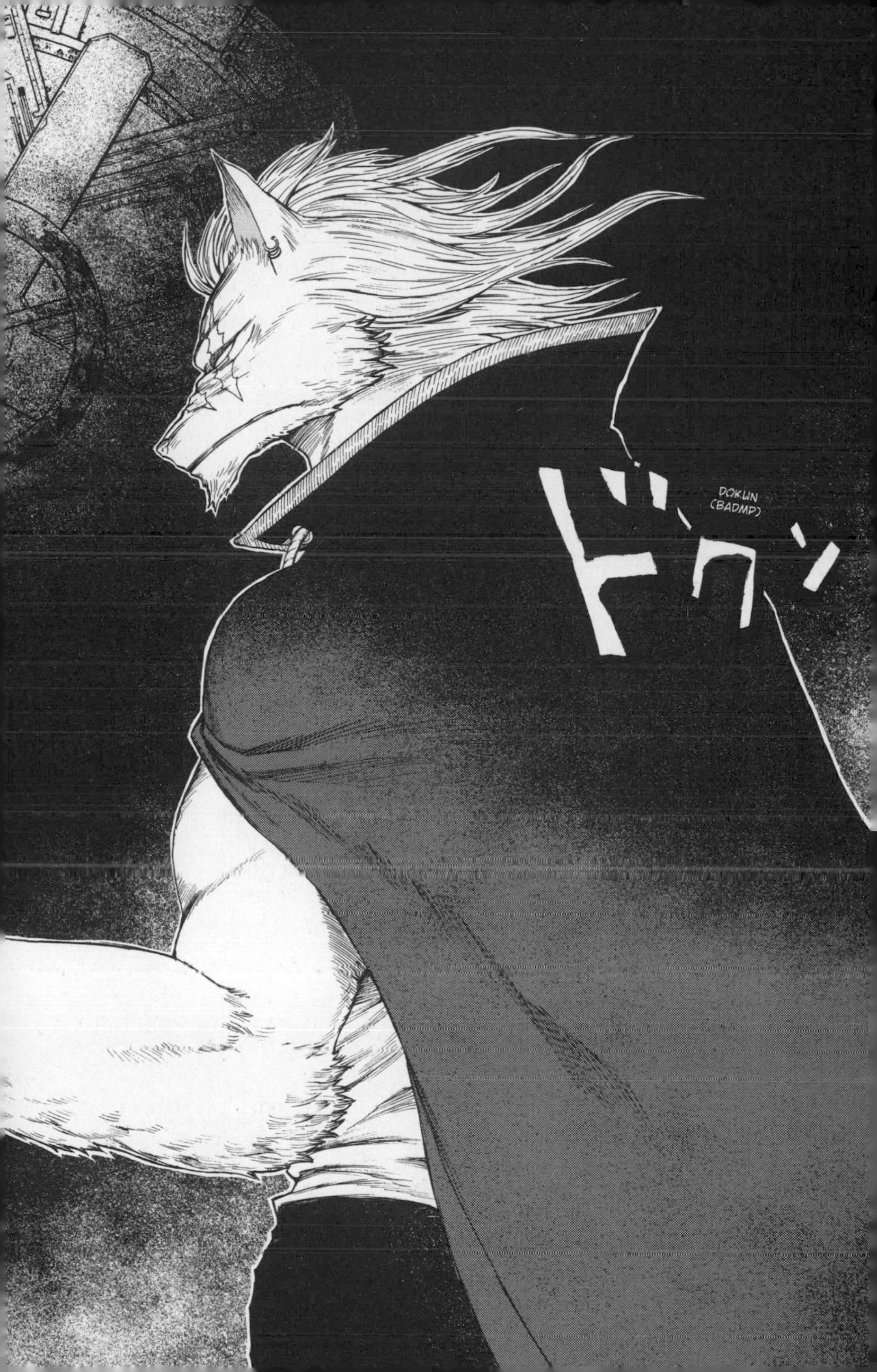
ドクン
DOKUN
(BADMP)

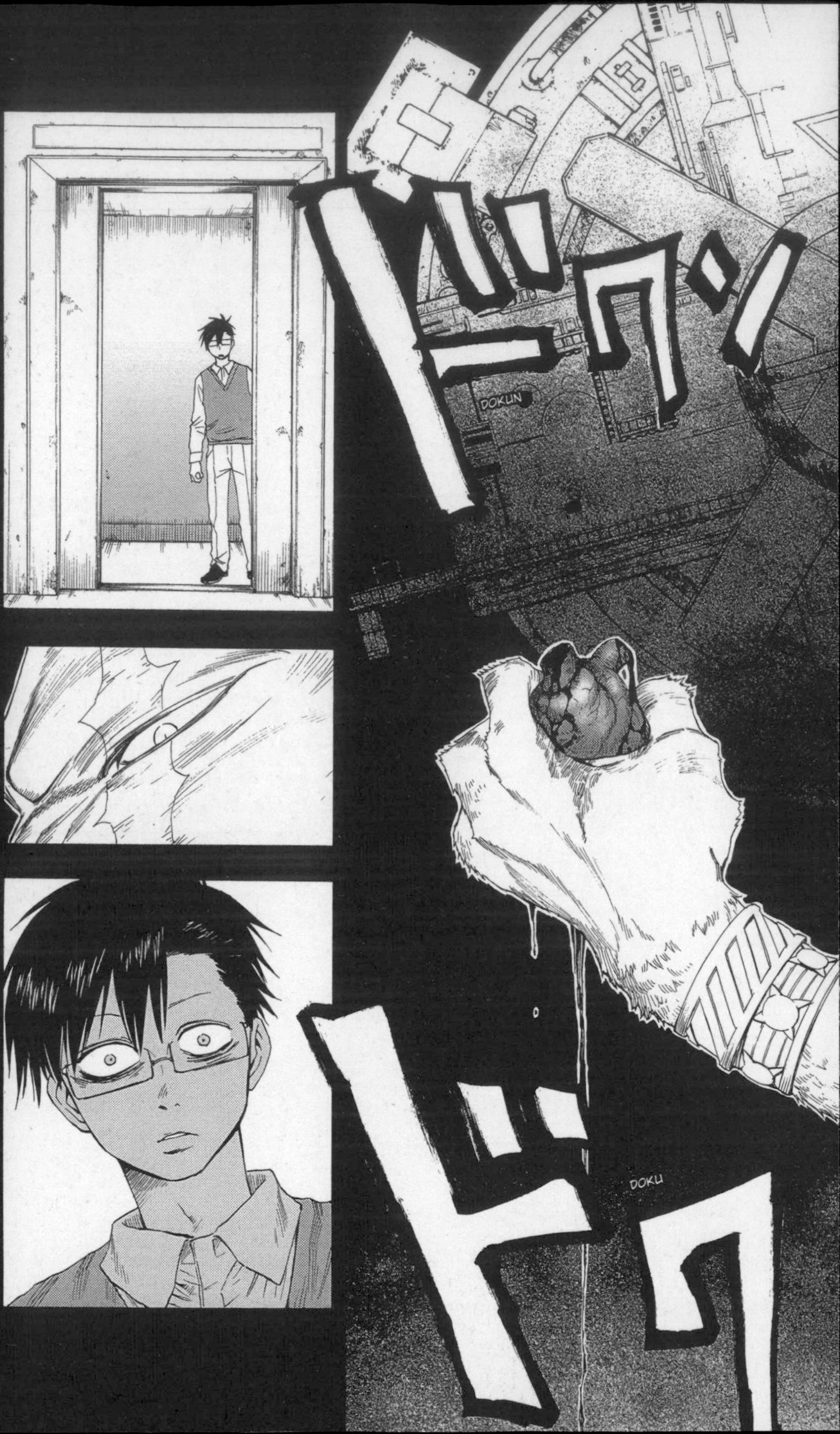
DOKUN
DOKU

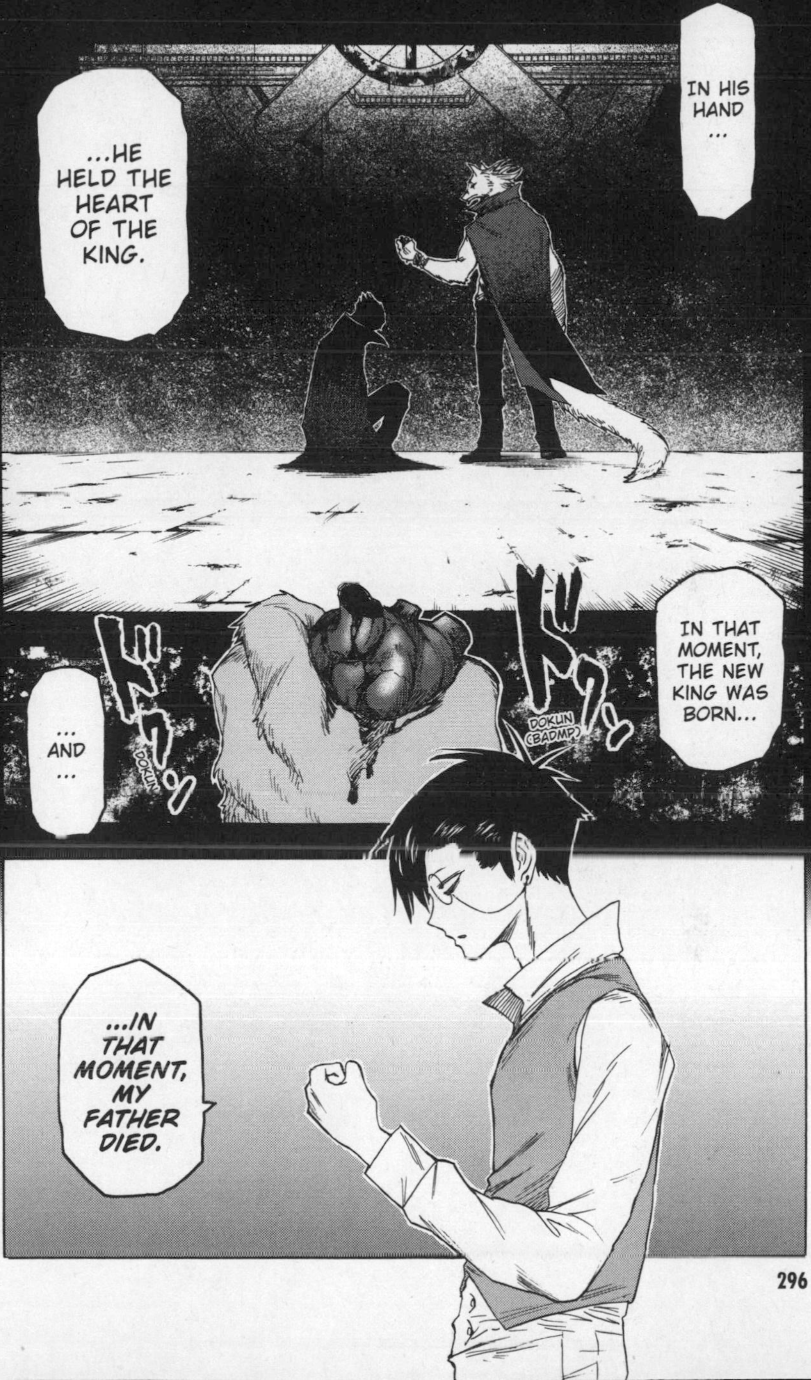
IN HIS HAND ...
...HE HELD THE HEART OF THE KING.
IN THAT MOMENT, THE NEW KING WAS BORN...
DOKUN (BADMP)
DOKUN
... AND ...
...IN THAT MOMENT, MY FATHER DIED.

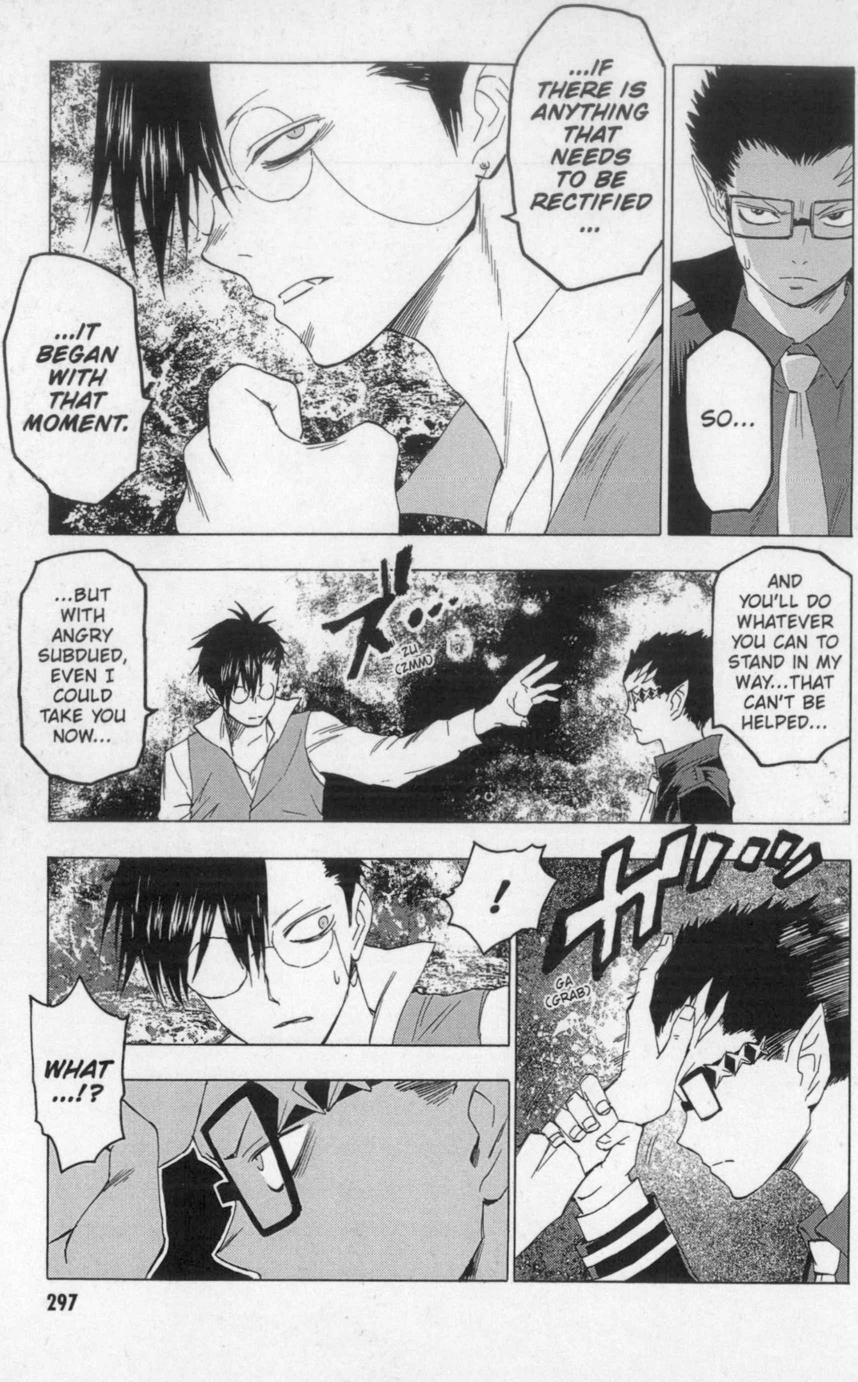
SO...
...IF THERE IS ANYTHING THAT NEEDS TO BE RECTIFIED...
...IT BEGAN WITH THAT MOMENT.
AND YOU'LL DO WHATEVER YOU CAN TO STAND IN MY WAY...THAT CAN'T BE HELPED...
ZU (ZMMM)
...BUT WITH ANGRY SUBDUED, EVEN I COULD TAKE YOU NOW...
GA (GRAB)
!
WHAT ...!?

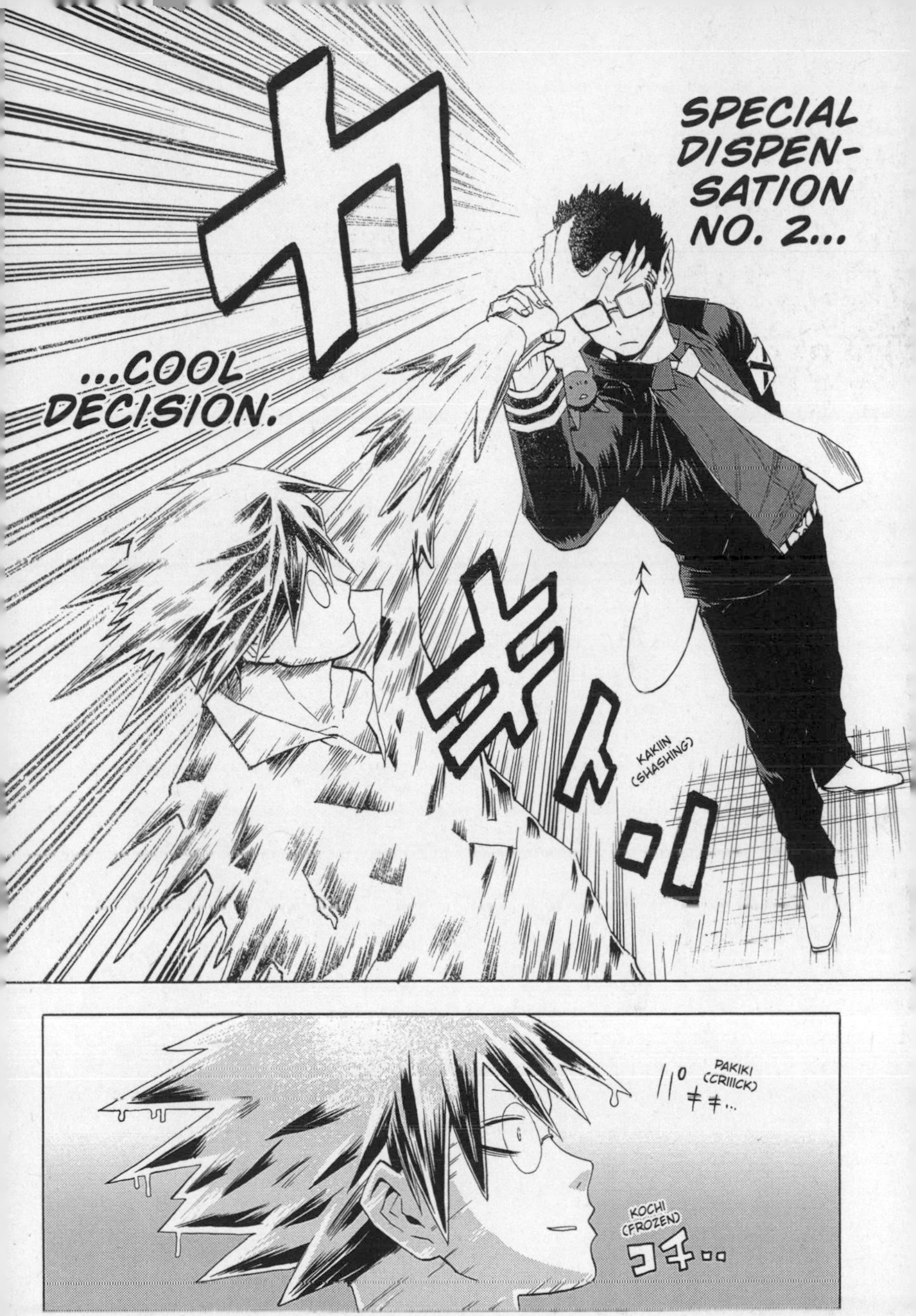
SPECIAL DISPENSATION NO. 2...
...COOL DECISION.
KAKIIN (SHASHING)
PAKIKI (CRIIICK)
KOCHI (FROZEN)

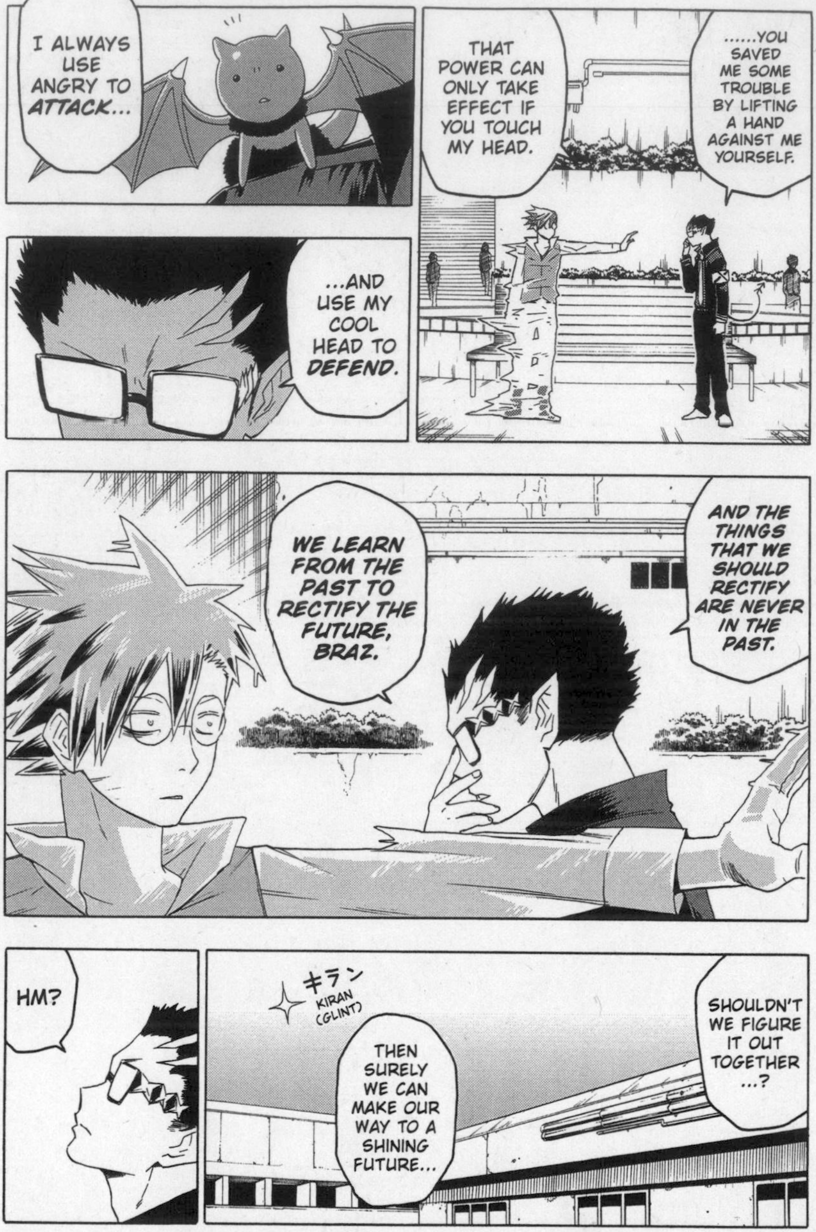
......YOU SAVED ME SOME TROUBLE BY LIFTING A HAND AGAINST ME YOURSELF.
THAT POWER CAN ONLY TAKE EFFECT IF YOU TOUCH MY HEAD.
I ALWAYS USE ANGRY TO ATTACK...
...AND USE MY COOL HEAD TO DEFEND.
AND THE THINGS THAT WE SHOULD RECTIFY ARE NEVER IN THE PAST.
WE LEARN FROM THE PAST TO RECTIFY THE FUTURE, BRAZ.
SHOULDN'T WE FIGURE IT OUT TOGETHER ...?
キラン
KIRAN (GLINT)
THEN SURELY WE CAN MAKE OUR WAY TO A SHINING FUTURE...
HM?

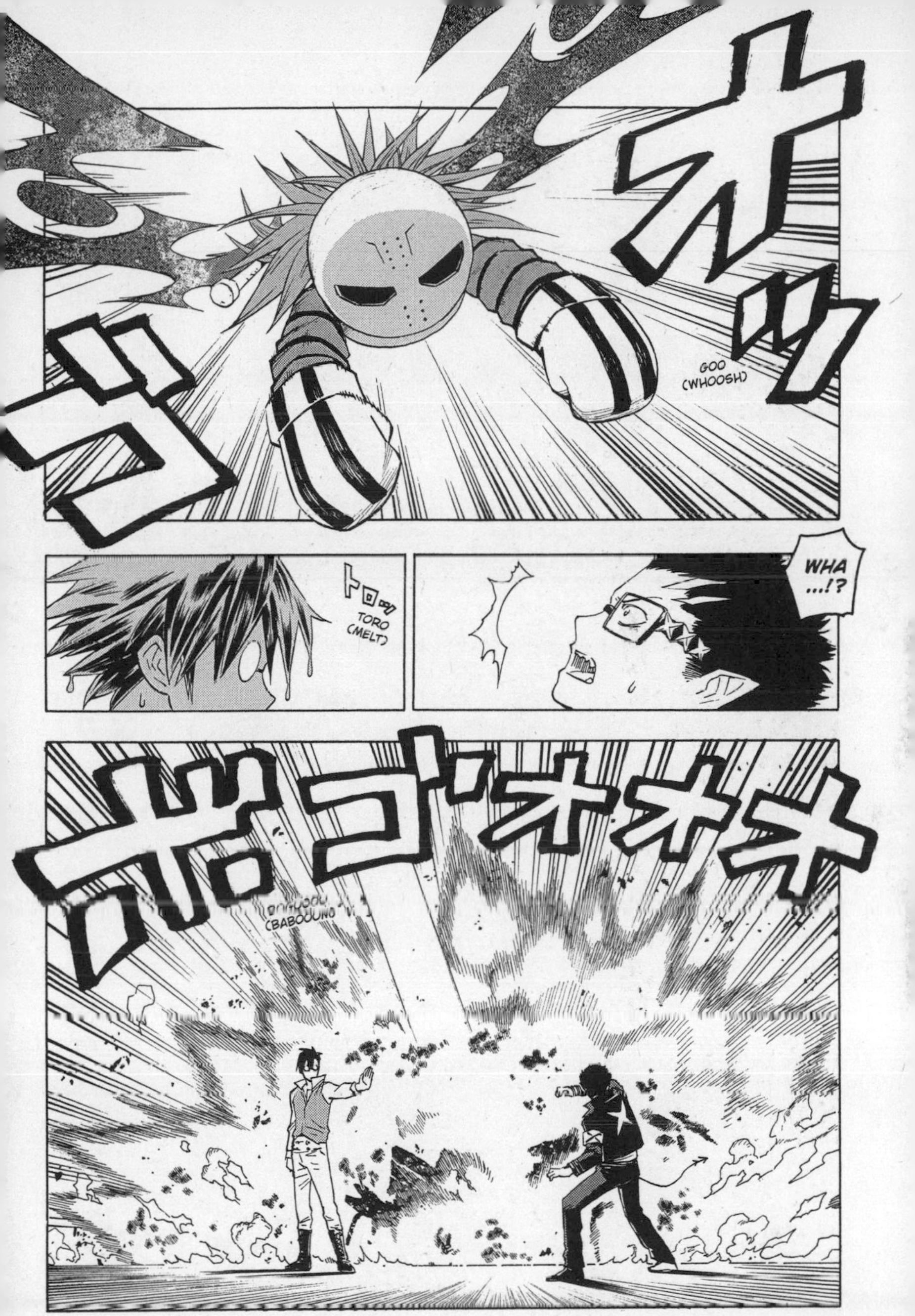

ゴオッ
GOO
(WHOOSH)
WHA
...!?
トロッ
TORO
(MELT)
ボゴオオオ
(BABOOUNG

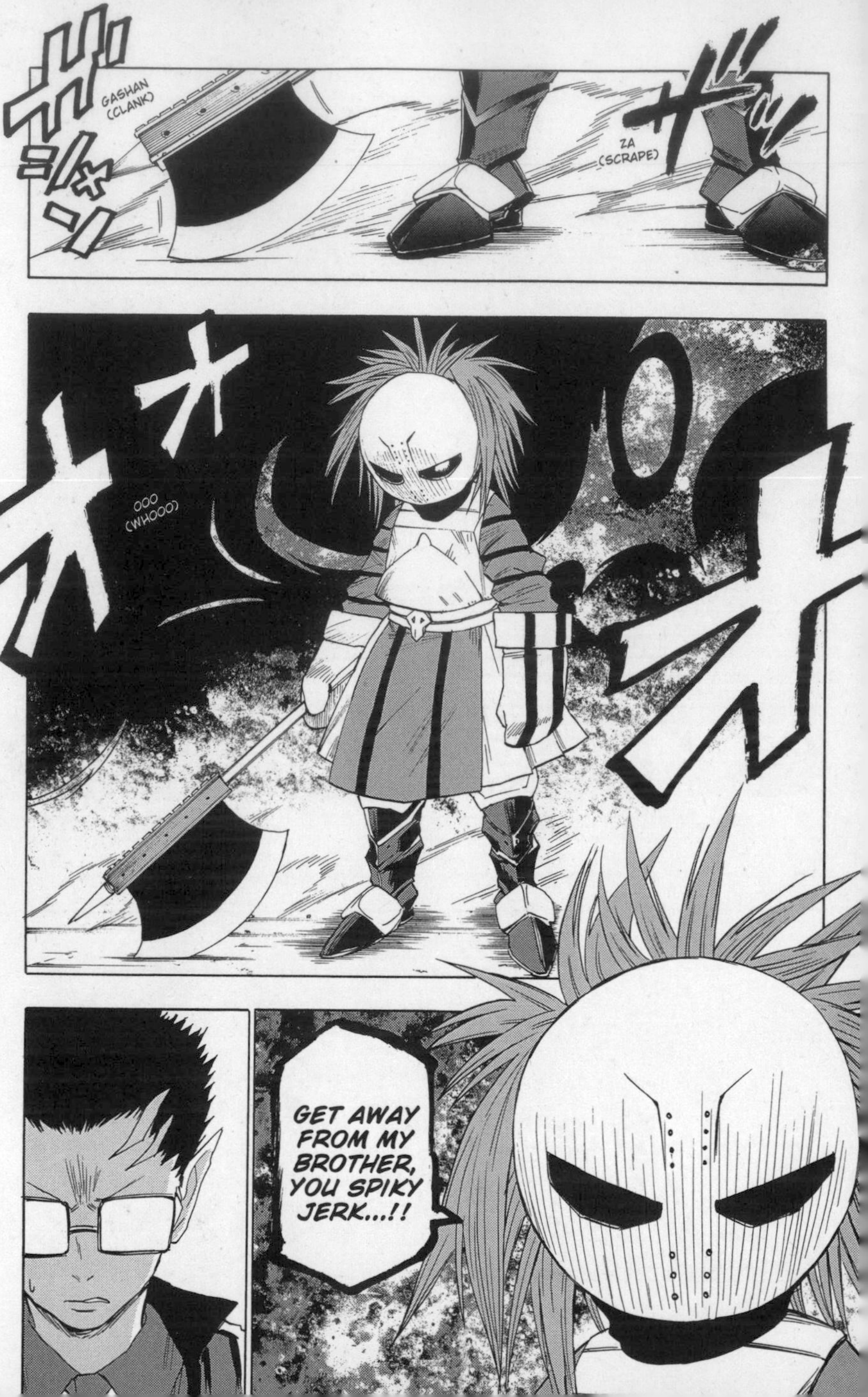
ZA (SCRAPE)
GASHAN (CLANK)
OOO (WHOOO)
GET AWAY FROM MY BROTHER, YOU SPIKY JERK...!!

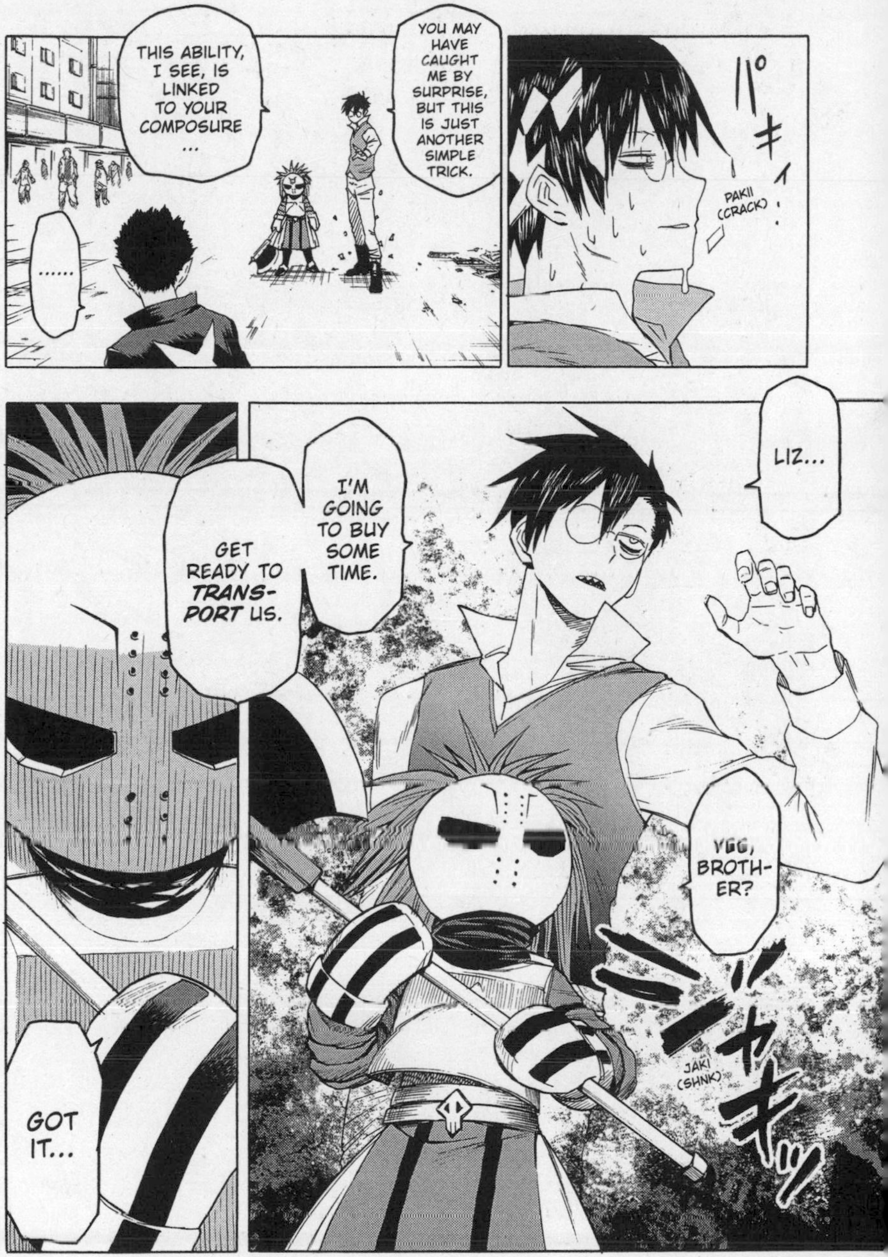
PAKII (CRACK)
YOU MAY HAVE CAUGHT ME BY SURPRISE, BUT THIS IS JUST ANOTHER SIMPLE TRICK.
THIS ABILITY, I SEE, IS LINKED TO YOUR COMPOSURE ...
......
LIZ...
I'M GOING TO BUY SOME TIME.
GET READY TO *TRANSPORT* US.
YES, BROTHER?
JAKI (SHNK)
GOT IT...

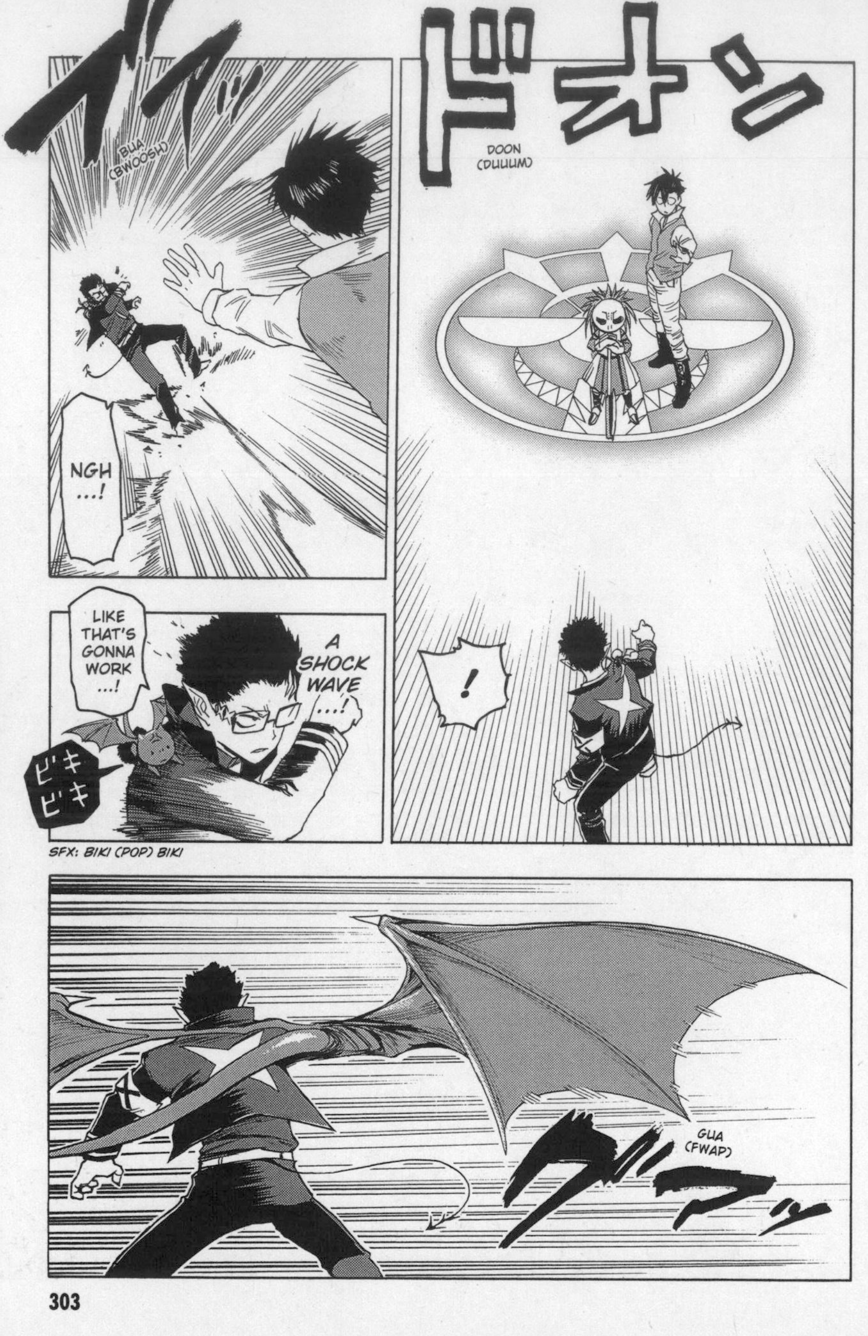
ドオン
DOON (DUUUM)
!
ブアッ
BUA (BWOOSH)
NGH ...!
A SHOCK WAVE ...!
LIKE THAT'S GONNA WORK ...!
ビキビキ
グアッ
GUA (FWAP)
SFX: BIKI (POP) BIKI

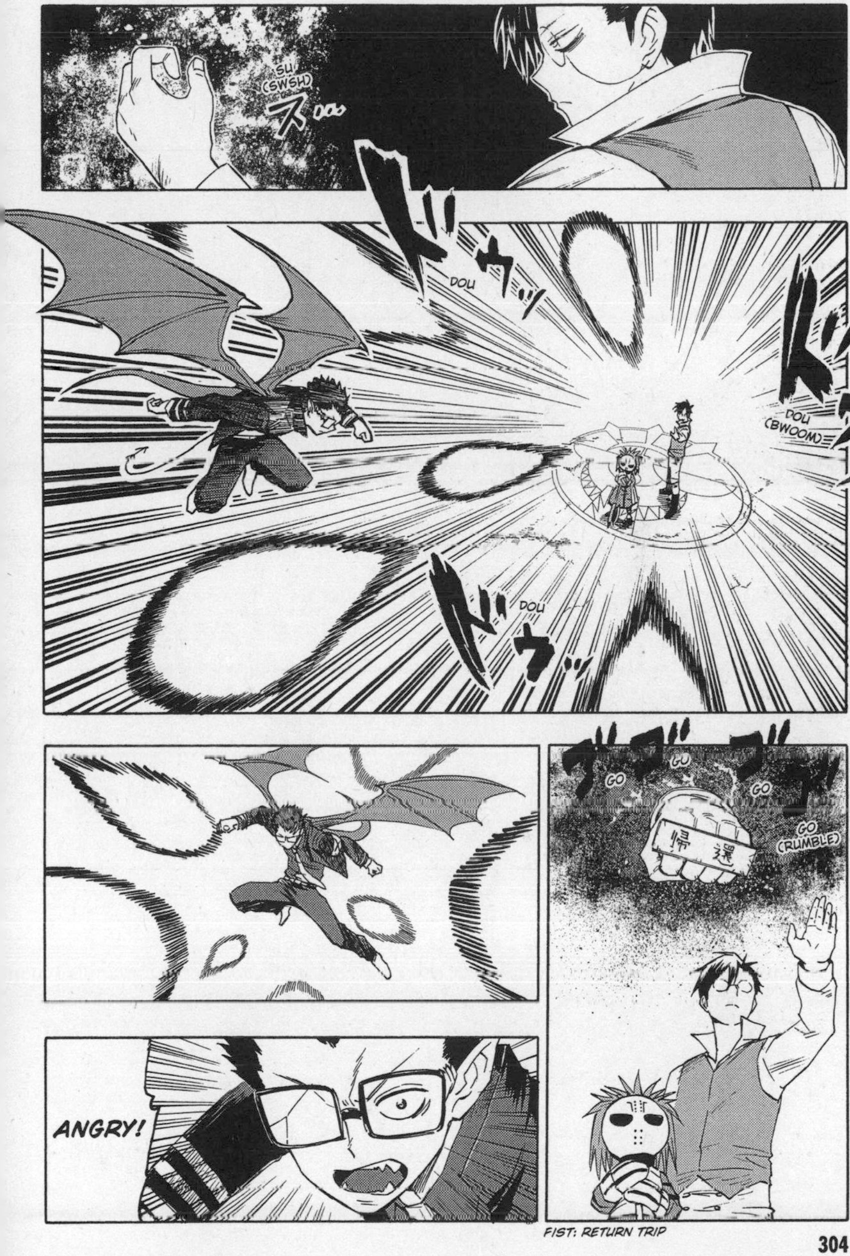
SU
(SWSH)
DOU
DOU
(BWOOM)
DOU
GO
GO
GO
GO
(RUMBLE)
ANGRY!

FIST: RETURN TRIP

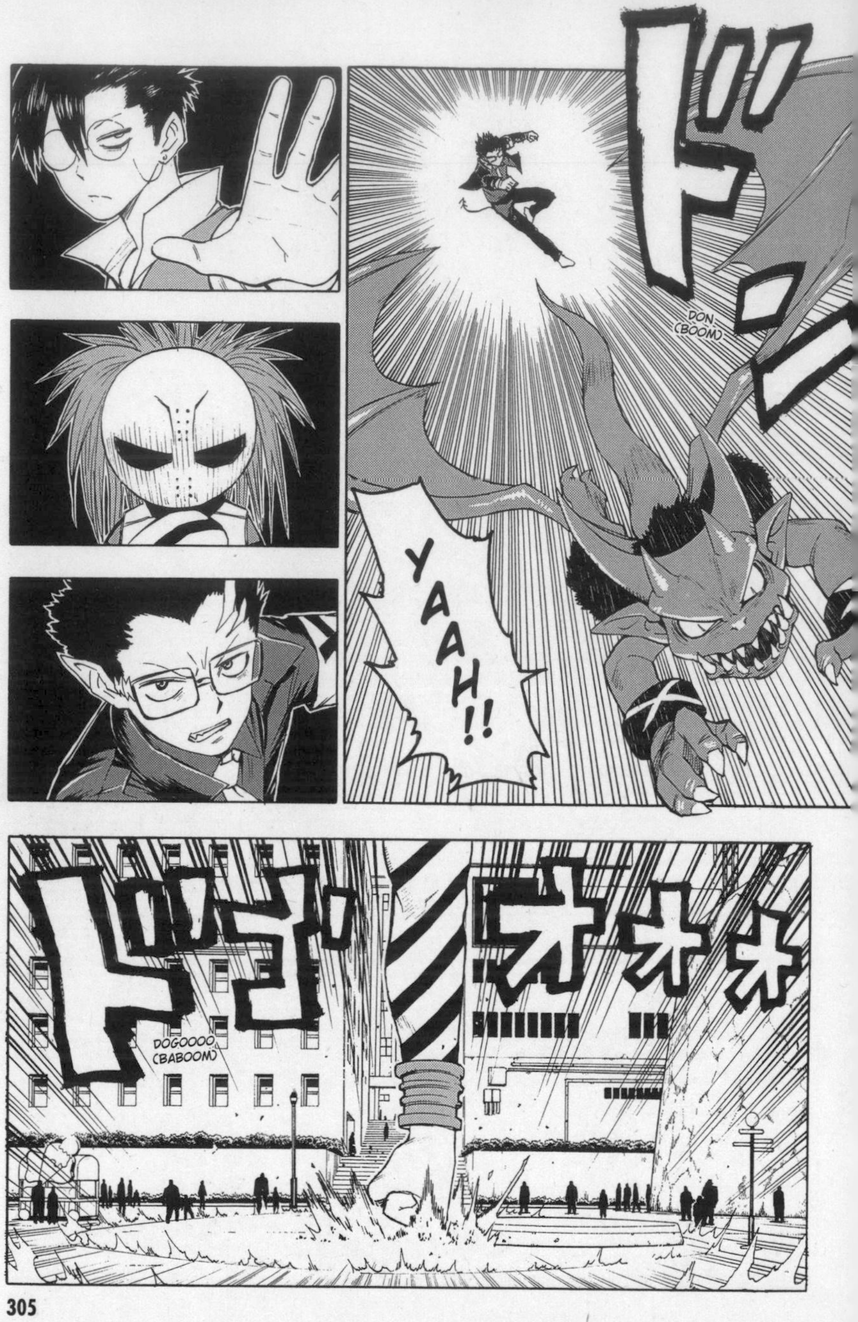
ドン
DON (BOOM)
YAAH!!
ドゴオオオ
DOGOOOO (BABOOM)

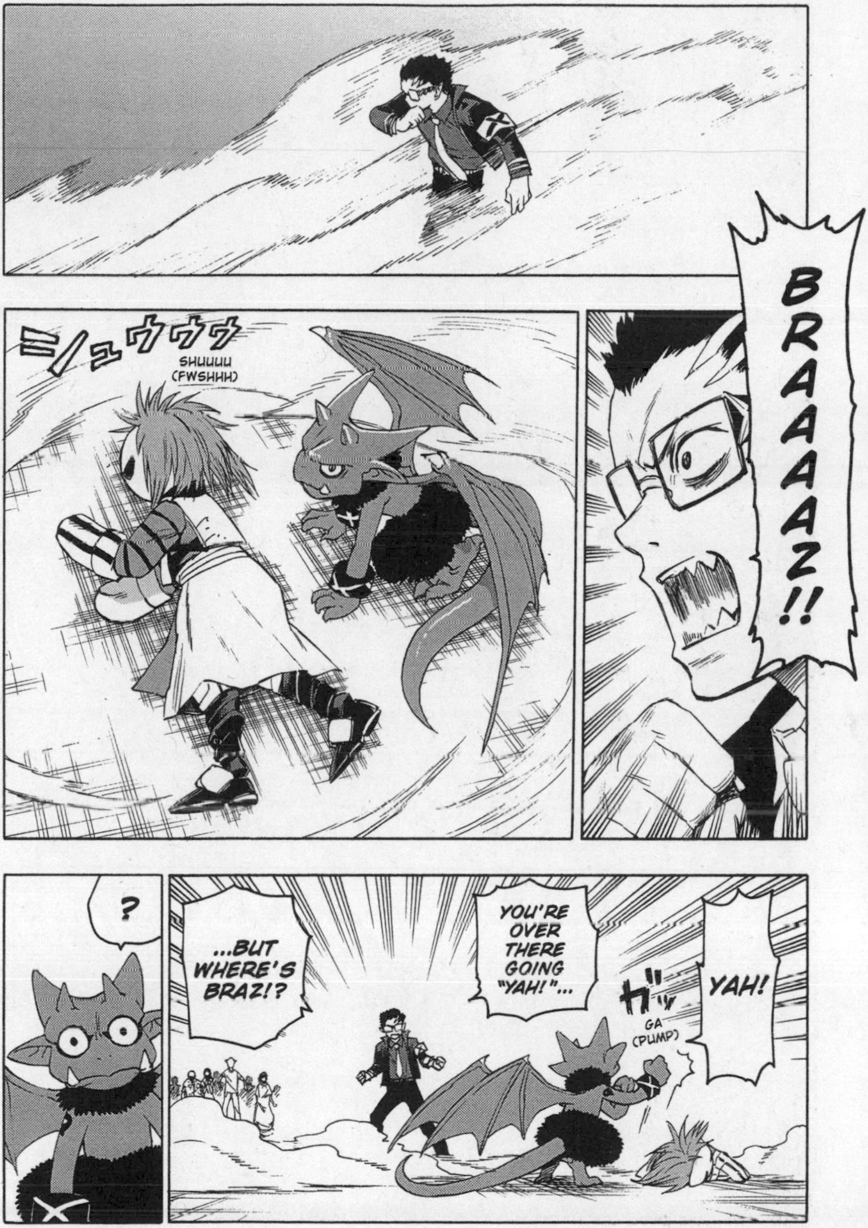
BRAAAAAZ!!
ニュウウウ
SHUUUU (FWSHHH)
YAH!
ガッ
GA (PUMP)
YOU'RE OVER THERE GOING "YAH!"...
...BUT WHERE'S BRAZ!?
?

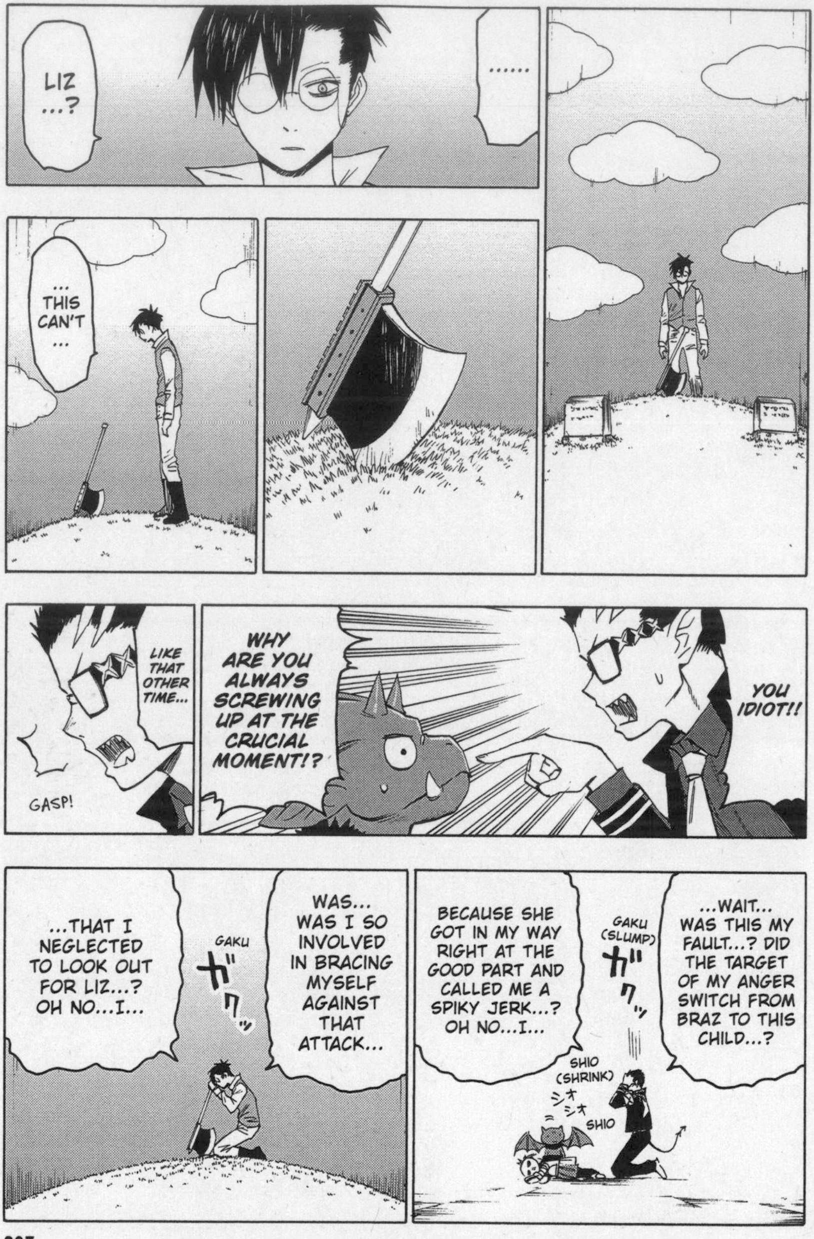
......
LIZ ...?
... THIS CAN'T ...
YOU IDIOT!!
WHY ARE YOU ALWAYS SCREWING UP AT THE CRUCIAL MOMENT!?
LIKE THAT OTHER TIME...
GASP!
...WAIT... WAS THIS MY FAULT...? DID THE TARGET OF MY ANGER SWITCH FROM BRAZ TO THIS CHILD...?
GAKU (SLUMP)
ガクッ
BECAUSE SHE GOT IN MY WAY RIGHT AT THE GOOD PART AND CALLED ME A SPIKY JERK...? OH NO...I...
SHIO (SHRINK)
シオ シオ
SHIO
WAS... WAS I SO INVOLVED IN BRACING MYSELF AGAINST THAT ATTACK...
GAKU
ガクッ
...THAT I NEGLECTED TO LOOK OUT FOR LIZ...? OH NO...I...

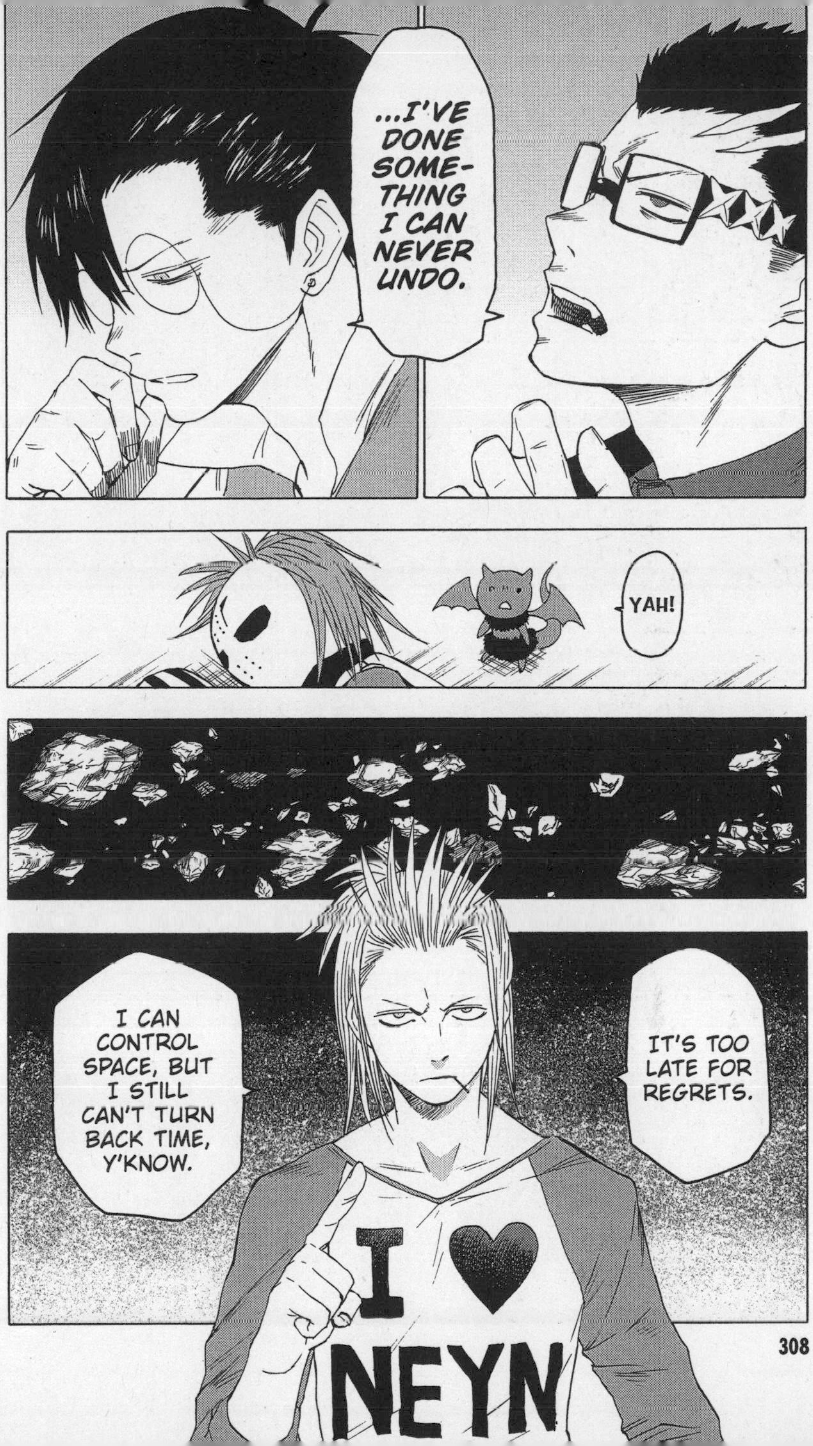
...I'VE DONE SOMETHING I CAN NEVER UNDO.
YAH!
IT'S TOO LATE FOR REGRETS.
I CAN CONTROL SPACE, BUT I STILL CAN'T TURN BACK TIME, Y'KNOW.
I ♥ NEYN

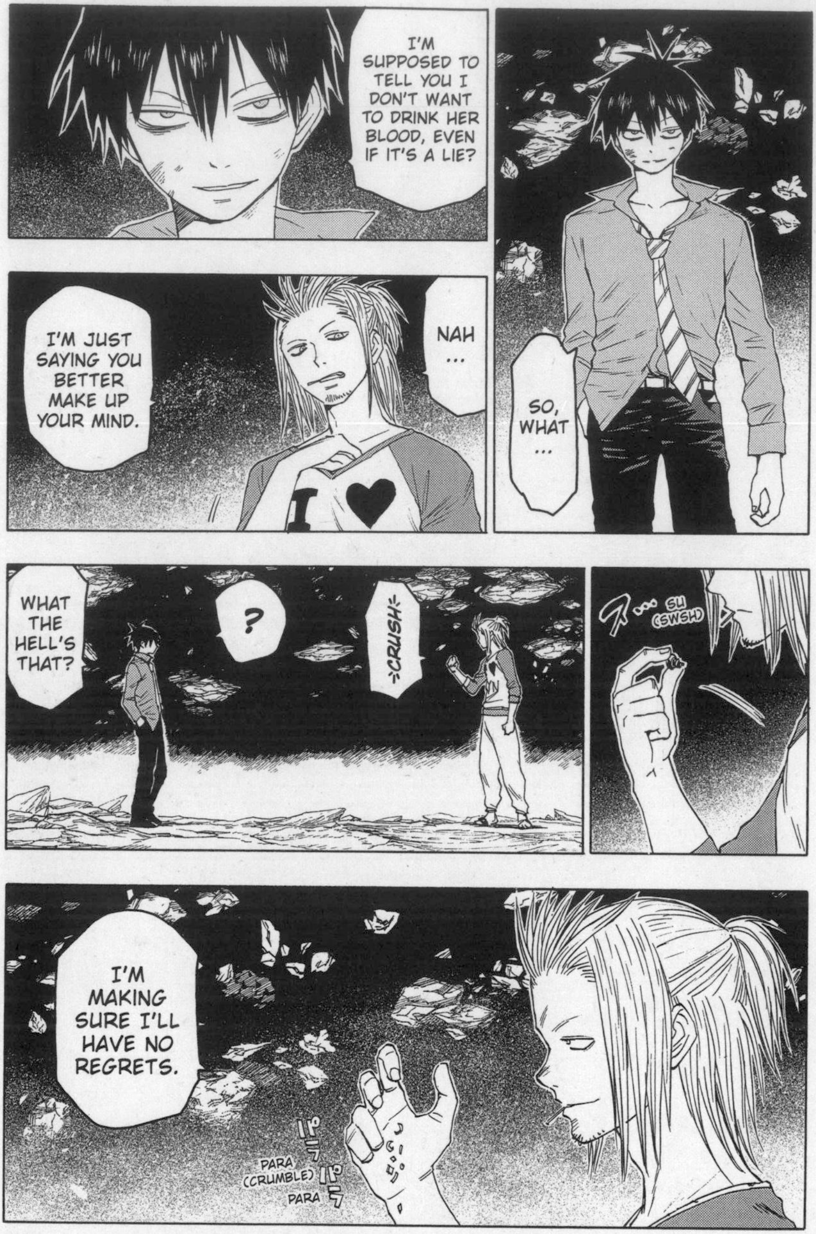
SO, WHAT ...
I'M SUPPOSED TO TELL YOU I DON'T WANT TO DRINK HER BLOOD, EVEN IF IT'S A LIE?
NAH ...
I'M JUST SAYING YOU BETTER MAKE UP YOUR MIND.
SU (SWSH)
-CRUSH-
?
WHAT THE HELL'S THAT?
I'M MAKING SURE I'LL HAVE NO REGRETS.
PARA (CRUMBLE) PARA

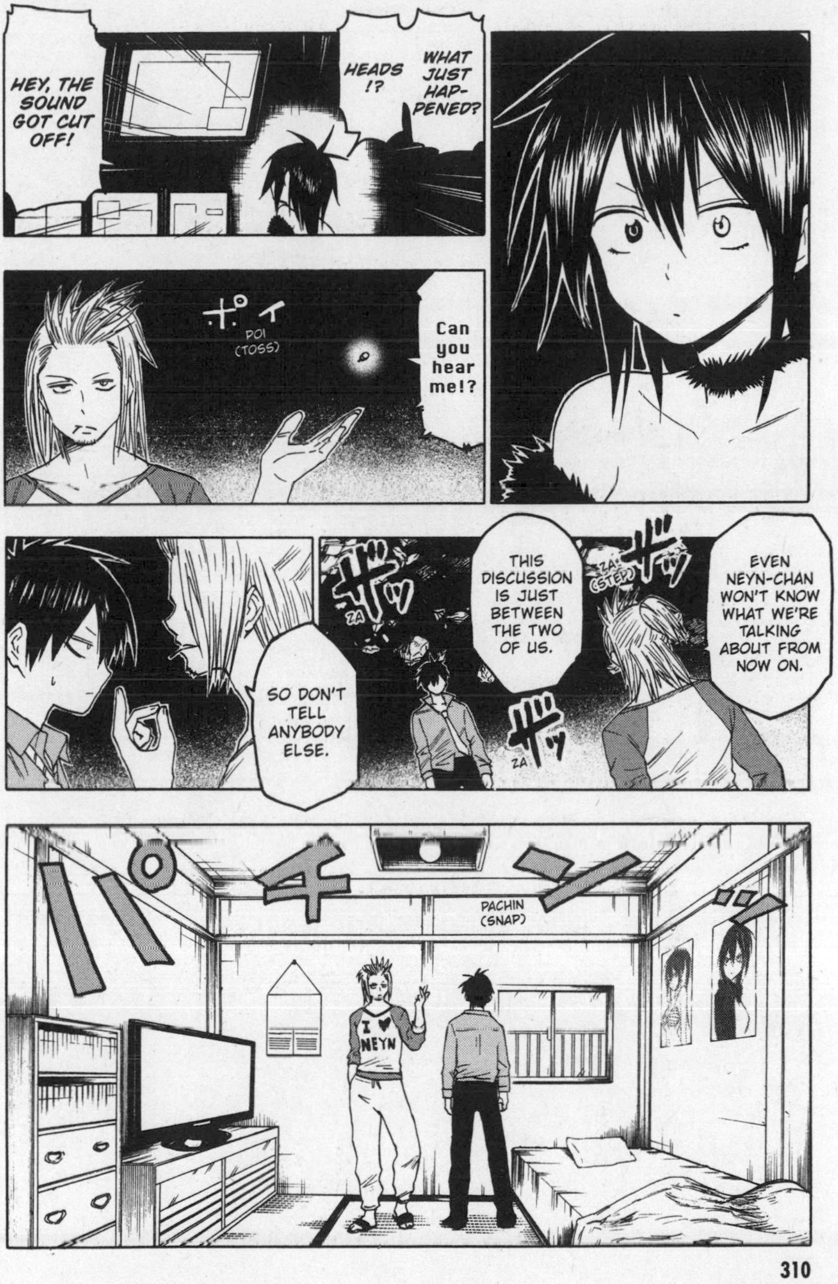
WHAT JUST HAP-PENED?
HEADS!?
HEY, THE SOUND GOT CUT OFF!
Can you hear me!?
POI (TOSS)
EVEN NEYN-CHAN WON'T KNOW WHAT WE'RE TALKING ABOUT FROM NOW ON.
ZA (STEP)
THIS DISCUSSION IS JUST BETWEEN THE TWO OF US.
ZA
ZA
SO DON'T TELL ANYBODY ELSE.
PACHIN (SNAP)
I NEYN

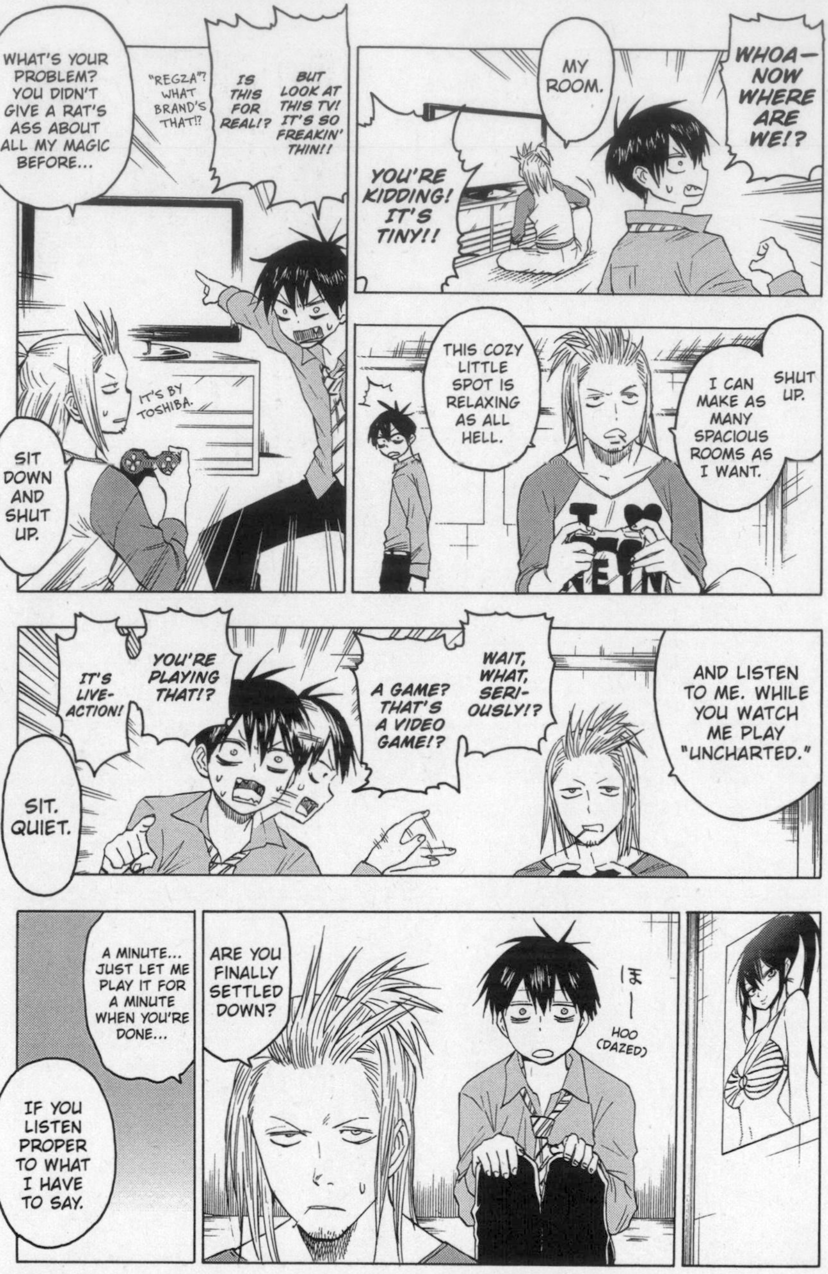
WHOA—NOW WHERE ARE WE!?
MY ROOM.
YOU'RE KIDDING! IT'S TINY!!
SHUT UP.
I CAN MAKE AS MANY SPACIOUS ROOMS AS I WANT.
THIS COZY LITTLE SPOT IS RELAXING AS ALL HELL.
IS THIS FOR REAL!? BUT LOOK AT THIS TV! IT'S SO FREAKIN' THIN!!
"REGZA"? WHAT BRAND'S THAT!?
WHAT'S YOUR PROBLEM? YOU DIDN'T GIVE A RAT'S ASS ABOUT ALL MY MAGIC BEFORE...
IT'S BY TOSHIBA.
SIT DOWN AND SHUT UP.
AND LISTEN TO ME. WHILE YOU WATCH ME PLAY "UNCHARTED."
WAIT, WHAT, SERI-OUSLY!?
A GAME? THAT'S A VIDEO GAME!?
YOU'RE PLAYING THAT!?
IT'S LIVE-ACTION!
SIT. QUIET.
ほー
HOO (DAZED)
ARE YOU FINALLY SETTLED DOWN?
A MINUTE... JUST LET ME PLAY IT FOR A MINUTE WHEN YOU'RE DONE...
IF YOU LISTEN PROPER TO WHAT I HAVE TO SAY.

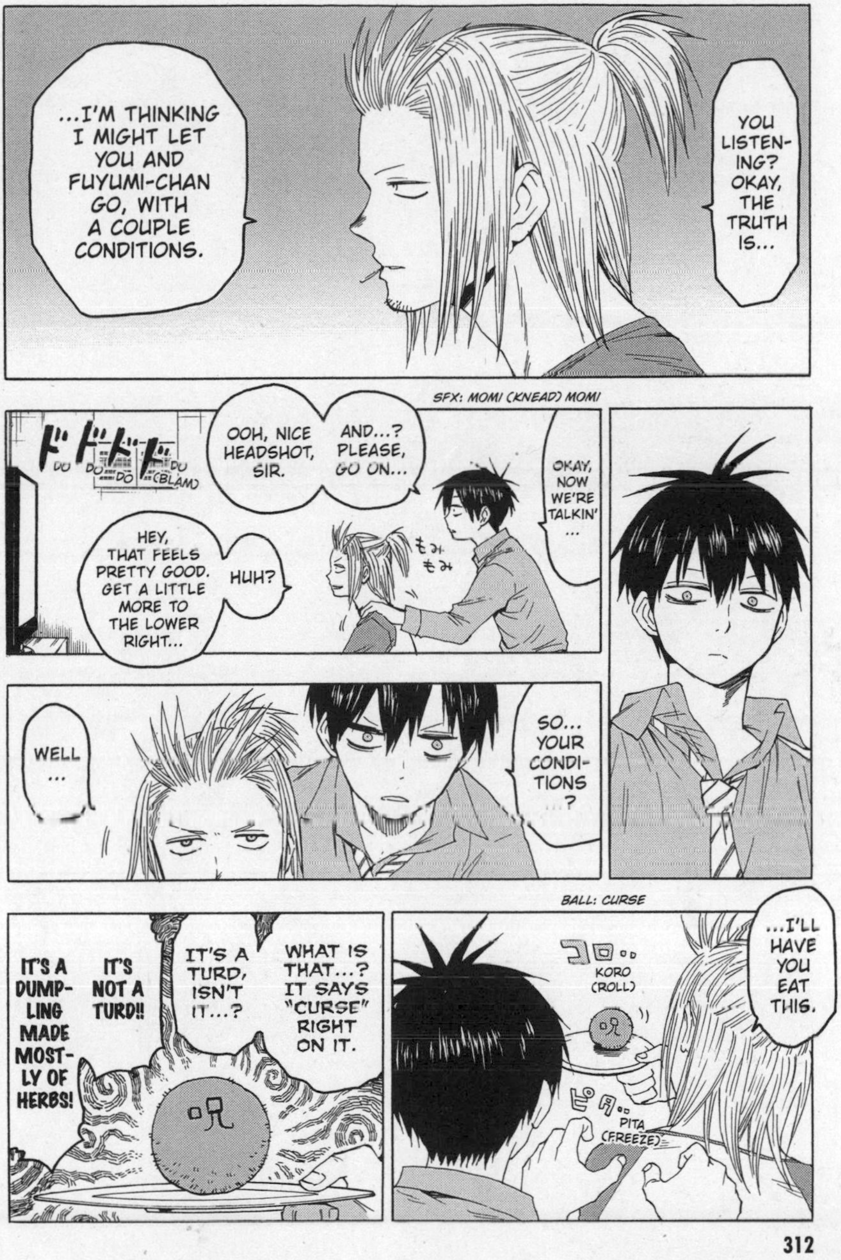
YOU LISTENING? OKAY, THE TRUTH IS...
...I'M THINKING I MIGHT LET YOU AND FUYUMI-CHAN GO, WITH A COUPLE CONDITIONS.
SFX: MOMI (KNEAD) MOMI
OKAY, NOW WE'RE TALKIN'...
AND...? PLEASE, GO ON...
OOH, NICE HEADSHOT, SIR.
ドドドド
DO DO DO DU (BLAM)
もみもみ
HUH?
HEY, THAT FEELS PRETTY GOOD. GET A LITTLE MORE TO THE LOWER RIGHT...
SO... YOUR CONDITIONS...?
WELL...
BALL: CURSE
...I'LL HAVE YOU EAT THIS.
コロ
KORO (ROLL)
呪
ピタ
PITA (FREEZE)
WHAT IS THAT...? IT SAYS "CURSE" RIGHT ON IT.
IT'S A TURD, ISN'T IT...?
IT'S NOT A TURD!!
IT'S A DUMPLING MADE MOSTLY OF HERBS!
呪

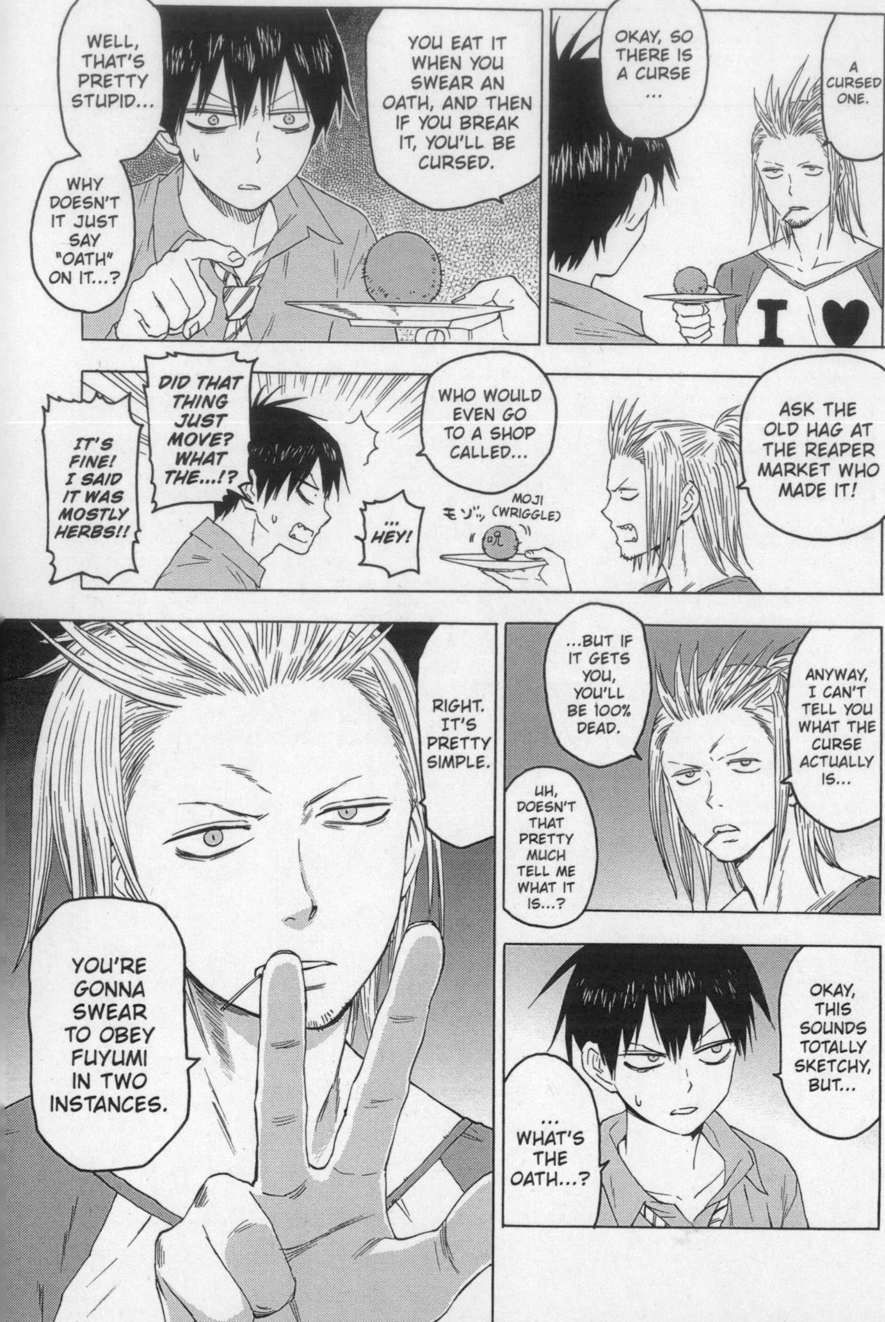
OKAY, SO THERE IS A CURSE ...
A CURSED ONE.
YOU EAT IT WHEN YOU SWEAR AN OATH, AND THEN IF YOU BREAK IT, YOU'LL BE CURSED.
WELL, THAT'S PRETTY STUPID...
WHY DOESN'T IT JUST SAY "OATH" ON IT...?
ASK THE OLD HAG AT THE REAPER MARKET WHO MADE IT!
WHO WOULD EVEN GO TO A SHOP CALLED...
モジッ
MOJI (WRIGGLE)
... HEY!
DID THAT THING JUST MOVE? WHAT THE...!?
IT'S FINE! I SAID IT WAS MOSTLY HERBS!!
ANYWAY, I CAN'T TELL YOU WHAT THE CURSE ACTUALLY IS...
...BUT IF IT GETS YOU, YOU'LL BE 100% DEAD.
UH, DOESN'T THAT PRETTY MUCH TELL ME WHAT IT IS...?
OKAY, THIS SOUNDS TOTALLY SKETCHY, BUT...
... WHAT'S THE OATH...?
RIGHT. IT'S PRETTY SIMPLE.
YOU'RE GONNA SWEAR TO OBEY FUYUMI IN TWO INSTANCES.

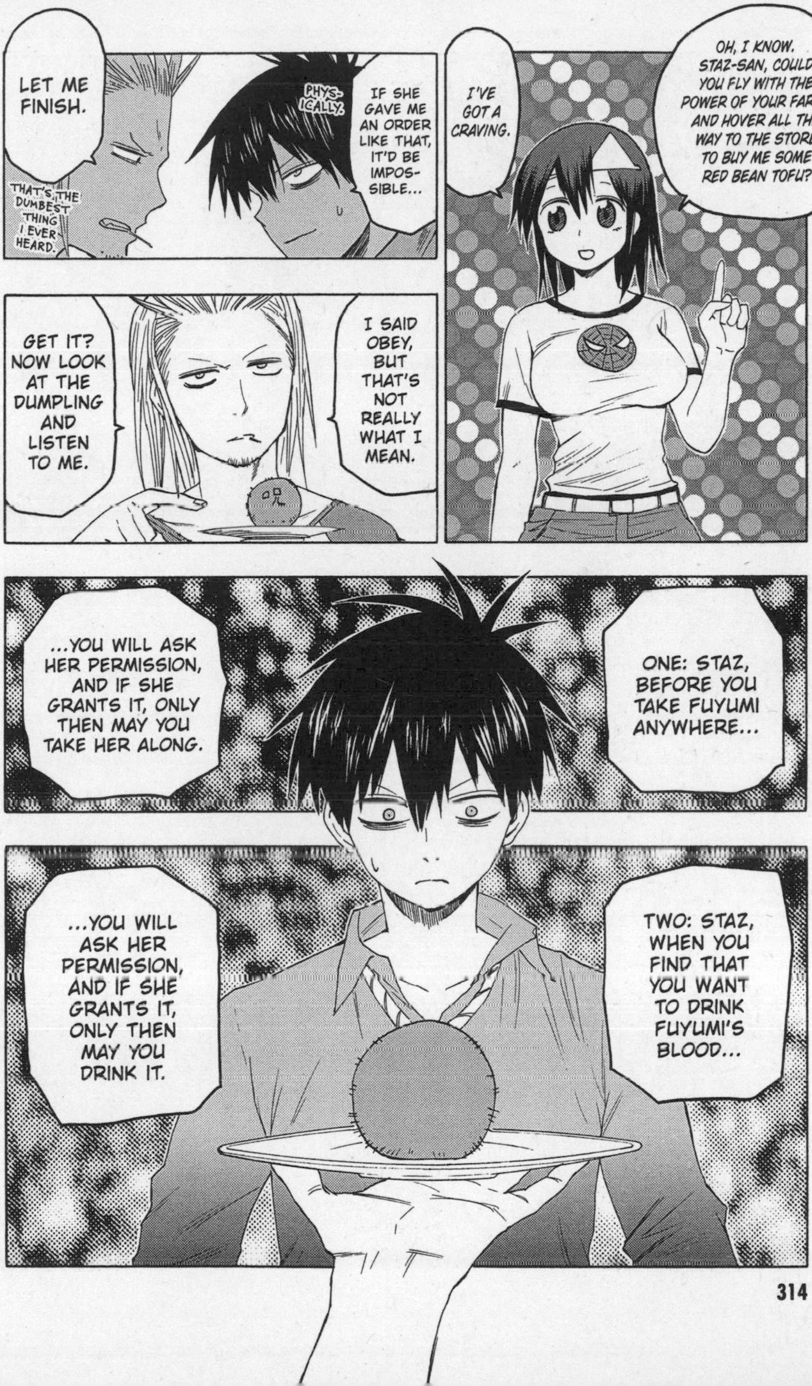
OH, I KNOW. STAZ-SAN, COULD YOU FLY WITH THE POWER OF YOUR FARTS AND HOVER ALL THE WAY TO THE STORE TO BUY ME SOME RED BEAN TOFU?
I'VE GOT A CRAVING.
IF SHE GAVE ME AN ORDER LIKE THAT, IT'D BE IMPOSSIBLE...
PHYS-ICALLY.
LET ME FINISH.
THAT'S THE DUMBEST THING I EVER HEARD.
I SAID OBEY, BUT THAT'S NOT REALLY WHAT I MEAN.
GET IT? NOW LOOK AT THE DUMPLING AND LISTEN TO ME.
ONE: STAZ, BEFORE YOU TAKE FUYUMI ANYWHERE...
...YOU WILL ASK HER PERMISSION, AND IF SHE GRANTS IT, ONLY THEN MAY YOU TAKE HER ALONG.
TWO: STAZ, WHEN YOU FIND THAT YOU WANT TO DRINK FUYUMI'S BLOOD...
...YOU WILL ASK HER PERMISSION, AND IF SHE GRANTS IT, ONLY THEN MAY YOU DRINK IT.

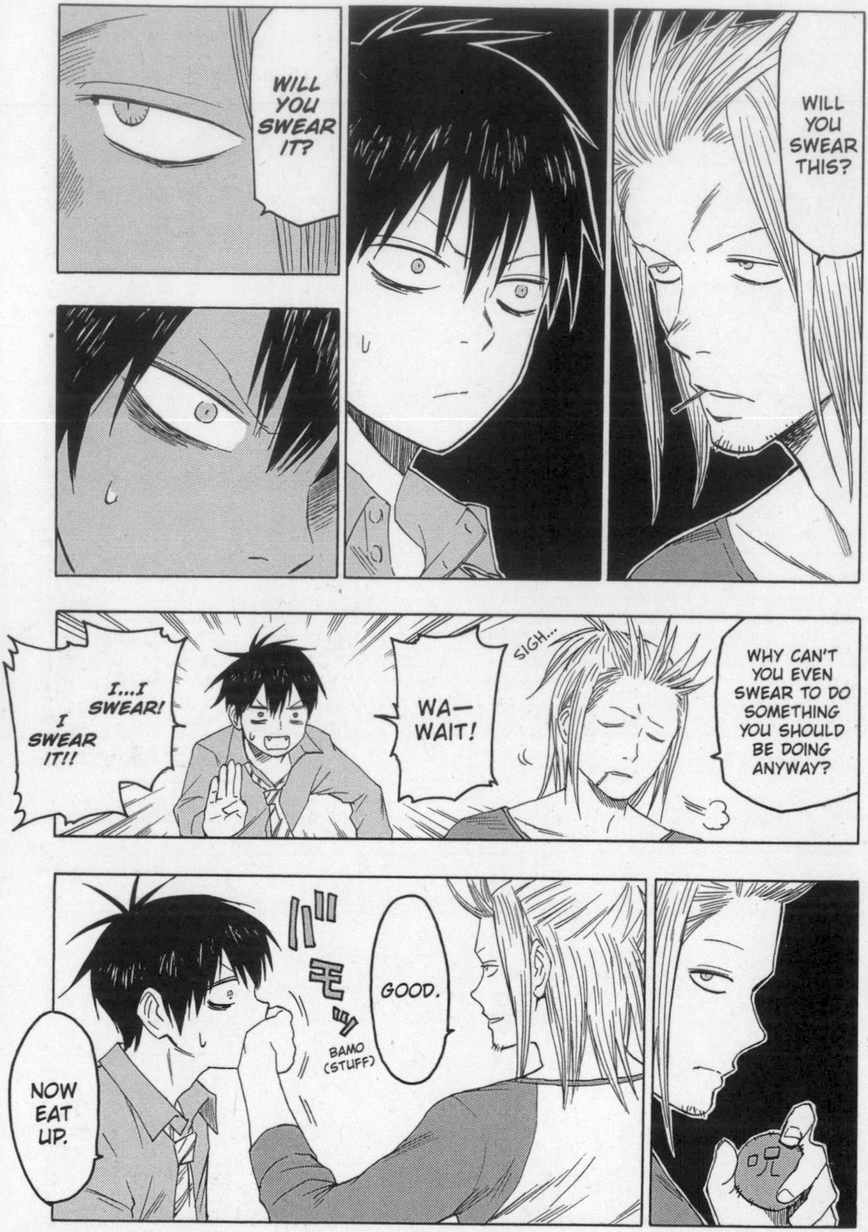
WILL YOU SWEAR THIS?
WILL YOU SWEAR IT?
WHY CAN'T YOU EVEN SWEAR TO DO SOMETHING YOU SHOULD BE DOING ANYWAY?
SIGH...
WA— WAIT!
I...I SWEAR!
I SWEAR IT!!
GOOD.
バモッ
BAMO (STUFF)
NOW EAT UP.

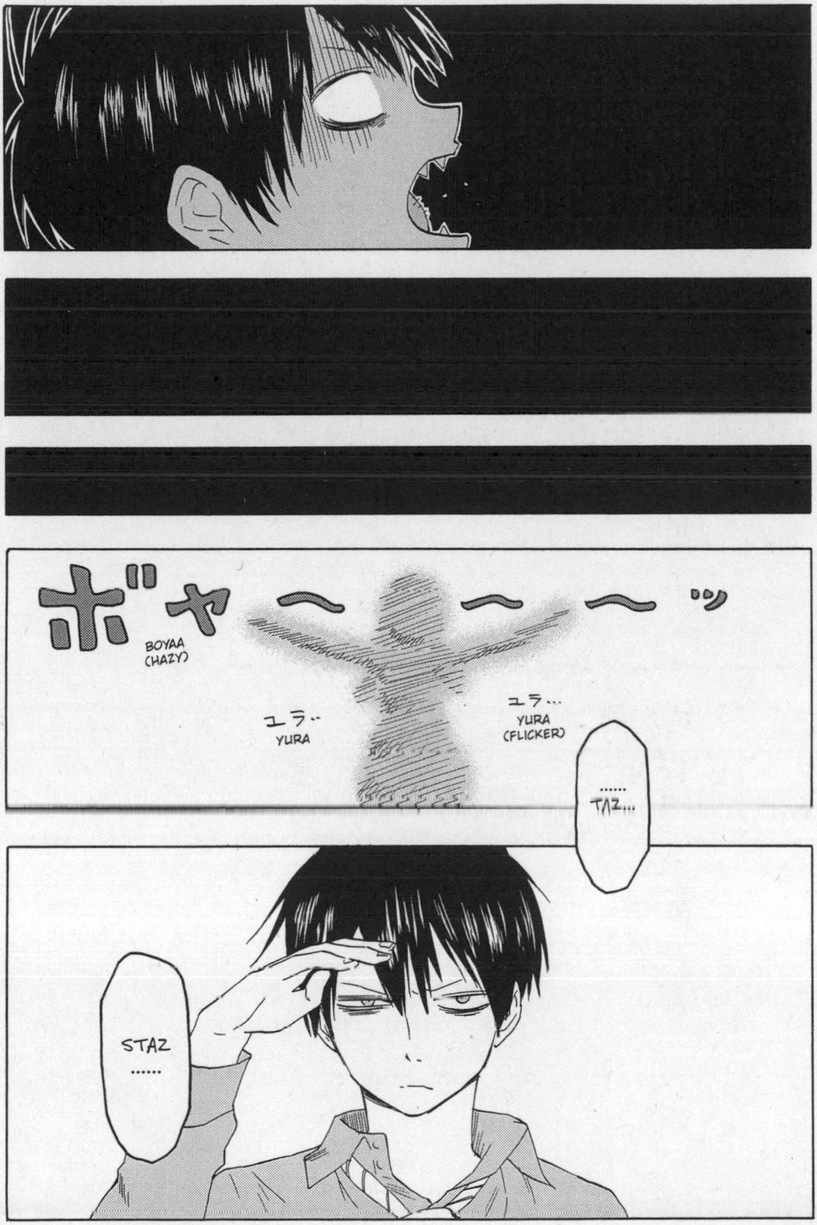

ボヤ〜〜〜ッ
BOYAA (HAZY)
ユラ… YURA (FLICKER)
ユラ‥ YURA
...... TAZ...
STAZ ......

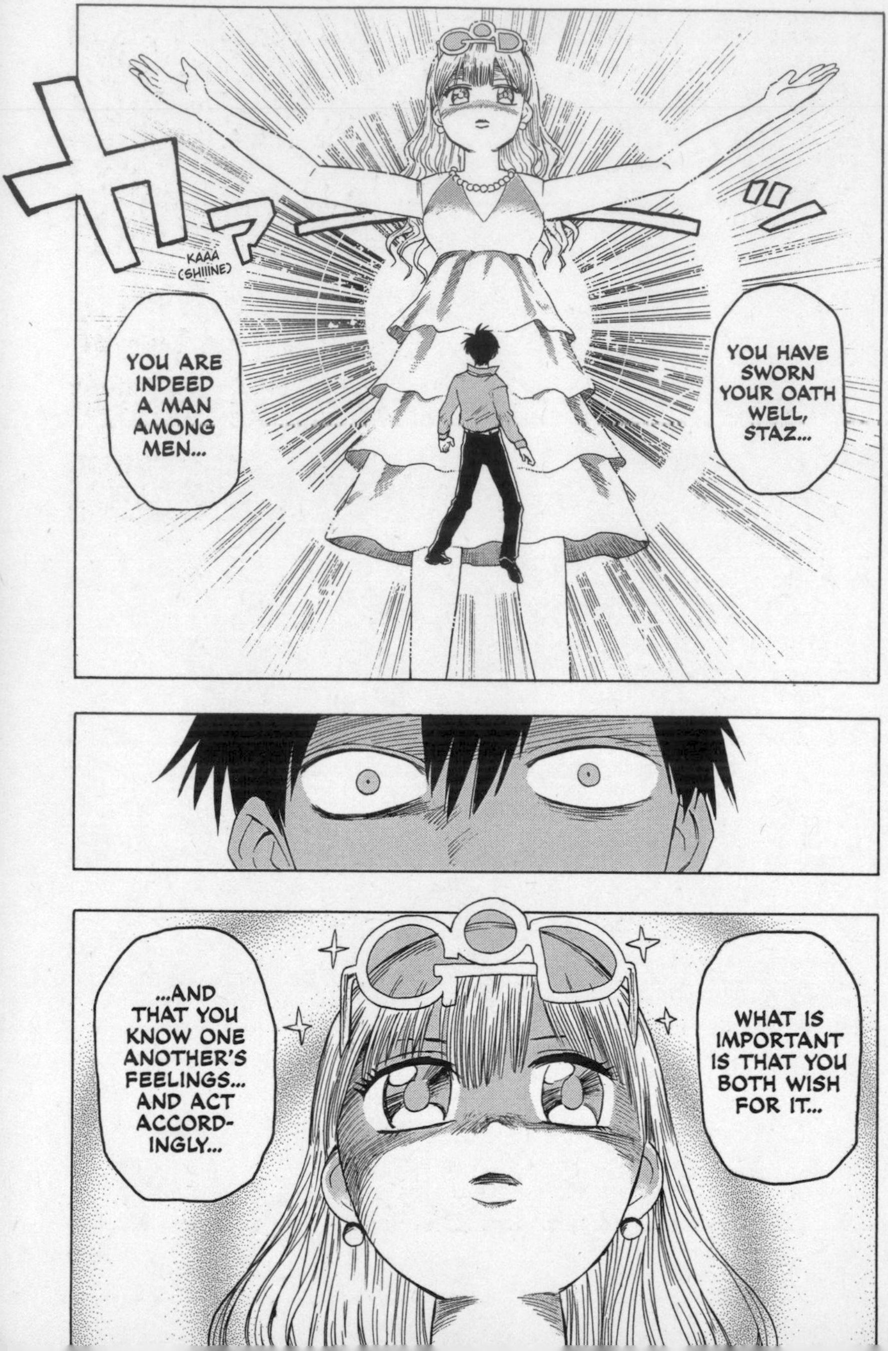
カァーーッ
KAAA (SHIIINE)
YOU HAVE SWORN YOUR OATH WELL, STAZ...
YOU ARE INDEED A MAN AMONG MEN...
WHAT IS IMPORTANT IS THAT YOU BOTH WISH FOR IT...
...AND THAT YOU KNOW ONE ANOTHER'S FEELINGS... AND ACT ACCORDINGLY...

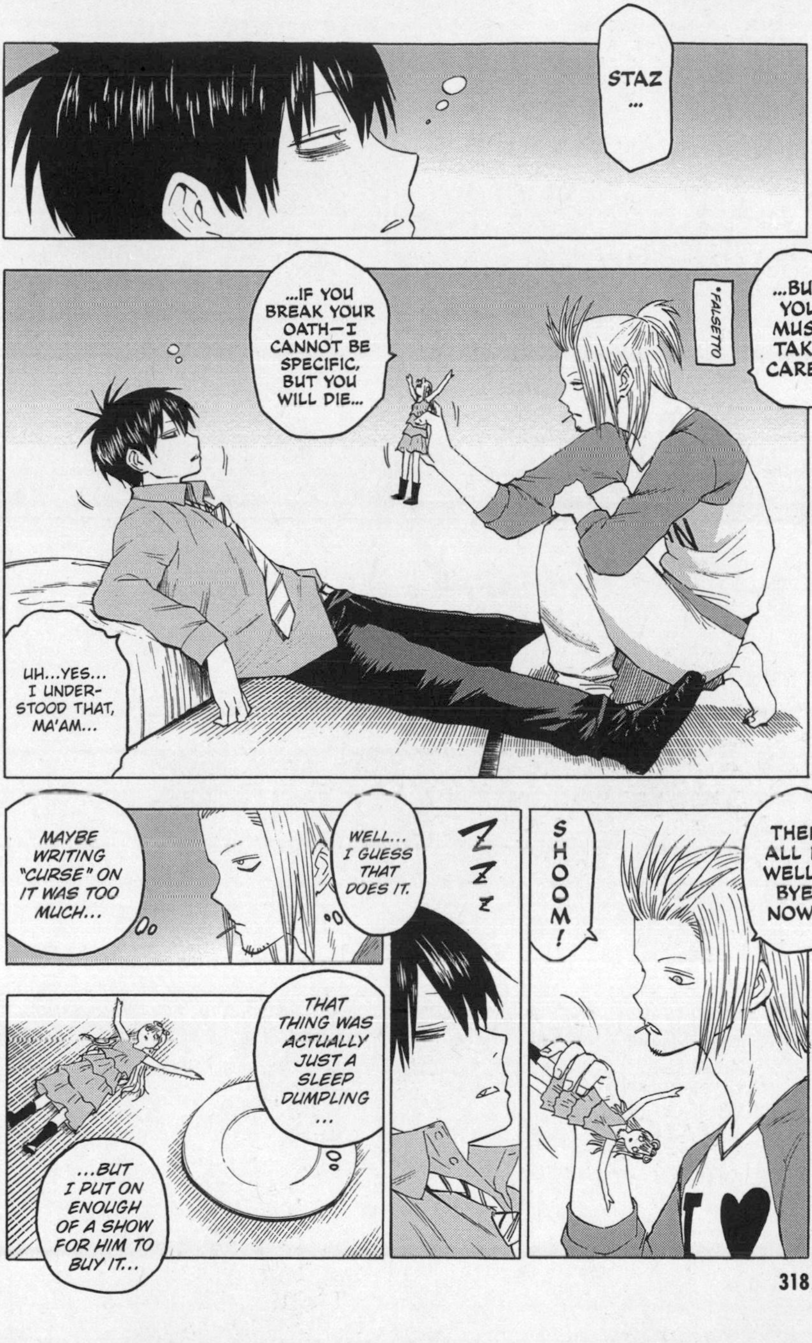
STAZ ...
...BUT YOU MUST TAKE CARE...
*FALSETTO
...IF YOU BREAK YOUR OATH—I CANNOT BE SPECIFIC, BUT YOU WILL DIE...
UH...YES... I UNDERSTOOD THAT, MA'AM...
THEN ALL IS WELL... BYE, NOW...
SHOOM!
ZZZ
WELL... I GUESS THAT DOES IT.
MAYBE WRITING "CURSE" ON IT WAS TOO MUCH...
THAT THING WAS ACTUALLY JUST A SLEEP DUMPLING ...
...BUT I PUT ON ENOUGH OF A SHOW FOR HIM TO BUY IT...

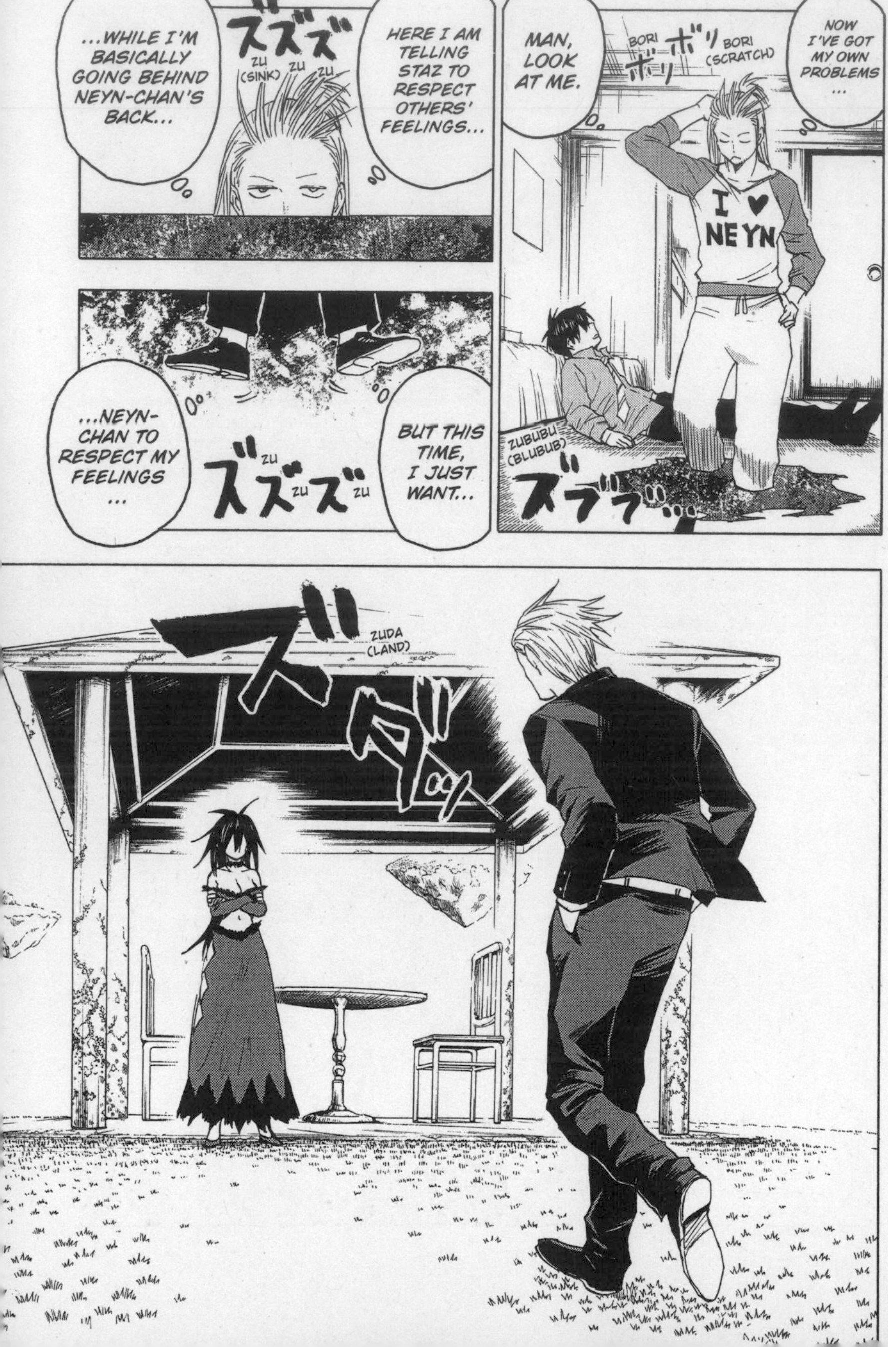

NOW I'VE GOT MY OWN PROBLEMS ...
BORI BORI (SCRATCH)
MAN, LOOK AT ME.
ZUBUBU (BLUBUB)
HERE I AM TELLING STAZ TO RESPECT OTHERS' FEELINGS...
ZU (SINK) ZU ZU
...WHILE I'M BASICALLY GOING BEHIND NEYN-CHAN'S BACK...
BUT THIS TIME, I JUST WANT...
ZU ZU ZU ZU
...NEYN-CHAN TO RESPECT MY FEELINGS ...
ZUDA (LAND)

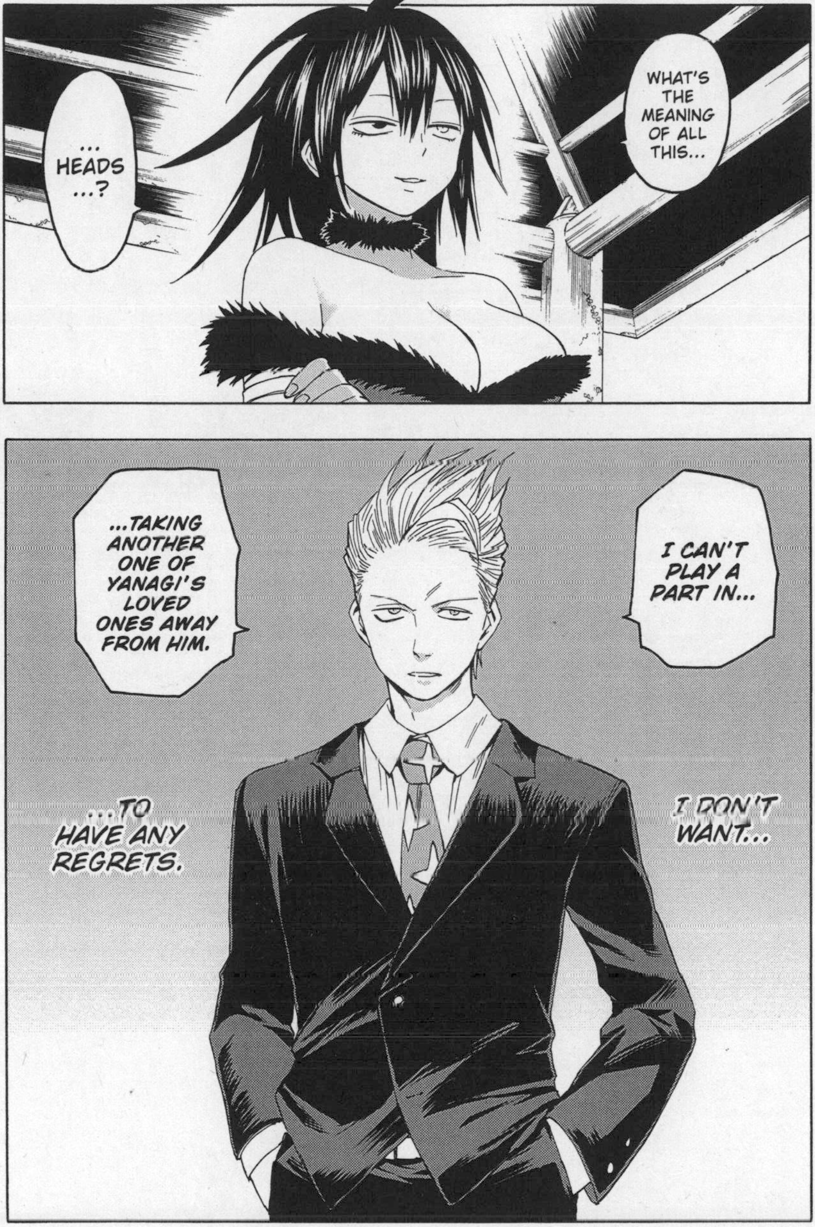
WHAT'S THE MEANING OF ALL THIS...
... HEADS ...?
I CAN'T PLAY A PART IN...
...TAKING ANOTHER ONE OF YANAGI'S LOVED ONES AWAY FROM HIM.
I DON'T WANT...
...TO HAVE ANY REGRETS.

♠ To Be Continued ♠

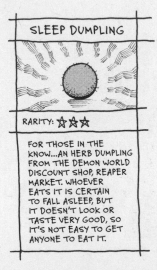

SLEEP DUMPLING

RARITY: ☆☆☆

FOR THOSE IN THE KNOW...AN HERB DUMPLING FROM THE DEMON WORLD DISCOUNT SHOP, REAPER MARKET. WHOEVER EATS IT IS CERTAIN TO FALL ASLEEP, BUT IT DOESN'T LOOK OR TASTE VERY GOOD, SO IT'S NOT EASY TO GET ANYONE TO EAT IT.

BLOOD LAD

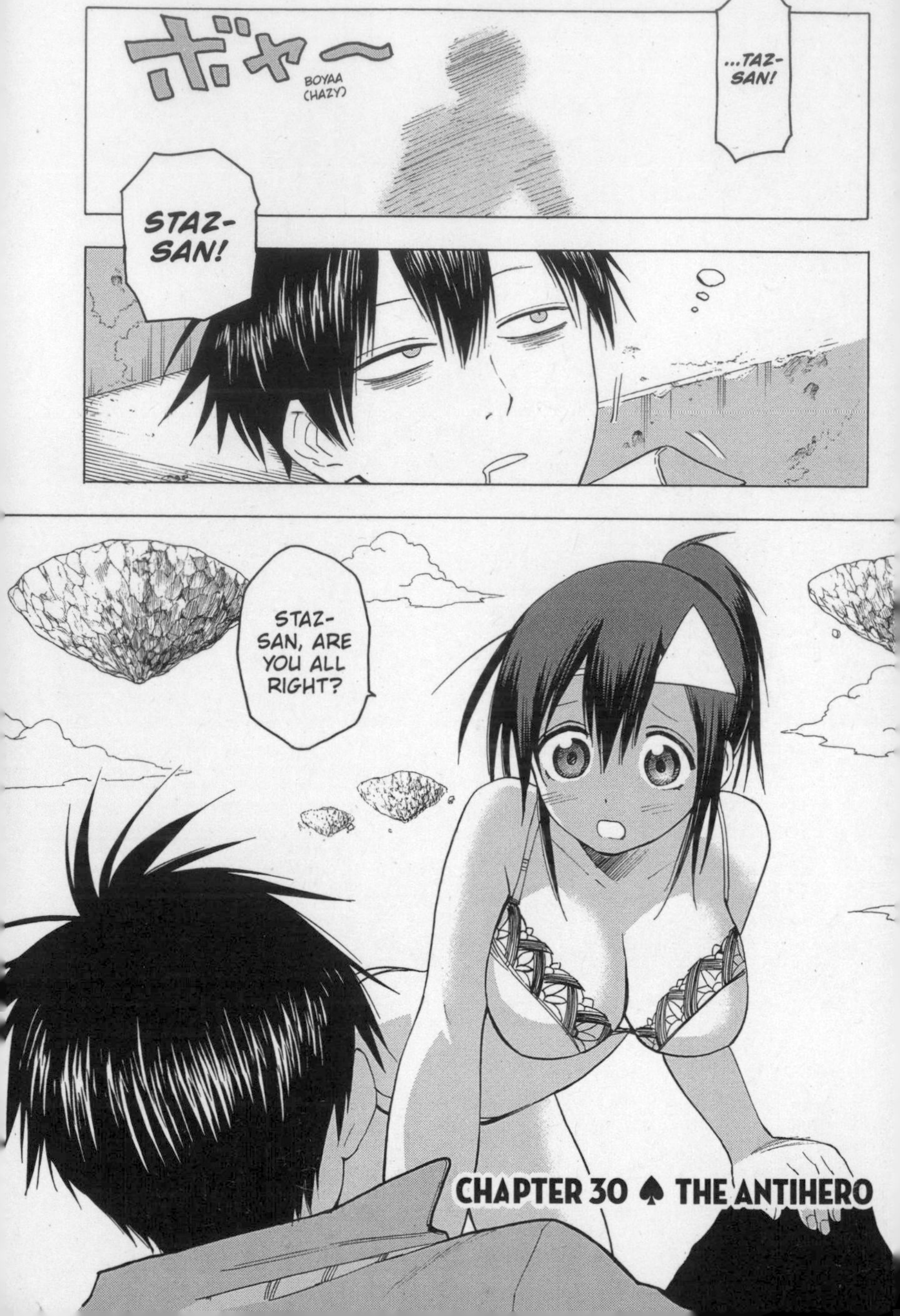
...TAZ-SAN!
ボャ〜
BOYAA (HAZY)
STAZ-SAN!
STAZ-SAN, ARE YOU ALL RIGHT?
CHAPTER 30 ♠ THE ANTIHERO

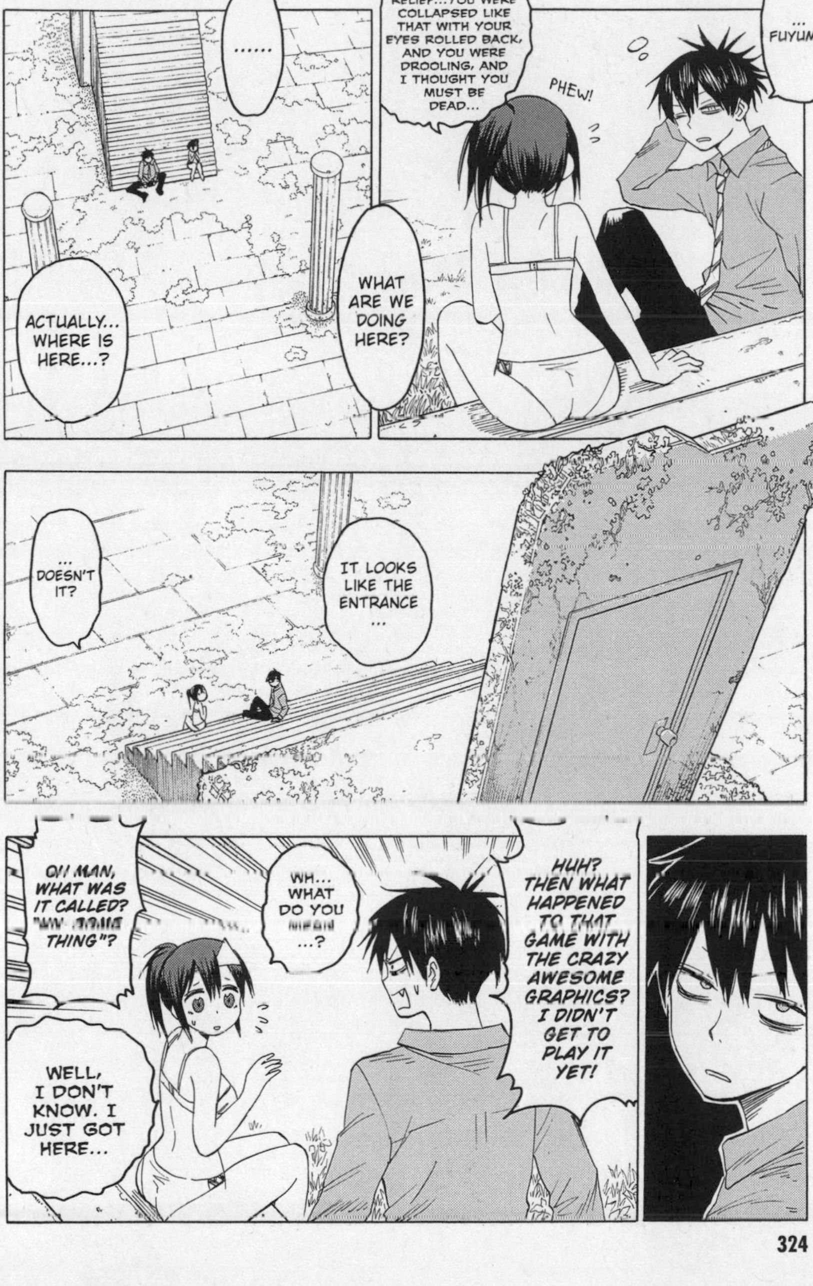
...FUYUMI?
PHEW!
WHAT A RELIEF...YOU WERE COLLAPSED LIKE THAT WITH YOUR EYES ROLLED BACK, AND YOU WERE DROOLING, AND I THOUGHT YOU MUST BE DEAD...
......
WHAT ARE WE DOING HERE?
ACTUALLY... WHERE IS HERE...?
IT LOOKS LIKE THE ENTRANCE...
...DOESN'T IT?
HUH? THEN WHAT HAPPENED TO THAT GAME WITH THE CRAZY AWESOME GRAPHICS? I DIDN'T GET TO PLAY IT YET!
WH... WHAT DO YOU MEAN ...?
OH MAN, WHAT WAS IT CALLED? THING"?
WELL, I DON'T KNOW. I JUST GOT HERE...

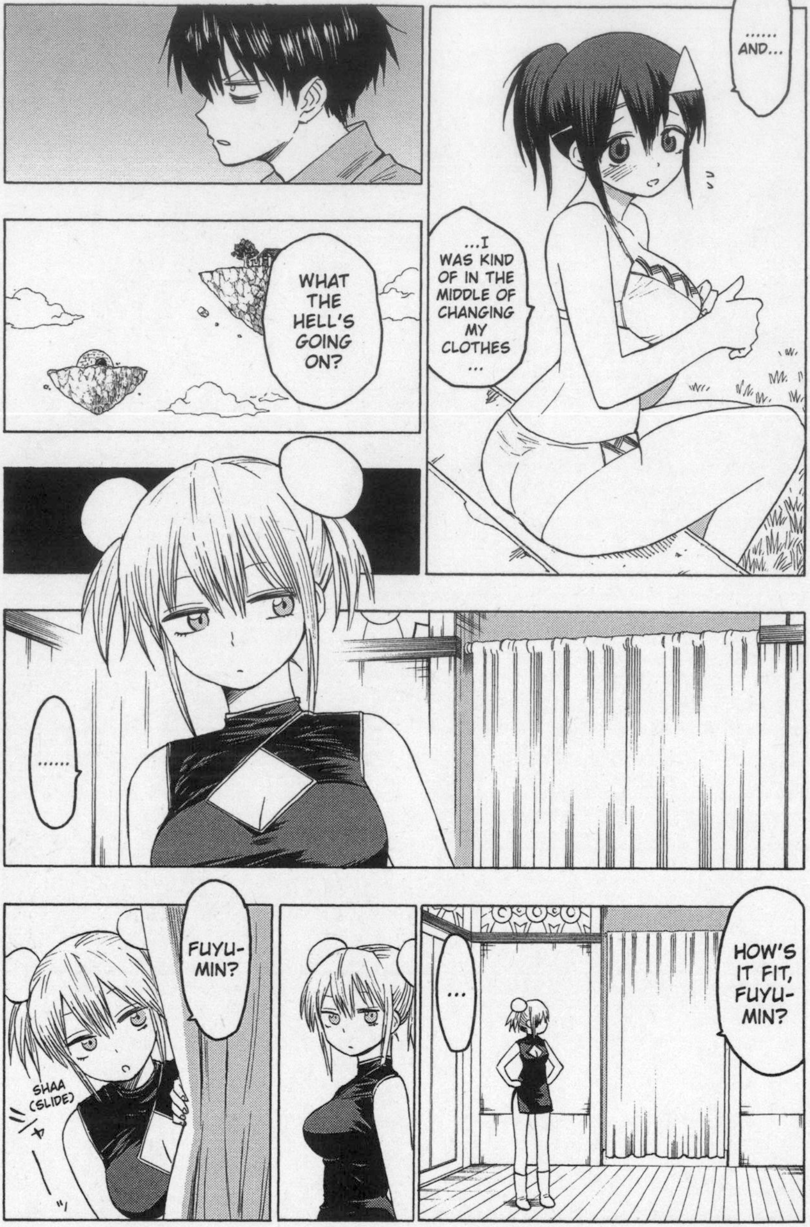
...... AND...
...I WAS KIND OF IN THE MIDDLE OF CHANGING MY CLOTHES ...
WHAT THE HELL'S GOING ON?
......
HOW'S IT FIT, FUYU-MIN?
...
FUYU-MIN?
SHAA (SLIDE)

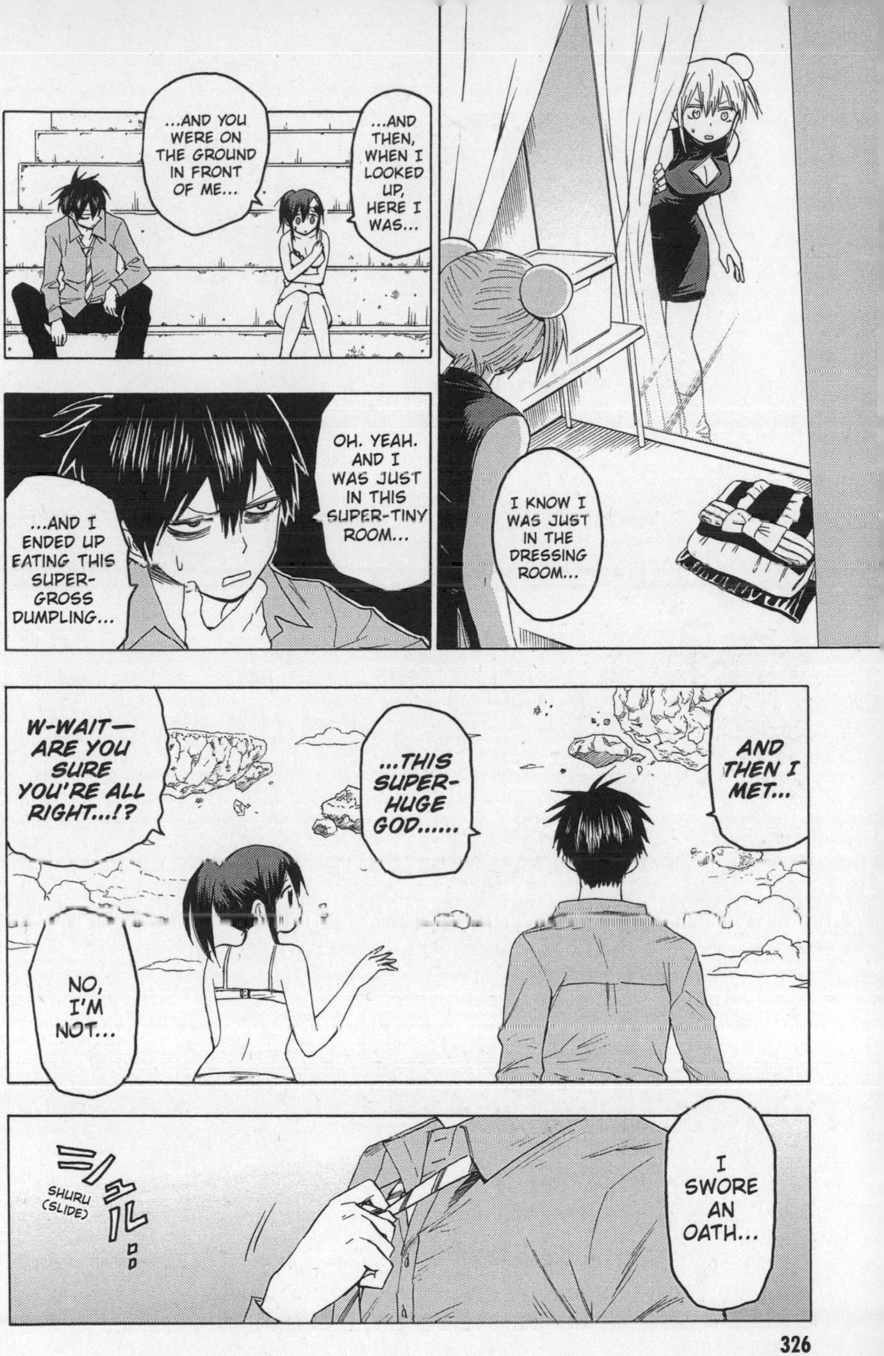
I KNOW I WAS JUST IN THE DRESSING ROOM...
...AND THEN, WHEN I LOOKED UP, HERE I WAS...
...AND YOU WERE ON THE GROUND IN FRONT OF ME...
OH. YEAH. AND I WAS JUST IN THIS SUPER-TINY ROOM...
...AND I ENDED UP EATING THIS SUPER-GROSS DUMPLING...
AND THEN I MET...
...THIS SUPER-HUGE GOD......
W-WAIT— ARE YOU SURE YOU'RE ALL RIGHT...!?
NO, I'M NOT...
I SWORE AN OATH...
シュル
SHURU (SLIDE)

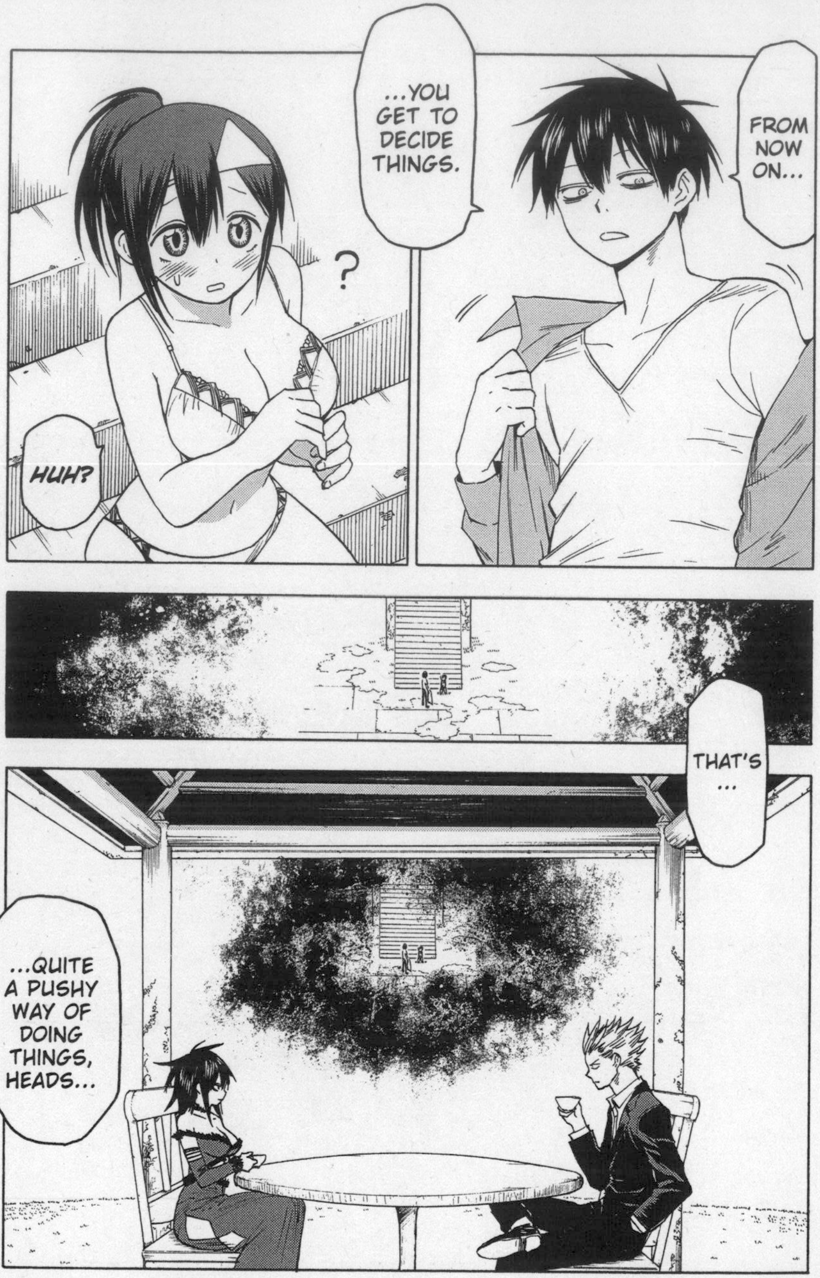
FROM NOW ON...
...YOU GET TO DECIDE THINGS.
?
HUH?
THAT'S...
...QUITE A PUSHY WAY OF DOING THINGS, HEADS...

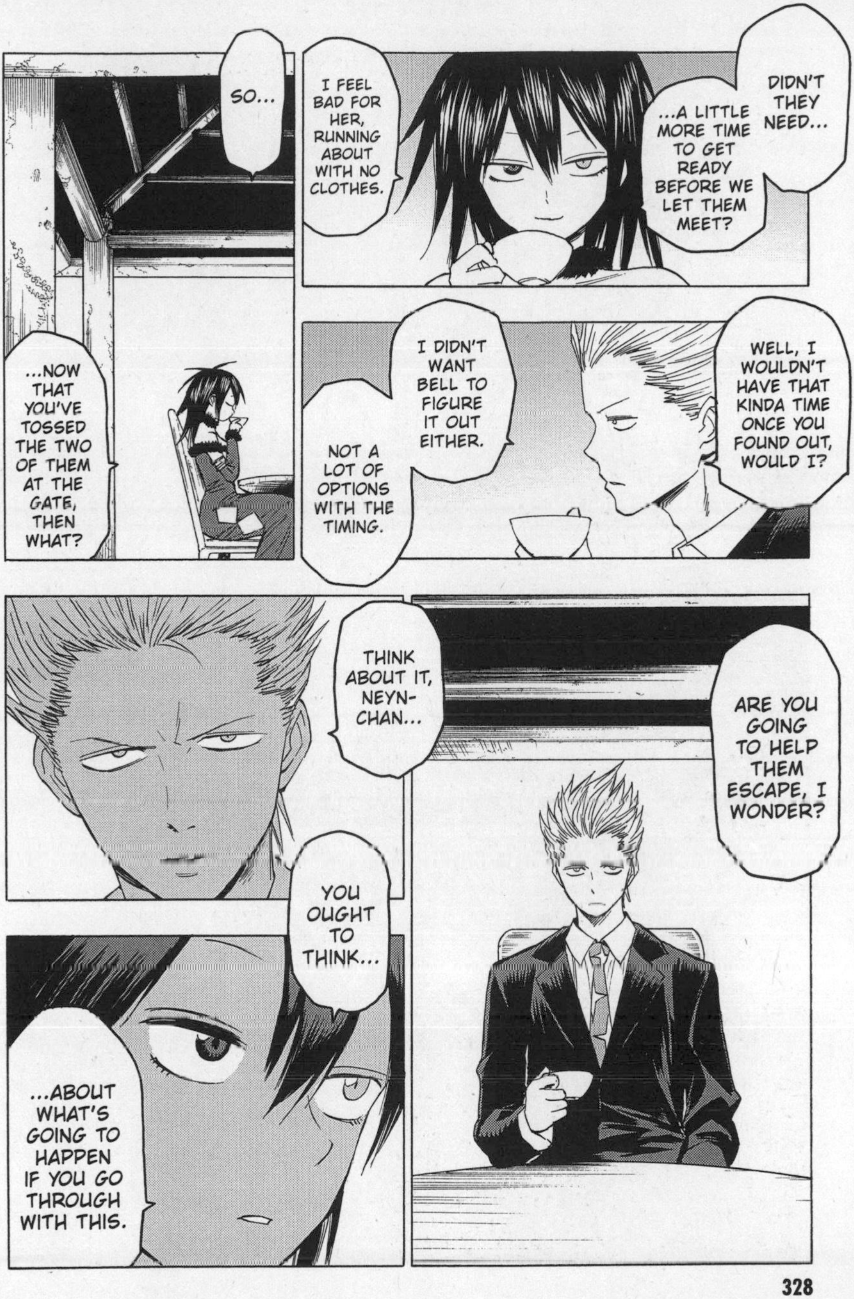
DIDN'T THEY NEED...
...A LITTLE MORE TIME TO GET READY BEFORE WE LET THEM MEET?
I FEEL BAD FOR HER, RUNNING ABOUT WITH NO CLOTHES.
WELL, I WOULDN'T HAVE THAT KINDA TIME ONCE YOU FOUND OUT, WOULD I?
I DIDN'T WANT BELL TO FIGURE IT OUT EITHER.
NOT A LOT OF OPTIONS WITH THE TIMING.
SO...
...NOW THAT YOU'VE TOSSED THE TWO OF THEM AT THE GATE, THEN WHAT?
ARE YOU GOING TO HELP THEM ESCAPE, I WONDER?
THINK ABOUT IT, NEYN-CHAN...
YOU OUGHT TO THINK...
...ABOUT WHAT'S GOING TO HAPPEN IF YOU GO THROUGH WITH THIS.

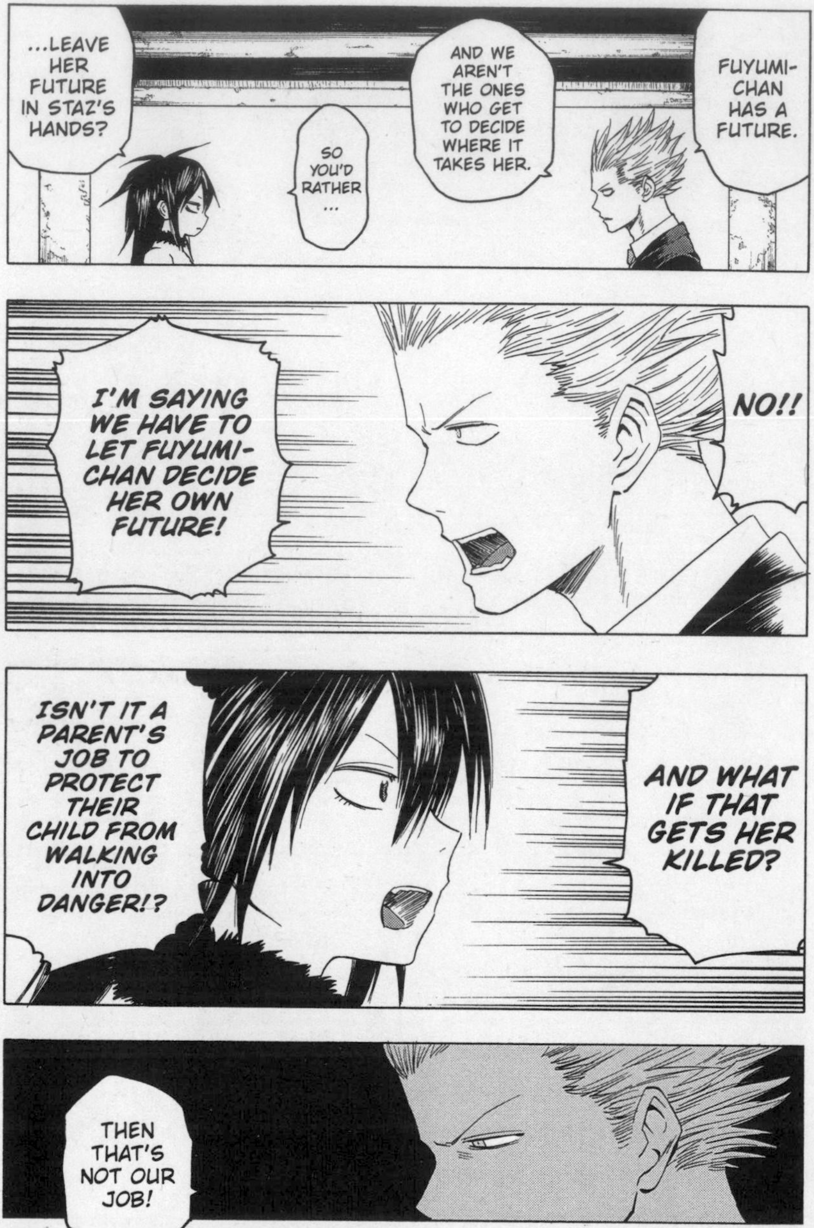
FUYUMI-CHAN HAS A FUTURE.
AND WE AREN'T THE ONES WHO GET TO DECIDE WHERE IT TAKES HER.
SO YOU'D RATHER ...
...LEAVE HER FUTURE IN STAZ'S HANDS?
NO!!
I'M SAYING WE HAVE TO LET FUYUMI-CHAN DECIDE HER OWN FUTURE!
AND WHAT IF THAT GETS HER KILLED?
ISN'T IT A PARENT'S JOB TO PROTECT THEIR CHILD FROM WALKING INTO DANGER!?
THEN THAT'S NOT OUR JOB!

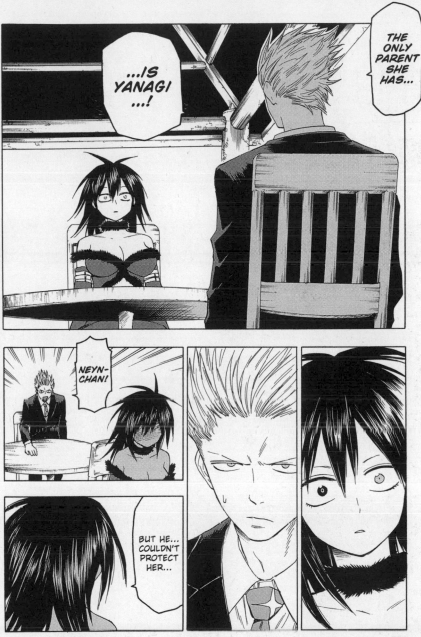

...IS YANAGI ...!

THE ONLY PARENT SHE HAS...

NEYN- CHAN!

BUT HE... COULDN'T PROTECT HER...

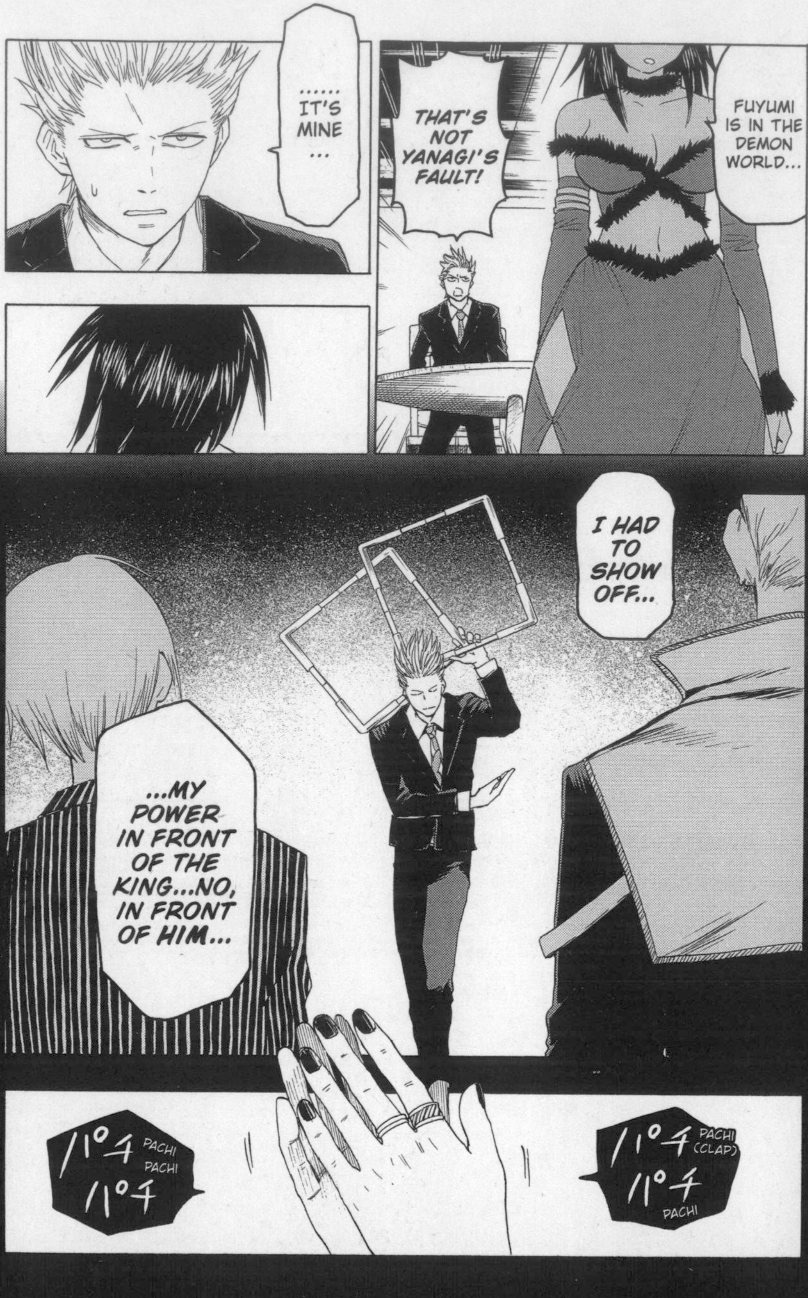
FUYUMI IS IN THE DEMON WORLD...
THAT'S NOT YANAGI'S FAULT!
......IT'S MINE...
I HAD TO SHOW OFF...
...MY POWER IN FRONT OF THE KING...NO, IN FRONT OF HIM...
パチ PACHI (CLAP) パチ PACHI
パチ PACHI PACHI パチ

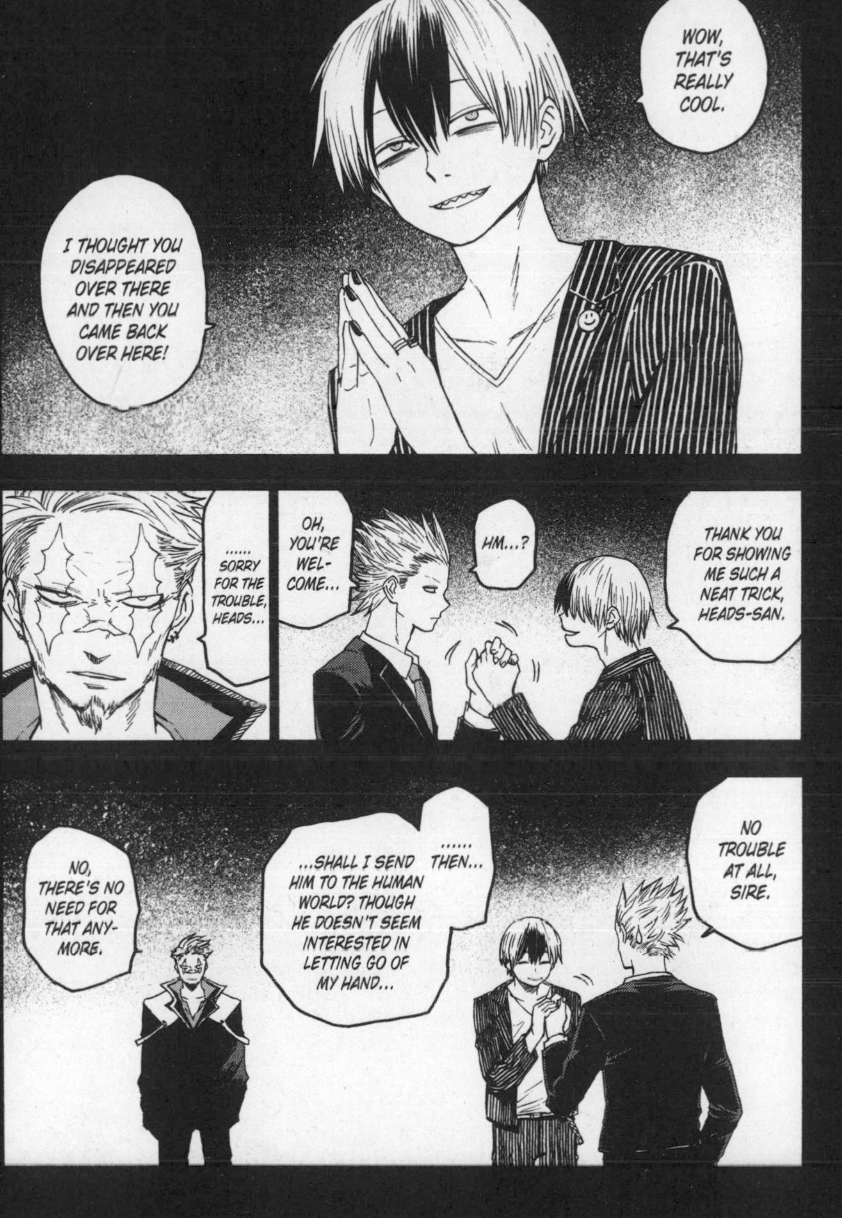
WOW, THAT'S REALLY COOL.
I THOUGHT YOU DISAPPEARED OVER THERE AND THEN YOU CAME BACK OVER HERE!
THANK YOU FOR SHOWING ME SUCH A NEAT TRICK, HEADS-SAN.
HM...?
OH, YOU'RE WEL-COME...
...... SORRY FOR THE TROUBLE, HEADS...
NO TROUBLE AT ALL, SIRE.
...... THEN...
...SHALL I SEND HIM TO THE HUMAN WORLD? THOUGH HE DOESN'T SEEM INTERESTED IN LETTING GO OF MY HAND...
NO, THERE'S NO NEED FOR THAT ANY-MORE.

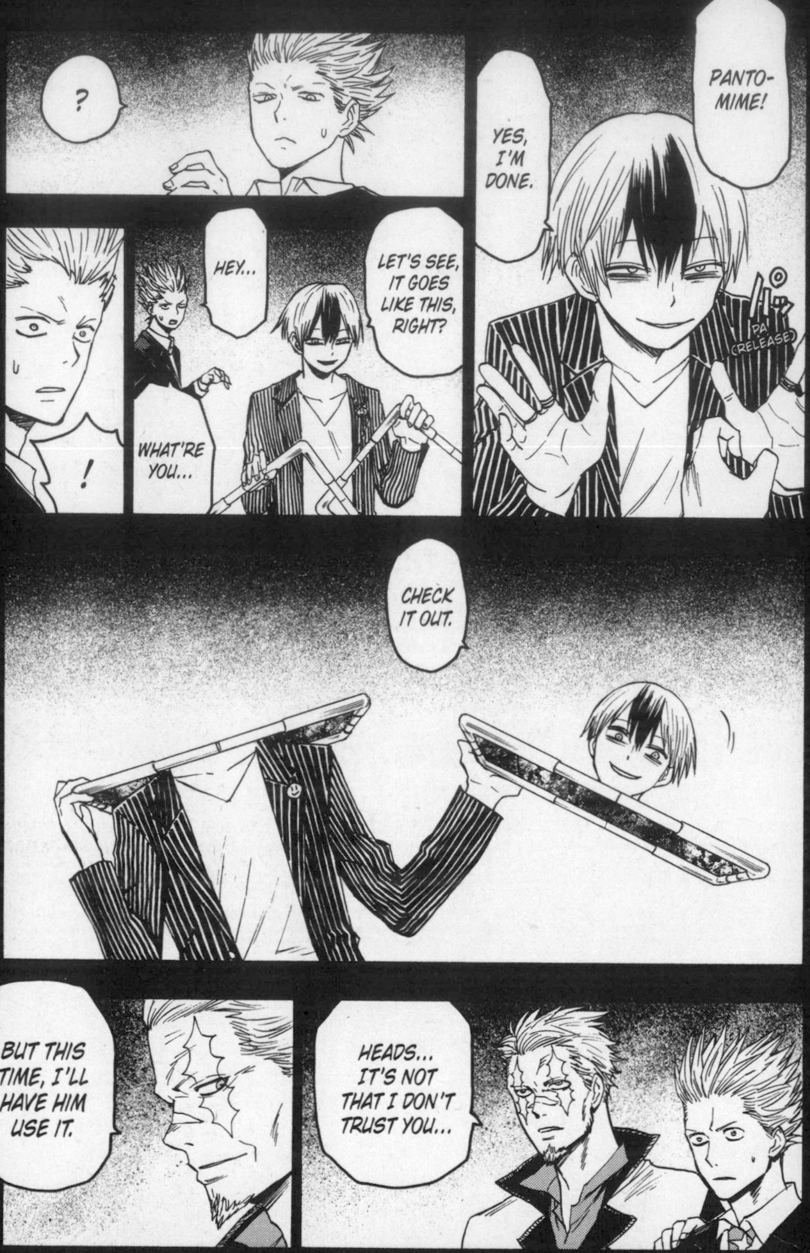
PANTO-MIME!
YES, I'M DONE.
PA (RELEASE)
?
LET'S SEE, IT GOES LIKE THIS, RIGHT?
HEY...
WHAT'RE YOU...
!
CHECK IT OUT.
HEADS... IT'S NOT THAT I DON'T TRUST YOU...
BUT THIS TIME, I'LL HAVE HIM USE IT.

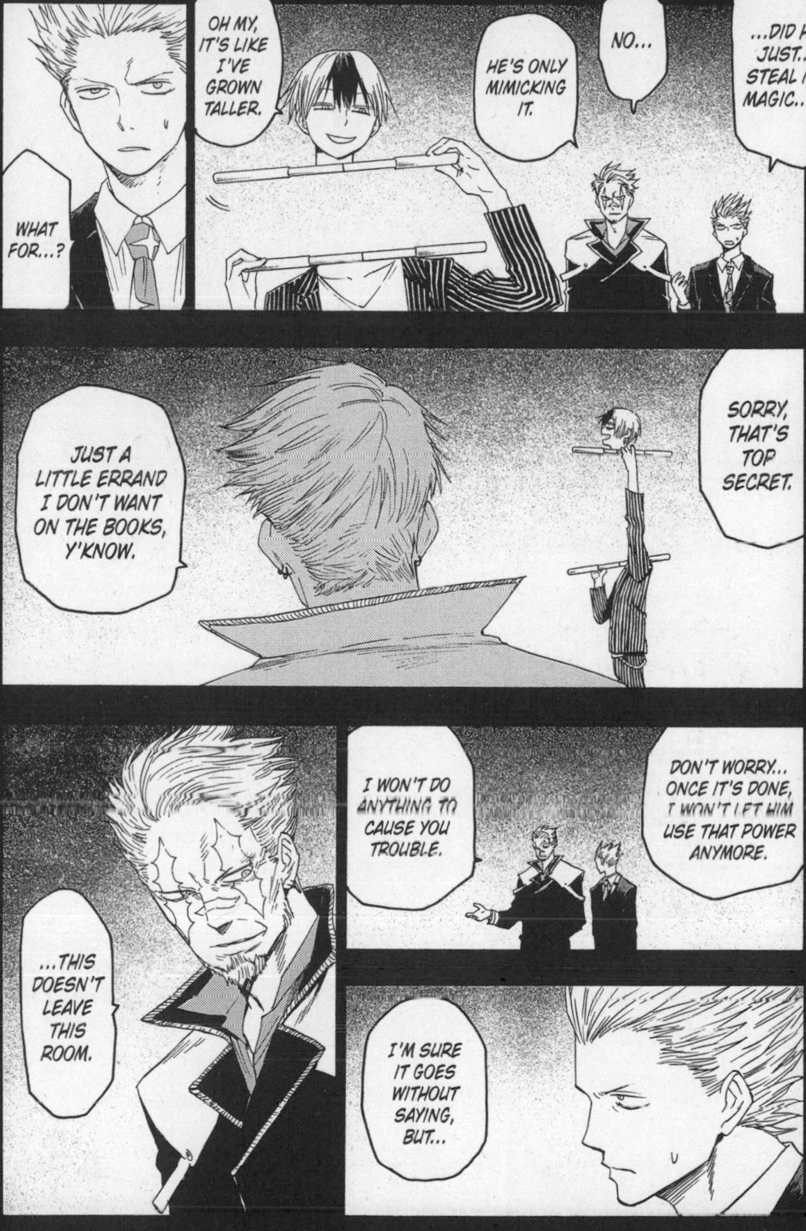
...DID HE JUST... STEAL MY MAGIC...!?
NO...
HE'S ONLY MIMICKING IT.
OH MY, IT'S LIKE I'VE GROWN TALLER.
WHAT FOR...?
SORRY, THAT'S TOP SECRET.
JUST A LITTLE ERRAND I DON'T WANT ON THE BOOKS, Y'KNOW.
DON'T WORRY... ONCE IT'S DONE, I WON'T LET HIM USE THAT POWER ANYMORE.
I WON'T DO ANYTHING TO CAUSE YOU TROUBLE.
I'M SURE IT GOES WITHOUT SAYING, BUT...
...THIS DOESN'T LEAVE THIS ROOM.

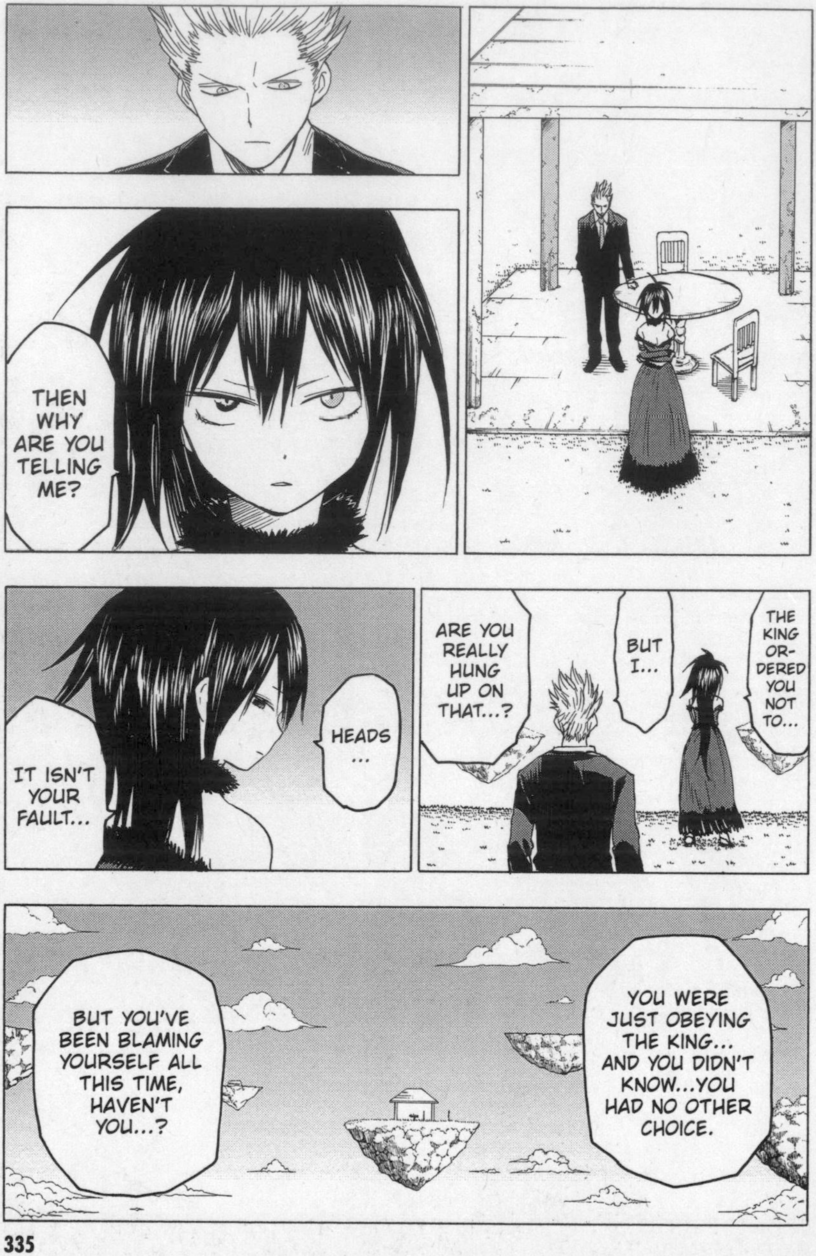
THEN WHY ARE YOU TELLING ME?
THE KING ORDERED YOU NOT TO...
BUT I...
ARE YOU REALLY HUNG UP ON THAT...?
HEADS...
IT ISN'T YOUR FAULT...
YOU WERE JUST OBEYING THE KING... AND YOU DIDN'T KNOW...YOU HAD NO OTHER CHOICE.
BUT YOU'VE BEEN BLAMING YOURSELF ALL THIS TIME, HAVEN'T YOU...?

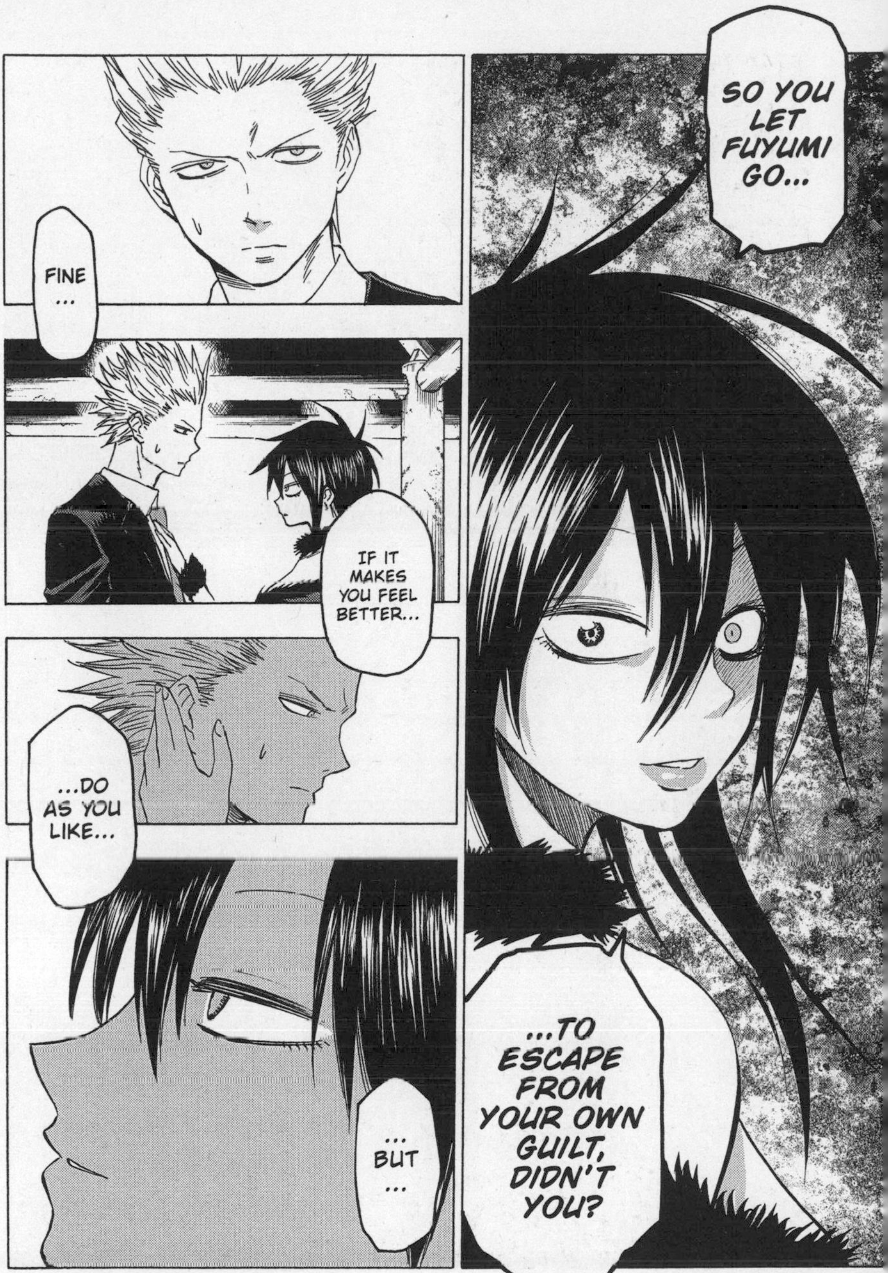
SO YOU LET FUYUMI GO...
...TO ESCAPE FROM YOUR OWN GUILT, DIDN'T YOU?
FINE ...
IF IT MAKES YOU FEEL BETTER...
...DO AS YOU LIKE...
... BUT ...

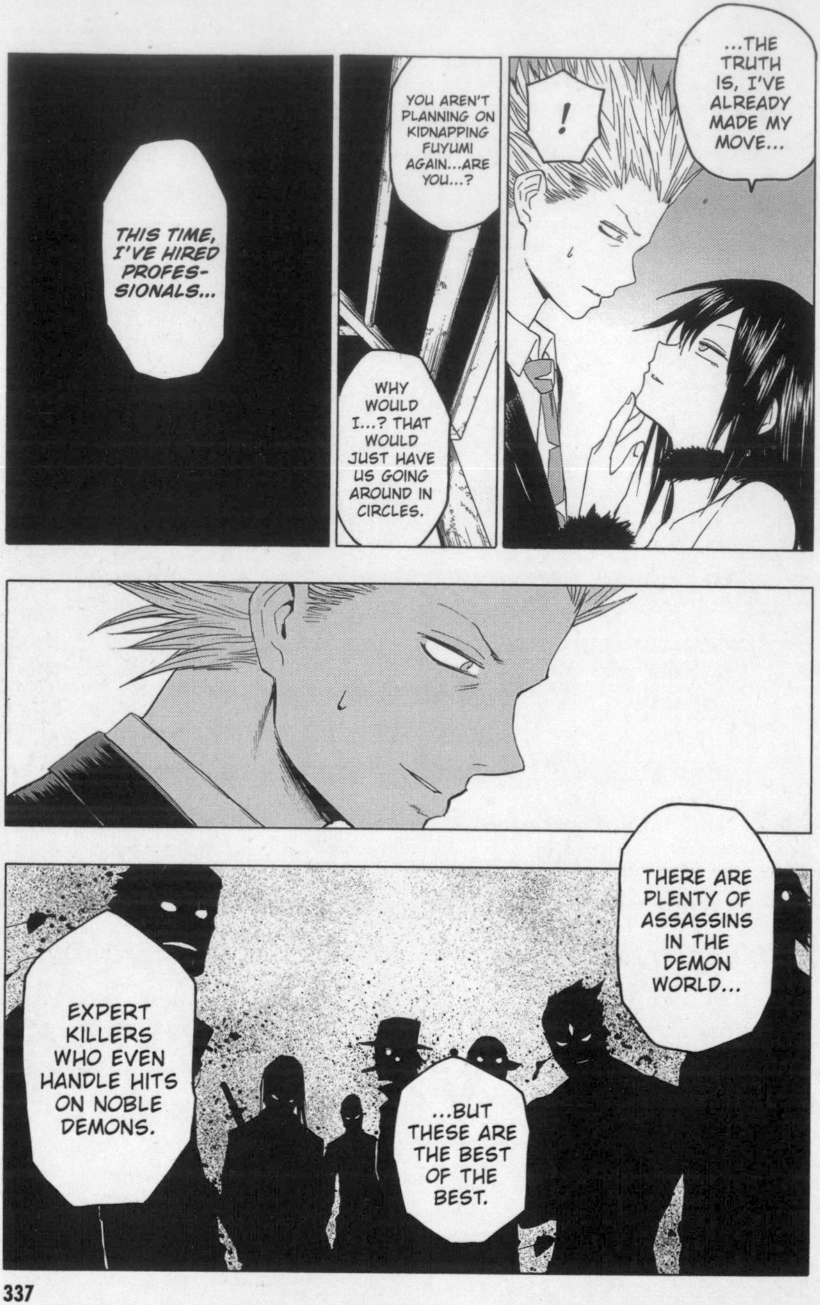
...THE TRUTH IS, I'VE ALREADY MADE MY MOVE...
!
YOU AREN'T PLANNING ON KIDNAPPING FUYUMI AGAIN...ARE YOU...?
WHY WOULD I...? THAT WOULD JUST HAVE US GOING AROUND IN CIRCLES.
THIS TIME, I'VE HIRED PROFESSIONALS...
THERE ARE PLENTY OF ASSASSINS IN THE DEMON WORLD...
...BUT THESE ARE THE BEST OF THE BEST.
EXPERT KILLERS WHO EVEN HANDLE HITS ON NOBLE DEMONS.

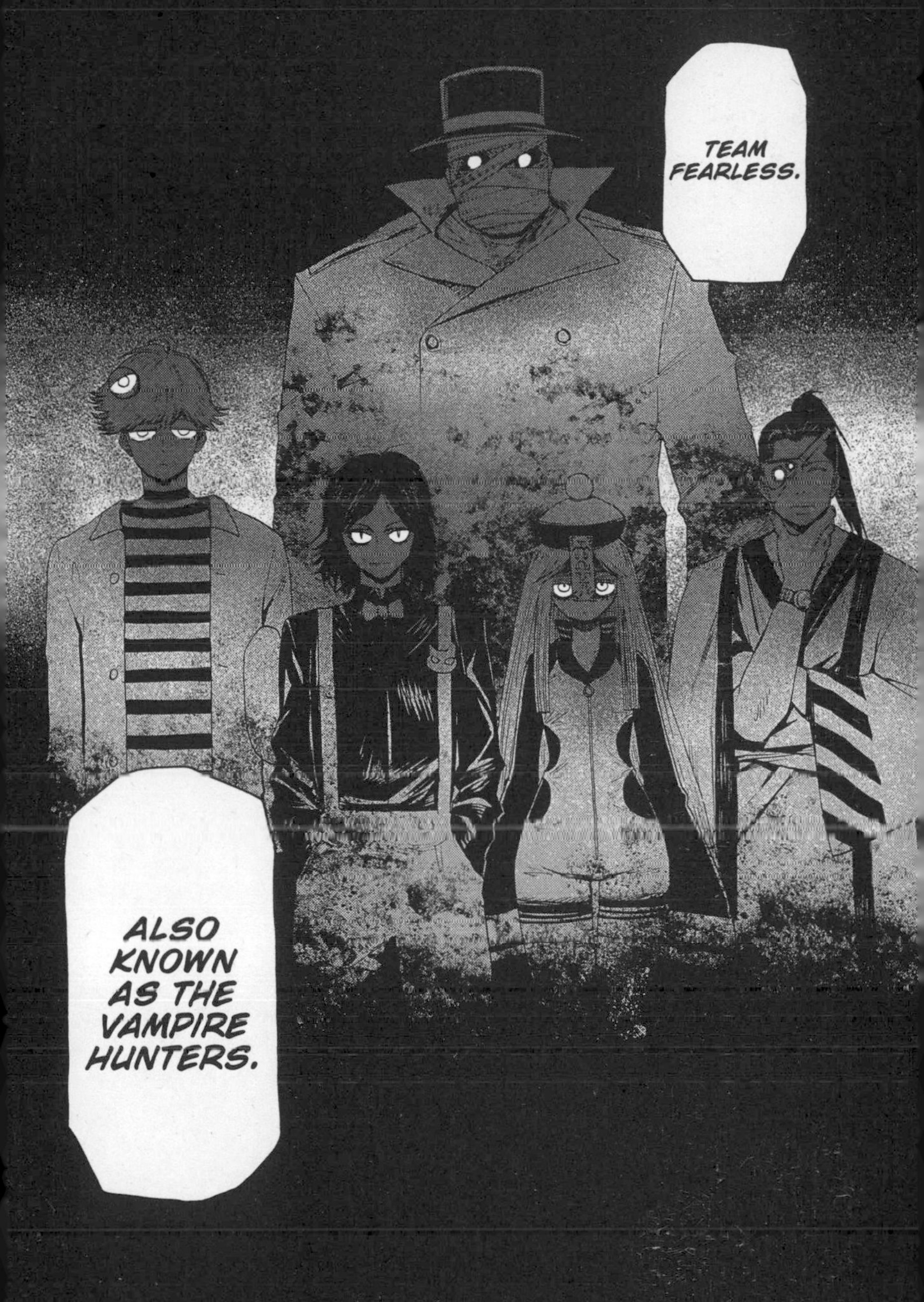
TEAM FEARLESS.
ALSO KNOWN AS THE VAMPIRE HUNTERS.

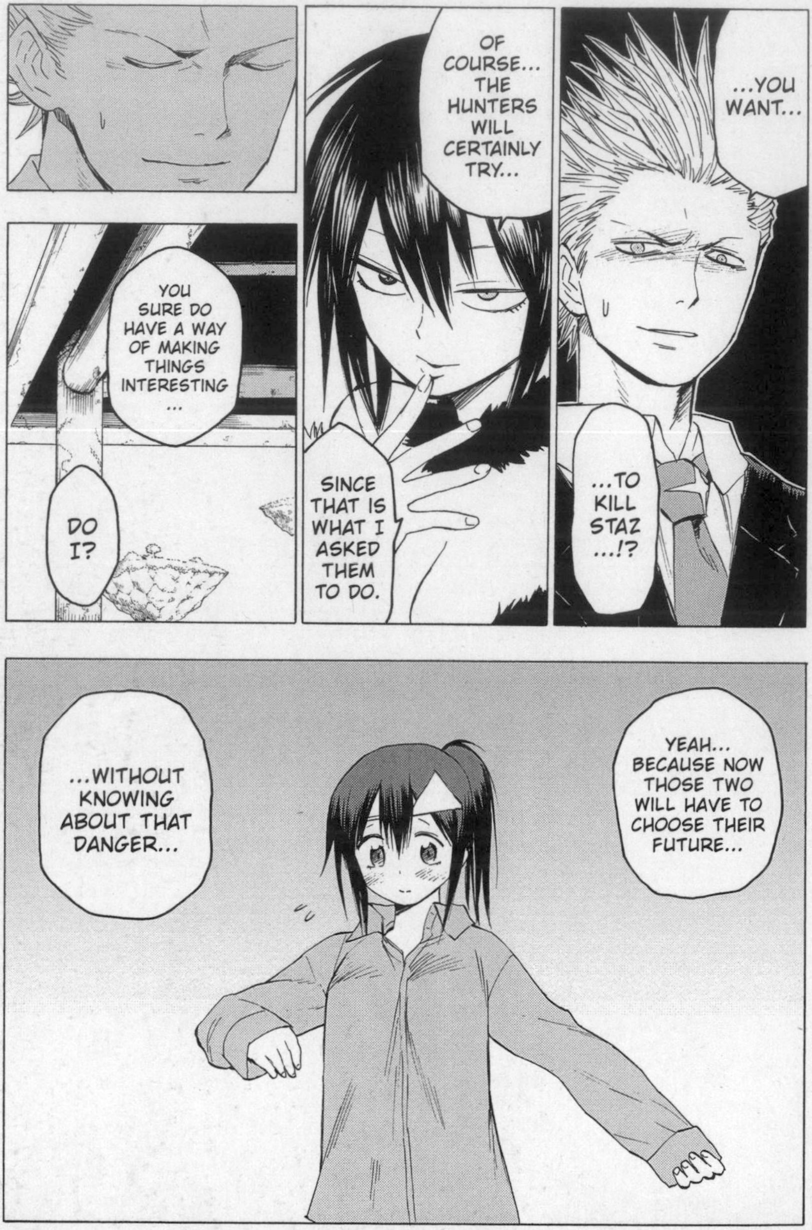
...YOU WANT...
...TO KILL STAZ ...!?
OF COURSE... THE HUNTERS WILL CERTAINLY TRY...
SINCE THAT IS WHAT I ASKED THEM TO DO.
YOU SURE DO HAVE A WAY OF MAKING THINGS INTERESTING ...
DO I?
YEAH... BECAUSE NOW THOSE TWO WILL HAVE TO CHOOSE THEIR FUTURE...
...WITHOUT KNOWING ABOUT THAT DANGER...

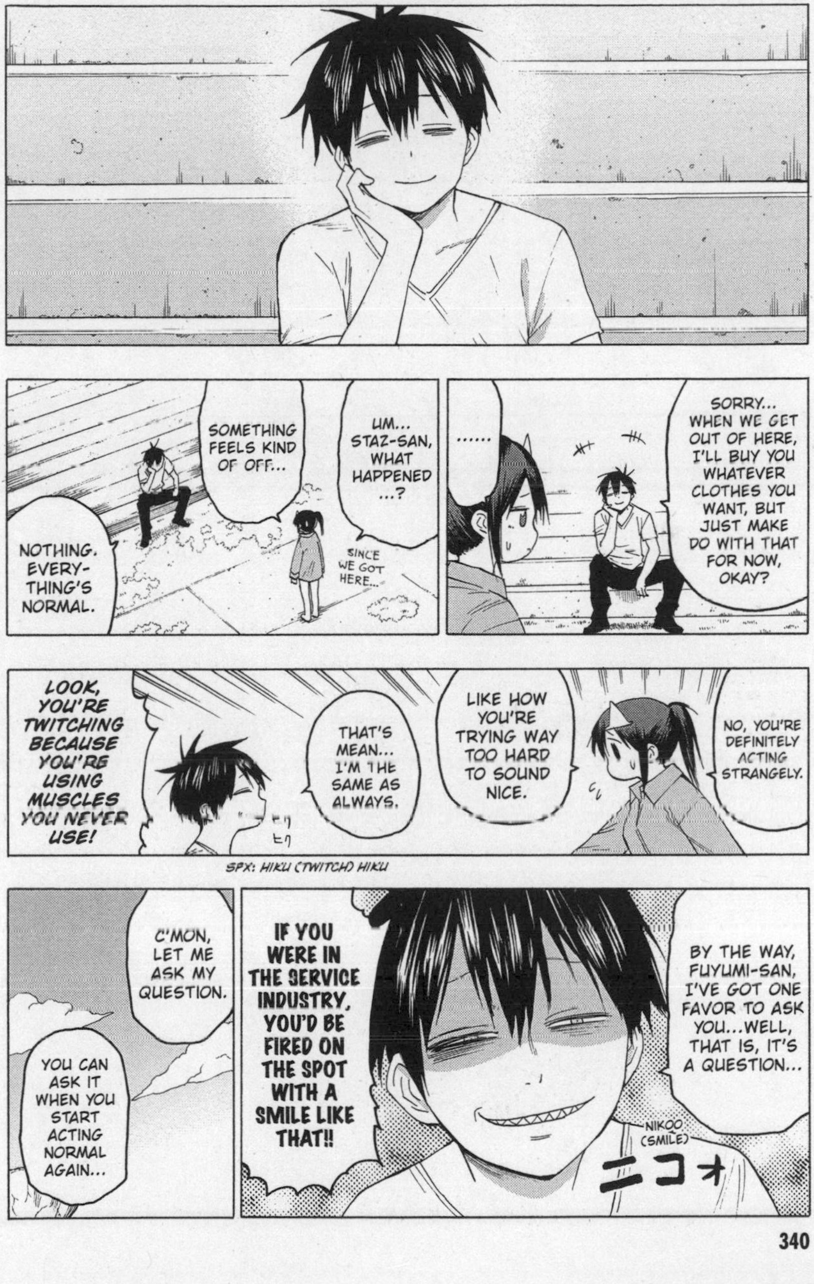
SORRY... WHEN WE GET OUT OF HERE, I'LL BUY YOU WHATEVER CLOTHES YOU WANT, BUT JUST MAKE DO WITH THAT FOR NOW, OKAY?
......
UM... STAZ-SAN, WHAT HAPPENED ...?
SINCE WE GOT HERE...
SOMETHING FEELS KIND OF OFF...
NOTHING. EVERY-THING'S NORMAL.
NO, YOU'RE DEFINITELY ACTING STRANGELY.
LIKE HOW YOU'RE TRYING WAY TOO HARD TO SOUND NICE.
THAT'S MEAN... I'M THE SAME AS ALWAYS.
LOOK, YOU'RE TWITCHING BECAUSE YOU'RE USING MUSCLES YOU NEVER USE!
SPX: HIKU (TWITCH) HIKU
BY THE WAY, FUYUMI-SAN, I'VE GOT ONE FAVOR TO ASK YOU...WELL, THAT IS, IT'S A QUESTION...
NIKOO (SMILE)
ニコォ
IF YOU WERE IN THE SERVICE INDUSTRY, YOU'D BE FIRED ON THE SPOT WITH A SMILE LIKE THAT!!
C'MON, LET ME ASK MY QUESTION.
YOU CAN ASK IT WHEN YOU START ACTING NORMAL AGAIN...

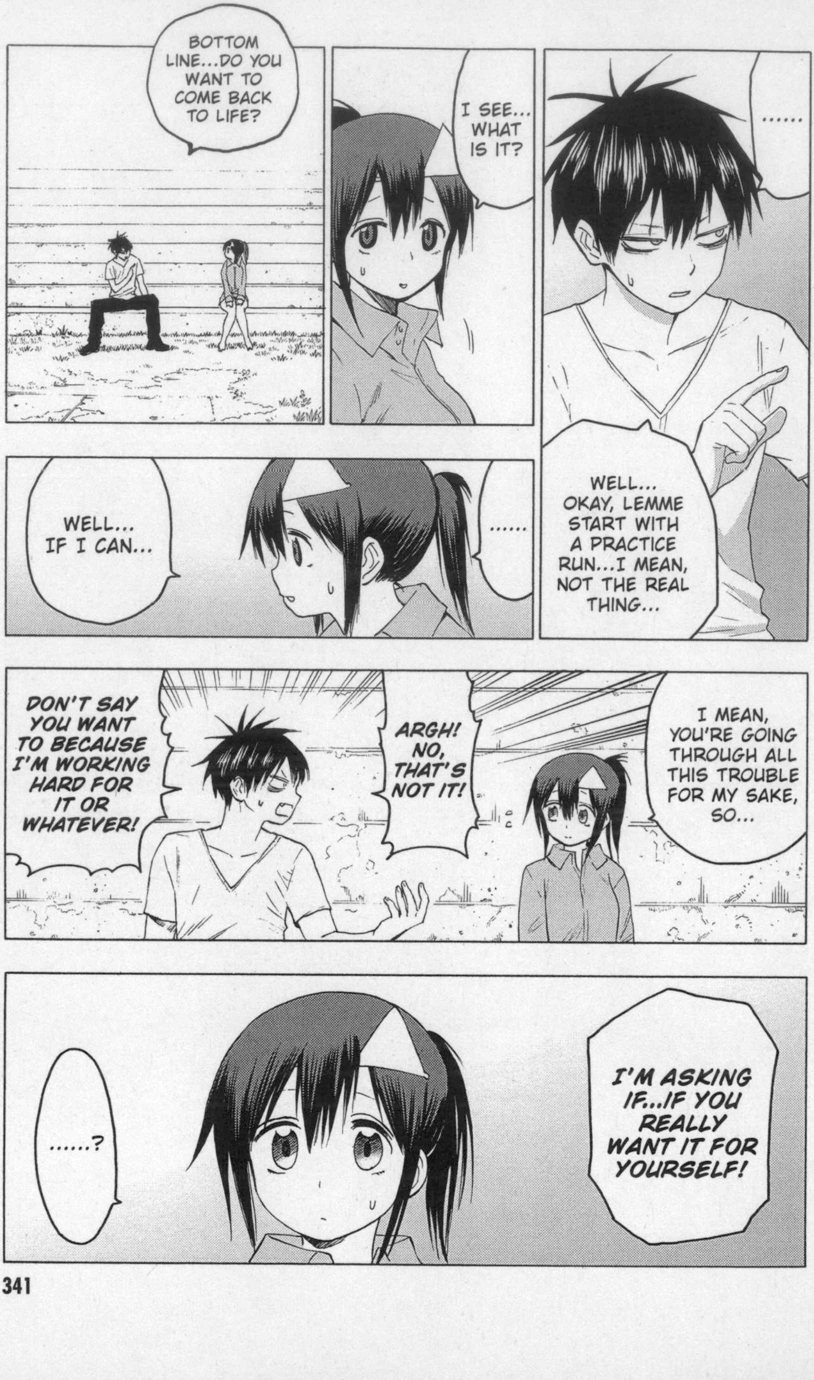
......
WELL... OKAY, LEMME START WITH A PRACTICE RUN...I MEAN, NOT THE REAL THING...
I SEE... WHAT IS IT?
BOTTOM LINE...DO YOU WANT TO COME BACK TO LIFE?
......
WELL... IF I CAN...
I MEAN, YOU'RE GOING THROUGH ALL THIS TROUBLE FOR MY SAKE, SO...
ARGH! NO, THAT'S NOT IT!
DON'T SAY YOU WANT TO BECAUSE I'M WORKING HARD FOR IT OR WHATEVER!
I'M ASKING IF...IF YOU REALLY WANT IT FOR YOURSELF!
......?

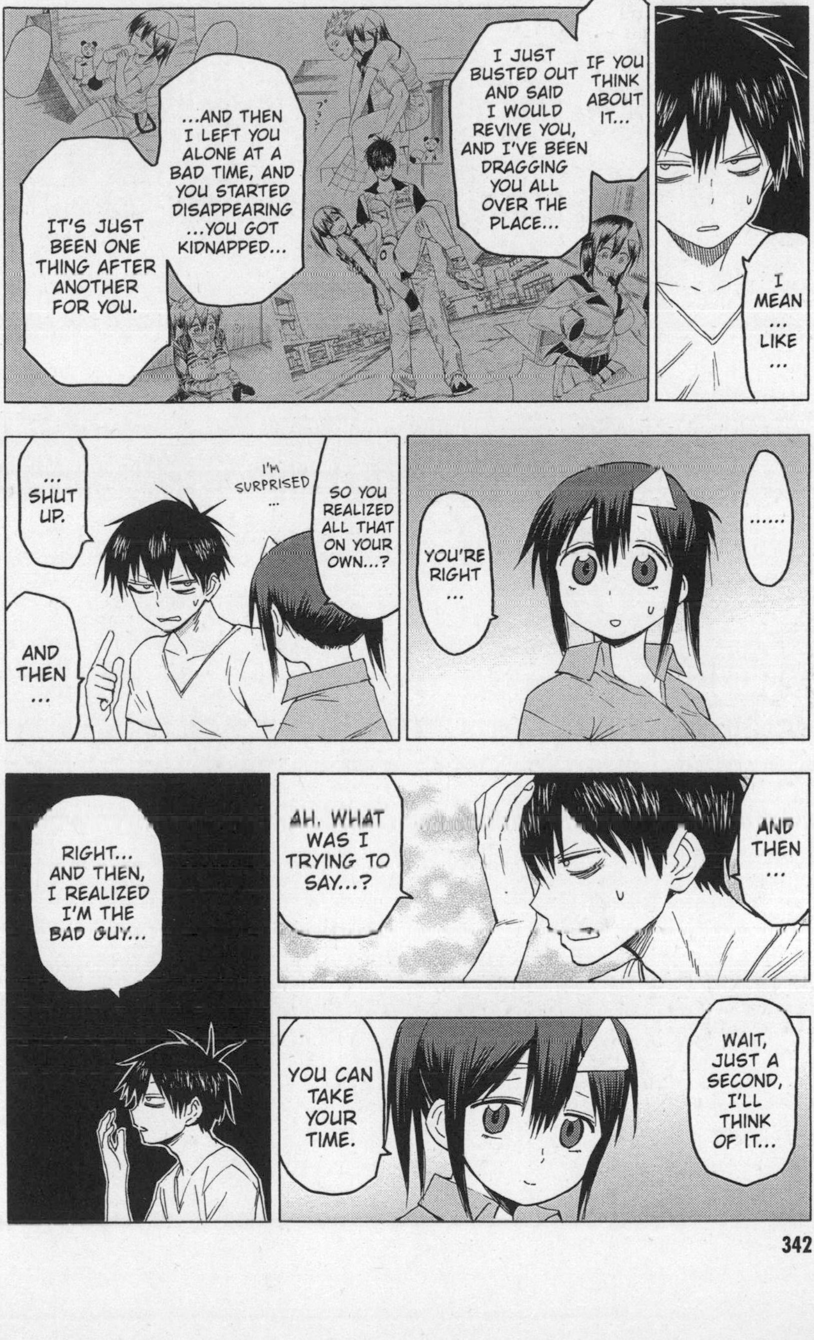
I MEAN ... LIKE ...
IF YOU THINK ABOUT IT...
I JUST BUSTED OUT AND SAID I WOULD REVIVE YOU, AND I'VE BEEN DRAGGING YOU ALL OVER THE PLACE...
...AND THEN I LEFT YOU ALONE AT A BAD TIME, AND YOU STARTED DISAPPEARING ...YOU GOT KIDNAPPED...
IT'S JUST BEEN ONE THING AFTER ANOTHER FOR YOU.
......
YOU'RE RIGHT ...
SO YOU REALIZED ALL THAT ON YOUR OWN...?
I'M SURPRISED ...
... SHUT UP.
AND THEN ...
AND THEN ...
AH. WHAT WAS I TRYING TO SAY...?
WAIT, JUST A SECOND, I'LL THINK OF IT...
YOU CAN TAKE YOUR TIME.
RIGHT... AND THEN, I REALIZED I'M THE BAD GUY...

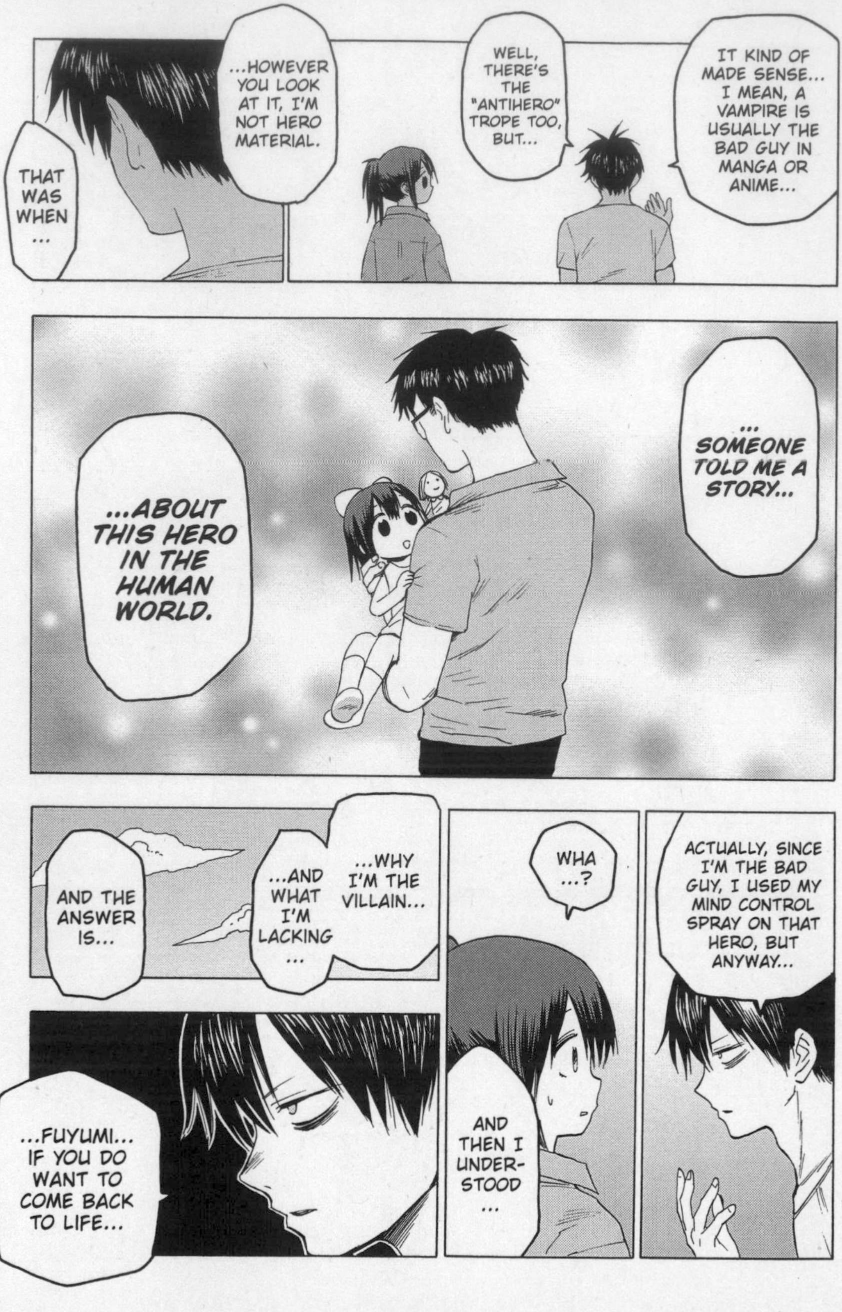
IT KIND OF MADE SENSE... I MEAN, A VAMPIRE IS USUALLY THE BAD GUY IN MANGA OR ANIME...
WELL, THERE'S THE "ANTIHERO" TROPE TOO, BUT...
...HOWEVER YOU LOOK AT IT, I'M NOT HERO MATERIAL.
THAT WAS WHEN...
...SOMEONE TOLD ME A STORY...
...ABOUT THIS HERO IN THE HUMAN WORLD.
ACTUALLY, SINCE I'M THE BAD GUY, I USED MY MIND CONTROL SPRAY ON THAT HERO, BUT ANYWAY...
WHA...?
AND THEN I UNDERSTOOD...
...WHY I'M THE VILLAIN...
...AND WHAT I'M LACKING...
AND THE ANSWER IS...
...FUYUMI... IF YOU DO WANT TO COME BACK TO LIFE...

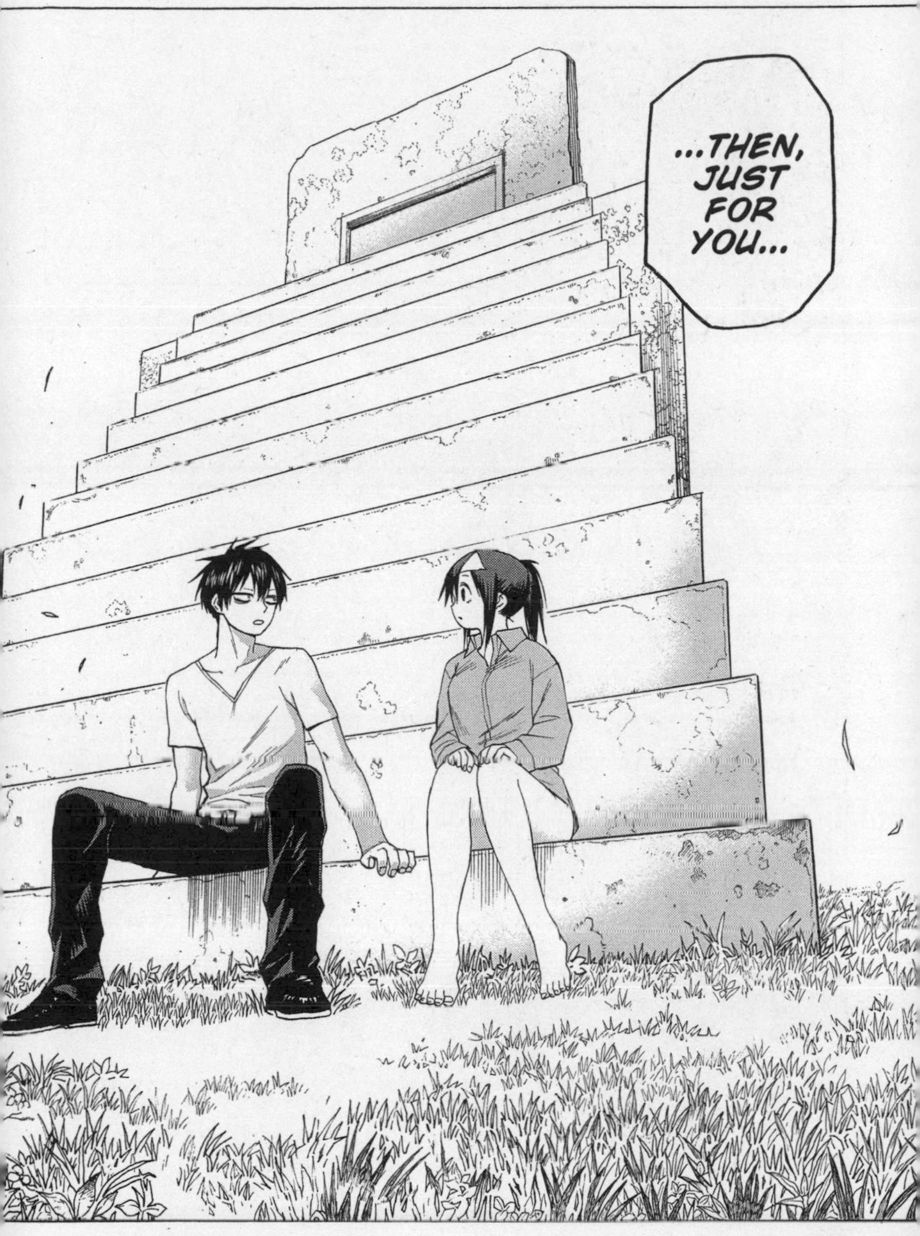
...THEN, JUST FOR YOU...

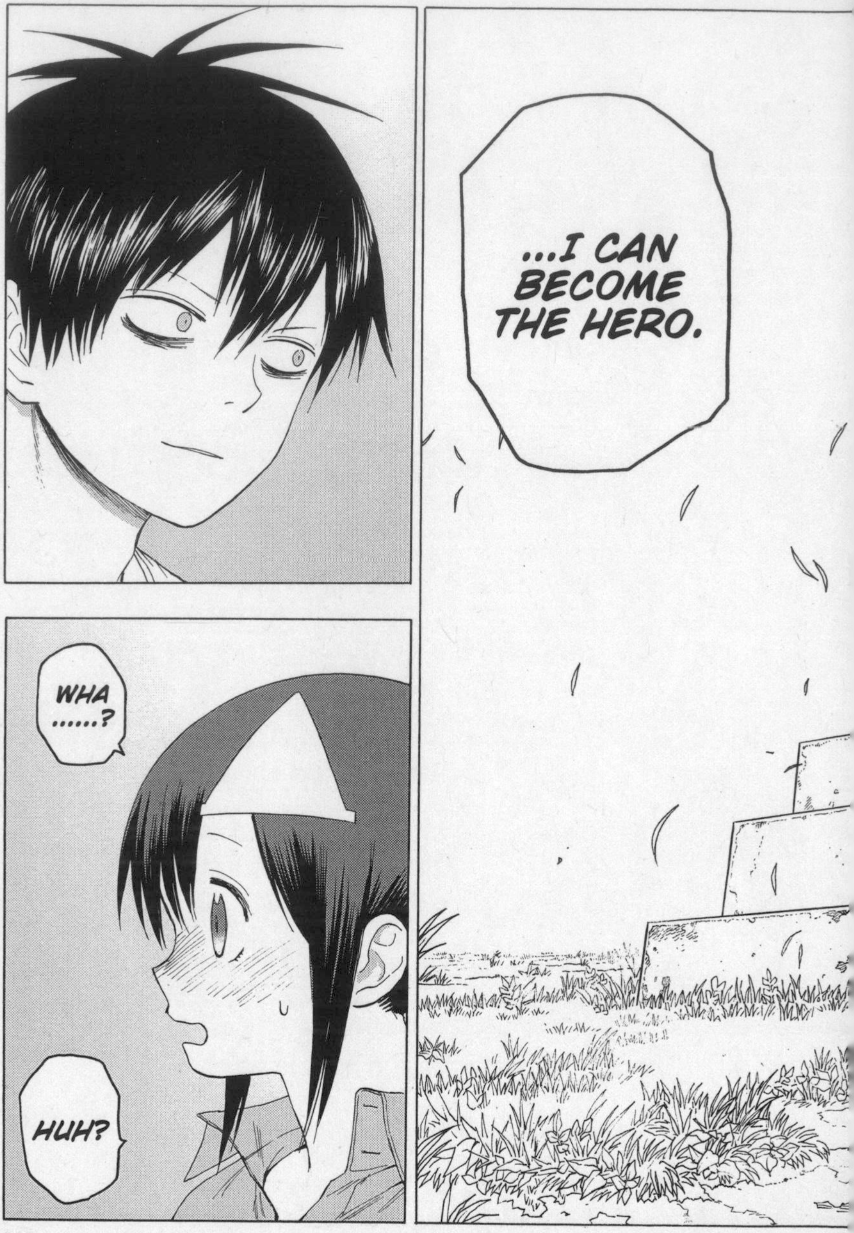
...I CAN BECOME THE HERO.
WHA ......?
HUH?

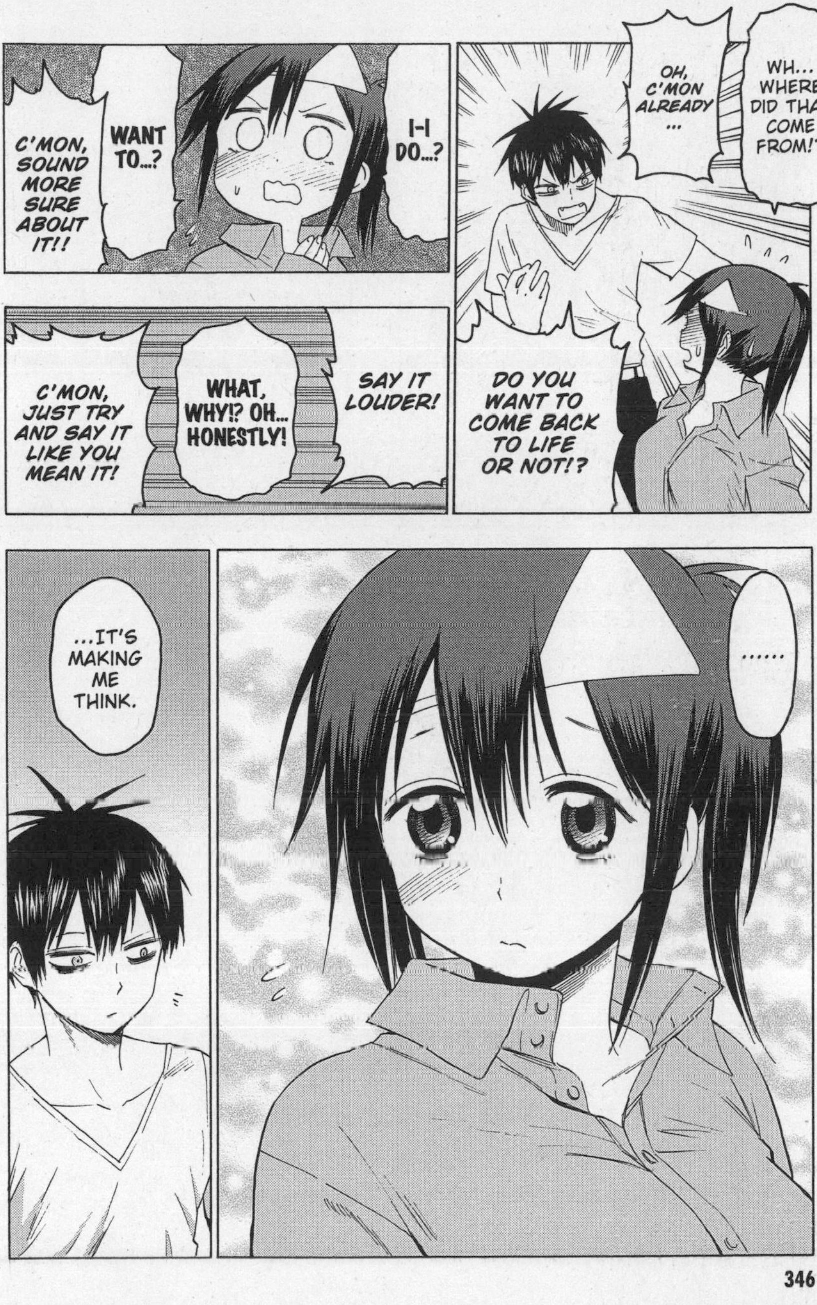
WH... WHERE DID THAT COME FROM!?
OH, C'MON ALREADY ...
DO YOU WANT TO COME BACK TO LIFE OR NOT!?
I-I DO...?
WANT TO...?
C'MON, SOUND MORE SURE ABOUT IT!!
SAY IT LOUDER!
WHAT, WHY!? OH... HONESTLY!
C'MON, JUST TRY AND SAY IT LIKE YOU MEAN IT!
......
...IT'S MAKING ME THINK.

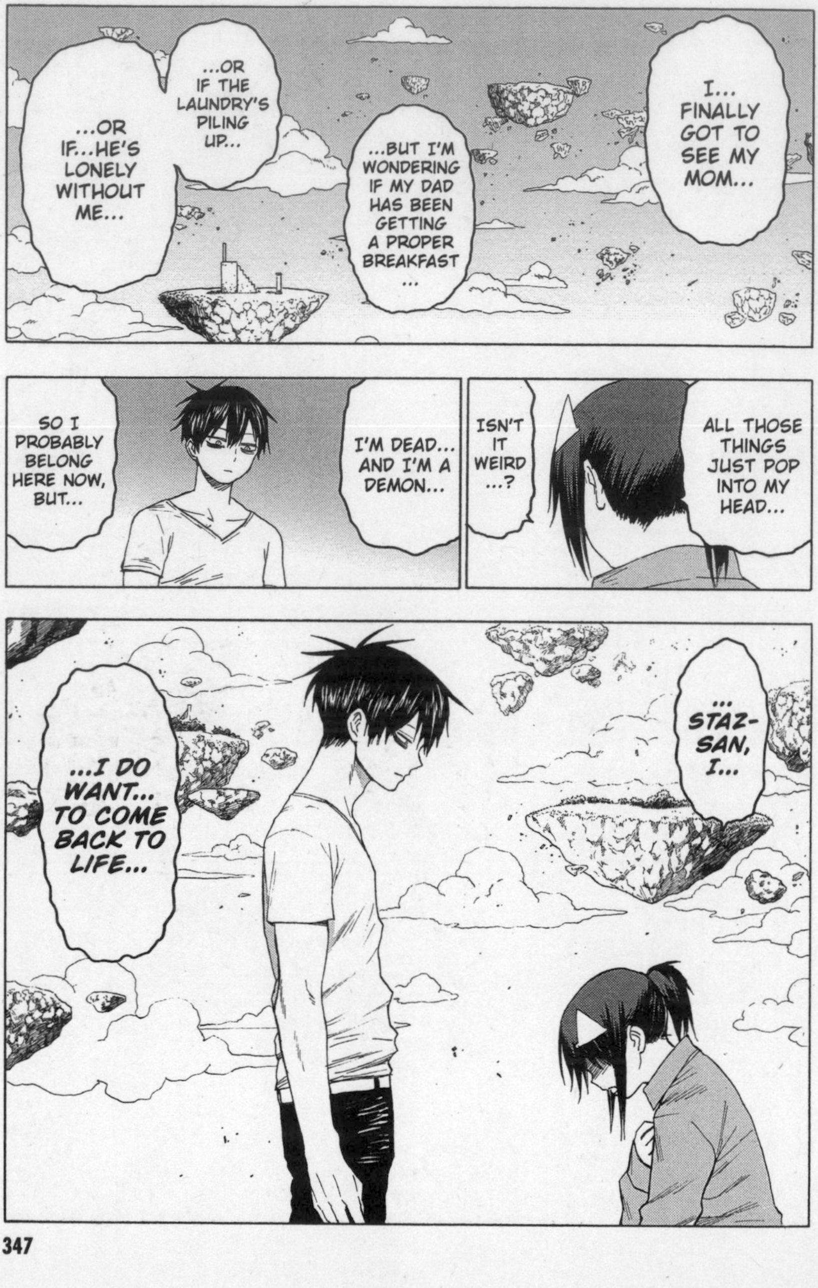
I... FINALLY GOT TO SEE MY MOM...
...BUT I'M WONDERING IF MY DAD HAS BEEN GETTING A PROPER BREAKFAST ...
...OR IF THE LAUNDRY'S PILING UP...
...OR IF...HE'S LONELY WITHOUT ME...
ALL THOSE THINGS JUST POP INTO MY HEAD...
ISN'T IT WEIRD ...?
I'M DEAD... AND I'M A DEMON...
SO I PROBABLY BELONG HERE NOW, BUT...
... STAZ-SAN, I...
...I DO WANT... TO COME BACK TO LIFE...

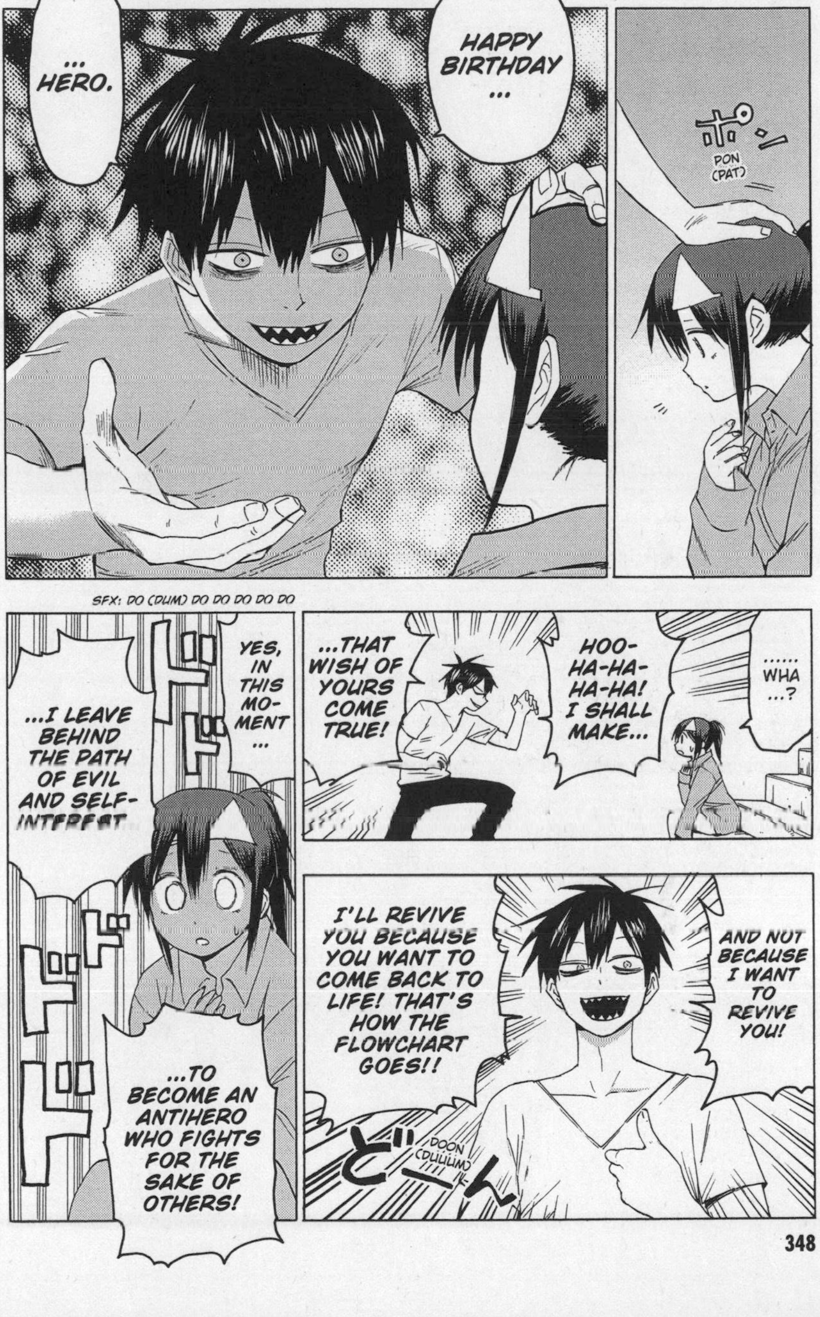
PON (PAT)
HAPPY BIRTHDAY ...
... HERO.
SFX: DO (DUM) DO DO DO DO DO
...... WHA ...?
HOO-HA-HA-HA! I SHALL MAKE...
...THAT WISH OF YOURS COME TRUE!
AND NOT BECAUSE I WANT TO REVIVE YOU!
I'LL REVIVE YOU BECAUSE YOU WANT TO COME BACK TO LIFE! THAT'S HOW THE FLOWCHART GOES!!
DOON (DUUUM)
YES, IN THIS MOMENT ...
...I LEAVE BEHIND THE PATH OF EVIL AND SELF-INTEREST
...TO BECOME AN ANTIHERO WHO FIGHTS FOR THE SAKE OF OTHERS!

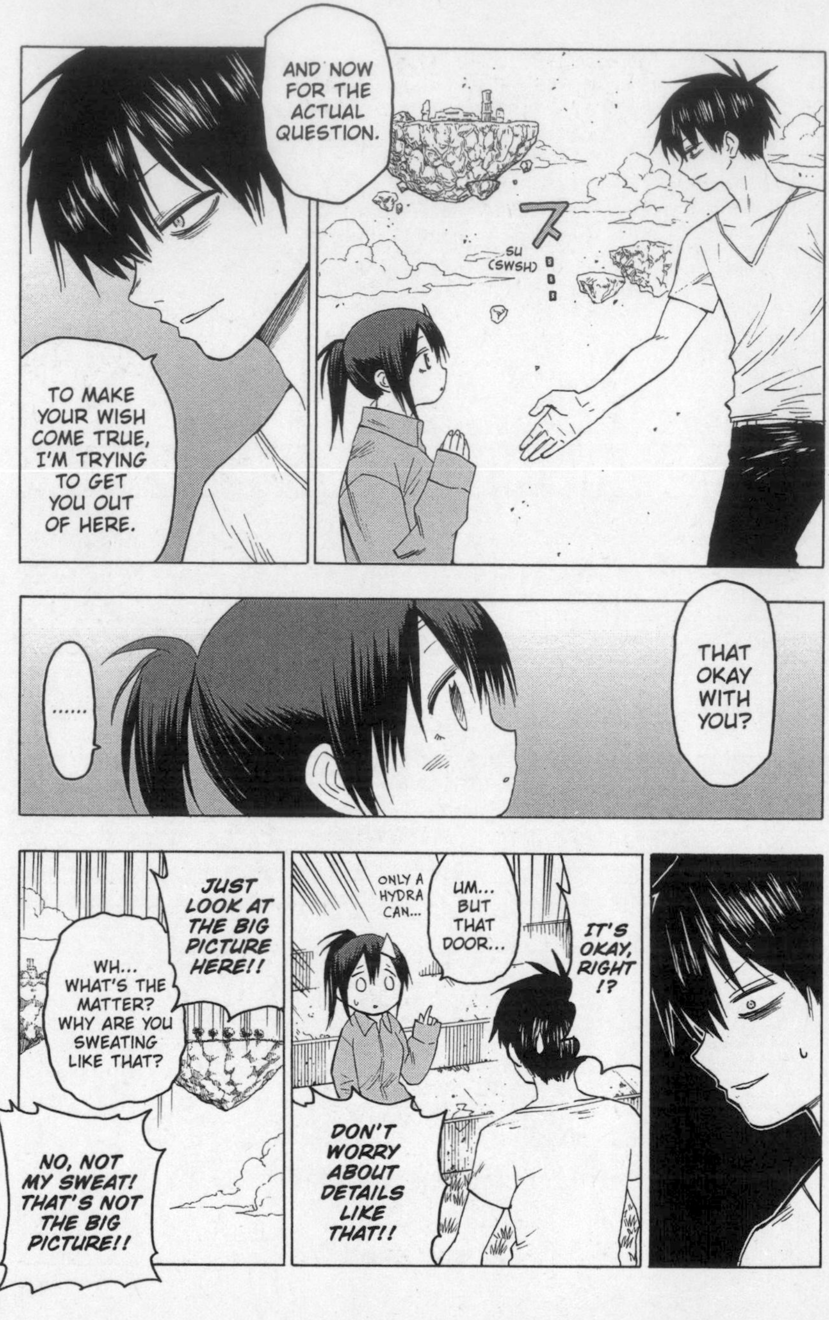
AND NOW FOR THE ACTUAL QUESTION.
ス
SU (SWSH)
TO MAKE YOUR WISH COME TRUE, I'M TRYING TO GET YOU OUT OF HERE.
THAT OKAY WITH YOU?
......
IT'S OKAY, RIGHT!?
UM... BUT THAT DOOR...
ONLY A HYDRA CAN...
DON'T WORRY ABOUT DETAILS LIKE THAT!!
JUST LOOK AT THE BIG PICTURE HERE!!
WH... WHAT'S THE MATTER? WHY ARE YOU SWEATING LIKE THAT?
NO, NOT MY SWEAT! THAT'S NOT THE BIG PICTURE!!

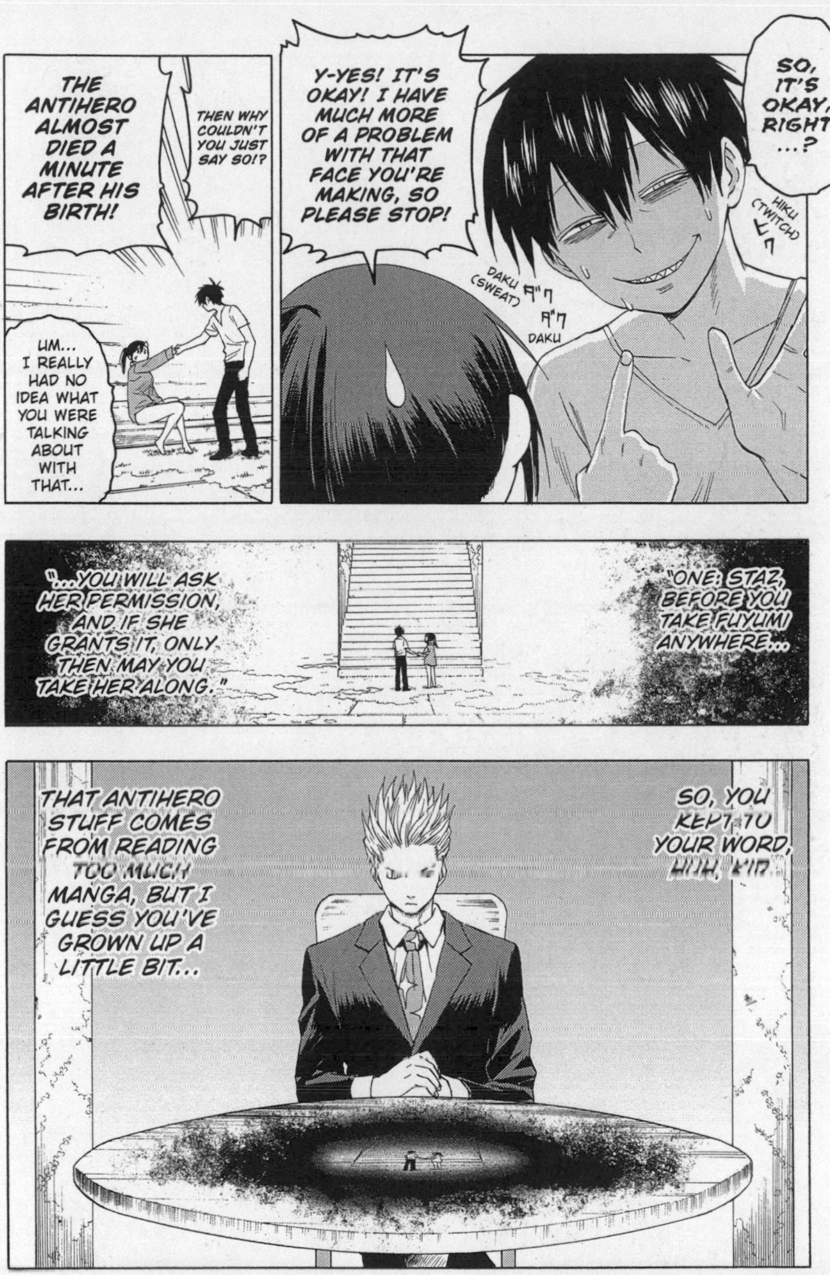
SO, IT'S OKAY, RIGHT ...?
HIKU (TWITCH)
DAKU (SWEAT)
DAKU
Y-YES! IT'S OKAY! I HAVE MUCH MORE OF A PROBLEM WITH THAT FACE YOU'RE MAKING, SO PLEASE STOP!
THE ANTIHERO ALMOST DIED A MINUTE AFTER HIS BIRTH!
THEN WHY COULDN'T YOU JUST SAY SO!?
UM... I REALLY HAD NO IDEA WHAT YOU WERE TALKING ABOUT WITH THAT...
"ONE: STAZ, BEFORE YOU TAKE FUYUMI ANYWHERE...
"...YOU WILL ASK HER PERMISSION, AND IF SHE GRANTS IT, ONLY THEN MAY YOU TAKE HER ALONG."
SO, YOU KEPT TO YOUR WORD,
THAT ANTIHERO STUFF COMES FROM READING TOO MUCH MANGA, BUT I GUESS YOU'VE GROWN UP A LITTLE BIT...

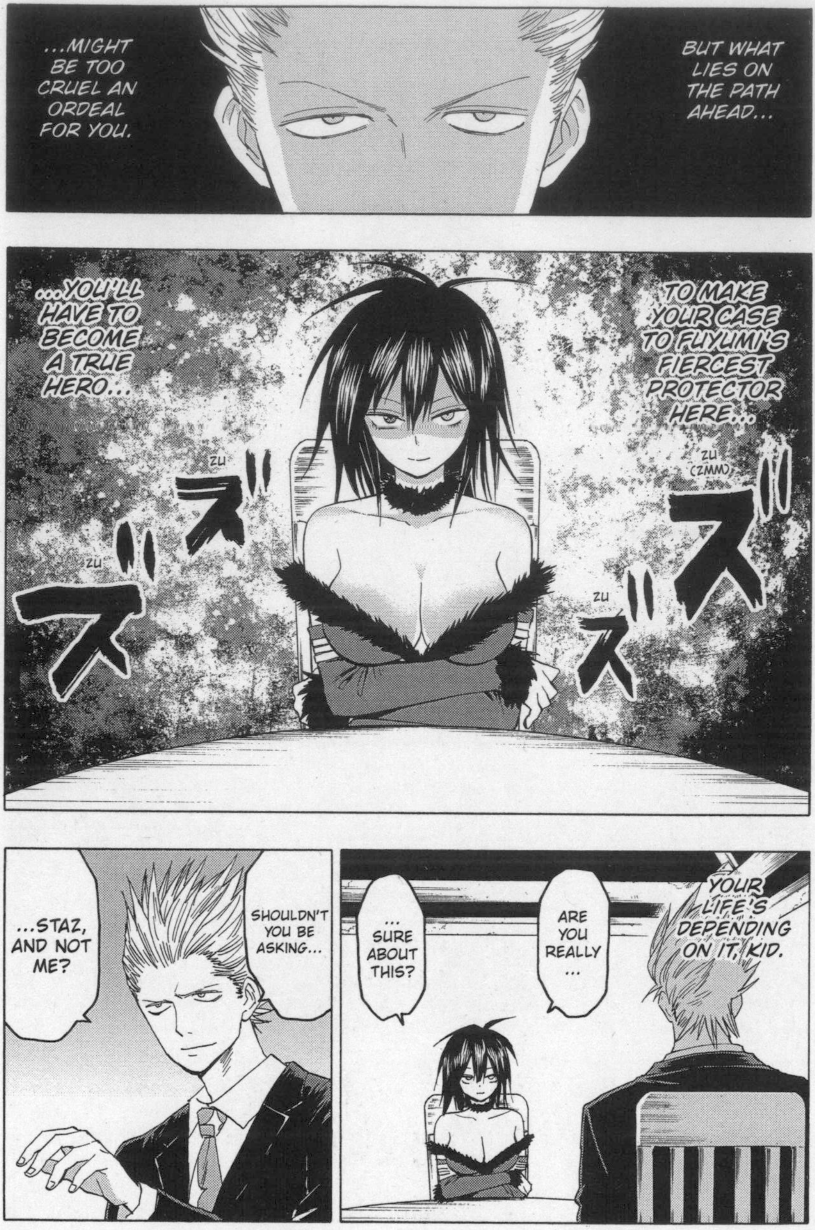
BUT WHAT LIES ON THE PATH AHEAD...
...MIGHT BE TOO CRUEL AN ORDEAL FOR YOU.
TO MAKE YOUR CASE TO FUYUMI'S FIERCEST PROTECTOR HERE...
...YOU'LL HAVE TO BECOME A TRUE HERO...
ZU (ZMM)
ズ
ZU
ズ
ZU
ズ
ZU
ズ
YOUR LIFE'S DEPENDING ON IT, KID.
ARE YOU REALLY...
...SURE ABOUT THIS?
SHOULDN'T YOU BE ASKING...
...STAZ, AND NOT ME?

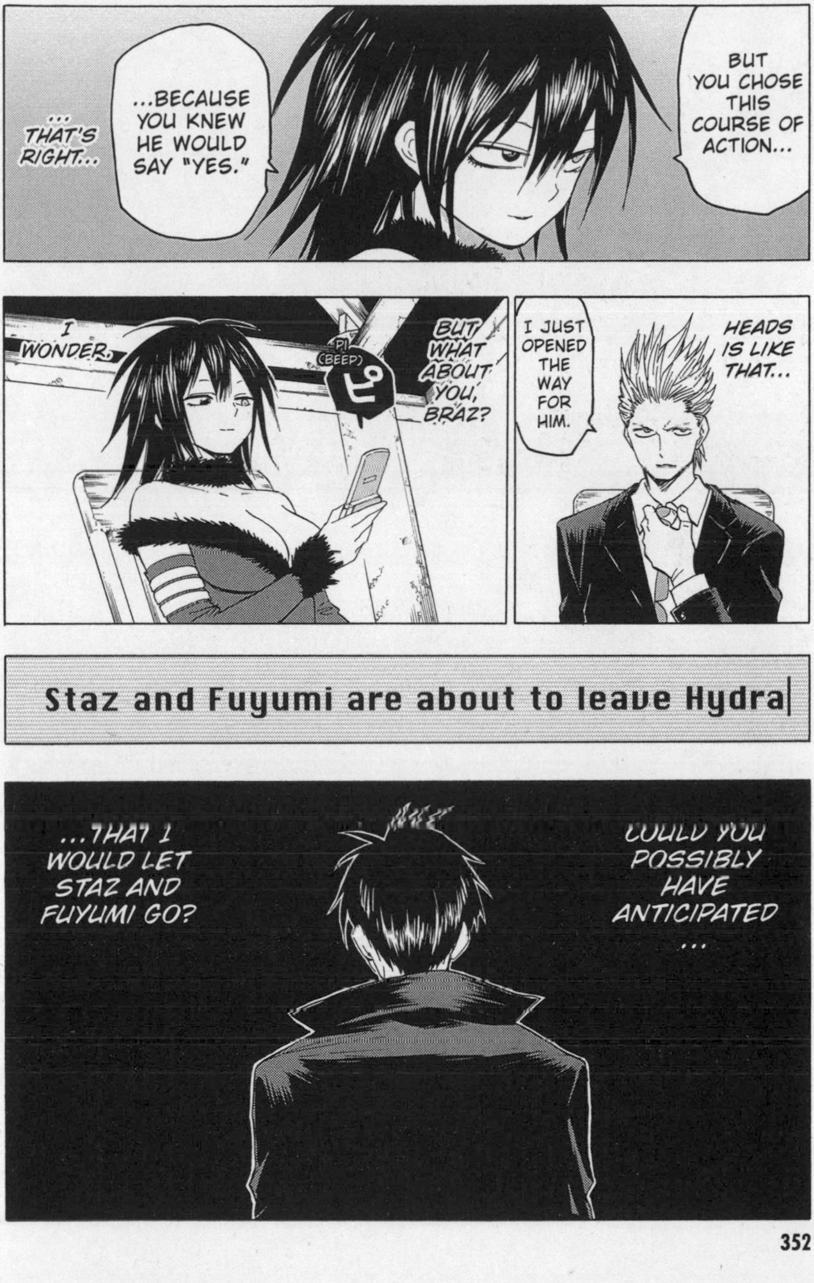
BUT YOU CHOSE THIS COURSE OF ACTION...
...BECAUSE YOU KNEW HE WOULD SAY "YES."
... THAT'S RIGHT...
HEADS IS LIKE THAT...
I JUST OPENED THE WAY FOR HIM.
BUT WHAT ABOUT YOU, BRAZ?
PI (BEEP)
I WONDER.
Staz and Fuyumi are about to leave Hydra
COULD YOU POSSIBLY HAVE ANTICIPATED ...
...THAT I WOULD LET STAZ AND FUYUMI GO?

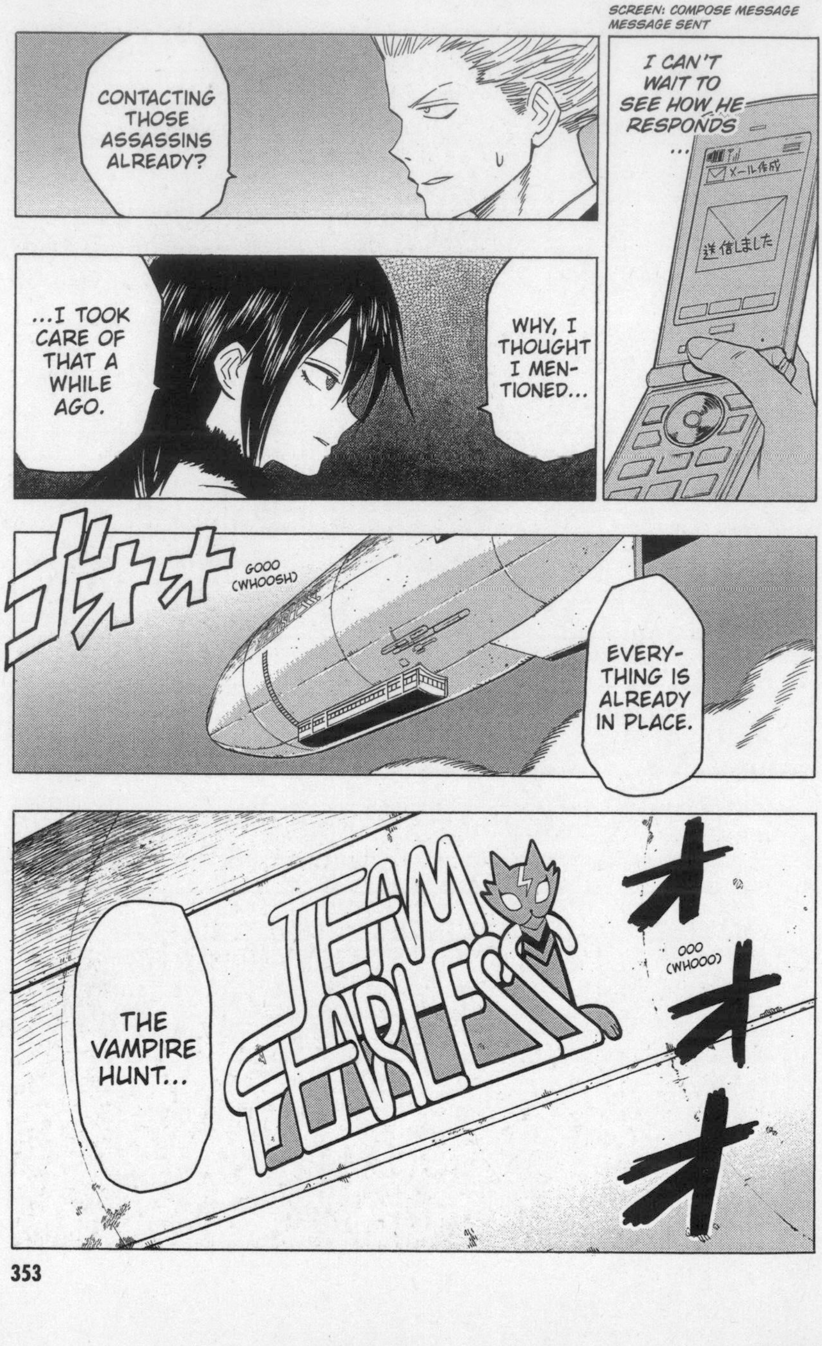
SCREEN: COMPOSE MESSAGE
MESSAGE SENT
I CAN'T WAIT TO SEE HOW HE RESPONDS ...
メール作成
送信しました
CONTACTING THOSE ASSASSINS ALREADY?
WHY, I THOUGHT I MENTIONED...
...I TOOK CARE OF THAT A WHILE AGO.
EVERYTHING IS ALREADY IN PLACE.
ゴオオ
GOOO (WHOOSH)
オオオ
OOO (WHOOO)
THE VAMPIRE HUNT...
TEAM FEARLESS

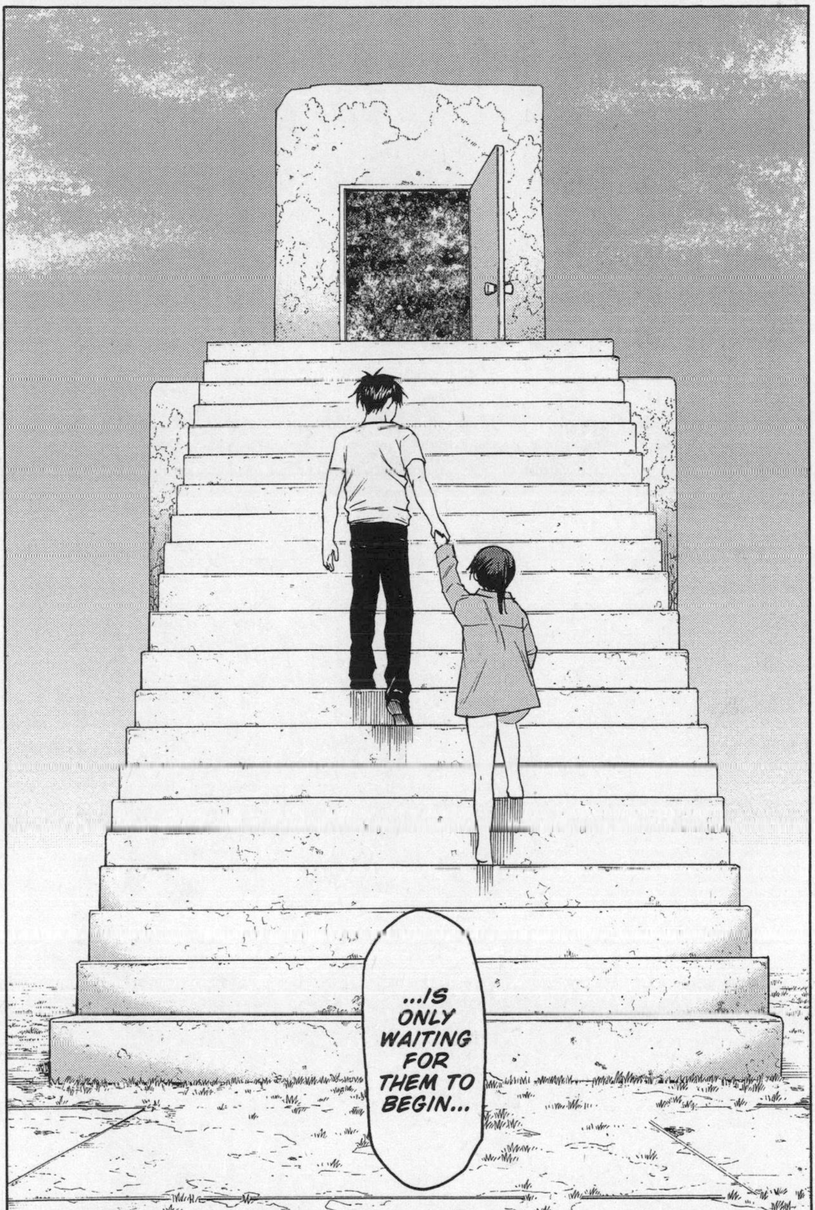
...IS ONLY WAITING FOR THEM TO BEGIN...

♠ To Be Continued ♠

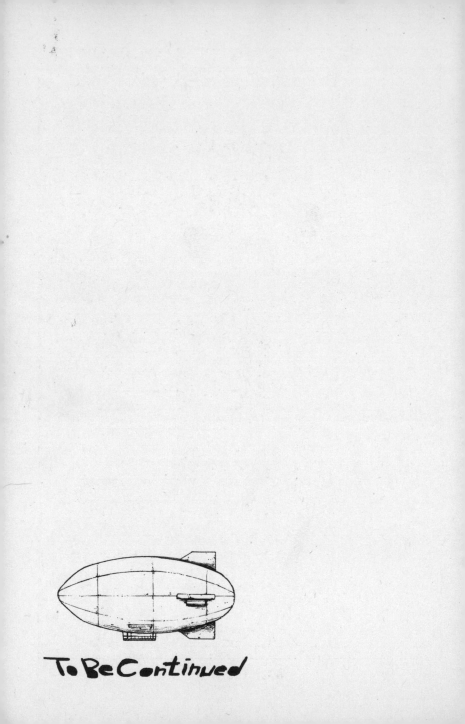

To Be Continued

BLOOD LAD

LIVING IN THE DEMON WORLD

BEROS'S EVERYDAY LIFE

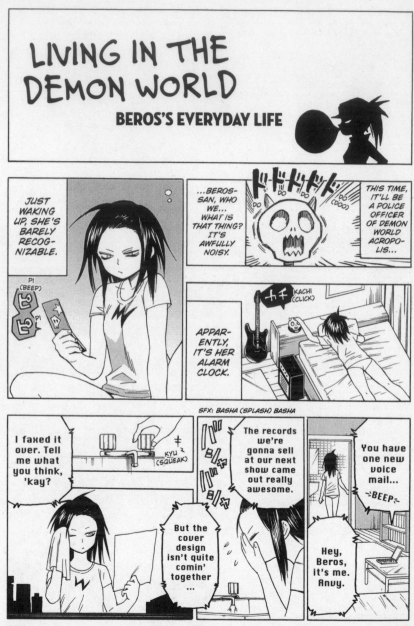

THIS TIME, IT'LL BE A POLICE OFFICER OF DEMON WORLD ACROPOLIS...
DO DO DO DO (DOO)
...BEROS-SAN, WHO WE... WHAT IS THAT THING? IT'S AWFULLY NOISY.
KACHI (CLICK)
APPARENTLY, IT'S HER ALARM CLOCK.
JUST WAKING UP, SHE'S BARELY RECOGNIZABLE.
PI (BEEP) PI
SFX: BASHA (SPLASH) BASHA
You have one new voice mail...
BEEP
Hey, Beros, it's me. Anvy.
The records we're gonna sell at our next show came out really awesome.
But the cover design isn't quite comin' together ...
KYU (SQUEAK)
I faxed it over. Tell me what you think, 'kay?

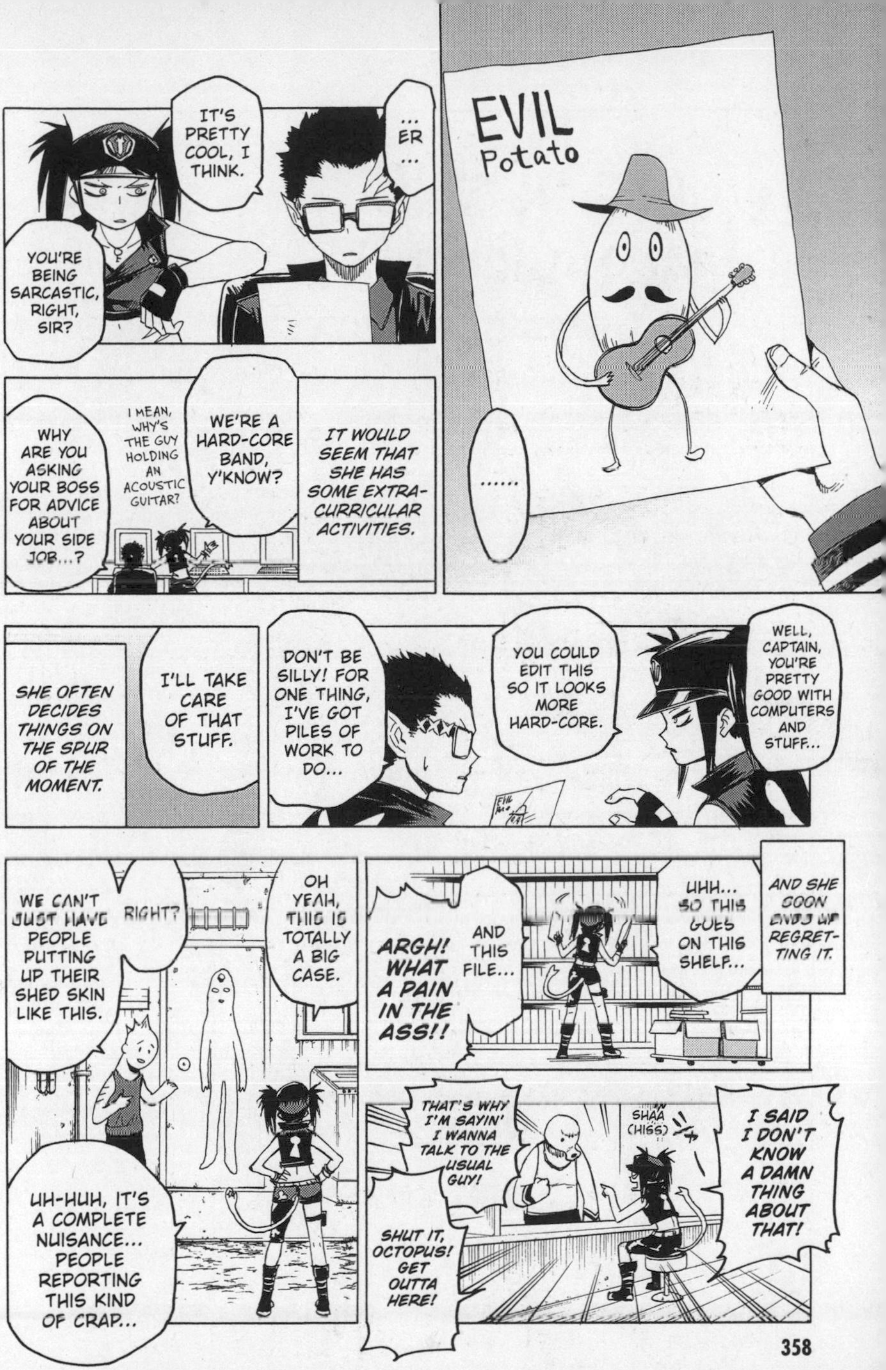
EVIL Potato
......
... ER ...
IT'S PRETTY COOL, I THINK.
YOU'RE BEING SARCASTIC, RIGHT, SIR?
IT WOULD SEEM THAT SHE HAS SOME EXTRA-CURRICULAR ACTIVITIES.
WE'RE A HARD-CORE BAND, Y'KNOW?
I MEAN, WHY'S THE GUY HOLDING AN ACOUSTIC GUITAR?
WHY ARE YOU ASKING YOUR BOSS FOR ADVICE ABOUT YOUR SIDE JOB...?
WELL, CAPTAIN, YOU'RE PRETTY GOOD WITH COMPUTERS AND STUFF...
YOU COULD EDIT THIS SO IT LOOKS MORE HARD-CORE.
DON'T BE SILLY! FOR ONE THING, I'VE GOT PILES OF WORK TO DO...
I'LL TAKE CARE OF THAT STUFF.
SHE OFTEN DECIDES THINGS ON THE SPUR OF THE MOMENT.
AND SHE SOON ENDS UP REGRETTING IT.
UHH... SO THIS GOES ON THIS SHELF...
AND THIS FILE...
ARGH! WHAT A PAIN IN THE ASS!!
I SAID I DON'T KNOW A DAMN THING ABOUT THAT!
SHAA (HISS)
THAT'S WHY I'M SAYIN' I WANNA TALK TO THE USUAL GUY!
SHUT IT, OCTOPUS! GET OUTTA HERE!
OH YEAH, THIS IS TOTALLY A BIG CASE.
RIGHT?
WE CAN'T JUST HAVE PEOPLE PUTTING UP THEIR SHED SKIN LIKE THIS.
UH-HUH, IT'S A COMPLETE NUISANCE... PEOPLE REPORTING THIS KIND OF CRAP...

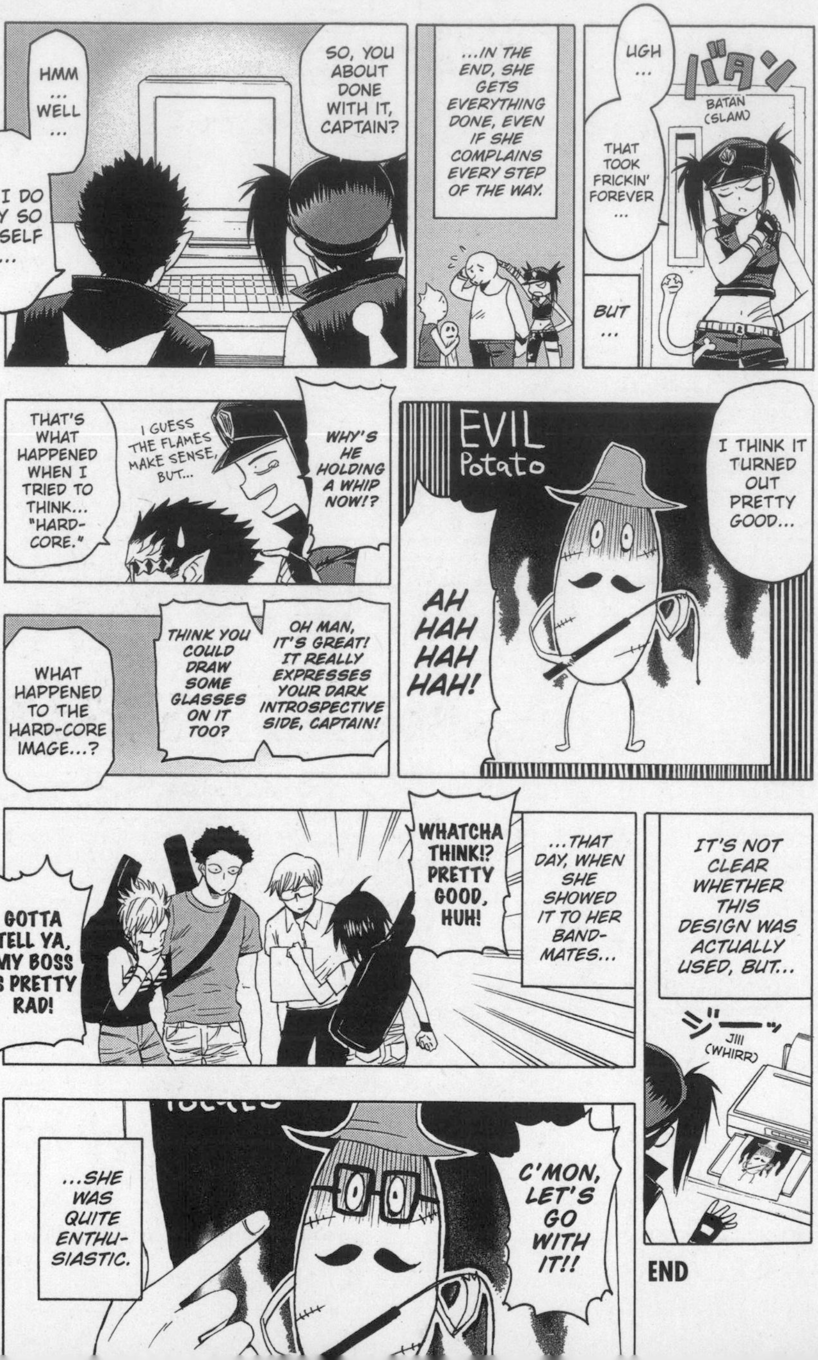

UGH ...
バタン
BATAN (SLAM)
THAT TOOK FRICKIN' FOREVER ...
BUT ...
...IN THE END, SHE GETS EVERYTHING DONE, EVEN IF SHE COMPLAINS EVERY STEP OF THE WAY.
SO, YOU ABOUT DONE WITH IT, CAPTAIN?
HMM ... WELL ...
IF I DO SAY SO MYSELF ...
I THINK IT TURNED OUT PRETTY GOOD...
EVIL Potato
AH HAH HAH HAH!
WHY'S HE HOLDING A WHIP NOW!?
I GUESS THE FLAMES MAKE SENSE, BUT...
THAT'S WHAT HAPPENED WHEN I TRIED TO THINK... "HARD-CORE."
OH MAN, IT'S GREAT! IT REALLY EXPRESSES YOUR DARK INTROSPECTIVE SIDE, CAPTAIN!
THINK YOU COULD DRAW SOME GLASSES ON IT TOO?
WHAT HAPPENED TO THE HARD-CORE IMAGE...?
IT'S NOT CLEAR WHETHER THIS DESIGN WAS ACTUALLY USED, BUT...
ジーッ
JIII (WHIRR)
...THAT DAY, WHEN SHE SHOWED IT TO HER BAND-MATES...
WHATCHA THINK!? PRETTY GOOD, HUH!
GOTTA TELL YA, MY BOSS IS PRETTY RAD!
C'MON, LET'S GO WITH IT!!
...SHE WAS QUITE ENTHUSIASTIC.
END

BLOOD LAD 6

These images appeared under the jacket of the original edition of *Blood Lad*!

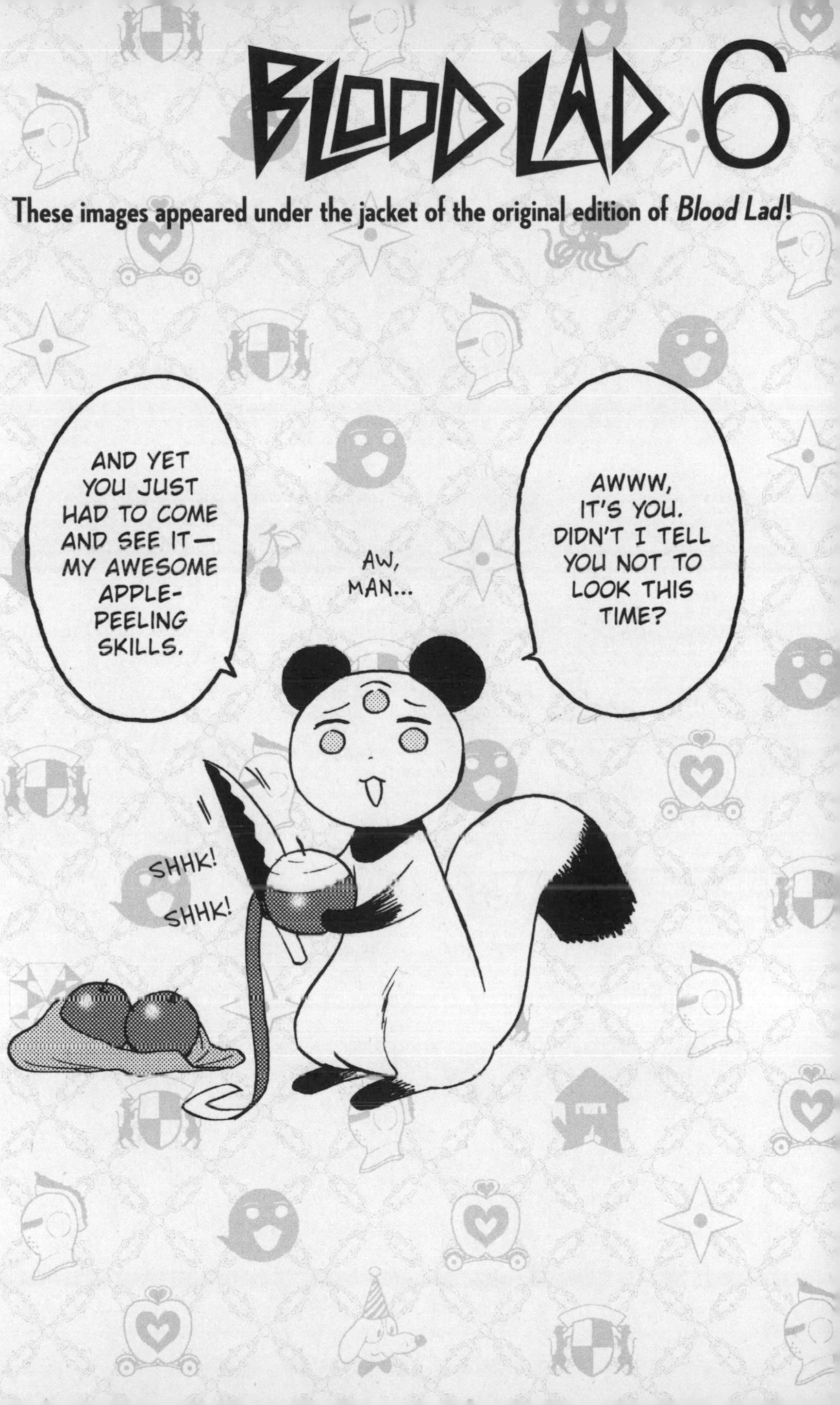
AWWW, IT'S YOU. DIDN'T I TELL YOU NOT TO LOOK THIS TIME?
AW, MAN...
AND YET YOU JUST HAD TO COME AND SEE IT—MY AWESOME APPLE-PEELING SKILLS.
SHHK!
SHHK!

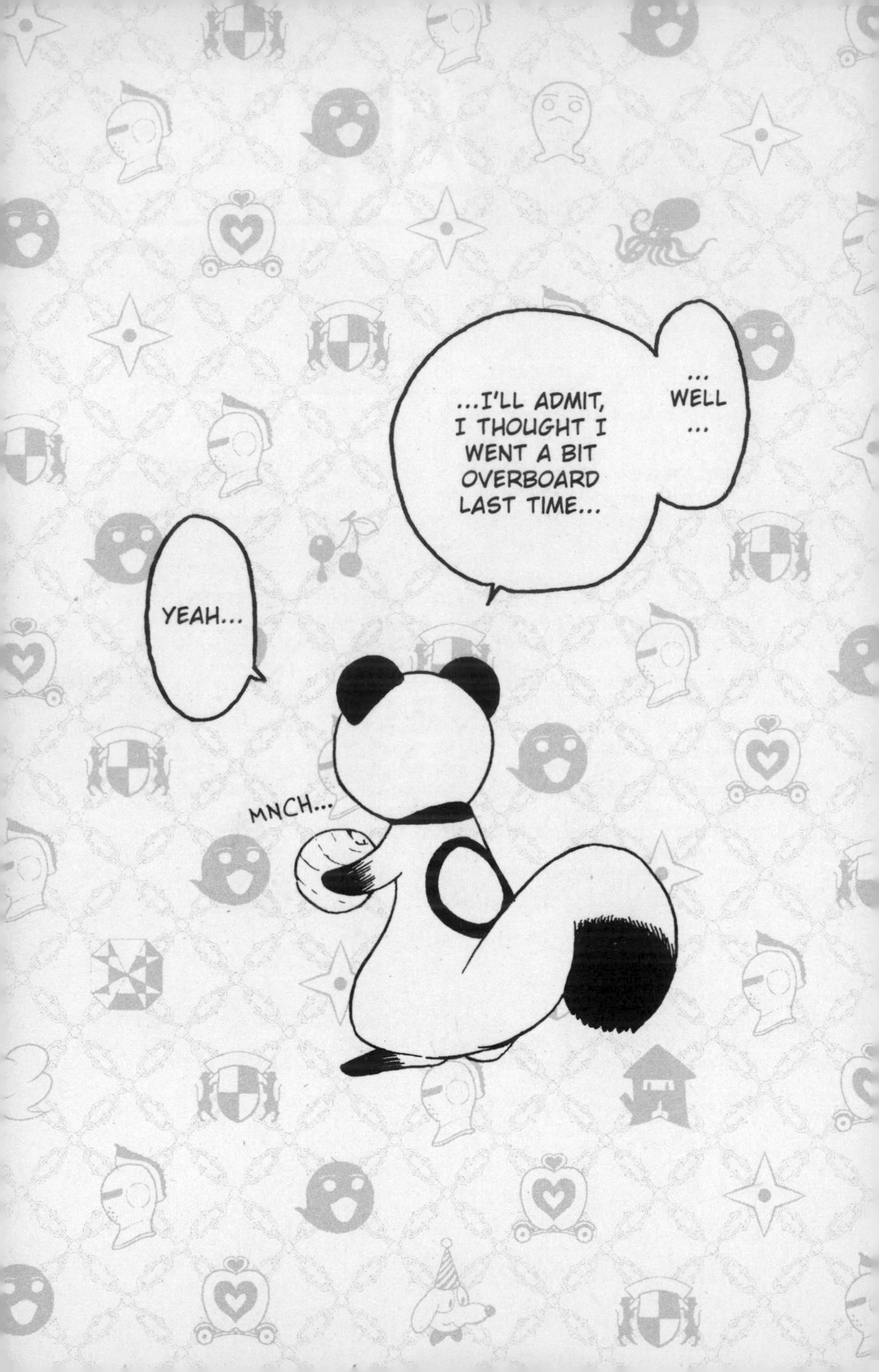
... WELL ...
...I'LL ADMIT, I THOUGHT I WENT A BIT OVERBOARD LAST TIME...
YEAH...
MNCH...

BLOOD LAD

YUUKI KODAMA

Translation: Melissa Tanaka

Lettering: Alexis Eckerman

This book is a work of fiction. Names, characters, places, and incidents are the product of the author's imagination or are used fictitiously. Any resemblance to actual events, locales, or persons, living or dead, is coincidental.

BLOOD LAD Volumes 5 and 6 © Yuuki KODAMA 2011, 2012.
Edited by KADOKAWA SHOTEN
First published in Japan in 2011, 2012 by KADOKAWA CORPORATION, Tokyo.
English translation rights arranged with KADOKAWA CORPORATION, Tokyo, through TUTTLE-MORI AGENCY, INC., Tokyo.

Translation © 2013 by Hachette Book Group, Inc.

All rights reserved. In accordance with the U.S. Copyright Act of 1976, the scanning, uploading, and electronic sharing of any part of this book without the permission of the publisher is unlawful piracy and theft of the author's intellectual property. If you would like to use material from the book (other than for review purposes), prior written permission must be obtained by contacting the publisher at permissions@hbgusa.com. Thank you for your support of the author's rights.

Yen Press
Hachette Book Group
1290 Avenue of the Americas, New York, NY 10104

www.HachetteBookGroup.com
www.YenPress.com

Yen Press is an imprint of Hachette Book Group, Inc.
The Yen Press name and logo are trademarks of Hachette Book Group, Inc.

First Yen Press Edition: May 2013

ISBN: 978-0-316-25092-4

10 9 8 7

BVG

Printed in the United States of America